The

Secret
Christmas
Library

Also by Jenny Colgan

The
Secret
Christmas
Library

A Novel

JENNY COLGAN

wm

WILLIAM MORROW
An Imprint of HarperCollins*Publishers*

HarperCollins books may be purchased for educational, business, or sales promotional use. For information, please email the Special Markets Department at SPsales@harpercollins.com.

hc.com

FIRST EDITION

Interior text design by Diahann Sturge-Campbell

Title page and chapter opener illustration © Tatiana Bass/Stock.Adobe.com

Library of Congress Cataloging-in-Publication Data has been applied for.

ISBN 978-0-06-343737-1
ISBN 978-0-06-345544-3 (simultaneous hardcover edition)

25 26 27 28 29 LBC 5 4 3 2 1

The
Secret
Christmas
Library

Chapter One

It was not London's fault, because London was looking beautiful in the frosty start of the festive season: huge red ribbons on display; little snowy houses that lit up in the shop windows; the great Norwegian-gifted tree in Trafalgar Square glittering mightily.

Each dark early evening, fogged-up pub windows showed people inside in the warm, chattering and laughing and toasting the season; men in black tie and women in beautiful jewel-coloured dresses alighted from black cabs in clouds of perfume onto wet pavements reflecting the shining fairy lights above them; skaters flew around the ice rink in the ancient cobbled confines of Somerset House.

No. It wasn't beautiful, glitzy, shining, expensive London, Mirren Sutherland knew, that was making her feel so down. It was her. And this time of year.

London turning sparkly and shiny and exciting just reminded her of other people's wonderful Christmases. Whereas her mum was working, her siblings were away, and she had made a stupid mistake by pretending to her friends that she was totally fine and had loads of plans and now it was too late to backtrack. Because last Christmas had been terrific, and this one was going to blow monkey chunks.

Mirren was a lifelong book obsessive, who never felt she had quite enough books, who could really only feel secure with half a dozen unread paperbacks propped up by her bedside table, three library cards, two Kindles, and an emergency set of Douglas Adams in the bathroom, in case the lock broke.

She had spent the previous Christmas on the trail of a book her great-aunt Violet had remembered from childhood and begged Mirren to track down at the very end of her life. Joined by the devastatingly handsome Theo Palliser, who worked for an antiquarian bookseller, they had searched bookshops up and down the country, before she had finally found it all by herself, hidden in her great-great-uncle's kit bag.

The book had turned out to be a priceless original, written by Robert Louis Stevenson and illustrated by Aubrey Beardsley, and its real owner, her great-aunt's childhood best friend June, who was related to Beardsley, had decided to donate it. There had been a fancy handing-over ceremony when it went on display, and Mirren had even received a small finder's fee, which everyone had told her to use as a deposit on a studio flat.

Theo hadn't come to the ceremony. Mirren had really thought they'd had something. But as soon as all the excitement had died down, he had ghosted her completely. Mirren had gone back to her job as a quantity surveyor, where nobody cared about books at all; her great-aunt had died, and frankly life now was much duller than it had been before her big adventure.

She had even had daydreams where she and Theo travelled the world, tracking down books together . . . but of course he had gone back to his posh world of hushed libraries and expensive first editions, and she had gone back to measuring up rat-infested warehouses for yet more student housing. There were not, she had discovered, a lot of job openings for book-finders. Having such a breathtakingly large mortgage on her tiny new studio meant it was difficult to even think about doing something else. It was childish, she knew, to wish for something magical to happen at Christmas.

Work was quiet, so she decided to take her lunch break early, and found her steps straying, as they often did, from her nondescript office on the Euston Road, across the heavy thoroughfare of traffic, past the gleaming white hospital and escaping into Bloomsbury, home of the British Museum, which in turn was home of her precious find, her most shining moment. The vast building took up an entire city block. Oh, how she loved Bloomsbury, the elegant area of London devoted to learning and books and study. It was stuffed with universities, libraries, publishing houses, and archives; beautiful squares and manicured gardens—and, everywhere on ancient buildings, blue plaques indicating the famous writers who had once lived there: J. M. Barrie, Virginia Woolf, W. B. Yeats, H. G. Wells, Charles Dickens . . . it went on and on.

Mirren examined the Christmas displays in the tiny shops she passed, many selling books and antiques, and cut through ancient cobbled passageways where stood great tall houses with large brass door knockers that were old when Dickens was young. It was raining, of course, and she tucked her curling chestnut hair under her mustard-coloured beanie and prayed it wouldn't frizz too much. She passed groups of happy shouting people on the way, heading into old timbered restaurants or wearing party hats. She wasn't looking forward to her own office party. They had had a very quiet year, and all the fun people who didn't have vast new mortgages had left. It would probably just be her and the accountants in the staff room with a packet of ginger nuts.

The museum, with its columns and vast steps at the front, supporting its iconic dome, was busy as ever. She loved the vastness of the museum, the overflowing nature of it. Locked doors with pictures of lions on them were full of precious items that must be saved in the event of a fire; there was a deserted Underground station beneath the building where they stowed even more. Tourists, keen to visit the mummies and the Anglo-Saxon burial ship, were getting their bags searched out front, and there were glittering Christmas trees standing by the tall entrance. Inside, everywhere were more trees and lights, as well as great swags of holly and ivy hanging around the top of the famous Round Reading Room in the Great Court, the enormous glazed white atrium that sat at the very heart of the museum. Mirren nodded to the security guards, who had got to know her as a regular. She loved the vastness of the museum, the overflowing nature of it. Locked doors with pictures of lions on them were full of precious items that must be saved in the event of a fire, she knew; there was a deserted underground station beneath the building where they stowed even more.

And in the very heart of it, up in the viewing gallery in the circular reading room, was her very contribution: her very own book. Well, the book she had found. Visiting it always reminded her, rather wistfully, how happy she had been last Christmas; it gave her a feeling of pride, before she went back to her sad office and contemplated spending three days on her brother's sofa this Christmas while everyone felt sorry for her and her mum fretted. Here was one thing she had. She hopped nimbly up the wide old stone steps, worn smooth by two hundred years of visitors, her scarf trailing behind her.

Chapter Two

Once inside, Mirren made her way quietly to a side room. Even though she came here often, it never ceased to impress. It was a cool, temperature-controlled space, in near-total darkness, where you could walk in—where, amazingly, anyone in the *world* could walk in—and see some of the most extraordinary books ever made.

A Shakespeare first folio. A fourth-century Bible. *Middlemarch*, written out by hand. It was a book-lover's paradise. And there, right at the end, sometimes with a huddle around it, was her book, on display: *A Child's Garden of Verses*, with original illustrations by Aubrey Beardsley.

She took a seat on one of the red hexagonal stools and waited for people to come and have a look. There were some bored children, of course, being hauled around the museum for their supposed improvement, but she wasn't interested in them; she was interested in the people who genuinely were excited to see it, who oohed and aahed over the fine lines of the beautiful drawings, the notes scrawled in the margin by Stevenson himself. She had not gone looking for treasure, but she had found it, and when things were difficult, as they were at the moment, it gave her a lot of pleasure to see other people enjoy it. There was even a sign—there it was, in tiny letters: *Kindly donated by June Wilson, great-niece of Aubrey Beardsley: found, Mirren Sutherland, London 2024.*

On this particular day, a tall, sandy-haired man in rather scruffy clothes—not, it had to be said, an unusual sight in the British Museum—was staring closely at the book. She smiled happily to herself, liking the man without knowing a thing about him, just because he was appreciating it. He turned suddenly and beckoned an attendant.

"When it says 'found' . . ." he said in an unusual accent Mirren struggled to place. She was eavesdropping furiously.

"Yes?" said the attendant, who, unlike the security guards, never noticed Mirren coming and going, or, if she did, never let on to the pale girl with the large grey eyes and russet-brown ringleted hair who was so often in the room.

"How did they find it?"

Mirren was surprised. Nobody had ever asked about *her* before. They normally asked if they had any of Beardsley's other work, by which they usually meant the naughty paintings.

"It was in an attic."

"Oh," said the man, sounding disappointed. "It's just, it says 'found,' as if they were searching for it."

The attendant shrugged. "Dunno. Maybe it was a really big attic?"

The man paused and looked at the book for a long time. Then he took out a phone that looked as old as a BlackBerry. The attendant gave him the Paddington Bear stare she reserved for everyone on their phone in the library exhibition, but he didn't notice.

"Ugh, you can't Google . . . him? Her?" he said. "Apparently Helen Mirren and Donald Sutherland made tons of films together."

Mirren's heart leapt suddenly. Wait. He was . . . he was Googling *her*? She blinked rapidly, feeling more like an eavesdropper than ever.

"Um . . . ?" she said quietly, clearing her throat. Neither of them turned round and she sank back into the gloom.

"Oh well," said the attendant, and walked away, leaving Mirren alone with the tourist, and that odd feeling she had, of having nowhere particular to be at that moment, nobody who would miss her if she was or wasn't there, among the nine million souls in the great city.

She had a loving family, of course, she always reminded herself. But it was also a family that would show quite a lot of that love by slagging her off and asking her when she was going to get a better job, and did she know that everyone she was at school with had a baby now, every single one of them?

"Excuse me," she said, stepping forward, speaking more loudly. The attendant looked back, and Mirren moved away from her and towards the man.

"Yes?"

The man looked down at her. He was in his early thirties, thin, in need of a haircut. He had a long, elegant nose and a strong chin and hooded hazel eyes. His hair was a sandy brown, thick and too long.

Mirren instantly felt herself flush with the sheer embarrassment of talking to a stranger in London. This was completely ridiculous. She shouldn't have said anything. But she was here now.

"Sorry . . . I'm Mirren. Mirren Sutherland," she added, for clarification.

"Eh? Who? What?"

Mirren looked at the display case and he followed her gaze then looked back at her.

"Erm, yeah . . . I couldn't help overhearing."

He looked even more uncomfortable. "So you're telling me you're . . ."

"I'm the person who found the book, yes."

He looked completely unconvinced. "So, er, you just happened to be passing . . . ?"

"Yes," said Mirren. "Would you like to see my driver's licence?"

He made a slightly wobbly line with his lips, because obviously he did want to, but was too well-mannered to insist. Fumbling, Mirren pulled out her wallet and showed him instead her British Library card, of which she was inordinately proud.

"Ah," he said, but he still looked puzzled. "And you were in the area? Just a massive coincidence?"

Mirren frowned. "I work not far away. And sometimes I like to visit my book," she said.

He grinned then and it changed his rather pointed solemn face completely; lit it up. Finally, this made sense.

"You come and watch people visiting your book?!"

"That's not all I do," said Mirren, suddenly slightly stung.

"Do you wait to hear them talk about it and then confront them? Weird hobby. Ooh—or do you wait for them to talk about you?"

"It's not a *hobby*," said Mirren, a little stiffly. He was taking the piss now and she didn't like it.

"It's something you repeatedly do of your own free will? Because I have to tell you, that does sound quite a lot like a hobby."

Mirren was annoyed suddenly. Who even was this guy?

"Well, I love that book, and I loved the person who asked me to find it," she said, her voice a little tight.

He held up his hands. "Of course. Sorry. Sorry. I didn't mean to tease. Did you really just find it in an attic, though?" His eyes were curiously searching, as if he wasn't just making conversation, he really wanted to know.

"No!" said Mirren. "I searched the entire country. That's just where it was, in the end. And by the way, half of the UK was looking for that book."

"I bet they were," he said. "But you tracked it down. Well, well."

He glanced at his watch and winced.

"Meeting," he said. Then he took out a small white embossed card with his name and number—nothing else—on it in raised black print.

"Jamie McKinnon?" she read aloud.

"Uh-huh," he said. "Non-finder of books, unfortunately."

She looked at him uncomprehendingly.

"Listen . . . if you're ever interested in a job, call me."

A job? thought Mirren. But also: A job?

Chapter Three

The next strange thing that happened to Mirren was this: the number on the business card he had given her was a home number. A proper, area-code-in-parentheses number, with a very long code and a very short number. Obviously the first thing Mirren did when she was back in the office was Google it, without success, except to learn that it was up in the Highlands of Scotland somewhere, up on the northeast coast, an area of the UK about which she knew precisely nothing.

The following day she saw the Christmas duty roster.

"There's only you on it now," her boss said, slightly pityingly. "Imran just handed in his notice."

"Oh my goodness," said Mirren. "Everyone's gone."

She'd needed the job to get her mortgage. She knew she ought to find something else. But somehow she hadn't found the energy to do it—to send thousands of CVs to thousands of inboxes, hoping she'd somehow hit the jackpot.

"Nobody needs an emergency quantity surveyor over Christmas!" said Mirren in despair, looking at the days she was meant to be on, which appeared to be all of them.

"We have to look like a full-service organisation," said her boss, who was not a bad sort, but very, very tired.

Mirren headed back to her desk grumpily. It was clearly Christmastime. Nobody needed anything surveyed. They were too busy watching perfume ads and complaining about how small the plastic tubs of Quality Street were these days, compared to when they were younger and they were apparently the size of gas boilers.

She sighed and stared at her computer screen. And now she couldn't even go back to the British Museum to look at her book, in case the attendant remembered who she was now. It would be too embarrassing to be caught lurking round her own exhibition.

On impulse, she decided to text the number on the card.

The text, of course, wouldn't send, to what was clearly a landline. This was ridiculous; he had to be doing it on purpose. He probably had a tricycle and thought they should bring back shillings and half crowns. Mind you, he hadn't had any peculiar facial hair. He'd looked pretty normal, if a bit skinny and scruffy. But even so.

THE WALLS OF the studio felt closer than ever when she got home, a long journey to south London with millions of other grim-faced puffa-jacket-wearing people all heading to the same place at the same time and wishing everyone else weren't heading there too.

Mirren checked to see if she had any food in the fridge that she'd forgotten about (she didn't), picked up her phone, then put it down again. She wasn't going to be a total weirdo and phone some creep who'd spoken to her in a museum.

She picked it up again. What else exactly was she going to do tonight? Browse Instagram to look at everyone else having an amazing time? Threaten terrible imaginary revenge to Theo bloody invisible Palliser? Go out in the freezing cold, trudge miles to the bus stop and go back out in town to a noisy overcrowded bar where she couldn't hear anyone, and it would cost her a fortune?

The phone rang out, for ages. There was no answering service, no way to leave a message.

Fine. He could keep his stupid antiquarian cool-boy fetish—who cared? She suddenly felt like having a bath, which was impossible as of course she didn't have one. Although she could already hear her next-door neighbour having a shower, which was not good news, as it was normally a precursor to him having rather loud sex with his boyfriend.

Then a long number appeared on the screen, and her own phone began to ring.

Chapter Four

"Ah, is that the book-finder?" came the voice at the end, sounding amused.

Now she was hearing it outside of the busy library, she realised the tinge in his voice was Scottish—but not Scottish as she normally thought of it, which was funny, loud Glaswegian. This was more of a burr, the words not elongated, more clipped. Once again Mirren found herself feeling annoyed. It was his tone of voice, as if he'd absolutely expected her to call, just because he had gone up to her in a museum. She searched for the word. That was it; he sounded *entitled*.

"You asked me to phone you!" she pointed out, sounding snippy.

"I did," he said.

"You don't have a mobile?"

"I do!" he said, his voice echoing on the other end of the line. "You saw it. What I *don't* have is reception."

"What do you mean?"

"I mean, you know when phone companies promise you ninety-nine percent coverage? Well, I live in that very special one percent."

"Aren't they making home phones digital soon too?"

"So they say," he said gloomily. "I'll have to go back to hand-written letters."

"I bet you wouldn't mind that," said Mirren, then could have bitten her tongue at how rude that sounded.

"What do you mean?" he asked reasonably.

"Oh," said Mirren, recovering quite quickly, "because you're looking for a book-finder. So you sound like a . . . a pen-and-paper kind of a person."

"Oh yes!" His laugh was easy. "So I am. Anyway. Yes. Hi. So, I need a book found. And according to this plaque I saw in the British Museum, you're the person to get in touch with."

"Why can't you find it yourself?" said Mirren.

"Well, that's definitely a hard sell," said Jamie. "I thought we'd just negotiate a price."

Mirren was quiet for a minute, then said, "Where do you think it is?"

"It's in my house."

"Are you being funny?"

"Sadly not," said Jamie.

"Are you just a massive weirdo who gets their rocks off by approaching strange women?"

He laughed. "In the *British Museum*?"

"True," said Mirren. "That is more of a London Library thing."

"Look. I have a really big house. And there's a book in it somewhere, left by my grandfather—I think—but I can't track it down."

"You think?"

"It's referred to. In his . . . notes." He sounded rather shifty.

Mirren couldn't help it. She felt a lurch of excitement inside. The adventure she had yearned for, the change to the daily routine. And books, of course; anything to do with books. She tried to keep the curiosity out of her voice.

"What's the book?"

"Ah yeah. Well."

"What?"

"I don't know."

"So you need me to find a book in your house but you don't know what it's called or where it is."

"That's very much about the size of it."

"And you are where . . . ?"

"In northern Scotland."

Mirren looked out of her window, at the long row of identical Victorian terraces, all chopped up into tiny studios and cramped apartments just like hers, small plastic Christmas trees glowing brightly, all the way up and down the extremely long road. The rain was coming down in that sullen way, as if it knows it has to rain on south London in December, obviously, but isn't any happier about it than you are.

This was something new. Something different. Different from work rotas and mortgages and . . . oh. She still had to think about all of that stuff.

"Is there money in it?" said Mirren suddenly. "Is it a paid job? Because I'm a surveyor really. And I'm at work. Or I'm supposed to be."

"Um," said the man. "Well, if you find it, there is."

"Okay, so you're asking me to come to a strange place in the middle of nowhere for free?"

"Oh, I'll get you here." He paused on the line. "You're right. I didn't realise how weird it sounds until you say it out loud. Do you want me to call your boss? Or . . . your dad?"

"I don't think so," she said, wondering what her dad, who lived three streets away and mostly showed her he loved her by coming round and informing her that the studio's electrics were a death-trap and didn't she know that, being a surveyor, would make of such a request.

A lot of her wanted to say yes. But she had to grow up, put away childish ideas of adventures and travel.

"It's a fun idea, but I just can't get away."

It was the right thing to do, she told herself. She had no business gallivanting off to the middle of nowhere in Scotland with a strange man without a mobile signal. Okay, so it was quite an elaborate murder scheme, particularly considering she'd approached him—twice, if you counted the phone call. But actually, that was maybe even worse. Maybe he hadn't even considered murder until she'd kept approaching him.

But she didn't think he was a murderer, not really. She assumed he was just some kind of eccentric book guy, and she couldn't afford to get caught up. Not again. Not when the last time she'd gone looking for a book she'd got her heart broken.

She'd had fun, though . . .

No! Bloody evil Theo Palliser. He'd love this, be all gung ho about it without a second thought. He'd probably have booked the job already. But she couldn't.

She wasn't a book-finder. That wasn't even a job. She'd been lucky once, that was all.

After they hung up, Mirren buried herself in her latest novel, getting caught up in a Christmas romance involving princes, again, and ordered a takeaway even though Takeaway Tuesday was absolutely not a thing, and it wasn't doing her any good, something she was well aware of even as she was ordering it.

SHE SLEPT BADLY and arrived through the filthy grey morning in a bad temper, late for work. Her boss was in an excellent mood, unusually.

"A job came in!" she said triumphantly. "In Scotland. I don't know why they didn't go local, but they asked for you. They want you to go up the week before Christmas."

Mirren's eyes went wide. "Oh yeah?" she said, trying to sound casual.

"You're to go and see if the property would be suitable for an extension, or demolition: actually, it's odd: he wasn't that specific about the details."

Mirren smiled. "Okay."

"And he sent a train ticket."

MIRREN COULDN'T HELP perking up after that. The studio was sad, her mum was busy, she was completely skint and it wouldn't stop raining—but at least she had a job on that looked as if it might be interesting. Which was, in the end, about books. She tried to fathom out what he might mean; perhaps it was a cataloguing and indexing job. Dull, but she could handle that. In her mind's eye she saw a lovely house lined with immaculate bookshelves, beautiful old editions of interesting things. She hoped he wouldn't expect her to be able to price up old editions; she couldn't do that at all. That was much more a Theo Palliser–type job . . . She tried not to think about him, even as her finger was creeping towards the Instagram search button. Which she had told herself never to do. She didn't follow him. But she . . . glanced at him from time to time.

Oh yeah, there he was. His dark hair was tousled over his brow, and he was holding up an ancient Henry Fielding novel and had made a little film about it. He had a tiny following as @thatlondonbookboy where he talked about new books they had in at the shop while looking soulful. It attracted quite a lot of book-loving girls and boys, and made Mirren furiously jealous and annoyed whenever she went to see it, plus she had to use a fake profile so he didn't know she was looking, which was even more of a pain in the arse. He looked great. She shut it down immediately. She had book stuff happening too! Cool stuff!

Mirren looked at the train ticket again. It was for a train she'd never taken before: the Caledonian Sleeper. It travelled overnight from London to the Highlands of Scotland, with sleeping compartments as well as seated carriages. The ticket, alas, did not include a sleeping berth, which was disappointing, as that meant sitting upright for ten hours overnight. It was supposed to be a lovely romantic journey, but that was probably only true if you had a nice bed to sleep in; then it would be lovely. Still, a journey.

Mirren put together a small case and grabbed an aeroplane pillow from her mother. She might ask Jamie McKinnon to fly her home, she mused, if she had any luck. She still wasn't very clear as to what on earth he wanted her to do, but she did find herself lifted out of her slump and gloom, at having something different, out of the routine in her plans.

Mirren remembered how after the pandemic she had made a promise to herself that she wouldn't just go back to her old ways—and then she had. She was too young to be stuck in a rut. This might be terrible—although she didn't think it would be dangerous—but it would be something. Maybe he did in fact want her for some actual quantity surveying—that had crossed her mind. Although that was even creepier. Well, it was a job, and if she felt remotely unsafe she would thwack him with her theodolite and get the hell out of there.

She shut up the studio, and headed off to the station, late at night, with excitement in her heart.

It did not last long.

Chapter Five

There are many beautiful railway stations in Britain. Euston Station, London, is emphatically not one of them.

It is a squat, grey, low-ceilinged box that smells of anxiety. Attempts to brighten it up—colourful pictures of happy blended families in the countryside; pianos everywhere—seem to do absolutely nothing except highlight the dinginess, the greyness of it all, as if the trains themselves still gave off thick black soot.

There are numerous fast-food concessions, and lots and lots of people staring at their phones and then peering upwards again at the departure boards, and if one person twitches as if they've seen the platform being announced, everyone else twitches, too, like a flock of startled birds. When the platforms finally appear, people run as if their lives depend on it, knowing that the crush will leave behind the burdened, the old, and the weak. This makes everyone feel slightly unhappy and ashamed, and these feelings run into the very concrete of the building, giving it a patina of greasy worry that you can sense the second you walk through the low, smeared doors, buses belching in your face as you do so.

On this cold, wet December night, it is freezing and filthy and not a very happy or Christmassy place to be, particularly if, like Mirren, you are standing outside it, currently collapsed in heaving fits of sobs, sobs which can be heard even above the optimistic

Salvation Army carol singers trying to raise some money from sentimental commuters on their way back from their office parties, bestrewn with defeated tinsel.

"But I'm *street-smart*," Mirren was sobbing. "I'm a *Londoner*! I *live* here! I thought those guys were meant to target green tourists who'd just arrived."

It had taken milliseconds. She had exited the tube, been crossing the road, pulling the ticket up on her phone, and—*whoosh*: a darting figure on an electric bike had zoomed straight past her and snatched the phone right out of her hand, disappearing into the mass of wet headlights and taillights bullying their way up the Euston Road.

The friendly Scottish British Transport policeman who was trying to help the crying lady at the end of a very long shift didn't think this wishing of bad luck onto tourists was a particularly charitable response, but he did his best.

"Yes, well," he said, pointing at a poster nearby informing everyone that Thieves Operate in the Area. "We do tell everyone to keep their phones out of sight."

"But I'm at a train station, and my train ticket is on my phone!" snivelled Mirren. "It didn't *feel* like a very controversial thing to be doing."

She sniffed loudly and other people looked at her. She tugged hard on one of the chestnut curls that was poking out from her beanie, an old habit.

"Would you like to come into the office, and we'll file a report?" said the policeman.

"I need my phone! Can you get it back?" implored Mirren desperately. "There's loads of CCTV around here."

"No," said the policeman. "You haven't had your phone stolen very often, have you?"

THE ROOM THEY TAKE you to at Euston if you have had something bad happen to you is, almost unbelievably, even worse than the rest of the station. There is a cheap box of tissues on a scuffed low table, and two chairs which have had the stuffing pulled out of them.

"So do you want to hear the whole story?" said Mirren, sitting down, as the officer took out a notepad.

"Not really," said the policeman. "I was just going to give you this for your insurance."

"But I really need my phone!" said Mirren. "It's like . . . having your daemon guillotined from your body—do you know what I mean?"

"Aye. No' really," said the man, as if he didn't have to listen to this exact same thing a hundred times a day.

"Why won't somebody *stop* it?"

"It's the wee lads on bikes," said the officer sagely. "They're pretty fast."

"You sound like you think they're cool!"

"I did not say 'cool,'" said the man. "I said 'fast.'"

"They should set up electrical tripwires," said Mirren, with unusual verve. Like most readers she was not, day-to-day, a cruel person. "And pull them up at the station exit."

"And catapult the wee laddies out into the traffic," said the man thoughtfully.

"Yes!"

"So. Capital punishment."

"It would stop the thefts," said Mirren sullenly.

"Well, there is that."

They sat in silence for a little longer and she cried on filling out the form for her insurance.

"Oh *God*," said Mirren. "This can't be happening. I have a train to catch. And the ticket's on my phone!"

"I anticipated that," said the policeman, holding up a docket. "Where are you headed?"

"Scotland," said Mirren.

"Och, lovely," he said. "On the sleeper?"

"Will you stop trying to pretend everything's fine?" said Mirren. "I've been robbed, I'm on my way to a new job, and it's all *terrible*."

"Nobody died . . ." said the policeman.

"That's because nobody will listen to my tripwire idea!"

". . . and you're off to Scotland at Christmastime," said the officer, with a friendly smile. "Could be worse."

THE NICE POLICEMAN waited while she canceled everything with her bank on a landline phone they kept for this purpose.

Now, stuck in this filthy, miserable room in Euston, Mirren just wanted to go home. Her studio might be tiny and have no sound insulation and be lying about its mezzanine pretensions, but it was hers. She could lock the door and be alone.

Then she remembered. Her Oyster card and all her contacts and her details and her life and her Uber and everything—*everything* was on her stupid bloody, bloody phone. She'd outsourced her entire brain in about 2009, and now she didn't even know her brother's mobile number, or anyone who could help her out.

But she had a job to do. They were expecting her. She'd better carry on.

"Okay?" said the policeman. "Your train is going soon."

"And I'll be all right without a ticket?" She held up the thin paper docket again.

He nodded his head. "You've got ID, haven't you?"

"They didn't get my wallet, just my phone. As you'd know because, if you wanted, you could just go and find it on Find My Phone."

The policeman cleared his throat. He'd had a very long day and had saved an errant buggy from rolling onto the tracks and arrested a flasher, so he didn't feel entirely useless, but there sure were a lot more disgruntled victims of cycle-by muggings these days.

"Well, let's go down to check in on Platform 1, miss; they'll sort you out. Then you can get picked up the other side, get a new phone, Bob's your uncle. Get a cup of tea on there too. Or maybe a wee dram?"

"Okay," she said, feeling cold and depressed and wretched. "I'll try that."

THE SLEEPER WAS tucked away in the far corner of the station. She looked with envy at the promotional posters of people tucking themselves up in clean white duvets.

The train was petrol blue and stood in its own corner as passengers made their way down the wide concrete gangway. The very first carriage, she saw, was half for seating and half for bikes and luggage. It looked reasonably comfortable as these things went, but she'd still be sitting upright all night, next to a total stranger—the train was always sold out. There were people already in there, mostly men, a pair of women knitting, men with large kit bags next to them, already fast asleep. A family were trying to wrestle a two-year-old and a baby into their seats and Mirren felt sorry for them and then, also, for herself. Whatever was up in Scotland, she was absolutely not going to be in the best state to get into it in the morning. She realised she hadn't checked to see if there was any information about when she was getting picked up. She was getting picked up, yes? She couldn't even remember the name of the stop . . . no, it would be okay. It would come to her, would be a new day. Someone would have a laptop, wouldn't mind her logging in. Perhaps even an adventure, she told herself, rubbing her arms to keep warm.

But nothing felt like an adventure right then. A group of clearly quite inebriated men clambered into the seated carriage and started to unpack cans and clinking bottles from thin plastic bags. Oh God. They were obviously planning a party.

"Thank you," she said to the policeman.

"Good luck," he said, and gave her a wink. "You'll like Scotland, I promise."

"MA'AM?"

The train attendant was in a smart green-blue uniform, with a tartan waistcoat and a box hat.

"Do you have a berth?"

"No," said Mirren sadly, watching the men marching up and down the aisle. She could already hear the baby screaming through the glass. "Just seated, I think."

The attendant took her docket, looked at her driver's licence and looked down at their clipboard for a long time while Mirren shivered. It was utterly freezing on the platform, and she was five hundred miles south of her eventual destination. She wondered if she should have brought a thicker coat than the green peacoat she liked so much.

"Ah yes," they said eventually. "Here you are. Follow me."

And they nodded to the other attendant and set off up the end of the train at quite a clip, Mirren moving quickly to keep up, the air getting colder and colder as they moved towards the outdoors, the train releasing gouts of steam, like a dragon warming up.

The train was extraordinarily long, carriage after carriage. Once past the start, and the seated areas, it grew quieter; Mirren looked sadly through the windows at people opening little doors into cosily appointed cabins, with tartan-carpeted rooms, and beds with crisp, clean duvets on them; tiny sinks and showers; bottles of water and toiletries neatly arrayed. Her heart sank. It looked so warm and cosy, when she was so freezing and sad. She was obviously being taken to another seated carriage, presumably at the other end of the train.

They were almost fully back out in the dark sooty air of the London night by the time they reached the very end of the train and the very last carriage. The final carriage, right before the engine, was not blue at all. It was a dark, rich red. Instead of large, rounded-edged windows, it had an old-fashioned slammable door and windows that could open. It had obviously been attached from a completely different train; it was a different make and model altogether from the sleek new Caledonian Sleeper. Oh, great. Maybe she had to sit all the way on an Underground seat.

"Ma'am," said the attendant, tipping their hat, as the door swung open.

Mirren mounted the steps, carrying her wheelie bag, and turned right into the carriage. She expected an electric door, but there was a handle. Then, when she got inside, she stopped dead.

Chapter Six

"No way . . ." she breathed, out loud. Then blinked twice. It had already been a very confusing evening. Was that . . . ? It couldn't be.

The small door opened out into a carriage with no partitions in it, so in fact it was more like a very long, if narrow, room. It was markedly bigger than Mirren would have imagined. Her brain still couldn't quite take in what she was seeing. But the carriage—room, home, whatever you wanted to call it—was done out like a . . . well, there was no other word for it. It was done out like a library.

There was faded cloth wallpaper on the walls around the windows, which themselves had proper burgundy printed curtains, with tiebacks. And around and above the windows there were books: old books, in careful bookshelves with high lintels, to keep the books safe on sharp corners. There were comfortable, rather chintzy sofas along the windows; an antique armoire for writing at, a baby grand piano at which Mirren stared in disbelief, and a small bar with old crystal decanters. Hunting scenes were on the walls, and brass lights let out a warm glow into the darkness. At the far end, with two chairs set in front of it, was an actual coal fire.

"*No way,*" she breathed.

A man wearing a tie came forward from behind the bar; she hadn't noticed him at first.

"What is this place?" she asked in wonder.

"Welcome to the McKinnon Carriage," said the man. "May I offer you a drink?"

Mirren was already walking forward into this extraordinary room.

"No way!" She was furious that she didn't have her phone to take pictures. "Is this . . . is this for people who are targets of assassins?"

"Ma'am," said the man, smiling indulgently. "Could I offer you a hot snack?"

But Mirren's attention was suddenly stolen by something else: a figure in one of the two seats next to the fire, which, she realised now, was electric, not coal, but remarkably convincing, and certainly gave out a good heat. Compared to the freezing railway platform the warmth was absolutely delicious, and she could think of nothing more appealing than sinking into an armchair with one of the books around the place.

The barman reappeared. "I took the liberty of making you a hot toddy," he said. "Many passengers feel like one when they board, but if you'd like anything else, just ask."

Whatever it was, it smelled like heaven.

"No, no, that's fine," said Mirren, gratefully taking the thick, warm glass and inhaling the mingled odours of whisky, brown sugar, cloves, and lemon gratefully. "Thank you."

The figure in the armchair turned round, and Mirren braced herself to say hello to the strange man from the library.

"Mirren bloody Sutherland! I wondered if I'd see you!"

It was the ghosting bookseller himself. Theo Palliser.

Chapter Seven

In what had already been an extremely surprising week for Mirren, this was perhaps the most surprising of all. Immediately she was furious that he was seeing her with a tearstained face, mascara all down it, a stupid neck pillow—a *neck pillow*—hanging off her, her coat dirty from the station and not warm enough for the weather.

Because she had forgotten how attractive he was. Devastating: so pale and thin, those great big dark eyes, the clever eyebrows permanently arched as if he was on the brink of saying something wicked, which he generally was. When Theo was about, with his courtly manners and sparkling black eyes, his quick wit and taste for adventure made him irresistible to be with. Of course, Mirren had realised painfully over the last long months, she probably wasn't the only one who thought so.

"What are you doing here?" said Mirren.

"Miss Sutherland," he returned, in his overly formal way.

"Why are you even . . ." She looked around. "Wherever the hell we are?"

"Book business," said Theo, smiling. "My uncle sent me."

"I thought you weren't working for him anymore."

"Ah, one last job and all that, you know . . . You're looking well." This was so clearly not the case that Mirren winced. She also suddenly wanted to say, *Why didn't you call me? Where the hell have you been?*—but instead she found herself holding on to her drink hard as, with a judder, the train started up and slowly pulled out of the station.

"What *is* this?" she said. "Am I being kidnapped?"

"I know," said Theo. "Isn't it marvellous?"

"But what *is* going on?"

"It's Jamie McKinnon," said Theo, as if this explained everything.

"Yes, *and*?" said Mirren.

"You don't know?"

"Wikipedia was not very useful."

Theo smiled. "No, it wouldn't be. That family is pretty good at keeping itself out of the papers."

"Okay, stop being so supercilious and posh," said Mirren, properly cross now. "Yes, blah blah, you know posh people."

Theo's uncle ran an incredibly smart bookshop in Kensington, acquired extraordinarily expensive books, often by dubious means, and had treated Mirren like something unfortunate he'd stepped in. Theo was his penniless nephew who relied on him for room and board—which also meant sometimes carrying out his dirty work.

"That's not . . . well," said Theo. "I don't know this guy. Except by reputation."

"Which is . . . guy who owns a mad train?"

Theo looked around. "Oh yeah. It's pretty cool, eh?"

"You're pretending to be unimpressed when basically this is JAMES BOND VILLAIN stuff."

"I am not," said Theo, smiling. "I am very impressed. I'd heard it existed, but I couldn't imagine they'd still let it run."

"What even is it?"

"Well, Jamie's family used to be incredibly wealthy. Owned half the Highlands."

"That sounds like a political minefield."

"Oh, well, absolutely, yes, quite right. Until Jamie's grandfather, a great learned scholar. He gave away a lot of the land and tried to make things right—but he kept the books and the libraries; he was a big fan of that. So basically, the family was left with a lot of books but without a bean. And the grandfather was quite *tonto*, estranged from Jamie's mother, let the estate run to rack and ruin. He died recently, practically a pauper."

"Oh," said Mirren. "But they still have the train . . ."

"Yes—private carriages used to be quite common. So the family allowed the railway to build through their land a hundred and fifty years ago if and only if they got a halt of their own, and a carriage at their disposal, for as long as the railway ran. And I suppose, one hundred and fifty years later, they still do."

"They just summon a train carriage, like getting a cab?"

"Seems about the size of it."

Mirren couldn't help breaking out into a huge grin. Deciding she would reckon with Theo's behaviour later, she plonked herself into one of the large, comfortable armchairs.

Theo for his part looked exactly as he had done a year ago: thin, tall, and pale, with deep-set black eyes, rather like a vampire if that vampire wore Adidas Gazelles and a slightly cheeky expression. Mirren informed herself quite sternly that he was a rat, and she was absolutely not under any circumstances going to find him attractive again. She sipped her drink carefully and warmed her freezing feet. The toddy was delicious.

"So, we just sit here all night?"

"Oh no," said Theo, rather smugly. "Go and have a look."

Past the fire was a sliding door through which was a further part of the carriage, with a narrow corridor and compartments, like in old rolling stock, except here the compartments were neatly made-up single beds; there were three compartments, each with two beds. Fresh white linen and a water bowl were laid out; at the end of the corridor was a bathroom with, astonishingly, a proper cast-iron bath in it. Mirren whistled.

By the time she returned to the main section of the carriage, a table had been set up with white linen. Theo was already there, and she noticed he was wearing a suit and tie.

"You're dressed for dinner?"

"Of course," he said with some surprise.

Mirren glanced down at her dirty shirt that she'd been wearing all day and rubbed her tearstained face. "Okay," she said. "Give me five minutes."

SHE UNPACKED HER suitcase on one of the pristine white-counterpaned beds, steadying herself as the train swayed along the tracks. To be inside both a house and a train at the same time was a discombobulating but enchanting experience. She stared out of the window in the dark, seeing, briefly, a lit-up platform, with "Watford" just visible as it flashed past. This was not at all the way she normally thought of the signage for Watford. She wondered what people thought when they saw the carriage. Or perhaps they didn't think a thing about it, didn't even notice. Perhaps there were private trains travelling all over the railway network all the time. The royal family had one, she knew. Maybe lots of people did, making their own way in the dead of night. The room had a faded tartan carpet on the floor and dull green walls, the same lowlight brass wall lamps, and real dark red curtains with tassels on them. *Goodness*, Mirren thought, looking longingly at the bed. She could get used to this.

She washed quickly and redid her makeup and pulled out the only dress she had brought, a lovely brick-red one, which she had figured could work for a Christmas event or a formal business meeting depending on what exactly was required. She pulled down her curly hair and added a bit of lipstick, then crossly took it off again. She wasn't putting it on for this guy, who last year had been absolutely charming, absolutely as interested in books as she was—and then had walked off without a second glance, back to his rich family and cosseted life.

THERE WAS A wonderful smell when she reentered the main salon, the train jolting quietly along. She found herself wondering how the drunk lads' party was going on, then found she didn't care, because, here, tinkling music was playing and the table was laid with white linen and it was all so lovely she could cry, again, but for different reasons from how her evening had started out.

The barman, who was clearly, in fact, a butler, drew out her chair. "Madam."

She glanced at Theo, half grinning, but his face was fairly straight; no doubt he was a bit more used to this kind of thing. Because he was an entitled doughnut, she told herself sternly. She had just forgotten what great hair the entitled doughnut had: a bit too long, sticking up here and there, little sideburns which might be out of fashion but she couldn't help liking them anyway. Argh. She had to stop this.

"Some wine, madam?" said the butler, uncorking a crystal decanter.

Well, that was well known to help her make good decisions, Mirren thought with a sigh.

"Yes, please."

THE DELICIOUS SMELL turned out to be French onion soup.

"You can have another course if you want it," said Theo, "but it's after nine."

"No, no, this is fine," said Mirren, taking in the delicious smell. It was covered in toasted French bread with melted Emmental and masses of black pepper. "Oh my goodness." She sighed. "This is so good."

"Isn't it?" said Theo. "It's basically a late-night cheese-on-toast delivery system."

She smiled. The butler came and refilled their glasses and set the decanter down between them.

"There is cranachan in the fridge, and help yourself to anything, of course," he said, indicating the bar area. "But if there's nothing further?"

"Thank you," they both said, and watched as he left the carriage, back into the main section of the train. For a moment as the door opened there was a noisy rattling sound of the wind, then all was sealed and quiet again.

They looked at one another.

"Did he just . . . completely vanish?" said Mirren.

"Oh yeah, I think every time they have one of these journeys, the butler has to throw himself off the moving train rather than get in the way."

"Oh, stop it," said Mirren, smiling despite herself.

She finished the soup, which was warming, with a good slug of brandy in it, and found herself scouring the bowl with the very good bread. Theo looked at her, smiling.

"You were hungry."

She frowned. "I'm not, usually, this time of night. But I've had a tough day."

She explained about the mugging and Theo made sympathetic noises in all the right places, even though Mirren was still thinking, *Well, that guy stole my phone from me. You stole my self-confidence, my faith in myself as someone worth dating.*

"So," she said, abruptly changing the subject. "Tell me about this missing book."

"Absolutely not," he said, sipping his wine with an amused

expression on his face. There was a rattle at the windows and Mirren glanced over. Hail.

"How can you lose a book in your own house?"

He shrugged, infuriatingly straight-faced. "Oh, well," he said, "you know . . ."

"I *don't* know."

"Well, that's good," said Theo suddenly. "Stop you getting to it first and taking all the credit."

"What?" said Mirren.

"Nothing," said Theo. "Nice plaque with your name on it at the British Museum, by the way. You know, for the book we both found."

"You didn't find it, I did! You'd given up and gone home!"

"I helped!"

"Well, they didn't ask me for a line about people who helped!"

"Would it have made any difference if they had?"

They sat there in silence for a few more seconds as the train's whistle blew.

"You never contacted me," said Mirren in a small voice. "You ghosted me."

"I was getting round to it," said Theo. "Then, I didn't want to interrupt your publicity tour."

"I didn't do a publicity tour!"

"Hope you did well out of it."

"Are you kidding? I waited for you to call; you didn't. I messaged you; you didn't get back to me. There's a word for that, Theo."

He looked sulky. "Well, I didn't know everyone was going to make such a fuss of you."

"Oh, boo-hoo," said Mirren. "And it wasn't a fuss. It was one picture."

"And a plaque."

"I'll make you a plaque."

There was a further silence.

"I see they didn't give you enough money to buy a new coat."

"Oh my God, shut up!" Then, after a moment: "No, they didn't."

"Well, that's one good thing."

"Oh yeah, thanks, yes, I'm still skint and I'm glad you're glad. I thought you were working in a bookshop anyway."

"I am," said Theo. "This is an extra job."

"For your uncle?"

He shrugged.

She looked at him again in the soft light. He looked even hotter when he was pouting, if that was even possible.

"So you don't know anything about this book either," she said.

He wouldn't answer either way, which she took to mean he absolutely definitely didn't know any more than she did.

"Fine," she said finally. "I found the last book first; I'll find this one too."

"Good for you," he said. Then he picked up his glass and wandered over to the nearest shelf, selecting an Edward Gibbon with a look of happy recognition and taking it to the armchair next to the fire. Obviously their conversation was over.

Mirren looked around to see if there was anywhere obvious to tidy up the plates—there wasn't. Then she remembered that this was a stupid posh world for stupid posh people who never considered even for a second clearing their own bloody plates, so she simply left things where they were and headed off for bed without saying good night.

Chapter Eight

It was, it turned out, quite difficult not to sleep after a delicious meal, a glass of wine, and a heavenly bed with its own rocking motion, and the comforting sound of *clickety clack, clickety clack* fading the world away. Mirren sank into oblivion in the dark carriage, the mattress firm yet yielding, the pillows perfectly soft.

At first, when she woke up, she wasn't sure where she was. Then the strangeness of the night and all her unanswered questions came back; the train was still moving, and she quickly nipped to the toilet and drank a glass of fresh cold water, before pulling up the blind. It was pitch dark outside, but she could feel from the glass that it was sharply cold. She squinted past her own reflection and caught glimpses of frosted white in the bushes beside the tracks and wondered where they were.

She sniffed—she could smell fresh coffee, and suddenly she wanted one more than anything, even if she did have to walk past stupid bloody Theo to get to it.

She was tempted by the bath, but coffee came first, so she threw on a jumper and jeans and headed into the main salon, as if she slept in private train carriages all the time.

Amazingly, the butler was back, looking immaculate; the room was cleared and the table was laid.

"Breakfast, madam?"

The newspapers had been picked up at Inverness, and *The Scotsman*, *The Times*, and the *Inverness Courier* sat, immaculate, on the side of the table. Theo was already behind the *Racing Post* as the butler set down a huge plate of bacon, sausage, tomatoes, and mushrooms in front of him, and he grunted his thanks.

"How do you stay so skinny?" said Mirren, hoping that at least they could be on speaking terms this morning.

"Someone found a priceless book and didn't cut me in," grunted Theo, and so she decided just to ignore him again and enjoy her breakfast of yellow-yolked soft-boiled eggs and lashings of coffee and hot buttered toast, which she did, enormously. Gradually, the first streaks of pink appeared across the sky and the stars began to disappear in the east, through the windows to the right of the train. Mirren watched, fascinated. The empty world was frosted, bright pink; they cut through vast plains; passed mountains dimly outlined against the dawn; trundled over viaducts and across bridges on vast lochs, ice just about visible, shifting in the water. It was an extraordinary sunrise. Mirren was again regretting the loss of her phone.

As the sun laid its first late winter rays across the snowcapped peaks, Mirren felt the train finally slowing beneath her feet and felt sorry. She wouldn't mind moving in permanently.

She glanced out of the window to take a look at the station name, but, as far as she could tell, they weren't anywhere. It wasn't a station, just a small platform, a halt, in the middle of nowhere, fields full of Highland coos with their twisted horns and bright orange hair; the harvest a distant memory, frost twinkling fields lying fallow, waiting for the old year to die and a new world to come, but not now; not for a long time.

The sun was almost up now, or as up as it got in December, which was hardly at all, and not for very long, but the ice danced like diamonds, making even the muddy ruts beautiful. Mirren watched as a pair of peregrines circled in the air. She had never felt further from London. There was the occasional stone farmhouse here and there but nothing you could reasonably call a town, or even a village; they truly were nowhere. Yet the train absolutely was stopping.

"Madam," said the butler's voice, and she saw to her horror that he was standing there with their bags, hers all packed up. She made a quick mental inventory of what he might have seen, but his face was impassive.

"Okay, thanks," she said nervously, going pink, to Theo's evident amusement. He took a last bite of sausage, then stood up in a leisurely way.

"Isn't this our stop?" said Mirren, already moving towards the door.

"It's *our* stop," said Theo, with some amusement. "They'll wait for us. That's the point."

Mirren felt annoyed with him all over again for being so supercilious.

"I can't believe I'm such scum I was raised without my own train," she said as she thanked the butler and wondered if she should tip him, then remembered she couldn't because she didn't have any cash, and then got even more annoyed with herself when Theo subtly did so.

Well, there was nothing to be done about that. She took a deep breath, pulled on her thin coat and a scarf in anticipation of the freezing air, and waited as the train powered down with a hiss. They unlocked the doors, and she found herself stepping down on to the halt, and into a whole new world.

Chapter Nine

With some clunking and kerfuffle, the train moved off, back the way they had come. They were obviously the very end of the line. To her surprise Mirren noticed that on the end of their special carriage was a small viewing platform—for nicer days, she supposed, or daytime trips where it could be attached to the end. She sighed watching it go. What a lovely thing.

The fading noise of the train disappearing left them completely alone in the crisp white day, and Mirren finally drew back to take in her surroundings.

The halt was made of old, pale wood with steps up to the height of the train doors, one on the up line and one on the down, with a wooden crossing point on the lines that didn't look remotely safe to Mirren. She turned slowly in a full circle. The view was sensational. Ahead, towards the mountains, were great patches of almost entirely faded winter colours: burgundy, almost blue. A dark thatch of evergreens sat in their neatly curated rows on the hillsides. A huge loch lay ahead, with birds circling idly above it, looking for their breakfast.

The side near to where they were standing was more cultivated. A road, completely empty at the moment, wound its way uphill through walled fields of sheep and Highland coos, into rolling hills much gentler and lower than the great mountains to the west. Just in the distance a house—a rather large house by the looks of things—was nestled between them, and, beyond that, glinting gold in the early morning light, was the North Sea.

Mirren had been to Scotland in wintertime before and had thought she was prepared, but she wasn't. She zipped up her pea-coat and tucked in her scarf, and plonked on her beanie, but it wasn't enough.

Apart from Theo, who looked like a man who wished he still smoked (he still carried a Zippo with him, in case the opportunity ever arose to be gallant to a model), there was not another soul to be seen, just the distant calls of birds and the rustling of the wind through the trees. Mirren took a deep breath. Even though it was cold, the air was fresh and clear, sharp and lovely. She took another, and gradually felt her shoulders unfurl just a little. She didn't have her phone to take a photo or talk to people or post anywhere—but, somehow, that felt all right. As though she was in a world out of time. Nobody, it occurred to her, knew she was here. Well, her mum had her address in case of emergencies, and she'd told her friends she was going to the Highlands, and work knew, she supposed. But really, nobody on earth knew *exactly* where she was right now. What a strange night had just passed. She felt, she realised, alive. For the first time in a long while.

Ignoring Theo, she looked up towards the road, not even worrying for once about whether they were getting collected or whether they were stuck out here.

"I wonder if we're stuck out here," said Theo, staring at his phone, and shaking it, as if that would help him get a signal. "Because I would have some doubts about Uber."

But at that very moment Mirren exclaimed and pointed. Along the narrow track road that led up the valley and into the rolling hills before the house was a tiny, moving dot, heading straight for them.

Chapter Ten

The tall, diffident chap Mirren had met in London appeared much more at home on this territory, as he pulled up in a filthy old Land Rover with canvas sides. A small black-and-white sheepdog leapt out like a flash, and Mirren oohed and smiled.

"Hello, sweetie pie! Hello, gorgeous!!"

The dog didn't approach her at all, and Mirren crouched down. "Hello, lovely!" She beckoned.

"Actually, he's a working dog," said Jamie.

Mirren fell silent.

"Hi," said Jamie, clearing his throat. "I see you guys made it."

Mirren was feeling squashed, but she still couldn't help herself. "Your train is awesome," she said.

Jamie smiled. "I know. We don't have a lot of perks left, but . . ."

"It's amazing, having a whole carriage to yourself!"

"Well, they got a big streak of our land, so I guess it works out. And you must be Theo Palliser?"

Theo stuck out his hand. "Nice to see you."

"I thought you two knew each other?" said Mirren, and they both turned round to look at her. Jamie was broader, with sandy brown hair, and a little older; Theo a little taller, with the black hair and the pallor. He didn't even look embarrassed.

"Oh, we've been at some of the same events."

"Have we?" said Jamie.

Mirren felt quite pleased. Obviously this was not going to be as much of a shoo-in for Theo as he'd thought.

"Well, anyway," said Theo, rubbing his long fingers together. "It's pretty chilly—shall we?"

INSIDE THE LAND ROVER was not noticeably warmer than outside. The dog took a crouching position by the open flaps at the back, scanning the horizon, it seemed, for any threats it might need to intercept. Mirren looked at him rather longingly. He was such a beautiful creature; she would love to pet his soft fur and scritch behind his ears, but she assumed that wouldn't go down well at all.

"What's his name?" she asked.

"Roger," said Jamie briefly.

"Roger the sheepdog? Are you sure?"

"All our sheepdogs are called Roger," said Jamie. "Since about 1840, I think."

"What . . . one dies, and you call another one Roger?"

"Yes," said Jamie. "They're working animals; they just need to be identifiable."

"Oh my God," said Mirren, quite horrified. "Poor Roger."

Roger turned his head immediately.

"I mean, I suppose 'Roger' to him just means 'dog,'" mused Mirren.

"I think that's how all dogs' names work," said Theo annoyingly.

Mirren ignored him and vowed to pet the dog if she got half a chance, although, given the dog's stoic expression as it surveyed the mountains behind it, this would be approximately never.

She looked out of the side window as they drove. The single-track road weaved from side to side up the hills until they got to a pair of vast rusted iron gates, held together with what looked like a cheap bicycle lock. Mirren watched, puzzled, as Jamie leapt out and opened it, and creaked back the great gates. Atop a pair of weather-beaten, moss-covered stone pillars were two vast, chipped stone pineapples. Mirren glanced at them.

"What's with the pineapples??"

"I'm not sure," said Jamie, "but they weigh about a billion kilos, so we're stuck with them unless I magically inherit a crane."

The road wound upwards, meandering up and through into a forest of bare-limbed oak trees, until they were perched on an outcrop. It had obviously been deliberately designed that way, as the road could have gone straight across from the gates, but from here, from a clearing through the trees, the road head was framed, and there, dead centre, was the house itself.

Jamie pulled up, and Roger jumped up and hared towards it, a manoeuvre he was obviously used to.

Mirren didn't want to say anything to betray her absolute astonishment at the vision ahead. She wanted to make it look as though this was nothing to her. She snuck a glance at Theo, who was looking nonchalant, although that was his default expression.

But this—this was something. When Jamie had said "my house," she hadn't for a moment imagined anything like this. *No wonder*, she thought suddenly. No wonder he couldn't find a book in his own house. Because it wasn't a house. It was a castle.

For a second, situated between two deep hills, with the sea unfolding behind them, it looked, to Mirren, like Cair Paravel, the citadel of Narnia. It was brown and white, and covered in small crenellated towers. The scale of it was hard to tell from this angle; it seemed to go on and on.

"Bloody hell." Theo whistled, and Mirren gave him a quick glance. He wasn't so unimpressed, then.

"Yeah," said Jamie. "Welcome to Forres. I promise you, this is very much the best view."

The icy sunlight glinted off the windows. How many were

there? Dozens and dozens. Mirren wondered who cleaned them. The main body of the house was square, but there was a long line of buildings behind that, some of which appeared to have been added as an afterthought. The windows were diamond-paned and ran around the turrets, following the spiral stairs. There were two square gatehouses at the front, in plain grey stone, linked by a bridge over the road, before the main building itself, and the white section was covered by a variety of low stone buildings: stables, barns, and cottages. It was more than a castle: it was practically a town. From the tallest of the turrets a Scottish saltire flew proudly, but from another was a long, fluttering pennant in red and yellow, following the breeze out to sea. Mirren couldn't take her eyes off it. It was devastatingly romantic. Her eyes followed it longingly. Imagine. Imagine having a tower with a pennant streaming, like a princess in a storybook. It was glorious.

"It's amazing," she said breathily.

"From here," said Jamie, smiling ruefully. He looked at them, shy suddenly. "I just . . . I suppose I just wanted to show it to you from its best angle. It's all downhill from here."

"When did you inherit?" asked Theo. Mirren was surprised to hear a pitying tone in his voice.

"This summer," said Jamie.

"And you're the eldest? Or just the eldest son?"

"Both. Also, literally nobody else wanted it."

"They must do!" interjected Mirren in astonishment, and both men looked at her.

"Nope," said Jamie. "They want me to sell it and get all the cash. Nobody wants it. But nobody wants to be the one responsible for letting it go."

"But why would you let it go?" said Mirren, still caught in the romance and the dream of it.

"Well," said Jamie. "Well. You'll see."

And, rather sullenly, he turned the key, the Land Rover sparked into life, and they rejoined the road and bumped their way up to the castle lodge.

THE CLOSER THEY got, the more Mirren stared. The palace—how on earth could Jamie call it a house, that was utterly ridiculous—loomed overhead as they drew closer.

It also became increasingly apparent what kind of state the place was in.

The window frames were peeling, the stone was chipped, and the pointing had completely come away on the stone buildings. The bridge itself looked scruffy and half falling down. The castle that looked white and glowing from far away—a glowing citadel between two hills—was dirty old white close-up. There were abandoned vehicles in the gravel, which had weeds growing up all around them. A dried-up fountain in the middle of the driveway, and the windows, close-up, answered Mirren's unspoken question as to who cleaned them: clearly nobody did.

Mirren frowned. With her surveyor hat on, this place wouldn't comply with building regulations. She didn't think it looked structurally sound; great cracks ran up the side of the exterior. She picked a section right off the wall and it crumbled in her fingers. Mind you, old buildings were built of sterner stuff. Some of the new builds she worked with would blow over in a strong wind. If it had stood for several hundred years, you were probably all right today. Even so, she wished she had a hard hat.

"You moved in?" said Theo.

Jamie nodded.

"Where were you before?"

"Edinburgh," said Jamie. "I worked in the Botanic Gardens."

"You're a gardener?" said Mirren. She thought that was quite cool, but it came out as if she was being sarcastic, and Jamie frowned.

Theo tutted at her. "He was biding his time," he said to Mirren, as if she should have known this, and then gestured towards the huge grounds. "Bringing back your expertise?"

Jamie grimaced slightly and didn't answer.

"And you live here now?" went on Mirren, embarrassed that he thought she'd called him the gardener.

Jamie pulled the Land Rover to a halt. "Well. Yeah. It was . . ." He looked awkward. "I'm the heir. I have to." He jumped out onto the gravel. "We spent all our time here when we were children. And now it's mine."

He didn't sound remotely happy about it.

Chapter Eleven

The front door creaked as if someone were streaming a sound effects playlist, a proper horror film screech. Mirren laughed rather nervously; Jamie didn't seem to notice.

They entered a vast hallway, with grey flagstones on the ground and a huge crevasse in the wall to their right. Above them, a minstrels' gallery, a long mezzanine space that ran the entire width of the hallway. The room itself was huge, triple height. Mirren smelled the slightly fusty but not unpleasant air and glanced upwards. The ceiling held a vast chandelier, shrouded in cobwebs. It was hard to see all the way up, but it looked as though, once upon a time, the ceiling had been painted a deep blue, and there were still the faintest traces of painted-on stars that must once have been bright gold.

"Wow," Mirren said again, then told herself to stop doing that. She closed her mouth; she was not a codfish.

A small side door opened, and a young woman came through, beaming. She was short and round and naturally pretty, with a large bust, round pink cheeks, and masses of soft russet-coloured hair. Her huge brown eyes looked amused.

"Master!" she said happily, then, at Mirren's shocked look, laughed.

"*Don't*, Bonnie!" said Jamie. "It's not funny."

"I know," said the girl, but the smile still played around her lips. "I'm just trying it out for size."

"Please don't," said Jamie. "It's already weird enough."

At this her face turned sad, and she went and stood beside him. "I know," she said softly. "I was just trying to lighten the mood."

She was wearing a plain black dress and had a tea towel slung over her shoulder, Mirren noticed. Did she work here? She seemed extremely confident if she did. Was she staff? Were there lots of staff? Maybe they hadn't noticed the windows.

Bonnie turned round with a slightly forced smile. "Welcome! Are you the crack discovery team?"

Theo, charming as ever, stuck out his hand. "Lovely to meet you," he said, smiling.

"I'm not sure if we're exactly a team," said Mirren, which came out as rather peevish and awkward, particularly as at the same moment Jamie said, "Yes!" Bonnie just looked confused.

"Well, welcome to McKinnon house," she said. Her voice was a lovely, musical burr. "Did you eat on the train?"

They both nodded.

"Then I won't make a second breakfast unless you're really hungry. But come, bring your bags in. I'll show you to your rooms and then I'll put the kettle on."

They followed her through the side door, and down a long passageway, with doors off the left-hand side and several large, square white shapes on the walls. Mirren looked at them curiously.

"Sold off?" said Theo sympathetically. Jamie nodded, looking sad.

"They were just all your face, going back four hundred years," added Bonnie cheerfully. "We'll simply take a new picture of you with a wig on. There's a wig box in the East Attic. If the mice haven't got to it," she added thoughtfully.

"Let us assume," said Jamie heavily, "that the mice have got to it."

Mirren wondered what their relationship was. The girl was obviously informal, almost sisterly. But she appeared to be working here? A girlfriend? Surely not, with the tea towel. But it was very difficult to tell.

Jamie carried on down another set of steps, then turned into a turret spiral staircase that seemed to go up three storeys; Mirren had completely lost her bearings. They emerged on to an extraordinarily long corridor, the walls covered in an odd red grosgrain material, which seemed to vanish into the distance. It felt cold and unloved and smelled musty, like a huge but spooky hotel.

"Wow," said Mirren again, but less emphatically. The other thing she noticed was that, here, each side of the corridor was lined with just one thing—bookshelves. Miles of them. There were bookshelves as far as the eye could see, overflowing with books. Mirren and Theo, bibliophiles both, immediately glanced at the piles. Everything was ramshackle, piled up without much order to it. The books were of all types: old law registers, hunting manuals, novels, memoirs, shopping lists, all of it thrown in hugger-mugger.

"Bloody hell," said Theo, looking up. "There's no organisation here at all."

"Nope," said Bonnie, reasonably cheerfully.

"We'll get to that," said Jamie hastily.

Bonnie came to the middle of the corridor, where there was a grand pair of double doors on the left, opening towards the front of the house. She flung them open, and Mirren and Theo moved forward, only to stop in amazement. They were standing once again on a gallery level above a vast room: a library.

Light streamed in through double-height windows, even from the ice-grey day beyond. A gilt spiral staircase led down from the gallery level to the endless units of shelving down below, with several fine desks dotted here and there. The books here were older, mostly hardbound, but, Mirren could tell from glancing to one side, as hugger-mugger as before, with no rhyme or reason applied that might explain why, for instance, an early set of Dickens was sitting next to a handwritten recipe book from the nineteenth century, which was in turn against a collection of 1970s Rupert the Bear and Jack Frost annuals, which frankly Mirren would happily have sat down and read right then and there, were it not so chilly in the library that she could see her breath in front of her face.

"The library," said Theo, impressed.

"No," said Bonnie. "The East Library."

They both looked at her, and she smiled her warm smile. "Oh, aye, you've got your work cut out. He was quite the man for books, the old laird."

This sounded like the understatement of the year.

They left the East Library, and continued down to the end of the corridor, where they went up and down various sets of steps, each with bookshelves, or simply piles, until they found themselves in another endless corridor, and it was here that Bonnie opened up two doors, opposite each other.

"How will we ever find our way back?" said Theo.

"You'll figure it out," said Bonnie, smiling.

Mirren followed her into the first of the rooms, on the right. It was filled with bookcases, naturally, with a huge Audubon book on birds on top of the pile on the low antique table. But her eye was caught instead by—it couldn't be—she couldn't stop smiling—a genuine four-poster bed.

"No way," she said. "I'm sleeping here?" Then, quickly, "Oh, this is nice," as she didn't want to imply that she didn't sleep in four-posters all the time. Secretly, though, she wanted to run up to it and bounce on top of it. A real four-poster bed! It had dark red sheets and hanging curtains, like the walls outside. A little dusty, perhaps, but she could handle that.

Bonnie didn't seem to have noticed her excitement. "I'd draw the curtains on it," she said. "Gets a bit fresh in here."

Mirren looked around. The room was absolutely freezing, but the windows were jammed shut—warped, she guessed correctly.

"Is it okay to . . . put the heating on?"

Bonnie smiled and Mirren realised what else was strange about the room: it didn't have a radiator.

"Aye, whenever you like," she said, nodding at the fireplace, which had a pile of wood next to it. "I'll start it off for you," she said, seeing Mirren's horrified face. "Don't worry about it. And I'll damp it at night."

The wardrobe, when opened, proved also to be full of books, plus a tiny electric heater, of uncertain vintage and frayed cord, which, in the huge room, with its long, moth-eaten curtains and uncarpeted boards, apart from a beautiful rug in front of the fire, looked about as useful as trying to heat the room with a hair dryer. Mirren figured she'd be better off with the actual fire.

"Thanks," she said.

"Do you want me to leave you to get settled in?"

"No! I'll never find my way back again!"

"Fair enough."

Theo's room, on the opposite side of the corridor, was much the same, only without the four-poster, and rather smaller, and it looked over an internal courtyard, choked with weeds. Mirren felt slightly superior, until she noticed Theo had a duvet rather than ancient, dusty blankets.

There was one bathroom, and it was miles away, at the end of the corridor. You would have to absolutely tear up there in the cold. Mirren regretted not having had a bath on the train that morning. The bath here was fitted with a handheld shower attachment made of rubber that went over the taps and didn't seem remotely up to the job of cleaning a person. There were two small thread-bare towels on the rack and the cracked black-and-white tile floor looked uninviting, but, as Mirren's eye followed the inevitable book pile leading up to a mullioned window high in the wall, she saw that the room looked out over the towers of the castle, pen-nants fluttering, and over to the steel-grey sea beyond. It was a vista of mind-boggling wild beauty. Mirren could almost imagine an old wooden sailing ship bearing men back from the rich worlds of Scandinavia along with wool and silk and pottery.

"It's lovely." She sighed.

Bonnie nodded. "Come on, I'll take you back downstairs for a brew."

Mirren still couldn't get her bearings. They went down a differ-ent set of stairs, set behind a door that was inlaid into wood pan-elling and hard to spot, and then moved into what was clearly a different part of the building. The ceilings were lower, the windows smaller, now looking out onto the forest they had come through on the way.

A city girl her entire life, Mirren didn't know if she had ever looked through a window like this before. There was not a single sign of modern life in the frame: fields and paths and forests and nothing else as far as the eye could see; not a car, nor a roof; not an aerial or a power cable. Somewhere out there must be the railway line, but it was invisible from here. She had never been further away from . . . well, everything. She instinctively reached for her phone to take a photograph before remembering that she didn't have it, which added to the unreality of the entire thing.

A large open door and a further three steps downwards—there seemed to be odd steps up and down all over the place—opened out into a very large kitchen, with a scullery leading off it. It was absolutely huge, with a vast scrubbed wooden table, and a sink the size of a trough. There was a large old range, and as Mirren drew closer to its cosy heat, with her hands outstretched, she realised quite how chilled she had become in the house.

"You'll get chilblains," said Bonnie and Jamie at the same time, then shared a look.

"What are those?" said Mirren.

"I don't really know," said Jamie. "Bonnie's grandmother used to say it all time."

There were dressers full of more crockery than Mirren had ever seen in her life: dozens and dozens of patterned plates, side plates, eggcups, toast racks. There were nine teapots displayed on a shelf and six silver coffeepots. Bonnie pulled one down.

"Sit," she said. "From the look on your face"—she was talking to Mirren—"Jamie hasn't explained a thing, has he?"

Jamie raised his hands. "They just got here!"

Mirren shook her head. "Not really . . . something about . . ." She wasn't sure how much Bonnie would know, and closed her mouth. It might not be something she should be talking about.

An ancient kettle started whistling on the stove, and Bonnie took it off and filled the teapot. She also opened one of the myriad doors on the range and withdrew a plate of warm shortbread, cut into fingers, lightly sprinkled with sugar. Even though Mirren had had a huge breakfast hardly anytime before, the smell was irresistible, and Bonnie pushed the plate towards her as they all sat around one corner of the vast table, Mirren gradually warming up.

"Come on, then, Master Jamie," she said, in her slightly teasing tone. "You tell it."

Chapter Twelve

"So," said Jamie, after he'd demolished a second piece of short-bread, "this house has been in my family—on and off—for, well, hundreds of years. A proper long time. They had some wars and whatnot and this and that . . ."

"Is this shorthand for 'killed lots of peasants'?" asked Mirren, and was silenced with a look.

"I'm not saying *here is our perfectly acquired fortune*," said Jamie. "One, because there is no such thing as a perfectly acquired fortune, and two, because we don't have any money anymore. But regardless, a couple of generations ago, the war did huge things to the staff and upkeep of the house. It just became impossible to maintain."

Bonnie nodded at this. "There used to be fifty people living here, running this place," she said. "But . . ." She raised her hands. She must, Mirren thought, be the last member of staff.

"We get a bit from letting people come and visit," said Jamie. "But most people come and see it and go, *Oh my God it's freezing, oh what a shame it's falling apart, seriously, £10, I don't think so, what are all these books doing here?* Our Tripadvisor ratings are awful. Then we failed a health and safety check."

"I am not surprised," said Mirren.

"Those reviewers were evil," said Bonnie darkly.

"They can't all have been evil," said Jamie. "I don't . . . I mean, eight hundred people can't all be born evil just because they gave us mediocre reviews on Tripadvisor."

"Yes, they can," said Bonnie stoutly.

"Anyway, after the war, everyone was so miserable—we lost four men off the estate, three under-gardeners and a butler."

"Those were Goodwin boys," said Bonnie.

"That was nothing compared to the first war. They lost over a dozen then. There's a memorial up by the maze."

"You have a *maze*?" said Mirren.

Jamie shrugged, in a kind of a *yeah, we have a maze but it's nothing really I'm embarrassed about it, to be honest* kind of a way.

"Anyway," he said. "My great-grandfather was really knocked by the war. And the house had been requisitioned anyway; they trained a lot of soldiers here. He was in the air force but he did his leg in and they shipped him home and he was stuck here. He kept track of all of them, or tried to. It was very bad for him. He had . . . I suppose what you'd call a nervous breakdown afterwards. The army gave back the house but they'd left it in a hell of a state, and there were no staff to come back. The men who'd come back from the war—they wanted better jobs, or to go to college or do something else. And some didn't come back at all."

He took a long swig of his tea and Bonnie topped up the kettle.

"He died . . . he died." He clearly didn't want to say any more about that. "And then my grandfather inherited. He was only young; he didn't know what to do, I don't think. I only knew him when he was old. I just know things got worse and worse. He got into book-collecting. We'd always been readers and I think he started selling off bits and pieces of the estate. He couldn't afford to look after it, and taxes kept going up and up. He'd sell something, like a painting, or some china, but then he'd buy books. Loads of them. It started off kind of famous books or good books, but it seemed to get more and more compulsive . . ."

"Like being a hoarder," said Mirren suddenly. "Except he never ran out of space."

"Yes, I think that's exactly it. It was never quite this bad, was it?" he said, glancing at Bonnie, whose face looked gentle. "Not when we were bairns."

"I don't know," said Bonnie. "My ma would complain about it then. Maybe we just didn't notice it."

"Maybe we liked it," said Jamie, and they shared a look.

"Aye, we did," said Bonnie.

"Forts, endless bloody forts," said Jamie. "And Esme kept making Wendy houses and boys weren't allowed in."

"I wasn't allowed in either," said Bonnie with a snort, and Mirren let them reminisce. *Upstairs, downstairs,* she thought, and wondered if there was more than that.

"Well, anyway," said Jamie. "He got married to my grandmother." Another look shared with Bonnie. "Who was, uh . . . anyway. And they had my mother, just before their marriage broke up."

"Goodness knows how," said Bonnie, and Jamie grimaced, but Bonnie didn't look as if she'd remotely stepped over the mark, even though dissing people's grandmothers tended to be on the avoidance list as far as Mirren had always been concerned. Maybe that made her common.

"And then she grew up and married and then divorced my dad, who lives in Dubai with his second wife, and my mum lives in Perth with her third husband, Plumber Boy Jim—Perth, Australia, that is, not actual Perth down the road. I have a clutch of half siblings here and there whom I don't know, and then there's me and Esme and, well, my grandfather died last month. And left . . ."

"A right bloody mess," said Bonnie.

Mirren frowned. "Your mum didn't inherit?"

"Primogeniture," said Jamie. "Sorry. It's about penises and stuff. They keep meaning to change it in parliament but then they find they have stuff to deal with that affects more than four families a year, so we slip down the list a bit." He shrugged his shoulders. "Mum didn't want it anyway. She spent everything she could find and buggered off. Hoarders, she and my grandfather both."

"And we don't blame her," said Bonnie stoutly.

"No—no, we don't," said Jamie. "But it's my problem now."

Theo looked around. "Right," he said, nodding. "I think I understand. I see this a lot."

Mirren was peeved that he appeared to be taking charge. On the other hand, it was true, he did have more experience than she did. His handsome face looked concerned as he picked up his hand and started ticking off on his long fingers.

"Would the National Trust want it?"

"The Scottish Heritage Foundation? Neh, we've tried. There are about two thousand castles in Scotland. It's basically the equivalent of trying to send a cow to a zoo. They like the back bit—it's ancient, the old stone towers and the chapel. But it's covered in the front bit: the turrets and the wedding cake stuff."

"Those are the bits I like," interjected Mirren.

"I know, but apparently it's vulgar and just gets in the way. They are *very* picky."

"Okay. Hotel chains?" said Theo.

"For various reasons, to do with kestrels and bats, you can build stuff—houses, or a hotel—but you can't put another road here."

Theo frowned. "So there's just that muddy path? Goodness, you are in a pickle."

"Uh-huh," said Jamie, the weight of the world on his shoulders. Bonnie patted him gently on the arm, Mirren noticed.

"But the train!" said Mirren. "The train is awesome . . ." Her voice trailed off as everyone looked at her. "Well. I mean. You can't be that skint if you have your own train."

"We don't," explained Jamie. "That's a perk; it doesn't belong to us. It's a contractual quirk of the railways. You couldn't actually have a proper station here. And even if you could, you can't have a road to connect it with everything."

"Because of the bats," said Theo, ticking off another finger.

"*Bats* are one of your fingers?" said Mirren.

"You don't know a lot about old Scottish houses," said Theo.

"And you do?"

There was a silence in the kitchen and Jamie and Bonnie looked at each other.

"Sorry, are you guys . . . married?" asked Bonnie.

"No!" said Mirren, too quickly, and everyone looked at her. It was more awkward than ever.

Theo didn't even look remotely perturbed. After a second, he held up another finger—"And kestrels, yeah?"—while Mirren felt herself go bright pink.

Jamie meanwhile was staring out of the window sadly.

"There's been a McKinnon house on this site for five hundred years. Every bit of this place was built at a different time. There's a fourteenth-century chapel, can you even imagine? What they were even praying for back then?"

"Was it maybe central heating?" asked Mirren.

Jamie rubbed his head.

"I can't . . . I can't bear to give it up. To lose it all. But the paperwork . . . the will." His face looked older suddenly. "The will . . . I thought there might be something left over. But there isn't. Not a bit of it. Just debts and bad memories."

Bonnie blinked. "Don't say that."

"You know there's nothing left," he said. "Nothing to keep it going. Nothing to pay you." He nodded at Bonnie, who rolled her eyes, as if that was the last of their worries. Ah, thought Mirren. Interesting.

"Oh, come on," said Theo, standing up. "Some billionaire will want to take this off your hands. It's breathtaking."

He stepped forward and, with some difficulty, opened the kitchen door. Up the steps, light flooded in. At the top of the steps was a kitchen garden, still neatly kept, with the peeling white crenellated wall above it, and a perfect wrought-iron gate giving a view of the grounds ahead.

"You'd think," said Jamie. "But it's too big even for them. And lots of them want to knock everything down and start again and they're not allowed to do that either. Our neighbours want to buy the halt, for the train link. But that's all they want: one field. One field that will block our right of way and ruin the grounds. And nothing else."

"So, hang on—you can't sell it, it can't be knocked down, it can't be used for anything . . ." said Mirren. "The government are not being very helpful, are they?"

"You could say that," said Jamie.

"The White Elephant," said Theo. "You should have elephants on your doorposts instead of pineapples."

Jamie smiled for the first time that morning. "Huh," he said.

"Well, you lot can carry on grousing," said Bonnie. "I've got stuff to do." And she vanished into the depths of the house.

Jamie waited until she had gone out of earshot, then lowered his voice.

"But there was one thing in my grandfather's papers," he said. "Just one thing."

Mirren, wanting to ease the atmosphere between them, glanced over at Theo. He didn't look back, concentrating fiercely on Jamie.

Jamie felt in an inside pocket of the old tweed jacket he was wearing over a jumper, then pulled out a long vellum envelope.

Chapter Thirteen

"So, my grandfather . . ."

"What was his name?" asked Mirren. Theo and Jamie just looked at her.

"Well, James, duh," said Theo.

"Stop doing this," said Mirren. "Duhhing me every time I don't know some stupid posh-people code thing. I don't even want to be in the posh Olympics, so you can just stop duhhing me about it." And she stuck her tongue out at him.

Jamie laughed. "You are completely right," he said.

"Yes, point taken," said Theo, slightly reluctantly.

"What was he like?" asked Mirren. "Your grandfather?"

Jamie smiled. "*Complicated*, the obituaries said. Crotchety. Obsessed with books and puzzles and crosswords. He could be kind, I think. But he just withdrew into himself. I don't know if anyone ever reached him, not really. I mean, I don't know how well we ever know our grandparents as people . . . Well, that's what I tell myself."

"Did he die here?"

Jamie nodded sadly. "He stopped taking his medication. Went out one night into the fields and died of exposure. Bonnie found . . ." He stopped talking.

"Oh, goodness!" said Mirren. "That's tragic!"

"He was old and sick," said Jamie. "I don't know if . . . well. I don't know. We never will."

Theo blinked. "Bloody hell." He looked around. "He never met anyone after his marriage broke up? There must have been *some* rich American heiress . . ."

Jamie shook his head. "No."

"Gay?"

"You're talking about my grandfather!"

"You're right," said Theo. "Nobody ever had a gay grandfather."

"*Theo!*" said Mirren.

"What?" said Theo. "It's not an insult."

"No, but it's personal."

Jamie was looking very awkward suddenly. "Um," he said, "I think he was just . . . I don't know. But I don't think so. I think just a bit odd, which is why . . ." He opened one of the ancient kitchen cupboards. It was filled to the brim with books on water-divining.

"God," said Theo. "Mind you, you wouldn't think that would stop those determined heiresses."

"Stop it!" said Mirren. "What's in the envelope, Jamie??"

He was still tapping the envelope thoughtfully. Carefully he wiped his hands on a clean dishcloth that was over the back of the chair. Then he pulled out a folded sheet of heavy paper from the envelope.

"He left this."

Mirren and Theo got up and stood behind him and read it over his shoulder, as behind them in the fields a lone gull cut through the penny-bright air.

To my heir,

Down these paths we all must tread,
There hides a precious book, unread;

At the star of neither land nor sea,
First take thy pen, go in, go see.
If you can bear to trace its line,
There it will be, now yours, once mine.
If you can understand, my friend,
Then time and tide must come to end.
The setting of the sun will show
The ancient routes stand fast;
The saddest tale of woe is told
When all the songs are past.
Then you must find a crown of gold,
And hopes will not be dashed;
Between the vellum sheets, dear James,
The answer shows at last.

THEY STARED AT it.

"That's it?" said Mirren. "That's all you have to go on?"

"A precious book?" said Theo, sizing up the situation and nodding seriously. "Among everything else."

James nodded. Theo looked around, his face doubtful.

"Oh my goodness," said Mirren. "Are you absolutely sure these aren't just—I don't know, poetic ramblings or something?"

"Oh no, he'd mentioned it before," said Jamie. "That there was an incredibly valuable book in the house. And I asked him what it was, when I was about eleven, and he said he couldn't say, otherwise my mother would sell it and spend it on clothes."

"Harsh," said Mirren.

"No, my mother *would* have sold it and spent it on clothes."

"What does the internet say?" said Theo, taking out his phone.

"Absolutely zero," said Jamie. "It talks about some old paintings we used to have, but that's about it. And before the war everything was carefully listed and written down by staff—how many bottles of Burgundy in the cellar, how many silver spoons, that kind of thing, and they kept all the receipts in account books. But then that started to go by the by once they lost all their staff, and after that I don't think my family kept receipts for anything. My grandfather would sell a painting for cash at lunchtime and spend it by the afternoon." He said this without bitterness.

"I thought it was kind of an essential part of the job, to look after places like this for the next generation," said Mirren, gently, not wanting to speak ill of the dead.

"I know," said Jamie. "I think he must have hoped I'd fix it." He opened his hands. "But I don't know where to start."

A broad beam of sun suddenly appeared behind a cloud, rendering the world dark and light all at once. Mirren couldn't help it: she stood up and walked to the kitchen door.

"Can I . . . ?" She indicated outside.

Jamie shrugged. "Be my guest," he said, although, of course, she wasn't a guest at all.

Chapter Fourteen

Jamie followed her outside. Theo was already flipping through his phone, trying to work out what precious lost book might theoretically have found its way to the remote northeast of Scotland. His face frowned at the lack of signal, but Mirren couldn't deny, much as she would like to, that it was quite attractive to see him take charge.

They were standing in front of the kitchen garden, which had a high wall, with a gate set low in it. It was surprisingly tidy, long rows of carefully planted carrots and cabbages, with nets over the fruit, and a small greenhouse where, in the summer, tomatoes must run free. Now it was full of herbs, great tubs of rosemary and mint. The gravel was neatly raked and from here it was almost possible to imagine the castle as it must once have been: filled with gardeners and footmen, chefs rushing to gather the ingredients for a ball or a party taking place that night, the rumble of the carriages coming up the long drive and great braziers lighting the way. Mirren followed Jamie through the open door at the far side of the garden, entranced by the world visible beyond it, like stepping through Alice's garden gate. There wasn't a croquet lawn, she saw, looking around, but long, unkempt fields, barley stalks left unharvested.

Jamie saw her looking.

"We've had tenant farmers, but . . ." He shrugged. "They need schools and supermarkets and their kids moved away and . . ."

Mirren nodded. She walked forward onto the little path. "I see what you mean."

You could hear the breath of the wind through the trees, the chattering of winter birds here and there, on their busy way, but apart from that, nothing. To Mirren, born and raised in London, it was an astonishing lack of noise. No sirens. No car horns or reversing lorries or screeching boy racers or rumbling Underground trains. A world untouched by time.

She headed on up the track, worrying that her trainers wouldn't stand up to the mud. The mud, it turned out, however, was crusty. She nudged a puddle with her toe; it was solid.

"It's getting very cold," Jamie said worriedly, looking at the sky and sniffing.

"What are you sniffing for?" she asked.

"Snow. It's a little early; it's normally February we're digging ourselves out."

"What does snow smell like?" she said, trying an experimental sniff.

"Hmm. Hard to say. Clean linen?"

"Huh."

She crested the little mound leading out of the field. Over on the other side—she'd known it was there, of course—was the sea, now at high tide, pounding against the rocks at the foot of the castle.

"*Whoa!*" she said, stepping closer to the edge, her eyes trying to take everything in. The sun was weaving in and out of clouds and the rays struck the ominous grey crags, illuminating the great height suddenly.

From the front entrance, the house looked posh, certainly—large but formal, a stately home designed to impress, to show off how much money the owners had, to be filled with expensive and fashionable things over the centuries: precious paintings, now sold; precious books, lost . . .

From here, though, from the back, it was a different story altogether.

Here was simply a great wet cragside rising from the churning water below them. The very oldest part of the castle, great big mossy stones, started here and emanated from the rock itself. The castle looked more grown than built. You could see this was not a place for people to attend balls in carriages; this was a defensive structure.

Mirren walked to the edge—there was a theoretical fence, but it was old and bendy.

"Careful," said Jamie suddenly.

She peered over. She didn't think of herself as scared of heights, but watching the sea crash into the rocks far, far below was genuinely frightening. She stepped backwards smartly, to Jamie's evident relief.

"I don't know what state those rocks are in," he said. "Another reason we can't really open the grounds to the public. Because, you know. They'd all die."

"Oh yeah," said Mirren. "Bloody hell, it's amazing."

Jamie smiled weakly. "Apparently bits of it were started to ward off Vikings coming from the east. It's *that* old."

"I bet it worked."

"I believe it did," said Jamie. Then he thought for a moment. "Well, I'd believe it a bit more if forty percent of people in the village weren't all called Anderson and six foot nine."

They carried on strolling the cliff head, keeping a safe distance from the edge. Despite the occasional glimpse of sun through the clouds, it had indeed got notably colder, even since that morning. Mirren pulled her jacket closer round her. Her short peacoat was fine for mild, wet London winters; she wasn't sure it would cut the mustard here at all.

Where the gorse bushes grew over the path, their prickles snagging Mirren's tights, they stopped and looked back.

From here, the entire castle was in sight: the glorious frontage, once again from a good distance looking fuzzily clean and white instead of dirty and old; the turrets gleaming in the sun, the pennant fluttering—and then the back, in plain stone, larger and heavier as they went on, outbuildings clear on the other side, as well as the small chapel.

"It's amazing," said Mirren dreamily. Jamie looked at her.

"I know," he said, kicking at an iced-over puddle with his heavy boot, watching as it fractured into thick slabs of diamond. "I can't . . . I can't bear, after hundreds of years . . . I can't bear to be the one who lets it go, who mucks it up."

"Couldn't *you* marry a rich American heiress?"

He looked at her. "I see you and your colleague have a playbook."

"He's not my colleague," said Mirren quickly, and he raised his eyebrows.

"Anyway, why do you think I went to St. Andrews?" he said, smiling and changing the subject. "This place was too crappy even for them, I'm afraid."

Another stray ray of low sun in the steely sky hit the windows on the south side and lit it a vibrant winter gold. Mirren could hear, now, the crash of the waves.

"What's going to happen to it?" she said.

"I don't know," he said. "The factor says we've got until January to settle the death duties—then . . ." He shrugged.

"Then *what*?"

"The council will faff about what has to be done with it, it'll go on the market, but because of the roads issue . . . nobody could buy it or make it a going concern, and there's money owing on it, so that won't help . . ."

"If you had the book—if you had the money," said Mirren, "then what would you do? Say it was a *lot* of money . . ."

Jamie turned, the sea at his back, and gazed back over to where they'd just come from.

"I'd love to open up the gardens," he said finally. "At least. Restore them to what they were. Grow the original plants that were brought here."

"Pineapples?"

"Maybe. But that's what I'd love. The house, the stuff, the money . . . it isn't as much fun as you'd imagine. But you could get kids up here . . . maybe run a small farm again . . ."

Mirren nodded.

"That sounds," she said, seeing his solemn face, "quite a lot like you'd end up running a cult."

He laughed, despite himself, and his worried-looking face softened considerably. "Ha. Oh God. The only people who do actually approach me are, yes, 'alternative lifestyles.'"

"You need us to save you from that," said Mirren.

"I do."

"Better get to it, then," she said, setting her face back to the castle.

Chapter Fifteen

They snuck in through a side door Mirren hadn't noticed before. It was barely warmer inside than out. They were in an older side of the castle, the corridors here rough-hewn and painted in a strange shiny industrial paint, in a dirty cream. Jamie caught her looking at it.

"Ah yes," he said. "From when it was requisitioned in the war. They painted the walls for us. We haven't quite got round to the touch-up."

Mirren blinked. "And I thought I was late getting my boiler serviced." She frowned as she looked at the pipes. "Where do they discharge to?"

"I was only kidding about hiring a surveyor," said Jamie, and Mirren smiled. "Also, never mention the B-word in this house. I think the boiler works by prayer."

Back in the kitchen, Mirren instantly went in and tried to get some warmth back into her fingers from the stove.

"Don't do that," said Jamie. "You just have to let your body adjust."

"You're telling me I have to activate Penguin Mode?" said Mirren. "I don't think so. We're only here for three days."

The size of the job suddenly struck her. This house was a town. It went on forever. Every surface of it was covered in books, and none of them in any kind of order.

Theo was no longer in the kitchen; his phone lay abandoned on the table.

They found him slumped in the laundry room on the other side of the corridor from the vast kitchen. This was equally vast; there was a mangle, a twin tub that looked older than Mirren's mother, and, in the high ceiling, a great long drying rack that was worked by some kind of odd pulley system, as well as various sinks, cupboards, and ominous-looking pipes. The door at the far end led to something which must, once upon a time, have been a storeroom for sheets—there were shelves covered in very faded paper, with neat labels in copperplate on each one—East Wing Blue, East Wing Red, and so on, shelf after shelf.

Except, unsurprisingly, only the bottom of one far shelf sported fresh linen sheets. The rest were filled instead with books, pushed all the way back, piled four lanes deep in every conceivable nook and cranny. Theo was sitting on the hard stone floor, at the far end, already among a discarded pile, his handsome face looking distraught.

"What?" said Mirren.

"There's . . ." He held up his hands in a gesture of futility. "Who buys three hundred books about *frogs*?"

Jamie picked up the nearest one. It was an ancient hardback by a reverend, entitled *Frogs and Amphibians of the Norfolk Broads, with many various illustrations therein*. "I didn't think the Norfolk Broads had so many different amphibians," he said, leafing through it. He glanced up. "I doubt this is the one we're looking for," he said, showing them a rather crudely drawn sketch of an unusually large and badly proportioned toad.

"But *why*?" said Theo. "I have done some house clearances, but this is pathologically *insane*."

There was a silence.

"Although I'm sure he was a very nice man and whatnot."

Jamie shrugged. "Oh, he'd buy anything, really. Auction lots. Charity shops. I think he was always . . . He loved books. I think he wanted to own every book in the world. It was a mission. While everything else fell down around his ears."

"I've got a lot of books about dragons," said Mirren, trying to be supportive. Both the men looked at her. "What? You shut up."

Theo took down another handful and flicked through them.

"No . . . no . . . lizards . . . no, no . . ." He stood up and dusted off his hands. "Laird McKinnon—"

"Jamie, please. People only use my title when I'm in trouble," said Jamie.

"Okay. Well, you know, I handle a lot of antiquarian books," he said.

"I kind of hoped you did," said Jamie.

"I have to say . . . a lot of these . . . they're old, but they're just . . ." Theo rubbed the back of his neck. "They're just old toot."

Jamie nodded.

"How many miles of corridor are there in this place? How many rooms?"

"Um. About two miles. And, I think, about sixty rooms?"

"Bloody hell," said Mirren.

"Plus . . ."

"Attics and cellars," said Theo. "Look, I'm sorry, but to do this properly would take . . ."

None of the three said anything.

"Well, then, let's get a move on," said Mirren, as cheerily as she could. She was worried Theo was just going to turn around and leave. She didn't want her trip to end as soon as it began. "Show me that poem again."

Chapter Sixteen

Jamie suggested they move to the Chinois Drawing Room, as it was one of the rooms Bonnie kept up; the place visitors were taken to, one of very few that was shown off and painted up and kept tidy.

There seemed to be endless other public rooms they glimpsed from the corridors. The huge spaces between the great double doors—with wood peeling; missing door handles sometimes, indicated the vast size of them. There was a long rug down this particular corridor; once, Mirren thought, looking at it, it must have been heavenly, with little birds, rooms in turquoise, and gold leaf intertwining to form the pattern, almost entirely obscured. The sides of the carpet were held down either side with more and more books piled up; it was like wading through a tide. Mirren glanced at titles as they headed past: a history of Raworth School, a guide to tea shops, and a recent Jack Reacher. Theo was right, the order made no sense.

Halfway down, Jamie stopped, and opened one particular set of double doors, with an anxious look on his face, as if he really wanted them to like it. How strange, she thought, to be what many people would consider to be the luckiest fellow in the world, inheritor of a huge country estate, and yet to be so worried and unhappy, for it to be such a burden. Feeling sorry for a posh boy was very far down her list of things to do, but she couldn't deny that she did.

The Chinois Drawing Room—"Colonial nightmare," Theo whispered to her in a rare moment of solidarity, and she could only agree—was undeniably beautiful. Turquoise, gold, and red wallpaper—antique, but its colours still vivid—covered the walls with bright, bustling bees and butterflies. There were brightly painted screens in several parts of the room, which was clean and clear of dust, and, thank goodness, a newly laid fire was burning in the grate. Mirren darted towards it gratefully.

She glanced out of the vast window. Every window showed a picture of the water, shimmering silver and pewter, under a sky that was already, in early afternoon, leaching light. The view, though, was still exceptional, a vision unchanged for hundreds of years. There were no oil rigs to spoil the vista; no tankers cruising the horizon, although they must be out there. It was just the tumbling cliffs beneath the beautiful drawing room, all the way down to the lapping water, and the sea in front of them, the Cromarty Firth below. Nothing between them and Norway. Once upon a time, she thought, ships would have come here; to trade, to fight—who knew?

She walked over and stood so close against the window that she could see her own face superimposed on the scene, feeling as though she was stepping into someone else's history, the history of the many, many people who had walked these halls; it was thrilling. The men of course had to go and do derring-do; but how many women and girls had stood here, looking out, dreaming of distant shores? The daughters, the brides, the mothers, the parlourmaids; the rich, the bored, the spoiled; the slaveys; the silent unvoiced legions of women who had come and gone across this room, once upon a time.

It occurred to Mirren suddenly that with her background—her ancestors were Scots who'd moved down south when the pits closed—she would not have been a lady in a long, pretty dress staring out and dreaming of voyages and dances. She would have been one of the staff. Just as she thought this, Bonnie pushed her way into the room.

"You didn't!" said Jamie, glancing at the tray then beaming at her. Bonnie beamed back at him and set the tray down. Mirren wondered once more about the relationship between them.

There was a large teapot, wearing a cosy—it was such a very long way from the kitchen to the room they were in, everything would get cold on the way without it—and a huge plate of raisin scones, puffy and floury and utterly delicious-looking; next to that sat an ancient glass dish containing jewel-like jam that was obviously homemade—gooseberry, Bonnie announced—and cream and sugar in beautiful blue-and-white Chinese willow-pattern porcelain, almost every piece chipped, and butter and clotted cream likewise.

"You haven't had any lunch," said Bonnie, "so I thought you might want your afternoon tea early."

"You thought right," said Jamie. Even Theo, whose interest in food was lackadaisical at best, perked up from the stop of a stepladder where he had been reading a Victorian book of childcare, eyes bulging slightly in horror at its contents.

They sat in front of the roaring fire and drank tea as the last of the light drained from the sky, and Jamie closed the shutters and the room became cosy and pretty much warm enough to take your jacket off, if not your jumper, obviously.

Mirren ate a scone hungrily, piled high with the jam from the estate, then another. The boys, too, were tucking in with goodwill when she pulled out the poem again. She moved across the room to a tiny escritoire. "Can I sit here?"

"Yes," said Jamie. "Rest assured, if anything was worth anything, it was sold off years ago."

"To buy more books," said Theo.

"So it'll be either reproduction or valueless."

"Okay," said Mirren, sitting down at the little table. It was still delicate and flimsy; she felt rather huge and inelegant sitting there. Opening up the tiny drawers that rose up from the polished table surface, she found, to her delight and surprise, proper vellum notepaper, an ink bottle, and an old fountain pen.

"Ooh!" she said. "Can I use this?"

"Again, just assume anything you find in the house you can use," Jamie said.

Mirren took the fountain pen and rinsed it in a bathroom down the hall, then had the satisfaction of drawing fresh black ink up through the balloon cartridge.

"Oh," she said in delight. "I haven't used one of these for years."

She started to write an elaborate *D* on the vellum paper. The nib was fine, and the paper slightly rough, but in a way that caught the ink beautifully. She smiled, pleased at her handiwork, and copied out the rest of the line in calligraphic script from the paper Jamie deposited in front of her.

"Where did you learn to do that?" asked Jamie, looking over her shoulder.

She went slightly pink. "I had a . . . well, I went through a phase in my adolescence."

Theo glanced at it. "My God, Sutherland," he said. "How nerdy were you? Did you learn how to do this by staying home on prom night?"

Mirren gave him a look and set about quietly picking out the nouns in careful script.

Lines . . . book, pen, line . . . setting of the sun—maybe that was to the west. Stars, land, sea; everything was in here. Ancient routes, though? Surely all the routes were ancient. Lines and setting suns. And crowns of gold . . .

"What does it *mean*? Have you got any *crowns of gold*?"

"I believe any crowns of gold would have been sold pretty much first," said Jamie drily. He ran his fingers through his hair. "It is possible he was just . . . I don't know. Wibbling. He loved games and puzzles, all those kinds of things. He was such an odd man. It's not outside the realm of possibility that he's just winding us up. From beyond the grave. Or thought he did have something—thought that he'd bought so many books, one of them must be worth something."

Theo blew out some air. "As an investment strategy, you're probably better off betting on horses. This is a wild-goose chase. Playing silly buggers."

"But . . . no. I can't think like that. He was absolutely adamant that he had something precious," said Jamie. "I didn't . . . I didn't have any reason not to believe him."

"Well, quite," said Mirren.

Jamie looked over her shoulder. "I thought *go see* might mean the halt. Because it's where you might travel from."

"There are no books there, though," said Theo.

"No, I know."

"*Go see*," said Mirren. "I mean, you don't really need those words in the poem. *First take thy pen, go in* works totally fine. *Take thy pen, go in, go see* . . ." She frowned. "What did you say before?" she asked Theo. "Just now."

"About playing silly buggers?"

"Before that."

"About being on a wild-goose chase?"

Mirren glanced down. She wrote the words *go see* then she wrote the word "goose." "Have you got any geese here?" she asked.

"We used to," said Jamie. "I think we used to have a goose girl."

"What's a goose girl?"

"It's someone who looks after the geese," said Jamie. "They'd have been down at the duck pond."

"Do you have books down there?"

"I suppose there's a summerhouse. It seems a bit . . . I mean, *go see* meaning 'goose'? It's a long shot, surely."

He got up, and Theo did too.

"What about *take thy pen*?" said Mirren.

"Yeah, well, I suppose if you were outside, but the ducks . . . you wouldn't need a pen . . ."

"Is there a duck pen?"

"Argh," said Jamie. "I don't know! I don't get it! It's unbearable. There is a sheep pen, but it's up on the side of the ben; nobody's used it for years!"

"*If you can bear*," said Mirren, writing the words in her beautiful script. "What does that mean? Like, just 'can you bear it'?"

"A bear. And a goose," said Theo.

"What do you mean?"

"*At the star of neither land nor sea.*"

"I thought that might be filler," said Jamie. "All stars are in space. It's just stupid."

Theo frowned. "But if you did have geese and bears . . . and *take thy pen, go in* . . ."

"PENGUIN!" said Mirren.

"What??"

Mirren flapped her hands. "If it was . . . oh my God . . . the north. The North Star! Over the ice! Not land, not sea—ice! Those are Arctic animals!"

"But we're already in the north," said Theo, puzzled. "It's freezing enough up here. Have you got bears?"

But Jamie wasn't listening.

"Bloody hell," he said. "I wonder if . . . I wonder if he meant the North Library."

Chapter Seventeen

They all jumped up, galvanised. Then Mirren glanced back down and grabbed the last bit of her scone. It had been a very good scone.

"Bring your notebook," said Jamie. "That method obviously works."

"I wouldn't say 'obviously,'" said Theo. "Seeing as, you know, we haven't actually found anything yet."

"Copying things out works?" said Mirren, ignoring him. "Do you think?"

"I've stared at that thing for three months without figuring a thing out," he said.

"Why didn't you just put it on the internet?" said Mirren, puzzled.

"Sure," said Jamie. "What I absolutely want is hundreds of weirdos turning up here and pulling the house apart. Thanks, that's exactly what I had in mind." He shivered. *"Oh, guess what, every rando on the internet? There might be treasure in my house and by the way, the doors don't lock because they're completely warped!"*

Outside the drawing room, the house felt colder than ever. The mercury really was dropping, and it was getting steadily darker. Following Jamie up the corridor, Mirren stopped and listened. She could hear the wind outside.

"It's over . . ." Jamie screwed up his face for a moment.

"You can't remember where a room is in your own house?" said Mirren, shaking her head in amazement.

"I absolutely can," said Jamie straightaway. "I'm just figuring out the quickest way to get to it. Right, follow me."

And he charged off to the left, past an old stand that was, according to the ancient, stained card next to it, where a suit of armour used to be. They followed him to the end of the corridor, then he made a sharp left and disappeared through a hole that turned out to be a door hidden in the panelling. They were now in a grey stone stairwell, a carved spiral staircase heading up and down, into gloom, where a clear dripping could be heard. There were tiny lead-lined windows cut into the wall and Mirren correctly surmised that they were inside one of the tinier turrets. The light was fading fast, though, and she couldn't see the bottom at all.

Their breath showed in front of their faces. Theo got his phone torch out. "This is literally all it's good for here," he said ruefully, checking his reception again: none. They followed Jamie as he scampered upwards, clearly very familiar with where they were, and came out goodness knew how many floors above.

Mirren was glad someone else opened the cobwebby door; it was extremely spidery in there. They were now on a quiet, dusty landing. The ceilings here were lower; this was a private, rather than public space. The great old wooden doors looked as if they hadn't been opened in decades. Mirren decided to ignore the cobwebs. She was broadly in favour of spiders, she told herself firmly, as long as they weren't dropping down her neck.

"Now, which is it?" said Jamie to himself. He counted four along and opened a door. Mirren screamed, and even Theo started back, until Jamie turned the lights on. It was a room entirely filled with taxidermied animals—badgers, raccoons, even a lion, staring back at them, glassy-eyed. Mirren took in a rearing cobra, poised to strike, and grabbed in alarm for the nearest person, which happened to be Theo—who didn't look much less shocked than she was. It was unbelievably unpleasant in there.

Behind the army of moth-eaten animals were, of course, more bookshelves. Mirren very much hoped she wouldn't have to clamber over the animals to get to those books, and in fact had absolutely no intention of doing so.

"Snakearoonie!" said Jamie to the cobra, in seeming delight. "Oh my goodness, it's been ages!"

"You guys are friends?" said Mirren when she'd got her breath back.

"Oh, Bonnie and I used to take beasties out of here and put them in people's rooms—we'd scare the wits out of them." He patted the cobra jar affectionately.

"I bet you bloody did," said Mirren. "Also, if you even think of doing that to me, I'm out of here in five seconds flat."

"As," said Theo, trying to sound dignified, "am I."

Jamie grinned and turned out the light and shut the door.

"I think that's worse," said Mirren. "Knowing they're all in there. In the dark. Plotting how to kill us."

"It's just a collection," said Jamie.

"Yes, of HORRIFYING THINGS."

But he was striding on.

"Where is it, where is it . . . ? Ah, of course."

In front of them was a pair of heavy wooden doors with black studs in them. Jamie rifled in the capacious pockets of his waxed jacket, which, like the rest of them, he hadn't bothered to take off, and withdrew a huge ring of keys.

"When's the last time anyone was in here?"

Jamie shook his head. "Not the foggiest."

"It sounds," said Mirren, "like your grandfather . . . he needed a lot of help. Like he wasn't well at all."

"It's hardly unusual for a McKinnon to turn eccentric in their old age," said Jamie. "And I was here a lot. But he didn't want any help. He just wanted to tell me about new books he'd bought, and crossword clues."

"Your mum didn't . . . ?"

"She sided with my grandmother in that particular divorce," said Jamie. "Hardly spoke to the old man at all. She'd leave me and Esme here for the holidays while she went swanning off on the proceeds of whatever there was left to sell."

He tried to sound cheerful about it, not entirely satisfactorily.

He finally found the right key—a large black iron thing with an elaborate rounded end—and the wooden doors creaked open.

THE AIR INSIDE the room was like a tomb. Jamie fumbled for the light, an ancient switch in a round setting. The bulbs had mostly blown; there were one or two weak bulbs left in a dusty chandelier hanging from the roof.

Just as before, in the East Library, this had two storeys, and they had entered on the mezzanine. They must have been designed this way. But the windows didn't face east, to the wild sea, or west, to the beautiful dying rays of the setting winter sun. They looked out on the harsh landscape of the northern hills, where there was no heather left now, so late in the year. Hardy sheep were dotted here and there; everything in shades of grey, cold and inhospitable.

Mirren shivered. The books here, as dishevelled as anywhere else, were covered in a thick layer of dust. Nobody had been here for years, surely. Thousands of volumes lined the mezzanine, then down below there was shelving and cupboards, all full.

"So . . . it's in here, whatever it is?" said Mirren. They stood staring around at the vastness of the task.

They decided to divide the room up methodically, and Jamie found a collection of Post-its in an old desk. Every shelving stack they'd finished needed a Post-it, and if they fell off, well, that would be a problem for another day.

Anything that looked vaguely old or precious or promising, they decided, they would pull out to examine properly later. Any famous editions of well-known books, they were to ask Theo, who had the expertise; anything local or handwritten, they would put aside in case that meant something, and if Jamie had written in it or on it, he could check the handwriting and confirm it either way.

Mirren wished she'd worn gloves—she was sure there was some disease you could get from handling old books, something to do with spores—but she wasn't sure how to politely bring it up. She had wanted an adventure, she reminded herself. A change in her life. And here she was, up in the Highlands in a crazy old castle. Okay, she had been anticipating rather less indexing of old titles about—she picked up one at random—great chess games from the International Bradford Chess Competition, but maybe people forgot about the slightly duller parts of adventures.

They got their heads down as dusk fell. Jamie went and scared up some light bulbs from various other rooms—Mirren hoped he hadn't annoyed the animal gods next door—to give them a bit of light, and plugged in an ancient radio on one of the desks, which pleasingly still worked, although the choices were limited to the local Gaelic radio station or Russian seafaring channels. They went for the former, which played enough jolly jigs and reels to keep them moving.

What, though, thought Mirren, as she sorted through the stacks, did Jamie mean? What could the book be? Really rich people did buy and sell books for absolutely loads of money, she knew that. Silly money, for things that nobody else could have, rarities or special things. Because, when they'd run out of every commonplace thing, every single normal mass-produced thing a human could ever want, they had to spend their money somewhere, so they spent it on pointless things nobody could possibly want or need: engagement rings the size of hens' eggs for marriages that wouldn't last; rocket ships that exploded all over the place; artworks that only existed on the internet, for heaven's sake. Houses so big, so impossibly huge and useless, that you couldn't even go in every room and you could get lost just looking around them. What on earth was the point of this, truly? she thought as the windows showed full dark outside now on the long, wild grounds of the north.

Oh, she didn't know. She didn't understand the world, not really. Maybe the old laird had given loads of his money away. Maybe he'd fed all the hungry kids in the villages all round, found good jobs for people to do. Or maybe she was naïve and studenty and didn't understand the world and all of that. But looking round at this dusty, forgotten, overflowing room, belonging to a man who seemingly, from the way Jamie told it, had died completely alone, his estranged daughter in a foreign land, his grandchildren passing the buck on the inheritance . . . well, she wouldn't say he'd been on top of it either.

"What was he like?" she called to Jamie, as she leafed desultorily through a selection of hardback guides to O-level mathematics in 1956. She could not deny, it looked a lot harder than her GCSEs. That was an entire puzzle on its own. Still, though, it was a treasure trove, and she remembered, looking round, how, when she was young, she'd thought, once, that she might read every book in the world, she loved them so. As she'd outgrown the tiny children's section in her branch library, she'd realised this was futile, but there was still something in her that wanted to sit down and not get up again till she'd read every single one; travelled to every single land within their pages; met their kings, learned about their strange ways; fallen in love. Perhaps the old man, too, really had thought he could possess every single book in the world. "Your grandfather. What was he like?"

Jamie frowned. "What do you mean?"

"Well, I mean . . . was he warm? Fun? You spent all your holidays here."

Jamie looked uncomfortable. "Well . . . he was head of the family, you know."

"I don't," said Mirren. "My parents are divorced, and I don't really see my dad's parents at all. I lost an entire set of grandparents."

"Oh, me too," said Jamie. He looked sad for a moment. "Well. He was . . . crusty, I suppose? Had his head in a book a lot of the time. Eccentric? You had to be quite quiet around him . . ."

"Was he fun?"

"The laird?" The way Jamie spoke his title said everything. "No," he said heavily. "No. He was not fun. No."

"But he liked games and puzzles and things . . ." Mirren gestured at the poem.

"Yes, he'd set us really hard puzzles then get annoyed when we couldn't solve them," said Jamie, wincing a little at the memory. "I was never exactly a Mensa candidate. He made it very clear what he thought about that. I like reading, but I'm not really into word games. He was a difficult man. I never understood him."

He looked down and they carried on. Some of the books half disintegrated when they picked them up. The room must be damp, thought Mirren; the beautiful, ancient mullioned windows were single-glazed, of course, and the moisture must get in. Another terrible note for the survey, if she had been doing her actual job. There must be mice too. This place would be a feast to them. Add them to the spiders and this castle was absolutely full of life. She made a promise to herself not to think about bats.

At the edge of the mezzanine, where the wrought-iron balcony creaked slightly and probably wouldn't handle too much leaning against, was a pile of old chests. One of them was full of magazines: old issues of *National Geographic* with their yellow borders, which might have been worth something if they weren't all warped and spotted. A second, likewise, but with a bunch of comics.

"*The Beano*!" said Mirren.

Jamie looked up.

"Hundreds of them!" she said.

He came up to inspect. "Well, there's some treasure," he said, and bounded up the curved staircase, which wobbled ominously at his large hands on it. "Ha. God, that old bastard."

"What?" said Mirren.

He shook his head. "It's funny really. He wouldn't let me have any comics because I should be reading 'real books.' And don't even start me on telly or internet. And he had all of these the entire time!"

He picked out the top one. "What was your favourite?"

"The Numskulls, obviously," said Mirren. "I feel sorry for kids today who only have *Inside Out*."

He laughed. "Quite right too. God, I used to look like Plug."

"I can't believe that."

"I went through a very prominent-Adam's-apple stage."

Jamie sat down excitedly to read them. Mirren carried on with the next trunk, feeling a niggling in her back and shoulders. Muscles that didn't get a workout very often were feeling the strain of a long day picking up and putting down.

"Ugh," she said. "Just school stuff."

Jamie ignored her. He was reading, and Theo had wandered up too.

"Do you know what we need?" he said. "A flask."

"I think there's about forty-two of them in the under-kitchen," murmured Jamie, handing over a *Dandy*. "They used to get used on hunting parties. Beef tea."

Mirren didn't know what beef tea was but it sounded disgusting, and she made a face as the boys sat down and started reading the comics like a couple of teenagers.

"Hey!" said Mirren.

"Come off it," said Theo. "We've been at it for hours."

"You're filthy," said Mirren. Theo was completely covered in dust, including a streak in his shiny hair.

"You should see yourself," he said.

"I can't," said Mirren. "Because I'm busy doing that job that I'm being paid for."

Theo groaned theatrically and put *Dennis the Menace* down.

Mirren carried on opening chests. The very smallest was at the back, a small brown case with *JWDMK* emblazoned on it as initials, plus a tiny golden coat of arms. It was so obviously a bag for a child going on a journey, it made Mirren feel oddly sad. Actual golden initials—but for what?

It creaked open, and the smell was of musty old ink. There were letters inside, on wrinkled old sheets of leaf-thin, see-through airmail paper, or crinkly proper stationery with the address emblazoned on it.

Dear James,

Thank you for your last letter. I will say, it is not to your credit to hear you complain. I have spoken to your housemaster, who tells me you have been coddled too much at home and are having trouble adapting. I see this as my own failing and feel it would probably be best—the master agrees—if you stayed on over the Easter break, as I shall be travelling to Capri and I worry the food may upset you.

THE LETTER WAS dated 1952.

Mirren stared at it for a long time. Obviously, these were letters received by the owner of the small, pathetic child's suitcase.

"Jamie," she said, glancing up, "when was your grandfather born?"

"Just before the end of the war," said Jamie, "1944. I had to order the headstone."

Eight, thought Mirren holding the letter. This was written to a child of eight. Telling them they couldn't come home for the Easter holidays.

"Where was your . . . Oh. Do you even know? Whose handwriting is this?" She passed it over.

"That's my great-grandfather," said Jamie, frowning. "You can see his signature."

"So, your grandfather's dad?"

"Yes."

"Also called . . ."

"James, yes."

She leafed through the pages.

We were disappointed to hear . . .

Unfortunately, we are unable . . .

Once again your headmaster . . .

Jamie got up and came over to examine the letters.

"He doesn't seem very happy," Mirren said. "They just seem to be a long collection of responding to complaints from your grandfather . . . Well, I don't suppose you'd like it if you were sent away from home at eight years old . . ."

"You wouldn't," said two emphatic voices. The boys looked at each other, surprised.

"You?" said Theo.

"Croffley," said Jamie. "Literally the same place these letters went to. Banged up at eight for a ten-stretch."

Theo nodded. "Dunner Hall."

"Isn't that for softies?"

Theo grimaced. "Apparently, yes."

"I am beginning to think," said Mirren, "that growing up posh is not quite as much fun as I imagined it might be."

Theo bent down and took a look.

"Oh my God. I can kind of understand keeping a kid's drawings—although probably not if you send them away, bloody hell. But this . . ." He pulled out a sheaf of ancient, flaking-away tracing paper.

Mirren looked at it. The old pages were such thin leaves, they looked ready to crumble into dust.

"*Trace its line*," she breathed.

Across the top, in a smudged child's hand, was written, *ANAN-MILS OF THE ARTIC*, and the tracings were of creatures—polar bears, Arctic foxes, and, yes, geese . . .

"No penguins, though," said Mirren.

"Wait—there actually aren't any penguins in the Arctic!" said Theo suddenly. "I forgot. How embarrassing."

"Oh! So he *did* mean *pick up your pen*!"

"Or he wasn't a very good student."

They leafed through the box, but it didn't seem to have anything in it other than the pictures.

Theo blinked. "Hang on," he said, and got up and jumped down the stairs and across the room. He waved a hand. "Over here," he said. "I'm sure I saw . . . somewhere around here . . ."

Just as he said it, the lights flickered, and they looked up.

"They do that," said Jamie. "Don't worry about it."

"Um, okay," said Theo. "Have you got a torch—you know, just in case?"

"No," said Jamie. "I can find my way round this place blind-folded. And have done, often."

"Well, that's okay for you," said Mirren. "I can't remember where my bedroom is when we're in broad daylight."

The lights flickered again.

"It's fine," said Jamie, and went towards the window, frowning. "Oh," he said. "That's earlier than the forecast. Oh well."

"What?" said Mirren, picking her way down the stairs towards the great high casement windows. The lights flickered again, and she could see it now: it had begun to snow. "It's snowing!" she said.

"It's winter in Scotland," said Jamie. "There are literally ski lifts one mountain over."

"Are we going to get stuck?" said Theo.

"Shouldn't think so," said Jamie, waving a hand. "Snow isn't what it was. I'm amazed we're even getting any in December. It used to show up in November, and you could be stuck for weeks after Christmas. It was great. If I didn't have to get back to school."

"Did you get to hang out with your grandad?"

"No! With Bonnie, of course."

They watched the flakes fall. It was cold and bleak out there; Mirren was happy she wasn't outside, even though the metal of the casement windows was freezing to the touch.

"Wow," she said. "It never snows in London. Like, five flakes, then it's all slushy and disgusting. This is . . . this is proper."

"It is," said Jamie. "We're going to have to get you kitted out."

The lights wobbled again.

"Is the power going to go off?"

Jamie shrugged. "Probably. Not yet."

"Not *yet*?"

"The electrics are . . . a little aged."

"I feel a Tripadvisor review coming on," said Mirren.

"So," said Theo, turning back to the matter at hand, "over here for some reason, mildly lumped together for once . . ."

He held up a front cover. They squinted to see it. *Bacteria of the Arctic*.

"I didn't think there were any bacteria in the Arctic," said Mirren. "I thought it was too cold."

"It's just an example," said Theo. "There are lots of books about the Arctic and Arctic animals over here."

Jamie glanced back. "You think they might have something to do with the tracings?"

"I don't know," said Theo. "But they were traced from somewhere."

"Fair point," said Jamie, and they started looking through the dusty old guides, Theo still using his phone as a torch. Jamie meanwhile had grabbed a stud of candle in a holder and was now reading by candlelight.

Mirren stared out a moment longer, letting her eyes adjust to looking at the swooping, dancing snowflakes blasting across the landscape. It was so lovely, the way they whisked and twirled in the air. As the boys leafed through the pages, occasionally making remarks like "Well, *someone* had never seen an otter before" and "Okay, I've gone bird-blind," she gazed into the lonely wilderness. She had travelled a little, she supposed—well, Ibiza with the girls, and France with her mum. But here, even though she was supposedly on the same island as London, it was hard to believe it. Not a speck of humanity or civilisation anywhere; nothing to be seen or heard; nobody else around. It was liberating, too, she supposed, to have this much space with which to do what you wanted. Although it hadn't seemed to make the old man very happy. Or the young one, she found herself thinking. Perhaps there was just too much solitude.

Just as she thought this, she saw a light blinking outside in the freezing dark.

Chapter Eighteen

"What's that?" Mirren asked, shielding her eyes against the black glass. There was a beam of light shining, flickering back and forth.

Jamie looked up from the scattered tomes and frowned.

"Probably lost tourists. They don't usually make it this far up the track, though. Plus once some kids thought it was deserted and came to do some kind of YouTube exploring thing and my grandfather threatened them with an actual blunderbuss."

"He blunderbussed YouTube kids?"

"Some of them are very annoying," murmured Theo.

Mirren looked at him.

"Come on, you know it's true. *Hey, you guys, like and subscribe as I break into this creepy mansion. Sure hope I get attacked by a guy with a blunderbuss!*"

"Well, if he did, how come that didn't go viral?" said Mirren.

"Friends in high places," said Jamie. "Old boys' network. Fortunately he was at school with the local paper's editor and they managed to get it hushed up. Sorry. I didn't invent it."

"Are they all *dead*?" said Mirren.

"No," said Jamie. Then, "I don't think so. And you're the one asking why I don't put the poem on the internet."

"In case *you* blunderbuss them?"

"It's definitely a car," said Theo with finality, pointing as, through the murk and the flurry of the blizzard outside, the glow separated itself into two separate beams: car headlights bending and moving as the light bounced off the snowflakes. It was being driven very erratically, though, rather too fast for the conditions and the state of the single-track road, weaving from side to side, occasionally mounting the bank. "In a hurry by the looks of things."

Jamie looked out at it and swore. "Oh, for Christ's sake."

"What?" said Mirren, as he turned and hurried towards the door.

Theo and Mirren looked at each other and kept watching as, eventually, the car drew up with a start outside a side door two storeys below them, and a furious-looking young woman with short hair jumped out.

Jamie came out from round the back and walked towards her, and she immediately started yelling at him, the Land Rover headlights still glowing, showing up how heavily the snow was falling.

"Cor," said Theo. "I thought living in the country would be quiet. This is like *EastEnders*, if *EastEnders* were set in a castle. Which I would very much watch."

"I can't work it out," said Mirren. "Girlfriend? Wife?"

"Sister," said Theo confidently. "She just got laid into him straightaway. Girlfriends lead up to it and pretend it's your fault."

"Had a lot of women shout at you?"

"You've done it yourself," said Theo.

The air in the room became even frostier than it was naturally. When Mirren spoke again, her tone had changed.

"I really thought you were going to call me," she said, and it wasn't with anger, or sarcasm, or implicit criticism. She spoke the truth, because it had made her sad. "And it made me really sad. I thought we had a good time."

Theo looked at the floor. "We did," he said. He scratched the back of his head. "I'm sorry."

He too looked up, his face open. It was as if the sadness of the North Library—the sad little boy, the unhappy family—had made them want to be better, to not waste as much of life as seemed to have been wasted here, in the piles of unread books and squandered paper. It had affected him, made him more thoughtful.

"I don't want us to squabble on this job," he said. "Not that I think it's going anywhere, but . . . even so."

Mirren nodded but didn't say anything. Theo took a deep breath, shook his dark hair to get some of the dust out of it.

"Look, Mirren, okay, fine. I was selfish. I thought I'd leave my options open. Then I felt like a shit, and it felt better not to get in touch because then I didn't have to think about myself being a shit." He winced. "And then, we always think bad things about someone we've treated badly. It's a horrible quirk of human nature. I felt like you were making me feel guilty by just existing, so I got pissed off with you."

Mirren almost laughed. "Oh *God*," she said. "That is *so annoying*. None of this is my fault. I didn't *do* anything!"

"I know," said Theo. "So saintly and nice. Drove me crazy."

She laughed properly then. "I'm not always nice," she said to him, in a slightly more challenging voice.

He looked back at her, those impish black eyebrows arched.

"I had forgotten," he said, "just how luscious-looking you are."

"Especially when I'm wearing all my clothes at once," said Mirren, but he didn't laugh back. Just fixed her with that intense, hot-eyed vampire gaze. Mirren felt her pulse speed up. It had been a long time—a very long time—since she'd had sex. Her body was reminding her of that.

"Well, I'm sure we could do something about that," he said.

The silence in the room was complete, apart from their breathing. Their breathing had become audible.

"Well, FUCKING HELL!" came a loud voice, and there was a huge bang, and the door of the library was thrown open.

Chapter Nineteen

"So this is where it's all going on," said the figure standing in the door with her hands on her hips.

Mirren and Theo whipped their heads round as if they'd been caught doing something they shouldn't.

Jamie was behind the figure, and squeezed past her, none too gently.

"Mirren, Theo—my sister, Esme."

"Yes, sorry, everyone, I've discovered your little game."

The voice was disarmingly posh—Jamie's voice was kind of posh, but Esme spoke like the late queen in old black-and-white broadcasts, before she got told to sound more like her subjects.

She was tall and slender, with a razor-sharp haircut that accentuated her high cheekbones. Her hair was tipped in purple in a way that 99.99 percent of mortals who weren't five foot ten wouldn't have a hope of getting away with, and she had tattoos almost everywhere. She was wearing heavy boots and combat trousers and was ever-so-slightly fabulous.

"There's no game, Esme," said Jamie. "I mean, apart from . . . well, there's some kind of riddle thing . . ."

"Why didn't you tell me about it?"

"Because," said Jamie, obviously trying to keep his temper,

"every time I mention anything to do with Forres you say *oh God, don't bore me with that shit*."

"Yes, and then I say, *sell the entire damn thing and send me my money*."

"There isn't any money, Esme."

"That's ridiculous. This place has thirty-six bedrooms; how can there be NO MONEY?" She glared at Mirren and Theo. "And you're obviously paying these guys. Someone told me they'd seen the train running, so I knew *something* was up."

Jamie scowled. "I'm paying them from money from the job which I had. How's your latest internship going? Or are you on another career break?"

"You have NO IDEA what it's like to try to make a living as a creative," said Esme.

"Neither do you!" sniped Jamie, and the atmosphere suddenly turned as cold as the snow outside.

The lights buzzed again.

"Oh yeah, the road's shut," said Esme. "They've closed the snow gates as well."

"You shouldn't have driven through it," said Jamie, his voice a little softer. "It's dangerous."

Esme snorted. "Don't be ridiculous. Me and the Landie know this place back to front."

Jamie looked outside. "Well, I wouldn't be too sure about that. I think 'the Landie' is going to be buried in about six minutes."

Esme cursed. Then she turned round and faced them all again.

"So, what are you looking for, then? This place has been picked clean by vultures for years, you should know. That's why there are all the gaps on the wall where pictures used to be. If there's anything of value in this house, our mother would have sniffed it out years ago."

"Esme—"

"Did he tell you the old laird was a lovely man?" said Esme, addressing them.

"I said he was complicated," said Jamie.

"He ran this place into the ground."

"But he had a hard upbringing," said Mirren, indicating the box of letters.

"That's actually quite offensive to all the good people in the world who had hard upbringings?" said Esme annoyingly.

While the siblings started bickering about light bulbs and where you could and couldn't take them from—the stairs, Esme arguing quite convincingly, being one of the places you should leave them in place—Mirren took the tracings over to Theo's pile of Arctic animal books. One of them, it turned out, was designed for children. *A Bestiary*, it was called; obviously a copy of a much, much older book—although between its dusty hard covers, closed with a clasp, it seemed quite old enough already. It was an engraved copy of a medieval manuscript. The pages were incredibly thick; double thickness really, many of them stuck together with age and, presumably, damp. The copyright page said 1928.

Mirren blew the dust off the gold-blocked pages. It was a true thing of beauty; a reproduction, but beautifully done, with strange creatures: plenty of dogs and horses, obviously, but unicorns, drawn as if real; curious-looking weasels and foxes with bounding tales and quizzical expressions; dragons of all shapes and sizes. The dogs were Mirren's favourite, often smiling, for some reason, and many with eyebrows that gave them distinctive expressions. There were hunting stags and does, flitting through gilt-embroidered apple trees, against rich backgrounds of forest trees latticing into repeating patterns. It was quite, quite beautiful.

"Cor," said Mirren quietly, and Theo leaned over to see. He grinned.

"No penguins."

"No penguins," said Mirren, smiling back

". . . but who can *bear* it?" said Theo, turning a page.

There was the most beautiful picture of a bear in the moonlight, rich in glowing reds and blues. The bear appeared to be mauling something, but it didn't take away from the loveliness of the drawing. Theo gently brought over the tracing paper from the old schoolbook and laid the bear picture on top. They looked at each other.

"Who's even going to pay the electricity bill?" Esme was shouting.

"Well, Grandfather left . . ."

"What?"

Jamie went quiet. "I don't know," he said finally.

Esme's sharp face was wintry. Theo and Mirren exchanged glances. He obviously didn't want to tell her.

"I heard you had people up here," Esme went on. "I figured you were up to something—selling the land or looking to cut your losses . . . What are you doing? What are you selling?" She looked around the messy library. "What the hell is this? For God's sake, Jamie."

"I didn't ask for this."

"Oh, come on; there hasn't been another boy born for thirty years! It was always going to be you! You should have been preparing for it all your life!!"

"Grampa didn't want to teach me and . . . Mum wasn't around."

Esme fell silent. "Well, no," she said eventually.

Mirren looked back down at the tracing of a bear. Theo moved it gently and, as they knew it would, it fitted exactly over the *Bestiary* bear, a perfect tracing, except, of course, with white fur instead of brown.

"This doesn't prove anything," whispered Theo, "not really."

They looked at it for a little longer.

"And it doesn't really get us anywhere."

Gently, Mirren pushed at the tracing, onto the book beneath. As the tracing paper hit the book and she pressed on it once again, she sniffed.

"What?" said Theo.

"I don't know," she muttered. Jamie and Esme were now having some sort of ding-dong about Scottish Power.

Mirren pressed a little harder and felt something give under her fingers.

"Careful!" hissed Theo; Mirren pulled back the tracing paper and they both stared at it. As they laid the tracing paper more carefully back over the outline again, the page below buckled. With great care, Theo touched it gently with one finger. Whereupon the bear, only just attached to the page, came loose, and within the thick old pages was revealed a small, empty compartment, which was bear-shaped.

Chapter Twenty

Mirren jolted with excitement. For a split second she didn't want—and nor, she sensed, did Theo—to tell the warring siblings, who were still fussing and squabbling. It felt like something so magical that neither of them quite deserved it, particularly the way they were so obviously used to behaving exactly how they wanted in front of the hired help. That was clearly a posh person characteristic: behave exactly how you like at all times.

Then Jamie said, "I'm sorry. I know this must be rotten for you as well. I'm doing my best, Esme. I can't make something out of nothing. I am sorry." And Mirren remembered, again, the haunted look on his face. He hadn't asked to be born into this ridiculous setup. He was making the best of it. He was, she realised, a gentler character than she'd thought at first. Such a contrast to confident, noisy Theo.

"You're as useless as every McKinnon man," spat Esme, and Jamie looked even more wounded.

"Ahem . . ." said Theo, commanding their attention.

"What is it?" Esme snapped.

"I'm afraid it's for Laird Jamie," said Theo, politely but in a tone that brooked no argument. Esme stared at them, as if about to order them to be marched off somewhere, but just at that moment the door opened. Everyone turned to it to see Bonnie's cheery, sweet face.

"Good evening, Miss Esme," she said, and even Esme couldn't not smile at Bonnie.

"Christ," said Esme. "I cannot believe you're still here."

"I'm not really," said Bonnie. "I died years ago in the attic and have come back to life as a ghost."

This would have possibly been funnier if the wind hadn't been whistling through one of what Mirren would later learn were thirty-seven chimney pots.

Esme laughed. "These guys are being absolutely *pissant* Secret Squirrels about something they're refusing to cut me in on. TELL ME you've got drinks."

"I've got drinks."

"Thank FUCK. Where are we down to, cellar-wise?"

"We haven't bottomed out yet. Plenty of grappa and absinthe."

"Perfect." Esme looked at them all and stood up, shaking her head. "Well, you guys keep grubbing about in this shit. *I'm* going with Bonnie. Is there a fire going anywhere?"

"The Chinois . . ."

"Yes, yes, the usual. Perfect." And she swept out of the room.

Jamie winced. "Sorry," he said. "Bit of a force of nature, my sister . . . Wait, what—you haven't *found* something?"

Theo held up the book. "Not sure," he said. "Well, yes, I think so. I think, though, that we could do with gloves and tweezers before we go ferreting around in there; it's incredibly old and fragile. Could all crumble to dust."

As he said this, the tracing paper, which had made contact with the old glue, started to curl up and almost disintegrate. They all watched it. Theo showed Jamie the bear-shaped hole in the book, and his eyes widened.

"Oh, wow!" he said. "This is amazing! You did it already!" He shook his head. "My bloody grandfather," he said. "All this effort and work put into this rather than, for example, teaching me some basic land management."

"Did you study it at university?"

"Yeah," said Jamie. "Then I dropped out and joined the Botanic Gardens and, well, here we are . . ."

Mirren was peering at the hole. "We probably do need tweezers, don't you think?"

"There's something that takes ticks off the dogs; that should do it," said Jamie.

"No!" said Mirren.

"It's all right," said Theo, pulling a box of disposable gloves and what looked like a small vanity kit—tiny scissors, needles, and indeed a pair of tweezers—out of his canvas bag.

"You came prepared, or just ready to exfoliate?" said Mirren.

"Mirren, I know you fell into this line of work, but I am actually someone who deals in antiquarian books," said Theo, with a faint edge of exasperation to his voice. "I came prepared . . . and actually, if we can reseal this book, I can probably get you a fair price on this as it is, without doing a thing to it. It's a curio."

"What's a fair price?" said Jamie, and Theo said a number, and Jamie said that wouldn't replace a pipe in the East Wing and Theo said no, and so on they went, and they let him put the gloves on, and Mirren, holding the torch, watched as he very carefully fished around inside the compartment.

At first he obviously couldn't find anything, and, as they watched, Mirren worried again that they were on a wild-goose chase, a pointless exercise designed as a last laugh from a troubled old man. But after what felt like the longest time, Theo's handsome face took on a set of deep concentration and stillness, which was not, Mirren couldn't help reflecting, entirely unattractive to witness, in the flickering lowlights of the room—and finally, with a steady hand, like a particularly tricky game of Operation, he pulled out a tiny, tightly folded piece of paper. As he held it up, it became apparent that it was in the shape of an origami swan, small and intricate. And it was equally clear that the paper had writing on it, in a tiny, cramped hand.

Chapter Twenty-One

Jamie whistled.

"What is it?" said Mirren in excitement.

They decamped to the nearest desk, an ancient wooden thing with drawers all over it, stuffed with feathers, thimbles, old fountain pens, blotting paper.

This time Jamie, the tallest, held his phone torch overhead as Theo carefully unfolded the object.

Flat out, the swan was a square of ancient heavy paper. It was completely covered in tiny letters, separated, in pale blue fountain pen ink. Theo took out a pair of black-rimmed glasses and put them on.

"Hmm," he said.

"Is that your professional opinion?" asked Mirren.

She looked more closely at it. In fact, they were not letters. They were minute, and each figure was either a zero or a one.

"Oh, *what*?" she said.

"Binary?" said Jamie. "What?"

Mirren screwed up her face. "I don't understand. He wrote computer code? But this . . . this looks really old. Like, before computers? Or did he work in early computers?"

Theo shook his head. "No, binary is a code that computers use, but they didn't invent it."

"It looks like *The Matrix*," said Mirren.

"It does," said Theo. "But it's ancient. We'll need to type it into a computer. And not get any of it wrong."

Jamie nodded. Suddenly, surprising two of them, a bell sounded, a deep clanging, somewhere far away. "This seems," he said, "like a job for tomorrow."

Mirren looked at her watch and was surprised to see it was six thirty. It had been dark for so long she'd lost track of time. And she was, after hours in the book stacks, completely and utterly filthy.

"Shall we dress for dinner? And meet in the Chinois . . . that room we were in before?" said Jamie.

"Oh, you are kidding me," said Mirren. "I don't have any more dresses! This is meant to be a work trip!"

Jamie shrugged. "Check the wardrobes. You never know." He turned to Theo. "You all right?"

Theo nodded. Well, he would be, thought Mirren.

"Okay, well, good luck with the hot water," said Jamie, then, as they left the room, "Don't . . . don't mention this to Esme. Please. I'm not trying to cheat anybody, but . . . who even knows what this is? If it's even anything?"

"It would seem a lot of trouble to go to for nothing," said Theo.

"You could probably say that about this whole house," said Jamie.

MIRREN FINALLY FOUND her way back to the bedroom. Second floor, east side, she told herself. It was easy to remember it was east, because it looked out over the cliff, onto where, somewhere out in the dark, the freezing North Sea was pounding, far below at the bottom of the dramatic cliffs. She was expecting the room to be freezing but to her absolute delight, Bonnie, true to her word had been in and lit a fire. There was a pile of logs next to it too;

tentatively she put one on it and it caught in an incredibly satisfying way. She smiled and nearly clapped her hands together. The lights buzzed ominously, but she was growing used to that.

Mirren glanced at the window. The snow was still swirling, in a way that now seemed more threatening than charming; Esme had already implied that the roads were impassable, and that was a couple of hours ago. And she'd been in a big car. Mirren wished she could phone her mum and let her know she was okay. Not that her mother would necessarily notice that she hadn't been in touch for a couple of days—in fact, she'd be horrified if Mirren rang her up out of the blue, and would assume something terrible had happened. Nora wasn't entirely convinced that Mirren qualified for adulthood, at thirty-one. Or ever would.

As she turned back from the window, she realised something amazing. A tin bath was set up in front of the fire, the metal warmed by the flames. There was a rough bar of soap, a flannel, and a large fluffy towel. The water was scorching.

You couldn't lie in it or even properly sit down, but Mirren managed a surprisingly adequate bath crouching in the hot water, scrubbing herself down with the warm flannel and drying herself off with the huge, washed-soft towel. Flushed from her unusual ablutions, she glanced around at the room. Indeed there was a wardrobe there. Jamie had told her to help herself . . . she couldn't help being curious as to what on earth was inside.

With the towel wrapped around her, she sidled over, her cheeks flushed from the hot water. It was one big wardrobe, the type that had a mirror in the door. Mirren tried the handle. She was quite sure it would be locked, and was surprised when it opened easily and two mothballs fell out.

The door swung open, and, as she glanced up, her face broke into a smile of pure surprise.

She had expected—well, nothing, really. She hadn't had a clue what Jamie was talking about. Maybe that there would be a bunch of old tweed mouldering away—more tat.

But no. The wardrobe was stuffed full of dresses. No, she thought again, these were not dresses; they were *gowns*. Wrapped in plastic, draped on soft padded hangers.

Mirren lifted them down. There was a '50s floral dress with a wide neck, in a stiff, shiny material with flowers appliquéd on to it. There was a high-necked, ruffled Victorian long frock that looked like the Vampire's Wife brand—ironic, thought Mirren, given who was across the corridor—but was far too old and frayed. There was a silvery '90s-style slip, a sliver of a thing which looked gorgeous but also freezing; and a bright orange, rather fabulous muumuu which came with a matching turban.

Finally she came across the simplest dress: a dark red, almost burgundy gown that was made of softest silk; it had little bell sleeves, and a full hem. She pulled it out and held it up against herself wonderingly. Whose dress was this? Whose had it been? Then she found a tag, still on it, with a designer label, and a breathtaking price. This dress had never been worn. They'd do better on Vinted than looking for a book, Mirren thought. She checked the others: many were the same. Someone had bought these and stuck them in a room and forgotten all about them.

Cut on the bias, the wine-coloured dress was also extremely forgiving, and she slipped it on and looked at herself in the mirror on the front and smiled. It was so utterly unlike anything she would ever wear; she looked like a flapper, getting ready to go down to the drawing room to find out who'd been murdered. She smiled to herself. She had one pair of black shoes, which were not ideal, being flat and rather sturdy, but actually, when she put them on, they rather added to the effect; they could easily be 1920s. She ran back to the bathwater and flattened down her curly hair behind her ears, then pulled out from her makeup bag a packed, but rarely used red MAC lipstick. Mixed with her regular browny lip gloss, it almost matched the colour of the dress. She lashed on some mascara, then picked up her black cardigan. It slightly spoiled the effect but there wasn't much she could do about that.

Then she put it down again. No. Things were a bit mad. She was hundreds of miles away from anyone who knew her, who would judge her—her family, her friends, her colleagues. This place was ridiculous—an endless crumbling castle—but it was magical too. It had a deep enchantment all of its own, in the ancient walls, the whirling snow, the empty spaces on the walls where the pictures had once been, the unhappy man and his unhappy antecedents, the endless, endless books. This was a holiday from real life, a different way of being, and she could behave however the hell she wanted. It wasn't as if she'd ever be in this situation again, being summoned in an ancient Scottish castle by a clanging old dinner bell.

She glanced around the room, spotting another bookcase, this time full of hardback fiction from the last quarter of the twentieth century—*The Thorn Birds*, *A Year in Provence*, *Lace*. Amazing! She could rifle through it later—and next to that, an old leather seat beside the window. On the back of the chair was an old tartan blanket, the deep red of the stripe, on a neutral background, matching her dress almost exactly. She gave it an experimental sniff, but it smelled absolutely fine, of soft lambswool infused with woodsmoke. She sprayed it quickly with perfume, then wrapped it around her elbows. That was more like it. She glanced at herself once more, almost lost her nerve, wondered whose dress it was, and if this was a completely ridiculous idea. Then she heard, once again, the bell clanging, deep within the building, summoning her, and without another thought, before she could change her mind, she opened the bedroom door.

Chapter Twenty-Two

The door opposite hers opened at exactly the same time, and she caught a glimpse inside; Theo's room was green where hers was red. She supposed that was how the household staff would have kept track of it, back in the day when they had a full staff, and not just Bonnie working wonders all on her own. She was perfectly friendly, but Mirren still found it creepy, as if, when there was nobody in the house, Bonnie simply shut herself away in a box.

Theo walked into the corridor. Mirren stared at him.

"You *brought* that?"

"Of course," said Theo. "Who comes to a castle without formal wear?"

He was immaculately attired in black tie, his bow tie a little floppy, his white shirt perfect. His thick hair was slicked back, making him look even more darkly handsome than usual, particularly when he smiled at her.

"You look very nice."

"Thank you," said Mirren. "I'm wearing a blanket; do you think they'll notice?"

Theo rolled his eyes. "Only if you insist on saying, *Hey, everyone, guess what, I'm wearing a blanket,*" he said. "I know you are very keen on reminding us how you're an honest working-class child of the soil or whatever it is, but we all get it: you hate the parasitical upper classes, even while you're currently working for them, so okay, Millie Tant, can we just go downstairs, with you looking quite lovely, and not be quite so chippy during dinner?"

Mirren gave him a look, stung.

"Oh, come on, don't give me that look. I just complimented you. Also, if you're going to be so insistent about the fact that you don't go to a lot of smart places, I should warn you in advance, dinner is going to be terrible."

And then, by way of consolation, he offered her his thick arm to go down the great, broad grand staircase, and, not knowing quite what else to do, she took it. The scent of his expensive Penhaligon's aftershave reminded her, briefly, of the year before. Why did he have to smell so good, dammit?

IN CONTRAST TO the rest of the house, which was now doused in gloom, presumably made even worse by Jamie taking out half the light bulbs from other places, the Chinese drawing room was easier to find this evening, blazing as it was with light. The faded turquoise and bright birds-and-flowers wallpaper glowed gently. An extremely old record player was playing jazz, rather fuzzily. Jamie and Esme were at opposite sides of the room, evidently still not talking to one another. Esme was standing by an open window as the storm raged outside, smoking furiously, even though the wind kept blowing her cigarette out. Jamie was by a wooden art deco cocktail bar, mixing some brown liquid in heavy glasses. He added maraschino cherries carefully.

"Old-fashioned?" he asked carelessly, and Mirren found herself beaming. Jamie looked at her rather strangely. In fact, had Mirren only known it, he was indeed finding it strange. Not many people in this house smiled for no reason. Not many people smiled, full stop. Plus, she looked different—Jamie didn't know much about women's clothes, but this was definitely something nice.

And the reason Mirren couldn't seem to stop this stupid grin from spreading across her face was similar. She hadn't been able to stop herself being excited by the fact that Jamie was wearing . . . well, of course he would be—why wouldn't he? This was just what dressing for dinner meant, up here. Nonetheless, he was wearing a real, honest-to-goodness, true-life kilt, without any self-consciousness whatsoever.

Mirren hadn't really ever given much thought to tartan, but this was a faded blue, green, and orange, a country-looking design, with a heavy old sporran on it. He wore it with a plain white shirt and a tweed waistcoat. Normally she would have thought of kilts as being quite funny, but somehow she really liked this. It suited him so well. He looked . . . he looked more at home. Not quite so anxious, rather more rugged.

He caught her eyes on him and looked up. "You look nice," he said.

"Thank you," said Mirren, blushing and accepting the drink he handed her. She bit her lip; she'd noticed him noticing her smile and didn't want to admit that the reason she looked so happy was that coming into a castle drawing room dressed in a beautiful dress and the lord of the manor handing her a cocktail felt like the stuff of fantasies.

"Oh," said Esme, turning in from the window. "That's a nice colour on you."

Mirren was even more surprised to get a compliment from Esme. "Um, thanks! There's loads of dresses up there."

Esme rolled her eyes. "Christ, yes. Another nail in the coffin of the McKinnon family coffers. Darling spendthrift Mama." She frowned. "Mind you, she doesn't need all that stuff where she is. I'm going to have a rummage. I bet some of it is worth a bit."

"That's what I thought," agreed Mirren.

"Esme!" said Jamie reprovingly.

"What? Shut up—you don't inherit everything IN THE WARDROBES!"

"Well, I do, actually, but I don't care about that. I meant, this is Mum's stuff."

Esme rolled her eyes. "I won't tell her if you don't."

"Where did you say your mum is?" said Mirren, smoothing down her dress, which now felt a little odd to be wearing. They were talking about her as if she was dead.

She sipped her drink, which was warming and utterly delicious, the whisky soft and smoky, not harsh and abrasive as she usually thought of it, with a bright edge of clementine. There were cloves in the glass, too, and the delicious maraschino cherry. Theo was already halfway down his.

"She got out," said Esme drily. "Sometimes being a girl does work in your favour."

"She had a small trust fund," explained Jamie. "She took it and went to Saint-Tropez . . ."

"Where she got taken in by an increasing pool of gigolos," said Esme. "Some of the oiliest men in the history of the universe. Then she got married and moved to Australia. I don't know how far the trust fund goes these days either. We certainly haven't got one."

"You don't see her?"

"Only when she wants something," said Esme. "I'm glad you found those gowns, actually; I can stave her off a little longer."

"But she's your mum!" said Mirren. She fell out with Nora all the time, but only because they loved one another so much.

The siblings looked at each other.

"She wasn't around that much when we were small," said Jamie. "That's why we spent so much time here."

Mirren felt it once again. Slightly sorry for these ridiculous rich people who had everything. It must have shown in her face because Theo gave her a stern look, then quickly raised his glass.

"To . . . a successful outcome," he said, that rather wolfish smile spreading across his face.

Esme closed the window and came into the centre of the room, then they clinked glasses. "Yeah," she said. "I notice you guys haven't told me how you got on today . . ."

Everyone went slightly quiet, looking at Jamie for a way forward. He looked torn; on the one hand, Mirren guessed, he wanted to share what they knew and what they had yet to find out. On the other, it was entirely possibly he didn't trust Esme one bit—he didn't seem to, didn't trust her not to behave exactly as her mother had, taking what she could get and then disappearing. She was very happy it wasn't a decision she had to make—and, thankfully, that great shuddering bell came once more.

"Lucky you," said Esme. "Saved by the bell."

Theo and Mirren followed the siblings as they trailed out into the corridor. It was ridiculous, Mirren found herself thinking, that it took so long to get anywhere in this building. As though they deliberately made life less convenient for themselves.

"What do you think about telling Esme?" Mirren whispered to Theo.

Theo glanced at the great arched window at the end of the corridor. The world remained a maelstrom, and they were still completely hemmed in by the falling snow.

"Well," he said, "nobody is going anywhere. She's going to be staying here. It'll be a bit daft if she just follows us about the entire time."

"But Jamie hired us. It's his house."

"I know," said Theo. "It's a bit of a shame, though: I think she'd be the brains of the outfit."

He glanced at Esme, in what Mirren worried was a rather admiring way, as she stalked her way down the corridors, utterly at ease in the half-light. She was wearing a pair of tight trousers teamed with a combat jacket and a light shirt and heavy boots; a bit piratical and very sexy, Mirren concluded, a little glumly. Her spiky hair stood up straight from her head: she looked remarkable. Suddenly Mirren's red dress felt absurdly old-fashioned, as if she was dressing up for a costume party.

They walked past shut-up rooms, and one with a door cracked open, which Mirren noticed was full of great dark shapes covered in white drapes. It was incredibly spooky.

"What's that? Ghost furniture?" she couldn't help asking.

"Music room," Jamie replied without stopping. "It's to preserve the instruments."

"It doesn't work," said Esme. "All the harp strings pinged aeons ago. If you hear music in the night, it's definitely the ghosts."

"There's ghosts?"

"Oodles!"

"Esme!" said Jamie.

"You didn't tell them about the ghosts?"

"No," said Jamie shortly. "Because it's absolute bollocks of the first order."

"Everyone thinks that, when there are other people around," observed Esme. "Once you're on your own in the middle of the night, well, it's a different matter." She looked straight at Mirren. "Listen for the floors creaking. The people who live here, who know their way around . . . we know how not to creak. But if anything unwanted shows up . . ."

Mirren couldn't help but shudder. They arrived at another set of double doors with light beneath them and she thought how strange it was to walk past the rows and rows of closed-off rooms, all dusty and miserable and spooky—then here and there find a tiny remnant of what the entire house would have been once, a room full of light and colour, clean and bright and lively and waiting for them: they had reached the dining room.

Chapter Twenty-Three

The dining room was dramatic, painted in a dark brick red. There were old glass cabinets lining the walls, some shelves empty, some with odds and ends of what had clearly once been beautiful sets of china but now only contained remnants; chipped willow-pattern saucers, cups without handles, whatever could not be sold. But the shelves were dust-free, the glass display cases unsmeared. Someone was looking after this room. No need to ask who.

Loveliest of all, in the corner was a vast Christmas tree, and the whole room was deeply scented with fir. It must have been quite a job to get it in, but now it was here it was beautiful; covered in ancient, cracked ornaments of thick glass or carefully hand-painted wood. There was no mass-produced tat here, no cheap tinsel. There were, amazingly, and, Mirren thought, incredibly dangerously, real candles lit, the candleholders carefully strapped to the boughs, and she stared at them in fascination.

The long table was set at one end with polished silver and old, thick glasses. A decanter of red wine stood open, and there were vases of winter ferns placed at intervals along the table. A huge fire crackled in the open fireplace, giving the gloomy room a cheery aspect; candelabra were lit and there was a delicious smell coming from somewhere.

Esme marched over to the carafe and poured wine for everyone, then handed out the glasses.

"Jamie is being a dick about this," said Esme, taking a long swig. "But I'm going to put it to you guys: you're trying to find something my grandfather left."

Nobody said anything.

"And all my grandfather left is a pile of bloody books. So, is it something to do with books? Am I guessing right so far?"

They all nodded.

"And you weren't going to tell me?" she said accusingly to Jamie, who went rather pink.

"Because you'd accuse me of stealing from you," he said, "and I really am not. And then you'd say it was a stupid idea."

"It is SUCH a stupid idea," said Esme. "Remember those treasure hunts he used to set for us?"

Jamie nodded.

"They were *impossible*," said Esme. "I don't think we ever solved one."

"One year Bonnie found the present by accident," said Jamie.

"What's that?" said Bonnie, pushing into the room from a different door, an inconspicuous swing door set in the side that must lead down to the kitchen. She was carrying a huge tray, which she set down on the embroidered tablecloth.

"The year you solved the treasure hunt."

Bonnie screwed up her face. "Oh, they were *impossible*, those things. Ridiculous."

"What was it?" asked Mirren, interested.

"Well, I was in the stables, and I found a parcel and I brought it in," said Bonnie.

"And Grandfather was FURIOUS," said Esme. "Absolutely furious. What were the clues, even?"

"There was a set of numbers," remembered Jamie, "that didn't seem to make any sense at all."

"Oh yeah," said Esme. "What were they?"

"It was celestial latitude and longitude," said Jamie suddenly.

"We were EIGHT!" said Esme.

"Apparently Grandfather knew about celestial navigation when *he* was eight. Or ten, at least," said Jamie. "I was ten."

"I was trying to cuddle a horse," said Bonnie.

"Then, if you figured that out and went to the telescope room . . ."

"You have a—" started Mirren, but Theo gave her a warning look, so she shut up again.

". . . and managed to figure out the really fiddly telescope, which we weren't supposed to touch anyway—it was completely ancient, so we didn't know how to use it. But if we had figured it out, it would have shown us a constellation that we would have had to identify and that would have been . . ."

"Pegasus!" said Mirren excitedly.

"Pegasus and Andromeda; there were two," said Jamie. "You would have had to figure out from there that Pegasus was a horse that had carried Andromeda. Then you had to find the horse that carried Andy. We had, like, thirty horses then."

"It was SO STUPID," said Esme.

"He got so annoyed," agreed Jamie.

"What was the treasure?"

"It was rather lovely," mused Esme. "Do you remember? A little gold horse. Absolutely ancient Egyptian or something."

"I'd rather have had chocolate," said Jamie.

"I thought I might get to keep it," said Bonnie. "But then, after your grandfather got so annoyed, my grandma snuck me away to the kitchen and gave me a mince pie and three Quality Streets for bringing it back and handed it in. So it worked out all right."

"It did for you!" said Jamie. "We just got a bollocking."

"What happened to the golden horse?" asked Mirren.

"God knows. You're probably wearing it," said Esme. She heaved a sigh. "So that's what this is? Another treasure hunt?" She looked around the table, but nobody replied.

They sat down to the loveliest thing: fresh brown bread and butter, and home-smoked salmon; great thick slices that Bonnie reluctantly admitted she'd smoked herself, remarking that not many people had an outbuilding just for smoking fish, so she might as well make use of it. Her uncle had taken a couple of salmon from their loch, so they were eating produce off their own land, something Mirren had never conceived of, if you didn't count her abortive attempts at tomato plants under her skylight. It was delicious.

Mirren would have asked Bonnie to stay and eat with them, but she had disappeared back into the kitchen already.

"I don't . . . Does she work for you full-time?" she asked, and Jamie and Esme both nodded.

"She nursed my grandfather, I suppose," said Jamie. "She's the only one left. Her family has worked in this house for generations."

"Her grandmother practically raised you," said Esme. "You were round there often enough, begging for scraps."

"She was a good cook," said Jamie crossly.

"But if you don't have any money, how do you pay Bonnie?"

"There's a trust," said Jamie, "set up for her family. Her family were always in service here; her great-grandmother started at ten."

"Oh, goodness," said Mirren, stricken.

"If you were from a poor family up here," said Jamie, "there were a lot worse places to be in those days."

Mirren nodded. "I know. My great-gran was in service in London. My cousin did one of the genealogy things in the pandemic."

"Well, then, various Airdries worked for us down the generations—gardeners and ghillies, they always had a home here. All of that gradually died out and they were the last to go, but there was a trust to keep servants in their old age, and, well . . ." Here his smile grew rueful. "They managed it well."

Mirren could barely suppress a smile. "You mean she has more money than you."

"*Everyone* has more money than us," said Esme.

"But she still works here?"

"It's her home as much as it is ours," said Jamie forcefully.

"And she has her own smoker," said Esme.

"Can't you ask *her* to buy the place?" said Theo.

"Unfortunately," said Jamie, "she would have very much done her due diligence as to whether or not it would be a worthwhile investment. What we really need is to find a billionaire who doesn't care that it's falling apart, just thinks it's cool. And to be able to keep going just a little while longer so that we have time to do that, by paying our taxes in January."

"And that's why you should count me in," said Esme. "More heads are better."

"Well, if that's the case, why don't we just send Bonnie off to the stables again?" chipped in Theo.

Mirren concentrated on the salmon. It was delicious; delicate and wild. Bonnie was very talented. The wine, too, tasted like nothing she'd ever had before: deep and velvety, with a peppery flavor. Esme took a sip and nodded appreciatively.

"I see we've made it to the better end of the cellars."

"Is there nothing down there you can sell?" asked Theo.

"Come on, my good man," said Jamie, with a rare smile. "One does have one's limits."

"Remember when Grampa sold all the whisky at auction?" said

Esme. "Nightmare. Load of crazies turning up like it was Drunk Disneyland."

"That actually sounds fun," said Theo.

"Esme had to help Bonnie mop up all the vomit," said Jamie. "Another brilliant Forres Castle idea bites the dust."

Esme shook her head. "Well, quite. So no more of that. If we have to go down, we might as well do it accompanied by a decent Burgundy."

Bonnie took the plates away, thanking Mirren when she complimented the fish effusively. She then brought in a huge china tureen, decorated with ancient hand-painted images of sides of the castle they were sitting in right then, and opened the lid.

"Venison again?" said Esme with a slight sigh, and Bonnie smiled.

"I'm afraid it's all off the land, Miss Esme. Our cheeseburger budget is unusually low this month."

"Yeah, yeah," said Esme, as Bonnie started ladling out large portions, with more of the wonderful bread, and dishes of fine green beans and a spinach with a sharp lemon dressing. The smell was heavenly, deep and rich and chocolatey, and Mirren inhaled deeply.

"This is fantastic," she said, and Bonnie laughed.

"I don't normally get so much appreciation."

"That's because Esme lives off the canapés she gets at fashion parties," said her brother.

"PLEASE," said Esme, waving her hands. "Who eats at fashion parties? Christ, Jamie."

With everyone served, Mirren made sure she was using the right fork and dug in carefully. It was just as delicious as it smelled; there were berries in there that added a sweetness to the dish, as well as more of the deep red wine to add body, and the meat itself was so soft, you could cut it with a spoon. She tried not to make more noise about it than was absolutely necessary, but she could tell by how quiet everyone was that there was a lot of general enjoyment going on; there was even a truce in the air, of sorts, between the warring siblings, and for the time being Mirren relaxed.

Chapter Twenty-Four

Everything always looked better after a good meal, and as Bonnie tidied away the amazing lemon tart she had served with crème Chantilly and which everyone else had eaten with a fork and Mirren had started, too late, with her teaspoon, they moved, replete, back to the drawing room, and took comfortable chairs around the fire.

Jamie had brought his laptop and plugged a router into the wall, which apparently would harness some tiny scrapings of internet every so often from a passing satellite, if nobody sneezed and a mouse didn't run across the road. Although the snow was not going to help.

Bonnie had announced that the kitchen door was jammed up already and if it didn't stop soon they'd all be climbing out of the first-storey windows. Mirren must have looked nervous, because Bonnie had smiled and said not to worry, there wasn't anything to complain about until it hit the third-storey windows, and Mirren had said are we going to be all right for supplies and Bonnie had said absolutely not, the castle had never been cut off by flooding, snow, ice, storms, harsh weather or war before and they had absolutely no idea what they were doing, what a great idea to think about stockpiling supplies, if only they'd thought of it . . . but she said it with such a sweet smile that Mirren couldn't take offence.

Jamie had opened up his creaking laptop and said, "Now, right," and Mirren was trying to pay attention, but it had been such a long day, with an exceptional amount of new things to deal with. Now, staring into the fire, the tartan blanket warm around her shoulders, her stomach full of good food and good wine, and with a wee dram of whisky sitting next to her on the flimsy lacquered table, she was in severe danger of falling asleep straightaway.

"So," Theo was saying. "It's numbers? Might it be celestial navigation again?"

"I wouldn't have thought so," said Jamie. "He didn't like to repeat himself."

"Remember Morse code year?" said Esme. "I thought he was going to cry."

"Fibonacci year was the worse," said Jamie. "I think he gave up after that. None of the adults could do it either. Mum started yelling at him. He ended up spending the whole of Christmas Day in his office on his own."

"Oh yeah!" said Esme. "And old Mrs. Airdrie—that's Bonnie's gran—let us watch *Top of the Pops* on the kitchen TV. That was a BRILLIANT Christmas."

There wasn't, Mirren now noticed, a television in the house, or at least not one she'd seen so far. In fact, there were almost no signs of modernity at all. There was the old gramophone, and an old wireless—not a router, an actual radio—in her bedroom, which she couldn't imagine how to use. There were no charger cables, apart from this old one Jamie had, no flat screens, no Xbox . . . It was a house stuck in the very distant past.

"Anyway, binary doesn't just mean numbers," said Jamie. "It stands for letters too. Just like Morse, actually. Zeros and ones instead of dots and dashes."

"Uh-oh," said Esme.

Theo fingered the tiny sheet of paper, frowned, and felt in his pocket for a thick pair of dark-rimmed glasses, which rather suited him. Mirren watched him sleepily. He was so attractive. But not a good prospect, she thought. Then she also thought, who cares about that? But that was what she'd thought when they met last year: that he was absolutely gorgeous and then everything else could sort itself out. So she'd thrown caution to the wind, gone after him for no other reason than that she found him attractive, and told herself that it didn't matter that she didn't want anything serious—and what had happened? She'd felt annoyed and miserable at being ghosted afterwards, for months. Completely not worth it. If a hangover lasted for an entire season, you'd never drink again.

She stared instead at Jamie, focusing so intently on his laptop, waiting for a connection. He was young, but his height and thinness made him look older than he was. His shoulders were broad—but not quite broad enough yet for the burden life had landed upon him. His open face and sweet turned-down eyes should have been very attractive, as well as his full lips—the gift of a fashion model or two somewhere in his family tree—but the worried look permanently lodged on his face detracted from the effect. Theo's devil-may-care stance would always be more appealing than Jamie's weight-of-the-world demeanour. Even when something undeniably nice was happening, like being served the world's best venison stew in front of a roaring fire in a Scottish castle in the snow, he still had the air of a man who was wondering if he'd left the oven on. Though Mirren would hazard a guess he'd never turned an oven on in his life.

He felt her eyes on him and looked up, and his first instinct, she noticed, was to smile. She liked that about him.

"It was," he observed, "a very stupid idea to try to start interpreting a tiny, decades-old binary code written on a swan after two old-fashioneds and half a bottle of Burgundy."

"Are the figures swimming?"

"The swan is."

Mirren stared into the fire as Theo intoned the numbers while Jamie typed them out.

"01010100 . . . 01001000 . . . 01010010 . . . 01000101 . . . 01000101 . . . oh God," he said, swiping off his glasses and rubbing his eyes. "I m literally going to send myself to sleep."

"*T . . . H . . . R . . . E . . . E . . .*" Jamie spelled out laboriously. "It says 'three'! Three wishes?"

"Three kings?"

"Three lions on the shirt," said Theo promptly. They all looked at him crossly, and the siblings looked very alike suddenly.

"Aye, that'll be right," said Bonnie, who was clearing away the coffee cups.

Theo bent back down to it.

"01001110 . . . 01001001 . . . 01001110 . . . 01000101 . . ."

"*N . . . I . . . N . . . E . . .*"

"Nine?" said Mirren, suddenly a little concerned.

"He wouldn't," said Jamie.

"He bloody would, that old bastard," said Esme, storming over. "He's using a number code to translate numbers . . . back into numbers. Oh my God."

"Maybe not," said Jamie helplessly. "Maybe it's an address. Thirty-nine Regent Street or something."

"Then you'd write 'thirty-nine.'"

They all stared at Theo, who cleared his throat and peered through his spectacles.

"01010011 . . . 01000101 . . . 01010110 . . . 01000101 . . . 01001110 . . ."

"*S . . . E . . . V . . .* Oh, bollocks," said Jamie.

"It's numbers? Is it all numbers? Give me that." Esme snatched the fragile swan from Theo's fingers.

"NO, DON'T!" hollered Jamie. "It's *fragile*!"

Just as he said this, the ancient, crumbling paper came apart in her long, pointed fingernails, the two halves of the swan dropping perilously close to the fire, the warm updrafts from the hot air refusing to let them come to land but instead drawing them dangerously close to the chimney . . .

It was Mirren who reached them first, hurling herself towards them and surprising even herself by grabbing both pieces, desperately holding on to one, the other just beyond her grasp if she could just . . .

BANG!

And, with an enormous crash of snow falling off the roof, there was a thud, a flash, a crackle, and every light went out.

Chapter Twenty-Five

The only light was the fire and the candles, but it took a moment for Mirren's eyes to adjust; she could see the flare of the electrics behind her eyeballs and squeezed her eyes shut. When she opened them, it was like a freeze-frame: nobody had moved, everyone straining, halfway through midair, trying to rescue the swan, or reach out, then finding themselves in the dark.

The corners of the room, anything not near the fire, vanished immediately. From deep in the castle there was the echo of a crash, almost certainly Bonnie and some plates, which shook Mirren from her reverie, the taut thrill of the four bodies, frozen there in the firelight.

"Crap!" shouted Jamie, with some feeling, as they all straightened up, Mirren breathless. "Oh God. Did you get it? Did you get it?"

For a second, Mirren was so shocked and confused, she didn't know what he meant. Then she checked her hand. To her total surprise, there was the other half of the swan; her hand must have closed on it automatically.

"Yeah," she said quietly. "I got it."

Esme blew air out. "Bloody electrics. Is it the weather or did you not pay the bill?"

"It'll be a fuse," said Jamie. "The solar pays the bills."

"Babe, it's been cloudy since . . ." Esme shrugged. "2020?"

"I'm glad we got to finish dinner," said Theo, lifting up the candelabra. "Should we go check Bonnie's all right and not broken her neck anywhere?" He opened the door, which led to the kitchen stairs. "Bonnie?"

The voice came from far away. "I'm here! I'm fine! But I think you might have to say goodbye to the last of the Royal Doulton."

"It's horrible anyway," shouted back Esme.

Slowly, a glow appeared in the stairwell, followed by Bonnie's cheerful face, candlelight flushing her a lovely pink. Mirren glanced at Jamie; she still couldn't quite understand the relationship between them. She didn't want to look at Theo, in case he had his wolfish expression on again.

"It's not the fuses," she said, coming in with an armful of extra candles under her elbow. She stuck them in various holders and in any saucer or plant pot she could get her hands on. By the time she'd finished, the room looked like a particularly incendiary place for a wedding proposal. "I checked them already."

"You're so practical," said Mirren.

"Uh-huh," said Bonnie dismissively, as if the very idea of the laird of the manor checking his own fuses was a ridiculous thing to think, as indeed, to Bonnie, it was.

Jamie frowned. "Not the lines, surely? They told us last time . . ."

"What did they tell you?" said Esme.

"They said they'd reinforce the lines, so that the snow didn't bring them down," said Jamie.

"Yes, but they have places people actually live, to do first?" said Esme. "We're at the very end of the line."

Jamie nodded. "You're right. It must be the lines. Okay. How are we for candles?"

Bonnie looked at him. "We're fine," she said.

He looked at Theo and Mirren.

"I'm so sorry," he said. "I really don't know when we might get out of here."

Theo shrugged. "If you're saying I won't have to spend Christmas Day at my uncle's watching the king's speech and everyone getting drunk and racist by three p.m., that's fine by me."

Jamie looked at Mirren, who had of course already known her Christmas wasn't going to be brilliant.

"I'd need to phone home," she said.

"Bollocks," growled Theo suddenly. "My battery is going to go. No phones. When will we get power back?"

"That's what we're saying," said Jamie. "Could be days. The snow has to stop, and the engineers have to come out. At Christmas."

Theo grabbed it out of his pocket. "I should not," he said, texting frantically, "have used it as a torch, in retrospect."

"You're not even going to call?" said Mirren.

"*You* don't even have a phone."

"Oh yeah," said Mirren. "Can I borrow yours?"

"Do you know your mum's number?"

"No!" said Mirren. "Oh, goodness. I'd better email her a message." She frowned. "Something that doesn't sound like I've been kidnapped."

"You kind of have," said Theo. "Maybe they did this on purpose."

"Yes," said Esme drily. "We've lured you both here for the fabulous ransoms you so clearly would generate."

Mirren didn't think that was very funny.

"I was rather hoping for sex slave cult," said Theo, and Esme snorted, the candlelight glinting off her nose ring.

Jamie took his old phone out of his sporran and handed it to Mirren. It felt like an oddly intimate thing to do.

"I don't know about a signal," he said, and sure enough, there was only half a bar showing. "But do what you can."

"My text went," said Theo helpfully.

Mirren looked at him. "Would you mind . . . Could you possibly ask your people to get in touch with my mum?"

She gave him the name of the care home her mum worked at. Her mum would probably still assume the worst, but then her mum assumed the worst when she called her literally going down the road to the shops, so she didn't think this would make that much difference. It was the best she could do.

"We've got plenty of goose," said Bonnie. "Never quite got the hang of downgrading Christmas in this place."

They had to abandon the translating of the clue for now; Jamie very carefully pressed the tiny swan between two pages of a heavy flower directory and put it on the top shelf by the Christmas tree. Esme poured everyone another whisky, which made Mirren sleepier than ever. She lay back on the old floral sofa and stared into the fire.

"If it's numbers," she speculated, "all numbers, what could it be? Latitude and longitude?"

"That seems a bit simplistic for Grandfather. Considering what he gave us when we were five."

"It would be ironic if it was a telephone number," piped up Theo. "You know. Considering the circumstances."

"Grandfather hated the telephone," said Esme dreamily. "Do you remember, Jamie? As if it was the police coming to fetch him or something."

Jamie shrugged. "I suppose he must have got a phone call at school, telling him about his dad. You probably wouldn't like it after that."

"No, I suppose you wouldn't."

They fell silent.

"It's kind of amazing," piped up Mirren. "You know so much

about your family tree. I have no idea who my grandparents' parents were. You've got portraits of all of yours."

"Well, the ones that haven't been sold. The really crappy ones," said Esme.

"It's like the royals," said Theo suddenly. "You know who King Charles's great-great-great-grandmother was."

"Do I?" said Mirren.

"Queen Victoria," said Theo.

"Oh, of course."

"But you don't know your own history."

"Do you know yours?" asked Mirren.

"A bit," said Theo. "Good minor gentry stock, and an unfortunate entanglement with a Romanian travelling circus."

Mirren burst out laughing.

"What?"

"Nothing," she said. "That sums you up perfectly."

"I'm not sure whether to be insulted or slightly titillated."

"Numbers," said Jamie again, as if he was trying to get them back on track. "What's numbered in the house?"

"The wine cellar," said Esme promptly. "It's got vintages chalked up everywhere."

"Oh Lord," said Jamie. "We've probably drunk the last clue."

"Wouldn't they start with one nine, though?" said Mirren.

"We used to have one eights," said Esme sadly.

Bonnie was watching over the candles to make sure the wax didn't spill over. She looked up.

"The birds are numbered," she said quietly.

Everyone turned to look at her.

"What do you mean, the birds are numbered?" said Jamie.

"The geese. Breeding pairs. And the homing pigeons. And the grouse for the ghillie."

"Well, that can't be it," said Esme. "These numbers in the clue were written ages ago. Any birds numbered back then wouldn't be alive now."

"Yes, I didn't mean the identified birds," said Bonnie patiently. "I mean the coops."

"Numbers printed on a bird . . ." said Theo thoughtfully.

"It might not even be all numbers," said Jamie. "We've only got three. It might still be an address."

"It started with three," said Mirren. "It might be the numbers of pi."

There was a massive groan.

"Oh GOD, please let it not be pi," said Esme.

"Well," said Jamie, standing up. Mirren realised he was a little tipsy, and at the same moment realised she herself was, too—her head was spinning. She drank some water and watched him cross the room to the window, carefully moving through the dark.

"I don't know if we'll find a damn thing tomorrow, in this snow. In the meantime . . ." He turned round. "We have jolly company. And we have music. We should dance."

"Jamie, go to bed," said Esme. "You're such a lightweight."

"We don't have any music," offered Mirren. "You know? Without electricity."

As she said that he beamed at her, then knelt back down to the old record player. To her amazement, she watched him crank a handle at the side and wind it up. Then he unsheathed an old heavy LP—incredibly large—and put it on at, amazingly, 78 rpm. It crackled and bounced and then, slightly too fast, on came an old jazz song.

"Aha," he said, then offered her his hand. "Madam."

"I can't dance to this!"

"Nonsense," he said, and took her in a formal waltzing position. "You must have learned at school."

"No," said Mirren. "We were too busy in shoplifting class."

"Hush. Follow me."

And, much more forward than he might have been without a couple of whiskies, he led her round the great rug in front of the fire, swaying her to and fro. Theo immediately jumped up and held out a hand to Esme, who snorted at him, then to Bonnie, who took him up on it, and the two couples took a spin around the rug, the flames casting their shadows against the high walls as they turned and giggled over the crackling old music. Theo bent Bonnie backwards in a dramatic arch and she laughed, her soft hair tumbling from its heavy bun. Esme meanwhile was still staring at her dead mobile phone crossly. Outside the snow fell and fell and fell, but the sitting room was, at last, cosy; a tiny spot of light, Mirren thought, in miles and miles of dark, all the way out across the sea; a tiny speck of jollity and warmth among the unforgiving landscape of the north of the world, the freezing waves still pummelling the rocks below.

Chapter Twenty-Six

It was hard to break up the party, but necessary. They had, Jamie observed, a lot to do tomorrow.

"Although we're all going to be stuck here till March, so I'm not sure why that's important," drawled Esme, yawning and heading for the door. "Bonnie, are you going to make it back to the cottage?"

Bonnie glanced out. "Nah, the kitchen door is wedged shut. I'm going to stay in the house till this is done. We'll do a joint effort tomorrow, dig it out."

Esme nodded.

"Everyone take a candle and a spare, and don't leave it burning, you'll burn the place down," said Bonnie.

"Hang on," said Mirren in a sudden panic. "I can't remember the way."

"Girls have no sense of direction," said Theo teasingly. Then, with a more flirtatious note in his voice, "I'll show you."

"Okay," said Mirren, as Bonnie blew out all of the candles save half a dozen or so and left the room with nothing more than the flickering firelight. It was hard, suddenly, to leave the warmth and head out into the long, cold red passageways, the dark corners, the empty, spooky, gloomy rooms containing nothing. She was glad she had Theo to accompany her; she would not have wanted to walk the passageways alone. Outside, the night sky was so thick with snow that there was not a drop of moonlight anywhere; it was so dark, you wouldn't be able to see your hand in front of your face.

Bonnie disappeared, Esme likewise, storming off with a full candelabra in front of her, even though she was so sure-footed she could probably find her way round the house blindfolded.

Theo headed out into the corridor. Jamie was still sitting, staring into the fire.

"Well, good night, then," he said, and his face suddenly looked tired and rumpled, and sad.

"Aren't you going up?"

"I'll stay here awhile," he said, nursing his glass.

Mirren nodded. Back in the doorway, Theo raised his eyebrow at her. "You coming?"

"Just a minute."

He grinned. "All right, then, I'm going down to the end of the corridor to jump out on you and give you a bluey."

"Well, I'm not going to have a bluey with all this warning," said Mirren.

"Yeah, you will, I'm very frightening." He headed off.

"Are you okay?" said Mirren to Jamie.

Jamie shrugged. "Och, yeah."

"We'll figure it out, you know," she said. "I'm very confident. Don't lose the bits of the bird."

"I won't," he said, shaking his head. Then the frown line was back. "Why," he said. "Why are all the men in my family such fuckups? This is just insane." He glanced up at her. "What kind of crazy mind does this, then goes out into the snow to die?"

"He got disorientated," said Mirren. "That happens with old people. And the puzzle—maybe he thought it would be fun for you."

"Maybe," said Jamie heavily. "Or maybe being crazy runs in families."

"You seem very sane to me," said Mirren. "But also, everyone's family is completely crazy."

"Is that true?"

"So, so true," said Mirren, thinking of her mother fretting about candied peel.

"But here I am, sitting in front of the fire in the middle of a vast pile I can't keep afloat, down to the bones of my arse, trying to chase down some binary code printed onto a swan to stop the council repossessing my home," said Jamie. "Is this *your* normal Tuesday?"

"Mirren, I can't keep up this bat pose for much longer!" came a voice from the end of the corridor.

"Off you go," said Jamie. "Don't keep him waiting, for goodness' sake."

Mirren wanted to say something more, but didn't know what would be appropriate. And now he was brushing her off, his gaze returning to deep in the fire.

"Okay," she said. And then, as she turned to go, carrying the candle in her hand, she paused.

"It wasn't my normal Tuesday," she said. "It was much, much better."

"WARRRGH!"

"Stop it, Theo, you're being ridiculous," Mirren said, but she couldn't help laughing. Theo had tugged his dinner jacket over his face like a cape, his handsome face laughing back at her. Mirren didn't want to admit that actually, advancing up the corridor lit only by a candle, with the house creaking and settling all around, the weight of the snow hemming them in and the air freezing, she had felt very frightened indeed, wondering constantly if she could feel unearthly footprints behind her. Passing closed door after closed door, not knowing what was inside, draped in sheets, shut away . . . The dying notes of the music on the wind-up gramophone still played in her head, conjuring images of other people, long dead, who must have danced through this house, full of conviction that they were living in the very latest way, that life would go on as it always had, not for one moment anticipating the house being filled to the brim with mouldering old books, crumbling away underneath their feet. She would have loved to see it in its heyday, bright-painted and bustling, filled with people, running like clockwork. But now, in its crumbling dotage, it was a frightening thing. And knowing someone was about to jump out on her also didn't help.

"Come on!" said Theo. "How often do you get to rampage around a stately home at night?!"

His eyes were so dark in the candlelight they were impossible to see.

Mirren thought briefly of Jamie, staring into the fire, far too young to seem so sad.

Theo opened a door she wouldn't have noticed, behind a curtain, and sure enough it was the turret stair. It was even colder here than it had been before; the windows were only single-pane, and none too new at that. They might as well have been outside.

"It really is freezing," said Theo as they ascended the stairs, Mirren trying to shield her candle and hold her tartan throw around herself at the same time. "If only one of us knew some way to warm up. At bedtime."

"Theo," said Mirren reprovingly. "We're here for work."

Theo shrugged and looked straight at her. "Actually, we're snowed in and off the clock."

"You're incorrigible," said Mirren.

"Thank you," said Theo, and pushed open a side door, then led them down another side of the building, and sure enough they were back on the bedroom corridor. It was annoying how he'd managed that.

At her door, she stopped. He stopped too and stood over her. They were intensely close. Once again Mirren could feel her pulse beating. It had been so long. She ached to be touched, to be held, to be wanted. She felt a flush rise in her cheeks. But she wouldn't fall for it again, she told herself. She wouldn't.

She hesitated. Too long; he backed away. She looked up at him in agony. If he had grabbed her, kissed her, right then and there . . . she didn't know what she would have done. Instead, taking her silence for a lack of assent, he took a step backwards, into the shadows.

"Well. You know where I am," he said quietly. "If you need anything."

Then he leaned in, very quietly, smelling of woodsmoke and whisky, and kissed her lightly on the cheek.

"Good night," he said, and turned and vanished across the hallway.

FEELING RESTLESS, TURNED on, and confused all at the same time, Mirren entered her own room. The fire was burning low, but it was still pleasant; there was hot water in the jug, and it was too dark to read, so she prepared herself to get into bed and stare into the fire. Steeling herself against damp sheets, she was surprised and delighted to feel them warm; Bonnie, bless her, had stuck in a hot water bottle. If she were that way inclined, she thought, untying the curtains around the bed but leaving a bit of the bottom open so she could see the fire, she would find Bonnie completely irresistible. She thought back to how she and Jamie were together. Like siblings, a little—more than Jamie and his actual sibling—or coconspirators, or something. It was odd. If she had her phone, and a charger, and a signal or an internet connection, she could have Googled him, seen what his relationship history was. He didn't seem to be someone who was on social media very much.

Even when the power was on, he hadn't kept feeling for his phone at odd moments, looking surprised when it didn't work or simply wasn't there. His phone didn't seem to be the reflex for him that it was for so many others.

But then again, a house this size . . . surely it would be in the news, would be of some interest? He must have a title or something. So there would be something online. But she didn't have access to it, or anything else—as it was, she was having to hope one of Theo's relatives would call her mother's workplace, so they didn't send a SWAT team out.

She thought about how strange it was, to meet someone and not immediately be able to find out anything about them; and she pictured his sad face in front of the fire. Bonnie, she was sure, would have come up to comfort him.

Mirren stared at the roof of the four-poster bed, wondering who had slept under this thick brocade canopy over the centuries. The shadows of the flames flickered up against it as she wondered about Theo. God, he was attractive. So attractive. And so close . . . but she shouldn't. She mustn't. Her long day overtook her; her limbs felt impossibly heavy, and, before she could follow her train of thought, it fell off the rails and she was asleep.

Chapter Twenty-Seven

Mirren knew it was late the next morning because it was almost light outside, and at this time of year—it was the twenty-third of December, just two nights after the very longest night—that meant it must be nearly nine o'clock.

At first, she couldn't work out where she was. She had had strange dreams of zeros and ones and books tumbling over and over, like Alice collapsing under armies of playing cards, and at first, looking at the red curtains all around her bed, she had panicked and thought she was buried.

Then it had come flooding back to her, that she was snowed in in a castle in Scotland, which, while obviously terribly inconvenient, was nonetheless rather exciting—and she leapt up immediately because—what had happened with the snow?

She realised two things as she got up. Firstly, the fire was flaming up again, which meant someone had been in to set it going; and, she noticed, there was a coffeepot on a tray, which was, to her slight embarrassment but also absolute delight, still hot. Bonnie must have come in when she was fast asleep and in fact that must have woken her, given how hot the coffee was. She wasn't at all used to this, and it felt extremely weird. On the other hand, it was such a treat. She poured herself a cup into another piece of extremely expensive china with a chunk out of it—there was a definite theme to the crockery in this house—and, pulling the tartan blanket around her again, she went to look out of the great old rattling window.

It had stopped snowing. At first, Mirren was slightly disappointed; it was a childish thing, to want it to snow and snow forever. But as she looked left out over the northern hills, then towards the water straight ahead, she saw a sudden pink beam of dawn reach out and hit the fields, and the scene, suddenly illuminated, was so extraordinarily beautiful it took her breath away.

Mirren had never seen proper deep snow before. Even on her one skiing trip, it had all been mostly melted in the huge mega-resort they were at, and she hadn't made it up much past the nursery slopes.

This was completely different. This was a thick fluffy blanket laid over the world. She could roughly gauge its extraordinary depth: it reached the top of the hand-built stone walls that demarcated the faraway fields.

Directly below the window were two completely concealed lumps that yesterday had been cars. The windows steamed up with condensation from her coffee cup and she rubbed it clean. She wanted to take a photo of it more than anything, then realised that, no, what she really wanted to do was to walk beyond the house and take a picture of the castle, in the snow, the pink light shining on its turrets, Cair Paravel by the sea. She looked at the rotting wood of the window frame and pushed her finger into it gently, watching it flake away. Yes. Definitely better from a distance.

But walking far looked like it would be out of the question; the wrought-iron gate showed the snow at waist height. Not a track despoiled the purity of the white, although the brown shapes of birds, looking for sustenance, could be seen here and there. It was utterly lovely.

Suddenly, she started. There was something on the horizon. She peered more closely. Outlined against the white, astonishing in its majesty and loveliness, was a huge stag, strolling nonchalantly out of the trees. His antlers reached up high out of his head; this wasn't a young animal. He sniffed the air, obviously finding his way in the new snow. Did he think it was beautiful? thought Mirren. Or a challenge, just as they did? Or both? He moved forward, in that silent world: the stag, the snow, the castle, the sea: every element frozen, like a huge chessboard of white fields and dark woods, waiting for the pieces to move.

She couldn't have said how long she stood there, watching the magnificent animal—and, who knew, maybe he was watching her, too—until something startled him, and his huge head turned rapidly, and he vanished back into the dark of the wild forest.

Conscious that presumably Bonnie had had to come wake her up because she was horribly late—and hating to be late—Mirren scampered down the corridor to the bathroom. Jamie hadn't been lying about the hot water, but at least there was some; there were still no lights working, so the electricity wasn't on, but the boiler seemed to be running. Hers at home wouldn't work without electricity, so she would have to assume this really was old. She got about two inches of water into the ancient vast tub that would just about double as a swimming pool and made do as best she could. There was no trace or sound of Theo but that didn't mean anything; the walls and doors here were so thick, he could be having a DJ party in his bedroom and she wouldn't notice.

Back in the bedroom, she made her bed and went back once again to the strange drawers. There was nothing else for it; she only had a couple of days' worth of clothes, and clothes appropriate for staying in a normal house at that, which, she now realised, was not good planning; but then, absolutely nothing so far had been remotely as expected.

In the drawer at the bottom of the wardrobe, amid quite a strong smell of mothballs, she discovered several old jumpers, huge chunky knits that were clearly handmade and nothing as chic as the party dresses hanging up. On the other hand, beggars couldn't be choosers, and actually if she donned an extra-bulky, rough oatmeal jumper and her jeans, and put on both pairs of socks she'd brought, she was almost warm, if not feeling quite as glamorous as she had the night before. She added a scarf, and wished she'd brought mittens.

She snuck out—there was nobody in the passageway, and the corridor was freezing; she was glad of the scarf. There was nothing to hear anywhere, and she wasn't sure where she ought to be. Life was odd when you didn't have your phone; you felt untethered from everything. She didn't even wear a watch, since her brother had bought her a smartwatch for Christmas one year and it kept bugging her about not answering her messages or taking enough steps or sleeping for long enough and basically it was like having a pass-agg small person following her about all day and as she'd explained at the time, if she needed one of those she could just go back home and live with her mum.

Now, which was the turret door they came through? It was down at the end of . . . This was ridiculous; she hadn't been that drunk last night. Although it had been very dark. Now light streamed in through the little arched windows, showing two rows of corridors going off at right angles to each other. The castle must be a square, which would put Theo's room overlooking the inside courtyard? And if she was looking out opposite to the sea . . . she must be on the east side. And the drawing room looked out over the front, which must be the south side . . . but where did that put the kitchen? She sighed; she would have tossed a coin if she had one. Then she headed off to her left. All the closed doors looked the same, one after another, like a vast hotel. But one where all the guests had left a long time ago.

Finally, she noticed that one door in the wall was set in the corner, at an angle. Surely this must be the one? She gave it an experimental tug; at first she thought it was locked, but it was merely stiff, and with a bigger pull it creaked open.

It was the turret with the spiral staircase. Pleased, Mirren stepped in and started to head down, around and around. Perhaps everyone had slept late, and there would be fresh eggs—Bonnie had mentioned birds, hadn't she? And more of that surprisingly good coffee. She should have brought her cup and pot down with her, but it was weird the vibe she got from Bonnie, a little bit kind of a *you don't belong here, don't try and pretend and don't think you're being nice by helping me* feeling.

It was probably her own paranoia, thought Mirren. Her own sense of inadequacy at being around people who, however financially embarrassed they might be now, came from great families, castles, and clans—a completely different way of living and being in the world. She and Esme were chalk and cheese; she could not imagine Esme ever entertaining any of the doubts Mirren had about her life, future, friends. Esme didn't seem to have a moment of self-doubt in her body. Just a clear belief that she was born slightly superior and therefore everyone should treat her correctly, and, amazingly, everyone did. No way would Theo have ghosted *her*, thought Mirren with surprising venom. She was suddenly very pleased that she hadn't given in to his tempting invitation last night. Only the last shreds of her self-respect had kept her from succumbing quite so easily. But she had been single for—well, if it was Christmas, then for a year. She missed human contact, quite desperately. And he was so terribly handsome, that wide clear forehead, the black hair flopping on his brow.

Completely lost in thought, she realised suddenly that she'd been walking down the steps for a long time. They were worn with footprints over hundreds of years; the multitude of feet that had trodden here, way back into deep time, had made indentations in the very rock itself. This must be the older section of the castle, the ancient part at the back. But she was surely further down than they had been the night before? She looked up at a sudden noise: a white bird far overhead flapped, then disappeared. They must be nesting in the towers. No wonder it was so freezing everywhere.

But when she looked at the walls she realised they were smooth: no doors anywhere, and the windows were fewer and further apart. Mirren frowned to herself. Well, it had to come out *somewhere*; this was ridiculous. There must be a fire exit. Even as she thought this, she figured that, actually, this building rather predated the existence of fire exits.

Curiously, she carried on, down and down. It became darker, and colder, but if she peered she could see a light below her. Perhaps they were right at the back of the house, and he stairs went down. She'd probably find herself by the bins.

She touched the walls to steady herself in the gloom. They were damp, and something slimy touched her fingers. She shuddered and rubbed them on her jeans. "Ugh, bloody hell."

But the idea of climbing all the way up hundreds of steps again didn't appeal, either, so she carried on down. The white circle of light grew larger, but it looked strange, bobbing in front of her eyes. She blinked, in case it was her eyesight, but no, something was definitely moving . . .

Near the bottom the steps were all wet, and dangerously slippery, and she finally realised—feeling quite the idiot as she did so, considering their geography—exactly where she was.

Sure enough, the steps coiled round a few more times, slippery with seaweed, and deposited her in the corner of a dark cave, the wobbling light being, of course, the shallow waves running up the shingle. She had come right out through the castle to the beach beyond; she had gone all the way down the cliffs, through a secret passageway that led here.

"Bloody hell!" said Mirren, first to herself, then out loud. The noise echoed off the close walls of the cave. "Hello? Hello . . . *hello?*"

There was no answer. She glanced over. The opening to the cave was small; it must be imperceptible from the other side. A secret escape route! It was rather thrilling. No wonder there weren't any more doors leading on to it.

Her eyes adjusted to the dimness, and, looking round, she saw, pulled up on the shingle, an old rowing boat, decayed and covered in barnacles. Goodness. She wondered if anyone ever came down here, or even knew it *was* still here. Well, they must do. She glanced at her feet. The waves were coming up to her toes. She supposed the tide must fill this place—that was an unpleasant thought. She glanced up just in case there were any rings drilled into the wall to chain unfortunates, but didn't see anything like that. But in doing so she leaned out, took two steps—and the door, which had been propped open, swung closed behind her.

MIRREN LET OUT a cry of dismay as the door slammed shut. It was completely smooth; the same colour as the rock—if you didn't know it was there, you would hardly be able to see it, tucked away behind a pile of rocks at the far back of a cave. Which of course was how it was designed, but her fingernails on the door didn't make the slightest bit of difference; there was no clawing it open.

"Oh, bollocks," she said, glancing at the tide. She was right: it was definitely coming in, washing further up than it had before. And she had no idea how deep this cave was. She might come out into full North Sea. In December. She could *die*. She was suddenly furious with Jamie and Esme for not warning her about this. It was so dangerous! What the hell were they thinking?

She was freezing now, and genuinely frightened, as well as feeling absolutely ridiculous—two days ago she had been cheery because she'd just got the last stamp on her coffee loyalty card, for goodness' sake, and now she appeared to be in danger of losing her life in a bloody cave in Scotland. Her body would probably wash out to sea and she'd never be heard of again. And *then* Theo would be sorry he ghosted her, she thought darkly.

She tiptoed gingerly to the mouth of the cave, the wind blowing fiercely outside. The waves were a steely grey.

She noticed, on the right-hand side, a slightly higher, climbable rock, and, splashing across the shingle, hauled herself up on it. From there, she could work her frozen fingers round the mouth of the cave, and she found, to her surprise, delight, and slight embarrassment, some cold grass—grass did not, of course, grow underwater. She must have reached the limits of the high tide, only a couple of feet above the floor of the cave.

There was another stone laid there, like a small stairway, and she heaved herself out onto that and found another one, and then another; casually laid, so they didn't look deliberate, just like random stones, but she was pretty sure they were there on purpose—and, with some effort, she managed to pull herself finally on to the little snowy outcrop of land.

Feeling rather foolish, she turned a hundred and eighty degrees and realised exactly what she was looking at. The sheer cliff ran straight up from the sea—when she had looked down from the drawing room side window, this was what she had seen. The castle, so formal from the front, from the back looked completely organic, as if it had grown out of the very stuff of the rock itself, a natural part of the crags. This must be the oldest section. The cave was well hidden at the bottom by this promontory of grass, presumably, underneath the snow; another one curved round the other side, forming a minuscule natural harbor. Brave would be the marauders who attempted to attack from the bottom, but you could nudge the boat out from the cave with complete and utter privacy and go—well, anywhere, she supposed.

She was truly cold now, and her wet feet were rapidly numbing. Her heart sank as she looked up the crag, but there was nothing else for it: she had to scramble her way up through the snow in an unusually undignified fashion. She found herself using muscles she hadn't for years; at one point she pitched forward headfirst and went knee-deep in the snow and head to foot. The ice scratched her face, and she was so annoyed with herself that she swore.

After what felt like an age, she finally made it to the foot of the castle, and headed round the back first, which for once turned out to be the right decision, as she soon found the kitchen garden and, from there, the kitchen door. She could even hear the chatter. The snow had been crudely pushed away from it, with a spade in the corner; footprints, human, dog, and bird, crisscrossed the area in between the door and the kitchen garden and beyond.

With a sigh of incredible relief, she pulled open the door and fell into the blessedly warm kitchen. Whereupon she was greeted with, first, total silence, and then, swirling up, a great roar of laughter.

Chapter Twenty-Eight

"Shut up, everyone!" said Mirren, still upset after her ordeal, and realising that she looked like a walking snowman. They were all gathered round the stove, looking cosy and well fed and self-satisfied. The end of a loaf of fresh bread was sitting on the breadboard; empty eggcups indicated she'd been right about the hens; coffee was still brewing on the stove, and crumb-ridden marmalade jars and butter tubs littered the large, scrubbed pine table.

"Skiing accident?" said Theo languidly, winking at her to show he was teasing.

"I NEARLY DROWNED, ACTUALLY!" spluttered Mirren.

"You got the bath working??" asked Esme in surprise, who was vaping furiously as if daring Jamie to tell her not to and leafing through a 1985 copy of *Vogue*.

"Why didn't you *tell* us you can get trapped in a cave at the bottom of the stairs?" asked Mirren. She had suddenly got very hot inside her wet clothes from the warmth of the Aga, something very unlikely to have a good effect on anyone's mood. Steam was rising from her body.

Jamie jumped up. "Do you want to . . ."

He gently unwound the scarf from round her neck. Great clumps of snow fell on the floor and they watched them melt. He then tugged at her snowy jumper, telling her to take it off.

"Come on," he said. "You're freezing."

Mirren felt like crying. She'd had such a shock, and his surprising gentleness undid her. She wondered where he'd learned it.

"Here," said Theo, taking off his expensive jumper and flinging it at her. "What on *earth* did you do?"

"I . . ." Mirren swallowed. "I went down the stairs . . ."

"Third floor," said Jamie, snapping his fingers. "Sorry, we should have warned you."

"Why didn't you just take the front steps?" said Esme, puzzled.

"Because I didn't grow up in a house with more than one set of stairs," said Mirren. "Nobody explained the rules."

"Those are . . . yeah, they're meant to be kept locked."

Mirren remembered how stiff the door had been. Perhaps, now she thought about it, it had been locked, and the wood had softened, just like the rotting window frame in her bedroom. "Ah," she said.

"Did you give it a *really* good tug?" said Jamie, his lips twitching.

"I thought it was the way!"

"Are you sure you weren't snooping?"

"Well, no. For one thing," said Mirren, "I wanted breakfast. And secondly, even if I were, I think this is a job about snooping, or am I wrong? Are we basically here to do snooping or not?"

"Fair point," said Jamie.

"But I wasn't."

"Okay."

"I wasn't!"

"Did it not occur to you that you might have gone down past the kitchen?" said Esme.

"There's nowhere to get off," said Mirren.

Bonnie snorted from the stove. "Come on, Esme, she was curious. You remember what we were like with that staircase."

"I'm glad they at least tried to keep children out of it," said Mirren, taking a long and very welcome sip of her coffee.

"Where does it go?" asked Theo.

"It leads down to a secret cave. In the cliff."

"*No way!*" said Theo. "Cool! For smuggling?"

"At one point, no doubt, but no, mostly for escape," said Jamie. "There were some . . . divided loyalties up here. For the king, for the Young Pretender, but even before then . . . there was some fairly emphatic landing of literature from the Netherlands, Germany . . ."

Bonnie sat Mirren down at the seat nearest the Aga and put a heaped plate in front of her. Sausages, bacon, eggs . . .

"Tea? Coffee?"

"You don't need to . . ."

Mirren tried to get up to help. Bonnie gave her a stiff look. "It's okay," she said. "You've shown everyone that you're a good and helpful person—it's fine. So just sit down and let me do my job."

Stung, Mirren sat down on her chair with a thump. The delicious breakfast, though—there were triangles of soft brown fried potato cakes, called, inexplicably, potato scones, which you spread with butter and salt and which were obviously going to decrease your life expectancy by half an hour for every one you ate but which were so uncommonly delicious she couldn't really complain about it. Bonnie put down a huge mug of tea, which warmed her from the outside in, and gradually her shivering subsided.

Theo was writing out the binary code by hand, and Jamie was translating it. It was number after number; ridiculous to use a number code to transcribe numbers, but, Mirren was starting to realise, wholly typical.

"Well, this is boring," scowled Esme, looking out of the window. The snow reached up to the window ledge. The day, though, was starting to clear; there was the slightest hint of blue sky.

Mirren finished her breakfast as the boys looked down the long list of numbers. The goose house theory seemed to be losing ground. She looked out.

There were two windows, one facing the front of the house with the buried cars, and one facing west, towards the kitchen garden. The freezing winter sun was gradually rising above what was left of what must once have been neatly trimmed topiary hedges; they were overgrown now, and scruffy, but their layout remained, and the sun marked bright lines through the gaps across the pristine snow. The light lay like diamonds, sparkling a full array of colours on this ground on which nobody had ever walked, in this silent world, without an engine, a police siren, or even a plane overhead. Nothing at all. A city girl all her life, Mirren leaned forward to breathe it in.

"I don't think it's boring," she said, putting her fingers to the window. Frost feathered the inside. It truly was cold. Esme looked at her with a curled lip, as if about to make a sarcastic response, then changed her mind and looked round at the boys. "What is it?"

"Just a string of numbers," said Jamie, looking frustrated.

"Well, have you tried phoning it?"

Theo was about to sneer but Jamie looked up. "Oh, that's actually quite a good idea," he said.

"What does it start with?"

"It doesn't really have a start. It depends which wing you're on; it covers every bit of it."

"Well, is there a bit that looks like a phone number?"

They studied the page.

"There's a zero then an eight . . ." said Theo eventually.

"Isn't that, like, a Freefone number?"

Esme snorted. "Grampa wouldn't have bothered setting up a free anything."

"But nobody's mobile has got a signal," pointed out Theo. "Plus, they're all dead, because I spent all day yesterday using mine as a stupid torch."

"House phone's working," said Bonnie, stacking plates.

"You're telling me your phone is so old it can survive a power cut?" said Mirren. "Does it wind up and have a trumpet on the end?"

Jamie was frowning at the numbers.

"I don't think so, but it doesn't start with a zero and a one."

"Maybe he made it before they did," said Theo. "What did they used to be like?"

"Forres Castle 74262," said Bonnie automatically. They all turned to look at her. "What?" she said. "That's how my gran had to answer the phone. That's how I'd still answer it if it ever rang. It used to ring all the time. We had an exchange."

They all followed her along the passage, Mirren heaving another blanket around her shoulders. It might look ridiculous, but remaining swaddled was the key to not gasping whenever you left the relative comfort of the kitchen or the drawing room.

The telephone, remarkably, was in a room of its own, which did indeed have a large bank of wires leading to various mysterious rooms Mirren hadn't come across yet: the Ladies' Smoking Room, the nursery, the dayroom, and the boot room all having their own connections.

"Wow," said Theo again. "This place must have been really something . . ."

"In its day, yeah, yeah," said Esme who had, nonetheless, come through to see if her hunch worked. There was indeed a dialling tone; it truly was that old.

Laboriously, Jamie dialled the numbers in every order they could think of. They got a Chinese restaurant in New York, lots of dead dialling tones, many "please replace the handset and try again"s, someone shouting "*QUE? QUE?*" down an intensely crackly line that felt as if you could hear the snow lying on the lines, and a friendly person in Australia who was extremely interested in what they were doing but couldn't actually help them in any way.

Mirren meanwhile was examining the telephone directories. There was none for London, but Mirren called Directory Enquiries, something she was astounded to discover still existed. She jotted down the care home number, then rang it while Jamie stared again at the numbers, puzzling over them. They couldn't call every combination; they'd be here till the heat death of the universe, as Esme had pointed out unhelpfully.

Mirren had never used a rotary dial phone before, and it took a while to get used to.

"Hello?"

"Yes, Bright Fields Nursing Home?"

Mirren recognised the voice of the receptionist; alas, it was the grumpy one. She used to be a librarian, and had left when she wasn't allowed to shush children anymore.

"Hello? Is Nora Sutherland working today? It's her daughter."

"Can't you call her mobile?"

"No," said Mirren. "I've lost my mobile and I don't remember the number. That's why I'm calling you."

"You don't know her mobile number?"

"What's *your* mum's mobile number?" said Mirren, stung.

The receptionist recited a series of numbers. "I'm very close to my mother," she said.

"Okay, well, is Nora there?"

"No, she's on her day off."

Mirren sighed. "Well, can you tell her I rang, and that I'm stranded in the big storm in Scotland?"

"What big storm in Scotland?"

"The big snowstorm that's cut off the electricity?"

"Not heard anything about that."

Jamie and Esme were making faces and shaking their heads.

"Oh," said Mirren.

"It's raining here."

"Okay. Well. Can you tell her I'll be home when I can? I'm just chasing down a book."

The woman paused for a moment. "You're the one who found that old Stevenson, aren't you?"

"Um, yes . . ." said Mirren.

"Yeah. I used to be a librarian. You were in all the library periodicals."

"Fame at last," said Mirren, as Theo, listening in, looked fierce.

"So you're looking for another one now, are you?"

"Yeah," said Mirren. Then, on impulse, "How would *you* track down a missing book?"

The woman laughed, and for the first time didn't sound grumpy at all.

"Well, I'd make a guess at some of the regulars . . . but then I'd put in the ISBN number, I suppose."

"The ISB what?"

Suddenly Theo's head shot up. He gesticulated madly for her to hang up the phone.

"Umm, thanks. Uh, just tell my mum I'm fine, okay?" Mirren managed to say, before Theo practically hung up for her. "What?" she said to him.

"The whole of Britain thinks 'weather' means London weather," Esme was grumbling, but Theo was still agitated.

"No. No," he said. "I'm an idiot. An *idiot*. Wasting time with this stupid phone . . ."

"Don't you want to call your family?"

"Shh. And stupid birds . . ."

"I thought 'wild-goose chase' was quite clever, actually," said Jamie quietly.

Theo took the piece of paper.

"Books have something called ISBN numbers. International Standard Book Numbers. Every book has one. Thirteen digits."

Everybody stared at him, then Jamie counted up the digits. "There are only ten of them," he said.

Theo shook his head. "It can still be an ISBN. Before 2007 they were only ten digits."

"I have to say," Jamie said slowly, "that this is kind of the thing you were hired to know before."

"I know, I know," said Theo. "Sorry. But we need to check. We need to check." He looked around at the piles of phone directories, leading onto another bookshelf crammed with road maps, atlases, and travel writing. "I don't think we could possibly find it by hand."

"If we had any internet, couldn't we look it up?"

"Yes, although even then," said Theo, "you'd still have to find it."

"But we'd have a title," said Mirren. They looked at each other, both full of excitement. She jumped up. "We have to find some internet!"

Theo laughed. "To the internet well!"

Jamie and Esme exchanged glances.

"I suppose . . . there is occasionally a signal . . ." said Jamie. "Out in the far woods."

"But nobody's got any battery," said Theo.

"Haven't they?" said Jamie, looking at Esme. She looked shifty and they all stared at her. "Only a tiny wee bit?" said Jamie in an imploring voice. "Please? We're stuck."

"Even my spare is nearly out," said Esme eventually, pulling out her phone, and a spare battery pack. "You had better be cutting me into this bloody thing, if it even exists."

Chapter Twenty-Nine

Jamie led them to the boot room, a large space with a stone floor, lined with Wellingtons in all sizes, and jackets on the wall—hunting, tweed, and old Barbours. There were boxes of gloves and riding boots too.

"Just pile everything on, I should say," said Jamie. "There are some waterproof trousers too."

Esme, it turned out, had about 6 percent left on her phone. There was a corner of the grounds nearest the village where there was occasional signal. Naturally it was absolutely miles away, at the very edge. It might not be possible to get there, depending on how thick the snow was . . .

Jamie disappeared suddenly while Mirren shrugged herself into even more layers of very old clothes. They smelled of the house itself; not a bad smell, not really. Just old. She added another jumper and a padded jacket and a huge overcoat, and Theo gave her something which appeared to be waders. She shook her head.

"Oh my God, I'm going to look like Coco the Clown," she said, laughing.

"Even more than you do already?" said Theo. "Anyway, I like it."

"You do not!"

"I do" he said. "It's very cute, plus it's completely impossible to tell what you actually look like underneath it all. Thrilling."

"Stop it," she said. He had found an enormous waterproof cape and swathed it around himself, and a huge soft hat. "You look like a Doctor Who," she said.

"Which one?"

"All of them put together."

"Good," he said. "I shall stride out for adventure."

Eventually, Jamie returned. He was covered in dust and had a spider's web in his hair.

"SPIDER!" hollered Mirren.

He frowned at her. "What?"

"You have a . . ."

He went to the old, spotted mirror above the butler's sink, then smiled and shook his head upside down, gently, letting the spider land in his hand. Then he popped it out of the door.

"See," he said. "Spider-free. For now." He turned back. "This is not really a house you want to be in if you're frightened of spiders."

Mirren winced.

"Spiders are great," he went on, suddenly enthused. "They eat bugs and keep flies away. What have you got against spiders?"

"Their terrifyingness?" said Mirren.

"Oh," he said, looking a little saddened.

This is a man who wouldn't kill a spider, thought Mirren. *Interesting.*

"I wouldn't kill them, though," she said quickly, not adding that this was only because she would be running too fast in the other direction. But he wasn't listening, instead bringing out, from a large wicker basket he had hauled down, something that Mirren at first took for tennis racquets.

"What the hell?" said Esme. "Oh, no way."

"Come on, Ess," said Jamie. "They're fun, remember?"

And he pulled out old, slightly busted snowshoes—wooden frames, with large leather buckles, designed to go over their shoes.

"They're not fun, they're ridiculous," said Esme.

"Can you think of a better plan?"

"Yes," said Esme. "Live in a city and go back in time and stop our stupid family squandering all our money."

Jamie smiled. There was no light in the boot room at all; the window was completely filled up with snow. It looked as if he was right: there was no better option.

"I'll have a shot," said Mirren, surprisingly anxious to get back in his good books after revealing herself to be a spider-hater.

Jamie smiled. "Come on, then. You won't need both jackets, I promise."

Esme smirked. "Oh, it's quite the workout."

"This is basically a north of Scotland striptease," commented Theo, as Mirren unbuttoned the sou'wester.

"Shut up, Theo!" said Mirren, smiling, but as ever he looked totally undaunted, and swished his cape behind him as he bent down to pick up his pair of snowshoes as if he'd been doing it all his life.

Bonnie was at the door as they left, carrying a scuffed silver tray. "Thought you'd . . ."

"Oh, Bonnie!" said Jamie. "I think I love being snowed in with you."

And Mirren wondered, once again, what exactly was going on between those two. Because she couldn't for the life of her understand why else Bonnie would stay in this tumbledown place, looking after it as best she could. There must be a million better jobs out there for a young woman, with lots of life and fun, and instead she had sequestered herself here like a nun. There must be a reason for it. Mirren found herself very curious as to whether that reason had sandy hair and a worried expression and an aversion to killing insects unusual in a gardener.

There were four mismatched small glasses on Bonnie's salver, filled with a reddish-brown liquid and steaming gently. Jamie, Theo, and Esme took one immediately and knocked it back. Not wanting to feel left out, Mirren did exactly the same thing.

It was like getting punched in the gut; the strange, hot drink went straight to her veins, making her shake and tingle.

"Bloody hell," she said.

"Well, quite," said Jamie, grinning at her.

"What is *in* that?"

"Venison stock, vodka, Worcestershire sauce, chilli . . ."

"I feel like I've just been punched in the face by a hot Bloody Mary."

"Yeah, well . . ."

"It's ten o'clock in the morning!"

"Best get going, then."

Mirren's head was still reeling as they forced back open the kitchen door.

THE SUN WAS low on the horizon, on this midwinter day, but you could see it, which was something in itself. It had formed a rime of frost on top of the endless acres of all-encompassing snow. Everything was still; there was not a breath of air through the trees, and even the birds had fallen silent.

The snowshoes were hard to adapt to. They sat on top of the snow—Theo experimented with taking a couple of steps without them and found himself stuck in snow up to his thighs, laughing heartily at his own predicament—and they would have had quite the job without them.

Mirren advanced very tentatively indeed. The shoes, worn and cracked as they were, did indeed hold her weight on top of the

snow. It was the oddest feeling, as if she were a bird or a tiny creature, rather than a ridiculous sight in someone else's jacket, a pair
of green waders, a pair of Wellingtons rather too big for her, and
two great tennis racquets strapped to her toes. She tried another
step tentatively, but it still worked: the snow scrunched satisfy-
ingly beneath her. She carried on further, as Jamie and Esme
lent a laughing Theo an arm to dig himself out. Even their noises
faded, as if folded into this big white world, and she found herself
eager to move on, even if she didn't know if she was going in the
right direction. She was now front left of the house, as they had
moved around again, and the boot room was at the bottom of the
south wing. In normal times, or once upon a time, this must have
been part of fine lawns to the front of the property, for ladies to
stroll in fine weather, giving the best vista as the carriages clipped
up the long driveway. The old Queen Mother had been a frequent
visitor, if the photos in the drawing room were anything to go by.
She stomped on—Esme was right, it was quite hard work—then
turned round to look back.

From this angle, covered in snow, the castle was so beautiful
it could break your heart. How could something so very lovely
be filled with such patent unhappiness? Mirren thought of the
house where she'd grown up, a terrace in south London, with her,
her mum, and her two brothers, with her aunties nearby and her
beloved great-aunt always swooping down to take her to visit a
museum or gallery. People in and out all day—it wasn't even that
unusual where she lived, to grow up without a dad; she had gone
to school two streets away, everyone lived in a house just like hers,
and she'd had friends of every race and type—although, she realised now, probably all of the same class. And it wouldn't even be
like that now; those same houses, with their handkerchief gardens
and three tiny upstairs bedrooms, were expensive these days, all
side returns and loft extensions.

But it had been fun; she had known she was loved; she had always had someone to play with, to watch YouTube videos with, to go up west to go stare at the big shops and visit the big Primark; she'd had a room full of Furbies and Christmas and a week in south Wales in the summer. It was a completely normal childhood, one replicated millions and millions of times over, and she had felt slightly bad at not having both parents living at home, but it was hardly unusual. It was hard to look at this gravely beautiful frontage, the perfect crenellated walls and of course those towers with their fluttering banners, and not think, *Why weren't you happy, any of you? Who couldn't be happy here, deep in the world of snow? What led your grandfather to die, alone, in miserable circumstances?*

She took a deep breath of the frosted air into her lungs, watched the others approach, with the funny shuffling gait you used as you managed the snowshoes for the first time. She had only met them the day before but somehow she couldn't help it . . . there was something unifying about all being trapped in together. She felt as if they were part of a gang: Jamie with his worried frown; Theo, full of cheek; Esme, tired of all of them. She looked at the boys for a moment, their arms swinging, Theo slipping and laughing. He took life so lightly, she thought, however annoying he was—even Jamie was smiling for a moment, his face brightening in the low winter sun. Her heart tugged suddenly. It made him look so different; she could almost see what Bonnie saw in him.

"JUST A MINUTE, I want to check my Insta first," said Esme, taking her phone out.

"*No!*" said Jamie. "Sis, you're being ridiculous. I thought you had nearly no battery left."

"I'm going to burrow into the car and charge it that way," said Esme.

"But we need this *now*," said Jamie. "Come on, sis."

"Why the great rush?" she said.

Jamie looked uncomfortable. *He doesn't want to tell her about the council rates bill being due*, thought Mirren suddenly. Goodness. The crossing of wires and secrets in this family could fill every book in it.

"Because these guys have homes to go to," he said.

"Not right now, they don't," pointed out Esme, not unreasonably.

Mirren was warmer after their tramp across the snowy fields, her gaze still turned up to the sky. A few moments ago, Jamie had quietly come up to her and touched her shoulder and pointed—she had followed his arm upwards and seen, to her amazement, what he told her were a pair of golden eagles, rising from the forest and making a circle in the blue sky.

"Oh, wow," she said now, as the sun glinted off their feathers. Their wingspan was vast and magnificent; they looked like creatures from another age, their profiles strong and cruel. All of a sudden, one of them vanished from view, diving somewhere out of their field of vision.

"That's one little mouse who won't be making it home tonight," said Jamie soberly.

"I thought you country folks loved killing things," said Mirren, surprised.

"He's a sentimental one," said Esme. "That's why we live in the largest spider colony in the western world."

"Yeah, all right," said Jamie, and then tramped on, but Mirren still felt touched by her small glimpse of these other creatures and their very different world. It applied to the McKinnons, too, she found herself thinking. A very different world.

RIGHT AT THE very edge of the field, to the left of the woods, Esme stood up in the corner, one foot on each of two wires supported between two posts, and held her head up high.

"Are we ready?" she said. "Theo, you have the numbers?"

Theo waved his notebook in his hand. He was wearing enormous mittens that looked like oven gloves, which slightly distracted from the dashing, saturnine air of the cape.

"Don't check your Instagram," said Jamie in a warning voice.

"I'm just going to upload a few TikTok videos," said Esme. "It's a relatable guide to being snowed in at your family castle."

"That does sound relatable," said Theo.

"You'd be amazed," said Esme snootily. "Lots of people like being considered to be in an algorithm of family castle owners."

"Not me," said Jamie quietly.

Esme showed her face to her phone, then held her long, elegant arm up in the air. "Okay, stand by . . ."

She pulled it down.

"It's 2G! OMG, I didn't realise they even still made 2G."

"Bugger," said Theo. "It'll probably give us the search results right back in binary."

"Just give me the number! I'm on six . . . no, now it's five percent."

"Okay, okay, quick . . .."

Esme finished and brought the phone down and they watched in silence as the phone took an age to search, a tiny circle going round and round.

"Gah," said Jamie. "I thought we could maybe check the news."

"Or the weather forecast," added Mirren. They both turned to look at her, as if confused. "What?" she said.

"Smell the air," said Jamie. "Can't you smell it?"

She did, and all she could smell was a slight icy, briny smell; the air had a foggy feel. She shrugged.

"Okay," said Jamie. "Well, it's going to snow again. In a bit. Look."

He pointed north, up past the house; low down on the horizon, thick clouds like duvets were gathering. They looked cosy. Mirren figured they would be anything but.

"Okay, it's coming, it's coming . . . YES! It *is* a book!"

Theo tried to look modest but failed.

"It is a house full of books, I suppose," he said, in case anyone had forgotten that it had been his idea.

"Well, bloody hell," said Esme. She showed them. "It's *Sunset Song*," she said, naming the famous Scottish novel.

"What?" said Mirren, who, having grown up in London, had never heard of it.

"Did you not do it for your Higher English?" said Jamie.

"What's Higher English . . . wait: sunset. Sunsets! *The setting of the sun*, Theo! In the poem!"

"But that's so weird," said Esme, displaying the cover on her phone. "It's a modern edition, that one, with the painting on the cover. You can still buy it. It's not that old."

Esme's phone suddenly collapsed into black. She stared at it for a second, as if she could will it back into existence, then sighed heavily and put the useless chunk of glass back in her pocket.

"There's hardly any modern stuff in the house," she said.

"Well, that's the book Google found for you—might it be a different edition?" said Jamie.

"All the editions have different ISBNs," said Theo. "But . . . oh."

"What?"

"Well, only books after—I don't know, but they're quite recent, ISBNs, I think. Old books don't have them."

"So," said Jamie, his voice going dangerously quiet. Mirren felt chilled suddenly, and stamped her booted feet on the crusting snow, putting her arms around herself. "So we just have to go round and look at every book in the house anyway."

"Um, maybe," said Theo, not sounding quite so triumphant. "But, you know—faster!"

"Exactly!" said Mirren. "We know the title of the book we're looking for."

Jamie turned sharply.

"In a houseful of books completely out of order . . . That *bloody* old man."

They snowshoed back to the house in silence, their breath visible in front of them. Jamie's gaze was distracted from the ground ahead only once, when a great hare bounded across the grass, beautiful, larger than Mirren would have thought possible. She had never seen a hare in the wild before. His face softened. Hers did too.

"What's the book about?" she asked Esme, crunching along next to her.

Unexpectedly, rather than being sarcastic, Esme, her cheeks pink from the cold, was thoughtful. "Oh, it's so sad. It's a big weepy love story and she loves him so much but they're so poor and the village is so gossipy and her love can't keep him sensible, and . . . it's really beautiful."

Mirren thought about it. "And it's set . . ."

"After the First World War. Up near here," said Esme. "It must have been a very familiar story to him."

"A love story?"

"I suppose," said Esme. "I never think of my grandfather as having had a romantic life beyond my grandmother, who he wasn't very nice to at all. After she left, he was a confirmed bachelor, back when that didn't immediately mean 'gay'—one of those men who's more interested in collecting and puzzles and old railway timetables than socialising. Neurospicy, I suspect we'd call him these days. Back then, we just called him an irascible old bugger."

She smiled.

"Not for want of trying by the good middle-class divorcées of the parish." She laughed in memory. "Rushing about in their best BHS, with the most god-awful homemade shepherd's pies."

"That sounds very snobby."

"Oh no!" said Esme drily. "You're going to have to report me to the *Guardian*."

She stalked onwards, her long legs making her look elegant even in the ridiculous snowshoes. Mirren didn't bother trying to keep up.

"I wish we could have called up all the covers," said Theo, as they sat around steaming mugs of tea and toasted sandwiches. The Aga was powering through, and its warmth was the most wonderful thing Mirren had ever felt. It was almost worth it, she thought, being constantly freezing and getting soaked through, for the joy of coming into the cosy kitchen. Maybe that was why people climbed mountains: for the sheer joy of stopping climbing mountains. That made a lot more sense.

"How many editions do you think there've been?" she asked.

"Over the years? Loads," said Theo.

"It's never off the school syllabus," said Esme. "Generations of girls have grown up sobbing."

"Did you sob?" asked Mirren of Jamie, who shrugged.

"That means yes," said Esme. "You should have seen him as a boy. Whenever they had to put a Roger down, he sobbed for weeks."

"I did not!" said Jamie. "Shut up." He glanced around nonetheless to check that Roger the sheepdog was still at his heels, which he was.

"You shut up!"

Mirren and Theo shared a look, that Jamie caught and immediately stopped himself. Mirren knew from her own family, particularly her relationship with her mum, how hard it was to break your old family dynamics sometimes.

"So it could look like anything?"

"I don't think *anything*, exactly," said Theo. "It's sad, and old, so it won't be bright yellow or have dogs on the front. We could each pick a corridor?"

"We'll have to speed down them," said Esme. "One, they're too cold to linger, and two, there's about two hours of light left. And I think, even before that, more snow will be here."

"It's practically the shortest night of the year," mused Mirren. *"The wolves are running."*

"Well, quite," said Esme, gulping down the last of her tea and pushing back her wobbly chair, which scraped across the flagstone floor. "I'll take west," she said. "Any last dribbles of sun, I'll get them. Plus, you know. Sunset is literally in the poem, so . . ."

Jamie rolled his eyes.

"I'll take east, then," said Mirren. "I like looking at the sea."

"Okay," said Esme. "Try not to get lost again and end up in a quarry somewhere."

"Right," said Jamie. "Quick as you can, every room, tear through and meet back here before it gets too dark. Take candles and matches. Good luck, everyone."

Chapter Thirty

Mirren had orientated herself properly now. East was always the sea, so at least she knew where to go. That meant the turret that led down to the cave must be at the northeastern corner, and her room on the opposite side. They were on a high floor, which meant, thinking logically—although nothing about this ridiculous house was remotely logical, so that wasn't necessarily a lot of use—if she could assume the servants' rooms were on the top floor, and the guest rooms where she and Theo were billeted were on the third, and the public rooms on the first floor, particularly facing the front, then it made sense that the family rooms would be on the second floor. She would have asked the others, but they had all dashed off, gung ho.

It was so odd to be so isolated, to not be just a quick text away from joining up or figuring something out. They needed walkie-talkies, really, but that, Esme had observed, would require a certain amount of foresight the family wasn't known for. She had also then announced that she was going to go out and hit the Landie with a spade till the snow fell off and she could charge her phone from the cigarette lighter, but, just as she'd said that, they'd looked out of the window at the lowering cloud turning the world into a black-and-white film and Jamie had said if she did she'd get trapped in her car and suffocate and die, so that had rather put the kibosh on that.

As they'd prepared to split up, Mirren had pulled on the heavy overcoat again, forgoing the waders, and Jamie had disappeared to grab her an extra jumper. Theo had looked slightly concerned. "There definitely aren't any ghosts really, right?" he'd said, and Esme had snorted.

"The only person who looks supernatural around these parts is you, Wraith Boy."

Theo had tried to look insulted, but failed.

"He does it on purpose," said Mirren. "He thinks he's in *Buffy the Vampire Slayer.*"

"I do *not*," said Theo, smiling. "I think I am in *Interview with the Vampire.*"

"I thought you were the count from *Sesame Street*," said Esme.

"Okay, enough of this," Theo had said, pulling his cloak around himself, which had the effect of making both girls burst out laughing at the same time. "I'm out of here."

"BAT FORM!" shouted Esme, which convulsed them even more. By the time Jamie got back with the jumper, they were still giggling. It smelled of him, Mirren had realised, putting it on: woody and rather comforting. She liked it. She'd jammed a woollen cap on her head.

"Okay," Jamie had said, glancing at his watch. "Come back when it's dark, I guess. Fast as we can." He'd glanced at Esme worriedly. "Good luck."

They had left the haven of the warm kitchen together, its candles a soft pool of light in the gloom of the corridors, the dull windows at the end letting in a grey light that only proved that the snow had started falling again. As they walked up the stairs together Mirren had been fine, but then they'd gone their separate ways, and their footsteps faded down the long-softened rugs, and Mirren had finally felt herself, completely alone.

From somewhere she could hear an ancient clock tick. Who wound it? she wondered. Bonnie, she supposed, nipping here and there on silent feet, treading in her own ancestors' footsteps just as surely as Jamie trod in his. It seemed a strange life. Mind you, being a quantity surveyor in London probably seemed odd to these people. It seemed odd even to Mirren now, the idea of a normal life with Starbucks and Korean chicken and the Overground and Wordle and Snapchat. As if the snow were a heavy curtain that had been drawn across her life, cutting off all that had been before. She stood on a floorboard, which creaked heavily. Only the ghosts creak, Esme had said. Mirren felt, fleetingly, as if she had always been here, as if she was the ghost.

She shivered. She was scaring herself, and that stupid clock wasn't helping.

She should have checked to make sure there weren't any more taxidermy rooms. No, surely there weren't. Steeling herself, she opened the first door.

The smell of dust was overwhelming. Nobody had been in here for a long time; this wasn't one of Bonnie's project rooms, that was for sure.

Her hand automatically tried the light switch before she remembered, and she blinked so she could see in the gloom. Big dim shapes covered in cloth: furniture, of course, packed away for some future use, as yet undecided.

She pulled off the cloth from one thing that looked as if it might be a bookshelf—and let out the most almighty scream as a figure loomed up out of the shadows, heading straight for her.

Chapter Thirty-One

It was several moments before Mirren's brain caught up with her terrified racing heart, her anguished scream caught in her throat, to realise what she was looking at was of course her own reflection, on the door of a wardrobe. "Bloody hell," she found herself swearing gently under her breath, then she looked up, ready to apologise to the others when they came running to help her. Of course nobody did, and she realised with a shiver that no one could hear you scream here, with the thick stone walls and miles of passageway between them all. No wonder Agatha Christie had murdered so many people in places like these.

She looked at herself in the old spotted wardrobe mirror. Her hair was wild and dark; the large jumper gave her a bulkier look. She looked like a terrifying stranger. She shivered again, just a tremor. A goose walking over my grave, she thought, then told herself to stop being an idiot. This was a quick rush-through.

But this was not somebody's bedroom, it was just "a" bedroom. Nothing personal in it at all; there was tapestry-style flock wallpaper that in a normal house would have been terribly naff but which here was magnificent; ancient dried flowers in the grate; a bed. She bravely opened the wardrobe; there was nothing but a dead bluebottle. She realised suddenly that she was disappointed.

If there was ever a magical wardrobe, surely it would be in a room like this, in a world of snow.

On the other hand, she thought, looking out of the window . . . She felt she was in Narnia already: the elusive grandfather was the mysterious professor, and Esme could be the White Witch, which would make Jamie Mr. Tumnus, she supposed, and she smiled at the thought. She wondered if Theo was Edmund.

She lit a candle and looked around but there was nothing else in here; she moved out and back into the corridor, listening for the others, but there was not a sign. They might be on different floors.

The next room was more promising: a study, rather tidy. Books were stacked high, but they were stacked rather than thrown in piles; she could run her eye and her finger over them. She realised suddenly she needed to mark which rooms she had seen and which she hadn't. She looked for Post-it notes on the study desk, and found only blotting paper. She opened one of the drawers: sheets of writing paper bloomed; old airmail envelopes, and thick, good-quality headed paper with the castle name engraved on the top, and *From the desk of Laird McKinnon* underneath. *His writing room*, she thought, looking around. Where he must have sat, probably made up this very game they were currently caught in.

Which meant, she figured, he wouldn't hide the book in here. Not if his tricksy ways were anything to go by.

She picked up a dusty old photograph on his desk. It was an angelic-looking baby in a dress, sitting on a tartan rug in the garden. She turned it over. 1943, it said. JMK. So it must be him—male babies used to wear dresses in those days, didn't they? She wondered why he kept a photo of himself as a baby on his desk. You would think his loved ones might make the cut, not just himself. What a peculiar sort of fellow he must have been.

"You're not going to beat me, Baby in a Dress," she announced aloud to the picture frame to give herself courage. "It's around here somewhere, and I'm going to find it. And I reckon if this is your study, your bedroom cannot be far away."

In fact, she realised, what she had taken for a cupboard was in actuality a connecting door. She pulled it open. How funny, she thought, to build a connecting room that wasn't a bathroom. Although the idea of having a bedroom with a study attached was not, she thought, a bad one.

The room she now found herself in was vast; you could play cricket in it. A large bed was at one end; to her surprise it was a modern bed, no four-poster here. Instead, this bed had a vast, comfortable-looking mattress and a thick modern duvet. There was a side table, piled high with books, of course, but also a box of tissues, and a remote control for a small, old-fashioned television sitting on a dressing table by one of the floor-to-ceiling windows. The only view from the bedroom was the pounding sea and the full vastness of the weather, beautiful and wild. The clouds were thick, the flakes dancing. The expanse of glass made the room cold; Mirren found herself huddling in Jamie's sweater. It could have been such a lovely sight, though, on this bleak December's eve. The drapes were not the old rotting curtains in every other room; they were thick and handsome and looked relatively new. The fireplace was large, though; if the fire was lit it would be pleasant, surely; homely almost, if you were warm and cosy in the bed, watching the freezing waves dance far, far beyond the window frame, safe and sound.

But then the laird had not felt safe, had he? He had been all alone. Out by himself, on a freezing night, one just like this. She stared again and shivered.

The surrounds of his bed were bookshelves, reasonably new again, at least compared to the rest of the house. This must have been the one place he could have things as he wanted them, rather than covering the ancient acquisitions of generations past in endless dumped tomes.

She looked at it. My goodness. To her surprise, these books were organised. From the very start: Ackroyd. Adams. Adichie. Alighieri. An extraordinarily broad but very high-quality selection, she noticed approvingly. Kept tidily and well, rather than just dumped willy-nilly. How very strange. She suddenly found herself smoothing the old duvet. There was a faint smell of pipe tobacco and stray cologne, which made her feel oddly sad; it was a grandfathery smell. But he should have been here, cosy in bed, fire blazing, moon up over the water, surrounded by a doting daughter and his grandchildren. Not out all by himself.

She lit the candle—it was still early afternoon, but dusk was already making its presence felt through the thickly falling snow—and scanned down the shelves till she reached *G*: Rumer Godden, Paul Gallico, Alan Garner . . . Lewis Grassic Gibbon.

And there it was. There it was. Tucked right away where you wouldn't notice it in a million years. *A Scots Quair. Sunset Song*.

This edition was green and white. The book felt . . . It felt heavy, as an old hardback would. But there was something else; it felt a little lumpy, misshapen, even.

The temperature in the room was absolutely freezing; it was ridiculous. Her hands were trembling too much to even open the book, and she fumbled it and nearly dropped it in her excitement. She should, of course, have run back down to the kitchen with it immediately, got Bonnie to ring the bell, informed the others.

But something stopped her. She found she wanted to look at it herself, before everyone started scrambling, and Theo swooshed in with his *I know everything about books* face on and Esme made smart remarks and wondered how long it would be before she could get her hands on her money. Mirren wanted to have a look, just her, before she announced it to the others.

She didn't think Jamie would mind. Would he mind? Surely not.

She could not have said what exactly possessed her. Getting into strange beds in strange houses wasn't something she made a habit of. But she found herself putting the candle and the book carefully down on the side table, shaking off her boots, clambering up onto the comfortable bed, and slipping underneath the soft duvet.

MIRREN SAT ON her hands till the feeling came back into them. She had been right: it was a wonderful cosy duvet, crunchy with goose feathers. She had taken her shoes off, obviously, but kept her jacket on, and she gradually felt herself beginning to warm up. She also felt rather sleepy—it had been hearty exercise, snowshoeing across the property; she was absolutely feeling quite ready for a nap.

But, just as her eyes were gradually drifting closed, she jerked them open again and sat bolt upright. The book!

She left the candle where it was and took her hands out of the bedclothes again, reluctantly. She let her eyes adjust for a moment then picked it up carefully.

"Okay, Baby in a Dress," she said. "Let's see, shall we?"

She opened the first page, and realised the book was in fact a compendium of three books in one, and *Sunset Song* was the first. It was obviously well read, and, as she flicked through, she saw bits of it were underlined. She hoped this did not make up the next clue.

But it was the second book, *Cloud Howe*, that made her stop. Because when she got to the first page—there was nothing there. Just as with the *Bestiary*, there was an actual, honest-to-goodness hole cut neatly out of the book, as if for a gun, or for a spy. Only this time it was much bigger.

And it was filled with letters.

She ought to take it to the others at once, she knew. But then she remembered Esme being so dismissive of the old man's sad experience at boarding school. She would go soon.

She glanced to the side of the bed and noticed a discarded crumple of paper that was covered in faded ones and zeros. He must have practiced his binary code up here, in bed. Esme and Jamie were so dismissive of him, but Mirren suddenly felt close to this old man who had filled his last days with something so intricate.

She unfolded one letter and began to read.

Once more they were replies; clumsily written, in a fountain pen that leaked quite heavily to the side. There was none of the refinement of the father's letters, but there was an envelope included—Sir James McKinnon, Faculty of Land Management, University of Edinburgh. So that was where they had found him. They were dated 1962. Such a long time ago.

Dearest James,

I hope youse are having fun in the big city. I know you say it is bad and you miss home, but I cannot imagine that. A fine fellow like you must be having a fine time, you and all your old friends from school. Bullies change, don't they? And so much going on all the time. You'll be having fun right enough, won't give us a thought.

Of course I miss you, my only one. But I want you to be having a good time, don't I? We were not a possible thing, now, were we? We could not have been, could we now?

So enjoy yourself, in the bright lights, please. I'll be waiting.

THERE WAS NO signature. Nothing to give the person's identity away. No return address. Mirren couldn't even tell from the blotted handwriting whether the author was a man or a woman.

She picked up the second. The tone was quite different.

> *I thought when you left for the university everything would change and it would be different and you would forget me and I could forget you.*
>
> *But seeing you again made that a foolish promise, every bit of it. All I wanted, all I want is you. I will say it, and I should not send this letter and I will deny every word of it if it is ever traced.*
>
> *But I want you and only you, James.*

I WANT YOU and only you, James, thought Mirren to herself.

Then, later, dated 1964.

> *You were so cold to me that day. I understand it, I do. And your friends . . . well, they're aye loud. I . . . no. You're all right. Just . . . I want to say that I'll always be here, but that's a ridiculous thing to say. I will always. I will. I would . . .*

THE LETTER TRAILED out, perhaps in tears. There was one after Christmas.

> *I can do nothing without you. To see you and not be able to touch you is torture, and I know you share it, I see it on your face. You think nobody knows you, but I do. All of it. Your funny ways. The way you light up when you see a new book. How much you love Forres, even if you don't quite know how it works. I know you; I love every part of you. And your father will not let you see me . . . well, I hope it is him. I truly do hope it is him, James, and not you.*

THERE HAD BEEN, then, a love affair. That had ended very badly. A school that had gone horribly wrong, then a love affair that had ended in disaster, in fact.

It occurred to Mirren, with some trepidation, that this man, who had walked out into an icy field to die alone, wasn't just leaving them a puzzle. He was telling them everything he hadn't been able to tell them in real life. A guide to his unhappiness, his eccentricities.

And then, at the very bottom of the hole in the book, a locket—not expensive, Mirren didn't think, by candlelight. A heart shape, in burnished gold. She held it up to the light to see if there was something engraved on it—

"What the hell are you doing?"

Chapter Thirty-Two

For the second time that afternoon, Mirren let out an enormous yelp.

Jamie had come in so quietly and stealthily that she hadn't even seen him. Night had descended as she'd become engrossed in the letters, across half a century; the very human pain and yearning written in them, as one might write a feverish Facebook post. Although that would be seen by everyone, and this had just been for one person. And then they had been left here, on purpose, a trail of breadcrumbs, leading straight to his bed.

She grabbed the candle back just in time.

"What the hell are you doing?" repeated the voice. Standing at the end of the bed, like a wraith conjured from the dark, was the tall figure of Jamie, holding his own candlestick.

"Bloody hell," said Mirren. "Don't do that! You look like you're going to show me Christmas Past! You should creak on purpose. No, then that would make you a ghost . . ."

Jamie frowned, not listening to her babbling nervously. "Why are you in *my grandfather's bed*?"

"Oh yeah," said Mirren, carefully setting the book and the letters aside and remembering where she was. "Um . . . because it's freezing?"

"But that's his *bed*!"

She jumped up and got out. "I'm sorry," she said, looking around at its messy state, slightly ashamed of herself now. "I'm sorry . . . I was so cold, and it . . . it was the only cosy bed I've seen in this place."

Jamie blinked.

"You should have said 'no getting in anybody's bed,'" said Mirren, going on the offensive, because she was feeling guilty. "I didn't think anyone would mind."

"It's really weird," said Jamie, backing down a bit.

"Not as weird as you creeping up on me."

"Oh yeah," said Jamie, looking at his feet. "I know where the creaks are, I suppose; years of practice. Not that I was ever in here very much." He moved over to the windows. "Ach, it's a hoolie out there," he said, then glanced back.

"I'm really sorry," said Mirren. "I realise this is your family."

"Och, no, you're all right," he said. "What does it matter, really?"

"It does matter," said Mirren. "I shouldn't have done it. I should have come immediately, as soon as I found this."

Jamie's face lit up as she proudly held up the book. "No way!" He dashed across the floor.

"Hang on, hang on, hang on," she said. "Be careful. It's fragile and there's a lot in it. We need to take it down to the kitchen and get as much light as possible and all look at it together."

Suddenly his head was very close to hers as he peered at it.

"Did you think of that too?" he said, sounding impressed. "That if it was a love story he'd want it near to him?"

"Why—is that why you came over here?"

"Yeah, it occurred to me. I thought, if it's something personal . . . Plus I got to the servants' rooms and he'd obviously never been in one of those, so it got a bit pointless. Well, anyway, we ended up in the same place."

"Apart from the getting-into-bed bit."

"No, no, now I think that that was quite sensible."

In the dark, the only sound the pair of them breathing, they both stood stock-still. The moon shone a faint bifurcated light through the huge windows; the snow kept on falling. They breathed in and out. So close, and so close to the fading warmth of the bed. Mirren held the book, full of passion and longing between its sheets, real and imaginary, both loves gone, and her fingers, in the dark, brushed Jamie's long ones, and his fingertips found hers. Would he be cruel, she found herself thinking, as his grandfather was accused of being? And then a thought to make her blush: Would she mind if he was?

"It's not just the book," she said. "There's something inside it."

"Really?" said Jamie, turning round to face her and get a better look at it.

"Yes. Loads of stuff."

"YOAH! HULLLOOOOOOOOO!"

There was a thundering noise suddenly outside the door Jamie had left open.

"I'M BORED, IT's FREEZING, AND MY CANDLE WENT OUT! WHERE IS EVERYONE?"

"Ah, your boyfriend," said Jamie, taking a step back.

"He's not my boyfriend," said Mirren, rather more decisively than she'd intended, in a way that made him look at her with a gaze she could not read.

Theo poked his head around the door. "Bloody hell, if I were a zillionaire robber baron who'd made my pile off the back of slavery cotton and other people's bloody money, do you know where I'd build my castle? THE SOUTH OF FRANCE. What are you two up to?" He blinked and looked at the unmade bed. "Oh, excuse me."

"Don't be *ridiculous*, Theo, and get your mind out of the gutter; this is the old laird's room," said Mirren, flushing.

"You're right," said Theo. "We've only been looking for two hours; that wouldn't even be enough time to undo all the buttons on the nine layers of clothes you're wearing."

She gave him a look.

"I'd still have a go, though, obviously."

"Actually, we found something."

"*Mirren* found something," said Jamie gallantly.

"Oh, thank Christ," said Theo. "Can I go and sit on the Aga? Or, possibly, in it?"

Chapter Thirty-Three

The sheer relief of being back in the kitchen was immense. Bonnie had found storm lamps and lit them, and they flickered reassuringly around the place, and made it cosier than ever. She had also lined the kitchen door to keep the snow and the draughts out. If she hadn't had exciting news to impart, Mirren would have been in grave danger of falling asleep the second she sat down.

They sat around the table, as Bonnie served them tea with a slug of whisky in it to make up for there being no fresh milk today, and black bun, a thick, treacly fruitcake that was absolutely delicious.

Mirren showed them the ingenious cut-out book.

"I wonder if he was ever a spy?" pondered Jamie, and Esme snorted and said, if he was he would have probably spent more time in the House of Lords, where he had once held a hereditary seat, and less poking around old secondhand bookshops buying stock by the yard, and Jamie had had to concede that that was probably true.

"Didn't he ever have a real job?" asked Mirren.

"The estate is a real job," said Esme quickly.

"That he was very, very bad at," added Jamie.

"Yes, bit of a family tradition," said Esme, holding up the locket to the light. "This is just cheap tat," she said. "Disappointing. I suppose if it had been worth anything Mummy would have sniffed it out a mile off."

"I think it's pretty," said Mirren.

"Do you?" said Esme, and Mirren felt that any warmth that had grown between them this morning had abruptly worn off.

"What's inside?" said Jamie. "I couldn't open it."

Esme, however, had perfectly manicured nails with neat edges, and with absolute precision she carefully found the latch and clicked it. They all leaned over, with Theo holding up the lantern to get a closer look.

Inside was a tiny picture.

But it was not, as Mirren had expected, a photograph of a young woman—nobody had recognised the handwriting of the letters.

Instead, it was a tiny, ancient painting. It was of a young man, but it wasn't James; it was a boy of a fashion many years ago, painted, with pink cheeks and blond hair, and an old suit with an Elizabethan ruff. Around his neck was an animal that looked something like a monkey. Both gazed out of the tiny locket with a cool, penetrating stare. The colours were crude—red, blue, and yellow—but they glowed bright. The style was very old indeed.

"What?" said Theo. "Who the hell is that?"

"It can't be someone from here," said Jamie. "It's much earlier."

All four of them stared at the picture. Theo once again took out his tweezers and very carefully worked the photo out of the locket. It was so beautiful and so strange.

Turning it over in the candlelight, they saw a faint trace of writing on the back. And sure enough, once more there they were: a series of numbers.

"Bloody hell," said Esme. "Grandfather, what the hell else did you have to *do* all day?"

Mirren read them out. "One, two, one, three, four, one, four, two." She blinked. "Oh God," she said. "Seriously, what now? Don't say Fibonacci."

"Fibonacci what?" said Theo. "What could it be?"

"A date? The day this was painted? The twelfth of the first, 1341?"

"Not very likely," said Jamie gloomily. "The fashion is Elizabethan."

"And it's printed, not painted," said Theo, holding it close to the candle, although wary of it. "Although that could be the original date . . ."

"But the clothes are too late; you'd need a five in there, minimum."

"Well, a date from another time, then?"

"Yes, but *where*?"

"Also, you know, this picture is almost certainly cut out of a book," ventured Theo, and they all groaned in unison.

"Oh *God*," said Esme. "For GOD'S SAKE. This is absolutely bloody ridiculous. I don't even think there's anything at the other end. I don't even think there's that. There's nothing. It's all been some completely futile *ha ha ha, make money on your own, you suckers, it's all gone*. If we ever get there, which I very much doubt, it'll be an empty jack-in-the-box. No wonder you didn't tell Mum about this stupid thing."

"Es," said Jamie, in a softer tone than he normally used.

"It's okay for you!" said Esme. "You've got a roof over your head. You've got it all! I'm the one bouncing about between friends I went to school with, spending half the year yacht-hopping!"

"I thought you loved yacht-hopping," said Jamie. "You're always going on about how great it is."

Esme rolled her eyes. "What, hanging on, being beautiful and elegant and delightful and entertaining and hoping for crumbs off their table? As every year the other girls get younger? Not particularly, no."

"Could you not just go and get a job?" said Mirren timidly. "You must have friends who work in film and fashion and cool stuff like that?"

Esme heaved a sigh. "Yes, I do. Those jobs don't pay actual money, you do know that? You can't live off them."

"Um," said Mirren, who did not know that.

"You don't search books for a living, do you?"

"I'm a quantity surveyor."

Esme snorted. "Exactly. I don't even know what the hell that is."

"It means she can tell you if your house is about to fall down," said Theo.

"Is this house about to fall down?"

Mirren made a wobbling *maybe* sign with her hand flat.

"Oh, that looks like an easy job," said Esme. "Better than wasting your time here with this nonsense. What do you think, Theo? You're meant to be the book guy."

Theo looked serious. "There's a lot of house clearance stuff here," he said. "I think when your grandfather . . . We see this quite a lot. When he bought a lot of stuff at auction, when people get really accumulative with book-collecting or anything else . . . they can get a bit less discriminating. Which means they'll buy anything. And collections that come to auction . . . well, usually those families have been through them first to see if there's anything truly valuable."

Esme folded her arms. "So it's only a heap of fucking junk," she said. "Just like I always thought." She kicked the wooden kitchen table leg in frustration. "And he just let these bloody books pile all their way up over here like a fricking . . . maze. The house is already a maze; he just made another maze. Out of garbage."

"Oh, Esme . . ." began Mirren, feeling sorry for the beautiful posh girl, which felt like a completely absurd position to be in.

"Shhhhhhh!" said Jamie suddenly.

They all turned to stare at him, Esme looking truculent: How dare her little brother consider giving her a telling off? But Jamie was screwing up his eyes as if trying to ignore everyone else in the room.

"A maze," he said.

"Yes," said Esme. "That's what I said."

He grabbed the tweezers from Theo and stared intently at the picture.

"What's that monkey thing?" he asked finally, screwing his eyes up even tighter and holding it right up to his face. "I don't think it is a monkey. It's got stripes. Monkeys don't have stripes."

"It's a bush baby?" said Theo. "Something like that?"

Jamie snapped his fingers. "It's a lemur."

They stared at him, uncomprehending.

"Hang on," said Mirren. "What about the boy with a ruff? Is he a fairy-tale boy? He's wearing a fairy-tale outfit. Like in 'The Elves and the Shoemaker.'"

"I think something like that . . ." said Jamie. "Oh Lord, it's on the tip of my tongue who he reminds me of."

They stared at it.

"Poem!" said Mirren, flapping her hand, then remembered it was still in her pocket. "*The saddest tale of woe is told,*" she said.

"Yes!" said Jamie, then thought for a second. "*For never was a story of more woe,*" he quoted, "*than this of Juliet and her Romeo.*"

Mirren grinned. The embroidered pantaloons, the dagger round his waist, the floppy hat . . . "It's Romeo!!!"

"YES!"

They practically hopped up and down in glee.

"And?" said Theo.

"Isn't it obvious?" said Jamie.

"Yeah," said Mirren. "Oh no, hang on, I don't get it at all. Why is there a locket with Romeo in it?"

"The one thing this isn't," said Theo, "is obvious."

"So it's Romeo. From *Romeo and Juliet*," said Jamie.

"Romeo and a lemur?"

"Exactly. Romeo Lemur."

"Who the fuck is Romeo Lemur?" said Esme.

"No. It's not a name. 'Romeo' is *R*. 'Lemur' is *L*. In the phonetic alphabet."

Theo scrunched up his nose. "'Lemur' isn't *L* in the phonetic alphabet. It's 'lima.'" He saw Mirren's surprised face. "I'm good in a pub quiz. Shut up."

"It's 'lima' *these days*," said Jamie, refusing to be put off. "It used to be 'lemur,' then they changed it because more people recognised it."

"They should probably change 'Zulu' now," said Theo, musing.

"Okay, let's not get into this," said Mirren, staring at the tiny picture. "Do you really think that's what it means? But then what do the numbers mean?"

"Well, it's possible . . . Look, this is a reach," said Jamie.

"YOU THINK?" said Esme.

"I think if you started with Romeo at the maze—and went one right, two left, one right, three left . . ."

They all stared.

"I haven't been in that stupid thing in years," said Esme.

"Well, that's not quite true," said Jamie. "Because someone used to go and smoke dope in it every school holiday."

Esme didn't deign to give this an answer, but Mirren, looking at her, could see she was working it out in her head, mentally tracing her steps.

Something occurred to Mirren. Even now, she still instinctively went to her pocket for her phone, before remembering.

"Jamie!" she said. "The poem. How does it go?"

Jamie took out the copy he was keeping in his back pocket and traced down the lines.

"*The ancient routes stand fast,*" he read.

"Oh yeah, those roots are ancient," said Esme. "They've been growing it for hundreds of years."

"No, not 'roots,' *r-o-u.*" Jamie paused. "Oh," he said. "Well, it could be. I mean, it could be 'roots' . . ."

"Sounds encouraging," said Mirren.

"Or rubbish," said Esme.

"Well, what's next?" said Theo.

"*A crown of gold,*" said Mirren. "Is there a crown of gold anywhere?"

Esme and Jamie looked at each other.

"It all got sold," said Esme. "Everything. This is so stupid. If we had any gold . . ."

"Well, we wouldn't, because it would have been sold," said Jamie.

"He should have put that in his stupid poem," said Esme. "*All the gold, which we accidentally sold. And now my stupid story is told and this house is stupid and old.*"

Jamie walked towards the kitchen window. The snow had stopped, and a vast oak moon hung over the gardens.

"I think we should probably call it a day before Esme goes bonkers," he said.

"Don't be so bloody bold," said Esme.

"If it doesn't snow tomorrow, we can probably get out. Sky is clear," he said. "That's a good sign. Hopefully everything will ice over. Shall we dress for dinner?"

"No, because it's TOO! FRICKING! COLD!" shouted Esme after him, as he disappeared upstairs.

Chapter Thirty-Four

They must be getting close, Mirren thought. They must be. What had seemed at first an impossible task—well, they had solved two clues today. They were doing it. There was going to be something there, out of the terrible jumble and mess of the house. She felt excited and rather proud.

Tonight she chose a plain black '20s-style dress, which cascaded straight down, with silver threaded through the fabric, and beautiful black-fringed shoulder caps that trembled when she moved. It made her stand differently, walk differently, to show it off. She put her curly hair in a low bun, pulled some ringleted strands free, added smudgy eyeliner to her grey eyes, and descended the front staircase this time, feeling unusually elegant.

There was nobody in the drawing room. The fire blazed high and she approached it gratefully. It was very strange being there by herself; where had the boys gone? She had thought she'd heard Theo zipping down their shared corridor to the bathroom.

She poured herself a very small whisky, topped it up with water, and pulled an Elizabeth Gaskell from the bookshelf; a fine edition, old but barely read. She settled into one of the brittle, stylised chairs; she'd rather have been stretched out on the rug, but the dress was too lovely.

Then she thought, who cared? Esme did whatever she wanted.

The dress could be cleaned; its owner didn't seem to care about it. She stretched out full length on the heavy rug in front of the fire, and lost herself in *Cranford* again.

Without her realising it, the whisky warmed her up, the flames popped and burned and she felt her eyes start to close again, just as they had in the old man's bed. It couldn't all be what they'd done that day, she thought, that was making her so sleepy. It was modern life that had made her tired. So, so tired. Here, the rules of modern life did not apply. And there was no doubt her body simply wanted to catch up. No phone. No internet dating. No being angry about Theo, or anyone else. No job stress. No pickpockets.

Her head nodded, and she found herself in that delicious halfway house between sleep and waking, where for some reason Mrs. Gaskell herself had turned up to help them with the clues, and they had all been very welcoming, except for Esme, who hadn't liked her shoes . . .

The next thing she knew, someone was licking her face.

She blinked blearily. "What . . . ? Oh, hello." It was Roger, Jamie's dog. "I thought you weren't allowed indoors."

The dog's tail was waving joyously.

"Once it hits minus four, he is," said Jamie's voice.

Mirren sat up and looked around, cuddling the dog, who, for a rough, tough working dog who had no time for any of that namby-pamby lifestyle, sure did suddenly seem to love being in front of the fire having a fuss made of him. Mirren scratched him behind the ears, and he practically whinnied in delight, showing her his belly and pushing his ear closer towards her.

"Roger, stop being ridiculous. You're being such a Pick Me," said Jamie's voice, and Mirren suddenly realised why she couldn't see him. He and Theo were carting in huge armfuls of mistletoe and holly, still festooned with snow.

"Oh my God," she said, jumping up. Roger jumped up with her, to make sure she didn't break any hand-to-ear contact. "You dragged in all that stuff!"

"It's nearly Christmas," said Jamie, going over to decorate the mantelpiece. "And I wanted to check if the ice was going to hold."

"I got dragged along against my will," said Theo, from the other side. "Bloody hell, it's freezing outside. And I thought it was cold to start with."

"Keeps witches away," said Esme, coming down behind them in a chic black minidress.

"Witches," said Theo. "I'll add it to my list of things to be terrified of around here."

"There's a big freeze tonight," said Jamie. "Better fill up the baths in case the pipes go. Might keep the kitchen one running; I'll tell Bonnie."

"How can this possibly still be the UK?" said Mirren, shaking her head.

"Excellent question," said Esme. "Come on, Theo, come to the cellar with me."

Mirren looked to see what he would do. To see whether his behavior towards her last night had just been timewasting for him, again. Or whether he would keep pressing her with as much ardour as he had then. He glanced over at her.

Esme blew her cheeks out impatiently. "Are you coming or what?"

And it seemed that she was asking for rather more than just some company in the cellar. It felt to Mirren that Theo was having to choose. There was a space next to her by the fire. She looked at him. For a second Theo said nothing. Then Esme made to move, and Theo got up and followed her, in her tiny dress, straight out of the door.

The strangest thing of all was how Mirren felt about it: uplifted.

Not at all what she would have expected. Relieved. All that time spent wondering what she had done wrong, whether or not it was a good idea; all that worry and fretting and headspace and thinking about it. All completely wasted. She had not, in fact, been in danger of passing up the love of her life with one wrong move. She had not been trying to land a good thing. She had been expending energy in the wrong direction, completely: a handsome, charming, fundamentally weak man who could never fully be there for her—or, she suspected, for anyone else. She prodded her heart, but even then all she could feel was clarity, and relief that she hadn't fallen deeper in, lost her pride even more. It was okay. It was done.

"WHAT ARE YOU smiling about?" Jamie asked, as Theo and Esme clattered out.

She shook her head. "Oh, things that used to matter but don't anymore," she said, cuddling Roger.

"Oh, good," said Jamie. "I would love to have things that didn't matter anymore."

Roger pushed his muzzle under her chin so she would pet him more.

"It's because you're stretched out on the rug. Roger thinks you're another dog."

"Or maybe," said Mirren, "Roger knows a sympathetic person when he sees one."

Roger looked at Jamie as if to say, *Why am I not in here every night?* and Jamie nodded briefly.

"Hungry?" he said.

"Incredibly," said Mirren, with some surprise, only just realising it. "We had a good day, don't you think?"

"I think so," said Jamie cautiously. "But who knows where it's all leading? It might just be on and on and round and round."

"Well, the poem comes to an end, doesn't it?"

"It does," he said. "Yeah." He looked around. "I think he did like us here at Christmas. My grandfather. Even if we moaned about his stupid treasure hunts."

"It's a shame he's missing this one when you're doing so well."

"Mmm," said Jamie.

Mirren leaned closer. "Do you think he really was just so unhappy?"

"It seems so, doesn't it? Sad at school. An unhappy love affair . . . it feels like he wants to explain his life to us. Well, to me. Why it all ended so badly."

"In a field, all alone," said Mirren sadly. Now she was here, it felt even sadder, his lonely death.

"Yeah," said Jamie. "In a field all alone."

They were quiet for a while.

"You never think grown-ups are unhappy, do you?" said Jamie. "When you're a kid. It never crosses your mind. You think they're having the best time."

"They can stay up as late as they like!"

"Ha, yeah. They can eat sweets *whenever they want*!"

"Drive cars!"

"Exactly. I cannot believe what we ever complain about."

They both smiled.

"I love going to bed early," confessed Jamie. "It's one of my favourite things."

"Mine too," said Mirren. "And if I eat a whole bar of chocolate I want to throw up."

"Me too," said Jamie. "Mind you, I used to do that when I was little as well. Plus, the cost of car insurance, oh my God."

"It feels . . ." said Mirren, then hesitated. "It feels like he really wants you to know. What it was like for him. It feels like he's seeking forgiveness maybe? For messing up your inheritance."

"I know," said Jamie. "I wondered that too. I think . . . I think that I never really knew him."

"Nobody knows their grandparents," said Mirren. "Maybe nobody understood him his whole life."

"I think the person who wrote the Sunset Letters to him did," said Jamie. "And for whatever reason . . ."

"Do you think it was a man?" said Mirren. "That seems the likeliest. Sorry and all that."

"That's what Mum thinks: that he was gay," said Jamie, rolling his eyes. "She'd love that: it would make her feel hip and down with things."

"So your mum just never visited your grandfather at all?"

He shook his head. "Once the money was finished, she was gone. I think . . . I think my grandmother and she were in fair cahoots about it. You get that in divorce, don't you? Sides get taken . . ." His voice trailed off. "My mum said some right awful things about my dad as well."

"There's a lot of broken marriages in your family."

"There are."

"So, who was your grandmother? Is she definitely not the letter-writer?"

"Definitely not," said Jamie. "I'd recognise her handwriting, from the disappointed letters she used to send me about my school report."

Mirren smiled. "Ah, a family trait."

"Yeah," said Jamie. "Anyway. She was a laird's daughter, from Lewis. It was kind of an arranged match between clans. I know some arranged marriages work fine, but this one . . . not so much.

She went back to Lewis in the end, couldn't bear the house or the east coast. I don't remember them ever exchanging a kind word."

He lay down on his back, his head near hers on the old rug. It was strangely intimate, but not uncomfortably so. He stared at the ceiling, and Roger sat on his chest in front of the fire. He appeared to have adjusted remarkably speedily to being an indoor dog.

"My mother grew up very like her. He was very short with her—though she gave as good as she got, mind you: she was vile back to him. And then she announced that her therapist had recommended family estrangement, and therefore she didn't have to contact him ever again. She announced it at Christmas, as well, right in front of us."

"Wow. You're not estranged from her, though?"

"Oh no, she still likes to get in touch to tell me what to do," said Jamie. "And how I'm going to make a mess of this place just like he did, and if she catches me reading it's because I'm too fond of books, and sometimes, when she's drunk, she needs to slag off my dad again. Or either of her subsequent two husbands, I can't quite keep them straight . . . Sorry, I'm going on and on and on . . . Tell me about your family."

Mirren stared up at the ceiling. It was incredibly high, with plaster moulding and a huge hanging crystal chandelier. There was a vast, soaring painted roof above a room full of beauty and treasure beyond imagining, or there had been, once upon a time.

"Um . . . pretty normal actually," she said awkwardly, suddenly realising she was lying down in a castle next to an actual lord, and trying her best not to make him feel bad. "My parents broke up when I was small—but I still see my dad a lot, he's just round the corner, and my mum is busy working; she's a fusspot. I've got two brothers, both married, one to a boy, one to a girl, and they're fantastic; they all gang up so my mum doesn't get *too* fusspotty, even though obviously she does. We tend to meet up on a Sunday, round someone's house—we try not to let Mum cook too much. I spent a lot of my childhood with my great-aunt; she was so kind to me. She's the one who made me go to university. And the one who loved books and got me to find one that was missing, so that's kind of how I ended up here."

"Because you love your family," said Jamie. "And look how *I* ended up here. Because mine all hate each other."

Mirren found herself stretching out and reaching for his hand and squeezing it.

"Sorry," he said. "Forget the self-pity. It's not very attractive. It's just this time of year."

Mirren was on the point of saying that he was perfectly attractive, but stopped herself just in time. The thought itself travelled up her like an electric shock and she was worried her hand would start to sweat. It felt nice in his large, comfortable one.

"It's okay," she said instead. "The idea that Christmas has to be super happy for everyone was invented by supermarkets to sell you stuff from September onwards. And it makes less-happy people even more unhappy. It's an arbitrary date."

"It's the deep heart of winter," said Jamie. "Not quite arbitrary."

"No, not quite," said Mirren. "I know. But you know, from Christmas onwards it gets lighter every day."

He squeezed her hand. "That's true," he said, glancing at her. Then he frowned.

"What now?" she said. "You've forgotten a small niece who betrayed you once?"

He actually guffawed at that. "Oh God, I really am terrible. You know, I have lots of nice friends who like me a lot."

"Really?" said Mirren. "Are you sure they're not just braying toffs you just happened to be banged up at school with?"

He covered his face with his hands. "Oh *Lord*, the abuse," he said, but he was smiling. "Anyway, that's all anyone's friends are."

"True," said Mirren, smiling to think of how her old, very dear school friends would take being described like that.

"And I didn't have an unhappy childhood, not really. It was normal to me. And I had the estate to charge about in, and Bonnie's grandmother was very kind to me—she grew up here too."

Mirren nodded.

"You seem close," she said carefully. She wanted to know.

"I've known her my whole life," said Jamie, and Mirren found herself suddenly feeling uncharacteristically jealous. "Actually," he went on, "I was thinking that if we end up spending Christmas here . . . I haven't got anyone Christmas presents."

"Oh Lord," said Mirren. "I have, but they're all in their hiding place at my mum's."

"What, for us?"

"No! For my family. I am going to be in such trouble for coming home late."

"Will they give you the silent treatment?" asked Jamie sympathetically.

"Oh God, no," said Mirren in surprise. "Though they won't be happy about having to move their Christmas Day to wait for me."

For a moment Jamie lay on the ground, slightly amazed. "Wow. They'd do that?" he said finally. "God. You are so, so lucky."

Mirren turned her head towards his. "But no," she said quickly. "There's all this other stuff you don't realise. Like my job doesn't pay enough. My company is going down the tubes. I can't live anywhere nice. I'm always late. I can't meet any men who want to commit. I don't know if or when I should settle down. I can't really handle modern life, I can't find a career I really love, and I'm never going to be able to afford to start a family or buy a proper house or retire. My life is a mess!"

Jamie screwed up his face. "Whereas I have too much sodding house and absolutely no choice in a career that isn't desperately clinging on by my fingertips."

They looked at each other, still lying head-to-head on the floor, and suddenly they burst out laughing. It was so unexpected.

"Oh my God, listen to us," said Jamie. He sat up. *"Boo-hoo, my house is too big even though I am relatively young and in perfect health and don't live in a war zone."*

Mirren sat up too. *"Boo-hoo, it's really annoying when your family loves you too much."*

He laughed. *"Oh my God, my nightmare happy childhood en route to growing up to be healthy and pretty!"*

Mirren fell silent. He'd called her pretty. Which . . . well. She was flattered. She couldn't help it. On his part, he looked as though he felt he had gone a little far and hadn't meant to say it.

She scrambled to her feet. "Anyway, that doesn't solve nobody getting any Christmas presents."

"I know." He jumped up, too, and stood a fair distance back from her.

Mirren looked around. "It may seem a little obvious," she said, "but we could *probably* choose books for everyone."

Jamie laughed. "Oh God. The last thing anyone wants to see. Ever again."

"I don't know," said Mirren stoutly. Nobody slagged off books in her presence. "A good book is a good book, regardless."

"I don't know what I'd get Esme," said Jamie. "She only reads *Vogue*."

"Oh, that's easy," said Mirren instantly. "Jilly Cooper. She'll love it."

"Have you seen any?"

"I think so, in the North Library yesterday . . . I did think it would have been funny if your grandfather hid his clues in something really sexy."

"Wouldn't be a bad place."

"Would be a *terrible* place," said Mirren instantly. "Don't put it in any books people can't stop reading if you want it to remain undiscovered."

He grinned. "See, that's why we need you."

She looked up at him then. His worried face, the slightly too-long hair, his fine brow and long nose. You could see his mother was a beauty; it showed in his fine features, his wide eyes and full lips.

The fire crackled behind them but there was no other noise in the room, and, quickly, the atmosphere had changed. Something about need: there was a hunger, now, in his eyes that Mirren hadn't noticed before. And in herself, too—she had felt something crystallise inside her; not because his story was sad, although it was, but because he had been able to share it with her, to talk, person-to-person, honestly and genuinely. She didn't find that in a lot of men. It made him attractive in a way she doubted he would understand; to explain to a man that it was strong to display vulnerability was not something, in Mirren's experience, that worked terribly well in this world. Theo never would understand. But she wasn't interested in Theo now. Not even the slightest. It had turned off like a switch. Because, suddenly, there was someone here she found herself far more drawn to.

He had felt it, too, she was sure of it. It felt like sparks flying in the heat of the room, his expression changing from worry to something like hope, as the fire crackled and he looked at her steadily.

"What kind of book would you choose for me?"

Mirren thought about it. "Something sad to begin with but ultimately . . . uplifting."

"With a happy ending?"

She looked at him directly then. "Why not?" she said, and suddenly her tone was breathy and unmistakable.

He moved forward, almost imperceptibly, just a little, and Mirren found herself, too, almost hypnotised, moving forward, just the tiniest bit, her entire body leaning towards him, wanting to be closer, immediately stopping as the door from the kitchen crashed open loudly and the rest of the party tumbled in.

Chapter Thirty-Five

The noise was ridiculous, and just seemed to get louder, as they both sprang apart as if doing something they shouldn't. Mirren felt her cheeks flame as Bonnie burst through the servants' staircase doors, followed closely by Esme and Theo, all of them shouting. Bonnie was laying down a tray full of cold cuts, cheese, and fresh bread, with chutney and pickled onions, for them to make a hearty ploughman's supper.

"I told them," she said to Jamie, her face pink and quivering. She stopped for a moment, looking at both of them, as if she could smell something in the air between them. Mirren frankly wouldn't put it past them: she already thought it entirely possible that Bonnie was part witch.

Esme and Theo were yelling incoherently, and, Mirren ascertained quite quickly, were absolutely roaring drunk. They must have achieved this with some speed. Although she wasn't wearing her watch. Time didn't seem to stick to its normal passage here; it wobbled in and out. She couldn't tell how long she and Jamie had been lying on the rug, talking of this and that. It could have been hours or minutes. She looked over to him. His sandy brown hair had fallen in his eyes, and the little frown line was back. She wanted to use her fingers to smooth it out, to calm him down. Then move her hand lower . . .

"What the hell?" he was saying.

"They've been all through the kitchen," said Bonnie, looking irritated for the first time. "Stuck their fingers in the Christmas pudding. They drank the cooking brandy! Now how am I going to set it on fire?"

"You were going to set it on fire?" Mirren was genuinely excited. "I love Christmas pudding."

"It was terrible," slurred Esme. "Or great—not sure."

"Not as great as the sloe gin," said Theo. His hair was awry, his chin unshaven, and his eyes weren't quite focused.

"You drank the *sloe gin*?" said Jamie. "That's been there for donkey's years."

"It gets stronger every year," said Esme.

"That's why nobody drinks it!" said Jamie. "It's rocket fuel."

"GOOD!" said Esme emphatically. "That's what this place needs. A FUCKING ROCKET. Explode the bloody lot."

Theo started tucking into the bread and cheese without even taking a plate. Bonnie folded her arms in a way that spoke volumes.

"Sorry," said Jamie. "I really am."

And he looked at her gently in a way that Mirren wished he were using on her.

"Just . . . keep them out of my kitchen," said Bonnie crossly.

"Oh, Bonnie Bonita, we are so, *soooo* sorry," said Theo, prostrating himself, his mouth full. "When you are so wonderful . . . you are wonderful, you know. So wonderful."

"Yeah, all right," said Bonnie.

"Almost makes me take my focus off my girlfriend," said Theo, his eyes sliding all over the place as he awkwardly segued across the room, all of him jerking about clumsily except for his glass of dark brown liquid, which remained miraculously upright.

"Your *what*?" said Esme, suddenly not sounding quite so drunk.

But Theo was, to Mirren's horror, already standing right in front of her.

"I miss you, my angel," he said, half crooning, to Mirren, blasting some boozy breath on her face. "Please come back to me."

"Wait—I didn't realise he was your . . . I thought you said . . ."

Jamie's face was suddenly a mixture of upset and confusion, which, if Mirren hadn't been so utterly horrified, might have answered a few of her questions.

"*No!*" said Mirren.

"Course you are," said Theo. Then, in a mock whisper to Jamie, "She LOVES it."

"I don't love *anything*!" said Mirren desperately. "Oh my God!"

"Course you do," said Theo. "You were giving me the come-on LAST NIGHT!"

The room fell silent, as Mirren boiled with fury. It had only been *flirting*. And she had had no idea that she would suddenly feel quite differently about her employer; she hadn't even noticed it creeping up on her. She had thought she would get her own back on Theo and, okay, had been feeling a bit lonely, but . . . well, that was yesterday!

Nobody would give her a chance to explain and she couldn't anyway without it sounding worse. Jamie was looking genuinely horrified, Theo was wildly swinging around, shouting, "Someone put that music on! It's too quiet in here and I want to dance with my baby!" and Esme was looking miserable and slightly more sober.

"Actually," said Jamie suddenly, "I'm not that fussed about supper. I think I'll just go to bed."

"Me too," said Mirren. "Theo, you're a disgrace."

"No, no, you stay," said Jamie, sounding tired.

"YEAH, STAY!" said Theo, grabbing her with one hand and some more bread with the other.

Esme was fumbling with the record player. "I'll dance," she announced boldly, and, as if things weren't already bad enough, as the old music came on—in a ghastly way, the needle speeding up on the record—she started to perform what was clearly supposed to be a very sexy dance, while Theo grabbed one arm, then held on to Mirren with another. The speeded-up waltz sounded gruesome but neither of them seemed to care.

"Get *off* me!" Mirren said crossly, pushing him away and running to the door. But Jamie had vanished into the gloom, and the spell was broken.

Chapter Thirty-Six

Mirren lay in bed, absolutely freezing and more than a little hungry. Even though she had stoked up the fire and closed the curtains, it wasn't enough. The temperature had plunged; she could see her breath in front of her whenever she moved away from the fire.

At first, running upstairs, she'd been hot, cross, and bothered, but she'd cooled down rapidly, still horrified by the double whammy of realising she felt something for sad, conflicted, handsome Jamie, and then immediately having those feelings dashed by that absolute *dipshit* Theo. Theo, who had now managed to make her this upset twice, which meant that the second time was absolutely her fault.

She groaned to herself in hopeless embarrassment. Oh God. Of course she shouldn't have flirted with him like that. She'd been trying to imply he was missing something, but it had completely backfired. For the first time, thoughts of the book completely fled from her head, and she lay down, staring at the draped curtains of the dark red bed, utterly frustrated with herself. And freezing. She would need to get out of bed and put her some extra clothes on before she got back into bed.

Of course, doing this made her instantly need a pee, so she zoomed down the corridor as if this was completely normal and she'd always done it. It was too cold to sit on the toilet seat. There was no noise in the passage, but from very far away she could still hear some strains of music. They must still be down there. Mirren smiled ruefully to herself, washing her hands in the freezing water. He'd never change. She hadn't wanted him; she'd just wanted . . . she had just felt . . .

Well, she could say it, here in this huge, rackety, empty palace, in the depths of winter. She'd felt so, so lonely.

She headed back from the bathroom, her eyes adjusting. With no more snow, and a full moon flooding in through the window at the far end of the passageway, you could see quite distinctly. The house made noises here and there, but she was no longer afraid. Sad, quite furious with herself, but not afraid.

BACK IN HER room, she stood gratefully in front of the fire and pulled open a drawer at random, finding some old jerseys inside, which she simply put on, as well as an old pair of socks. Normally putting on some absent or dead stranger's socks would have freaked her out. Not anymore.

She grabbed a blanket off the bed to go and look out of the window. The moon was absolutely ridiculous. If she'd had her phone she would have been tempted to take a picture. Which then, of course, wouldn't have come out—would have been as crap as everyone else's pictures of the moon always were.

But it was extraordinary. It had opened up a silver road on an unusually calm sea ahead of her; it was flat, like a pond. Looking at it, Mirren thought of old stories about creatures from other worlds walking down moonbeams like this, and realised she was just going to scare herself.

But it was clear enough outside to see the snow, sparkling in the moonlight; the sheer edge of the cliff, just below her. No birds were abroad, no creatures, everything tucked away cosily, hibernating in caves and holes, covered in leaves, or safely far away in southern climes. There would be badgers, she supposed, snuffling through the dark winter woods; a fox, left thin in the cold. But here, at the very end of the world, there were only grey bumps on rocks far, far below, which might be seals, or could be nothing at all.

It was a world full of mystery and magic, that felt better to Mirren. It was so much bigger than her own worries. Just as being here at Forres had made her feel far distant from her petty problems in London, looking out onto the broad, pitiless stars gave her, at least, a sense of perspective. There were, after all, far worse places to be.

She glanced at the door and thought, at last, of Jamie. Of when they were lying side by side, his long legs stretched out, Roger curled up affectionately on his chest in complete defiance of his stated treatment of the dog as a working animal, the worried look on his face chased away by sudden starts of laughter, like sunshine after clouds.

Oh, it would have been stupid anyway, she told herself. She was basically trade: a shopgirl, a maid. The idea of her, Mirren Sutherland from south London, and Laird Jamie McKinnon of Forres Castle—it was laughable and absurd. She didn't even know where in this place he was sleeping. Miles away. In a completely different part of the castle from the help. Or he might be in Bonnie's bed right now. They were miles apart. Miles.

STANDING RIGHT OUTSIDE her door, Jamie once again cursed his cowardice. He had loved chatting . . . He had found her so easy to talk to. No falseness, no pretending to be interested in hunting and fishing and shooting, or horses, or money, or the city, or what Lady So-and-So was doing, or capital gains tax, or laying down bottles . . . the kind of people he normally met; the women who showed an interest until they got up close to the house and realised it wasn't at all what they'd hoped for, and neither was he.

He wasn't a romantic laird in a book. He was a slightly messed-up bibliophile with a tendency to look on the negative side of things.

But with Mirren, they could talk about books. And puzzles. And real things. She was just so easy to be with, and such fun. She cheered him up. And when he had seen her all curled up in his grandfather's big bed, so immersed in her book that she hadn't even heard him come in . . . well, it was cold, but it wasn't that cold. She'd given him an absolute jolt; he'd felt, suddenly, incredibly attracted to her.

And on the other hand he'd met a million Theos. He didn't think a single one of them was good enough for her. But her reaction . . . it had given him hope. Had it? The way she'd looked at him; the outraged denials. Was he being ridiculous, thinking there was something there? He envied Roger, who had known straightaway he liked her and just gone and sat on her chest.

He didn't even know what he was doing in this corridor. Just a stupid urge to be nearer, really. To continue their conversation, now it had started. As he approached, silently, he realised how ridiculous an idea it was. Theo might even be in there now, although the faint strains of music from downstairs suggested not. God knew what he was getting up to with Esme—although better that than Mirren, he supposed, and at least if he was with Esme he wasn't annoying Bonnie.

But even so. He was also being completely inappropriate. She would be fast asleep, and think he was an intruder. Because he was behaving like one.

With a lump in his throat, Jamie took one last longing look at Mirren's bedroom door, and retreated on soft feet, not realising someone was on the other side of it, staring at it with equal, fervent longing.

Chapter Thirty-Seven

There were some slightly shamefaced looks next morning at breakfast, which Mirren, despite her sadness, tucked into with a will.

Esme and Theo had sidled in at different times, Theo looking rough, Esme looking fabulous, the slightly weary cast to her face only making her sexier than ever. The fact that they made a massive point of arriving at different times made it even clearer to Mirren that there was a very strong chance they'd got up to *something*. Theo didn't seem ever to be able to not at least give it a go.

Jamie was up, quietly pacing, looking at the poem and waiting for the sun to rise. Nobody seemed to have remembered what day it was, until Bonnie appeared, bright as a button, smiling and with a packet of batteries.

"It's Christmas Eve!" she said. "And I thought of something."

And she slotted the batteries into a small transistor radio and tuned it in.

Theo groaned. "Is it going to be the emergency broadcast network telling us the rest of the world is enjoying a zombie invasion?" he said, but instead it crackled into life with carols—from King's, in fact, the voices of the young choristers ringing out high and sweet: "Unto us is born a son."

Theo buried his head in his hands. "Owwww," he said.

Mirren smiled tentatively. "Is this your way of telling us we're not getting out today?"

"Fraid so," said Bonnie. "They haven't opened the road yet. Unless you've got a friend with a helicopter."

"I do!" said Esme suddenly. "Oh no, hang on—I slept with his sister."

"And that annoyed him?" said Theo curiously.

"I know—I was surprised too."

"It's going to be a funny old Christmas," said Mirren.

"No stockings," said Esme, sighing.

"No big boxes under the tree," said Mirren.

"No mother drunk by lunchtime," said Jamie. "Thank heaven for small mercies."

"No mum throwing the gravy on the floor because someone said it was lumpy." Mirren nodded.

"No church!" said Theo. "This is looking up. Where is the church anyway?"

"Oh, we have our own."

"You have your own church. Of course you do."

"But it's probably rather snowed in."

"And we don't have a vicar," added Esme. "Since the last one was caught doing un-vicary things."

"Actually, these days I think those are very vicary things," said Jamie. "Oh, Bonnie, is that bacon?"

Bonnie unveiled a large silver container, with a lid that was obviously from something else.

"Oh God, I love you," groaned Esme.

"I thought you were vegan," said Jamie.

"You're the animal-lover!"

"Yes," said Jamie. "Kindly and organically reared animals are okay to eat."

"Says you."

"Lots to do," said Bonnie, beating a retreat.

"Can we have Buck's fizz?" asked Esme. "As, one, it's Christmas Eve, and two, I need a hair of the dog."

No one stood up, so Esme made it in the end. She added a very small amount of orange juice to each glass, topped them up with fizz, and handed them around. Theo looked at it as if trying to figure out whether that would make things better or worse, then obviously decided it was worth the risk and necked it.

"Okay," Esme declared. "That feels better."

She glanced at Jamie, who was still very focused on the sunrise. "*Please* tell me today is the day we finally get our present?"

"I hope so," said Jamie, who was holding on to Mirren's copy of the poem as if it was something precious. "If we're right about the maze."

"What else can it be?"

"Anything," said Jamie. "Someone's old dry-cleaning receipt."

"Argh, don't say that. Please don't say that."

The delicious aroma of bacon spread as Theo made himself a sandwich and looked at it contemplatively. Esme reached for the dish herself.

"You're the worst vegan ever," said Jamie.

"I'm eating the bacon," said Esme. "It's my Christmas present to myself."

"But not that poor pig?"

"Everyone stop talking about pigs," said Theo, "or I might throw up."

Esme refilled his glass.

"Kill or cure," he said, and downed it.

Mirren came over and stood behind Jamie. The sky behind the trees was bright pink and gold—breathtaking colours. As she stared, the stag appeared once again, his horns high in the trees, part of the wild forest itself. She noticed Jamie incline his head, ever so slightly, as if nodding in respect—and it didn't seem weak or ridiculous; it seemed absolutely right.

"It's going to be the most beautiful day," she said, quietly amazed, really, that she would ever say that on a day so cold you could quite clearly see where Jack Frost had been, his fingers leaving traces all over the insides of the windows. But she meant it. "Happy Christmas Eve."

He turned to look at her, and his eyes had their sad look back. "Yeah," he said.

"I think we will find it," said Mirren, trying to be optimistic. "Look out there."

The first golden beams were bouncing off the ground; the snow had hardened into solid ice, glistening like diamonds, crunchy and solid.

"The whole world new," she said, still quietly, as if trying not to startle a shy creature. "That's the promise of Christmas, isn't it? Whatever you believe. The whole world turns shiny and new again, a brand-new year, a brand-new baby. It's always the same and always new."

Jamie nodded. The shadows of the trees on the white lawn were incredibly long.

"My grandfather never managed to make everything new."

"You're not him," said Mirren. "You're not, Jamie."

He smiled ruefully. "Got that same name."

"That doesn't matter," said Mirren. "At Christmas, everything old is new again."

He looked at her. "Did you choose me a book present yet?"

She smiled. "Yes."

"I want it!" he said. "I want my present. Can I have it today? We can pretend we're European."

And, because his smile was finally back, Mirren reached into the pillowcase she had filled when she hadn't been able to sleep the night before, and pulled it out.

Jamie beamed when he saw it. "I haven't read this in years!" He opened the first page. "'In a hole in the ground there lived a hobbit . . .'" He smiled. "I loved this book."

"Good," said Mirren.

"Hang on," said Esme. "You got up last night and went and looked at *more books?*"

Mirren looked back at her. "You don't know how lucky you are," she said. "It's a treasure trove here. I found the South Library. The moon was so bright, and I couldn't sleep. And I was hungry. You didn't leave me very much."

Theo and Esme had the grace to look shamefaced. Mirren didn't mention that she had secretly rather hoped she might bump into Jamie, wandering about in the halls at nighttime. She hadn't.

She handed over a book to Esme.

"'*Valley of the Dolls*,'" Esme read. 'The book too hot to publish.' Ooh!" she went on. "This looks like it would be just my kind of thing. Although I don't read much."

"You'll still like this."

"What happened to that other one you mentioned, the sexy one?" asked Jamie.

"I kept it for myself. Shh," said Mirren, and Jamie let his smile out cautiously.

Theo crossly flapped his hands in her direction when he saw his book, the second glass of champagne having fallen out with the first one, and being in no mood to make polite conversation.

"*A Rake's Diary?*" he said. "That seems harsh."

"*Au contraire*," said Mirren sternly. "If you'd been living back then, you'd have done some terrible harm."

"I'm not sure whether to take that as a compliment or not," he said, flipping through the illustrated plates.

"Not," said Mirren, and Jamie glanced at her, wondering.

"Bonnie?" said Mirren, as Bonnie set down steaming plates of black pudding, haggis, and eggs. Esme's eyes grew moist with longing. Theo, on the other hand, looked rather green. Bonnie looked up.

"This is for you. It's not much," said Mirren.

"And also not yours to give," pointed out Esme.

"No, I realise that," said Mirren. "I thought we could read them here." It was a copy of a book called *Longbourn*. "I wasn't sure if this was appropriate," said Mirren. "If it isn't, I'm really sorry. I just work here too."

Bonnie turned it over. It was *Pride and Prejudice*, written from the point of view of the servants. Mirren tensed in case she was offended—but Bonnie immediately softened.

"Thank you," she said, looking Mirren in the face for what felt like the first time. "Thanks for this. I think . . . I will read it."

"You don't have to," said Mirren.

"No, I will, thanks," said Bonnie, holding it close.

"Come on," said Jamie. "Hurry up and eat! The sun is up! Well, nearly."

"Where is this maze?" said Theo. "Maybe it's so far away that one of us should actually stay back here and, you know, hold the fort."

They looked at him.

"The fresh air will do you good," said Mirren, with no sympathy whatsoever.

Esme sighed. "It's on the far side of the loch," she said.

"Why is everything so far away?" groaned Theo. "We have a London garden square. Everything's *right there*."

Mirren's mum's suburban garden was the size of a pocket hand-kerchief, so she didn't mention it. "We could do with a tramp," she said. "Christmas Eve morning walk after our huge breakfast."

It was indeed huge, and after several refills of tea even Theo looked as if he might be ready to go.

"I know what we need," said Esme, nodding towards the boot room.

"No, don't," said Jamie. "You're terrible anyway."

"I am not!"

"You are! Always used to lean on the gardeners!"

"Oh, well, yes," said Esme. "But that was before I spent that winter in . . ." Her voice trailed off as she mumbled something that might or might not have been "St. Petersburg."

"What are you talking about?" said Mirren.

"You'll see," said Esme.

"You'd better check it," said Jamie, the little furrow appearing.

"If there's ice on the inside of windows, then you know it's fine," said Esme. "Come on, you old woman! Let's GO!"

And she leapt up, Theo groaning in her wake.

Chapter Thirty-Eight

All trussed up, Jamie flung open the boot room side door onto the gravel driveway. Esme looked at the sky, then at her still-buried, now-frozen car, and sighed.

Jamie hefted up a bag and stomped out, without his snowshoes today, just thick boots.

"We need crampons really," he said.

But actually, the thick layer of ice that had formed on the snow was both fairly straightforward to walk on—certainly easier than the thigh-deep snow—and oddly satisfying as it crunched beneath their heavy boots.

The sun made all the difference, though it was now straight in front of them, blinding them. Theo reached into a pocket and brought out a pair of sunglasses, which made the girls laugh. And suddenly, in the very far distance, they heard something.

"Shhh, listen!"

It was very faint—and not their church—but the bells were ringing, and the day was so still that the sound had carried all across the valley.

"That must mean *some* people have made it to church," said Esme.

"Don't make me feel guilty," said Theo.

"No, it means some roads must be passable! If they're ringing the bells. I mean, ours won't, but other people can't be in such desperate straits."

"Are they real bells?" said Mirren. "Not just recordings?"

"Recordings?" Esme sniffed, as if she'd never heard anything more ridiculous.

"Well, if it were recordings," said Jamie comfortingly, "that would mean their power was back on. Which would be great too."

It was rather lovely to hear the sound of the pealing bells bouncing off the crackling white world as they began to scrunch their way across the lawn, in a direction Mirren and Theo hadn't been before. With the sea behind them, the forest ahead, they bore far to the right. Again Mirren turned back, trying to imprint the house, outlined in ice and sun, into her memory, in case she never came here again . . . Well, of course she would never come here again, she remonstrated with herself. Why would she? She should consider herself happy that she'd found it, and seen it. And met . . . him. She looked at Jamie, marching out, in his element on the difficult ground, perfectly at home.

They passed the low settling of outhouses on the side, with smoke coming out of one chimney.

"What are those?" asked Theo.

"Oh, the farm cottages—abandoned now," said Esme airily.

"That one isn't abandoned."

Jamie tutted. "It's Bonnie's, obviously."

"Oh yeah, of course," said Esme.

"Didn't you know?" said Theo.

"I've never been in those buildings," said Esme.

"You have buildings on your own property you've never been in?"

Esme shrugged. "Do we have to go through the whole raised-in-a-castle thing again?"

"Have *you* been in them?" Mirren asked Jamie, not sure she wanted to know what the answer was.

"Oh yes," said Jamie. "When I was small. Bonnie's gran, Mrs. Airdrie, lived there. She was really kind to us. Bonnie's mum worked up in Aberdeen—still does—so old Mrs. Airdrie raised Bonnie, really. Her dad was a ghillie, moved on . . ." His face twisted. "Bit of a theme."

"Isn't it?" said Mirren, with some feeling. "So, you guys played together?"

He nodded. "Yeah. Mrs. Airdrie was an amazing baker too. Bonnie got it all from her."

Mirren frowned, crunching on. "When . . . when did you and Bonnie realise, though? That you would own the house, and she would work in it?"

Jamie smiled at the memory. Theo and Esme were hanging behind; Esme had conjured up a vape from somewhere and they were sharing it.

"When we were about nine or so? She went *mental*. I can see that wee face now."

"So what did you do? What did people say?"

"Oh, my mum didn't care, didn't know why I was hanging around with her in the first place, and of course everyone—we all—assumed Bonnie would leave, go to college, so it didn't matter. Nobody thought she'd grow up to work in the house; that was a ridiculous idea in this day and age. But Mrs. Airdrie was very good. She pointed out that they own their house outright—they do, and it's all stipulated to Bonnie. And that she could go to college, too, if she wanted. And we had a stupid cold big house, and they had a small cosy house and Pot Noodle and a big telly." Jamie smiled ruefully. "I think we both knew she had the better end of the bargain. I practically lived in there."

"What changed?"

"I got sent away to school," said Jamie. "And then . . . it was different after that."

"Why *does* she stay working here?" said Mirren, still wondering if the answer to that question was standing right in front of her.

"I genuinely don't know," said Jamie, in a way that made Mirren's heart pound. Either he was telling the truth—in which case, they had never dated—or he was the biggest cad of all time. And she didn't think he was. Mind you, she had been wrong about Theo too. She wasn't the best judge of character. "She nursed her gran all through her last illness. There's nothing keeping her here now."

"You guys are close," ventured Mirren.

"We were when we were children . . ." said Jamie, then trailed off and seemed unwilling to say any more.

He glanced up, even as Mirren was wishing she had brought her sunglasses too; the sunlight on the ice was blinding. But, inside, hope was leaping in her heart.

"You're easy to talk to," said Jamie shyly.

"Enough with the crazed flattery," said Mirren and he smiled. "Maybe she just loves the house that much," she suggested, looking back at the house, sparkling in the bright, multifaceted, frosted morning. "I could see why."

"Maybe she does," said Jamie. "And she doesn't need to find a way to pay for the roof." And the frown was back.

THEY LEFT THE cottages behind and crunched down a path. The snow was nearly level with the old stone walls. London snow was thin and wet and never lasted—it never even turned up till March, usually, and plenty of years it didn't turn up at all. This was the real thing: huge slabs of icing, not made grey by lorries or murky by feet. It was pure white, spoiled by nothing but tiny bird footprints and occasional glancing hooves. Roger was plocking along behind them, his claws clacking on the icy surface.

"What's up here—the maze?" said Mirren. She was enjoying being out of the gloomy castle, enjoying the sun on her face, swathed in every layer she could dig up, old wool made for the low temperatures. When you were warm enough, and you didn't have a wind blowing straight in your face, it was genuinely glorious, the only sound the crunching on the icy surface; the giggling of Theo and Esme some way behind them; the *skritch, skritch, skritch* of Roger's paws.

"No," said Jamie, smiling and taking down his rucksack. "There's a swimming pond. You go round it to get to the maze."

"Okay," said Mirren.

He pulled something out of his rucksack. It looked like a weapon of some kind . . . old steel.

"What's that?"

He handed it to her. It was a pair of ice skates, with a metal blade underneath, but the tops were simple wooden frames, designed to be buckled on top of the shoes you were already wearing.

"Oh my God," said Mirren. "You are kidding. These are *death-traps*."

"Neh, they're fine," said Jamie. "They just take a bit of getting used to and they don't go as fast as modern skates, but speed isn't really the essence."

"No, I mean, you are stark raving crazy," said Mirren. "You're going out on . . ."

They had reached the swimming hole now. As Jamie had said, it wasn't very big, and it had frozen, end to end. It looked absolutely solid.

"No," said Mirren. "I've read *Little Women*. Don't be an idiot."

"That was on a river," said Jamie. "This is a tiny freshwater pond. Completely different situation, believe me."

As if to illustrate matters, Roger ran out onto the ice.

"No!" shouted Mirren. "Roger! Come back! Come back, sweetie!"

Roger wagged his tail furiously as if to say, *Thanks so much for mentioning my name, I'm fine.* Then his back leg gave out from under him, Bambi-style, and his face took on a comical expression as he scrabbled back to the safety of the white-frosted fronds surrounding the pond.

"Okay, it's still a definite no," she said.

But Jamie had perched on a rock and was tying on his skates. "Come on," he said. "It's perfectly safe." As if to illustrate this, he bent down, grabbed a rock, and hurled it onto the middle of the water. It bounced off as if he'd thrown it at the wall. "I've done it all my life."

"I can barely skate on the Christmas rink at Somerset House," said Mirren. "And there they have people who push you around on a penguin."

"So you're trained," said Jamie.

Esme was behind them and was pulling out her own boots from Jamie's bag—she had proper black, professional-standard ice dance boots. Mirren felt Esme's scorn—she didn't even bother trying to persuade Mirren to come with her. She didn't give a toss either way, Mirren realised. And Theo, naturally, would absolutely have to ape the poshest people in the place at any point, so he was strapping up his shoes as well.

"Oh, for goodness' sake," said Mirren, grumbling as Jamie, with a smile, offered to tie her laces too. "This is like when your mother says *would you jump out of a window because all your friends were doing it?* except in this case it's *would you sink to an icy freezing agonising death because your boss gave you something from a hundred years ago when they were all totally used to icy freezing agonising deaths?*"

"Your boss?" said Jamie.

Esme and Theo were clanking noisily towards the rink. Theo had gone rather pale; Mirren wondered if he was going to throw up.

She looked at Jamie. "Just being literal," she said.

"Uh-huh," he said, and once again she was conscious—warmly,

embarrassingly conscious—that she had absolutely no idea where the line was between them; if there was something there, or if she had imagined the entire thing.

Taking off her mittens, she fumbled with the straps with cold fingers, and nearly fell over.

"Come here and sit down," he said. "This is a very comfortable . . . um, rock . . ."

She did so, and he knelt on the ground and started tying the buckles together tightly to make her shoes secure.

It felt oddly personal, him on one knee down by her feet. She looked at his bent head, the sandy hair falling over his face, and thought, what would it be like? What if he were bending over her feet . . . and leaning down to kiss her ankle . . . which would be brown, and pedicured, somehow, obviously . . . and then he would kiss her, gently, taking his time, bit by bit, slowly moving up her body, looking up at her with his piercing eyes, that smile that went right through her. She felt a blush rise to her cheeks, suddenly in that instant wanted nothing more than to be held, tightly in his arms; to crush herself against him; lift her legs around his long, lean torso . . .

"What?"

"What?" she said, startled, as he did, indeed, fix those hazel eyes on her. There were flecks of green in them.

"You looked absolutely miles away."

"Nothing!" Suddenly, Roger came over and licked her hand and for reasons completely mysterious to Jamie she burst out laughing. "I *was* miles away. Never mind."

She was still pink, and he looked at her curiously and straightened up, blocking out the sun in front of her. "Ready?" He held out his hand.

She looked up at him, took a deep breath, and grabbed hold of it.

"To *die*? Always."

DOWN ON THE pond, Esme was already circling, and as she stood up, Mirren stopped for a moment to watch her, her long, slim body encased in high-end ski gear, making her look chic, rather than, for example, like a woman who wore all her clothes at the same time to avoid budget airline charges, the way Mirren did.

She was a lovely skater, could turn and go backwards, and Mirren, watching her, couldn't help but feel a tug of envy. Theo, it was becoming obvious, didn't really have a clue what he was doing, and was clumping extremely nervously around the side of the pond. There was a wooden deck, for jumping and diving in the summer, and he was holding on very hard to that and stumbling forward, still looking very, very wan. There were no ominous creaking noises, Mirren noticed.

"Is the ice definitely okay?"

Esme heard this and rolled her eyes. She stood right in the middle and stomped loudly with her skates on. "Come on, City Mouse," she said. "It's perfectly safe."

Mirren took a step and skidded, went slightly off balance and put her arm out. Jamie caught her effortlessly.

"Come on," he said, tucking her arm into his left elbow, and leading down to the side of the dock with his right hand. "Okay," he said as they stood, the ice solid under their feet, with a leaf and a few twigs here and there that Esme was picking up. "You ready?"

Mirren smiled.

"My icy doom," she said, and held on tight, as he skated out, firmly, to the middle of the lake.

THIS ICE WAS different from skating-rink ice: it was bumpy, where the water had formed in crenellations, and it was dirty, but the old skates were solid and square and non-aerodynamic, designed instead to cut through debris; they worked surprisingly well.

The real surprise, though, was Jamie. He led them to the other side, far away from Esme's antics and from Theo, who was still holding tightly to the dock and looking very uninspired. Keeping close to the centre, where the ice was smoothest, Jamie started to pull Mirren round in vast circles. It was quite the contrast: his nervous demeanour in the house, compared to here, where he moved confidently, freely. He was fast, and Mirren was soon breathless trying to keep up with him—but she *could* keep up, she found, to her amazement, once she stopped worrying about twisting her ankle or the ice cracking, and simply let herself go. Once she relaxed into his grip, they became even faster and he passed her from hand to hand, simply because he could, and she found herself laughing out loud, staring up at the blue sky, her cheeks pink, her breath white, and felt something she couldn't quite put her finger on, and then realised: it was joy. It was a joyous thing to do on Christmas Eve morn; a joyous crisp, sunny, icy day to be abroad, to forget everything else in her life and just enjoy, for once, this moment, with no phone, no photos, no worries, no family, nothing except a strong hand in hers; a place where it felt completely natural to be. She heard the scraping of the metal blades on the hard-frozen lake—*Earth was hard as iron*, Mirren found herself thinking, *water like a stone.* She felt the cold air in her face, the laughter and fresh air in her lungs, as he spun her under his arm and somehow, miraculously, she managed it and ended up back there, facing him, both of them laughing at one another.

"Oh my God, are you guys *waltzing*?" came Esme's voice, breaking the spell, and they started to slow their turns, both of them pink-faced and out of breath and staring at one another. "And what the hell is that?" said Esme suddenly, and they both turned around, Mirren afraid once again that the ice was going to crack.

But it wasn't. It was just Theo being copiously sick by the side of the dock, and the spell of the morning was broken.

THEY PACKED THE skates away at the far side of the little loch.

"Thank you," said Mirren, meaning it. "That was a lot of fun."

"Did it make up for the fact that there aren't going to be any presents apart from the books?"

"The books are enough. Plus, that was a gift," said Mirren, quite seriously.

He grinned. "Not everyone thought so." Although Theo, it appeared, was much recovered after his spew and was marching on happily. They went to catch them up. About two hundred metres due north of the swimming loch was a gate that led out to the clifftop, the sea far below them on the right. And there, beyond the gate, was the twisting, turning, white-fringed deep green of a hedge maze.

Chapter Thirty-Nine

"This is amazing," breathed Mirren.

"It's just like *The Shining*," said Theo, looking concerned. "Oh my God—it has icicles and everything."

"Who looks after it?" Esme looked at Jamie. "You?"

"No, I . . . well, I try and keep it trimmed."

"So you know it back to front?"

"I don't," said Jamie. "I just trim the outside, keep my fingers crossed for inside."

The blue sky was clouding over and the temperature dropping by the minute. Now that she was no longer whizzing round the ice, Mirren started to feel cold, and found herself wishing profoundly that her hand were still in Jamie's.

Jamie tried the gate; it was locked.

"You lock the maze?"

Both the McKinnons looked faintly embarrassed.

"Have you got the key?" Esme said to Jamie.

Jamie pulled out the ring of jingling keys he'd had before but it was obvious none was nearly big enough for the large gate. "Nope," he said.

The hedge walls around the gate were far too high to climb, and Mirren started to feel like the prince in *Sleeping Beauty*, expected to fight his way through one hundred years of growing brambles.

"Huh," said Esme. She pushed at the rusty old gate, but, although it made a creaking noise, it didn't give.

"There must be a way in," said Theo, starting to push his thin torso against the hedge walls. "There must be a gap."

They followed the perimeter round. The square of the hedge reminded Mirren of the maze of the house itself, with its four points and long corridors.

Finally, two-thirds of the way round, they halted when Roger vanished, disappeared, and then could be heard, barking furiously, from the inside.

"Roger!" shouted Jamie.

"Yeah, Roger, open the gate," shouted Esme, then, to the others, "What?"

"How did he get in?" Jamie felt along the hedge until, almost imperceptibly, he came across a small gap in the hedge at the bottom. "Well," he said, ducking down and disappearing. Two seconds later he threw his hat in the air from the inside. "Yeah, that works!"

"Why is there a gate, though?" asked Mirren, as Theo got down on his hands and knees and pushed his way through.

"Don't spew again, Theo . . ." Esme was calling, and then, to Mirren, "Oh, we tried at one point to charge admission. You can imagine how well that went down with the locals."

"So badly that they made a tunnel into it?"

Esme smiled tightly. "Jamie has really been trying, I think. When the National Trust didn't want it, and the hotel groups didn't want it, and the army didn't want it . . . He has tried. To save the place. That's why you're here."

Mirren glanced back at the big house. "Do *you* want to save it?"

Esme didn't answer, but instead ducked down and, as elegantly as she did everything else, shimmied through the hole.

Mirren looked at the grey clouds gathering on the horizon—surely not more snow—and shivered, pulling the huge coat closer round herself. Then she, too, crouched and squeezed herself through the narrow hole in the hedge wall, thinking, not for the first time, that this was quite the oddest Christmas she'd ever known.

"FIRST PROBLEM," JAMIE was saying. "We're already lost."

Inside the maze it felt cold and gloomy; there was snow that hadn't iced over because the hedges were too thick, and the sky really felt grey now. It wasn't pleasant at all. Long passages ran in both directions, the hedge a dark green with a topping of white. In the summer, Mirren thought, it must be magical. But now, with the sky darkening, it felt threatening. Not a sound could be heard that wasn't the crackling of snow and ice beneath them.

"What do you mean? Isn't this your maze?" said Theo.

"Yeah, explain to me how your phone works," said Jamie. He glanced around. "The thing is, if we have to follow the locket's instructions that means we have to start from the entrance, and I'm not sure . . ."

"Don't be ridiculous," said Mirren. "It's over this way."

And she set off confidently back in the direction of the loch, only to find herself, two seconds later, in a cul-de-sac which contained a mildewed stone statue of a griffin. She came back and went the other way, with the same results.

"Oh, for God's sake."

"My great-great-something-grandfather designed it," said Jamie. "There was a great fashion for mazes, the more complicated the better. They were like the roller coasters of their day."

Mirren stomped back crossly. "There is an incredibly big streak of nonsense in your family tree."

"When I was small," said Esme, with an uncharacteristically romantic cast to her voice, "I used to come here and think the maze went on forever. I used to think I would pop out at school, or in London."

"That would be cool," said Theo, and for once he didn't sound as though he was just agreeing to agree. "Isn't the answer 'always go left,' or something?" he added.

"At Hampton Court it is," said Jamie. "This is much bigger."

"Can't we just smash through the hedges?" said Esme. "It's our bloody maze."

They looked at her, appalled.

"You sound like Mum," said Jamie.

"That would be terrible," said Mirren. "We just have to keep heading east. Someone keep in charge of where east is."

"Where is it?" said Theo.

"Where the sea is," said Mirren impatiently, shivering, even in her big jacket.

By popping his head over the hedge like a friendly otter, Theo managed to steer them more or less in the direction of the starting gate, and when they were only one hedge away they crawled underneath it as best they could, and stood, wiping the snow off themselves. Everyone was mucky. But they were on the right side of the gate. Now, maybe, they could begin.

Chapter Forty

"Okay," said Jamie, taking out the locket, his hands trembling slightly.

"I'm still not sure about your lemur hypothesis," said Esme. "What if it's a badger or something?"

"I don't know what you want me to do about that information," said Jamie. "Seeing as your contribution so far has mostly been 'please buy me some shoes.'"

Esme tutted. "Isn't getting to the centre . . . Doesn't it start with a right?" she said.

"Yeah," said Jamie. "Yeah, it definitely does. I remember that much. Okay," he said. "One right, two left."

"What's in the middle?" asked Mirren.

"A fountain," said Jamie. "Well, there was. I don't think it's working anymore."

"You wouldn't hide a book out here, surely," said Mirren.

"Oh God," said Theo. "If this is another nine clues . . ." He jumped up and down to get warm. "Seriously, I don't know how long I can stay up here. Cool as it is to miss family Christmas, obviously."

Jamie looked down and set off, and, for want of a better idea, they all followed him.

They trudged on, her head down, all feeling the cold now. The snow which had not formed an icy crust reached over the top of Mirren's boots and slipped in, and even two pairs of socks couldn't keep her toes dry; her feet started to get wet and then numb, which meant she felt absolutely dreadful.

The scale of the maze was insane. She couldn't see above the high hedges, piled with snow, just the threatening sky above, and wetness underfoot. The fun of the snow had gone. Esme was still needling Jamie about whether they were actually doing anything useful.

Mirren turned her head as they did indeed walk past the centre of the maze. She stopped for just a second to take it in: there was a fountain there, and it was frozen. It was an extraordinary-looking thing, the water cascading down, clear and hard, and then just stopping, piled on top of itself, over and over on its way to nowhere. It looked like a strange alien, bulbous and unexpected.

Jamie watched her looking at it. "Weird, eh?"

"*So* weird. I want to touch it. But I also really don't. It's like we're in the upside down."

"Where strange things happen."

"Where angels fear to tread," she said, and he looked at her curiously, and suddenly she felt it, just as she had before, getting dressed, or looking at her own reflection in the window: that the gossamer-thin line of present reality shimmered, between times and between old worlds and new, and that normal rules did not necessarily apply, down here in the very depths of the year.

He smiled. "You can tread, I think," he said. "Just don't lick it."

She burst out laughing, her reverie broken. "Okay!" she said, and laughed, her cheeks pink, her eyes sparkling.

He screwed his eyes up, staring at the locket. "We're not done," he said.

"I reckon we're going round in circles," hollered Esme. "And I'm getting frostbite."

"Yeah," said Jamie, not sounding very sure of himself. "Come on, then."

They marched on, but the one reassuring thing was that they didn't end up in any more cul-de-sacs; they never quite stopped, even though Esme insisted they were going nowhere.

Mirren's toes were freezing now; they were sore to the point of pain. She was getting seriously worried they'd never find their way out. She was, she realised, indeed marking well in Jamie's footsteps, just like the song.

Finally, he came to a stop, up against a leafy corner, snow heaped high. Mirren was distracted and stumbled into him.

"Whoa there," he said, holding her up. Then he looked at her closely. "You're freezing, aren't you?"

She nodded miserably.

"Oh Lord," he said. "I'm so sorry. Worst Christmas Eve ever." He cast around for the best thing to do. "Let me see your hands."

She looked at him, but he seemed entirely serious. She held out her hands and he took the mittens off, as well as his own.

"Yes, they're wet," he said, frowning, then rubbed her pale white hands, trying to get the life back into them, then put her hands into his own warm gloves and squeezed them tight.

Mirren looked at him. The warmth of his hands on hers felt so good, even if it hurt a little as the blood pulsed them back to life; his gloves were far better than hers.

"Thank you," she said, looking at him, and suddenly the fact that they were lost in a freezing, spooky old maze in the middle of nowhere didn't seem to matter so much. It didn't matter at all.

She was about to boldly ask for a hug, to step forward, ask for more than just his hands; ask for his arms, his long, lean, warm body—suddenly she wanted this more than anything, anything in the world. She craved it.

"Come *on*!" yelled Esme. "It's completely freezing!!"

"And I want to be sick again," said Theo unnecessarily.

Esme marched forward, kicking her way through the snow, and they meekly broke apart and followed.

"One more right," said Jamie. They were, as far as Mirren could tell, far away from the centre now, closer to the northeast edge, trees looming up ahead of her, making everything even darker. This end of the maze was neglected; presumably people made it to the centre then went back out again the same way, or bumbled about the beginning half. This was a distant corner, which presumably would look beautiful and symmetrical from above but was even more neglected than the rest. Piles of dark, rotting leaves were submerged in snowy corners, forming sinister outlines in the dirt.

Mirren's mood changed. She didn't like it, suddenly. Being so lost. So far away from home. They were incredibly far away from the house, even; what had felt like a nice walk on that nice, sunny morning now felt like a horrible trek back. And she was hungry, despite their good breakfast. They'd missed lunch completely, she'd had no dinner the night before, and all the exercise had given her a huge appetite. She wanted to be somewhere cosy, in front of the fire, with Jamie telling her things or, even better, both of them curled up with a book. Peace and quiet, and cosiness.

"Come ON!" said Esme again.

They turned the corner all together and found themselves at a dead end: the very farthest corner, Mirren thought, of the maze. Like the one they'd come in next to but on the opposite corner of the diamond. It, too, had a small statue in a little grotto.

"Is this it?" said Esme suspiciously.

"Well, there are no more instructions on the locket," said Jamie, looking relieved. "So it obviously brought us *somewhere*."

"If this is one of those things where you have to wait for the sun to hit a certain point . . ." started Esme, "or, like, an eclipse or something, I'm going to kill you."

But Jamie knelt down and cleared away some of the muck from the statue. It wasn't a griffin this time, but instead, of all things, a stone carving of a pineapple. It was weather-worn and chipped, but unmistakably a pineapple.

"Why on *earth* is there a pineapple here?" said Mirren, startled.

"Oh, they're quite common in Scotland," said Theo, and Esme shot him a withering glance.

"It's true," said Jamie, wincing slightly.

"Why? You can't grow pineapples here."

"No," said Esme. "But you can grow them in the Caribbean, thicko."

"Oh," said Mirren. Then, "*Oh*."

"Quite," said Jamie, rubbing the back of his neck. "They are a symbol of national shame. There aren't many still left."

Mirren stared at it.

"You know . . ." she said slowly, screwing up her eyes. "You know, if I'd lived all my life up here, and someone showed me a pineapple—a golden yellow pineapple, with fronds coming out of the top . . ."

The others stared at her.

"*A crown of gold*?" said Jamie. "Do you think?"

"It's the colour of gold and it looks like a crown," said Mirren obstinately.

They all stared at it.

Jamie tried to heave it up, but it wouldn't budge. There was nothing around it, just a stone plinth on the paving stones beneath their feet. Together the two boys tried to shift it, but nothing doing.

"Bloody hell," said Esme and gave it a good boot with her foot. Nothing happened, except she hurt her foot and swore in a way you presumably only learned how to do at either really posh boarding schools or at sea in the nineteenth century.

"Bollocks," said Jamie, looking around. "There's nothing else here! Nothing!"

Theo started searching the heavy hedges, which helped not at all, except he managed to scratch his face. Esme was still hopping. Jamie started exploring the ground, pushing leaves aside with his feet, the back of his neck going red. It got even darker overhead.

Mirren stepped forward, holding up the torch, and examined it closely.

She took her newly warmed hands out of the first set of mittens, keeping on the liner gloves, and knelt down. The pineapple stood about a metre high on its plinth; its stone was green and covered in moss and bird droppings, and worn away on its north and east sides, where the winds swept down. The lines of the rind had been etched into it with a chisel; it was fine work, or had been, once upon a time. Each had a dot in the centre or raised stone, just like the fruit, and its leaves, slightly broken now, made a profusion at the top. For an instant Mirren wondered what it must have been like, to live in the depths of the Scottish winter and taste a pineapple for the very first time. It must have been unimaginably exotic and extraordinary. She thought, too, of the awfulness of the trade that went to the Caribbean; that built this beautiful house and its grounds. No wonder its inhabitants had felt themselves cursed, at one time or another, down the years. No wonder.

Experimentally, she pushed one of the pineapple's buttons. Nothing happened, of course. But as she looked across the surface she saw one that did not look like the others. It almost did, but as she peered at it closely she could see it was not stone but metal, painted to look like stone but slightly worn on one side, where the metal gleamed through. She looked up. Esme and Theo were arguing about something. Jamie was just looking lost. Bending her head in an act of supplication that did not seem out of place, Mirren scratched away the ice around it until it was clear, then pressed the button hard.

And the top of the pineapple made a heavy grinding noise, and the leaves began to move.

Chapter Forty-One

The effect on the group was electrifying. Esme darted over, her sore foot forgotten. Theo managed to swallow down whatever had been threatening to reappear. Jamie looked up, his face full of hope.

They all shuffled forward. The leaves had moved a few centimetres to the right, but no further; the mechanism was obviously old and stiff. Jamie pushed it further, until it hit a point where the hole was large enough to insert a wrist; a slender one, at any rate.

"Mirren," he said. "Would you like to do the honours?"

"No chance," said Mirren. "I've seen *Indiana Jones*. That thing is *fizzing* with snakes."

Jamie laughed, surprised. "Living on what, exactly?"

"Other snakes! They're *cannibal* snakes! *I'm not doing it!*"

"Oh, for goodness' sake," said Esme. She pulled off her gloves just as Theo hissed loudly, and she started. "Stop it," she said. "I mean it."

"Let's drop a stick down," said Jamie, "if you guys are really that scared."

"What's the use in that?" said Mirren. "They're cannibal snakes. They'll eat it or have sex with it or both."

Jamie shone his torch into the hole. "See. No snakes."

"Yeah, obviously they've gone quiet *now*."

"I've got thin wrists," said Theo, rather annoyed he had to own up to this. "I'll put my hand in." He looked at them. "Would your grandfather booby-trap it, though?"

Esme and Jamie looked at each other, and Jamie shook his head decisively.

"He was eccentric . . . and unhappy . . . but he wasn't *cruel*. Not deliberately."

Theo rolled up his sleeve and stuck his hand all the way down into the middle of the pineapple. They watched him as he groped around.

"ARGH! SNAKES!" he shouted, his hand dropping and his shoulder heading down to the stone as he suddenly got pulled in. Mirren gave a small shriek before he burst out laughing and she gave him the V sign, even as he very carefully brought up . . .

"Oh, for God's sake," said Esme. "Seriously. Grandfather. GIVE IT A REST!"

"He wouldn't have put a valuable book out here in the wind and the weather," said Jamie, taking a worried glance at the clouds.

Theo had withdrawn another wrapped pile of letters, thickly encased in wax paper, presumably to protect them from the elements.

"We live like this now," he said ominously. "Tramping about, picking up old rubbish."

"It's not rubbish!" Jamie and Mirren said at the same time.

"What if there are forty-five clues," said Theo. "I bet they're all just school reports."

"Come on," said Mirren. "This is great! Jamie, your locket was right!"

Jamie carefully closed the pineapple's crown back over. "I know," he said, shaking his head.

Esme looked up. "Oh, crap," she said.

First one snowflake, then another. Then, suddenly, a thicket.

They headed forward, instinctively, but the snow came down thicker and thicker.

"Hang on," shouted Jamie. "We have to reverse the instructions to get out."

"Don't be daft," said Esme. "We'll find it!"

But Esme was dangerously wrong. She charged off down a promising-looking passage—only to hit a thick dead end, just as Mirren had. Visibility was so bad, they lost sight of her.

"Can't we follow our own footsteps back?" said Theo.

And indeed, that would have been an excellent idea, had the snow not been covering every trace of their paths the second they stepped onwards.

"ESME!" hollered Theo.

"I'm here," she said sulkily. "Stupid bloody place."

"Torches on," ordered Jamie. "Come on, let's be organised. Let me see . . . If it was third on the right, that must be . . ."

Hands shaking, they set off and trooped down a path. Before too long, though, it became obvious, as they hit one dead end after another, that somehow Jamie had miscounted or they'd got turned around, because they weren't getting out of there; they couldn't see the end, and on one turn they got straight back to the pineapple grotto again. The pineapple was almost totally obscured by snow. If they'd been ten minutes later, they'd never have found it at all.

They set out again, but with hideously the same result, no matter how carefully they tried to reverse the instructions, or how many times Esme announced she was sure she recognised this or that path, or Theo kicked at the undergrowth to try to find more hidden entrances. Visibility was genuinely very poor now.

"Bugger," said Jamie.

"*Shit*," said Esme. "Oh my God, we're going to freeze to death out here!"

Mirren didn't say anything. She was too cold. She felt rather strange, as if she was floating; barely there at all, a ghost in the maze. It wouldn't bother her, she thought, if she were to tear her clothes off; run barefoot, a nightgown flapping around her, nothing more; explore the maze, getting further and further in, deeper and deeper down. That, in fact, seemed to be a very delightful idea indeed. Sleepily she pulled the zip down a little on her jacket.

Beside her, the boys appeared to be having an argument, even as the snow continued to come down.

"Come on," Theo was saying, holding up a lighter. "Come on. We'll just burn a hole that we can crash through."

"You'll burn the entire damn thing down," Jamie was saying. "It's been here for hundreds of years!"

"Yes, and so will our corpses if we don't get out of here quickly!"

"Don't be ridiculous," said Jamie, but he didn't sound convinced. "Come on, let's go again, one more time. We're back at the start. Third on the left . . ."

He turned round and caught sight of Mirren, who was swaying slightly, then made a decision.

"Christ," he said to Theo, who was still waving his Zippo around. "Oh, for God's sake. Okay. Try it."

Theo bent down and flicked at the lighter, which made a tiny spot of yellow light in the darkening afternoon, in the thick snow. He held it to the wall of the maze. One tiny stem caught, and then another, coaxed by Theo, who tried to keep the snow off it. Jamie and Esme joined in, trying to make a barrier against the wind. The tiny stalks crackled, until a large pile of snow collapsed on them and put them out.

Theo frowned and started again. "Have we got any kindling? We really need something a bit more flammable."

Jamie looked worried. "Well," he said. "There's the letters . . ."

"Use the envelopes," said Esme impatiently.

"But it's someone's personal mail . . ."

"I feel warm already," said Mirren in a slightly dreamy voice, and they all looked at one another.

"Fuck it," said Jamie.

"Actually . . ." said Esme and pulled out a hip flask.

"Esme!" said Jamie disapprovingly.

"Oh yeah, like you've got a better way than watching your future fall apart in real time!"

They scrunched up some envelopes, doused the roots in alcohol, and the old paper, fine as an onion skin, blazed immediately. Enough little branches caught for them to enjoy the blaze—Jamie pushed Mirren out in front of it, and she felt herself swim in and out a little, not sure why there was a fire there—until there was finally enough burning for them to start kicking at it. The fire reared back like an animal, and grabbed other branches and roots inside the hedge, the ones inside that were protected from the rain and had stayed dry. It was surprising how fast they caught, and Theo shot them a worried glance. But there wasn't time; he had to boot through. Very nervously, the men used their gloved hands to pull ashy branches apart, as Esme hopped from foot to foot and told them to hurry.

Crawling through the bottom of the hedge with fire on either side of her to get out of the castle maze confirmed to Mirren that this was a very strange dream of some kind. Jamie was concerned and kept prodding her to go faster, and she didn't know why he was doing that; she didn't mind being there. She wouldn't be surprised at this point if a white rabbit turned up and she had to play croquet with a flamingo.

Once they were all out and found themselves on the far east side of the maze, miles away from the entrance, or the hole on the other side, Esme set out apace to the castle. Jamie looked back, worried, at the smouldering ruins of his hedge.

"The snow will put out the flames, right?" he said.

Theo was already heaping snow on the remaining fire. "Of course," he said. "You keep moving. I'll make sure it's out, and it'll be easy to repair."

"I'll add it to my list," said Jamie. "You know the way back?"

Theo nodded towards the direction of the house. No electric lights could be seen—the world around them was dark, lit only from the fire and the torches—but they could just make out—only just, through the thick snow—a tiny flickering glow: candles, it must be. But not one or two. All of them. Bonnie had lit all of the candles she could find, to light their way home.

Chapter Forty-Two

Later, Mirren couldn't remember much about that journey. People seemed to be shouting at her, Theo was there, then he wasn't, then he was again, and it took a long, long time. They skirted the loch, covered in snow on top of ice now; it got harder and harder to move, as the snow settled on the crust, piled up in corners, and rendered slippery sections invisible and incredibly dangerous. They slithered their way home, half shoving Mirren ahead of them, Esme cursing colourfully in their slipstream. It was so, so far, and even with the pale glow of the castle ahead they still lost their bearings in the deep dark, as the batteries of the torches started to fade and fail. Jamie constantly worried they would stray towards the cliffs, urging them on while staying on their left. He half carried Mirren up through the gardens in the end, she was in such a bad way. It had been a strenuous expedition.

"Bonnie!" he hollered, as he finally, at last, at last, turned up at the kitchen door, looking as if they'd all just come back from the South Pole. Every bit of them was covered in snow; Jamie had it in his eyebrows.

They fell in through the kitchen door, into the blissful warmth of the Aga-warmed room, which had something delicious-smelling cooking on the stove. Bonnie was nowhere to be seen.

"Oh God," said Jamie, propping Mirren up on the chair nearest the Aga. She looked up with a start.

"Oh God," she echoed. "What the hell?"

"Don't . . . it's okay," said Jamie. He found, suddenly, that he wanted to weep. It was a ridiculous sentiment, and he tried immediately to swallow it back. Mirren, he realised suddenly, had noticed.

"Do you know, I could cry," she said immediately. "God, that was so weird."

He knelt down, to keep himself busy.

"What are you doing?"

"Taking your boots off," he said. "You need to warm your feet up."

"Christ, I really do," said Mirren.

He carefully pulled them off and once again she was watching his sandy head. She was very tired, suffering from the effects of exposure, underslept and overstimulated, and she had seen the tears in his eyes. That was her excuse, anyway, for pulling off her mitten with her teeth, taking her frozen hand, and running it softly through his hair.

He looked up at her, his hazel eyes brimming with unshed tears, and blinked a couple of times. Then he put his hand on hers, drew it to his head.

"I was worried about you," he said gently.

"Ow!" said Mirren suddenly. "OW OW OWOWOW!"

"What?"

"My hand! It hurts like *buggery*." She shook it hard.

"That's the circulation coming back. You really are a softy southerner, aren't you?"

"*Yes*," said Mirren. "If I ever, ever get out of here, I am going to send up a prayer to the God of Central Heating every night."

He pulled off her other boot and put it to one side. "Give them to me," he said. "You have to rub them really hard. We can do it together."

"Is that even legal?" Mirren said, but she found a smile from somewhere within herself, as he took both her hands between his own and started rubbing them together fast, as if he were rubbing two sticks together to make a fire. Esme had headed off to the bathroom and to find Bonnie; there was no sign of Theo, and Jamie mentally gave him fifteen minutes before he went back out in the storm to look for him. He didn't even take his own boots off.

The feeling gradually came back into Mirren's hands, but she couldn't say she was entirely happy about it; she liked Jamie's hands on hers, liked him kneeling before her. The slightly cloudy feeling that had hit her out in the garden hadn't gone away; instead, it had transferred to this beautiful kitchen, the old clock still ticking on the wall, the candles fluttering everywhere, the pot on the warm stove. Inside, as the cold finally began to subside, the warmth she felt was from being indoors, somewhere dry and cosy—but also, from being near him.

I want this man so desperately, she found herself thinking to herself, very clearly. *I want him so much*. He looked at her, and she worried suddenly that she'd said it out loud, but instead he was saying, "I'll go and check for Theo in a minute . . . Here. You get started, *compadre*."

And he handed her the letters.

He trusted her so much, he'd simply handed them over. It was extraordinary. Mirren held the thin leaves in her hands. Jamie was going through the drawers until he found replacement batteries for his torch and put his gloves back on again.

"I may be some time," he said.

"Don't you dare!" said Mirren.

"I'm kidding," he said. "I'll be five minutes and haul Theo back.

He'll probably be doing his favourite thing: throwing up by a hedge."

Mirren nodded. "You're sure you don't want me to wait?" she said, waving the letters.

"Absolutely not," he said, rubbing his hands together and smiling, and she was so happy that he was as excited to get on with it as she was. "You can précis them for me when I get back. If it's really good, *don't* come and find me! I order it. You basically nearly died just now."

"I did not!"

"You did so."

"Well, then," she said, "you saved my life. I owe you a life."

He didn't answer, just looked at her for a long time. Then he strode across the kitchen floor, leaving puddles of melted snow in his wake, and opened the door again, to head out into the howling blizzard.

MIRREN MOVED TO the Aga, luxuriating in its heat. The opening of the kitchen door had sent a freezing wind through the space, revealing how very awful it was out there.

She unfolded the letters, but before she did, she already had a sense of them, in their tired old paper, their running ink. The paper felt heavy with disappointment, with frustrated hopes. She glanced at the writing; she recognised it. Sure enough, it was the father—Jamie's great-grandfather, his grandfather's father. Once more it was rejection letters: a sternly worded missive that he must give up this ridiculous idea of writing, of working in books; a further one, heartbreakingly pointing out that it was unbefitting to his status to be applying for a job as a librarian, that he was not paying attention to the accounts or the farm; that the factor—Mirren wasn't sure what this was, but it appeared to be some kind of estate manager—was disappointed in his lack of application, unpaid bills, invoices . . .

And on and on and on it went. And there wasn't a word from James, not a single word. When she thought of his room, with his books and his things—there was something about having felt so close to him. The crusty, unhappy person that Jamie and Esme had known—Mirren didn't think he was like that at all. Mirren thought he'd just been disappointed, thwarted at every turn.

But there was, thought Mirren, there was . . . this stupid bloody house.

If he didn't want it, he could have walked away.

And she thought about that again. What these letters were trying to say. That he should have walked away. That he should have had the life he wanted, the person he wanted but had given up.

That there was a chance for the person the quest was for.

That if Jamie didn't want it, he could walk away.

SHE WAS STARING into space when there was a crash at the door and the two men tumbled back in, Theo so covered in snow he looked like a yeti.

"Bloody hell," said Mirren, as Jamie pushed him towards the Aga.

"I was fine!" said Theo.

"He was heading straight over the cliffs," said Jamie shortly. He picked up the boiling kettle off the top of the stove.

"I should probably have some whisky," said Theo.

"That's the last thing you should have," said Jamie, pouring him a cup of Bovril.

"Oh, *yuk*," said Theo. "I hate this stuff."

"I don't get a lot of thanks around here," mused Jamie. "Where's Esme?"

"She said she'd gone to steal all and any hot water."

"Fair enough."

Jamie looked at Mirren, as Theo chittered and sipped his Bovril and made a face by the Aga. He nodded at the pile of letters. She looked back at him.

"Well?" Jamie said quietly.

"They're a message," said Mirren.

"Well, yes, I gathered that."

"No, I mean—a message to you."

Jamie grabbed the papers. "Really?"

"No, I mean, they're just a bunch of letters from his dad telling him he has to look after the house and he can't do what he wants."

"Which is what?"

"Well, I only have one half of the correspondence, but it looks like he applied to libraries, publishers, that kind of thing, and his dad is telling him he can't take up any jobs because he has to stay and work the estate."

Jamie blinked several times. "Right," he said.

"I mean," said Mirren, looking at him sideways, "I don't know if you feel that is something that applies to you?"

"Huh," said Jamie. "No. He couldn't have left. He had his duty . . ."

He read a few of them.

"He really . . . he hated it," he said. "He didn't get to be with the person he loved. He didn't want to work the estate. His life . . . He really did not enjoy it."

"He must have liked some of it," said Mirren, thinking again of the huge windows and the great moon in the sky. "He did the best he could. Surrounded himself with things he loved. His books."

"Why didn't he . . . why didn't he tell me before?"

Mirren looked at him. "Are you talkers, your family?"

Jamie laughed hollowly. "Then why did he tell me to do my duty?" He thought about it. "Mind you, that was mostly Mum. And my grandmother, I suppose."

"Not him?"

"No, that's why I'm always complaining. He didn't teach me anything—nothing about land management or how it was meant to work. I thought he just didn't trust me."

"Do you think he was maybe leading you another way?"

Jamie didn't say anything.

"I understand about duty to a house like this," said Mirren. "I mean, lots of people do think it's your duty. Maybe he thought you thought it was too. That everyone else was right; that it was just him who had failed."

"Until the very end," said Jamie, and Mirren suddenly felt so sorry for him. "Until the end, when he thought, *I've wasted my life. That's it. It's done.* And walked out into a field."

There was a silence then.

"I think this is actual filth," said Theo loudly, banging down the cup of Bovril. "I'm going to find Esme. I think she absolutely would prescribe some whisky. Es!" And he left the kitchen.

Jamie and Mirren both looked again at the papers.

"Is there another clue?" said Jamie, and they both sifted through. "Was there nothing else there?"

"I don't think so," said Mirren. "Theo brought it all up in one, the wax paper bundle. He fished down again afterwards for snake eggs or something but that was definitely it."

They leafed through the letters, but they all seemed normal.

"Shit," said Jamie.

"What?"

"You don't think it was on the envelopes?"

"What do you mean?"

"The envelopes we burned."

"What do you mean? How?"

"Well, people write tiny clues under stamps and things. This is just . . . these are just letters."

Mirren screwed up her face. "Oh God," she said. "Oh no."

"If we've literally burned the last clue. After all this."

"Everyone nearly dying of exposure," said Mirren.

"God," said Jamie, staring at them. "No. Surely not. Come on."

"What's that spooky thing people use? Like lemons or invisible ink?"

Jamie held the paper up to the Aga and shone a torch behind it. "Anything?"

"Nope."

"Oh Lord," said Jamie, scratching his head. "Maybe that's it. Maybe we've torn it."

Oddly, Mirren didn't feel as bad as she thought she might, not finding it. She wouldn't have changed what they'd done for anything.

"Does it matter?" she said. "You've got the point."

"I've got the *point*," said Jamie. "I haven't got the book."

"Oh yeah," she said.

She set all the sheets out on the kitchen table, and they moved them around, rearranged them. Jamie put on a pair of horn-rimmed glasses that were rather fetching, although he looked embarrassed when she noticed and took them off again.

"No," she said. "I like them."

And he didn't make a joke or brush off her remark; he put them back on, and stood over her shoulder, so close she could feel him breathe.

It was odd. It was while she was thinking about him—about the proximity of him, his soft, tweedy scent that she liked very much, the brush of his jumper against her hair that made her want to lean back, very much, into him, made her feel almost faint for desire for him simply to put his arms around her from behind, wrap her up in his coat, keep her warm, keep her safe, let the rest of the world fall even further away for him . . . it was then, when her mind wasn't focusing at all on the task at hand, that she saw it. It was almost as if it was something you could only spot when you weren't paying attention, where you had to rely on looking out of the corner of your eye.

"Look!" she said. "Why does your great-grandfather sometimes put dashes at the start of his new paragraphs and sometimes not?"

It was true. He had a black, thick hand, slanting forward, the fountain pen occasionally blotting as he constantly made heavily underlined points to James about not neglecting the estate, not getting caught up with unsuitable people, not complaining about school, not choosing a life of his own. But sometimes these paragraphs started with a dash, as if he were saying, —*and another thing*, like a drunk unable to give up an argument. Others simply did not.

"Probably no reason," said Jamie, but she already knew him well enough to tell when there was mild excitement in his voice.

Mirren pointed out one.

"Here you are: —*Really this is unacceptable* has got one, but *This is quite appalling* doesn't."

Jamie picked up the paper carefully, squishing his glasses up his nose and studying it carefully.

"Oh," he said. "I think . . . What do you think?"

Mirren had picked up another sheet, where the paragraph —*Wait until you have managed the estate successfully, then you'll find you know everything you need to know and won't waste your time with those ridiculous books* had a dash, but *You need to live in the real world* did not.

"I think . . ." said Jamie slowly. "I don't think those dashes are from my great-grandfather. I think they're written in a different hand. Look. It's not even a fountain pen."

"*Hopes will not be dashed*," whispered Mirren, "like in the poem!" She felt a twinge of excitement. She was so out of practice reading handwriting at all, but now that he mentioned it she thought he was right. The ink wasn't thick and fresh-looking; it wasn't a ballpoint, but it did look more like a marker.

"Jamie," she whispered, fingering the poem and repeating, "*Hopes will not be dashed*."

"Hopes will not be dashed!" he repeated joyfully. "Dashes! It is! You're right!"

"Really?" she said. "Or are we imagining it? Is this letter *graffitied*?"

"This is all a feat of imagination," said Jamie, sounding excited. "But it's taken us this far."

"Fair enough," said Mirren. "So, what should we do?"

"Well, the dashes point at capital letters. Let's write them down."

They worked through the pages in companionable silence. The wind still howled outside, but inside in the kitchen by the stove it was quiet and cosy.

"Okay," said Mirren finally. "I have *O-O-U-T-D-S*. Outside? Outdoors?"

"*R-N-W-A-R-J-Y*," read Jamie. "Oh, that's nothing, it's just rubbish."

"Well, it's rubbish *now*," said Mirren. "Maybe it's an anagram of some kind."

"Warts?" said Jamie. "War doubts?"

"No *B*," said Mirren. "We'll need to do it on paper." She drew a circle of all the letters. "This is why I've never been on *Countdown*," she said.

"What's *Countdown*?" said Jamie.

"You're too posh for *Countdown*?"

"Oh no, hang on, I know what it is. We just can't pick up Channel 4 here."

Mirren rolled her eyes. "Okay," she said. "Solve the anagram. Let's try with the *J* first; not many words begin with *J*."

"'Joust'?"

"If we have to joust, I'm out of here."

"'Jar'?" he suggested. "Something could be in a jar."

"True. Can it make 'Jamie'? Nope, sorry, no *M*, *I*, or *E* . . . You can get . . . 'joy.'"

"Hmm . . ."

"That's encouraging," said Mirren. "It being Christmas and everything." She crossed off *J*, *O*, and *Y*, and they stared and doodled some more.

"And 'run,'" pointed out Jamie.

"Oh yes!" said Mirren. "'Run owt joy' . . ."

Jamie almost leapt up in excitement. "It does spell something! Look!"

And he wrote, carefully:

RUN TOWARDS JOY.

THEY STARED AT it.

"We were right," said Mirren. "It's life advice. He's telling you that you can get away. All those messages about things he shouldn't do and couldn't do and didn't want to do. He's telling you to do something different."

"Seize the day?"

"More or less."

"Why couldn't he just write that? Instead of a stupid poem?"

Mirren thought of the bed, the beautiful view, the cosy space.

"I think he had a lot of time on his hands," said Mirren. "I think he enjoyed doing it. And he means it. And also . . ." She paused, thinking. "He might have wanted you to explore properly, explore the whole house, and see that you couldn't save it, maybe."

"Huh," said Jamie. He leafed through the papers. "There's nothing else," he said. "This is it. No more clues."

She looked up at him. "It's really not bad advice."

"I know. I totally get that," he said. "But . . ."

They pulled up the original poem again. *"Understand, my friend . . ."* He frowned. "Do you think this is it? This is the end? He just wanted to be understood?"

"Run towards joy," said Mirren. "I think that's not a bad outcome."

Jamie's face was a mixture of bewilderment and hope.

"I could just . . . walk away?" he said. He looked at Mirren. "Do you think I could?"

Mirren shrugged. "I bet there's a botanical garden somewhere that needs its spiders saved."

"But where would I live? What would I do?"

"Those are questions," said Mirren, "that, believe it or not, most of us deal with every day."

He blinked, and Mirren thought she could see new possibilities dancing in his eyes. "God," he said. "Esme is going to spit."

"Did she think you were going to find a pot of treasure and buy her a yacht?"

"It's not outside the realm of possibility."

"But there wasn't really a book," said Mirren. "Or rather, it was a book of his letters. And valuable advice."

"Goodness . . ."

Jamie looked around, stricken. *Do it now,* Mirren told herself. *Take him by the hand. Kiss him if you have to, before you get interrupted again.* And just as she had this thought, Bonnie walked into the kitchen, holding a live duck by the neck. The duck was loudly unimpressed.

Chapter Forty-Three

Mirren squawked almost as loudly as the duck and jumped backwards. Bonnie shot her a look.

"Come on! This is Quackers. Don't startle her, you'll make it worse."

"You *know* this duck?" said Mirren.

Bonnie ignored her. "Jamie, could you . . ."

"Can't Esme do it?" said Jamie, walking over and reluctantly holding the bottom half of the duck. "Didn't you want to do this outside?"

"No, they've unionised," said Bonnie.

"Are you going to . . . *What are you going to do to the duck?*" asked Mirren.

"Oh God," said Bonnie. "I really don't have time to explain the countryside. Jamie . . . Jamie . . ." she said in a warning tone of voice. "Would you *stop* being soft. *Esme!* ESME!"

Esme, as it turned out, was heading in, dressed in a sleek trouser suit. "Yes, yes, no need to holler," she said, then grinned. "Oh God, is my brother being pathetic again? You'll still eat it."

"I know," said Jamie. "I just don't . . ."

"Come on, Bonnie, we'll do it outside."

"Maybe the larder . . ." said Bonnie reluctantly.

"Out!" said Esme, opening the door, and letting the full force of the wind in. It wrenched the door open, smashing it all the way around against the wall. In the commotion, Jamie dropped his end of the duck, which took immediate advantage of the situation, pecked Bonnie hard on the arm, and flapped out into the dark, snowy sky.

THEY SAT AROUND the table.

"The thing is," said Bonnie, "it took me half an hour to get hold of that duck. And now it will fly back and warn the others and they'll all be in a flap."

"You are so pathetic," said Esme to Jamie.

"I know," said Jamie.

"If you can't catch it or kill it, you shouldn't eat it."

"That wouldn't work for Jamie," said Bonnie. "He thinks plants get upset when you pick them."

Jamie went red. "Shut up," he said.

"Well, anyway, that was our Christmas Eve supper," said Bonnie. "I'll have a look in the morning, but I'm not going out there again tonight."

"Quite right," said Theo, who had joined them and was finally looking rather better.

"I'll cook supper," said Jamie suddenly. "I'm sure there's stuff in the larder."

"Well, yes, obviously," said Bonnie. "We're managing fine without refrigeration, amazingly." She bustled out; Jamie got up and headed over to the larder and returned as the others settled around the fire and Mirren filled them in on the letters.

Esme, as predicted, was not happy about it.

"*Run towards joy?*" she said, sceptically. "That sounds like something someone would have on the wall of their new build in Slough!" She shivered.

"You are such a snob!" said Mirren, whose mum had Live Love Laugh up and Mirren didn't mind it in the slightest.

"Yes," said Esme. "Thank God somebody is, or we'd all be sitting round here eating Super Noodles."

Jamie was chopping garlic, rather efficiently, on a very old board.

"What does it even mean?" said Esme. "If I ran towards Tiffany's, they'd catch me and then they'd say, thanks, Lady Esme, we'd like some money now, please. This is a really bad show, Grampa." She frowned and leafed through the letters again. "Thanks for your legacy of total failure."

Jamie added a little butter to a huge old pan, heated it, and let the garlic sizzle into it. The smell was instantly intoxicating. Mirren remembered she was absolutely as hungry as she had ever been in her life. Starving, in fact.

Bonnie pushed open the door.

"Time for gin and tonics?" she said, carrying a tray.

"Oh God, yes. YES. Can I have one so strong that it will basically make me pass out?" said Esme.

"You want a tonic-flavoured martini?"

"That is exactly what I want."

Bonnie smiled indulgently. She even had ice cubes.

She had also baked some little cheese puffs, warm from the oven and light and delicious as clouds. Despite their dead end, Mirren couldn't help being delighted. Jamie had chopped a bunch of misshapen tomatoes that had obviously been grown in the grounds and added them gently to the garlic with a sprinkling of ground chilli, and Mirren's stomach growled. The wind howled round the house and there was a crashing noise. Mirren, who had been feeling woozy, and Theo, who was making good headway with his G and T, both started. Nobody else moved at all.

"What the hell was that?" said Mirren.

"Another tile off the roof," said the others, almost at the same time.

"The snow weighs them down," said Jamie, looking up.

"I know I didn't come here to do quantity surveying," said Mirren, "but this place really is falling down, you know. We'd probably condemn it."

Everyone laughed, but Mirren frowned. There surely wasn't a book in the world that could save this place.

The big water pot boiled, and he emptied some pasta into it.

"Be careful you don't harm that pasta!" said Esme. *"Oh no! I'm getting all hot and bendy!"*

"Shut up, Esme!"

"I think *you're* hot and bendy," said Theo.

"You shut up," said Esme, but she smiled.

This is joy, Mirren found herself thinking suddenly, completely out of the blue. Sitting in this kitchen with these odd people, and a warm oven, and a gin and tonic, and food on the way. *This is joy, and it's nearly ended.*

It was such a simple meal—rich, garlicky pasta with a squeeze of lemon; a leafy salad from the greenhouse; Bonnie's heavy sourdough bread with thick, salty butter; red wine that tasted as old and deep as mined jewels—but it was one of the best Mirren could remember. Jamie persuaded Bonnie to join them, and for once she acquiesced, pointing out that she would have to, as he had done for her roast duck, and they all reminisced about Christmases past, when dozens of people would come to the castle, when great braziers would line the driveway for the carriages, or cars with chauffeurs, or just people driving drunk, as they did in the country in those days.

Bonnie could remember stories of how downstairs, in the old days, they would have to put up the visiting maids and footmen, and how there was all sorts of funny business. And of course then there was Boxing Day, the day after Christmas, when the staff got their boxes, or gifts, and had a day off to spend with their own families after waiting on the great house. It felt so long ago. And yet so close: in the walls and the floors and the endless rooms for guests and staff and dogs and horses and noise. Now the castle felt so empty; people preferred mod cons, and hotels, and the distractions of a city, and ready access to the internet. Mirren thought of her own little box bedroom in London, so far away, so near to so many people, their noise, their cooking smells, their fuss, but still feeling so alone. Whereas here, she felt so much freer. And it was true: she had barely been alone for a second.

But great homes like this, off the beaten track—built before there was even a track to be off—what would become of them? Of all of them?

As everyone chattered away, and Bonnie brought in a beautiful Yule log cake, Mirren looked at the storm outside and grew wistful. She wouldn't see these people again. Jamie had a new road to plough, in the Botanic Gardens, she supposed. Esme would vanish back into her glamorous world, hoping to marry well. Theo might have to up his game if he wanted to keep hold of her, Mirren thought, but now without rancour. Bonnie would be fine, she sensed.

And she, Mirren . . . She glanced at Jamie's reflection in the window, only to see, with a start, that he was looking back at her. Their eyes met. When she turned back to the table he was glancing down again. Esme had dragged out Scrabble, much to Theo's protests.

"No," said Jamie. "No. I'm done. No more word games."

His face looked sad suddenly.

"I hope you guys . . . I'm so sorry. I hope the snow stops soon and you can get home. I'm sorry it hasn't worked out. I'm glad you came, though. It has genuinely helped me decide a few things, even if it doesn't feel that way. Thank you. Thank you all." He raised his glass. "To running towards joy."

"To running towards joy," they all repeated, raising their glasses.

"What's that about joy?" said Bonnie, pushing open the door from the larder.

"Oh, we're meant to run towards it," said Theo, frowning. "Grandfather James turned out just to have left some kind of hippie bollocks of advice. He's probably laughing his head off up there."

"But why does he mention Joy?" said Bonnie, looking annoyed. "What's she got to do with it?"

"What's *who* got to do with it?" said Jamie.

"*Joy*," said Bonnie, as if he were being particularly stupid. "My grandmother!"

Chapter Forty-Four

The room stared.

"Mrs. Airdrie?" said Esme stupidly.

"Mrs. *Airdrie*?" echoed Jamie.

"You didn't know your housekeeper's first name?" said Mirren.

"But that wasn't her name!" said Esme, screwing up her face. "Her name was Joyce."

"Yes, which she hated," said Bonnie. "Everyone called her Joy." She paused. "Everyone who knew her. Knew her well."

Neither of the McKinnon children said anything to that.

"Hang on," said Theo, looking excited. "Where is she now?"

Bonnie shook her head, and the other two looked stricken. "She died. Years ago. Breast cancer," said Bonnie shortly.

"Oh, I'm sorry," said Theo.

"Your grandfather was very good to us," said Bonnie. "Left us the cottage. Left the trust for me. It's why I still work here."

They looked at her.

"His room," said Mirren suddenly. "His lovely room. Fire, and pictures, and cosiness, and no dust or anything. You made it lovely."

Bonnie smiled sadly. "I wanted to."

Jamie looked confused.

"The night—the one night I went out," said Bonnie, going white suddenly. "That was the worst night of my life. Apart from when

I lost my gran. You don't know. None of you really knew him. He was the best, kindest man I ever met in my life."

Theo looked confused.

"So how could we . . . What does he mean? Did he know she died?"

"Of course," said Bonnie. "He was never the same after that. Not that anybody asked, or cared. He started hoarding, piling stuff up. He was obviously grieving, obviously deeply sad."

Mirren looked at Jamie, who had come to exactly the same thought at the same point. He nodded, and rooted in the box by the side of the table. He pulled out one of the letters from the bedroom and held it up.

"Bonnie," he said gently, "is this your grandmother's handwriting?"

Bonnie looked at the letter and grew very pink.

"Of course," she said. "And I don't think you should be reading them."

"How old was she when your mother was born?" said Esme, trying to soften her demanding tone.

"None of your fucking business," said Bonnie. And with this, she disappeared back into the scullery.

"Bloody hell," said Theo.

"Run towards Joy?" said Jamie. "He must mean . . . I wonder. Bonnie took the smaller cottage after Mrs. Airdrie died . . . we thought it was being kept for other staff. Who never came, of course."

"Hang on," said Theo. "You know what this implies."

"If she was . . . I mean, Bonnie's mum wouldn't have had to work as a skivvy, would she, if she was the laird's daughter?" said Mirren. "That would be really . . . I mean. That wouldn't happen. Would it?"

Esme and Jamie looked at her.

"Bloody hell," said Jamie.

"What?"

"Bonnie's mum *didn't* work here. She was sent away to school; we never knew how or why. She got a great job in Aberdeen. It was always a surprise that Bonnie loved being back here so much—that she ended up spending all her holidays and most of her childhood with her grandmother. Nobody was more surprised than us when she applied for the job when her grandmother retired . . ." His voice trailed off. "We grew up together."

"You behave as if you used to date sometimes," said Mirren.

"Do we?" He looked confused.

"Or . . . like family?"

Jamie laughed ruefully. "Oh my God," he said.

"And nobody knew?"

"There are always rumours in a big house," said Esme succinctly.

Jamie was rubbing the back of his neck. "Kids don't understand anything, do they? It's like trying to work out life from a poem. It's exactly like the stupid acrostic. Nobody explains anything."

"What do you mean?"

"We grew up together. We were in that cottage all the time. Playing there all day. Then when we got to, like, thirteen or so . . ."

He looked embarrassed.

"Uh-oh," said Mirren.

"No, no, nothing like that—Mrs. Airdrie took me aside and said Bonnie was busy every time I went over and then . . . well, then I got sent away to school."

"Does Bonnie know?"

Esme's voice was uncharacteristically soft. "She's the one who nursed him. This house flows through her veins, upstairs and down."

"So odd," said Mirren. "You desperate to escape the place, her desperate to keep it."

"Who's older?" asked Theo. "Your mum or Bonnie's mum?"

The siblings looked at one another.

"Bon," said Jamie, calling her. She came.

"I'm not talking about it," she said fiercely. "My own dad was a ghillie. It's all ancient history."

"I'm not . . ." Jamie said. "Okay. I just wanted to ask. Your gran's old house . . ."

"The laird gave it to her and offered me the other one," said Bonnie immediately.

"No, I'm not accusing you of anything . . . I'm just asking. How was it left?"

"Just as it was," said Bonnie. "I would have cleaned it out if new staff had come but . . . they never did."

There was another cracking tile on the roof.

"It's full of ghosts," she said.

"Happy ghosts," said Jamie, remembering.

"Oh yeah," said Bonnie, looking at him. "A lot of happy times in *that* house."

"Did they . . ." Esme asked. "Did they rekindle their relationship?"

Bonnie shook her head. "He was . . . I mean, his family was here."

Jamie bowed his head.

"And by the time everything got settled . . . I think by then it was just too late. Too much had happened, too much time had passed. I think he was beginning to get really eccentric then, and my gran was busy with me and the house and, well, then she got sick, she had cancer on and off for years. He always tried to keep wooing her, though. Would always bring her things he thought she would like."

Mirren understood immediately. "Books," she said.

"Books," agreed Bonnie.

They were silent for a moment or so. Then Esme asked, "Is the cottage kept locked?"

"Well, no," said Bonnie. "Generally, I feel if burglars *were* to stop by, they'd start at the place with the ballroom."

Chapter Forty-Five

The wind was still howling; the snow was still up.

"We can't go back out in this," said Theo, with feeling. He was remembering his time out in the maze, and not with relish. "We'll die. It's over a kilometre away. In the pitch black and a howling storm."

"How you can have a house on your property that is so far away you can't get to it?" said Mirren. "Every time I think I've got my head around it, I forget again."

"Nobody's doing another Captain Oates," said Jamie. "We'll get a good night's sleep, and we'll look in the morning. All of us, Bonnie."

Bonnie nodded. "Aye," she said.

MIRREN'S HEAD WAS whirring. She knew she wouldn't get a moment's sleep. Her fire was burning once again—once again laid by Bonnie, the room made nice by her. How could she work all hours, looking after this house for ungrateful people who . . . well, she supposed the grandfather had not been ungrateful; he'd paid for her education, bequeathed her the trust fund Jamie had mentioned, the house that was hers outright, the running joke that she was actually better off than any of the legitimate McKinnon offspring.

But that had not been the real reason, had it? She had stayed to look after her family. Both sides.

Mirren washed up and, as usual, got into her pyjamas, then added socks and two jumpers before hopping into the four-poster, but it was no use. Even her book was no good. She tossed and turned, and got warm, but not sleepy, not at all.

Above the persistent wailing of the wind, she stiffened. She had heard a creak. Definitely a creak. She sat up, wide awake.

If it was Theo, *still* chancing his arm after all his nonsense, she was going to tell him a thing or two about backing off. Bonnie would be gone, or busy downstairs.

Which left one person. Or about five thousand angry ghosts, or a witch, or even that stupid duck, back for revenge. But she didn't think it was any of those.

Mirren's heart started beating faster. She got out of bed, glad of the firelight, and picked up her torch again. She advanced towards the door.

"Hello?" she said quietly. "Who's out there?"

There was another creak, very close, but no response.

"Enough," said Mirren and threw open the door.

Standing there, looking sad but defiant, was Jamie.

"I thought you didn't creak" was all she could think of to say.

MIRREN GLANCED UP and down the corridor. He was alone.

"Is this a bad time? Were you asleep? Sorry, I didn't mean to wake you."

"You were creaking about outside my door!"

"I know. I figured if you were really asleep you wouldn't notice, but if you weren't, you'd hear me."

"No," said Mirren. "I wasn't asleep."

"Can I come in? It's freezing out here." He looked at her pyjamas, socks, hat, and two jumpers combo. "Although I don't want to impose on a lady when she's in her nightwear."

Mirren looked back at him for a moment. Thought of all the reasons why this was a bad idea, all the reasons it couldn't work.

And then she told herself, well, if it was just a dream, a sojourn, a break in her normal, quotidian city girl life, then she was going to make it count.

"You can come in," she said and swung open the heavy door.

MIRREN DREW BACK towards the fire; Jamie followed her without saying anything.

"I couldn't sleep."

"Me neither."

He looked at her with those warm hazel eyes and suddenly she knew the answer.

"I thought we could just talk it through," said Jamie. "I find . . . I like talking to you."

"Well, no," said Mirren. "We can't do that."

"Oh, okay," said Jamie, looking confused. "I'm sorry I bothered you."

"Because . . . I want to do something else," she said. And then he understood.

The flames crackled high in the grate as he moved towards her. He was so tall she had to reach up to meet him, and, just as she had thought about—dreamed about—his lips were soft, even as his long, wiry body was hard.

For the first time in forever her head went blank. Every thought of everything—her phone, her flat, her family, her job, her Christmas, the book, the messages, everything . . . everything left her. She was conscious of nothing but sensation, her mind a pure blank with nothing—no anxiety about kissing him, about whether they were doing it right; no worry about how she looked—she was in two jumpers and bed socks, after all. If she could have seen herself, she would have seen her very shoulders unfurl, her whole body sink into his embrace, until she was utterly languid in his arms, her hair glinting in the firelight, her eyes closed, even as he clasped a strong arm around her waist, the other stroking her face with the gentleness she had noticed in him from the very start.

"Oh," he said, breaking off temporarily, his eyes distant and unfocused. "Oh, Mirren, you are the sweetest, the very, very sweetest . . . I have wanted to do that for . . ."

"Well, you only met me ten days ago," she joked, but her voice was trembling; her legs, she was surprised to discover, were entirely unstable; even her breathing was faster than normal.

"I thought you were with . . ."

"Christ, no," said Mirren. "And . . ." She flushed. ". . . he doesn't compare to you."

"Oh, goodness," he said. "You are the only good thing to happen to me in . . ." He shook his head.

"Shall we talk less?" said Mirren, so he kissed her again, slowly and gently, as if they had all the time in the world; as if they were cooped up in a Scottish castle, hemmed in by snow, in the depths of the year, on Christmas Eve.

Ordinarily Mirren would be worrying if there had been the right number of dates or what his intentions were or even whether she liked the person that much, quite a long time before she ever slept with them, and even then it could be extremely awkward and sometimes just plain drunken.

Tonight was not going to be like that.

"Come to bed," she said. "It's warmer."

She expected him to be anxious, apologise possibly, worry that he was taking advantage of her. He did none of those things. He simply took her hand, took off her ridiculous hat and threw it across the room, then kissed the forehead he had removed it from.

Then, holding her hand, he drew her steadily towards the bed, and she followed, hypnotised, happily surprised, entirely willing, overwhelmingly excited.

Jamie opened the bottom curtains, the ones that faced the fire, so she could see him in the flickering light. They knelt, face-to-face, and he kissed her lips, then her neck, and started down her chest, so softly, so sweetly, that she let out an involuntary sigh, then opened her eyes.

"It's all right," he said. "I don't think anyone can hear you."

"I heard you making a *tiny creak*!"

He smiled. "Yes, well, you aren't one of the wine cellar twins."

She smiled, and he returned, unhurried, to the matter in hand.

She hadn't known what she had expected, barely knew what drew her to him so strongly. But his gentleness, the obvious abhorrence he had for hurting things, showed itself clearly here. His soft lips were light and teasing, unfurling her like a butterfly, making her push herself towards him, desperate for his teasing lips to find every part of her body. Carefully he pulled off her final vest—she wasn't wearing a bra and he smiled happily.

"Look at you in the firelight," he said. "Look at you."

"I am mostly goose bumps," said Mirren.

"Oh no," he said. "Let's see if we can do something about that."

"I think," said Mirren, her voice muffled, "you might be causing them."

But then he drew her full breast into his mouth, still with that maddening slowness and care. Mirren found herself thinking about his gardener's hands, gentle and strong; what an exceptional amount of patience that might require. Then she found it impossible to think of anything at all; her mind went white, entirely, as his head went lower, gradually kissing down her torso, and down between her legs, and she drew in a breath as she felt his lips slowly move between her thighs. She let out a small moan, and caressed his head, pulling him closer towards her, hearing the fire crackle, as heat flooded her entire body. His tongue was searching for something, found it, and she felt her head fall back behind her, the sensation incredibly intense, after so long.

"Oh my God," she said, then reached down. "No . . . later. For now, I want you here. Right here. Now. Please."

Again with teasing slowness he kissed all the way back up her body, until little spasms of delight were coursing through her.

"Tell me you were incredibly presumptuous and brought a condom," she whispered. "Because I don't think we can nip to the all-night garage."

He laughed, looked a little rueful, and confessed that he had.

And then they continued, staring into each other's eyes in the flickering firelight, completely naked and, unusually for Mirren, completely unembarrassed, completely unselfconscious. He covered her, and, still looking into her eyes, slowly, and totally in control, he entered her, just the tip. Her eyes widened at the width of him. But he didn't smile or apologise.

"It's okay," he said. "It's okay. Just . . ."

She felt her breath coming fast now, feeling so close to him; he laid his body full-length on hers and she felt his heart beat faster, and a groan escaped him, and suddenly she was sweating all over. She held on to him closely as he pushed further, breathtakingly deep, all the way inside her, both slippery now, the heat and the pressure overwhelming.

"Oh God," she said, looking up at him, the two of them caught in a red-curtained four-poster world of their own, and they waited, frozen for a moment, until she couldn't help moving, her hips urging him forward, until with a huge thrust he pushed them both over the edge, and before she knew it she was clinging to him, muttering words as he crashed down on her like a wave and she followed him, matched him, until they were completely one and she found her back arching, her body completely possessed by another, and slamming down again and again and again, until she felt herself lift, stretch, electricity powering through her veins to the very tips of her toes, even as he roared above her and reared up.

Neither of them spoke afterwards, both a little startled by what had just taken place. They swapped shy glances and giggled a little. Mirren felt sweat drying on her skin but also felt the urge to touch him, again, to stroke his hairless chest, to make sure in a way that he was still real. And yet even touching him set her off again, astonishingly, once more with longing. He looked at her, equally astonished, then pulled her towards him. He sat back against the headboard of the bed.

"Here," he said. "Come and sit on me. I want to see . . ."

He pulled her onto his lap, astride him, fondled her heavy, swollen breasts, as she squirmed, still flushed with the excitement he awoke in her. He hoiked her closer, looked up at her, his beautiful sandy hair falling over his forehead, the green highlights glowing in his hazel eyes. She pushed herself against him.

"This isn't getting the book found," she said, trying to lighten the mood.

"What fucking book?" he said, taking her face in his hand once more, crushing her tightly to him with the other hand, refusing to loosen their tight connection, to relinquish his hold, until once again, hard against him, she found herself holding one of the curtains, screaming hoarsely as her curls cascaded down her damp back while he rammed her steadily, taking his time, refusing to relinquish his hold, even as she cried out, over and over.

Afterwards, still warm, sore, still feeling as if inside she was entirely melting, Mirren stood up and walked towards the window, conscious he was watching her move, and of the power that it gave her, that she had over him in that moment, even as she knew he must be falling asleep. She glanced back and the fine eyes were already drooping, the long lashes shadowing on his high cheekbones, and she felt a bolt of both joy and alarm: joy at his beauty; alarm that this might be—would be, must be—part of a short-lived thing, a sojourn from real life, where normal rules applied, where he would marry someone posh and annoying, and she would save up to try to soundproof the connecting wall.

She turned back towards the window. The snow had stopped, finally; finally the storm had blown itself out. Which was good, of course, but it meant . . . at some point they would inevitably have to go home. This spell would come to an end.

On the other hand, would she have missed it? Would she ever have missed this? An evening that she already knew she would re-member for the rest of her life. Would probably, she thought, spend the rest of her life trying to equal.

The moon shone strongly now through the clearing sky, casting its light . . . She moved closer to the window, dreamily taking in the view.

Then, suddenly, she stopped short.

"Jamie!" she hissed loudly. "JAMIE!"

"What?" came the amused voice, sounding sleepy. "I mean, I can *probably* manage another time. You are just so unbelievably fuck-ing sexy . . ."

"Jamie! Come and see! NOW!"

Chapter Forty-Six

From the window, Mirren pointed. Her tone woke Jamie up fully, and he leapt up, grabbing a blanket to wrap them both in.

"If this is just a really good moon, could you take a bad photo of it and show me later?" he said, but as he crossed to the window he fell silent.

"What is it?" said Mirren. "Is it something totally normal that happens here all the time and I can just ignore it because it's some weird country thing I just don't understand?"

Jamie didn't answer her at first and just leaned over.

"Crap," he said. "No. No. I think . . ." He got even closer to the window. On the horizon to the north was a steady orange glow. "Crap," he said again. "You know what's there?"

Mirren looked at him, shrugging.

"I think it's the maze."

"Oh God," she said. "Theo didn't get the fire out?"

"Theo got completely turned around in the snow," said Jamie. "I was lucky to grab him. But I didn't think to go back . . . I thought if I couldn't see any flames then, it must be all right; it's so cold and wet. Mind you, the snow is dry, and there was fuel on it . . . It must have got inside the roots, and there was enough left when the snow stopped to smoulder . . . oh God."

"Oh no," said Mirren, then she frowned. "But it will just be the maze, won't it? It can't reach the house; it's too far away. Can it?"

"No, it won't reach us," said Jamie, shaking his head. "Although it is a shame about that old thing . . . but . . ."

Suddenly his body stiffened, and Mirren looked at him.

"The cottages next to the maze," he said.

"Bonnie's cottage."

"*Joy's* cottage," he said desperately, and she suddenly realised. The place they had been intending to head to at first light.

"Do you think?"

"It has a thatched roof," said Jamie.

"Oh no," said Mirren. "Oh Lord."

He looked at her.

"Should we phone the fire brigade?" she said.

He shook his head. "How would they even get here?"

They stared at it.

"The actual forest won't catch," he said. "Far too much snow, too wet. But the cottage . . ."

"Bonnie's here in the house, though?"

He nodded. "But Mrs. Airdrie's place . . ."

"Run towards Joy," said Mirren. It wasn't a question.

"It would be foolish," said Jamie. "It's still dangerous out there."

"Yeah, it is," Mirren said.

THEY DIDN'T WAKE the others. They threw on every piece of clothing they could find. Jamie grabbed a couple of fire extinguishers from the laundry and flung them into a backpack, and they put new batteries in the torches and pulled on the snowshoes. They worked quickly, in perfect harmony with each other, but there was no laughing, no joking. Just before they left the kitchen door, Jamie pulled Mirren towards him and kissed her fiercely once more, and once more she felt her insides melting.

"If I say fall back, we fall back, okay?" he said. "I've seen thatch go up before, and it goes *quick*."

Mirren swallowed. "Okay," she said. "No heroics."

"Nope," said Jamie. "Right." He took her hand. "Let's go."

THEY DIDN'T NEED the torches. The cold and the wind were biting as soon as they left the house, great drifts of snow piling up from the latest dump. But the scent of the fire was on the wind as they came round the north side of the house, moving quickly this time, towards the flames, skirting the loch. The noise filled Mirren's ears, and, when she looked up, a starry night brighter than any she had ever seen filled her vision. The cold stars glowed above, the full moon shining across the waves as they tore along, as fast as they could snowshoe, her hand in Jamie's strong one. It felt like a dream. Even the cold barely touched her, as they worked up a sweat moving hard through the terrain.

The maze was aflame, a pattern of fire. It must look extraordinary from above, the hidden rows and secret ways aglow. Mirren couldn't help looking at it in sadness, even as she felt the warmth on her face, her relief that it had not yet touched the cottages.

They looked at each other, nodded, and Jamie quietly turned the handle of the door.

IT WAS DIFFICULT not to at least try the light switch out of habit—it was much darker inside the cottage than outside—but, of course, there was no power. Their torches made Mirren feel like a burglar. From the back windows of the cottage the maze fire seemed much more pronounced, the smell of smoke terrifying.

The door opened directly onto the main room off the cottage; it was a clean-swept room, with rugs on the flagstones, a wood-burner in the stove, and comfortable old armchairs arranged around it. A small kitchen opened to the side, and there was a small, scrubbed

wooden dining table. It was nice; old beams held up the roof and
the entire place felt cosy, even when it was freezing, unlived in,
and unheated. Bonnie hadn't been lying about leaving it as it was;
there were family photos on the wall. Jamie held the torch up to
one of them—Bonnie as a baby.

"Gosh," he said.

"What?"

"She looks exactly like Esme at that age."

"You never came over here?"

"I practically lived here. But it wasn't something I was ever
looking for." He looked at the tiny winding staircase. "And I never
went upstairs. That was Mrs. Airdrie's domain."

The large sitting room was tidy and devoid of clutter; there were
no papers, not even any books. There was cutlery in the drawers in
the kitchen; obviously discarded pots and pans that were huge for
a tiny family of two; chipped crockery from expensive sets. Jamie
grabbed a small fire extinguisher from the side of the tiny kitchen.
It was designed to put out cooking fires, not what they saw through
the window.

"Maybe it will blow itself out," he said. "It won't spread, I don't
think. There are no more trees, and the ground is rock-solid. We
should save what we can, then leave."

But they both slowed down on their way up the creaking dark
wood stairs, breathless, wondering what they might find.

There were two doors at the top of the stairs; the smaller, to the
left, clearly Bonnie's childhood room. Jamie took a deep breath in
front of the other—if it hadn't been creepy, Mirren found herself
thinking, he might have knocked. And then he pulled down the
latch and opened it.

The room was simply furnished but quite, quite lovely. A large,
soft sleigh bed; a thick, fluffy red rug covering dark wooden floor-
boards; a tiny fireplace filled with dried flowers; beautiful pale white

furniture. This room was a haven, everything carefully chosen and looked after. There was good art on the walls and an immaculate little bathroom off to the side. And there were three windows in total, all the way around, and even lovelier than at the castle, because the view from the southern window was the castle itself.

"I wasn't expecting this," whispered Mirren. The flames were making a glow against the window frames. She glanced out. The maze still held its shape; she couldn't tell if the fire was spreading.

"This reminds me of somewhere," said Mirren. Then it came to her. "Your grandfather's room. It's the same bed! The same bedside table! Oh my God, the same lamp. I wondered why it was all so modern!"

"Oh yes," said Jamie, frowning. "Of course. He wanted . . . he wanted it replicated. Up there in the castle."

"The place where he was happy," said Mirren.

"Yeah."

He rested his hand on the top of the beautiful dresser by the bed. Then he glanced at his watch. "Huh," he said.

"What?"

"It's . . ." He showed her the time. "It's Christmas morning."

It was one minute past midnight.

He pulled her to him, the fire apparently forgotten. "Can I open my present?" he said, trying to undo her top button.

"I'm a scarecrow." Mirren laughed. "Seriously, one of these days you're going to see me in mascara and lippy and have a heart attack."

"I would like that very much," he said, and they both paused at the idea of a future event, a future of any kind.

"Anyway, no, we can't, we're on fire!" said Mirren.

"Yeah, we are," said Jamie. "Although . . . I don't usually show off like this, but I can be very quick . . ."

She laughed, then looked at him. "God, with you, me too," she said, and by the time he'd kissed her, deeply and passionately, she had half realised that she absolutely would let him, again; that she had to, was utterly compelled; and it was only as they fell back onto the bed, totally carried away, completely caught up in one another, that Mirren landed rather heavily on top of something.

"Ow!" she said.

"What? My darling, what is it?"

"Um," said Mirren, feeling behind her. If she hadn't been exactly there, in that exact position, they would never have found it. It was a small lump, book-shaped, sewn deep inside the mattress.

THEY SAT UP, staring at each other.

"No," said Jamie.

"Oh my God," said Mirren. "Do you think?"

"What else could it be?"

They stared at each other in the faint glow of the flames.

"This is it," said Jamie. "I can sense it."

Mirren nodded. "I think so."

He tore the stitches of the mattress cover apart, and fished inside, until he pulled out a soft, faded old Jiffy bag.

He handed it to her. "You open it."

"Absolutely not. You do it."

In the end, they tugged at it together, carefully opening the bag, and pulled it out. It was well wrapped up, covered in layers and layers of bubble wrap.

"Is it more letters?" breathed Mirren. Jamie looked at her and shook it.

"I don't think so," he said.

And that was the moment the flaming branch fell against the roof.

Chapter Forty-Seven

Mirren screamed and Jamie looked up.

"Come on," he said. "Out! Out! Get out! Run back towards the house!"

"Not without you," said Mirren. "I'll run across the loch and die."

"Okay," he said, tucking the parcel carefully into an inside pocket of his jacket. "Follow me."

Outside the house, they ran around the back, and he handed her another fire extinguisher. "Know how to use one of these?"

"I absolutely don't!"

"Okay, well . . . don't open it in your face."

He showed her how to pull off the black safety guard, and they directed the foam towards the branch on the roof, which lay there smouldering among the thatch. Mirren's aim was terrible, but Jamie managed to bank it carefully, smothering the flame and adding as much of the spray as he could for good measure.

"Okay," he said, as it finally damped down. "Okay."

He was breathing hard as he put down the fire extinguisher, just as Mirren turned round to see that a line of low hedging had caught on the side of the kitchen garden—and was racing closer to the castle. They could hear Roger outside somewhere, barking his head off.

"Quick!"

But they couldn't move quickly with their stupid snowshoes—or at least Mirren couldn't. They forged their way ahead as well as they could, hot and red-faced, Mirren's muscles all screaming at her as she deeply regretted not paying attention to the CrossFit machine.

"Bloody hell," she said.

Jamie was looking at the smouldering hedge. "You go ahead! Wake up the others! We'll get them out!"

"*Where?*" said Mirren.

"Well, we'll get them downstairs. Just in case. It's not going to make it to the house, though. It won't. It can't."

"We didn't think it would make it to the cottage!"

Jamie frowned, looking back. The maze was still ablaze; the cottages seemed safe for the time being. "I'll bring the fire extinguishers up. Every one we can find. We'll need to wake everyone. Buckets too. Cover it in snow."

THEY WENT IN the main door, the big old wooden entrance creaking furiously at being opened, as it so seldom was. Jamie left it open, then found the huge old gong and started hitting it. Roger stayed outside, as if astounded that the humans could be so stupid.

"EVERYONE! UP! UP! EVERYONE!!"

Mirren stood behind him. "Oh God," she said suddenly. "Do you think Theo and Esme . . ."

Jamie covered his face with his hands and almost started laughing. "Oh, please," he said. "What are we like?"

But Esme came running down by herself, nightgown flying behind her.

"The maze is on fire!" she shouted.

"Really?" said Jamie. "That's a coincidence; we were ringing the bells for fun."

"It won't reach the house," said Esme bullishly.

Then they all turned as Bonnie ran up to them, and finally Theo, down the main stairs, rubbing sleep from his eyes.

Bonnie stared out of the main doors. "The maze . . . It'll hit the cottages!!"

"No, the cottage is fine," said Jamie. "I checked."

"You've been up to the cottages?" said Bonnie.

"Yes," he said. "It was looking bad for a minute there but it was just a flying branch on the roof and the wind direction has changed now. It's not going to spread in that direction."

"Okay," said Bonnie. "But what *is* it doing?"

"What do you mean?"

"It's dying down?" said Theo optimistically. "I'm really, really sorry. I thought it was out. I thought I'd got it."

Jamie waved it away, not making a big deal out of it. "You did your best," he said, and Mirren had a little start in her heart—that she thought well of this man.

Bonnie shook her head. "It won't be enough," she said.

"I know," said Jamie. "We're just down to round up all the fire extinguishers."

Bonnie nodded. Then, suddenly, she stopped and cocked her head. "Can you hear it?"

They all stopped then and listened. There was a cracking sound, a creaking and a twisting noise.

"What's that?" said Esme.

Bonnie looked at her.

"It can't be the thaw," said Jamie. "It's still freezing outside."

"I think . . ." said Bonnie. "I think it's worse. I think if there's anything you need . . . you should probably grab it."

And, in the second of stunned, disbelieving silence that followed, Jamie grabbed Mirren and held her close. He didn't know.

But Mirren, the quantity surveyor—she knew. She looked at Bonnie and nodded in agreement.

"What are you talking about?" said Esme.

The cracking grew louder. There was a creaking everywhere. Something was very wrong.

"It's the pipes," said Mirren quietly.

Bonnie nodded. "They're unbelievably old. And the stress they've had on them—the snow, then the ice has frozen them, then more snow's warmed them . . . I mean, we've had bad years before . . ."

"And the flames have stretched them, and the cold must have pulled them about like billy-oh."

The two girls nodded.

"The pipes run up the north side; it's a long branch off the mains water. Your great-great-grandfather got us off the well system about the same time as the railways came. And I don't think anyone's looked at those pipes since . . . Well, Jamie, have you even looked at the schematics?"

Jamie looked very guilty as the creaking grew louder. "They've burst before," he said defensively. "Loads of times."

"And been patched up, here and there. But they haven't been heated over a flame before."

The creaking and crackling was growing louder. And then Mirren turned behind her.

From the laundry behind them, where the scullery and storerooms were, came a faint trickling noise. And suddenly she could see it: a line of water, moving terrifyingly quickly, seeping under the door.

"Okay, no time to grab anything," said Bonnie authoritatively. "Let's head out."

"*Where?*" said Esme. "The cottages are closer to the fire."

"I know," said Jamie, "but if we take the extinguishers . . ."

Already one side of the kitchen was covered in water, moving at lightning speed, like a living thing, spreading over the floor, and they ran through to the main section of the house to leave by the front door.

What they saw there dismayed them utterly.

There was water cascading down, pooling at the bottom of the staircase; desperately flowing downstairs, looking for an exit.

But that was not the worst of it. Years of neglect, of lack of money, lack of care—centuries of the house being there, put up in bits and pieces—meant that it was bodged, crumbling, held together with sticky tape and hope, birds' nests and layers of peeling paint and wallpaper.

They watched, horrified, as cold water cascaded around their heels, at first very slowly then faster and faster, and then, horrifyingly, a crack appeared above the ancient door, running swiftly upwards, straight to the ceiling.

Jamie rushed forward and pulled at the great front door, but the water pounding against the wood that had warped was holding it fast; he twisted the great handles, without success.

They charged back to the kitchen, just in time to see a huge eruption of black, filthy water from the butler's sink, pounding against the ceiling with full force. The ground was trembling now beneath their feet.

Jamie looked at Mirren. "Might this . . . come down?"

"I said we all needed hard hats," said Mirren.

They turned backwards, pursued by the filthy, sticky water that had started to move things—chairs, plates, and most of all books, coming at them menacingly out of the dark. Mirren gave a silent prayer of thanks that the electricity was not on, to spark, but as it was things were bad enough.

"Break the windows?" said Theo, but the water was now over their knees, kept pouring out from every sink, every loo, every hole in the place, like a river breaking its banks.

They waded back to the main hall, where things were worse than ever: the grandfather clock had lifted off the floor, was slowly subsiding in the water.

"Oh God," said Esme. "Quick. Up the stairs."

Nobody had a better idea, and they ran up, against the water crashing down. The smell was terrible as water cascaded through every wall or ceiling with a crack in it, which was all of them. Masonry was tumbling now, falling from the cornices, the elaborate plasterwork on the ceiling. A large chunk caught Theo on the head, and he cried out.

"We have to get out of here," said Jamie.

"The turret," said Mirren and Esme both at once. With a tremendous bang, a picture fell off a wall that was cracking in half. Jamie's torch was wobbling, its batteries running low.

"Quickly then," said Bonnie, and they tore along the corridors, wading through the water and a sea of books. Mirren's heart was sad to see them floating by: a life's work; a memoir of a great hero, now forgotten; a history of wars in which nobody now was left alive; incomprehensible jokes from long ago; compendiums of butterflies; stories of kings and queens of foreign lands, unimaginably long ago. An *Alice's Adventures in Wonderland* crossed her vision, looking surprised to be off on an adventure of its own; great long lists of cricketers eddied around her; a Shakespeare floated past peaceably, as if content to know that nothing could sink him forever. She passed the door of the East Library just in time to watch the great chandelier come crashing down.

The small door in the corner was also jammed, but all five of them together hurled their weight on it, and they spilled through it, almost falling down the stairs in their eagerness. This was the far corner, the very far edge of the castle, and it was built of ancient, thoroughly solid stuff, stones laid hand over hand. There were no curlicues, no plaster cherubs or fancy borders, no light fittings to crash, no pipes to unleash chaos.

Even with the torches it was black as pitch down the hole, and the noises from the rest of the house were harrowing.

"Nobody lose their footing," said Esme as they started down the spiral stair. "You'll fall all the way down."

Her voice echoed, and Mirren shivered, terrified, holding tight to the external wall, even as, on the other side of it, all hell was breaking loose. She couldn't feel her feet—the water was cascading all down their ankles—and she couldn't see them either in the dim light, but she felt, all the way down, the comforting hand of Jamie's in hers, pulling her onwards. He never let her go, even if he would have balanced far more easily on his own.

They carried on so long, their footprints sloshing, that Mirren started to get very scared, particularly when Bonnie slipped and Jamie only just managed to shoot his other hand out in time to catch her.

"I got you," he said, and, as she turned, Mirren caught her face in the wavering torchlight.

"Thank you," Bonnie said, and for a second she and Jamie looked very alike. And then they continued on.

Chapter Forty-Eight

When they finally made it to the bottom of the stairwell, the salty, briny smell hitting them hard coming off the water, they touched down on the sand. "I feel," said Theo, "that your draught issues may have something to do with this."

Water was still tumbling down from the castle above, as if it were raining. Jamie didn't pause, but immediately waded in to grab the dilapidated rowing boat tied to the chain on the wall, completely impervious to the freezing water. He hauled it over and helped them in one by one before pushing it off the tiny shoreline at the bottom of the castle, setting them out to sea. The boys rowed with all their might onto the cold, calm sea; everyone now had stopped moving, utterly chilled and suffering the aftereffects of shock.

The full moon was bright above their heads, and they could see it all, with amazement, watch in real time from fifty metres out as the house crumbled like a wedding cake left out in the rain. With a great juddering roar, the front section of the building collapsed, the turrets dropping down, the pennants fluttering vertically before dissolving in a heap of dust.

"Oh my God," said Mirren.

"I know," said Jamie, looking stricken. "Hey, Roger will have been far enough away, right?"

"Dogs aren't stupid," said Mirren.

"Some of them are," said Esme, but she was just as awestruck as everyone else.

But the back section—the ancient chapel, and the stone-built tower that had held off Vikings and marauders down the centuries—that stayed, strong and true, finally revealed, ruins among the landscape, lit by the huge moon. Silence fell, only the plashing of the oars by the boat audible, as the two of them stared, incredulous, at the great thing that was no longer there. Mirren moved closer to Jamie and put her arms around his waist. He leaned his head, very gently, on top of hers as they bobbed along in total silence.

Eventually, Jamie considered it safe for them to find a place to land, and started to pull—but, just as he did so, from nowhere, there was an enormous roaring noise, and a dark shape loomed, seemingly out of nowhere, and a huge light beam shone in their faces, and a broad Scottish accent shouted out:

"YOUSE OKAY? YOUSE OKAY DOWN THERE?"

Chapter Forty-Nine

The power was back on in Buckie, where the RNLI station was. The blessed warmth of the cabin of the boat, the hot tea they were given, the warm red blankets they were all wrapped in, felt heavenly. A medic checked them out, bandaged Theo's poor head and announced them shocked but otherwise very lucky. A passing tanker had called in what they thought was a fire. Mirren kept apologising to them for its being so early on Christmas morning, and a few of the kindly men and women laughed and one or two said their kids would be up already so it didn't really make much difference, but that the rest of them had volunteered that day, and would they like to stay and share their Christmas breakfast?

None of them could sleep and nobody had anywhere to go. Theo, though, had thought to grab his phone, and he plugged it in. There were a zillion messages for them, and he looked at it, grimaced, and was tempted to switch it off again.

There were boiling-hot showers and fresh T-shirts with RNLI written on them and clothes that went in a tumble dryer and came out fluffy and delicious and everything they needed to feel cosy again, even though Mirren occasionally shivered despite herself. She kept seeing the castle, outlined against the starry sky.

They all devoured an enormous amount of porridge with thick cream and a slug of whisky for Christmas; then sausage, haggis, and potato scones, washed down with mug after mug of tea and thick slices of pan bread toast. It was the most delicious meal she had ever tasted. Jamie clearly agreed with her, and Esme didn't even make any remarks about whether anyone was being a vegetarian or not, so that was something. Apart from that, they hardly spoke, each counting up the cost of what had happened, and what was left. As if they even knew.

"I'll need to call Mum," Jamie murmured to Esme.

"She won't care," said Esme, and Mirren squeezed his hand, sad that it was true.

"So it was all for nothing," said Theo eventually. "We didn't find anything."

Jamie glanced up from the table, where he'd been eating a fourth slice of toast.

"Oh my God," he said. "I nearly forgot!"

He reached into the inside pocket of his jacket, hanging on the wall.

"Thank God I didn't put it in the tumble dryer," he said, and he took out the little packet. "Have you seen this before?" he said to Bonnie, who shook her head.

They all gathered round.

"It might be nothing," warned Jamie. "More letters, or directions to something that might not be there anymore."

He unwrapped the envelope, which was padded.

"Hang on," said Theo, feeling in his trouser pocket. "I think I still have . . ."

"You rescued your *gloves*?" said Mirren.

"I'm here in a professional capacity!" said Theo. "Are you?"

And Mirren blushed, even as he grinned at her to let her know he was only joking.

Under the utilitarian bare bulb of the lighthouse common room,

Jamie donned the gloves and unwrapped, carefully, the layers and layers of bubble wrap. Inside, there was a small, crumbling, ancient book. On the wooden cover was the rough outline of a bearded man, in what had clearly once been gold, and some lettering Mirren couldn't make head nor tail of.

None of them touched it; they just looked at it. It was beautiful, the lettering carefully placed and stamped, even though faded to a dull dried blood colour, the cover ancient painted wood. It was clearly terribly, terribly old. The drawn man's face was serious; hooded eyes looked out from down the centuries.

"I don't even want to . . ." Jamie started, obviously loath to open it.

"Don't touch it," said Theo suddenly, his voice stricken, all his playfulness gone.

They all turned to look at him.

"What is it?" said Jamie.

"I don't know for sure," said Theo. "I don't know, but . . ." He pulled out his newly charged phone. "I think . . . It can't be." He did some frantic Googling. "Oh," he said. "Ooohh! No. It can't be."

"*What?*"

"The Protoevangelium." He shook his head. "No. No. I don't believe it."

Mirren looked at the incredibly ancient thing, amazed it could cause such a reaction.

"The proto what?" said Esme.

"The Protoevangelium." He looked at them. "It's a gospel."

"What, like Matthew, Mark, Luke, and John?"

"Yes," breathed Theo. "But not by them. By James."

"*Which* James?" said Esme. "Grandfather?"

"Oh no," said Theo. "I mean James. James, the brother of Jesus." There was silence.

"Jesus had . . . ?"

"It's controversial," said Theo, "to say the least. It's a nativity gospel. The story of Jesus's birth."

They all stared at it.

"From that time?"

"No, no, we don't have . . . This is a printing. This is it printed. It was printed . . . in 1552. The Church suppressed it. Too much Mary in it. There is one—one—extant in the entire world. It's in the Musée National du Moyen Âge in Paris. It's a Greek translation from the original Syrian, from a long, long time ago. Which is—well, people think it's very like what they might have spoken in Galilee. It might be as close to a contemporary account as we have."

They all stared at it.

"It's from *1552*?" said Mirren.

"We don't know," said Theo. "But it's very important that we get it to someone who does."

He swallowed hard. Bonnie patted him.

"I don't think I've ever seen you emotional," said Mirren.

"This is something very, very special," said Theo, in awe, wrapping it up carefully. "Can you look after it?" he said to Jamie.

"God, no," said Jamie. "We've already lost something precious tonight. Mirren, can you hold on to it?"

Mirren looked at Theo.

"You take it," she said softly. "Then you can have your name in the British Museum too."

Chapter Fifty

Roger came bounding up delightedly as they returned; the road had been ploughed to let the fire engines through, and they had successfully secured everything. The hedge was a black ruin, and the smell hung heavy, but the shape was still there. It could grow back.

Jamie made such a fuss of the dog, Mirren couldn't help but laugh. "I thought he was a working dog!"

Roger came up for his rightful cuddle from her too.

"He is," said Jamie. "From now on he's working as a petting animal."

They advanced cautiously towards the ruins, having been warned by the fire brigade not to go anywhere near it or inside. It was a huge mass of rubble and mulch: all that money, all that wealth and power, now just so much muck and dust.

Esme had spirited Theo and the book off to the halt in the Land Rover. Just before they'd left, there had been a roaring noise from the gates, and, charging up, there came a huge black motorbike ridden by someone in a leather jacket. The noise was incredible as it came to a stop that sprayed ice everywhere.

"Ian!" came a yell as Bonnie, normally so staid, careered towards him.

The tall youth pulled off his helmet, revealing a shock of bright red hair, grabbed Bonnie as she ran to him, and gave her a full deep-throated snog in front of everyone. They eventually came up for air and Ian gave them all a cursory glance. "Aw right, aye?" he said nonchalantly, as if he'd just popped by on his way somewhere else. Bonnie put the spare helmet on excitedly, hopped up on the back of the bike, and they'd departed in a roar of smoke and gravel and snow.

"What is it?" said Jamie, seeing Mirren's face.

"I just . . . At one point I thought maybe she kept working here because she was in love with you."

Jamie had thrown back his head and laughed. "Oh my God. No. No, I don't think it was that."

"I don't know," said Mirren, moving closer to him again. "I don't know why you think someone liking you is that funny."

And he'd pulled her to him, very tightly.

AFTERWARDS, BACK AT Joy's cottage, where they were staying, he paced up and down.

"What are you thinking?" she asked. "You need sleep."

"I can't sleep," said Jamie. "I'm too wired."

He looked at the photos on Mrs. Airdrie's old dresser.

"You know," he said, "Bonnie's three months older than me."

Mirren raised her eyebrows. "Uh-huh," she said.

There was a pause while she processed what he was trying to tell her.

"Are you sure you don't want to sleep on it?"

Jamie shook his head.

"She tended him every day. My—*our* grandfather. She kept the house going, kept his room warm, tended him while the rest of us just complained. This is her home. What's left of it."

Mirren smiled. "Are you sure she won't think you're just giving her a pile of old rubble?"

"I'm not so sure about that," said Jamie.

"What do you mean?"

"I told you about the heritage people—they'd liked the back, but not the front?"

"Yes."

"Well, now it's all the back."

"Oh!"

"I really think they could do something with it."

"With the ruins?"

"Uh-huh."

WHEN SHE CAME back the next morning, looking sleepy and happy, Bonnie listened for a long time, nodding seriously. Then she and Jamie made a plan together.

They would use the sale value of the book to pay off the council bill, then generally clean up, then lease the ruins to the heritage people, but it would be hers, and she would run it. They would keep a cottage each, and Esme could have the gardener's lodge, if she wanted it.

"What are you going to do for a real job?" asked Bonnie.

"I don't know," said Jamie. "I've never had to think about it before." He looked at Mirren. "What's being a quantity surveyor like?"

"I can't remember, and I've probably been fired," said Mirren.

"Don't start a podcast," said Bonnie.

"Huh. Okay. Well, I'll think about it."

"That maze needs to be regrown," said Bonnie thoughtfully.

Jamie smiled. "Are you going to hire me as a gardener?"

"Got any better ideas?"

"What are you going to do when he won't kill the snails?" said Mirren.

"Turn him out of his house," said Bonnie. "Kidding!"

Mirren picked up an old photo again. Joyce as a young woman: she was lovely, with the same round cheeks and soft brown hair as Bonnie. "Do you think . . . afterwards . . . ?"

Bonnie shrugged. "I think . . . I don't know. Who knows? I know he loved her all his life. And she loved him, too, once." She gave Jamie a sideways look. "But sometimes, women are tougher."

"You'll get no argument from me," said Jamie.

"But you stayed," said Mirren. "How could you bear it? Weren't you bitter?"

"The old laird—he offered me all what youse had. The schools and university and that. I went to cooking school in Edinburgh, and I got homesick. I didn't like the big city, don't know how you can stand it."

"Hmm," said Mirren.

"And the cost of finding a place to live! And all the apartments are just horrible! I mean, shoeboxes!!"

"Hmm," said Mirren again.

"Why would you do that, when you've got a lovely cottage for free, and you're surrounded by such a beautiful landscape? And I got to be with my family and Ian's got the next farm over, and all my friends are here, so . . ."

Mirren was rather regretting ever starting to feel sorry for Bonnie.

"He was kind, you know," said Bonnie to Jamie. "I know your mum told you all sorts of things and had all sorts of issues with him, and those kind of got passed on to you, but if you were patient and gentle and saw through the crustiness . . . he was just a little . . . different, that's all. There'd be a name for it these days."

Jamie nodded. "I feel sorry I didn't know him properly."

"Better late than never," said Bonnie, and Jamie nodded emphatically. As she got up to go, he stood instinctively.

"I'm sorry if I ever made you feel . . ." he began, and Bonnie shook her head.

"Naw, don't worry. We were always friends, eh? But when I knew and you didn't . . . well."

"And we're cousins!" said Jamie, beaming. "That's kind of cool. You're much nicer than my sister. Don't tell her I said that."

"I might introduce Esme to Ian's biker gang," mused Bonnie. "If we're all going to be family."

"That I want to see!" said Mirren.

"DON'T GO," SAID Jamie the next morning, kissing Mirren's naked body all over, as the sun beamed in, reflecting off the melting snow, and she was reading him a Burns poem from the compendium on the shelf, and he was laughing at her terrible pronunciation.

"I have to," said Mirren. "My mum will literally kill me, and I feel I am currently quite sorted for near-death experiences, on the whole."

"You know," said Jamie, "there's a ton of books left over. In outhouses and stuff."

"So?" She looked at him.

"I'm just saying . . . enough to start a bookshop. You know. If you knew of anyone who liked doing that kind of thing."

"Don't tempt me."

He pulled her back towards him in the warm bed.

"Oh, my darling," he said. "I think that's all I ever want to do."

"Run towards joy," said Mirren sleepily. "Run towards you."

Epilogue

It is spring, and Mirren is back at the cottage. She has let the unfortunate London flat out for an incredible amount of money. She felt so guilty about it that she told them about the bad sound-proofing and the bad water pressure and they said it was still a lot nicer than anything else they'd seen, thanks. She bought, rather reluctantly, a new phone, but fortunately the internet in the cottage was completely nonexistent, so she didn't feel as if it was dragging her back too far. And in January her nice boss had called her into the little office, saying that she was really, really sorry, the office was going to close, but they should be able to offer some redundancy money, and Mirren had done her best to put a very sad face on.

There are all sorts of interesting things sprouting in the kitchen garden on the grounds of the estate. Jamie is working hard on re-establishing the garden's original footprint.

The children who arrive to inspect the ruins very carefully on the permitted school trips up the bumpy track are generally more interested in the secret cave, for obvious reasons, or Bonnie's scones, for equally obvious reasons. But there are often one or two who sidle up quietly and watch as Jamie explains how he is trying a new humane slug-removal system, or admire the pathway full of daffodils he has planted along the outlines of the old house, still visible. The maze is still recovering, but recover it will.

But today there are no visits scheduled, and they have something to do.

Mirren comes down from the cottage, where she has been trying to file even more paperwork and carry on with the leftover books. It has been quite the job, but Jamie is going to build little shelves into the old stable block and that should work. As well as the redundancy and the rent from her flat and the money from the sale of the book, Jamie had also tracked down, astoundingly, an extant insurance policy from 1896, which was honoured by a two-hundred-year-old insurance company in Edinburgh. Unfortunately it covered the entire property for £18,000, but it has still come in extremely handy.

Esme has arrived back, too, fresh from the Australian sun. She is having fun with her share of the windfall, and Mirren sees no harm in that.

The four of them, plus Roger, who is now an indoor dog and in some danger of getting rather fat, walk round the back of the building, towards the ancient chapel.

Today, the sun is shining gently on the sea, and the light is dancing on the waves. Everything grows so quickly up here, and once the snow had gone, snowdrops and early daffodils had appeared everywhere; the place is a riot. Soon, moss will reclaim the last of the stones still visible; nature will take over and it will be as if the great house never existed.

Ian joins them, along with Bonnie's mum—she is so like her daughter but also so like them all, Mirren thinks. She is a lovely woman, still rather taken aback by their change in fortunes. She tells Mirren she has "never seen young Jamie so content," which in turn makes Mirren so happy she thinks she's going to bubble over. Nora and her brothers are arriving for Easter, and she cannot wait to show them everything. But this is for Jamie's family.

Behind the churchyard is the graveyard, and Joy Airdrie is buried there, as are generations of staff, and there is a war memorial to the young men who worked at the big house and never came home from fighting. There is a fancy mausoleum for family members, which rather made Mirren shiver, but Jamie has sorted things, and has (rather bravely, Mirren thought) gone in and retrieved the silver urn that held his grandfather's ashes and scattered them—not all of them, just a few—by, but not on, Mrs. Airdrie's grave. They want to be respectful to both of them. The wind blowing off the sea is cold, as it often is in May, and suddenly Mirren gets that sense she sometimes gets, of being out of time. She feels she can see the house behind her again, and almost as if there were snow on the ground—and an old man, who remembers it buzzing with light and life, and now sees it empty and hollow and hopes he can do better for future generations; who hopes something better will come, and dies knowing he has done his best, in his own way, to save his heir, if he wants to be saved.

"'The saddest tale of woe is told,'" read Jamie, off the sheet Mirren had copied out by hand; he carried it everywhere with him in his wallet. "'When all the songs are past. Then you must find a crown of gold, and hopes will not be dashed.'"

Then they turn back from the chapel and wander back in the sunshine, looking at the ruin, still marvelling at how very, very strange it is that the house simply is not there, and more than that—that in the end it barely matters. They are holding each other, and looking forward to scones—the cast-iron range survived, and has been moved with great difficulty and the help of Ian's biker gang—who, as it turned out, Esme did like, very much—and laughing when Bonnie's mum says actually her mum might have been furious that there was dust around her grave now, having spent a lifetime waging war on the stuff, while the sea continues to crash against the cliff walls, while the grass grows, while their footprints on the ground press on the dew, which then dries, and their footprints disappear.

Author's Note

This book is a fairy story, of sorts, and I really hope you will enjoy getting swept up in it as much as I enjoyed writing it, which was very much indeed.

If, however, you know London, you probably thought, "But special books are kept at the British Library, not the British Museum!" as you were reading the first few chapters of this book.

That is absolutely true. But I love the magic of the British Museum—the British Library casts a spell of its own, but it is redbrick and square and not quite as romantic as when I first arrived in London and found the British Museum Reading Room like something out of a fairy tale itself. Because of this, I felt I had to include it in Mirren's story. In reality, most of the books in the British Museum's Reading Room were rehoused in the newly built British Library building from the late 1990s. Now, the British Museum Reading Room is only open to the public for guided tours.

So I hope you accept this explanation and forgive the artistic license—and happy holidays!

Acknowledgments

Thank you to: Jo Dickinson, Sarah Ballard, Deborah Schneider, Rachel Kahan, Liv Bignold, Kate Burton, Katie Espinall, David Shelley, Jen Wilson, Helena Fouracre, Alainna Hadjigeorgiou, Fiona Brownlee, Kirsty Theocharous and Wendy McLay, Lauraine Harper-King, Katy Archer, Linda McQueen, Rachel Eley, Juliette Winter, Tom Holland, Cesar Castañeda Gámez, Sam Downs at C&W, and Victoria Haslam and Bekah Graham at Amazon.

About the Author

JENNY COLGAN is the *New York Times* bestselling author of numerous novels, including *The Christmas Bookshop, The Bookshop on the Corner, Little Beach Street Bakery*, and *Christmas at the Cupcake Café*. Jenny, her husband, and their three children live in a genuine castle in Scotland.

READ MORE BY
JENNY COLGAN

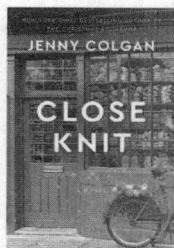

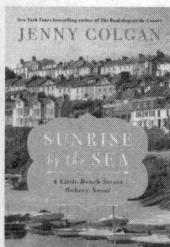

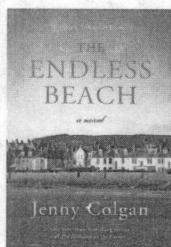

JENNY COLGAN
CLOSE KNIT

Jenny Colgan
The **Summer Skies**

An Island Wedding
JENNY COLGAN

JENNY COLGAN
Sunrise by the Sea
A Little Beach Street Bakery Novel

JENNY COLGAN
The Bookshop on the Shore
A Novel

THE **ENDLESS BEACH**
a novel
Jenny Colgan

JENNY COLGAN
The Cafe by the Sea

The **BOOKSHOP** *on the* **CORNER**
A Novel
JENNY COLGAN

Midnight at the Christmas Bookshop
A Novel
JENNY COLGAN

The Christmas Bookshop
JENNY COLGAN

Christmas at the Cupcake Café
JENNY COLGAN

CHRISTMAS *at the* ISLAND HOTEL
A NOVEL
Jenny Colgan

Christmas at Little Beach Street Bakery
A Novel
JENNY COLGAN

JENNY COLGAN

Jenny Colgan
CHRISTMAS *on the* ISLAND

the Southern region of
Aldinnia

Scarlor's
Landing

Roadside Respite

Linnevel

N

To Oshador and Tibia

www.mvixen.co.uk
Instagram: author.mvixen
Bluesky: mvixen.co.uk
Threads: author.mvixen
TikTok: m..vixen

Map by M. Vixen
Original illustrations by
The Map Effects Fantasy Map Builder

The Druid's Bindings

M. Vixen

To Jade ♡
Never trust
the Devil!
M Vixen

Midnight Tide
PUBLISHING
www.midnighttidepublishing.com

A catalogue record for this book is available from the British Library.

Paperback ISBN 978-1-964655-28-4
Ebook ISBN 978-1-964655-44-4

1st edition 2025

Edited by Meg Dailey
Book Cover by R. Anderson
Map by M. Vixen, original illustrations by The Map Effects Fantasy Map Builder

Excerpt of the Hex Next Door by Lou Wilham

For Ryan
Always and Forever

The Southern region of Aldinnia

Dewhaven

Scarlor's Landing

Roadside Respite

Linnevel

N

To Oshador and Tibia

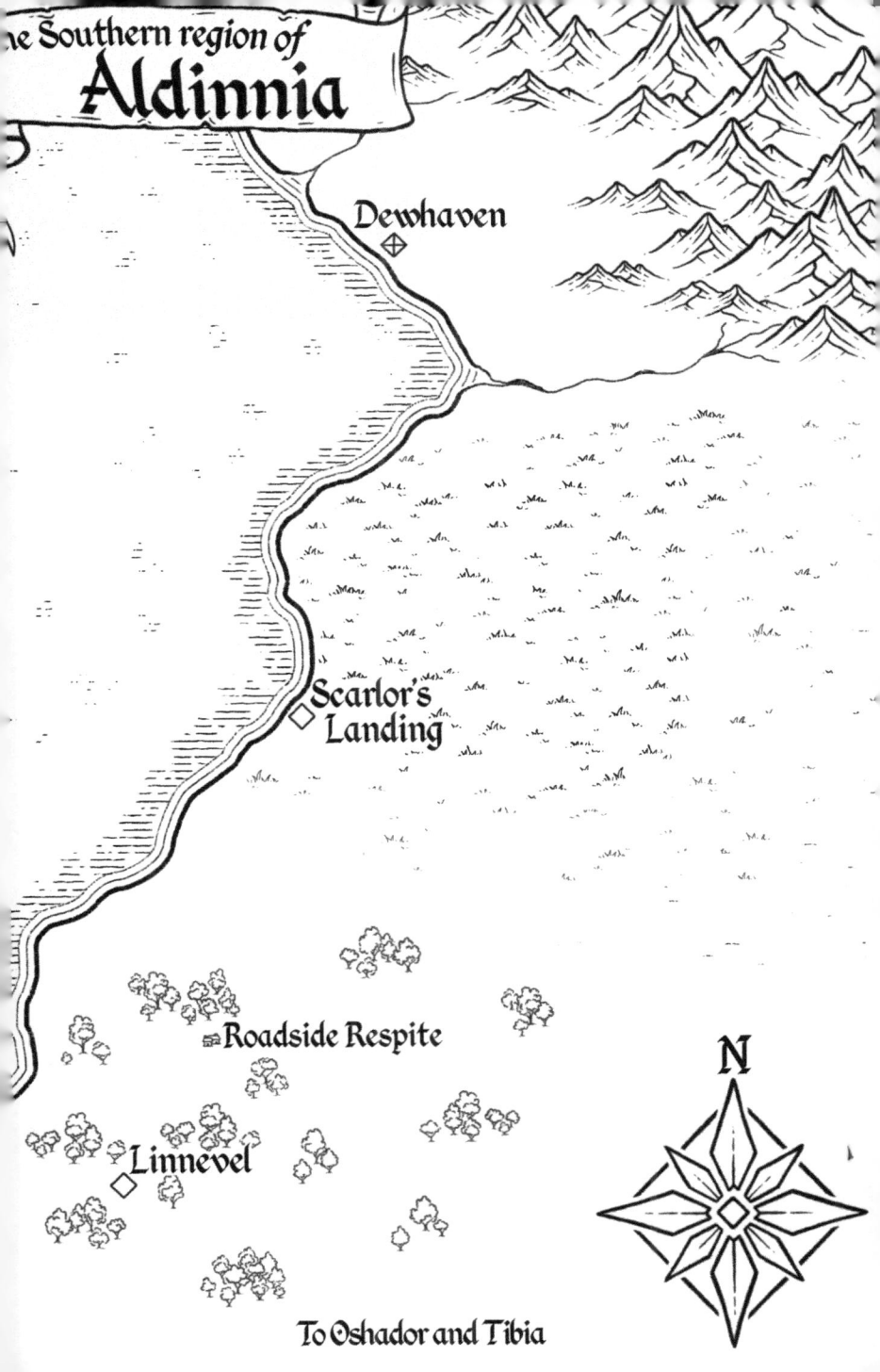

CHAPTER 1

"Really? You're going for the pins? Just rake it."

Ailith rolled her eyes, adjusting the torsion wrench, trying to focus on the pressure of the pins.

"Cut it out, you two. We don't have time. If you don't open that lock in the next ten—"

"Got it." Ailith shot Jay a triumphant look as the lock clicked open. "Raking feels cheap."

Amelie scoffed. "Nothing cheap about knowing when something is too easy to put in the effort."

She took Ailith's place at the door, very gently trying the handle. Ailith watched her work. In their crew of three, Amelie was without a doubt the best thief. She looked unassuming enough; her simple black clothes and the plain protective leather she wore over them meant she could easily blend into any crowd. Her short blonde hair was just long enough to be braided back against her head so she could keep it out of the way as she checked the door. With expertise, she tried the door for tension, resistance, noise—anything that could indicate a trap. Even if Ailith had seen her work many times before, it was never not impressive. When Amelie was done, she nodded at Jay and Ailith.

All clear so far.

Gently, she pushed the door open. Both Jay and Ailith stood at the ready. Jay's eyes flashed purple, ready for any magical trickery on the other side of the door, and Ailith was prepared to intervene should anything go wrong. She didn't really expect there to be any traps protecting the room. The wealthier the owner, the stronger their initial security. Anything behind that was often free game.

It seemed she was correct. Both Jay and Amelie nodded curtly to signal everything was clear.

The trio carefully moved into the chamber. It was small for a wizard's vault, even one that lived in a remote village. Ailith lifted the lantern. Only a few coffers lined the stone walls, and they were small, at that.

Instead, the value was in the display cases sat atop a large rectangular table in the middle of the room.

They were looking for a book. It had been described as having a red velvet cover, with a silvered clasp keeping the book locked. With a quick gesture, Ailith pointed the other two towards the display cases.

"Let's try there first," she signed.

They walked over to the table. The collection was about what she had come to expect from wizards. Many of the display cases held books. Some held wands, and others held more arbitrary artefacts. Ailith spotted a matching silver ring and amulet, an hourglass in which the sand seemed to move of its own accord, and a small simple wooden box.

"Here," Amelie gestured, pointing at one of the cases.

Jay walked over to her, moving his hand in a horizontal cutting motion.

"Trap."

If he had spotted it, it had to be magical. Ailith raised her eyebrows at him in silent query. Jay pointed at the base of the display case. The magical runes there were barely visible, blending almost perfectly with the decorative filigrees. Ailith studied them briefly. They were entirely arcane in nature, not her school of magic. She stepped back so Jay could get to work. Slowly, the young man started pulling at the magical threads of the trap, a faint purple glow illuminating his tan face and dark hair. The sleeves of his navy robe billowed slightly as he worked his magic.

This was the exact reason they never took artefacts outside of what they had been hired to take. Far too often, they were magically protected and not worth the risk. Much better to retrieve only what they were hired to and take the payment in gold. It was safer, a lot easier to carry around, and didn't bring the risk of pawning traceable items.

Ailith and Amelie waited patiently while Jay worked, watching the door, ears perked for any disturbances. They all felt the current of magic before they saw it. Even Amelie, who didn't have a single magical bone in her body, turned around. A bright violet light illuminated the room, slowly forming a solid circle that gradually became bigger.

"Portal!" Jay shouted in alarm. All three of them dove under the table, Amelie covering the lantern as they went. With a soft tearing sound, the violet circle tore in two, revealing the silhouettes of two figures behind it.

Ailith gripped the edge of the table, trying to find the remnants of the original tree in it. It barely responded.

Come on. Listen to me!

With a quiet groan, she forced the wood to expand, the top of the table slowly curving downwards, shielding them from view. It had only come halfway down the table legs when a pair of boots stepped through the portal and Ailith was forced to stop, lest they be discovered. The three of them froze, holding their breath as a second pair of boots stepped into the room.

"It is here," a gravelly voice said above them.

"Careful," a younger voice responded, "it looks warded."

"Can you undo it?"

Silence. One pair of boots, a light brown, slightly dirty pair, remained stationary while the black pair started pacing. Every time they rounded the corner of the table, Ailith held her breath, praying that the shadow gave them enough cover, that the intruder would not look down.

"Done." The black pair of boots rushed over to the other. She heard the sound of something heavy being moved and then the sharp inhalation of breath.

"Careful, don't open it! What are you—?" The younger voice sounded panicked. Something fell to the floor.

A black fabric? No, it was smoke. But it did not behave like smoke at all. It seemed alive as it spread itself across the floor, the edges of it almost like fingers, reaching for something. Behind her, Amelie grabbed her shoulder as the smoke reached them. They dared not move as it coiled around them. In horror, Ailith watched it whip towards her, crawling up her body, tendrils reaching for her face. Her lungs burned with pain as an ice-cold fire spread through her chest. She bit her lip to keep herself from making a noise. Behind her, she heard Jay gasp.

Nervously, she looked up. Neither visitor seemed to have heard. She noticed that the smoke was curling up the body of the owner of the brown boots as well.

The black boots walked towards the portal, then turned.

"Sorry kid."

Ailith closed her eyes at the familiar sound of a sickening thud, followed by the louder noise of a dropping body. She looked up. The eyes of a young elven man looked back at her, panicking as he clasped at the dagger in his chest, too panicked to be surprised by her small troupe under the table.

As the black boots stepped through the portal, the black smoke followed, then the violet light disappeared.

"What the fuck was that?" Jay exclaimed, alarm audible in his voice.

Ailith ignored him and rushed over to the dying man. He was convulsing, coughing up blood. Without hesitation she drew on her healing magic and sent it into his body, closing her eyes. It was bad. The dagger was wedged just above the heart and had severed the arteries there. She could maybe save the man, if she was fast.

As she sent her healing to the damaged areas, told the arteries to reform and reconnect themselves, she noticed something else. Something deeply wrong.

Carefully, she reached out to it. It was all throughout the elf's body. Like a sickness gnawing at him, yet like no sickness she had ever seen before. She couldn't tell exactly what it was attacking. Gently, she prodded it. Almost instantly the disease prodded back, like a hundred gnashing teeth biting into her healing magic. With a cry she withdrew herself, scrambling away from the dying man. It wasn't eating at his body. It was feeding off his magic, feeding off the very arcane essence in his body. It felt awful.

With sorrow in her eyes, she moved back to the man, holding his hand.

"I'm sorry," she whispered as he struggled for breath. But she didn't dare to dive back in.

"Dorian Redwing," he gasped, pointing at where the portal had vanished as he violently coughed up blood. Then he stilled.

Softly, she closed his eyes.

Amelie grabbed her by the arm. "Real sweet of you, but we have to go. Now."

"But what about the job?"

"Fuck the job. I want no part in whatever this was. And this man,"—she gestured at the dead elf—"people will start looking for him. We are thieves, not murderers! I am not going to jail for this!" There was a frantic note to her voice.

Ailith conceded. They didn't have much gold left to fall back on if they didn't do this job. They would just have to make do.

"Let's go then. Quietly."

It felt wrong leaving empty-handed. She looked back over her shoulder at the dead man. Then closed the vault door behind her.

CHAPTER 2

News of what had happened in the vault must not yet have reached the surface, for the way back was blissfully quiet. They walked past the vault door without issue, ignoring the traps that Jay and Amelie had disarmed, stepping gingerly over the few they hadn't. They left behind the gold and less valuable items in the first room and found themselves back in the basement of the wizard's home. The window they had unlocked was still open.

A tension Ailith didn't realise she was feeling immediately dissipated the moment she stepped out into the cobbled street, even as she shivered in the cold night air.

"Please tell me one of you understood what happened in there?" Amelie's quiet voice held a note of manic desperation, her blue eyes darting about frantically.

Ailith shook her head and looked at Jay, who mirrored her movements.

"Let's not panic, though," he offered as Ailith gave him a nudge. "Facts. Let's go over the facts." His voice, too, sounded slightly strangled.

"Someone else broke into the vault," Ailith started as they began walking to the inn they had been staying in the past few nights.

"Two someones," Jay added, "one of whom was a powerful caster. The type of portal they came in via? I've been trying my hands at it for years. And if we presume for a moment that everything was similarly trapped, he disarmed that trap in half the time it would have taken me."

"Do we know what they stole?" Ailith asked. She had been so disturbed by what she found in the elf's body, she had forgotten to look at what might have been taken.

"A box." Amelie finally seemed to have regained some semblance of control. "It was the only missing item."

The simple wooden box?

"Now." Jay's voice shook. "Please tell me if what you saw was different. But I saw a black smoke come down. Only it didn't look like smoke. More like . . ."

"A sentient creature," Ailith finished for him.

"Did it also—eh . . ." Jay hesitated. "Go up your nose?"

"What?" Amelie exclaimed, then looked around to make sure no one had noticed.

But Ailith nodded.

"It felt awful," she whispered, "as if—"

A scream sounded in the distance. They all looked up.

"We need to get back to the inn," Amelie said, her face pale. Quickening their pace, they walked through the waking town. Dark windows lit up around them. People had noticed something was amiss.

As soon as they entered the inn, Ailith realised it had been a mistake to return. A group of the town's guard stood at the bar, all eyes turning to her little group as they entered.

"She does magic!" the innkeep exclaimed, pointing right at her.

Great.

She had conjured a flower for a young girl one day prior. So much for kindness. The guards approached her. Ailith sighed and raised her hands, dropping her pack in the same motion and swiftly pushing her thumb and ring finger together as the bag slid down to let Amelie and Jay know it was fine. She was usually prison bait. Her grey skin made her stand out in a crowd, and she was more experienced in surviving prison life than the other two. There was no point in struggling or pleading innocence; if these people needed a scapegoat, they would try and arrest her one way or another. It was easier to play along and break out again.

The guards escorted her towards the door, one of them walking over to her friends. They would still be questioned. Amelie subtly extended a finger at her. They would try to break her out after one night.

Ailith wasn't too worried. Linnevel was a small enough town that she didn't expect bars to give her too much trouble.

She was led out of the inn with a hand on each arm.

"We caught the caster. Return to your homes."

Whoever was in charge clearly needed to be seen taking action. Ailith sighed as she resigned herself to a cold night with little sleep.

The prison was much like she expected: a long hallway of stone cells with single iron-barred doors. In addition to the door through which they entered, there was one other door leading out at the other end of the hallway, which Ailith guessed led to an interrogation room. Once she had been deposited into a cell, the guards left her without much ceremony. It was too early for everyone, it seemed.

The prison was quiet. There were no other occupants, and the stone walls muffled any outside noise. Ailith shivered. A wooden cot stood in the corner, but no blanket lay on it. Rubbing her arms, she cursed her body. She was almost always cold, her blood circulation not quite what it should have been. Often, she wondered if that was why her skin was so faded, so grey in colour. And it wasn't just her skin that seemed to have been drained of it. Both her hair and eyes lacked colour too. Her green tunic and the browns of the leather armour she wore over it were the only bits of colour on her. But she couldn't complain too much. The same incident that had left her body malfunctioning had also unlocked her affinity for druidic magic. She wouldn't give that up for the world.

Briefly, Ailith contemplated making a small fire in the cell. But with no chimney, she would only be smoking herself out. So she inspected the cell door. It was nothing special. Either these people knew that she was not the culprit they were looking for, or they were not very smart. Sinking down into a cross-legged position, Ailith leaned back against the wall.

What had happened in that vault? What had the smoke been? No matter how hard she tried to focus only on the facts, the events did not make any more sense to her.

Calm down.

She sat up straight, focusing on her breath. They would figure it out.

"What an unfortunate predicament."

Ailith's eyes shot open. A figure was leaning with their back against the bars of her cell. With some alarm, she realised she had not heard them approach.

Her eyes snapped to their boots. Well-tailored leather. She should have heard their footfall. The rest of them seemed equally well dressed. A white shirt tucked into black trousers, partially covered by a purple waistcoat with ornate gold brocade embroidery. Their dark brown hair was tied back at the nape of their neck, cascading just below the shoulder. Who wore a suit to a prison? A nobleman?

Her experience with the nobility had not been great. They usually demanded the nearly impossible but were never willing to pay appropriately. Either that or they tried to double-cross after the deal was done.

This felt different, though. Something felt wrong, made the hair on the back of her neck stand up. Every part of her body screamed at her to move away, to create as much distance between her and this figure as she could.

"Is it?" she finally responded.

Her visitor turned around.

Ailith tensed, drawing in a sharp breath, left hand ready with magic. She had been right to trust her gut. He was definitely not human. His cheekbones were *just* too sharp, his eyes an odd amber colour. His face had an agelessness to it, the look of someone who had lived for centuries, yet he had not a single wrinkle on his face. She glanced at his ears. They appeared human. But he was definitely too handsome, too beautiful, to be mortal.

"Oh, not this cell. I am well aware you could shape the wood of your"—he wrinkled his nose—"*cot* into a set of lockpicks." His quiet voice was low and smooth, and full of confidence. Something about the timbre of it caused goosebumps to crawl over her skin.

The general air of arrogance he exuded told Ailith he was used to being obeyed without question. It immediately irked her. She got up and walked over to the door. Even after straightening herself, she only reached his collarbone. She still had to look up to look him in the eye.

How annoying.

"What do you want?" She was in no mood to play games.

He raised an eyebrow at her, moving his hand to his heart, the wide fabric of his sleeves billowing slightly with the movement.

"So impatient."

Ailith rolled her eyes as he bowed.

"I'm here to propose a potentially mutually beneficial agreement."

A deal? Offered by someone masquerading as human? Fey or fiend?

"I don't deal in firstborns or souls."

Something flashed across his face. Too quick to read, but long enough for her to know she was correct. He offered her a smile that didn't quite reach his eyes.

"How convenient, then, that I'm not here for either. But I can see that you are in no mood to talk business." He bowed again. "To your good health. I'll be there when it changes."

Ailith wasn't quite sure whether his words sounded like a promise or a threat. With that, he turned around and walked away. Audibly so, she noticed, until the hallway went quiet again.

A sense of dread came over Ailith. She turned her attention inwards. It was there. Quietly lurking. So silent, she barely noticed it, but it was there all the same. The same gnawing teeth she had felt in the dying man's body.

"Fuck."

She tried to draw it out like she would draw poison from her body. It did nothing. The teeth gnawed and gnashed at her insides. She sent healing magic its way. A trickle at first. Then a wave. The teeth happily devoured the magic she sent it.

Panic gripped her body.

Ailith screamed. Something was inside her, and she could not get it out. She screamed until she had no voice left to scream with.

She had to get out. Escape. Run.

With shaking hands, she turned to the wooden cot.

Look for the tree inside it.

There was nothing. Not a single trace of life left in the small stone cell. Wildly, she threw out her magic, looking for anything natural nearby

You are never going to get out.

Her breath started to come in short spurts. She grabbed the bars of the door, pulled at the heavy metal. It clanged loudly in the silence of the hallway but didn't give.

That was when the thought hit her. She had never heard the hallway door open again. Her visitor had left as mysteriously as he had arrived. The realisation halted her frantic thoughts somewhat and pulled her out of her panic.

"Calm down. Facts."

She sat down again, breathing deeply. Whatever had ailed the elven man, she had contracted it too. *And he knew.* The alluding to her good health, the offer to help her with a predicament. It could not have been a coincidence. *How?*

She shook her head. It was a worry for later. Her thoughts were running far too wild to do any deducing now. Getting out was her first priority, plans be damned. She was not waiting around in a cell while something unknown ate at her body. She needed to calm down. Return to rational thought. Try to remind herself that she did not need nature to survive.

Inhale. Hold. Exhale.

Focus on the flow of breath.

What could she feel? The cold stone floor under her.

In. Hold. Out.

She could smell the slightly damp stone. The mildew from the wooden cot.

Her heart rate slowed to a more regular pace.

Another deep breath.

The jail was so quiet, her own heartbeat seemed deafening in her ears. But she was calmer.

Panic won't help now.

She laid another hand on the cot, extending her awareness to it once more. The wood still had life in it. Now that she was calm and more focused, she could feel the gentle thrum of its energy. From there, it was easy to shape a splinter of the wood into a set of lockpicks. The cell's lock was easily opened.

Ailith walked over to the entrance and laid her ear against the door. There was noise on the other side, the muffled sound of movement. She didn't want to fight anyone if she didn't have to. These guards weren't guilty of anything.

Quietly, she walked over to the other door. She heard only silence. Ailith tried the handle. She didn't quite have Amelie's touch, but they had worked together long enough that Amelie had taught her more than a few basics. There was no odd pressure, no unnatural resistance. The door swung open without issue. The room behind it was shrouded in darkness, barring a slim sliver of orange light. A single high window.

Ailith looked around. The room may once have been an interrogation room, but the chair that had been used for that had been pushed to the side, the manacles attached to it long since rusted over. Instead, boxes and crates filled the space.

In the dark, she could just make out the silhouette of a wall sconce. Mindful of tripping hazards, she walked over to it and tried to conjure a small flame in her left hand. It took her a few attempts to bring it to life. As a druid, she was supposed to be able to command all elemental magic, but she had never quite reached that level of control. Give her plants or air to command, but when it came to fire magic, she could barely conjure the smallest of flames, and even that often eluded her.

With the room now slightly lit, Ailith started quietly stacking boxes and crates until she could reach the window. It was conveniently at street level, a lantern just outside it casting its dim light into the room.

At a guess, she would just fit through. Another jab at her abilities. If she had been a better druid, she would have been able to change her form, transform her body into that of an animal. She had never mastered that skill either.

No use lamenting it now. Think practically.

The window needed opening, for a start, and she didn't see any hinges. The window frame, however, was wooden. That could be used. On the other side of the glass, she summoned a small bed of thick vines, then examined the wood of the frame. Most of it had been touched by damp. It didn't take much to magically warp it a little.

Once she thought she had created enough space, Ailith braced herself and pushed against the glass pane. With a grunt and a quiet screech, it came loose and fell backwards onto the vines she had summoned. They would crumble into dust before long. No conjured nature was ever permanent.

Swiftly, she hoisted herself up and crawled through the empty frame. She barely fit, ignoring the splinters that wedged themselves into her leather doublet.

The street had remained quiet, despite the little noise she made. Gingerly, she took the glass pane and leaned it back against the frame. It wasn't in properly, but it would look the part for anyone walking by. She just needed it to hold up until she had left town.

CHAPTER 3

The streets were mostly empty again as Ailith rushed back to the inn. Clearly the arrest of one scapegoat had been enough to send people back to bed. She walked as quickly as she could without being too suspicious.

At the inn, she went directly to the stables and saddled three horses, picking the ones that looked fastest and healthiest. A better druid may have been able to speak with the animals, or at least get a sense for their health, but animals had never been her forte. They would have to make do with the ones she picked. In the distance a bird sang its morning song. She had to hurry.

Walking around the building, she looked for the window to their room, then examined the wall below it. The grey brick was far from smooth, but she was not enough of a climber to scale that wall. Again, she drew on her magic, and a wave of exhaustion washed over her. She had done so too many times already today without resting. *Just once more.*

From the windowsill itself, she conjured up a vine, trailing it down and wrapping the end of it around her wrist.

A second bird joined the first, announcing the coming dawn to the world. Ailith gritted her teeth. Almost there.

Planting her feet against the wall, she slowly started pulling herself upwards. By the time she had reached the window, beads of sweat dripped from her forehead. The other two would have set some form of alarm trap around the window. Gently, she knocked on the glass. Amelie's tired face appeared behind it after she had pulled back the rag of a curtain, expression changing from alarmed to concerned as she unhooked a tripwire and opened the window.

"What are you doing here?" she hissed quietly.

"The plan has changed." Ailith sat down on the windowsill. "We're leaving *now.*"

Further into the room Jay opened his mouth to speak, but he must have seen something on her face, for he closed it again and nodded. "Are you okay?"

Ailith shook her head. "No, but it can wait. Horses are ready."

Her team didn't need much time. They always kept their bags packed in case they needed to make a quick escape. Without a word, they followed her back out the window, leaving the town as the first rays of sunlight crested over the horizon.

They took the busiest road out of town, northwards, urging their horses into a quick step. Not only would a busy road mean that any tracks they left would disappear in the crowd, but they were also desperately running out of food, and this road would lead them past the Roadside Respite, where they would be able to resupply.

Ailith doubted anyone would come after them. A small town was like a small world of its own, and outsiders were best forgotten quickly. Whatever had happened during the night would soon be nothing more than a rumour. And with her arrest happening in the dark, Ailith doubted anyone would recognise her on the road.

Only when nothing but trees surrounded them did she slow down to tell Jay and Amelie what had happened. She left nothing out. From the disease in the dead elf to the otherworldly visitor in the prison to the panic when she discovered that she, too, was a carrier. To their credit, neither of them reprimanded her for panicking. Instead, they listened quietly until she had finished her tale.

"I couldn't sleep after everything that happened. And I have a theory." Jay moved his horse next to hers and held out a hand to her. "A theory that I truly hope is wrong. If you don't mind, have a look at my general health."

Ailith took his hand. It was shaking slightly, she noticed.

He's scared.

She knew the answer even before she called on her magic. Jay had a brilliant mind, and his theories were seldom wrong. Knowing what to look for, she found the anomaly immediately. A thousand tiny mouths clung to the magical energy in him, ripping and tearing. Biting back the immediate feeling of panic, she tried to study them without drawing nearer. Although something seemed to be eating at his magic, it didn't seem to immediately consume it. Instead, it seemed to be trying to tear it or change it. She had never felt anything like it, and she didn't understand it either. It scared her. Bile rose in her throat, and she withdrew herself from his body, squeezing his hand.

"I'm sorry."

He tightened his jaw in response. "If I'm correct, Amelie should be clear of it."

Ailith looked over at the other woman. "Do you want me to look for you?"

Amelie nodded. When Ailith took her hand, she found nothing. A bruise where Amelie had bumped her elbow into the door frame. Otherwise, she was in perfect health.

"It's attached to our affinity for magic?" Ailith looked back at Jay, who nodded.

"I realise it is based on very little, but it is the only theory I have for now. What else sets us apart that a magical smoke could be attracted to?"

So if she looked inside her own body . . . She turned her magic inwards, only to immediately withdraw again. It had gotten worse since she checked in the cell, the gnashing teeth doing *something* to her magic. What exactly, she didn't want to think about. The thought alone that her magic could be affected like that was too terrifying to contemplate.

"So what do we do?" Ailith struggled to keep the panic out of her voice. Exhaustion was making it hard to think rationally, and the night's events were rapidly catching up.

Jay nudged his horse a little closer, putting a hand on her arm. "No matter how scary this is, I'm sure we can find a healer who can help us. First, we stay the course. We go to the Roadside Respite. We have enough food left for the few days it will take us to get there, and we can replenish our supplies. Then we travel to the nearest big city and look for help."

Ailith tried to calm her mind, focusing on what Jay proposed. It was a solid plan, and she desperately needed a heading.

The day passed as if it were a fever dream. The excessive use of magic, the panic, and the lack of sleep made her brain so foggy, she could barely stay atop her horse. The banter between Jay and Amelie completely bypassed her. The blossoming trees around her that she usually loved so much left her unaffected.

It was only after a night of cold and restless sleep that Ailith felt slightly more human. The first thing she did upon waking was turn her energy inwards. The gnawing blackness was still there, but she noticed no difference in her body. Whatever this disease or curse was, it seemed to be content to just linger in the background. She prayed it would stay there.

By the time Jay and Amelie woke, she had saddled the horses and concocted the very loose beginnings of a plan.

They would indeed travel to the Roadside Respite. Once there, they would ask around for Dorian Redwing, the name the dying elf had given them, and give chase. They needed answers, and he was the only lead they had. If that trail went cold, they could always travel to Dewhaven. Ailith knew a healer there who would be willing to help them.

With that, her spirits raised a bit. They had a solid plan, this odd disease seemed happy to remain dormant, and the sun was out for once.

It was easy to join Amelie and Jay in their back-and-forth, if only to temporarily forget about the darkness that waited inside her.

CHAPTER 4

The first symptom of the disease showed itself on the third day. Ailith woke up drenched in sweat, the fingers of her left hand cramped and swollen. Her knuckles burned as if they had been pressed with a hot iron.

One look at Jay confirmed that he was suffering the same.

Anxious for what she would find, Ailith let magic run through her body. The disease was there. And it had grown, slowly but surely making itself more present.

How long until she could no longer ignore it? How long before that strange darkness inside her was larger than she was?

She tried not to ponder it too much. Nothing could be done about it immediately. There was no point in panicking herself even further.

"And so, our good health changes," she said wryly over breakfast, eating the last of their rations with trembling hands.

Before they left, she drenched some cloth in water and froze it to try to numb the pain somewhat, offering the same cold compress to Jay.

Their usual banter was notably absent that day, even if Amelie did her best to distract them all with small talk. The reigns burned in Ailith's hand. Every movement seemed to only intensify the fire in her fingers. To deal with pain, she would normally disassociate herself, distance her body and mind, trying to reach a state of near meditation. But that was difficult to do when Amelie was trying so hard to make them feel better.

By the time they reached the inn, both of Ailith's hands were on fire. Yet where she gritted her teeth and bore the pain, Jay had no such success. He had been continuously rubbing his hands the last part of the journey.

"Don't touch it. It will only make you focus on the pain more," she told him repeatedly. But when he snapped back at her a third time that he wasn't touching it, she let it rest.

The Roadside Respite was a welcome sight. The promise of good fresh food alone quickened Ailith's step. But the moment they entered, Ailith knew something was off. A shiver ran down her back.

They were being watched.

Her eyes scanned the room. The big fireplace in the centre cast dancing shadows across the walls and patrons. It was busy; the Roadside Respite usually was. Lying next to one of the busiest trade roads, it catered to a steady stream of customers all desperate for fresh food and a soft bed. Most patrons looked like the sort Ailith expected: small groups of merchants, a family here and there, all sat around a collection of mismatched tables. But she spotted him immediately, even though he was sitting at one of the darker tables in the corner. The man from the prison.

"On our eleven, danger," Ailith muttered, making sure to not let her eyes linger. Her group had worked together long enough that neither Amelie nor Jay looked over immediately as they walked to the bar, only glancing around as if looking for an empty table.

"Who is he?" Jay asked.

"The man from the prison," Ailith responded under her breath before ordering a room, food, and drinks.

Amelie sucked in a breath. "Do we engage?"

"What if he isn't here for us?" Jay butted in. They all exchanged a sceptical look, and Jay shrugged. "A man can hope."

Ailith sighed. "I'll get it. Jay, watch my back. Amelie, go after the mark. See if you can learn anything."

"Be careful." Amelie touched her wrist briefly. "Both fey and fiend are dangerous, and you are not as sharp as you usually are. No gambling."

Ailith winked back. "Only if I know I can win." She took her tankard and walked over to the stranger.

He was wearing the same suit as last time, she noted. And like last time, the hair on the back of her neck stood up more the closer she got to him.

Only when she sat down did he acknowledge her presence by looking at her. Something about his amber eyes made her heart skip a beat. And not just because they were beautiful. He seemed to look right through her, as if he could see her very soul.

Was he a mind reader? In her head, she screamed loudly. No reaction.

What is he?

Despite her entire body telling her to run, she didn't break eye contact as she sat down. Instead, she cocked a challenging eyebrow, sipping from her tankard.

Let him make the opening move.

"Well, well. Already coming to me voluntarily? I expected a bit more resilience from you." He spoke quietly despite the noise of the taproom, but his voice still held that same air of confidence. As did the smile he flashed her. All arrogance and no warmth.

Ailith offered him a cold smile in return. "I usually prefer to smother potential threats before they get close, but this scenario seemed to call for a different approach."

He spread his arms. "Potential threat? You wound me. My intentions here are nothing if not benevolent." He leaned forwards. "I told you I would be there when your good health changed, didn't I? And I never lie. *That* I can promise you."

Only when he leaned back again did Ailith realise she had been digging her nails into her palms. Slowly, she let go; it had only made the burning in her fingers worse. Why was this man so intimidating? *Because he is not a man,* she reminded herself. *Focus. Every game has rules. You just need to determine the rules of this game.*

With a deep breath, she forced herself to appear more relaxed.

"Which leaves me the obvious question. What are your benevolent intentions?"

She held up a hand as he was about to respond, earning herself an annoyed glare.

He's used to deciding when to speak.

"And although my curiosity has been piqued, I would much rather know exactly who I'm talking to." Her turn to lean forwards, both eyebrows raised.

"Simply Arkhael will do."

Was that amusement in his eyes? He, too, leaned in closer, and for the briefest moment, she thought she saw the fire reflected in his eyes, his teeth sharp as he smiled at her.

Just as quickly, it was gone again.

Fiend. Her heart beat in her throat, but Ailith maintained her position. *Definitely fiend.*

Devil or demon? Ailith had encountered only a few demons. They were unpredictable, wild, and dangerous. Threats best killed swiftly. Devils were even rarer, more of a subject of folklore. And if those stories were to be believed, they were a lot more cunning. Even in the secluded grove where she had grown up, there were tales of promises that could not be broken. Binding contracts and deals that always ended in stolen souls.

She looked at him with this in mind.

Not a single wrinkle on his clothes, not a hair out of place. She decided to take the gamble.

"So, what are your benevolent intentions, *devil*?"

She had struck home. The mask dropped. Only briefly, but long enough for her to see the annoyance.

Confidence rushed through her. This man—devil—might be terrifying, the power and arrogance that radiated off him making it clear he was not to be taken lightly, but this game of words and masks, that was one Ailith could play.

She leaned back, taking another sip from her tankard.

"How are your hands, *druid*?" He mimicked the same tone she had just used. "Not yet sore enough that you're tearing the skin off your flesh, I see."

"Is that it? The cure for our souls? Neither my friend nor I are that stupid."

Arkhael laughed. "My dear, you have contracted a sickness so serious, even I cannot cure it. And after the next full moon, there will be nothing left of you to cure." Ailith's blood went cold. He seemed dead serious in his taunting. "But I do know what the cure is, what the symptoms are, and how to suppress those."

He extended a hand.

She eyed it as if he had offered her a poison dagger blade-first. Only benevolent intentions, he had said. If he was indeed a devil, she believed he couldn't go back on his own word.

Carefully, she put her hand in his, magic tingling in her fingertips. If he tried something, she was ready.

His hand was hot to the touch. If she hadn't already known he wasn't human, she would have been concerned for his well-being. He closed his fingers over hers, bent forwards, and brushed his lips against her knuckles.

"It won't be long until the second symptom shows itself. We can discuss less altruistic intentions then."

And with that, he was gone, vanishing into thin air in front of her. Leaving her utterly confused and with her fingers still burning. She clasped them in her other hand until the feeling subsided, then looked at them. The cramping was gone. She flexed her hand. Closed her fingers. No pain.

So he couldn't cure it, but he could suppress the symptoms? She rubbed her hand where his lips had brushed her skin. It was still tingling slightly.

Suave arrogant bastard.

Standing up to rejoin her companions, Ailith realised her legs were shaking slightly.

Fucking terrifying suave arrogant bastard.

"All good?" Jay's voice was full of concern as she joined them at their table. Ailith shook her head.

"Fiend. Not fey. Devil, to be precise. And he's after something."

She shared the details of the conversation with them.

Jay paled. "Until the next full moon gives us precious little time."

Ailith nodded, ignoring the terror that gripped her very soul. Less than twenty days. It wasn't a lot of time at all. With a deep breath, she grabbed the table. Devil be damned. They had a plan, a solid plan. It was going to be fine.

Amelie leaned back. "Any idea what he wants?"

"Not really."

The three of them fell silent.

"Let's go over what we *do* know first," Jay offered, always the pragmatic.

Ailith held up a finger. "He's been watching us. These two meetings, he was prepared for them, and he seems to know the details about what ails us. So one, he wants something from us." She raised another finger. "And two, he's powerful enough to suppress the symptoms, even if he can't cure this disease. And he made sure we would be aware of this. This entire meeting seemed like a power play."

Amelie nodded along. "He's trying to gain at least some modicum of trust, making sure we know what he's capable of so that, when he plays his cards, we'll play the game with him." She looked at Ailith. "Do I sound like you yet?"

They all laughed, despite everything.

"We can play along for now. If there is indeed something he wants from us, that gives us leverage, and he clearly has information that could help us. So we try and learn what this leverage is. Just . . ." Jay gave both Amelie and Ailith a stern look. "Watch your words. Don't accidentally agree to something."

Amelie scoffed.

Ailith looked offended. "I never make accidental deals."

"No, but you like gambling too much." He raised an eyebrow as she was about to protest. "This is not some nobleman, Ailith. Deals with a devil are irrevocable. Any agreement made with them, however accidental, is binding. And the stakes are often souls, not just a few coins."

Ailith rolled her eyes but conceded. Jay was right.

"What do you know of devils?" she asked him. Out of the three of them, he was the only one who had received a formal education.

"Enough to know that their power isn't something to be scoffed at. Not enough to feel comfortable dealing with one," Jay grumbled, but then he sat up a bit straighter. "I have only little knowledge on fiends in general. From a wizard's perspective, neither demon nor devil is particularly interesting as their magics are inborn rather than learned. Even so, we had a few classes on the infernal."

Ailith listened attentively. It wasn't often that Jay was willing to talk about the schooling he had once received.

"From what I can recall, devils are proud creatures. Their lives in the Hells follow a strict hierarchy and rule system. Some of those rules are magically binding. Don't ask me how it works, I don't know," he added as Ailith opened her mouth. "But it is because of this that devils can be dealt with, whereas demons can never be trusted. A devil cannot lie, cannot go back on their word, and a contract made with them is binding. Again, magically so. That is why they are master wordsmiths. Even before I learned this, I was told tales of people bargaining away their souls to devils because of their trickery with words. Always be specific when talking to them." The last was aimed solely at Ailith.

Ailith smiled at him. "Don't worry, I wasn't planning on making these chats a regular occurrence."

With that, the matter was settled.

"Anything from you?" She turned to Amelie.

"The regular inn gossip. Supposed merrow attacks further north. Talk of a war brewing in the southeast. But we're at least on one trail. A man by the name of Dorian Redwing travelled through here. Without asking too much, I got the impression he must be nobility or otherwise in high standing. He's travelling northwards, which is conveniently in the same direction as Dewhaven." Her shoulders sagged a bit. "But it sounds like he has a good two days on us."

So no way to catch up. Even if they crippled their horses, they wouldn't be able to close that distance. How had he gotten so far ahead?

"At least we can hold reigns again without pain," Ailith tried.

"About that . . ." Jay raised his hands. His fingers were still red. "I had hoped that maybe it would take some time, but it looks like your new friend only cured your symptoms." He smiled wryly, and Ailith did not begrudge him the note of envy in his voice.

If there was one thing Ailith loved about paid accommodation, it was the baths. As someone who was often cold, there were few things she liked better than the hug of hot water around her body.

She sighed and pulled her knees up in the small tub of the shared bathroom. What an absolute mess they had found themselves in. A magical disease and a devil, all because they had been in the wrong place at the wrong time. She looked at her hand and shivered slightly at the memory of his lips on her fingers.

"You okay?"

She jumped at the sudden noise and looked up with a scowl. Amelie walked over to the tub next to hers, towel around her waist, giving her a very pointed look.

"Where were your thoughts? Either you have finally found yourself a bath that runs hot enough, or you are blushing." She lit the fire under her bath and sat down on the edge while she waited for it to heat up.

"I was not blushing."

"Of course not. And neither did you speak to an incredibly attractive man earlier today. I noticed how you couldn't take your eyes off him. Am I wrong?" She wiggled her eyebrows at Ailith, who huffed in response.

"Not man, devil. Very different. And weren't you supposed to be gathering information?"

Amelie let herself glide into the water and put her hands on the edge of the tub, resting her chin atop them.

"Listen, I don't judge your fantasies. I'm sure there's something to be said for a forked tongue. It's been a while for all of us." The woman looked around the empty bathroom. "I mean, if you are really desperate, I could share a tub with you."

"Amelie!" Ailith splashed some water into her friend's face. "Of course I didn't take my eyes off of him, he's a *devil*." She rolled her eyes when Amelie only raised her eyebrows further. "*Fine*. Yes, he is good looking. And yes, you are right, we all need to visit a brothel sooner rather than later. But now is hardly the time! And I most certainly was not thinking about his tongue, forked or otherwise!"

Amelie giggled. "Have we finally found your type, then? High cheekbones, well dressed, and dangerous?"

Ailith scoffed. "You're drunk." But she smiled despite herself.

"Only a little." Amelie turned her back on Ailith, sinking further into the water.

For all her brazen comments, Ailith appreciated the woman. Leave it up to Amelie to make people smile even in the worst of times. Briefly, she considered taking her up on the offer. It wouldn't be the first time they had found pleasure in each other's bodies. She rubbed her hand. It would be unfair to the other woman to do anything with her while thinking of someone else. *And you really shouldn't be doing so.* She kicked herself mentally. How did one kiss on the hand get her so flustered?

"You know," Amelie's voice broke the silence again.

"Hmm?"

"I think Jay was jealous."

Ailith sat up. "I know. I genuinely felt so guilty when I realised the devil had cured my hands but not his."

That earned her another eye roll. "That's not what I meant, you absolute oblivious beansprout." Ailith raised her eyebrows at the choice of insult but let it lie. Amelie's words were becoming more slurred. There would be no point in arguing with her at this stage.

She stepped out of the hot water, goosebumps immediately covering her body, and wrapped a towel around herself.

"I'm off to bed. Try not to drown in a tub."

Amelie gave her a wink. "Don't have too many sex dreams while we're sharing a room."

Ailith only shook her head. *Incorrigible.*

CHAPTER 5

The next two days were gruelling. Not only did they push their horses in an attempt to close at least some of the distance, but Jay was struggling. In the mornings and evenings, Ailith did everything she could to numb the pain with what was available to her. She made teas and tinctures. She froze water and wrapped it in bandages to make a cold compress. She tried to block the pain magically. All to no avail.

What little relief she could bring during these moments was immediately undone on the road. The wizard's fingers were raw and cramped at the end of every day. To his credit, he didn't complain. Jay bore it all with gritted teeth, knowing full well that they couldn't afford to slow down. But his usually witty responses had become short and snippy, to the point that even Amelie stopped trying to take his mind off the pain.

So they travelled in tense silence, only stopping long enough to keep the horses from going lame and to sleep. Amelie and Ailith took a little time to either hunt or gather every evening, adding some fresh food to the rations they had bought at the inn. Ailith was also fairly certain that Amelie had swiped a bottle of wine, but the mood for a drink never struck.

Even the hours of rest brought no respite. Guilt gnawed at Ailith. She was much better at bearing pain. Every jerk of the saddle, every grimace Jay made, only increased her guilt. And when she kept watch in the quiet hours of the night, she couldn't help but regret that she was the one who had spoken to the devil, not Jay.

You're better at negotiating, she told herself over and over. There was a reason she usually did the dealing, but it didn't make her feel any better.

It didn't help that she could still feel the devil's lips on her fingers. At first, she had tried to tell herself that it must have been whatever magic he had used to cure her hands, but she couldn't keep that pretence up for long. She knew her own body too well for that.

It was the adrenaline rush she had gotten when that facade had dropped, however briefly. Ailith wanted to be angry at him. Demand that he help Jay as he had helped her.

But she was much more ashamed of the part of her that wanted to sit at that table again. To play that game of words. To see if she could crack those defences one more time.

You're exhausted, and he's a devil. Of course you're fascinated. It's part of their nature.

No matter how often she repeated it, it did not diminish the burning shame she felt. Maybe she truly did have a gambling addiction.

The second symptom hit them as unexpectedly as the first had. One moment, they were riding in tense silence; the next, Jay gasped and fell off his horse. They were with him immediately, Ailith putting a hand on his forehead and closing her eyes. Bruises from falling. That alien gnawing darkness. Nothing unexpected. She trickled some mild healing into the bruises regardless. The man was in enough pain already; he didn't need more.

"Anything?" Amelie asked as Ailith opened her eyes. She shook her head. Jay lay gasping under their hands. As soon as it had started, it was over. His breathing steadied, and he sat up shakily.

"Fuck," he said, then proceeded to retch up the remnants of his lunch.

Amelie got up. "I'll find us a spot for the night."

Ailith didn't argue. It would cost them an hour, but she preferred that over risking Jay's life. Gently, she rubbed his back, trying to relax his body with both her physical and magical touch. Otherwise, she remained quiet, knowing Jay would speak when ready.

By the time he calmed down, Amelie had returned. "There's a clearing just off the path."

They made their way over to set up camp. Amelie exchanged a glance with Ailith. They wouldn't hunt or forage tonight. Instead, they ate their dinner in tense silence. Jay was the one who finally broke it.

"Leave me."

Ailith nearly dropped the stale bread she had been chewing. He had been quiet and withdrawn after his blackout. To hear him start a conversation with something so incredibly stupid was the last thing she expected from him. "What?"

"Leave me. I'll follow your trail. But right now, I am only slowing you down."

"You can't mean that." Even in the warm light of the fire, Amelie's face had gone slightly pale.

"I do." He rubbed his swollen fingers. "I'm a liability. Unless you have any more otherworldly miracle cures." The faintest hint of irritation laced his tone, and he narrowed his eyes at Ailith. But before she could respond, he continued, "I'll follow your trail. Catch up with you when I can."

"Out of the question. You're part of the team." Ailith's tone was firm. "We can tie you to the horse if we need to. But we need your mind if we are going to figure out how to solve this. Plus." Her voice faltered. "The devil healed my fingers, but he didn't cure me. It's only a matter of time before I fall off my horse too."

Amelie put a hand on Jay's arm. "We are stronger together."

The wizard opened his mouth to speak, then closed it again.

Amelie smiled at him, squeezing his arm. "I'll take first watch."

Ailith felt like she had barely slept when Amelie woke her.

"Anything?" she mouthed, nodding in Jay's direction. Amelie shook her head.

No changes. That was good, at least.

Quietly, Ailith sat up, her back to the remnants of the fire. One eye on Jay, the other on the forest. Its health was comforting. The trees around her had strong roots and thick bark. It made her feel less fragile, less out of control while a mysterious disease ran through her veins. How long until she, too, blacked out? The anticipation was nerve-wracking.

Ailith reached out. With her next heartbeat, she and the forest were one. She was the roots digging down for water, keeping the soil together. She was the new growth that had sprouted at the edge of the clearing and had only seen the sun twice. Regardless of her turmoil, the forest was stable. At peace.

Ailith had heard of druids who had linked themselves with a forest and never woken again. It was easy to see why. She had always felt nature's pull especially strong. Where most druids were able to link themselves with all the elements, she had never felt the same affinity. Never understood what they meant when they spoke of "losing themselves to the fire" or "being one with the wind." Even if her command of air magic was strong, it had never held her in its stormy embrace. It was the greenery around her that drew her in. And maybe it was because she was unable to connect with the life in the other elements that she clung to the growing parts of nature with something akin to desperation. It had always been her comfort in even the loneliest hours, her shield against the world. The one reliable constant. With something so very foreign in her own body, it was tempting to remain a part of the strong trees. If it hadn't been for the soft breathing of her friends nearby, maybe she would have.

Slowly, she drew back into herself, shivering slightly at the cold chill of night and taking a deep breath. They could do this.

A shrill ringing pierced her ears. Followed by pain. Her vision blurred. She couldn't tell if it was her or the world that was spinning. The ground met her and flung her around. Through her blurred vision, she watched the sky come down as she herself fell upwards. She wanted to scream. To warn the others. But her body seemed out of reach no matter how hard she tried. And she was dizzy. So dizzy. Her head pounded with it.

Roots.

Ailith blinked.

The world was below her again. The sky above her. Where it should have been. As suddenly as the episode had come on, it was gone again.

She was on the ground, panting. Her cheek was pressed to the cold forest floor, its beating, thriving heart an anchor she desperately clung to. As she willed her breath to slow, she became aware of her stomach protesting the unnatural movements of the world.

Gently, she calmed it down, focusing inwards. Her body was fine. Upset as if she had just been jostled about, but fine otherwise. She shivered, suddenly aware of the sweat on her skin and how cold the soil was below her.

Planting her hands firmly on the ground, she opened her eyes again.

From the corner of her eye, she could just see a pair of very finely made boots.

Now, of all times.

Of course. It was no coincidence.

With a groan, she pushed herself off the ground. He was leaning against a tree. Arms crossed. The hint of a smile on his lips.

Ailith narrowed her eyes. He was watching her struggle and had the gall to smile. *Devil,* she reminded herself. Not known for their kindness. But she was not in the mood for his games.

"Do you want me to get back on my knees for your entertainment, or are you here to talk?"

His eyebrows shot up in surprise, and briefly that smile curled into something . . . else.

It was long enough to set Ailith's pulse racing, earlier annoyance gone.

But then that perfectly sculpted mask took its place again.

"I thought we might converse. And maybe in a more . . ." Arkhael glanced around the camp. "Appropriate setting."

That fucking honeyed voice. She shivered.

"I'm on watch duty. Afraid I can't just leave on a whim."

"Hmm." Arkhael raised his hand and made a circular gesture. Despite herself, Ailith watched curiously. She had not seen this style of casting or this type of magic before. As Jay had mentioned, it seemed like more of an inborn skill than a studied ability, but nothing like her own.

Flames sprang up out of the forest ground, creating a perfect circle around the small campsite, before dying back down. Rather than the expected scorch mark, glowing red runes remained in their place.

"They are protected." He turned back to Ailith and snapped a finger. The air next to him started to shimmer before igniting into a small circle of flames, slowly expanding until a person could easily step through it. A portal. A very fiery portal. Through the shimmer, the faint outline of a room was visible. She could just barely make out a large table in front of a fireplace.

Bowing slightly, Arkhael gestured at the portal. "Shall we?"

It was an invitation only in form. His smooth, quiet voice was full of confidence and command.

What if Jay had another fit? Would this circle of runes protect against magic? Against arrows?

But she voiced none of her concerns. Instead, Ailith nodded. There was not truly a choice. Her group needed his knowledge. She stepped through.

It was warm. Blessedly so, after the cold night air. That was the first thing Ailith noticed.

The room she found herself in took her breath away. It was a large circular chamber with walls that looked to be hewn out of a dark stone. An ornate dark-wooden table stood as the centrepiece. The plates, the cutlery, the goblets—all were either silver or silvered. The mantle above the fireplace held two golden candelabras. Several lacquered cabinets stood against the walls, each with some form of display piece. She saw a collection of crystal decanters holding liquids in one. Another displayed what looked like a horned skull encrusted with gems. Yet another held a large shining purple rock. Almost everything in the room that could be lifted would fetch her a very decent price.

Above the mantle hung a large painting. It was meant to be a centrepiece, an eye catcher, Ailith realised with some amusement. Clearly she was not the correct audience. Only after she had appreciated the gilded frame did she take in the actual painting.

But she could recognise quality, even if art was something she didn't deal in. The painting showed a figure flying against a darkened sky. Below him, a city burned. Whoever the artist was had created a masterpiece. The flames almost seemed alive on the canvas.

Before she could have a closer look at it, Arkhael pulled back a chair for her.

"Please, have a seat."

Briefly the sound of moving flames increased as the portal behind Ailith shrank, then disappeared.

No unnecessary risks, she reminded herself, or at least not until after she got some relief for Jay.

As if being here was not the epitome of unnecessary risks.

She sat down, watching Arkhael closely. Her magic was brimming just below the surface, ready should she need it. Walking over to one of the cabinets, Arkhael retrieved one of the crystal decanters and poured an amber liquid into two glasses on the table.

He sat across from her with a smile. "Welcome, druid, to my home." He raised the glass at her, looking very pleased with himself.

Without taking her eyes off him, Ailith picked up her glass and sniffed the contents.

Whatever it was, it was strong. The smell of it alone made her eyes water. Any poison in it could easily have been masked. Carefully, she took a small sip, rolling the liquid over her tongue. If the liquid contained poison, her body could neutralise it, but it would take time and magic. That was a risk she didn't want to take. Not here. Not with this devil.

The flavours were rich and warm. Unfamiliar, but she tasted nothing that didn't belong, and her magic detected no immediate threat to her health.

The liquid burned on the way down, making her eyes water. Arkhael put his own glass down, smile still on his lips.

"You can relax. I would hardly poison you now."

Ailith narrowed her eyes. "What do you want, *devil*?"

He flashed her a toothy grin. "I believe you offered yourself on your knees?"

"A one-time offer only."

"Pity." He took another swig from his glass. "But not what I invited you for." He leaned forwards. "How is your head?"

"About as good as my hands were last time."

"And how are those now?"

"Fishing for gratitude?"

"Merely reminding you."

"You invited me into your home to fix my headache?"

"Do you want me to?"

Danger.

Ailith bit back her response just in time. Her face mere inches from Arkhael's.

When had she moved forwards? She realised her breathing had quickened as well. She had gotten too caught up in their back-and-forth.

Relaxing her shoulders she leaned back, slowing her breath and taking another sip to steady her shaking hands.

He knew. There was no change to his expression, but his eyes glittered with satisfaction. Carefully, she put her glass back down, ignoring her watering eyes and burning throat. "You never named your price."

He nodded. "Good. It wouldn't do for you to give in too easily." He rose from his chair. "The cure lies with that beautifully unassuming wooden box you saw in that sad excuse for a vault. I know its exact whereabouts and, more importantly, where it will be before your time runs out."

Ailith glared at him, eyes full of suspicion. "You don't seem like the type to volunteer information."

"I most certainly am not. All information comes at a price." Arkhael walked over to her, putting one hand on the table, the other on the back of her chair. It meant Ailith had no choice but to look up at him.

How had he gotten the upper hand so quickly?

"I am showing you how serious my offer is." He leaned closer as he quietly added, "But make no mistake. It is also the only offer, your only chance, to get rid of this disease before it consumes you alive. Before your magic burns you up from the inside, taking with it anyone you care about."

The intensity in his voice stunned her into silence. His amber eyes seemed to reflect the flames. No, they *were* aflame.

Ailith gasped audibly. She couldn't help herself. The devil had finally dropped the illusion of humanity. The hair, the suit, the arrogant facial expression, they were the same. But the hand on the table now ended in long, sharp claws. His face was even less human, somehow even more unnaturally beautiful. His cheekbones were slightly too high, his teeth pointed, his skin no longer tanned but dark red. Atop his head, emerging from his brown tied-back hair, was a large set of horns that curled back over his head. And behind him, Ailith could make out a set of large, dark, leathery wings.

Yet somehow no less enthralling.

"So, *druid*, will you listen to your only chance of survival?"

Ailith swallowed, her throat suddenly dry. What had she gotten herself into?

It doesn't matter, she told herself, *stay calm.* These were the cards dealt. Call or fold. And she never folded. Digging her nails into her palms, she took a deep breath.

He's intimidating. He knows he is intimidating. Don't let it get to you.

She stood up, forcing Arkhael to take a step back lest they bump heads, and straightened herself.

Fuck, is he even taller like this?

She barely reached his chest.

"I'm willing to listen, devil, but nothing more."

For a moment, they just stared at each other. A quiet challenge for either to avert their gaze. Neither did, even if Ailith felt as if her heart might leave her chest.

Arkhael's lips curled into a sneer. "False courage won't save you. But very well. The box is being brought to a strongly secured location. In said location, another item is also being held." He snapped his fingers. Above his hand appeared a floating piece of rolled up parchment. "To save your life, you will sign a contract agreeing to retrieve this item and deliver it to me. In exchange, I will give you the location of the box and tell you how to use it to cure yourself."

An infernal contract. He wanted her to sign an *infernal contract*?!

Ailith had no witty remark.

As if reading her mind, he added, "I don't even require your soul."

She fell back down into the chair, rubbing her temples. It was exactly as she had suspected in that small prison. Some arrogant bastard offering a job. A job that could save their lives.

Her mind raced. Jay would tell her to approach it like any other job. To look at the facts.

What was certain? The devil needed them. Meaning he couldn't get the mystery item himself. How? Seeing him in this form left her no doubt that he could raze entire villages to the ground. What would stop him?

She lost her trail of thought. It was hard to focus with said devil looming over her. If only she had more time to think.

And why not?

"I don't work alone." She looked back up. "If you want to employ me, then you employ the team with me. Especially if this is a high security . . . vault?" Arkhael narrowed his eyes at her, his face betraying nothing. Ailith shrugged. "And we won't function if two of us are constantly falling over."

"Are you haggling with me?"

"Do you want me to bring your proposal to my team, or what?"

Please be as desperate as I think you are. Why else would you bring me here?

Arkhael crossed his arms, the parchment disappearing as if it was never there.

"Don't try your luck."

Ailith rose up again and walked up to him until they were almost touching. She might not be as intimidating, but she could at least stand up to him.

"Get rid of this symptom for both me and Jay. Cure his hands like you did mine, and I will bring your offer to the team. We'll discuss it like we would any job."

Arkhael uncrossed his arms. "You treat this as if you have a choice." His voice was low, almost a whisper. "But you *will* come back to me. And the longer you wait, the deeper in the dust you will be before you come crawling back on your knees, begging for my help."

Ailith snorted. "I will never beg." But as she said it, a shiver ran down her spine at the way he looked at her. She chose to ignore it.

The shiver became more violent.

No, not now.

The room spun as pain lashed through her head. No matter how hard she tried to hold on, to focus, to block the dagger that cut into her skull, the pain became unbearable until the room, the fire, the devil all became one blur.

She screamed noiselessly as she was whirled through darkness.

There were no roots here to ground her. Instead, she clawed her way back to consciousness through the thick molasses of her mind. She told her stomach to settle before it had a chance to lunge. This was neither the place nor time.

Her magic found no bruises. She hadn't fallen. That gave her pause.

Was she leaning against something? Slowly, she opened her eyes. Dizziness still danced at the edge of her vision. She tried to force it away. Her forehead was resting against something warm, gold reflecting the flames of the fireplace.

Realisation started to settle in as the surface she was leaning against moved. Something firm loosened its hold on her back.

Fuck.

She unclenched her hands, let go of the fabric that she was holding, and shakily lifted her head from the devil's chest, the heat of his body palpable even through his clothing. She refused to look up. Refused to meet his gaze. His arm was still around her, she realised, holding her upright. Tentatively, she took a step back, and immediately he loosened his grip on her. It was a mistake.

With his support gone, she swayed on her feet, not having realised how unsteady her legs were. Instinctively, she reached out to stabilise herself. As her hands clutched the fabric of his shirt, his arm came back to catch her.

Ailith closed her eyes, trying to steady her breath, to stop the trembling of her body. To no avail. She was an outsider looking down on herself with no way to reach in.

Fuck. Fuck. "Fuck." The whispered word escaped her, and she immediately cringed at the display of weakness.

Ever so slowly, she tried to open her fists. Palms flat against his chest. Moving with the rise and fall of his breath.

In. Hold. Out.

Ground.

Flow.

Listen.

She could hear the sound of flames crackling nearby. The devil's deep breath above her.

In. Hold. Out.

Ground.

Flow.

Inhale.

Warm air filled her lungs. With it came the scent of alcohol, as well as something like dark chocolate, and an undertone of sulphur.

Gently out.

Feel.

She felt the devil's firm form under the soft fabric. The arm around her loosened its grip, no longer carrying her full weight as she regained some semblance of control.

See.

She opened her eyes and looked up. Fiery eyes met hers. No smile, no cocked eyebrow.

"Thank you." It was barely a whisper.

A log fell in the fire, throwing sparks up into the air, emphasising the silence between them.

Embarrassed and at a loss for what to say, Ailith tried to avert her gaze. Only to have Arkhael's arm tighten around her again, his other hand reaching for her chin, forcing her to look up.

"Deal." The smile was back as he moved a clawed hand to her cheek. Briefly, the pain in her head returned, his touch fire against her skin, until it was gone entirely.

Arkhael stepped back, letting go of her. "I'm sure we will meet again soon. But should you and your team reach a decision sooner, you're welcome to grace my doorstep." He handed her a small ruby-like gem. "You merely need to crush it."

Arkhael snapped his fingers, a fiery portal whirling into existence next to them.

"And you know *how* I'll be expecting you." Before Ailith could say anything, respond to the cocked eyebrow, he pushed her backwards through the portal, never breaking eye contact, until it whirred out of existence.

The forest air was cold on her skin. Every moving critter, every creaking branch, seemed deafening in the silence of the night. Shaken to the core, Ailith sank down onto the log she had been sitting on earlier.

CHAPTER 6

She stared into the darkness of the night for a long time, replaying the meeting over and over in her head. The surprise on his face at her challenge, the sparring with words, the devil hiding underneath the human facade, his arm around her waist, the way he had held her chin . . . A nervous nausea twirled in her stomach, and her heart was pounding. Only when the first rays of sunlight caressed the horizon did the adrenaline start to settle. And with it came the return of rational thought.

A blush rose to her cheeks. What had she been thinking?! Had she really flirted with a devil just to get under his skin?

And had Jay not specifically told her that she should *not* be making deals with a devil?

"*Deal.*" The memory of his voice was vivid in her mind. *Fuck.*

She rubbed her temples. Was it truly that bad? Unnecessary risk to herself aside, she considered what she had agreed to: to approach his offer with her team as they would approach any offer. In exchange for physical relief for both Jay and herself. She couldn't find any downsides to it.

With the rising sun, the runes that Arkhael had left around their little camp slowly dissipated, until no trace of them remained. Almost mechanically, Ailith went through the motions of making a small breakfast. Her long hair had escaped the bun she usually kept it in. With deft fingers, she put her hair back up before preparing tea and pulling out some rations for them all, giving the other two a chance to wake up.

They joined her around the dying fire, Jay examining his hands and looking deeply contemplative, Amelie with her usual morning face that meant murder for anyone who spoke to her.

Surprisingly, she was the first to open her mouth. "Jay, you are too quiet. Ailith, you are even paler than usual. At this rate we're going to have to explain to people you're not a walking corpse. What is going on this morning?"

"What indeed, Ailith? How did I have such a restful night?" Jay demanded, surprisingly hostile. Amelie raised her eyebrows at him in confusion.

"It's fine," Ailith conceded, "something did happen." She stared at the ground in front of her, wondering where to start.

"I had an . . . episode. Similar to yours." She looked at Jay. "After which the devil paid us a visit. Long story short, he has a job for us. I agreed to bring it to the two of you in exchange for suppression of symptoms for Jay. Like he had done for me."

"And the longer story?" Amelie asked hesitantly, as if she was afraid to hear the answer.

"He invited me to his home. Told me that the cure for this disease lies with that stolen box, which we already suspected. He knows where it is being brought. A secure location somewhere. In return for giving us the location and telling us the proper way to cure ourselves with it, we would retrieve another item for him from said location. Other than that, he was mostly littering the conversation with the kind of threats you might expect. 'Do this or else,' 'I am your only chance,' the usual."

"You are getting too comfortable speaking to that devil." Jay's tone was sharp.

Ailith understood his hesitance; she did not understand the sudden hostility. "You're welcome. I tried my best on your behalf. Great to hear it is being appreciated."

"You're dancing to its pipes."

"Don't you think that's a bit unfair, Jay?" Amelie seemed equally as baffled by his tone. "It sounds like Ailith managed to buy us time, information, and a little respite."

"And the vaguest promise of a job. You did exactly what I warned you against, Ailith! Tell me that you at least brought some kind of proposal back with you, something in writing so that we have a measure of guarantee that the devil will keep its word."

Ailith bit her lip. "There was a contract, but I didn't get a chance to read it. And isn't that what you would have done? You told me to stay away from further deals. I did. I bought us more time and didn't sign anything."

Jay narrowed his eyes at her. And to her surprise, it was annoyance she saw on his face. "You don't know what I would have done because I wasn't there. Why didn't you wake me?"

"I . . ." Ailith hesitated. Why hadn't she? "I went with him to protect you. First you blacked out, then you offered to stay behind because you thought yourself a liability. I didn't want to risk bringing you into something when you weren't at full strength." Ailith tried to keep her voice calm. It wasn't a lie. If she had considered her options, she would not have taken Jay because she *had* been worried for him. But if she was honest, the thought had never crossed her mind. The moment she had gotten under the devil's skin, all she had focused on was the thrill of it. Guilt gnawed at the back of her head. She couldn't even say that she had been careful with a clear conscience.

With a deep sigh, Jay rubbed his hands together. The pain of the disease might have been gone, but they were still visibly raw. He looked to be struggling with something, and when he finally spoke, he sounded oddly defeated. "Fine. You're right. If I had been in your shoes, I wouldn't have brought anyone either. Just . . . Just wake me next time. For now, let's make the best of this opportunity." He looked up at Ailith. "You usually spearhead our plans. So, what is the plan?"

Ailith exchanged a look with Amelie but decided to drop the matter. If Jay wanted to talk about what he was struggling with, he would do so in his own time.

"I've had some time to think this morning, and I have the loose beginnings of a plan. Whatever he wants, it must be truly valuable and well protected if he is willing to risk hiring a group of thieves for it. Otherwise, a devil who can seemingly appear anywhere would surely have just retrieved it, which means the world as a whole would probably be better off if he did not have this item. So we hear the devil out, but don't follow through. That would be the ideal scenario."

"We're going to trick a devil? I never doubt your negotiation skills Ailith, but you have to admit that sounds a little . . . silly." Amelie's voice implied that "silly" was putting it mildly.

Ailith shrugged. "If you have a better plan, then I am all ears. But I say we join the game but play by our rules. We continue our journey to Dewhaven. It has no shortage of wealthy organisations that could all possibly have secure vaults. Let's hope that it is where this Dorian is travelling. If not, we'll still have been following his journey north, and at least there is a healer there. If we travel via Scarlor's Landing, we might even be able to take a boat and make up for some lost time. We pray the devil shows up if we go the wrong way. Otherwise, we ignore him. We wait until he shows himself when the next symptom appears and hear him out. Ideally, he tells us everything we need to know so we don't have to agree to his deal. Thoughts?"

Both Amelie and Jay were silent, but Ailith could tell from the furrowed brows and distant stares that they were thinking.

"Scarlor's Landing is a risky manoeuvre." Amelie frowned. "Ignoring the devil for a moment. Taking a ship from there will cost us more than we have right now. Stealing that amount of money might take as much time as we would gain."

"It might; it also might not. I agree with Ailith on this. Scarlor's Landing could be a shortcut that buys us valuable time, and we are rapidly running out." Jay rubbed his hands again. "I don't like the plan, but I don't see a better alternative. As far as I can tell, we have three options. One: we agree to the devil's contract. We have the highest chance of surviving this illness, but if something has been specifically put out of the reach of fiends, then I would rather not steal it for them. Two: we try and solve this problem ourselves. I don't know if we have the time for that. We would have to figure out where this box is held and what the secrets to it are without having any solid leads. I don't foresee a high chance of success. Three: we go with your plan," he said, gesturing at Ailith. "Worst case scenario, the devil gets angry and kills us, but we might die regardless. We could even sign the contract if we find that we are truly stuck."

And the longer you wait, the deeper in the dust you will be before you come crawling back on your knees.

Somehow Ailith didn't think that Arkhael would allow them to reject him only to then sign the contract as a backup option. Or if he would, she suspected the price would not be the same.

But she said none of that. There was no need to sow doubt when they were already clinging to a precariously small amount of hope.

Amelie sighed. "Well, at least we finally know what exactly is going on. Let's go."

As they mounted their horses Ailith fingered the gem in her pocket, unsure why she hadn't told her friends about it.

CHAPTER 7

A rkhael looked at the eclectic group through his silver scrying mirror as they set up their small roadside camp. He had studied them all carefully, never leaving anything to chance.

The whispers of success for Dorian Redwing, the fake job opportunity for the book that same night, the specific thieves that job was offered to. It had all come together precisely as planned.

He had gathered as much detailed information on them as he could, and his spies had been watching them carefully. To the thieves' credit, it hadn't been an easy job. He had condemned three of his spies for failing to gather anything useful on them, their souls now added to his collection, and he had only sent those who he had judged capable in the first place. The trio was well trained in covering their tracks. And no wonder with their history.

He focused on the tan wizard. The young man's long black hair was tied back into a long ponytail. The hems of his dark blue robe were grey with dust from the road. Jarlayval Lansith, who ran away from university after he was caught using illusion magic to lead a fellow student to their near-death. Rather than facing trial, knowing execution was not unlikely, he fled. Arkhael shook his head disapprovingly. So much wasted intelligence. With the right drive, the youngster could have achieved great feats. Instead, he wasted all his magical prowess on thieving jobs.

Then there was the only truly trained thief among them. Amelie Stirling. Runaway from a noble home. With her short blonde hair and the simple leather armour she wore over her black tunic, she barely stood out. But she had been the master thief for the Swiftforce and so good at her job, she had found her guild master's dirty secrets, a profitable agreement between him and the city guard. The discovery would have led to her execution—had an unexpected saviour not shown up. Eyewitnesses spoke of a woman of grey skin accidentally appearing in the right place at the right time, and of the sudden collapse of the guild's hideout.

He focused the glass on the druid. Her nearly silver hair had escaped the bun she had put it in and hung around her face in messy strands. It bothered him that she hadn't fixed it. That she didn't at least tug the loose strands behind her slightly pointed ears. There clearly was some elven heritage there, even if it was very diluted. But he knew of no people, elven or human, that had her odd ashen skin colour. Not even the elves who resided underground were as pallid as she was. If it weren't for the green colour of the tunic she wore under her armour, she might well have been part of the shadows that danced over her face.

The druid was the one he knew the least about. Her grove had exiled her, and she had never stayed in one place long enough to leave much of an impression. That, combined with druids not keeping written records, meant he barely had anything on her. From his spies he had learned that she was the leader of their little group and that she did most of the talking, even if they pretended to all be equals. But he had no idea how far her power extended, how much of a liability she could potentially be. Even one weak link might ruin his plans. He had watched her perform a variety of magics he expected from druids. Nothing extraordinary. However, she had also seemed certain that she could save the dying man in that vault from a knife to the heart. That would have required a powerful feat of healing. And she didn't look physically weak like most casters did either. Not to mention how confidently she had stood her ground against him.

How unexpectedly and delightfully challenging she was.

She had also been a mistake. The plan had been to speak to the wizard. Reports from his spies and his own research all pointed towards the man being susceptible to bribery when his own life was at stake. He would have been a perfect target. A guaranteed road to success. Instead, curiosity had gotten the better of him, and in a terrible lapse of judgement, he had spoken to the druid instead.

Or maybe he was due some amusement. He did prefer his prey fighting back, after all. And she had not disappointed.

He shook his head again.

Too much time and effort had been put into this plan to let it fall apart over some short-lived entertainment.

And yet.

And yet, here he was pondering her. How infuriating her retorts were. She wasn't the first to try and haggle or negotiate. But not many were so annoyingly confident while doing so. Or so perceptive. Arkhael understood the reports now. Why she was the one to represent their group. Her read on people was phenomenal, and he had not expected her to have such a keen mind. Then again, he barely dealt with druids. Not many things could tempt a people who mostly just desired to live amongst trees. If anything, *she* was the one who had thrown out the temptation. And stupidly, he had briefly considered it. Briefly entertained the idea of having her on her knees, breaking her until that annoying, smug, cocky expression was wiped off her face.

Pinching the bridge of his nose, he forced the image from his mind. He had tried to bait her into an agreement, and she had seen through it almost immediately. *That* should have been his focus. So far, she had been less than receptive, damn her. Instead, he had agreed to *her* deal.

It had been sensible. Show her that he had enough power to live up to his end of the bargain, even if she saw through the illusion of trustworthiness. And if she still wasn't willing to deal with him, she would at least convey his message to the wizard. In the end, he didn't need her. The young wizard had suffered the pain longer. Arkhael had no doubt he would have agreed to the deal. He just didn't know if Jarlayval would be able to convince Ailith.

Ailith, who had asked for his name and then refused to use it. Who had quite literally stood up to him even though he could crush her slim neck with one hand. Who he had caught before she keeled over. It hadn't seemed right to him to let her just fall to the floor. Not after she had shown such annoying, defiant strength. He still felt the way her hands had clutched at him, her quick breath against him, could vividly remember the feel of her cheek under his hand, the temptation to press her body against his. A sudden heat rushed through him.

By the Hells, she had gotten under his skin.

Abruptly he put the mirror down. Other jobs needed doing.

CHAPTER 8

I f the mood had been tense before, it could have been cut with even a butter knife by the time the group arrived at Scarlor's Landing. Any immediate relief from finally having formulated a plan was tempered by Jay's brooding silence and Ailith's distracted thoughts. Her nights had been restless. Her dreams would wake her multiple times, leaving her covered in sweat that quickly chilled her in the already cold nights. During the day, she had been haunted by their memories. Brought back repeatedly to that warm dining room, a devil's arm around her. Sometimes the dreams would stop there. If she was unlucky, the sickness took over in the dreams, leaving her wiped out and weak on the floor while the devil stood over her and laughed. But worse were the dreams where he lifted her up on the table and did unspeakable things to her. Or bent her over it. Or forced her to her knees.

She kept her eyes downcast in shame, worried her friends would be able to see the thoughts on her face.

Meanwhile, Jay's mood was straight up foul, even though he was no longer in pain, and he seemed almost hostile towards Ailith. Why remained a mystery to her. She had expected him to be at least somewhat grateful after she had bargained for him with the devil, but instead he only seemed angered by it. Amelie's words came back to her, but she couldn't tell if Jay's foul mood was indeed due to jealousy. And if so, she couldn't fathom what she had to be jealous of. A devil was toying with her; that hardly seemed worth being envied.

Even Amelie had started to share in their morose mood. Her attempts to make conversation fell on deaf ears, until she stopped them entirely when the responses became too strained. And Ailith was well aware that Amelie was watching her with a worried brow.

The silence was aggressively broken just before they rode into town. They had exchanged the blossoming forest for budding meadows as they got closer to Scarlor's Landing. For once, the afternoon sun had managed to get through, and Ailith welcomed the warmth of it, turning her face up towards the sky and ignoring the chill carried by the sea breeze.

Amelie, who rode next to her, smiled at the gesture and opened her mouth to speak just as Jay's horse stopped in front of them.

"All good up there?" she shouted.

There was no response. Exchanging a worried glance with Ailith, Amelie kicked her horse forwards.

Ailith smelled the fire before she saw it, felt the alien feeling of Jay's arcane magic raise the hair on her arms.

"Amelie, wait!" she cried out. A vine burst forth from the ground next to her, reaching for the other woman and pulling her backwards off her horse just before Jay set the sky alight. With a guttural shout, he sent fire streaming from his hands. Another shrill cry pierced the air as the horse he was riding was caught in the blaze, the stench of burned hair wafting over them. It flailed wildly, throwing its rider off its back. Jay's head hit the ground with a resounding crack, the inferno from his hands halting briefly.

Seeing her chance, Amelie threw herself onto the other man, trying to pin him to the ground. She was the stronger one by far, but she shouted for help as Jay struggled below her.

Ailith rushed over. The wizard's face was contorted in fear, eyes rolled back into his head. With a hand to the ground, she conjured up her vines, restraining his hands and fingers to prevent him from casting any other spells.

"Snap out of it, Jay!" Amelie slapped him in the face, and Ailith winced. Whatever had possessed the man, it refused to let go of him. Dreading what she might find, she touched his forehead and sent forth her magic. The disease was gnawing at him, his magic struggling against it as they warred within him. It had grown, she realised. Its sickening black tendrils seemed to envelop the magic inside him, tearing it apart as he lay writhing on the ground, and forcing it out of him. She felt a strength well up in him, his magic flashing and dispersing the teeth, sending them back to the edges of his awareness. Even there, the disease seemed bigger as it lay in wait, ready to strike again.

With shuddering breath, Ailith withdrew. She hadn't dared to look at her own health for the last few days in fear of what she might find, and this did not inspire her to do so. It filled her with revulsion at what was thriving inside her own body.

Jay slowly opened his eyes under Amelie, his breathing laboured, his face clammy. The expression of rage on his face swiftly replaced by one of absolute terror.

He groaned and closed his eyes.

"Are you okay?" Amelie's voice was quiet, tinged with hesitation, as she slowly moved herself off the wizard.

He shook his head. Unable or unwilling to speak. Ailith closed her eyes again and briefly checked him for injuries, urging the bruises from his fall to heal and soothing the burns on his arms.

"A new form of attack," she whispered quietly once done. "It's getting worse."

Slowly, Jay sat up. "I saw . . . something. An illusion, I guess." He looked around as if to verify that whatever he had seen was truly gone. "It was terrifying." The words came out slowly, his voice hesitant, and it was hard to miss the undertone of terror. "I thought I was defending myself."

It was all he said about it. No matter how much Ailith and Amelie pressed him, he refused to talk. Instead, he requested that they tie his hands together, ensuring he couldn't cast any spells should another attack hit him.

They walked the remainder of the road to Scarlor's Landing. Ailith and Amelie's horses had bolted. Jay's they found further down the road, succumbed to its burns. A group of travellers stood around it, wondering who could have committed such cruelty. Ailith thought she caught the words "magic" and "casters," and gestured to the others to keep a low profile, their heads bent down until they finally passed through the city gates.

Scarlor's Landing hadn't changed much since Ailith had last been there. It reeked of fish and perfume to her, of wealthy merchants vying with poor fishermen. The smell seemed to be trapped in the weathered wood that the houses were built out of, and the strong breeze brought in the occasional spray of sea foam when they veered too near the coast. It was a chaotic town, with no real structure or organisation to the buildings. Instead, they seemed stacked on top of one another, and Ailith wondered how some of the buildings had not toppled over already under the constant wind.

They veered to a part of town that was far enough away from the harbour but low enough to not be too expensive and found an inn that offered big private chambers. Amelie opened a tab with an advance that she had swiped off the streets with a deft hand.

"You and Jay retreat," she sternly ordered Ailith. "I will inquire as to the prices and times of potential passage and get food ordered up to the room."

CHAPTER 9

Despite the soft beds, Ailith couldn't bring herself to sleep that night. Jay's expression plagued her. The genuine anger and fear on his face had been frightening, and his refusal to talk about what he had seen only increased her anxiety.

In addition, Amelie had told them that rumours had reached the city about a mysterious disease down south, where they had come from. One that made mages go insane. A group of experts had been dispatched to help "contain" magic users in that area.

Ailith shivered. It was a fancy word for an execution. Once these experts learned that the mages couldn't be cured, they would choose the greater good. They always did.

She turned over in the bed, rolling her shoulders. The restraints around her wrists pulled them forwards slightly, and it was starting to grate on her already tense nerves. It had been Jay's idea that both of them should have their hands tied, just in case, and Ailith had begrudgingly agreed. The last thing she wanted was to accidentally hurt Amelie. The poor woman had suffered through so much with them already. And if rumours of mad casters had reached the city, they hardly needed to draw more attention to themselves.

Ailith felt bile rise in her throat. Their plan had seemed so clever a few days ago. But that had been before Jay had set his horse on fire, before they had heard of the witch hunt. She realised that in less than a day, Arkhael had suddenly gained the upper hand again. If they wanted to leave the town alive, they needed to get rid of this symptom. They might have to consider the devil's offer after all. Her stomach twisted itself into a knot. When would she start hallucinating? So far, her symptoms had shown up either with or just after Jay's. Would Arkhael be there again afterwards? She felt like she might throw up.

Please don't let him appear while my hands are bound.

"Why not? Did you not offer yourself on your knees?"

Ailith shot up.

The devil was sitting at the foot of her bed. In the darkness, she could just make out his silhouette. She narrowed her eyes at him. Something felt different, but she couldn't quite make out what.

"As I said before, one-time offer only."

The goosebumps on her skin had little to do with the cold. He moved closer and pulled her up by her bound hands, forcing her onto her knees.

"Beautiful." His quiet voice seemed loud in the silence of the room. He stroked her cheek with the back of his hand. "I know you've been dreaming of me."

Ailith felt her face flush, too embarrassed to speak. *How did he know?* Her body seemed paralysed, unwilling to protest. *Why?*

He brought his mouth to her ear. "I know you've been wanting to taste me." He bit her earlobe, traced her jaw with his tongue until his lips were on hers.

Ailith knew she should do something—*anything*—to regain at least some semblance of control. She couldn't just let him get away with this. So why wasn't she?

Yet instead, she opened her mouth for him, gasping into his as his other hand trailed down her body. To the waistband of her trousers. Past it, down between her legs.

"So, this is how much you've wanted me," he murmured against her mouth, and she closed her eyes in shame, unwilling to look at him while her body betrayed her. His breath ghosted over her lips. She shivered.

He isn't warm enough.

"This is a dream." She pulled back from him. It wouldn't be her first dream about him, but something felt so terribly wrong.

"Is it?" He withdrew his hand and held it in front of her face. Sudden flames licked up his fingers. "Do you want to test that theory?" The expression on his face seemed cruel.

Ailith narrowed her eyes. "You have no reason to hurt me."

"Other than my enjoyment." His hand came closer to her cheek, the heat of it burning slightly. "There are so many ways I could inflict pain. And not just physical." His voice quieted to a whisper. "I know why your grove cast you out."

Ailith jerked away from him. "You do not. They would never share that information with a devil."

"Wouldn't they? They told me all about your guilt." The flames in his hand brightened, grew in size. She smelled burning hair as he scorched the side of her face. "Now sit still for me, druid."

"No!" She rolled backwards off the bed, raising her hands in self-defence.

When were they untied? she wondered as she called forth her magic.

Pain shot through her head.

She tried to scream and was immediately cut off by a hand covering her mouth.

"Quiet, druid."

Ailith opened her eyes.

She was still lying in her bed, the blanket tangled between her legs, skin covered in a thin sheen of sweat, her tunic plastered to her body. It *had* been a dream.

The hand on her mouth seemed very real though. And very warm.

She shot up in a weird reflection of her dream when she saw Arkhael's silhouette next to her pillow, twisting her head away from his hand.

"Prove to me that you are real." She didn't need to see his face to imagine his raised eyebrows in the silence that followed. That in itself was almost proof enough to her. A spark briefly lit up his features, and with a hiss, the lantern next to her bed sputtered to life. Ailith realised that she could feel him almost more than she could see him in the dim light. He radiated power and danger. Even if she had grown somewhat used to it, the hair on the back of her neck still stood up with him so near.

"And how do you imagine I should prove myself to you?" His voice was barely above a whisper.

He looked immaculate as ever, eyes almost glowing in the darkness of the room. It was easy to imagine the horns atop his head, now that she knew. Easy to see through the illusion of amber and know that a fire burned in his eyes.

A blush crept up her cheeks now that she could see his face.

Oh gods. How long had he sat there? Had she done or said anything in her sleep? How much did he know?

She nearly forgot to answer him her own demand.

"Tell me what just happened." Her voice was equally quiet. Partially so she wouldn't wake the rest of her group and partially to mask the tremors in it.

Arkhael raised his eyebrows. "And how does this prove that I am not a manifestation of your mind?"

It didn't. But she was aware enough of him to no longer need an answer to that. She needed to hear him say that he had just arrived. That he hadn't watched her. That he didn't know what part he had played in her nightmare.

"Humour me."

"You were about to set fire to the sheets and collapse the roof. It seemed a waste for my potential employee to die before she had even had a chance to work for me." He leaned back, shadows playing across his perfect face. "Happy?"

Far from.

Only now that he had pointed it out did she notice the smell of smoke in the air. She looked down. The ropes around her wrists were smouldering slightly. Even in the dim light, she could see the red welts on her skin. She had never even noticed the pain.

Holding up the ropes to Arkhael, she raised a questioning eyebrow.

He shook his head in response, bringing his mouth close to her ear.

"I would have kept them on you."

A smile curled his lips as he stood and extended a hand. Narrowing her eyes, she took it and let him pull her up. Only for her to nearly lose her balance when the inn disappeared around her.

She found herself in a dimly lit room next to a red, soft-looking sofa. The walls were made from the same black stone as she had previously seen. Right across from the sofa hung a painting almost as tall as the wall itself. It showed Arkhael in all his fiendish glory, sitting on what looked like a golden throne, staring directly at the painter. Despite everything, Ailith had to bite back a brief smile of amusement. Of course the devil had a giant painting of himself. Arkhael followed her gaze, looking frustratingly pleased with himself when he saw what she was looking at.

"Enjoy it, druid, I don't usually invite mortals beyond my dining chambers."

The rest of the room was equally lavishly decorated. On the other end of it, she saw a dark wooden writing desk and two large, cushioned chairs around a table. A mirror with an ornate golden frame hung next to the sofa. Long windows of stained glass decorated one of the walls, but no light shone through them. Apparently the Hells, too, knew nighttime.

Every inch of this room exuded Arkhael, reflected him in how meticulously everything was placed, how fine the quality seemed even at a glance. But why had he brought her here?

"You stopped me." Reality finally caught up with Ailith. It hadn't been *just* a dream. That's why it had taken such a weird turn. Why he had appeared to her. "But how did you wake me from it? When Jay was hallucinating, there was nothing we could do to shake him out of it." She took her eyes off the decor and looked back at Arkhael, her breath catching only a little when she realised that he had turned back to his true form.

He gestured to the sofa, and she sat down without thinking about it, frowning as everything slowly caught up with her.

"Don't insult me by asking redundant questions, druid." He sat down next to her. "Or I'll return the favour and ask you why your cheeks were so flushed when I woke you." His eyes glittered in the torchlight as Ailith felt her cheeks do exactly that. She opened her mouth to respond, but he continued, "I expected you to visit."

Ailith decided to ignore her burning cheeks and cleared her throat. "It's only been a few days, and we've been busy." Her thoughts were racing. The plan. Get information on the job. *Jay wanted to be here.* Her mind seemed to take forever to catch up. "But we're interested."

She pulled her legs up onto the sofa, turning to face him, choosing her next words carefully.

"I understand you won't give us all the information, but we want the details of the job at least. Where are we going? What are we stealing? We need to know how and what to prepare. And one of my friends, Jay, he wanted to take part in the negotiations."

Could he tell how fast her heart was beating?

"I invited you, didn't I? Not mister Lansith." Guiltily, Ailith realised she wasn't sad at all that Arkhael wanted to be alone with her. The devil looked her in the eye, suddenly all business. "Are you agreeing to the terms?"

"Not without more information." Ailith stood her ground, even if nerves made her hands tremble slightly. She clasped them together.

"Hmm." Arkhael leaned forwards, elbows on his knees, chin on his intertwined fingers. "And how do I know you won't abuse said information?"

"You wish to hire us? This is how we work, regardless of who our client might be."

He didn't respond, so Ailith said nothing, watching him contemplate. His wings moved slightly with his breath, she noticed. She wondered what they felt like, if they were as warm as the rest of him. Her gaze went to his long, folded fingers. The memory of the hallucination, of those fingers between her legs, was far too fresh in her mind.

". . . that agreeable?"

"What?" Ailith blinked, bringing her gaze up to meet Arkhael's. He slowly raised an eyebrow as she felt colour rise to her cheeks again. Unfolding his hands, he leaned back, the ghost of a smile around his lips.

"You seem distracted."

"A magical disease has been eating away at my body, I have limited time left to find the cure, a devil is talking small print with me, and I just woke up from what I thought was a nightmare to learn I nearly destroyed our room." Ailith sat up straight, trying to seem more confident than she felt. "I am a little distracted indeed."

He didn't buy it. She knew it before he even responded. He leaned towards her.

"Did you bind your wrists despite knowing I would be there tonight, or did you bind your wrists *because* you knew I would be there?"

Her mouth fell open at his words. *The audacity.* She leaned back, away from him, pretending he didn't set her entire body aflame with his words and his voice alone.

"How dare you! I was protecting my friends."

As he continued to move closer, she moved back, until her back hit the armrest and she could retreat no further. Her heart beat in her throat when he brought his face close to hers, his body hovering over her. She could feel the heat radiating off of him, his breath ghosting over her lips as he spoke.

"You are lucky, druid." He brought his hand to her face and traced the line of her cheek with his nails. "I do not combine business and pleasure."

Ailith let out a long shaky breath as he moved back. That *fucking* devil. She dug her nails into the palm of her hand. *Get a hold of yourself girl. Take back control.*

"Good. It wouldn't do for a devil to give in that easily."

He narrowed his eyes as she threw his own words back at him, and a small surge of relief rushed through her. Some control was hers again.

"I would be greatly obliged if you could repeat your earlier words." She smiled sweetly.

"You have a day to discuss my offer, and then I will demand an answer." All earlier traces of humour were gone. His face was back to that jovial but cold mask.

"Two days," Ailith countered. "Time is running out on us, and we need tomorrow to sort our means of transport."

"The lack of time shows a flaw in your planning. That is your problem, not mine. You *will* have an answer by tomorrow night if you want the information."

She had regained control but lost his goodwill. *Fuck.*

His offer made sense, and it was more than generous, all things considered. She still could not shake the feeling that they were backing themselves into a corner that they wouldn't be able to run from.

"Tomorrow night. After midnight."

Arkhael rolled his eyes at her.

"If you think a few hours will save you, I will let you have that illusion."

"Deal, then?" Tentatively, she extended a hand.

He took it with none of his usual flamboyance, roughly pulling her towards him instead. "Whatever game you think you are playing, ask yourself if you can afford to lose it." His eyes bore into hers, and Ailith swallowed hard. When he let go of her hand, the mask was back in place.

"The box you are looking for is headed for a vault under the Chambers. In that—"

"The Chambers?!" Ailith interrupted him without thinking. She sucked in a breath and ran a hand through her hair. "You want us to break into the vaults of the Children of Illumination? The biggest group of fanatics in the country?"

The Children of Illumination were one of the biggest religious factions in Aldinnia. Ailith had always found their dogma extremely black and white. And the clergy, the "Children", were known to commit questionable acts of what they called divine intervention.

Arkhael glared at her, and Ailith shut her mouth.

"In that same vault lies a mummified hand. *That* is what I am after."

Impossible, she wanted to say. But it made sense. A cathedral. If the ground around it was properly consecrated, anyone of fiendish nature would be unable to enter the premises.

"How close have you gotten?"

"I fail to see how that is relevant."

Ailith gave him an annoyed glare. "Could you treat me like the professional that I am and quit the games for one moment if we are talking about the job?" The outburst earned her a look of genuine surprise. "Your personal experience with this makes all the difference in whether we think this is at all doable and what our chances of success are."

"There are three vault doors. Someone of . . . my calibre can get past the first two. But not without attracting attention." His hesitation told her two things. He didn't want to admit weakness. She could see it in the aversion on his face and hear it in the distaste of his words. And she had been wrong to call him a devil. She was dealing with an archdevil. One powerful enough to be able to step foot on at least some consecrated ground.

Ailith pulled her knees to her chest. Three vault doors protected by divine magic. Could they do it? For all her bravado, she genuinely did not know. Divine magic lay closer to her domain than it did to Jay's. Nature and divinity were somewhat entangled. The arcane schools of magic and the divine had a . . . tenuous relationship, to put it mildly. If divine magic protected the vault, it would be up to her to dismantle the traps. Could she manage that?

She chewed the inside of her cheek. And if they did find themselves having to agree to a contract with this devil—*archdevil*—could they truly trust him with what sounded like a divine reliquary? Did they have any other options? Was she willing to die for a world that had done very little for her, to prevent a devil from getting something powerful?

Yes, she realised. But she also knew that she could not condemn her friends to that same fate.

"What are your thoughts, druid?" Arkhael's voice cut through her contemplation, and she looked up to find his eyes trained on her.

"Honestly? You have likely condemned us to die, one way or another." She laughed mirthlessly. "But a deal is a deal. I will bring it to the group, and will have an answer for you tomorrow night." Ailith leaned back against the armrest of the sofa, suddenly tired, rubbing her temples.

"I started planning for this before your parents even thought of your existence. Consider it my life's work. I wouldn't have offered you the job if I didn't think you could fulfil it."

His faith in them was oddly encouraging. And Ailith felt like she needed all the encouragement she could get. Her limbs felt heavy. How long had it been since she had had a good night's rest? One without fear, without cold? She shook her head. Soon. One way or another.

"I need to sleep."

Arkhael nodded, snapping his fingers. "Go then. I will see you soon enough."

Ailith dragged herself off the sofa, looking at the inn's dark interior through his portal in distaste.

"After midnight," she repeated, before hesitantly stepping through.

CHAPTER 10

E ven though the difference in temperature was expected, it didn't stop Ailith from shivering. Before crawling back into her bed, she threw her cloak on top of her blankets. *Next time, you should bargain him for some heat.* The sudden urge to laugh hysterically came over her. The whole situation was ridiculous. With some desperation, she reached out around her. There was no nature nearby. Only the dead processed wood and cold cobbled streets of a human settlement. So she clung to her blanket, pretending she was still on his sofa and that the air around her was warm, pointedly ignoring the very vivid image he had left in her mind.

When the sun finally rose, she felt like she had one foot in the grave already.

"So, how bad is it? Are we selling our souls, or is there some hope for us?" Amelie had brought breakfast up to their room. The coffee was old, but Ailith clung to her mug like it could solve all her problems.

"I'm that transparent?"

"You look like shit and like you haven't slept. He shows up every time you two develop something new. It doesn't take a genius, dear." Amelie sat down next to Ailith on her bed. "And you keep staring off into the void with a very specific look on your face," she added in a near whisper. "Us girls are going to talk about that later."

Ailith groaned. "It's pretty bad."

Amelie raised an expectant eyebrow in response.

"Not *that*, you insufferable woman!" She rolled her eyes. "The job he's offering us, it's pretty bad." Jay slowly sat up at the other side of the room, now also paying attention. He looked possibly worse than Ailith felt, even his usually tanned skin slightly pale. "Before you say anything, I asked him to bring you, Jay. He refused."

The wizard's shoulders dropped. "Well, let's hear it then."

"He wants us to break into the Chambers."

"Impossible." For once, there was no trace of humour on Amelie's face.

"Concur," Jay added, "that's suicide."

"I said as much. Apparently, there is a vault under it with three doors. The devil couldn't get past the last one, which is why he needs us. He is certain that the box is headed there and wants us to retrieve him a mummified hand."

With a loud clang, Jay dropped the mug he had been drinking from. "The Hand of Saint Argon?" His tone was almost reverent.

"You know of it?"

He nodded. "Of course. The Hand was said to belong to a man who had managed to master both arcane and divine magics. And used both in harmony. It's a highly contested story, of course. Saint Argon was an incredible threat to the dogma of the fanatics who see the divine and arcane as opposites."

"But why would a devil be after it?" There was no small amount of scepticism in Amelie's voice. She had never been a fan of the divine, one way or another.

Jay got up and started pacing, carefully stepping over the spilled coffee. "Legend has it that Saint Argon was eventually hunted down by those who opposed him. Before he was captured, he cut off his own hand and gave it to his apprentice. On this hand, he inscribed a powerful incantation, one that was supposed to be powerful enough to open the gates between the different Realms so his apprentice could broker a peace between the divine and the arcane. All legend, of course. The Hand has never been found. But even if the incantation proved to be an exaggeration of time, the existence of the Hand alone would throw several of the ruling religious powers into complete disarray."

Ailith was starting to see the bigger picture. If the Hand was real, it would entirely undermine some of the major political players on both the arcane and religious side of the debate. That in itself was a powerful tool. And if the legends were true, they would be delivering an archdevil a skeleton key that would allow him to travel beyond just their Realm. And not just him, Ailith realised. The Hand could throw open a gate that would allow an army to follow him through, should he desire it.

"And the Children have had this the entire time?" The scepticism hadn't entirely left Amelie's voice.

Jay ran his hand through his hair. "That surprises me too. But it makes sense, all things considered. They notoriously dislike anything arcane. Aaah . . ."

Ailith could practically see his mind working.

"I am willing to bet that Dorian Redwing is one of the Children. A disease that drives magic users seemingly insane? I would not be surprised if they found a way to protect themselves from it, or to ensure that it doesn't affect users of divine magic." He nodded as he spoke. "Which might well be why your symptoms are taking longer to develop than mine." He looked at Ailith. "Your magic has the smallest touch of divinity, does it not?"

He finally sat down. "Naturally, this is all speculation and hypotheticals. But, pfff," he exhaled deeply, "that is one hell of an item to steal."

"Wait, you are actually contemplating this?" Amelie's voice was nearly an octave higher, and both brows were raised.

Jay shrugged. "If that is where our cure lies, we're going to have to go to the Chambers regardless. I will not die sitting idly on my hands. We might as well add another item to the list."

Ailith's mouth had fallen open at his sudden eagerness. She narrowed her eyes. "What are *you* hoping to gain from it?"

"If we brought the Hand to the right organisation, we would be hailed as heroes. No more need to steal. Past sins would be forgiven. Devils aren't the only ones dealing in favours and bargains."

She had nothing to say to that. Her sin had been failure and its deadly consequences. There was no organisation, no place of fame, that she wished to return to. But she sympathised with the other two. They had both lost positions of prestige, and even if they all had an unspoken agreement to not talk about the past, she knew that especially Jay was still bitter about lost opportunities.

Silence filled the room.

They were going to try. Even if no one had spoken yet, Ailith could feel the change in tension, could see from even Amelie's posture that she was considering the implications.

"Alright, let's start planning, then." Ailith rubbed her temples. Usually she loved this part, but this felt like planning for her own demise. "Our immediate problem is getting a boat to Dewhaven. We can either try and sneak aboard, or we get some coin somewhere and buy passage."

"Are we not forgetting something?"

Ailith looked up at Amelie. "Are we?"

"Our very hellish problem?"

"I presumed we were going to refuse him." She looked at the others. "Are we not?"

Jay nodded. "Of course. We cannot let him get his hands on a reliquary that powerful."

"So we're just letting Ailith deal with an angry devil?"

Ailith shrugged. She had expected she would need to do as much since the beginning.

Jay nodded. "She's been doing fine so far."

Ailith couldn't tell if he was sincere or trying to make a point. "Listen, Amelie," she started before the other woman could speak. "This was always going to end poorly. One way or another. I have no illusions that refusal is not something he will take kindly to. The two of you have a real opportunity here. Even if it doesn't end well for me, I would be happy knowing you got something good out of all of this."

She looked each of them in the eye. "Genuinely. He wants our answer tonight. I have bought us until after midnight. If I don't return from that meeting, I want you two to carry on. Go get this gross Hand, get cured, and get yourself the life you have always wanted to live."

Stunned silence met her. It made her uncomfortable.

Amelie reached over and laid a hand on her arm. "I owe you my second chance. You know I would kill for you, if you asked me to."

Ailith smiled. "I know. Please don't try and go after the devil if—" She paused, then looked at Jay. "I may have just had my worst idea to date." She threw him the ruby Arkhael had given her. "Don't crush it. Can you decipher the magic in this?"

His eyes widened when he realised what it was. "Why do you have this?"

Ailith shrugged somewhat guiltily. "In case we had an early answer."

"So, you know where it brings you. What exactly are you thinking?"

She hesitated. *This is for all of us, not just to sate my curiosity.* "I've seen two rooms in his home. Both of them held more riches than we could possibly carry between us."

"You're mad."

"Possibly." She smiled wryly. "But we all agreed not to do robberies, so we're not getting our coin during the day. Amelie is the only one who can reliably pickpocket, and I doubt even she could gather enough money in just one day. The next transport leaves"—she looked over at Amelie—"tomorrow morning, you said?"

The other woman nodded.

"And I have an appointment tonight. We could maybe have attempted some nighttime burglary otherwise, but even then, we would have to be certain we could hit multiple places to ensure we have enough coin for passage. As it stands, why not try it? We don't take anything obvious. With that much decoration on display, he has to have some coin lying around. A quick in, run through, and back out. If he turns out to be home, I'll say we were there to give him his answer." She was starting to feel the familiar pre-heist adrenaline rush.

"And if he catches us?" Amelie's face had lit up, though. She enjoyed the rush almost as much as Ailith did.

"Then I'll deal with it. I am going to have to regardless."

Jay shook his head. "You're both mad. You realise that it could still force you into a contract?"

She had considered that. "You say other organisations are also looking for this Hand? It would certainly be a shame if they received it first." She raised an eyebrow at Jay. He caught on immediately and nodded at her.

Amelie did not. "Are you saying we should—"

Jay interrupted her. "The less said about this, the better. Just in case."

Ailith nodded, ignoring Amelie's offended expression. She trusted him to come up with a contingency plan, just in case she was forced into some form of contract. The less she knew about it, the less she could give away. "So, the ruby. Is it a one-way trip, or can we use it as a return?"

"Why don't I look at it while you bring our empty mugs and plates downstairs?" Jay gave her a meaningful look. Ailith took the hint.

There were a few patrons in the taproom already. Ailith made sure to walk near enough to the burly woman standing at the bar that she could cut the coin purse off her belt. Enough for a dinner and not much more.

What are you doing?

Taking risks for her friends, she told herself firmly. She had always known that she had no dreams of grandeur, no ultimate goal, but only at Jay's words had she realised how much that set her apart. Ailith was far from happy with her life as a thief, but it was a life she knew and one that she was good at. And she would be lying if she didn't admit that she loved the thrill. Putting that on the line for Jay and Amelie's dreams and aspirations seemed a small sacrifice. She firmly avoided thinking of what the consequences could be for her.

But what of the contract?

Putting her dishes on the counter, Ailith ordered their group a bottle with her newly acquired money and slowly walked back up to the room.

She had no idea if it could be avoided. Initially, it had seemed so simple. Just fool the devil into believing they were working with him. But the more she spoke to him, the clearer it was that he was ready for them at every turn. Rubbing her pale arms for warmth, she knocked on their room's door to announce her return.

She would try her very best and deal with the consequences as they happened.

When she opened the door, Jay was deep in thought, carefully studying the ruby between his fingertips. Occasionally a flash of blue or purple would spring from the fingers in his other hand as he studied it.

Amelie gave her a very pointed look and immediately took her aside. Ailith prayed the woman understood what Jay had hopefully told her behind closed doors.

With a look at Jay, Amelie lowered her voice. "Two things. One: I have never trusted someone like I trust you, Ailith. I hope you know that."

Ailith raised her eyebrows at that, but the intensity in Amelie's gaze softened the look immediately. She put her hand on Amelie's.

"Two: you are going to have to tell me if you have at least seen the devil naked yet."

"Amelie!" Ailith hissed.

Amelie's eyes glinted with mirth. "Come on, we're about to do something stupidly dangerous. Fess up."

"Of course I have not." Ailith rolled her eyes in response, then threw her hands up at Amelie's sceptical look. "Everything so far has been bargains and threats."

"But you want to?"

"Gods, you are such a child sometimes."

"Not an answer."

Ailith glanced over at Jay. He seemed oblivious to the world still.

"I may have thought about it. Can you blame me though? He's a devil; they are made to be perfect, if the stories are to be believed."

Amelie grinned. "I knew it. I wonder what type of lover he would be."

Ailith snorted. "I doubt he would be a 'lover' at all. Are devils even capable of that? And he seems like the type that would care only about his own pleasure." She gave Amelie a stern look. "I don't have a death wish."

"You are lying." Amelie was still grinning. "If he offered, you would *so* take him to bed. I have never seen you this distracted."

"I am not about to lose my soul over a shag," Ailith answered indignantly. "And he doesn't combine business and pleasure," she added.

"Aha, I knew it!" Amelie exclaimed. Then immediately lowered her voice again, apologetically looking in Jay's direction.

With another roll of her eyes, Ailith shared some of the details with Amelie that she had omitted from her previous stories. That she may have flirted with the devil; how he had caught and held her, and how it made her skin burn; how he had threatened her just the previous night.

"Don't even think about it, though," Ailith hissed at her. "For all your jokes, I do prefer to keep both my life and my soul. Fantasies are one thing, but there is absolutely no chance I would take that risk."

Amelie leaned back. "Fine by me. I have enough to tease you with for the next three years, if not more."

"I've got it." Jay's voice cut through their chatter. Both women shot up, Ailith's face reddening, Amelie with a big grin still on hers.

The wizard ignored both of them. "I think you could learn this, Ailith." He held the ruby up at her. "It's a very different magic from anything I have seen. But yours might be related to it. In a thrice-removed distant cousin sort of manner. It draws more on primal forces."

She listened with interest.

"Although, even if you were to learn this, you would still not be able to create a portal to this exact destination. This devil of yours has done something to hide the location from the magic. We can use this to travel, and I can manipulate the magic to last longer. However, I wouldn't be able to replicate it or travel to the same location again."

Ailith nodded along. "I don't think we'll need to travel there more than once. I certainly hope not."

Jay shrugged. "So, whenever we are packed and ready, we can go. Once we're there, we'll have one hour before our way out disappears."

They packed little. Rope, lockpicks, oil, Amelie's carefully put-together disarming kit, and a crowbar. They left most of the space in their packs for whatever treasure they could carry back with them. Ailith's heart was in her throat, adrenaline making her hands clammy, an excitement that was entirely inappropriate considering the stakes quickening her breath. There were so many ways for this rushed plan to go wrong. She glanced over at Jay, noticing the set of his jaw. He caught her gaze and nodded. Even if there was only a slim chance of success, he had a plan prepared for if they failed.

With a final deep breath, Ailith locked the door to their room, pulling a bed in front of it to ensure no one could accidentally enter. Just a quick in and out, fast enough to have an answer by the time the devil expected it of her. Jay started chanting, hands weaving a set of complicated gestures, before he crushed the ruby. It went up in flames, spreading until they formed the shape of a familiar portal. Behind it, they saw only black. Ailith stepped through.

CHAPTER 11

Even before Ailith felt the now almost familiar heat, she was hit by wind. A strong gale almost blew her off her feet, and she heard the scared gasp of Amelie next to her.

They found themselves on a plateau on the side of an ink-black mountain, the portal mere inches from the edge. How far down the ground was they could not see. A thick, impenetrable fog or cloud cover lay far below the plateau. It was not reassuring.

"Jay, are you sure this is right?" Amelie shouted over the wind.

But Ailith looked ahead. The plateau led to a set of stairs hewn out of the mountain's stone. Carefully, she bent down to touch it. It was warm and smooth. Despite her knowledge of nature, she realised it was almost entirely unfamiliar to her. She had seen it in only one other place. The stairs led up to a door, carved slightly further into the mountainside, and the moment she laid eyes on it, she knew it was right.

"We're here," she said quietly.

The doors, too, appeared to be made of the same black stone, but they had been smoothed entirely, until the surface was almost reflective. A relief had been carved onto it and painted golden, of flames and devils flying over them. It bordered on kitsch.

Relieved to be moving away from the edge, they headed towards the door.

"Wait!" Jay held up a hand, pointing at the edges of the relief. Subtle runes were woven in amongst the depictions of flames. They looked vaguely like the runes Arkhael had conjured up around their little camp in the forest.

"Do you recognise them?" Ailith queried.

Jay didn't respond. Instead, his eyes glowed faintly as he muttered under his breath. Eventually, he shook his head.

"They are magical, but I have no idea what their purpose is or how to get rid of them. It might well be an alarm."

Ailith hesitated, then clenched her jaw. "We're only at his front door. If an alarm goes off, we'll fall back on the excuse that we're here to sign." She nodded at Amelie. "Just tread carefully and be ready to run."

Amelie took her usual position at the head as she inspected the door. They all held their breath as she neared the runes, but they remained inert. Finally, she nodded at the others. It seemed clear. Carefully, she pushed it.

Nothing happened.

Both Jay and Ailith looked at her expectantly.

"It's too heavy," Amelie mouthed at them, expression incredulous.

Jay rolled his eyes, and Ailith bit back a chuckle. Of all the obstacles to come across.

She walked forwards and carefully tried the door. It was heavy indeed. Digging her heels down on the stone, she put her weight into it with Amelie, attempting to open it without pushing it too far. Instead, the force of their shove opened the door suddenly, and they nearly fell forwards through the doorway.

Ailith cursed under her breath and froze.

Nothing happened. No trap sprung, no guards appeared, no obvious alarm was rung. Instead, she found herself on the doorstep of an empty hallway.

As she stepped forwards, she felt a rush of nostalgia. This almost felt like old times. It reminded her of her group breaking into castles and sneaking through long, empty hallways.

Amelie and Jay followed behind her, and between the three of them, they managed to close the door relatively quietly.

"*One hour,*" Jay gestured as they entered the devil's lair.

The hallway itself was short. The ground covered in a red carpet that they gratefully used to quiet their footfall. On either side of the hallway hung a large painting flanked by unlit wall sconces. One depicted a large room of kneeling figures, some with horns and wings, in front of a large golden throne. The other showed Arkhael overseeing a large battle. Were these based on actual events?

Ailith breathed a sigh of relief. If the sconces were unlit, he might not be home.

They made their way over to the ornate door at the other end of the hallway.

Amelie went through her usual routine of checking the door for traps before cracking it open. The room behind it revealed itself to be a circular dining room.

"I have been here," Ailith breathed, barely audible. She gestured at the silverware that lay on the table and the golden candelabras.

Jay tapped her on the arm. "We don't find loose gold quickly enough, we take this and run."

They took the other door out of the dining room and found themselves in another hallway. The walls still seemed to be carved out of the mountainside itself. Ailith wondered why a devil would choose to live here. It was nothing like the grand mansions she had heard of in the folklore.

The three of them halted. To their left, they saw a set of the most ornate and ostentatious vault doors they had ever encountered. Even with none of the wall sconces lit, its gilded decoration shone.

"Well, he's just asking to be robbed," Amelie murmured quietly. She immediately walked over to the doors and carefully started her examination of them.

Ailith gestured at the door straight ahead, then to her ears. "*I'll listen to make sure it's clear.*"

She tiptoed over. No light seeped through any of the cracks around the door, but that didn't mean no one was in the room behind it.

She pressed her ear against the door and calmed her breathing. Not a single sound came through from the other side. Carefully, she cracked the door open. Behind it lay Arkhael's chambers. Her heart skipped a beat as she spotted his sofa to the right and remembered how he had cornered her on it. She peeked over her shoulder just as Amelie stepped back, bewildered.

"He hasn't trapped it?"

Jay shrugged. "Who would be foolish enough to break into a devil's home? Shall we?"

But Amelie had joined Ailith at the door and was peeking in next to her.

"Just a quick look?"

Ailith's heart beat in her throat, but she looked at the other woman and nodded.

"Are you mad?" Jay hissed.

Amelie winked at him. "Just a peek! How often do you get to see a devil's home?"

She slipped through the doorway, Ailith following close behind her, nearly bumping into her back.

Amelie was staring at the large portrait of the devil on his gilded throne. "He's very vain, isn't he," she whispered.

Ailith nodded and advanced into the room with quick step. They didn't have long and certainly didn't have time for this. Curious, she took in the rest of the space now that she had a chance to do so. The corner of the room housed a massive bookshelf of dark polished wood. Books lined the shelves, many of them looking like they would put a collector to shame. But to Ailith's surprise, an equally large number looked old and worn. She ignored the titles, instead looking for any that might hide a switch. Nothing. Just an ordinary bookshelf. It was almost disappointing. Next, Ailith tiptoed over to the writing desk that stood under the large stained-glass windows and opened it just enough to peek inside. A large stack of parchment lay neatly in one corner, a variety of quills, sorted by size, next to it. On the other side lay a small silvered mirror and a handful of rubies like the one they had used to get here. With deft fingers, she pocketed one, closing the desk again and peeking out of the windows. The door to the left of the desk seemed to lead to a balcony. Through the glass, she could make out another set of comfortable-looking chairs and a table. They were of little interest to her, so she went to a door in the left wall. Amelie appeared behind her, and with a nod, Ailith let her test the door before opening it.

They found themselves in a bedroom. A large bed stood against one side of the wall, the black sheets on it perfectly made. It, too, was made of dark wood, the headboard covered in a gilded brocade. Directly in the middle hung a big brass ring. Amelie wiggled her brows at Ailith and walked over to the nightstands.

Ailith rolled her eyes, turning the other way. Her mouth dropped. Opposite the bed hung another massive painting of the devil, but in this one, he appeared to be entirely nude.

Ignoring the heat in her cheeks, she looked at it curiously. The devil was lounging on a bench, wings folded against his back. If the artist had made a true rendition, then his chest was toned with a little hair in the middle. Her gaze went down to the trail of hair on his lower abdomen. His left leg was just raised enough that anything too explicit was hidden from sight. Even so, she felt her breath catch in her throat and a heat pool between her legs.

"Ailith. Look at this!" Startled, she turned around. Amelie was gesturing at the contents of one of the nightstands. All forms of rope, chains, and restraints were carefully sorted and folded inside. She bit the inside of her cheek, refusing to think about what those were used for.

"Are you blushing?" Amelie whispered at her with a wink. Only then did she spot the painting. Gently, she closed the nightstand and got up to look at it. "Oh, I see why."

"I don't know what you are talking about," Ailith whispered back, tearing her eyes away. There was one other door leading out of the bedchamber. She walked over to it before she lost control of her thoughts even further and cracked it open after a brief inspection. Steam wafted in her face, and she blinked in surprise. Almost the entire room consisted of a large, lowered pool, the steam making it hard for her to see any further.

Briefly, she felt a moment of envy. Soaking in a pool like that must have been amazing. But then she closed the door again, turning to Amelie and gesturing that it was time to leave. They carefully made their way back out, finding a very annoyed Jay in the hallway. Although he said nothing, Ailith knew that he would be reprimanding them for this later. She didn't care; they hadn't taken long.

He tapped the vault door, and Amelie rolled her eyes, retrieving her lockpicks. With a pointed look at Ailith, she took her rake out first, but even she looked surprised at how quickly the pins clicked into place.

The door opened. All three of them held their breath as Amelie gave the all-clear signal and gently pushed it inwards.

It was not the biggest vault Ailith had ever seen, but it was certainly the most well laden. Chests and coffers lined the walls, and at the very back, she saw a cabinet holding hundreds of scrolls. Curiously, she stepped over to it, scanning the ground for tripwires, runes, or any other indication of a trap. Nothing.

She opened one of the scrolls and almost immediately dropped it. A contract. All of these scrolls were contracts. She could only imagine how many people, how many souls, were indebted to the devil. She rolled it back up and returned it to its original place. This was something she did not want to mess with. Instead, she joined Amelie and Jay in opening the chests. The glint of gold met them as soon as they lifted the lids, more than they could ever carry back, and they wasted no time in loading their packs with it. Amelie also found a chest containing a collection of jewellery and decided to pocket some of it as well. Worst case scenario, they could sell it; best case scenario, it turned out to be magical, and they could sell it for more.

They closed the chests again when they were done, ensuring everything looked as they had first encountered it. Just as Amelie closed the door again and locked it behind her, a wailing moan resounded from the one path they hadn't gone down. The three of them looked at each other.

"Whoever they are, we can't help them," Ailith started. But Amelie was already making her way over.

"If you had said that a few years ago, I would be dead now," she quietly called back.

It was a fair point.

They followed the curving hallway to a much duller door, Amelie making quick work of another lock, and found themselves in another circular room. But this one lacked all flair and decor that the previous ones had had in such abundance. Manacles hung from the stones in the wall. A large table stood against one of them, a variety of torture instruments neatly sorted on it, a chair in the middle.

Amelie froze. A man hung suspended from one of the walls, his arms shackled above his head, body emaciated and bloodied, both legs broken in varying places.

"In case you needed a reminder that we are dealing with a fucking devil, despite how it may appear," Jay swore behind them.

The man opened his eyes at Jay's quiet voice.

"Please. Please, you have to help me." His voice echoed against the stone walls.

Ailith gently took Amelie's shoulders.

"There's nothing we can do here," she whispered, turning the other woman around, exchanging a glance with Jay. There was no way that they could save this man, and he was a witness now that he had seen their faces.

Jay nodded grimly at her and led Amelie away by the shoulder.

Ailith took a deep breath.

"I'm sorry," she mouthed at the man.

"No. NO! MASTER. HELP ME! PLEASE HELP!" His screams echoed through the room, and Ailith cursed, summoning a vine from the wall next to him and breaking his neck with one swift tug. The sound was abruptly cut off, the body going limp. Just as she dared to exhale, the wall sconces in the room flared to life.

Fuck.

She bolted down the hallway after the other two and caught them disappearing into the dining room, also running through the now-lit hallways.

The devil had returned home.

CHAPTER 12

Even as she was running, Ailith made sure to close the doors behind her, praying that the devil wouldn't be on their trail immediately.

She ran through the dining room, the last hallway, and finally to the front door.

"Run. Just Run!" Ailith called out as she saw the other two turn to wait for her.

To her alarm, Jay slowed his pace. "I can talk to him."

"Are you mad?" She grabbed Jay by the arm, pulling him down the stairs with her. "That was a last resort, remember? We can still get out."

Jay wrestled his arm free, but he didn't stop running, keeping pace with her as he spoke. "You just betrayed his trust by breaking in, Ailith. I've not spoken to him yet. There's a better chance he'll be amicable to our terms if I do the talking."

The portal through which they had come still glimmered where they had left it on the plateau. Ailith could just make out the vague shimmering shapes of the grubby inn room on the other side.

"We might yet escape, Jay."

They were so close to a way out. Her heart was pounding in her ears as she bolted down the stairs with Jay.

A loud slam resounded behind them, echoing against the rock walls.

Ailith froze, Jay halting with her. The hair on her neck stood up, a cold shiver running down her body despite the heat. For a brief moment, Ailith considered the distance between her and the portal.

It was too far. If she ran, she would leave her back exposed for too long. She was too experienced a spellcaster to know what that meant.

So she swallowed, tried to still the swirling nerves and fear in her stomach, and turned around to face the dreaded consequences of her actions.

Ailith knew it would have to be him. But even though they had discussed the eventuality, she couldn't quite believe that he had caught them, and she suddenly felt woefully underprepared.

Despite the anger that radiated off him in waves, Arkhael looked his usual immaculate self. Not a single speck of dirt to be found on his boots. Not a single strand of hair had escaped its confinements. It was as if no time had passed since their meeting last night. But never had she seen such an obvious display of emotion on his usually perfectly composed face. And even while still looking human, he commanded the space.

Despite herself, her eyes flitted down his body.

How true was that painting?

The thought came to her unbidden, and she quickly pushed it aside. This was not the place and most definitely not the time. They were all in very real danger. Taking risks with her own life was one thing, but she didn't want to endanger the others.

"Well, well. After everything I have done for you. The generosity I have shown you. *This* is your answer."

The tone in his quiet voice was one of unmistakable disdain. Almost instinctively, Ailith took a step back. Slowly, he walked down the stairs, his eyes locked on hers.

"I would not only have led you to your cure, your actions would have made you saviours. You could have been celebrated, rewarded even. Instead, you chose to lose your souls to hellfire. I would say it was a waste, if I wasn't the one claiming them."

At that, Ailith shook herself back into action, ignoring how his voice made her shiver.

"Wait! I am willing to strike the deal with you."

He shook his head at her, still approaching at a slow pace, as if he wasn't threatening her with eternal damnation. "Oh no, my dear. The time for deals is over." His voice was quiet, the smile on his lips full of malice as he walked up to her.

"Then deal with me." Jay took a shaky step forwards. "I have not—"

"SILENCE!"

Ailith stood her ground. "I can get you the Hand of Saint Argon. I'm your best chance at it, and you know it."

Turn the tables. He's a devil. As long as you are worth more alive than dead, he won't kill you.

Arkhael hesitated. It was only a second, but it was enough for her to know she had a chance. She raised her hands, palms bared.

"Let them go, and I promise you a deal, one way or another." *Promise*—she knew it was a magical word here, binding. She hoped it would be enough to at least buy the safety of her companions.

"Ailith, no! You know this won't end well." Jay turned to face her, but she ignored him. Her eyes remained trained on Arkhael. She raised an eyebrow, inviting him to rise to the challenge, lest he hurt his pride. He narrowed his eyes.

"Out, then." The quiet words may as well have been shouted for how they echoed across the plateau.

Ailith was careful not to show the intense relief she felt on her face, careful not to break eye contact as she spoke. "Go, it's fine. If I don't return, the plan still stands."

Amelie sounded like she was about to protest, her weak voice barely audible over the howling wind, when Arkhael's voice thundered over the space.

"*NOW!*"

Ailith nodded and stepped forwards, away from the portal. "Go."

Devils were true to their word. She might die later—or worse—but she knew he would at least have to hear her out now.

Her companions stepped through the portal. She heard their footsteps recede, then watched the familiar snap of Arkhael's fingers. From behind her came the sound of whirling flames. The noise slowly dissipated until nothing but the howling wind remained. No way out now.

She allowed herself one second to let out a long, shuddering breath before composing herself and lifting her chin. Arkhael's face was contorted with anger, but he kept his word as he opened the doors behind him again and jovially gestured for her to go through. With some alarm, she noted how easily he had pushed open the heavy doors. But she entered, cocking a challenging eyebrow at him, heart beating rapidly, never having felt less in control.

In silence, they walked through his home. Her heart raced as they walked past the vault doors. With every step, she could feel his anger increase. She was going to have to drive a hard bargain if she wanted to get out of here alive and with her soul intact, and she really only had one bargaining chip in hand. The reliquary, what he had called his life's work. She had no doubt he already had plans for it once it was his, and she was certain that it would spell nothing good for the world. At the same time, she didn't have the Hand yet. So much could still happen between now and then. She might yet find a way out. *Jay might have already thought of something.* Quickly, she pushed that thought away. If she had to sign something, it would be better for her to not even consider that possibility.

Approaching the doors to his chambers, she paused, waiting for Arkhael to open them and wincing slightly as she noticed how his knuckles tensed on the handle.

Yes, she was going to have to bargain away the reliquary. There was no way he would let her go for anything less. She just hoped it was enough for him to restrain his anger.

"You must be very confident in your offer to think it will compensate for this."

His anger lowered his voice even more, causing a shiver to run down Ailith's spine. She looked him in his eyes as she entered the room and couldn't help but pause in her step. If they hadn't just agreed that he would at least hear her out, he would have torn her soul from her body right then and there. The fire in his eyes, the tension in his jaw, it was barely contained.

And he could if he truly wanted to.

She knew her improvised promise wasn't without loopholes. He could keep her here. Tie her up and torture her until she begged for mercy and signed herself away for a painless death. A deal was a deal; she hadn't specified anything. Technically, it still fell within the terms of her proposal.

He was a devil. If she had realised there were loopholes, he had been aware of them the moment she had suggested her parlay.

He must be more desperate than you thought.

And with that thought came the realisation of power. The familiar feeling of adrenaline slowly replaced the dread. She dug her nails into the palm of her hand. Provoking him now would be suicide.

Ailith realised she had paused mid-step for too long. No turning back now.

"I think we're both equally confident in my offer, or you would have had me in chains already," she said, smiling slightly, unmoving. "I have seen your prison. There is room."

It took all her effort to stand her ground as he grabbed her by the throat, all instincts screaming at her to get to safety.

"Don't push it, druid. The ice you are treading is thin enough as it is." He tightened his grasp, claws digging into her skin until she felt it break.

His hand was hot against her, almost burning. Nearly breathless, Ailith pushed forwards into the choking grip he had on her, feeling a trickle of blood run down her neck, until their bodies were almost touching. Up close she could feel the heat that radiated off his body, how hot his breath was as it ghosted over her skin. She wanted to challenge him, to break that perfect composure. She wanted him to *want* her.

The last thought caught her off guard entirely, and she pushed it away, refusing to let it throw her off her game. She needed to bargain.

"If you had been able to obtain the reliquary without my help, you would never have offered me a deal in the first place, *devil*," she bit back breathlessly, the cocky smile never quite leaving her lips.

The reaction to her mockery was instant. As if she weighed nothing, Ailith was hurled across the room. She barely had time to curl up and protect her neck before her back hit a small table, knocking the wind out of her, the furniture breaking behind her.

Immediately she assessed the damage: a small fracture in one of the shoulder blades. She trickled some healing magic towards it. Enough to get her back in fighting condition. Any superficial bruises or bleeding could be dealt with later, when she actually had time.

Hearing the rush of fire before she had a chance to focus her vision again, she rolled to the side, then to her feet. Flames of an immense heat barely missed her.

Hellfire.

If that had hit her, it could well have been fatal. Maybe she had pushed him too far. And yet, she felt a small thrill of satisfaction as she realised she had gotten under his skin again. After all his taunts, she felt like finally, she had the upper hand. If only verbally.

Still, she preferred to come out of this alive.

Meanwhile, Arkhael had lifted another hand, flames already licking his palm.

This time prepared, Ailith conjured up a vine out of the ground behind him, grabbing his hand with it as he was about to throw the fire at her. It went wide, briefly covering the stone wall of the room before dispersing harmlessly. He growled, burning the vine around his wrist as leathery wings appeared on his back in a whirl of flame. The long horns on his head visible as Arkhael dropped the illusion of humanity. The sight still filled her with the same awe.

Ailith considered going on the offensive. She had an opening if she struck now. She decided against it. She doubted it would improve her situation. Angering the devil any further by actually hurting him might spoil what little chance she had. So she steeled herself as she watched the devil beat his wings once and move over to her with surprising speed.

He was on her in an instant, claws going for her face. But she was ready for him. Ducking out of the way, she started the conjuration of another vine, only to be interrupted by him grabbing her hand. Before she could consider casting with the right hand instead, she felt his claws around her wrist. Both hands now restrained, he pushed her back. Ailith had no choice but to let him. Magically, she suspected she could have held her own for a little bit, but physically, he easily overpowered her. He was *strong*. She could either walk back with him with her head held high or let him drag her. It wasn't really a choice.

So she was sure to make and maintain eye contact as she almost tripped over the broken furniture before he slammed her against the wall, knocking the air out of her, her hands restrained on either side of her head.

She tried straining against his hold briefly, but he only tightened his grip.

Stalemate.

If he let go of her hands, she would have her spellcasting back, but holding onto her as he was, he wasn't able to attack her either. And so they found themselves frozen for a moment, breathing heavily. And he was close to her, *so very close.*

Ailith couldn't help but lower her gaze briefly to his slightly parted lips. The faintest outline of sharp teeth glinted behind them. She wondered if his tongue was forked.

Immediately, she forced her gaze back up to his eyes, the yellow more pronounced next to his now dark red skin.

Focus.

Had he noticed? Was there something other than anger on his face?

Ailith took a deep, shuddering breath, her voice a near whisper as she spoke. "I'm willing to offer you what you desire. You know that I am capable of retrieving it for you." She tried to still her racing heart.

"Is that so?" His voice was quiet, dangerous.

He moved her hands, forced them from next to her face to above her head. Ailith was immediately aware of the danger, knew he was about to have the advantage. But no matter how hard she struggled, she could not free herself from his grip as he took both her wrists in one clawed hand. In a desperate move, she tried to kick him in the shins. All it did was make him move closer, his eyes flashing with anger as he lifted her wrists higher, forcing her to stand on her toes.

With his free hand, he grabbed her by the chin and brought his face close to hers.

"Looks like you've been outmanoeuvred, druid." His lips curved into a smile. "Let's start talking contract."

He was right. And so close. She could smell the faintest trace of sulphur on him, almost shared his breath with how close he had brought his face to hers.

Fuck it.

She had gambled and was about to lose; she might as well go all in. If she didn't act now, the victory would certainly be his.

"Or maybe I'm exactly where I want to be," she breathed.

His face betrayed nothing, but she felt the claws around her wrists slacken briefly. At least she had caught him off-guard. Then he surprised her by fully closing the distance between them, his body pressing into hers. She bit her lip when she realised that he was hard, pressing into her through the fabric of their clothes. Was it the fighting? Or was his desire for her?

"You play dangerous games," Arkhael whispered in her ear. And then everything happened all at once.

Chapter 13

He bit down on her neck, hard, as Ailith wrangled one of her legs free so she could hook it around his hips. She moaned at the sudden sharp pain, arched her back, and pressed her hips against his. Still holding her wrists, he used the claws of his other hand to tear at her clothes.

There was no ceremony, no untying of knots or undoing of buttons. It was a frantic tearing of fabric.

The part of Ailith's mind that governed rational thought noted Arkhael's almost desperate rush and was surprised by it, but that part had been pushed very far away. All she could think to do was curse the devil holding her hands. She wanted—no, *needed* more, and even at his rapid pace, he was moving too slowly.

She jerked her hands down, and this time he relented, using both of his instead to claw at her leggings. Finally free, Ailith tore at his shirt until it hung open around his shoulders, wrapping her arms around them and lifting herself off the ground the moment her leggings came off, hooking both legs around his hips. He obliged instantly to the unspoken invitation.

She never noticed him lowering his trousers until she was aware of his hot skin pressing against her. She wanted to move back, finally sate her curiosity and see what was under those layers of clothes.

Instead, his hands moved to her waist, lifting her, barely giving her time to hold on before she felt him line up and enter her. She dug her nails into his back at the suddenness of it, heard his moan in response as he worked his way in, barely giving her time to adjust.

Fuck.

Her world was on fire. Everything about him burned. His skin, his breath, the way he moved inside her until he filled her entirely.

And *fuck* did it feel better than she had imagined it would.

There was no tenderness. It was all the desperate longing, all the dreams that she had awoken from in a cold sweat and with quickened breath. And clearly she was not alone in needing the gratification.

At the pace he set, all she could do was hang on and move her hips with him, digging her nails into his back over and over again, and listen to his moans in her ear every time she did so.

She could feel a climax building that felt like it had started the very first moment they met. Ailith gritted her teeth. The barely lucid part of her mind urged her to hold on, that she couldn't give him that satisfaction.

But it had been so long, and *fuck* did he feel good inside her. Every thrust was fire as he pulled out almost entirely before slamming back into her.

Then she felt him shudder, his hips tensing against hers as he buried himself in her, and there were no thoughts left as she realised she could feel him come inside her. She bit his shoulder to stop herself from crying out.

Had he? She couldn't tell. The pounding of the blood in her ears seemed deafening. They could have stood there against that wall for centuries or mere seconds, frozen in mutual ecstasy.

Ailith was the first to move, loosening her grip on Arkhael's back, leaning her head back against the wall, eyes closed and breathing still heavy. She felt him shift, couldn't help the quiet moan that left her lips. A shiver ran down her body as his tongue went over her collar bone, a sharp nail tracing its path from there to her throat.

"So exposed and vulnerable. One small snap, and you would be snuffed out forever." His voice was slightly hoarse, rougher than it normally was.

Ailith resisted the temptation to lean into his touch, the words sending goosebumps up her body.

Instead, she opened her eyes, searching for his. "You won't kill me before we've agreed on a deal. And . . ." She tightened her legs around his hips, biting back a moan at the feeling of him still inside her. "I think you enjoyed my body too much to rid yourself of it that quickly. How long have you been thinking about that?" She couldn't stop the satisfied smile as he tensed against her.

He cocked an eyebrow. "I'm a devil, dear. Temptations are what I deal in."

"Then tell me, *devil*," Ailith said, leaning forwards and bringing her mouth to his ear, "how tempting am I to you? Because if your body's reaction is anything to go by . . ." She lifted her hips ever so slightly, enough to let him know she was well aware of him hardening inside her.

He said nothing. Instead, he grabbed her tightly and moved them away from the wall, beating his wings and lifting them off the ground until he suddenly dropped her. She yelped in surprise but hit something soft before she had a chance to react otherwise.

Has he brought you to his bed?

And then he was on her, pinning her down below him, claws on her wrists again. She parted her legs for him to settle between them, moaning as his mouth roamed the area around her neck. He moved slower this time, biting and licking a burning trail over her throat, her shoulders, her breasts. All the while, he kept her hands pinned down, his hard lid pressed against her, never quite entering, rubbing against her with every move he made.

She realised it was payback for her earlier retort, but if this was his idea of punishment, she would gladly take it. She had looked into his eyes. The need there had mirrored her own. She knew he would only last so long before he, too, would have to give in.

That did not stop her from being reduced to moans and whimpers under his torture. Ailith bit her tongue. She couldn't—*wouldn't*—ask him for anything. But *fuck*, she needed him to touch her. Or move. Anything but this teasing that left her wet and needing more from him. Desperately, she tried to get at least a part of her brain to function.

Leverage. Think. Anything!

He took a nipple in his mouth, pointed teeth scraping her skin as he pressed down just a little between her legs. Not enough to enter her, just enough to make her shudder and arch her back.

"Fuck, Arkhael."

It left her mouth before she could stop herself. He froze, and she could feel him stifle a moan against her skin.

Leverage.

"*Arkhael,*" she moaned his name again, tasting it in her mouth before letting it roll off her tongue. The claws holding her wrists tightened. Closing her eyes, she shuddered under his continued ministrations, which now had a frantic urgency to them.

Would it be too desperate?

Fuck it. Once was not nearly enough.

"Take me, Arkhael."

For a brief second, he stilled, and she opened her eyes to find him looking down at her, an unreadable expression on his face. Finally, he had dropped that mask he held onto so tightly, and what she saw underneath only quickened her heartbeat even more.

Then he complied. Slowly, too slowly, he pressed forwards, until he was finally fully sheathed. Time stopped. It was pure torture. His face reflected the need on hers as he held her gaze. Ailith bit the inside of her cheek hard enough that she could feel it bleed.

She caved. Or maybe he did. It didn't matter.

He took her. Again. Aggressively and quickly. She had engaged in longer sex in a brothel.

Then why does it feel like so much more?

She clung to him as if her life depended on it, wrapping her legs around his hips as he moved inside her. With one of her hands, she grabbed his dark hair, the strands soft around her fingers as he bit her neck again. The sharp pain of it only emphasised how sweet the pleasure was he gave her. With one arm, he lifted her up slightly, pressing her against his body, her sensitive nipples burning at the touch of him.

Every thrust set her body aflame, until she was certain that all coherent thought had left her.

What happened after was a blur of sweat and moans.

He took her until he filled her, holding her up with one arm, her arched back pressing their bodies together. Stars danced across Ailith's vision. Her head spun with the lack of oxygen. The devil still inside her, holding onto her, as the world slowly disappeared around her.

It took a while for reality to come back to Ailith. When it did, her entire body hurt. She took care of it quickly. Superficial burns, bruises, and cuts. Nothing that needed urgent tending or would hinder her in a fight. And she might yet need to be ready for one. Opening her eyes, she assessed her surroundings. She was still on the bed, lying on her side. Next to her Arkhael was somewhat more gracefully reclined against the many pillows at the headboard.

Was this bed just used for sex, or did devils sleep?

His eyes were closed, his chest moved rhythmically, yet she dared not move too much, unsure if he was asleep or merely resting. Instead, she took the opportunity to shamelessly take in his body. The painting had not been a lie. If anything, it had not done reality justice.

He took great care in his appearance, that much was clear. His chest was toned, ever so slightly covered in dark hair near the centre. Shame he always hid it under so many layers of clothing. His dark wings lay splayed out on the bed next to him. She had underestimated how quickly they allowed him to move, a mistake she wouldn't make again. Her eyes travelled to the dark horns on his head as he rested it on one of his arms. Everything about him implied power. From the muscle she saw under his skin to the casual confidence with which he lay there.

Resisting the temptation to reach out and touch him, Ailith instead cast her mind to the future. She was still alive, which was a pleasant surprise. She still had to make a deal with him. Nothing had changed.

If only you could enjoy this a little longer.

That thought caught her by surprise, and she reprimanded herself immediately. He was a *devil*, of course he was going to be a good lay. And objectively, it hadn't even been that special.

Don't make it more than it is just because you fantasised about it.

She wondered what she looked like right now, if the marks of pleasure were clear on her body and if she could pretend they were battle scars should she not get the chance to heal them. Her friends were going to kill her when she managed to make it back. *If.*

Her gaze was drawn back to him. Would she dare take one more risk? He didn't seem particularly alert. The places where she had broken skin were already starting to heal. From his neck, her eyes travelled to his face, the cheekbones just too pronounced to be human, the dark red colour of his skin, back to his lips. He hadn't kissed her, she had noticed, and the desire for it overcame her. Like a forbidden fruit, now that she had had a small bite, she wanted all of it. What would he taste like?

Could you make him . . . ?

Stop it! she interrupted the train of thought. *Look at what you already got and how much you nearly paid for it. You are still alive! Do not take another unnecessary risk!* But even as she said it to herself, she knew she had already made up her mind.

"Gold piece for your thoughts?"

So much for having the upper hand. It felt as if his fiery eyes pierced right into her soul, the hint of a knowing smile on his lips as he caught her staring. Ailith knew she shouldn't, but she would be damned before she turned back, and the timbre of his voice alone was enough to remove rational thought from her mind and quicken her heart. So she lifted herself up, bringing her body close to his atop the torn sheets.

She felt him tense as she raised a hand and realised it wasn't in anticipation. The shift of his body was defensive. He was ready for combat, ready to stop her should she try any spellcasting. Ailith couldn't help the small sense of pride she felt at that. It meant that, to some extent, she was powerful enough to be a threat to him. But that wasn't what she was after.

Ignoring his question, she brought her hand down on his chest. Slowly, making sure to make no sudden motions. She traced her finger up to his collarbone, to the already healing bite marks she had left, then back down over his chest, through the small amount of hair there. Under her touch she could feel him relax a little, though the situation was no less tense.

This was no desperate sex. No redirected anger or desperation. No sudden fulfilment of a forbidden fantasy. He was letting her explore his body. She shouldn't have been as interested as she was, and he shouldn't have been so compliant. Yet here they were, the silence between them deafening, the tension palpable.

Lower, Ailith traced her hand. Learning that along his abdomen were hard ridges, three thin lines of leathery skin starting on either side at his midriff, disappearing towards his back.

Definitely not human.

She had never admired a body as much as she did his.

Lower still, she let her hand wander, down his stomach, over his pronounced hipbones, following the trail of hair until she traced a single finger up his hard lid. *No wonder he felt so good.*

The tension dissipated. They were back in familiar territory. She felt the small tremor run through him at her touch. Replaced the single finger with her hand, then looked up at him. His eyes were intently trained on her, lips slightly parted, an almost pained look on his face. Then she moved her hand, slowly, and watched him exhale shakily, saw one of his hands grip the bed from the corner of her eyes. She felt him shift, but this time, she moved quicker than he did. Throwing her leg over his hips, she straddled him, trapping him between their bodies, both her hands now on his chest, pushing him down. Again, he let her, but she had felt the tension in his legs, saw the brief bulging of his shoulder muscles. He didn't trust her to not suddenly turn against him.

She dug her nails down until she drew blood, and his gasp was music to her ears. If he was worried about how she moved her hands, she would make sure he knew where they were.

Leaning forwards, she brought her mouth to his ear.

"I want you to kiss me."

He hissed as she dug her nails in deeper and rocked her hips slightly, making sure he knew exactly how much she wanted him.

"And why would I do that?"

Her head was jerked back as he grabbed her hair, pulling her up, his other hand on her hip, eyes full of challenge.

"Because I, ah—"

He had let go of her hair, instead moving both hands to her hips, forcing her to move. For a moment, she could focus on nothing but the feeling of him trapped between their bodies and her own betraying how much she wanted him as he moved her over him, spreading her arousal between them. It was the moan he let out that brought her back some semblance of control.

"I think you enjoy me—ah—moaning your name too much to not—" Her sentence was cut off entirely as he lifted her just enough to slip inside her. Filled her just enough to leave her wanting more. If her hands hadn't been on him already, she may have fallen forwards. Instead, she caught herself on him, leaving bloody fingerprints as she moved her hands to support herself. Through half-lidded eyes she saw the pleased expression on his face. If anything, it strengthened her resolve.

Getting herself back in a more upright position, she started slowly moving her hips, taking him in deeper with every thrust, making sure to look him in the eye before letting her head fall, and arching her back. But every moan that threatened to leave her lips she bit back.

He knew her terms.

Their tempo was slow this time. She wouldn't be the first to relent. Even when it became increasingly hard to hold back. With every thrust, she was aware of how deep he was inside her, and she couldn't stop the occasional moan from spilling. But she could tell from the steely grip on her hips and the pained look on his face that he was struggling more than she was.

There was a sudden gust of air as Arkhael used his wings to manoeuvre himself into a seated position, one arm behind Ailith to prevent her losing her balance, claws digging into her back, face close to hers.

She made sure to look him in the eye as she bit her lower lip, stifling the sounds she was making as she continued to take him in, legs on either side of his hips. He growled in response, grabbed her chin with his free hand, forcing her mouth open with his thumb. She brought her teeth down, then took his thumb into her mouth, moaning around it instead, tasting her own blood on his finger.

He withdrew his hand as if she had burned him, his rhythm faltering briefly. Then he grabbed her by the back of her head and kissed her.

Like everything else he had done, it was aggressive, demanding, and slightly painful. And immediately addictive. And *fuck* if it wasn't better than anything she had imagined it to be.

Ailith responded with a hunger that she thought should have been sated by now. She tasted him in her mouth as he forced his tongue in, biting her lip as she moaned against him. No longer holding back.

They parted, gasping for air, close enough that their lips still touched.

"*Arkhael,*" she quietly moaned against his lips, and to her surprise, he kissed her again. Their mouths clashed as their bodies frantically moved with each other. And then again. And again. Until her world consisted of him inside her, his taste in her mouth, and his name on her lips. They collapsed together onto the torn bedsheets, one of his arms still around her, her head on his chest, vaguely aware of his quickened heartbeat.

CHAPTER 14

Ailith could feel herself drifting off. How long ago it seemed that she had sneaked into this very room.

No. Stay awake, you fool. You cannot afford to let your guard down.

Bit late for that, she thought wryly.

What about Arkhael, was he awake? The light filtering through the windows had dimmed, but she had no idea how much time had actually passed.

The heartbeat under her ear had definitely slowed to a more normal pace, but otherwise he hadn't moved.

Briefly, she closed her eyes, allowing herself to enjoy the feeling of his naked hot skin against hers. The warmth of him, the knowledge of how far she had pushed him, how good everything about him felt. With a start, she opened her eyes again.

Pull yourself together, girl. There is no being comfortable with a devil. The moment you show any vulnerability, you become prey.

Resentfully, she lifted her head to look at him. He seemed equally as spent as she felt, barely opening his eyes to look back at her. For a moment, she thought the arm around her tightened, but then he removed it altogether.

"Do devils sleep?" She sounded tired even to her own ears.

The corners of his mouth pulled up into a faint smile before he opened his eyes fully.

"We rest. We don't sleep like most mortals do." He stretched, muscles rippling under his skin. "You, on the other hand, must be exhausted."

The words spelled danger, and the glint in his eyes promised he would follow up on them. She couldn't give him that opportunity.

So she didn't respond, instead sitting up fully and rolling her shoulders. She was going to feel this for a few days at least.

With a sigh, she swung her legs over the side of the bed, avoiding eye contact.

"So, the reliquary . . . In exchange for my freedom to leave, life and soul intact, and the cure." She hesitated, then added, "And removal of the current and future symptoms for me and Jay, so we can actually retrieve it?"

She could hear him get up behind her and turned her head to watch him walk over to one of his wardrobes and pull out a set of clothing identical to what he had been wearing before. She wondered how many of the same pieces he owned.

What had happened to her own clothes? She stepped out of the bed, stone floor warm under her bare feet, and found her legs dangerously wobbly.

Steady.

She took a few deep breaths, then straightened herself. Something on her back started bleeding as she stretched the skin.

The first of her garments she spotted just outside the bedroom doorway. She picked up the pieces of her leather armour. The ropes that had held it together were beyond repair, but the armour itself had survived. The lovely green shirt that she had worn under it kept her decent, but that was about all it did. The fabric had been torn to shreds.

Her leggings had been torn open entirely down one side. Trying not to damage them any further, she managed to mostly get them on. Then carefully and gently started the conjuration of small, wiry branches of ivy to keep the torn material together. It didn't need to last long, just long enough.

From the corner of her eye, she saw Arkhael walk into the room, immaculately dressed as always already. Pretending to focus on her work, she watched him sit down and unfold his writing desk, carefully laying out the quills in them, a different quill entirely appearing in his hand.

To business then.

She judged her improvised repair job. It would have to do. Her eyes scanned the wall for the mirror. Dreading what she would see, Ailith walked over to it.

Her grey hair was loose and dishevelled, but she hadn't expected otherwise. The side of her chin was bruised, and her lips were cut in many places, but that seemed to be the worst of it on her face.

The rest of her, however . . . Every visible patch of skin seemed to be either bruised, cut, or burned. Bite marks covered her neck and shoulders. Long grooves left by his claws ran down her arms, down from her throat to between her breasts.

The bite marks she healed right then and there, too tired to have *that* conversation should she return. The remainder she just gave a small push to encourage their natural healing. Just enough that it wouldn't scar.

Then she walked over to Arkhael. Rather than standing next to him, she sat on the armrest of his chair and leaned down to look over his shoulder. He briefly paused the quill, then continued his writing. No ink was used. Instead, the letters seemed to burn themselves into the paper where he wrote.

An infernal contract.

Ailith started reading.

She didn't have much experience with infernal contracts, but the beginning seemed fairly straightforward, though it used too many words to lay out basic terms. To her surprise, he had complied with her request. "Suppression of current and future symptoms should the immediate curing of them not be possible due to the magical nature of the illness."

She read on.

"No. This section here." She pointed at the parchment. "If I fail to retrieve the reliquary, my soul will not be yours."

Arkhael paused again.

"If I want to cure myself, which I most certainly do, I'll need to get to it either way. If I fail, it won't have been for lack of trying but because something will either have outsmarted me, or because I'm dead. I will not be held responsible for the former, and I have no desire for the latter."

She caught the sly smile on his face before he scratched out the sentences, the letters turning to ash and falling off the paper. The remainder of the contract seemed worryingly straightforward to Ailith. She read it again, trying to pick out any hidden tricks, only to find none. Her requests in exchange for the reliquary. No attempts on one another's life until after the contract had been fulfilled. If she worked against him, the cure would be destroyed.

He had added a clause that prevented her from stealing or destroying the contract, something she couldn't blame him for considering the circumstances. With the one passage removed, it never once mentioned her soul.

Arkhael held out the quill to her with a gleam in his eyes. All she needed to do was sign.

With her heartbeat in her throat, she took quill and paper from him, then read it again. This was no longer a wild dare or stupid gamble.

Touching nib to the paper, she realised one thing: *This archdevil is too powerful already. You cannot let him have the reliquary.*

She signed.

Her name burned into the parchment before both it and quill vanished.

What had she done?

It's just another problem that needs a very creative solution. We're good at those. We were prepared for this eventuality.

She looked at Arkhael, his expression almost as pleased as it had been just a few moments ago.

"Now then, let's look at you." He pulled her down from the armrest onto his lap, putting his sharp nails against her temples.

Before she had a chance to react, she was on fire. And not the good kind. A pain inside her head that slowly spread through the rest of her body. It burned, too hot to think, too hot for her to survive, surely.

The fire ate at her insides, gnawed on her flesh. A thousand tiny flames devoured her. And just as suddenly, it was gone, leaving her gasping for air, rolling backwards off the chair and into a defensive stance.

"What—" Her body felt lighter. Whatever he had done, the disease didn't feel as oppressive, as threatening, as it usually did. With a start, she realised he must have suppressed whatever symptoms it had been about to assault her with.

"Fuck. You could at least have given me a heads-up!" She dropped her stance.

He got out of the chair and retrieved something wrapped in cloth out of a cabinet, ignoring her entirely.

"Close the box, then destroy it with this. That is the only way to cure yourself." He handed her the item, and Ailith unfolded the cloth gingerly. In it lay a single golden feather with a sharpened pin. She gasped. She was holding the feather of a Celestial. How a devil had gotten his hands on it she didn't dare ask. With great care, she folded the cloth again and watched Arkhael snap a finger. Swirling into existence next to him was a fiery portal. Through it, Ailith saw the vague outline of the inn room. Two silhouettes looked up.

"I believe that is my half of our bargain fulfilled."

Just like that, huh.

Ailith stared at him, then back at the portal, suddenly unsure of what to say.

You got what you wanted and more. There's nothing left for you here. She straightened, then nodded at him.

"Pleasure doing business."

As she walked to the portal, he held out a hand. Hesitantly, she extended her own, ignoring the immediate reaction her body had to his touch as he took it and bowed down to kiss her hand.

"Anytime."

A shiver ran down her back, but she said nothing, pretending she didn't want his lips in other places. Instead, she stepped through the portal into the cold night air.

CHAPTER 15

"Aaah you're alive!" With a cry, Amelie threw herself around Ailith's neck. Ailith nearly lost her balance and fell backwards. Having stepped back into her own Realm, the shock at her actions started to kick in. Despite that, she hugged her friend back tightly. "I know we agreed to continue without you, but . . . Gods, I am glad you are not dead."

"I don't think any of the gods were responsible for that." Jay's voice was quiet behind Amelie. He was sitting on one of the beds, surrounded by riches and giving Ailith a wary look. "I presume that it is done, then."

She nodded. "I'm sorry Jay, there was no way around it."

His lips tightened into a grimace. "You're right. I had hoped there would be. But ever since we've had that devil at our heels, I knew it could only end one way." He leaned back against the wall and sighed. "You look awful. Are you very hurt?" His brow creased with concern.

Ailith gently wrestled herself free from Amelie's hug. "Nothing that won't heal quickly. I . . ." Heat threatened to crawl up her cheeks. She changed her approach. "I did what you so often accuse me of. My first words were maybe not the most tactical, and I very nearly did not make it out."

She just hoped he would buy that that was what caused her blush.

Amelie swung an arm around her waist. "Jay, while you continue counting our haul, I'll bring this one to a bath."

Ailith's eyes swept over the bed before she let Amelie take her away. Arkhael could have demanded that she return the stolen goods to him. She doubted he had forgotten about them.

Jay met her eyes. "Go and get some rest. We have already paid for transport, leaving tomorrow morning. You took one for the team. You deserve the break."

She nodded and let herself be ushered out of the room. With the shock slowly settling in, the world seemed to pass her in a daze, her mind reeling, exhaustion sinking its relentless claws in deeper and deeper.

". . . Ailith?"

She blinked, trying to focus as Amelie readied her a bath.

"Yes?"

"Your bath is ready, dear. Get in, you're shivering."

Ailith smiled through her exhaustion. "I can't tell if it's the cold air or just how tired I feel."

She started removing her ruined garments.

Amelie clicked her tongue. "These will need to go."

Her eyes narrowed slightly as she saw the many claw marks on Ailith's form. Carefully, she followed one near her shoulder with a finger.

"I meant what I said, Ailith. I would kill for you. I owe you my life. So tell me one thing." She tapped the wounds on Ailith's back. "Were these received in pleasure or torment?"

"Amelie!" Ailith managed to muster enough energy to sound indignant.

"I mean it. Do you need me to kill him." The other woman's voice was dead serious.

Finally, the exhaustion caught up. Tears came to Ailith's eyes.

"I don't deserve you." She hugged the woman again. The leather of Amelie's armour almost painful against her naked breasts. "There is no need for killing," she whispered in her ear and could feel Amelie's tense form relax.

"Good. 'Cause I would have tried, but if he's a match for you, I don't believe I would have stood much of a chance."

Ailith let her friend go and got into the warm water. The burns and grazes on her skin stung sharply, and she hissed.

Amelie sat down on the side of the tub, one eye on the door, just in case.

"You know, if the circumstances had been different, I would have told you it was about time."

"I am too tired to properly retort, and you know it." Ailith glared at her. The spark had returned to her friend's eye. It was a comforting sight.

"Exactly. Which means you are too tired to protest when I say that I told you so. Dangerous and handsome." Amelie grinned wickedly. "Turns out that your type is not human at all. Was there any truth to that painting? I bet he was huge."

Ailith just groaned, too tired to argue or even be too offended. The bathwater felt cold compared to Arkhael's halls. She shivered and quickly washed herself. For once, she was even too tired to enjoy a long soak.

"Are *any* of those actually from you fighting?" Amelie wiggled her eyebrows.

Ailith rolled her eyes. "You know I don't lie. I'm not good at it. And yes, I'm fairly certain he threw me through a table. Although I have no idea which exact bruise that caused."

"So, all of that is . . . ? I did not know you had it in you." Amelie handed her a robe as she got out of the bath, her face growing serious. "Take my advice, Ailith: don't tell Jay. He's been in an odd mood all day. It's nothing more than a gut feeling, but I don't think it would go down well with him."

Ailith shook her wet hair, her teeth almost chattering. "I wasn't even planning on telling you, you annoyingly perceptive woman. So don't worry. And for what it's worth, the contract is very real and very scary."

Amelie hooked an arm through hers, giving Ailith a chance to lean on her.

"You look fucked." She snickered slightly at her own joke, and Ailith punched her side. "Scary contracts can wait until tomorrow. You need sleep."

Arkhael had let them get away with quite a haul. If they survived past the full moon, they would have money enough to live luxuriously for a few months, at least.

The gold had certainly been enough to buy them passage on an actual ferry rather than just a merchant's boat, which meant they had their own cabin and more than just hardtack for food in the evenings. It was almost a shame that it would only take them four days to reach Dewhaven.

The first day, they had gathered in their cabin and Jay had dealt out their haul. Any coinage had been evenly distributed. Most of it they had put in the group fund that Jay kept in a small satchel he magically made to look like a water flask, but they had had enough left that they could each take a cut as well. There was also a variety of valuables that they could sell in Dewhaven, but they all took a moment to rake through it first.

Ailith picked out an intricate golden necklace for herself. Golden interwoven chains sat high around the neck like a choker, with longer chains creating an intricate pattern down her chest, small rubies woven into the gold. It was a beautiful piece, one she highly doubted she would ever have an occasion for, and certainly not something she could wear daily. She picked it as her own regardless.

Jay had taken a look at it and told her the piece was magically protected. The gold couldn't be damaged or torn, but otherwise, it held no function. She could tell that he thought it was a waste of magic.

He and Amelie had kept a few items as well. Small pieces of jewellery, that could easily be pawned, but most of their valuables they decided to sell. As travelling thieves, they had little use for such riches.

The sea travel brought a much-needed respite from the constant haste they had known the past few days. Even Ailith, who was usually nervous being too far from land for too long, found herself relaxing just a tad. There was little they could do while aboard the ship, and with Jay and Ailith no longer needing to be on guard for the onset of new symptoms, a little bit of their old banter returned.

They discussed their plans as much as they could while aboard the boat. Three days of information gathering and preparation once they reached Dewhaven. On the third night, they would strike. It should see them cured one day before the full moon.

Ailith had also suggested they approach the archdruid Nial. He was an old acquaintance of hers and might well be able to help them find their way in the city. He was an extremely skilled healer. After everything Arkhael had said, she doubted he would be able to help them, but it was worth at least asking him about it. Plus, he held a position of some influence, being an ambassador between the groves and Dewhaven. If they failed to retrieve the box, he might be able to use whatever power he had to go after the Children, or at least spread the word of what they had unleashed on the world.

Their short peace was only interrupted by the rumours that floated among the passengers. During dinner, Ailith overheard more talk of magic users who had lost their minds. And much as she tried to close herself off to the chatter, she couldn't stop herself from listening in on the conversation. A well-respected healer had been thrown into jail after attempting to burn down the hospital she worked in. Before the woman could face trial, she had disappeared from her cell, leaving behind only ash and smoke. Ailith's stomach turned as she wondered whether the ash had been caused by the woman, or was all that remained of her. It wasn't the only horror story that reached their ears, and from the grim set of his jaw, Ailith could tell that Jay was also trying his best to ignore the feeling of urgency.

Amelie called them all above deck in the evening. The breeze immediately caused Ailith to shiver, and she pulled her cloak closer around herself, cursing slightly as her hair fell out of the bun she had put it in. Then she saw what Amelie wanted them to see. Dewhaven lay in the distance, the lights of the city twinkling in the water, the surrounding mountainscape creating a dark silhouette against the darkening sky. It was beautiful. They would make port there in the morning. In a moment of impulse, she hugged both her friends close. Even in this stressful race against time, not everything was bad. They would get through this, and take a well-deserved break before taking on the next job.

And what of the devil?

With a frown, she pushed the thought away, casting her eyes downwards. A dark shape in the water caught her attention. A fish?

Then she went pale at the sound of wood splintering.

CHAPTER 16

He had been angry the last few days. Angry, annoyed, and so very distracted. There weren't many rules he lived by—he was the one who had created most of the damned rules, after all—but one he had always honoured was to never combine business and pleasure.

Arkhael sat down at his writing desk, unfolding it with great care, carefully laying out his quills and inks, then laid out the contract he had been working on. It was a good one. Either a strong soul to add to his collection or a good bit of political influence. His quill hovered above the paper as his eyes were drawn to the small silver mirror that lay on the corner of the desk. He sighed.

Get the druid out of your head.

He looked back down at the paper, but the words he needed suddenly escaped him.

"I want you to kiss me."

His nails dug into the wood as he tried to drive the memory of her out of his mind. She was infuriating. First she dared to challenge him at every turn, and now she couldn't even let him work in peace.

His eyes flitted to the mirror again.

Just one glimpse of her. To ensure she is still doing her job.

The job he had contracted her to do. It felt weirdly surreal that, after everything, he had gotten her to sign. And an expensive contract it had been too. Not only had she cost him a valuable prisoner and potential loyal spy, she should never have gotten as much control as he had let her have. Even when he had her cornered, when he could have plucked the soul from her body with just a snap of his fingers, she had dared to challenge him.

Infuriating. And beautiful. And so strangely intoxicating.

A groan escaped his lips. He should never have kissed her. It was not proper. Something they did in the upper circles of the Hells, where the succubi and incubi lived. One tryst of indulgence in mortal flesh every once in a while could be condoned. Partaking in their other physical frivolities was below him.

So why could he still feel where she had dug her nails into his chest? Remember so vividly what she looked like above him with her back arched, hair spilling down like a silvered waterfall? Teeth on her lip as she tried to defy him even then. She had tasted sweet, dangerous, and forbidden. Like poisonous berries that seemed enticing but would kill you if you dared to take a single bite.

He stood up and grabbed the mirror, squeezing the handle of it so hard, he could feel the silver dig into his flesh.

Just to ensure she is still working for you and not against you.

He knew full well the contract prevented her from doing that. Even so, he conjured up the image of her in the small mirror. It came into view slowly.

Something was wrong.

The mirror showed her swimming frantically through a wooden hallway.

Where is she? Floating in the water next to her was a piece of fabric, more of it coming into view as Ailith swam closer. The blue fabric became a dress attached to a woman who floated in the water, a cloud of red spreading around the body.

Ailith ignored her, instead focusing on a door, pulling it open. The image followed her into a cabin with several people treading water, trying to reach for air near the ceiling.

The boat she had been on. Something must have happened. But why was she not swimming to the surface? The confusion was quickly replaced with anger. She did not have time for this. *He* did not have time for this.

And judging by her lack of usual grace, the situation was not going well. He watched her speak, expel precious air, before the water was suddenly forced out of the room. Arkhael breathed a sigh of relief. Not for the first time, he wondered how powerful she truly was.

How long could she do this for? And how often? And what else could she do that he hadn't seen yet?

Other people flitted through the image, leaving the space as he watched her strain to hold the spell. He imagined sweat mixing with the salt water on her forehead. She faltered. He watched her gasp, imagined the sound leaving her lips, as water rushed back into the room, the force of it pushing her against a wall.

He watched her protect her face as a painting came at her with speed, dragged by the current. Muscles straining, she gestured into the tide. It appeared to slow. She had created another bubble, although Arkhael noted with concern that this one was much smaller. Her lips moved—Who could she be talking to?—and he watched her kneel down as a child entered the image.

Disgusting.

Ailith picked it up, closed her eyes, and the bubble seemed to fade. Child in one arm, he watched her swim, unnaturally fast. She must have cast something that altered the flow of the water. In her arms, the child began to struggle, and she paused, creating the smallest of bubbles around both their heads. He saw the barely veiled panic on her face. It was an expression he was all too familiar with. That of someone who knew there was no way out.

He was usually the cause of expressions like these, and took great satisfaction in them. Seeing it on her face, however, he felt a strange chill in his heart.

Of course. You still need her to break into the vault.

In the small mirror image, Ailith's journey had continued, her brow furrowed with determination. She had reached open waters, leaving the sinking boat behind her. Arkhael watched her suddenly let go of the child and push it upwards. Other figures entered the image.

Merrows. She didn't stand a chance. Their webbed fingers reached for her legs, pulling her back down.

Entranced, Arkhael watched the tragedy unfold before his eyes. Watched the realisation set in on Ailith's face. She stopped struggling. He watched air bubbles leave her mouth, her eyes spark and turn a violet white as lightning came down from above. The webbed hands disappeared from the image.

It was just Ailith, body doubling over, trying desperately to gasp for air when there was only water around her. She stilled. Arkhael sat frozen, contract on the table entirely forgotten.

With his lack of focus, the image faded. He threw the mirror across the room in sudden frustration, wincing as it shattered, immediately annoyed with himself for the mess he had created in his otherwise perfectly tidied chambers. Mortals. No matter how powerful, they remained only mortal.

But she hasn't fulfilled her contract yet . . .

He would have to start over again. Find another candidate with her unique skill set. Could he sway the wizard still?

Would there even be others like her? He had waited multiple centuries already; he could wait another few. No mortal was ever entirely unique.

"Arkhael."

Like a slap to the face, the memory hit him. That annoying, cocky little smile wiped off her face by ecstasy. The way she had so brazenly explored his body. How her voice sounded when she finally called him by his name, as if she tasted his very essence on her tongue.

You haven't made her squirm enough yet.

Fury ignited in him. If anyone deserved the pleasure of her demise, it was him. With a flick of his wrist, he summoned her contract. The scrawl of her name seemed aflame to him. If the contract still existed, then she was still alive. He pushed away the hesitation, his distaste for large bodies of water. She was his best chance of getting the reliquary. Squandering that would be folly. He transported himself to her body.

For a moment, everything was silent, sound dampened by the water around him. She floated, eerily quiet, eyes shut, hair moving with the current. An illusion of peace.

He took her in his arms, took her back home.

The illusion immediately shattered, replaced by a rapid urgency. She wasn't breathing. Arkhael was no healer, but he was an expert in the application of pain, and they were surprisingly similar subjects. Dropping her on the floor, he bent her head back and breathed hot air into her mouth.

She is a druid. Surely her body will try its hardest to heal itself?

He pressed down on her chest. Nothing. He breathed into her again. Her body convulsed. He moved away just before she coughed water and bile onto his floor.

Disgusting.

The pit in his stomach relaxed, and he unclenched his jaw, watching her wretch and heave until she finally steadied herself.

"Arkhael?" Her voice was barely audible. He could see the obvious confusion on her face as she took in her surroundings. Watched her struggle as she tried to speak, tried to stay conscious, and failed.

He caught her before she could collapse into the mess she had made. She was vile. He grimaced, realising that meant he was too.

What now?

Lips curled in disgust, he brought her over to his bathroom and gently lowered her into the warm water, clothes and all, rinsing the filth off of her. Once satisfied, he carried her still-dripping body to his bedchambers.

Leaving her with her companions would have been considerably less work.

But they clearly could not be trusted to look after his asset.

After putting her down atop the sheets, he took a moment to just watch her. Her wet armour clung to her. The rise and fall of her chest was slightly quicker than he wanted it to be, and despite the warm ambient temperature, she seemed to shiver.

He hesitated only briefly before he started undoing the ties that held her armour together, carefully and meticulously removing the wet garments, folding them in a neat pile next to the bed, until she lay mostly naked before him.

The art he had made on her body had already mostly faded. He traced the lines with his claws.

She looked stunning when the wounds were still fresh.

A foolish thought to entertain, he reprimanded himself. Indulging once was more than enough. Business and pleasure were best kept separate.

He removed his hand, reaching for the bedcovers, when he noticed the more permanent scars that littered her body. A small circle of white skin on the right shoulder, unmistakably an arrow wound. Some form of blade had left a long line across her abdomen. Her upper left leg was covered in old burn scars, ones that looked to have been applied deliberately. *Who could have tortured her?* And there were numerous other traces of recklessness on her body that could not be identified as easily.

She must only have learned her healing magics more recently.

He pulled the covers over her. His hand moved to her face, her mouth. He traced her lips with his thumb, remembering how she had bitten down. Abruptly he withdrew his hand and left the room.

His chamber was a mess. He shouted into the hallway for Marius, his chamberlain. The man appeared within moments, bound to tend to Arkhael's every need. He barely paid the man any attention. Marius's soul was so tightly bound in clauses and subclauses, he would almost say he trusted him. Almost.

Arkhael ordered the fluids and broken glass removed, then stalked back through the bedroom to change into a clean set of clothes before finally settling on his balcony. He knew he wouldn't be getting any more work done today. Pouring himself a glass of fragrant red wine, he sat down in a chair, the strong winds whipping around him, and plotted.

The sunless yellow sky had turned dark, lit only by distant fires, when he heard movement from inside. Violent coughing cut the silence. He got up.

Ailith was sitting upright in his bed, clutching her bared chest. Her eyes immediately found him as he entered, then she closed them, muttering quietly, fingers moving ever so slightly with complex gestures and glowing faintly. A healing magic of sorts. He sat down next to her but said nothing, waiting for her to finish as he allowed himself to take in her body. She had such an odd appearance, her grey skin so pale compared to his own. His gaze came to rest on her heaving chest, the skin slightly pinker where he had raked his nails over it. So oddly beautiful.

Slowly, her breathing became less laboured, and she opened her eyes again, frowning.

"Why am I here?"

Not the immediate outpouring of gratitude he had expected.

"You have not yet completed your half of the contract. It seemed wasteful to let my most promising employee drown."

Her frown deepened. "But wait. I was under water when . . ."

He saw her confused thoughts fall into place.

"*You* saved me?" Her mouth dropped open, eyes wide as reality sunk in.

"Rest. I'll ensure your safe return before the first light of dawn."

He got up, leaving her in his bed, and returned to the balcony.

The air never cooled in the Hells, yet there was still something soothing about the nighttime air. Perhaps it was the reduced visibility of the landscape below, he mused.

With a sigh, he let his head fall back against the chair. What was he doing? All of this was so unlike him.

He could hear the loud rustling of sheets inside, followed by the sound of his wardrobe door. Was she trying to rob him while he was at home?

He barely noticed her quiet footfall until she was right next to him, dropping herself down into the other chair. His breath caught in his throat despite himself. She had walked out in nothing but one of his white shirts. It was both too large for her, and not long enough to cover her entirely. She had left the top few buttons open. But even if she hadn't, he would have been able to see the clear outline of her breasts through the fabric, the curvature of her waist. Frantically, he reached for the control that was slowly trying to escape him, that he normally held in such an iron grip. What was it about her that made it so easy for his restraint to slip?

"Rolling up the sleeves like that creates wrinkles." He cleared his throat, watching as she tucked her legs in under herself, following the line of her thigh.

Ailith shrugged. "As does wearing the fabric in general."

Somehow, seeing her so poorly covered in his clothes, he found her more alluring even than when she had been naked in his bed just a moment ago. He tore his eyes away.

"Should you not be resting?"

"Turns out it's hard to relax if you nearly drowned earlier in the day." She stared off into the distance, then turned back to him after a moment of silence. "Do you know if the others survived?"

He shrugged. "I saw no other bodies in the water, but I didn't look for them either."

"Then I can't stay."

See? Mortals. They always disappoint, sooner rather than later.

Why? What were you expecting her to do?

The answer to that question he quickly silenced. "Just give the word and I'll return you to find your loving companions."

She nodded, yet she didn't get up immediately. So they sat in silence, avoiding each other's gazes.

Finally, she sighed and rose, returning to his bedchambers to gather her belongings. He watched her leave, watched his shirt ride up a little with every step she took.

She emerged not too much later, dressed in her own clothing again, with some of the wet pieces of leather draped over her arms.

As she emerged, he got up, snapped his fingers, and opened her a portal.

Ailith walked towards it, then stopped.

She hesitated, opening her mouth to say something. "Arkha—"

He pushed her through before she could speak, watched her and the portal disappear from sight.

With a scream, he hurled an orb of hellfire off into the distance.

Chapter 17

Ailith stumbled through the portal, a bitter taste in her mouth. Somehow the entire encounter had felt like missed opportunities and unspoken words.

Too late for regrets now. Straightening her shoulders, she looked around. The sky was dark around her still, and she cursed her lack of vision. *You should have stayed with him till morning.* Regardless of where her friends were or what state they were in, there was nothing she could do for them if she couldn't see. Vaguely, she saw the movement of water. He had dropped her off on a beach or a riverbank. As she inhaled deeply, the smell of salt water tickled her nose. A beach, then.

She looked around. In the distance, she saw lights reflected in the water. Dewhaven. She couldn't be far. Putting her pack down, she reached into it. Everything was soaked. There was no way she would get any of her torches to light. Blindly, she reached around the sand until her hands found what she was looking for. A piece of wood. Bringing her hands together, she tried to focus her magic. A small spark shot between her fingers. It landed on the wood before its glow slowly faded. With gritted teeth, Ailith tried again. An equally weak spark sprang from her hands. With a frustrated cry, she reached up. Lightning flashed down from the sky, almost instantly burning half of the branch. But the other half caught fire. She sat next to it with clenched fists.

Compose yourself.

Her magic reserves were nearly depleted. Between the water she had tried to stave off and the lightning she had used to get rid of the merrows, there was little energy left in her. Wasting it on calling down lightning when she should have focused and persisted in trying to create a small flame was foolish. She forced herself to her feet. If she couldn't create a torch, she could at least get a fire going. There was plenty of other driftwood around, and it didn't take long before she had created a small fire that lit up her immediate surroundings. The beach she had found herself on was small. Almost immediately behind her was a large cliff face. Without magic to draw on, there was no way for her to safely scale that in the darkness.

"Where have you put me, Arkhael?" she muttered under her breath, sitting herself down next to the fire. She laid her wet armour out on the sand to dry and sat as close to the flames as she could without burning herself.

Had he put her here purposely, knowing she could get nowhere? With her chin on her knees, she recalled his face after he had saved her. If she didn't know any better, she would say he had looked concerned.

Ailith shook her head. Initially, she had thought she was dreaming, but then she had woken up in his bed with his smell all around her and him sitting by her bedside. Her stomach fluttered, and with a groan she let herself fall backwards, immediately regretting it as her back hit the cold sand.

With begrudging resignation, she prepared herself to spend the night on the cold beach, cursing the merrows, the arrogant devil, and mostly herself for leaving so swiftly.

To her surprise, barely any time had passed before she heard a voice.

"Ailith?"

Startled, she sat up.

"Amelie?" She looked around for the source of the voice. A light shone at the top of the cliff.

"You're alive? Jay! She's here!" Amelie's face disappeared before returning again, accompanied by a very tired looking wizard. He rubbed his temples before going through a series of complicated gestures with his hands and drawing what looked like a door in the air. Stepping through it, he appeared next to Ailith, hand outstretched.

Gratefully, Ailith took it as he teleported both of them to the top of the cliff.

"And that's all my magic depleted," Jay smiled weakly. "I'm afraid you'll have to bear with me being grumpy for a day."

Ailith hugged him. "I'm so glad to see you both alive. Thanks, Jay. If you need me to provide any pain relief, just let me know." She knew his head would ache in the morning.

The moment she let go of Jay, Amelie came in for a hug.

"We have a camp set up a little further down." She pulled Ailith along.

Ailith frowned at the darkness surrounding them. "Where are we?" She glanced up at the stars.

Jay sounded exhausted when he answered. "The nearest shore that we could reach when the ship sank, slightly more than a day away I'd guess."

More than a day away . . . Any time they had hoped to make up for by taking the boat they were now rapidly losing. Ailith tried to keep her mind off the consequences.

Amelie's voice pulled her from her thoughts. "How did you survive? Jay and I both saw you go under."

Ailith was grateful for the many shadows the flickering torches cast. "The devil saved me."

"It did what?" Jay's exclamation was somewhat dulled by the exhaustion in his voice.

"I know." Ailith shrugged, avoiding eye contact. "He said it was a waste to let a promising employee drown."

"Was that why you summoned the lightning?" he asked warily.

"No, that was frustration at finding myself stranded on a beach with no way out," she admitted a little awkwardly.

"Well, I am glad you lost your temper," Amelie spoke up. "When I saw it, I immediately recognised it as yours." She smiled as a small campfire slowly came into view. "I can stay up tonight," she offered, "both of you look drained, physically and magically. All I had to do was swim."

Ailith took the offer gratefully, wrapping herself in her cloak next to the fire. Thinking of the devil's lips on hers to keep herself warm through the night.

It was late afternoon two days later when they finally passed through the gates of Dewhaven. Ailith instantly felt a familiar dislike for the city. It was too loud, and it reeked of too many bodies and their waste. The stone buildings towered over them the moment they passed through the gates, guards eyeing them warily. Large cities offered a sense of anonymity, but they also demanded constant wariness and distrust. Immediately, Ailith was aware of people lurking in the dark alleys and shadows next to the large houses. The sudden lack of greenery around her only fuelled her sense of unease.

They had agreed to find Nial before doing anything else. Last she had spoken to him, he had lived in a large park in the city centre, but that was some time ago now, and the city had changed much since. A few times, she took a wrong turn before finally finding the park she remembered. Admittedly, it was beautiful. A patch of green, a breath of fresh air, in a city of stone. The centrepiece of it was a large willow next to a pond. Around it grew a wide variety of plants, flowers, and smaller trees. It was also clearly well loved. The park was full of people sitting on benches, reading next to the pond, or simply strolling through.

It wasn't hard to find Nial among them. There weren't that many druids, especially not in cities. She sensed his druidic magic almost immediately. If not for that, he would have looked unassuming. He was a wiry older looking elven man. His long grey hair stood out above the red poppies he was working on. At her approach, he looked up, a surprised smile curling his lips.

"Well, well, look at what the wind brought in." With a groan, he rose.

Ailith returned his smile. He hadn't changed a bit since she had last seen him. "Bad tidings, I'm afraid."

"Ah, what else is new." He gave her shoulder a squeeze. "And who are your friends?"

"Jay and Amelie," Ailith introduced them. Amelie gave the man a nod. Jay shook his hand. "Can we talk somewhere private?"

"Of course." Nial beckoned for them to follow as he led them to a small cottage near the park.

It could not have been clearer that a druid lived there if he had written "druid's cottage" on the front of it. The walls were lined with shelves holding potions, jars, and other containers that were filled with what looked like dried herbs. Bundles of plants hung from the ceiling. Exotic plants that definitely shouldn't thrive in the colder climate flourished in tall pots, bathing the entire space in a sweet scent.

"So, what can I help you with?" Nial leaned against the small table that stood in the middle of the room.

Ailith told him everything. From the meeting in the cell to the discovery of the weird disease, to the deal she had signed. Only the more intimate details were left out. Nial listened to it all stoically, and when she was done telling her tale, he stood for a long time in silence. Thinking.

When he finally spoke, his voice was firm.

"Let me look at you."

Ailith gave him her hand hesitantly. She hadn't meditated for days, scared of what she would find within her own body. And even as she felt Nial's magic course through her, she didn't follow it, fearing what she would see. With a curse, he withdrew.

"And they brought this here, you say?"

Ailith nodded, and he cursed again.

"Can you help us?" There was a desperate note to Jay's voice as he spoke.

"I don't know." Nial sank down onto a stool. "The devil was right about at least one thing. There is no easy cure. I can't rid you of this. And you know how I feel about your . . . other ventures, Ailith. I cannot advise you on how to break in. You are the expert there, not me." He rubbed his face. "But I am well aware that this could be a threat to other magic users in the city."

"When we last spoke, you were an ambassador for the groves. Surely that gives you some influence, or at least some useful contacts here?" Ailith felt her hope dwindle. Nial was the one person she had been counting on. If not to provide them with a solution, then at least with a helpful opportunity.

He huffed. "And what do I say to my contacts? That one of the biggest and richest organisations in the city is trying to secretly murder all magic users of a non-divine nature? It sounds ridiculous." He raised a hand when he saw that Ailith was about to protest. "It doesn't matter how true your story is. Without proof, it sounds ridiculous. I can try and get word to the right people, and they might be willing to consider investigating your claim, but there is no chance of that happening in the next few days. And I don't believe you have the luxury of waiting around."

"So what do we do?" Amelie looked around the group.

Jay had put his head in his hands, and Ailith felt close to doing the same. It would be so easy to let herself be overwhelmed by everything, to give in to the doubt and fear. She pinched the bridge of her nose. If she gave in now, they would definitely not make it. So she straightened her shoulders and took a few deep breaths. Could they organise a heist into the Chambers in two days?

"I can help you with one thing." Nial walked over to one of his cabinets and fished from it a rusty key.

"I own a second house in the city. I don't really use it, and it is mostly unfurnished, but you can stay there if you wish. It will give you a safe place to work from, and it will save you needing to pay for accommodation."

Ailith took it from him gratefully. He gave her a sad smile.

"Plan your heist. I will do what I can for you, but don't count on my help. If you can bring me the remains of the box after destroying it, I might be able to get an investigation started then. I'm sorry I can't do more."

"I appreciate your honesty." Ailith gave him a forced smile. "We'll get settled tonight, get our bearings and some supplies. Thanks, Nial."

Nial's house lay against one of the hillsides. It could have been a decent home if it had been furnished. As it was, it was mostly empty rooms. Only the kitchen held a small dining table and a few chairs.

Ailith sat down on one of them, looking at the tired faces of Jay and Amelie. They just needed to keep going for a few more days. After that, their troubles would be over. One way or another.

"Go out tonight." She broke the silence with a tired smile. "There is not enough time left to do anything productive, and we are all tired. Find yourself a distraction. Some entertainment. We meet back here for breakfast tomorrow, and we'll plan. We have earned one night of joy." They hadn't just earned it; they *needed* it. The defeated looks on the faces of her friends told her that they all needed a moment of reprieve, however brief.

"Are you sure we have time for this?" Jay queried.

"No." Ailith looked at him, the set of her jaw grim. "But we won't be productive in this state either. We have barely had a single moment's rest since this started. Let's give ourselves one evening to take our minds off things. We can start fresh tomorrow."

Amelie nodded and got up. "She's right. I'm going to find either a brothel or a big bathhouse. I'll see you both tomorrow."

CHAPTER 18

Much as Ailith loved her friends, it was almost a relief to walk through the city alone. Their company had been strained the last few days, the strong sense of impending doom putting everyone even more on edge than they already had been. Whatever moment of peace they had found on the boat had dissipated entirely.

The evening crowds granted her a sense of anonymity that made it easy to forget her worries. Walking between them, she could imagine herself as just a woman going out for the night. She tugged her cloak closer around her body, shielding herself from the wind and hiding her coin purse from any greedy hands. Living the life of a criminal meant that she was always wary of other people, never trusting them to not be guilty of the same crimes she had committed. She veered into a street that housed the fancier brothels, the "bordellos" as they called themselves. The only true difference was that the hygiene increased with the price.

The street was filled with a mixture of music. The sound of quiet harps clashed with the lively notes of a fiddle, increasing in volume whenever a door to one of the establishments was opened. Ailith sighed at the auditory overload.

What did you come here for?

Distraction. She needed to get the devil out of her head. Giving in to her desire for him had not quelled the fire like she had thought it would. If anything, it had only added more fuel to the flames. The last thing she had expected was for him to mirror the hunger that she had felt, that intense and burning need.

Ailith stared at the posters on one of the bordello's facades. The courtesans advertised were beautiful, but the thought of sharing a night with them left her body coldly unaffected. Turning away, she quickened her pace as she heard moans trickle through an open window.

He hadn't just used her body, he had *enjoyed* her body. And she had finally managed to bring him low. A shiver ran down her spine as she remembered the feeling of his mouth on hers.

Turning on her heel, Ailith left the street. There was nothing for her here this night. She should just return to their small, borrowed home and sleep, use the opportunity to get some much-needed rest. But she knew she wouldn't be able to sleep, even if her body was struggling to keep her going. Uttering a curse, she straightened her shoulders. If she could not sleep, she might as well do something somewhat practical.

Which was how she found herself in a tailor's rather than a bordello. The spare clothing Amelie had gathered back in Scarlor's Landing functioned well enough, but she needed some garb that actually fit properly and was her own. As the tailor took her measurements and presented her with his wares, Ailith's hand went to the small ruby in her pocket.

She hated how she hadn't said goodbye to him after he had saved her. He had almost seemed disappointed when she had told him she couldn't stay, and she hadn't even properly expressed her gratitude. Even if it wasn't out of altruism, he had still saved her life. There was no way she would have survived the merrow attack without his intervention.

Maybe you should thank him.

She almost dropped the ruby at the thought. Would she dare pay him a visit?

"Do you do evening wear?" When the tailor gave her a sceptical look, she shook her coin purse, and rolled her eyes as his entire demeanour changed.

If she hadn't been in a sudden unexpected rush, she would have found herself a different shop. As it was, she showed the man the golden necklace she had stolen.

"Preferably something that would showcase this well."

The man returned with a variety of gowns. His sudden willingness to help sickened her.

She ended up choosing a dark green dress with a tight bodice that fell to the ground loosely. It was the simplest piece he had laid out and the only piece she felt comfortable wearing. Everything else seemed too ostentatious, too bold for an already daring occasion. The plunging neckline of the dress accentuated the golden necklace nicely, and the rubies stood out starkly against the dark green.

Satisfied, Ailith paid the man for her regular clothes, the dress, and a nice thick black cloak, the last of which she immediately put on.

Before she left, she asked him if there were any proper liquor merchants nearby.

Quickly walking down the street, she chewed the inside of her cheek nervously.

What are you trying to achieve?

Heat coiled in her stomach. There was no point in lying to herself. She *wanted* to see him, needed to know if that hunger still burned in his eyes. If that lust for her was due to more than a heated argument.

At the merchant's, she picked up a unique bottle of red wine. Apparently, it was the surviving bottle of a brewery that had gone up in flames. She was far from an expert on alcohol, but the man seemed honest enough, even when he asked her for enough gold to feed a small family.

Ailith paid him without question. She had no use for more gold than she needed for the bare necessities. She could always get more.

By the time she arrived back at the small, borrowed home they were staying in, the evening was well underway. Neither Jay nor Amelie seemed to be in, she noted to her relief.

Quickly, she washed herself, letting her hair hang loose for once, and donned the dress. Her heart beat in her throat as she threw the cloak over her shoulders, covering up the necklace. Doubts flitted through her mind.

What if it had just been battle lust? Or lust for a contract? He was a devil, after all.

Enough. She straightened her shoulders. Only one way to get an answer to these questions. Before she could have any other second thoughts, she crushed the ruby.

It's just another gamble.

Well aware that it was a shallow lie to comfort herself, she stepped through the portal.

Nerves battered her stomach as she found herself on the plateau in front of his doors, wind immediately grabbing at the loose strands of her hair. She briefly considered sneaking into his chambers. There was still time to change her plan. Nothing was set in stone.

No, she would stick to it.

So, much unlike last time, she walked up to the big doors and lifted the heavy gilded door knocker. It fell down with a loud THUD.

Her heart skipped a beat as the doors opened, only for her to be immediately disappointed. It was a man who opened the door. Well dressed in a simple black suit, his greying hair combed back. A doorman or servant, she surmised, and mortal by the looks of it. Surprise was clear on his face.

"Can I help you, miss . . . ?"

They clearly don't get many visitors.

"I'm here to see Arkhael."

"My lord is not in, miss. Shall I leave a message?"

My lord? She huffed. Would she turn back? *No.* She had all night.

"Then I'll wait for his return. I'm sure he'll want to see me."
She pushed herself through the door and could see the poor man's hesitation.

Not her fault he had sold his soul to a devil.

"I'll make sure he knows you are here, miss." The man hurried off.

She made her way over to the dining room. Despite Arkhael's absence, the fire under his portrait was lit and the table set, empty plates and goblets ready for the next unlucky guest. She hesitated. Should she push further into his home?

She decided against it. She intended to visit him as a guest. It would hardly be appropriate for her to barge into his chambers.

So she moved some of the tableware and sat down on the edge of the table, staring at the portrait above the fire, pretending her heart wasn't trying to beat itself out of her chest.

Behind her, the doors opened.

"To what do I owe the unexpected delight of your company?" Arkhael bowed deeply. There it was. That shiver up her spine he alone seemed to be able to cause. He looked human still, his skin a normal tan, his features smoothed over, more distinguished but not less dangerous. And his voice was just as smooth as his eyes trailed along her legs where the dress was visible below the cloak. "You look positively marvellous."

Ailith smiled. "We finally cashed in on our last heist. I figured I would treat myself." She jumped off the table. "And I brought a gift."

He raised his eyebrows in surprise. "Have you indeed? Come, then. Let us retire to a more appropriate setting."

He gestured for her to follow, leading her to his now familiar chambers. Inside, he pulled back a chair for her.

"It's not often I receive voluntary visitors bearing gifts." He sat down opposite her.

Ailith smiled. "I don't often get fished out of the water. I believe I never properly expressed my gratitude. Consider it an owed favour.

Within reason." Before Arkhael could respond, she pushed the box with the wine in his direction. "And a gesture of goodwill."

"A thief in a generous mood? How very ironic." He searched her face for a hidden catch. Ailith merely shrugged, expression carefully neutral. Opening the box, Arkhael chuckled at the contents.

"An Ardinger Red, a rare find indeed. You know, I witnessed the incineration of the—"

He stopped mid-sentence. Ailith had taken off the cloak, revealing the dress and necklace beneath it.

"That is a *very* bold move." His voice was dangerously low, all traces of joviality gone, even as his eyes flashed down below the necklace.

Nerves flared in Ailith's stomach, followed by the thrill of satisfaction knowing she had gotten to him. Again. She stroked the golden chains.

"It's a very pretty piece."

"It was once a queen's necklace." He leaned forwards, drawing his eyes back up. "What is stopping me from retrieving it back from you?"

Ailith leaned back, an expression of mock-horror on her face. "We call that a 'hard job' in my line of work. It's considered very distasteful."

"And flaunting stolen goods in front of their owner isn't considered distasteful?" Slowly, he got up, abandoning the illusion of humanity as he did so.

"No." Ailith rose as well, clenching her hands to stop them from shaking. "But it is considered unnecessarily foolish." She stood her ground as he took a step forwards. "Besides, are you truly still the owner if they have been successfully stolen?"

Arkhael narrowed his eyes at her, then his hand shot forwards. Ailith was prepared. She caught it mid-air, cocking an eyebrow, smile still on her lips. His fingers closed around hers, and he jerked her forwards, towards him.

Time seemed to stop. So close to him, Ailith felt her skin tingle. His eyes met hers, and she saw reflected in them the same hunger.

Then time resumed, and the necklace was forgotten. His lips were on hers, his body pressed against her, and *fuck* she needed him with a desperation that frightened her. He guided them backwards until his legs hit the sofa and they all but fell onto it, tearing at their clothes as they went.

The moment his trousers were gone, Ailith sank herself down onto him, the dress around her waist. Uncaring that she was revealing exactly how badly she wanted him, needed him. How wet she had already been for him. She didn't stop until she could feel him deep inside her, her legs on either side of him, her hands on his back.

Finally.

His mirrored hunger only increased her need. Arkhael groaned.

She was barely aware of his hands on her hips, slipping under the material of the dress, of his mouth on her neck and her breasts as the bodice fell slack around her. All she could feel was him inside her again and again, faster and faster. The world ceased to exist until it was just the joining of their bodies and the moans leaving their lips. Every thrust sent sparks through her. Until she shuddered and tensed way too soon and felt him tense against her.

If the circumstances had been any different, she might have been embarrassed. Instead, she leaned her forehead against his, panting heavily, feeling mostly overwhelmed with how suddenly everything had happened, trying to steady her breathing. Finding a sliver of comfort in the fact that the desperation had seemed mutual. She was nowhere near done wanting him, but the desperate pain had dulled.

He pulled back slightly, the unreadable expression on his face quickly replaced by one of smug satisfaction. Before she could be too alarmed by it, he pulled her in for a kiss.

There was a sharp, burning pain at the nape of her neck.

Immediately, she tried to pull her head back, only to find that Arkhael held her in a vice-like grip.

"And now both jewels and thief belong to me."

Ailith reached behind her until she found his hand. He took her fingers, led them to where the clasp of the necklace had been. The gold there felt hot still, and there was no sign of the clasp, only solid metal.

How? It was meant to be magically protected.

Hellfire.

She couldn't stop the look of shock and indignance on her face, made worse by the smile he returned.

How dare he?

"Just because you collar something does not mean you own it," she spat at him.

She struggled off of him, and he let her go, still looking annoyingly pleased with himself. Nearly, she tripped over the dress as it fell down around her, the bodice torn entirely at the back. She walked over to the mirror that hung against the wall and inspected the necklace. There was nothing she could do about it; the clasp had been melted into a solid piece. She knew there was no point in trying to break it either. Something imbued with magic like this wouldn't break easily. Not without specialised magical tools.

She heard him get up behind her, watched him walk over in the reflection.

"I'll find a blacksmith with a forge hot enough."

He only smiled at her as she turned around.

"You're mine."

She took a step backwards.

"You wish."

He laughed.

"I'll have you begging to be mine."

He was on her in three swift steps, pressing her against the mirror.

No, he had gone too far.

Then why did her heart flutter so?

The stone floor behind Arkhael cracked before a thick vine wrapped itself around his neck. Ailith closed her fist, pulling him away with it.

He tutted, burning it away with ease. "We both know you will have to pull out a lot more than that if you truly wish to stop me."

Ailith tried to sidestep him as he stalked forwards again. She knew he was right, and yet she hesitated. Slowly, Arkhael closed the distance between them.

"But you won't." He lowered his voice and let the quiet implication hang in the air between them.

"Or maybe I have no desire to gravely harm you." The retort sounded hollow even to her own ears.

He had cornered her again, but this time, he didn't touch her. Instead, he just stood, arms crossed, giving her a chance to move or act. His spread wings cast a shadow over his body, but Ailith didn't need much light to eye him up.

He had given her an opportunity.

Why didn't she take it?

Her eyes went from his wings to his toned chest, couldn't help but briefly flick down to see how erect he was.

As her eyes trailed his body, he uncrossed his arms and extended a hand. An invitation.

A point of no return.

"This changes nothing." The moment her fingers touched his outstretched hand, he pulled her in, kissing her lips, her jaw, her neck.

"Indeed it doesn't. You'll still beg," he whispered against her ear.

He spun her around, and she barely caught herself from slamming into the bottom of the painting, the wood of the frame catching her in the stomach, knocking the wind out of her.

A hand on her back pushed her forwards, claws digging in slightly. Everything he had said about begging, all her curses directed at him, were forgotten when she felt him press against her.

She clawed at the wall, the canvas. Ended up gripping the painting's frame as he entered her painfully slowly. Ailith tried to move her hips back to meet him, but both his hands were on them in an instant, stopping her from moving.

She was aware of every single searing inch of him as he moved into her at a pace that made eternity seem short.

By the time he had entered her fully, she was sweating and trembling, straining against the iron grip Arkhael had on her hips.

He let go of her with one hand and moved it to her throat, forcing her to arch her back, bringing her face closer to his. She shuddered as he kept her hips in place, so desperately wanting him to move.

"What are you?"

When she didn't respond immediately, he started pulling back out. At the same excruciatingly slow pace.

"Fu . . . Not that—ah—easily . . . swayed," Ailith managed through gritted teeth. Her fingers started cramping from how tightly she was gripping the frame.

The hand at her throat suddenly let go, and she gasped for air. Only to have it knocked out of her again as he slammed back into her, setting an unrelenting pace. A string of curses left her lips despite herself at the sudden change. She felt his hands move from her hips to her breasts, his claws digging in around them, sinking in a little bit deeper with every thrust. The pain only added to the pleasure. Behind her, Arkhael groaned, his breath hot on her neck. Every time he pushed back in, a little more of her sanity vanished. Just as her body started to shake involuntarily, he stopped moving, almost entirely withdrawn.

"What are you?"

Ailith swore loudly, tried to push back against him, struggled with the grip he had on her. To no avail. He kept her right on the edge of her climax, giving her enough to bring her to the brink, not enough to push her over the edge.

Almost gently, he pulled out entirely, turning her around and lifting her again. Eagerly, Ailith let him, hooking her legs around his waist. Gasping as she felt him press against her, then push in. Leaning her against the painting, he dug his claws into her thighs. Was pain meant to feel this good?

His pace was more lavish now, every thrust a searing fire through her body, as if he knew exactly how he tortured her and wanted to take his time doing so.

She clung to him, and again he denied her as she raged, biting and clawing in desperation. Her attempts only darkened the fire in his eyes, and she hated how much he was enjoying it. How unfair his physical advantage over her was.

"What are you?"

Ailith had no idea how long he tortured her for or how often he brought her to the very edge. Every part of her body cried for release. She seemed to exist on the brink of pleasure, painfully close, hyperaware of every single place their bodies touched.

"What are you?"

How often had he asked her that? And would it truly be so bad to admit that she was his?

Admit?

Something told her she should feel alarmed, but rational thought had long since left her, and the one voice in her head she should have been listening to was drowned out by the sound of moans.

Just give him . . . what he wants . . .

His claws dug into her back—when had he moved his hands?—as he held her still again.

No.

She must have uttered the word out loud, for he leaned back a bit to look at her.

"No?" There was sweat on his face, she noticed, and his usually neatly tied hair had broken loose from its bonds.

"You love how I feel inside you." Even he was taking heavy breaths between words. "You want nothing more than for me to fill you. To claim you."

One of his hands moved down between them, sliding between her legs.

"At this point, you are just lying to yourself."

For the briefest moment, he put pressure on her while slowly sliding in, then removed his hand again. She might as well have died. The last of her thoughts left her at his touch, black spots dancing across her eyes, her hands searching for purchase, nails digging into the canvas behind her, his shoulders. She needed him to continue. She needed *him*. Her voice was hoarse when it came out.

"I am yours." She bit the inside of her cheek at Arkhael's questioning eyebrows, his knowing smile, and closed her eyes, unable to look at him. "Please. Make me yours."

It was barely audible. Even with her gaze averted, she couldn't miss the victorious smile on his face. His movements resumed, and this time, he didn't withdraw his hand.

Stars danced across Ailith's vision as her climax finally washed over her so violently, she forgot to breathe. The absolute bliss almost painful, only accentuated by the sting of his teeth breaking the skin above her collarbone.

Vaguely, she was aware that Arkhael had stopped moving too, buried inside her, tremors wrecking his body.

Together, they fell. In a pile of limbs, sweat, and blood, they crashed to the floor. Her head swam. Ailith felt like she might pass out. Survival instinct kicked in.

Blood loss.

Where from? With great effort, she tried to locate the source. Her entire body hurt, muscles burning from the repeated strain. Her thighs were bleeding, as were her chest and shoulders. Enough to scar, not enough to justify the dizziness.

Her focus shifted to her back. The skin was in shreds.

How had that happened? She remembered him raking his claws down her back, she had arched into it, and he had bitten her breasts in response. Never had she noticed the cuts went that deep.

A little healing magic would do, enough to stop the bleeding. The skin itched as it knit itself back together.

A clawed finger traced the necklace on her chest. Outrage and nerves flaring back to life, Ailith opened her eyes. Arkhael had propped himself up on his elbows next to her, wings folded on his back, an expression of utter satisfaction on his face.

"You were bound to lose one at some point."

Ailith narrowed her eyes. "Just enjoy your one victory while it lasts."

He brought his face close to hers. "I fully intend to."

She shivered in response and sat up abruptly. "My soul?"

"Oh, don't worry. Unfortunately, it is still entirely in your possession. If souls could be so easily acquired in the throes of passion, the Hells would be ruled by succubi instead."

Ailith breathed a sigh of relief and straightened her shoulders.

He's right. You can't always win if you gamble with such high stakes. Get up. Show him you're not defeated.

Without a word, she stood and stretched, legs still shaking. As she walked, she could feel the evidence of his earlier words between her legs and barely managed to bite back a moan at the realisation. He didn't need to know how right he had been.

No wonder her head was spinning. The bottom of the painting had been ruined. The canvas below the throne was in tatters, and it was covered in streaks of blood, as well as the occasional handprint. Amused, she snorted—so much for his vanity—then turned to Arkhael.

"I need a bath, and I've wanted to try yours ever since I broke in here. So if you truly intend to enjoy your victory all night, I suggest you follow." She didn't wait for his response, instead walking to where she knew his bath chambers to be, strutting like she owned the place and hadn't just begged to be his.

CHAPTER 19

The bathroom seemed even warmer than the other rooms, no doubt thanks to the steam that came off the perpetually running hot water. She reached down. The water was scathingly hot. Perfect. Gingerly, she stepped down into the pool and almost fully submerged herself. The wounds on her skin burned in the hot water. Hissing slightly, she gently started washing herself, turning the water immediately around her red with her own blood. She watched it go down a drain at the other end, then sank down onto the bench near the edge.

Devils and contracts aside, Ailith immediately knew she would never find another bath as good as this. The water felt truly hot against her skin. She didn't have to sit still for fear of disturbing a cold patch. With a sigh, she let herself relax, wondering briefly what Arkhael was up to.

She must have dozed off slightly, as the sound of the door opening startled her back to reality. Arkhael walked in, a bottle and two glasses in hand. Wordlessly, he joined her in the hot water, pouring them each a glass.

Ailith took it with narrowed eyes and sniffed the liquid suspiciously. A sweet-smelling wine.

"An older vintage, but still just wine." Clearly amused, Arkhael put his own glass down, then leaned back in the water.

Ailith carefully sipped from hers. The drink was delightfully sweet, and not that heavy on the alcohol, she realised. Gratefully, she took another swig before setting the glass back down.

They sat in silence for some time. Closing her eyes, Ailith wondered if he was as sore and exhausted as she was.

When she felt his arm sneak around her, she tensed.

She didn't expect him to simply pull her closer to him, resting her head against his chest, arm still around her. Slowly, she relaxed again, allowing herself to lean against him, heart beating frantically at this odd moment of intimacy.

His other hand came up and stroked the skin of her arm.

"How does one get such an unusual skin colour?" he murmured. Ailith opened her mouth to answer, then changed her mind.

"Was it not you who said information should never be given freely?"

"Hmm, then ask," he breathed against her hair.

She could play this game, even tired as she was. Tit for tat. A piece of information of equal worth.

"Do all devils have this much stamina?" she asked, unable to keep the mischief out of her voice entirely.

He chuckled. "We are creatures of sin. If we couldn't outdo mortals, we wouldn't be very tempting, would we?" He bit her earlobe to emphasise his point.

Ailith failed to bite back the small gasp that escaped her, then looked down at her ashen hand. "Are you familiar with Nimble Weed?"

"Slightly magical, a hallucinogenic popular among the nobility. Lethal in high doses. Not known for changing one's skin, though."

She nodded. "Grown as a small flower in cities, but it naturally grows in big clusters. Over the summer, the plant produces hair-like seeds, highly coveted by druids. They burn them during rituals. Apparently it deepens their connection with nature." She shrugged. "I was a small kid when they found me in a Nimble Weed cluster. Hairs clinging to my skin." She chuckled. "Probably stoned out of my mind. They had no idea how long I had been in there, and I have no memory of it."

Ailith raised the hand, flexing her fingers. "Supposedly, they tried their best to cure me, but some parts of me were forever changed."

Arkhael took her hand in his and brought it to his mouth to kiss.

Where had this tender side of him come from? She closed her eyes, determined to enjoy it while it lasted.

Danger, her mind whispered. She stilled the voice. Why shouldn't she allow herself a moment of joy?

"So, how does an orphan turned druid become a thief?" A touchy subject.

"Why did you refuse to kiss me until I made you?"

He froze, and she immediately regretted her tone, fearing the moment would end.

"Pass."

The silence returned, and Ailith scrambled for something to break it with.

"What will you do once you have the reliquary, oh archdevil?"

Arkhael nearly snorted. "You truly think I would share that with you?"

"Why not?" Ailith opened her eyes so she could look at him, eyebrow raised. "You know I can't work against you. I'm just curious."

"As if you wouldn't still try." He huffed at her, but a faint smile curled his lips, and Ailith allowed herself to relax again. The earlier tension had dissipated.

"Tell you what, thief. Swear to me you will share neither word nor thought of what I am about to tell you with others, and I might just answer you."

Ailith barely considered it. With her bound by the contract, it was up to her friends to try and thwart him, not her. In a way, it was almost freeing.

"An easy promise to make." She brought the hand that was holding hers up and kissed it. "I swear to share neither word nor thought of your plans for the reliquary with others."

Arkhael tightened his grip on her hand slightly. "You should swear yourself to me more often," he murmured before clearing his throat. "When you close your eyes each night and let the day disappear, what is it that you chase in your dreams? What is it you truly desire?"

Ailith was so taken aback by the question, she almost forgot the game that they were playing. In Arkhael's eyes burned a hunger that had nothing to do with her body, a stark reminder that she was sharing a bath with a devil. One who knew too much about her already. She bit her lip, averting her gaze. Answering his question truthfully would be dumb. It was clearly meant to test her. How badly did she really want to know? But when she raised her eyes again, she realised it didn't matter. He expected her to back down because they both knew how stupid it would be to give him this information, which didn't really leave her a choice.

Hesitantly, she opened her mouth. "To find a home where I can truly be happy."

Arkhael's eyes bored into hers. "What's stopping you from finding it?"

"That's elaboration. If I tell you, I get an extra question as well."

"Fair enough."

Ailith sat up slightly to take another sip from her glass, ignoring how easy it was to lean herself back against him again. How nice the arm around her shoulders felt.

"I . . ." She laughed awkwardly. "I don't know. I guess I don't know what I'm looking for exactly. There are parts of my life that I don't want to give up, so as long as I don't know what I want, I am scared of losing what I have." Her eyes went to Arkhael's again. "And I know full well I shouldn't have told you any of that," she added with an eyeroll before he could look too pleased with himself.

"You play a dangerous game; you should have expected dangerous questions." He smiled in response, his eyes glittering with satisfaction. "The reliquary would allow me to bring a large host into the Hells, which could get rid of some inconveniences for me."

Cryptic. "Wait, into the Hells? You're not going to use it to invade our Realm?"

Ailith raised an eyebrow when Arkhael hesitated, feeling rather smug with herself when his smile turned wry. "Eventually. Some other pieces need removing before I would be able to do so. It would be well past your lifetime."

"As if that makes it better," she responded drily.

"You presume I would make your Realm worse, but so far you seem to have enjoyed what you have seen here." *I dare you to disagree with me.* He didn't need to say it. The unspoken challenge was right there. And Ailith knew she had nothing to counter it with.

She let her head fall backwards against him, closing her eyes, choosing not to dignify his statement with a response.

His hot breath ghosted over her skin as he whispered in her ear.

"Enough talk of politics and plans of world domination." With his mouth he traced the curve of her neck, his teeth scraping over the skin until she found herself tilting her head for him. His hands had started wandering again, tracing something. From the pattern of it, she guessed it was the old scars on her arm.

"I find it hard to believe you are that bad a thief."

Her eyes shot open, and she looked up at him. "I am deeply offended."

"Then explain the many scars."

"How come you have none? I understand violence doesn't seem to be your first choice per se, but I don't believe you've never been hit."

Arkhael raised his eyebrows at her. "Only weapons of holy or divine nature can scar me, but surely that's not something you needed to ask?"

Ailith shrugged. "Until I met you, I had a very sensible approach to anything fiendish. Kill them before they get a chance to speak, in any way possible. Not that I encountered that many."

Anything holy or divine. Her stomach filled with a sense of foreboding.

"A sensible approach."

He nudged her when she didn't speak.

Ailith shook off the feeling of dread and smiled. "I think you'll find I am an excellent thief. So excellent in fact, that a few times we were hired to acquire some extremely sensitive items from extremely powerful people. And they often have enough money to hire some magical lapdog to track you down and bring you in." Then she laughed and pointed at a thin line on her left leg. "Except for that one. The first few times, I was indeed awful. I suppose we all start somewhere. But once I got shanked in a prison fight, I decided to properly get better."

"That's . . . a lot of scars still." He traced the outside of her thigh.

Ailith looked away, remembering. "A lot can be done in two weeks. I learned how to withdraw from my body during that time. Separate my mind from the pain. Numb myself to the fear of what comes next."

"And this?" Arkhael traced the big line across her abdomen.

"A trap of razor wire. I saw my insides that day, one of the few times I actually feared for my life." She smiled. "And a good incentive to get better at healing myself."

He pointed at the white scar in the palm of her left hand.

"Torture. They drove a blunt stick through it with a hammer." She turned her hand around, the skin unblemished on the other side. "I killed that man before he could finish."

"And what about these?" He traced the fresh lines around her breasts. Ailith rolled over, straddling him, aware of how obviously he desired her again already.

"A crazy devil who decided that he just had to have me."

His eyes glittered dangerously. "A crazy devil, hmm?"

She leaned forwards, her voice quiet. "Who else would try to own a thief, just so he could hear her cry his name? *Arkhael*," she added.

His reaction was instant, lifting her and bending her over the edge of the pool. His hands slid down her back to her legs, spreading them. Ailith felt him press against her, then rub himself along her. She bit her lip at the friction. He had no right to feel so good while doing so little. Her nails scraped along the stone floor every time he stroked his length across her.

"Again." His voice was hoarse behind her.

"Again what?"

She knew well enough what he wanted. But the memory of him making her beg was too fresh in her mind.

He bent over her, pressing against her just enough that she could almost feel him inside her, and brought his mouth to her ear.

"Say my name, and I will make you mine until you can no longer stand."

Ailith's arms nearly buckled at his words, and she let out a strangled moan.

"Arkhael."

He eased into her until his hips were flush with hers, pulling her back by the necklace, forcing Ailith to hold his hand to stop it suffocating her.

"Mine," he grunted as he buried himself inside her, withdrawing just a little only to move inside her again.

To deny him would be lying. She knew it in her heart. In this moment, she was his. Wanted to be his.

"Yours," she whispered, and felt his rhythm stutter before he picked it up again, faster.

Once she had said it, it was as if a barrier had been removed.

She repeated it. "Yours, Arkhael."

He let go of her, pulled out so she could turn over, the stone floor bruising her already sore back. Ailith parted her legs for him. He held her chin, looking her in the eye as he entered her again. Forcing her to reveal to him exactly how much she enjoyed the feeling of him sliding into her.

"Mine," he whispered.

Fuck, what is this?

His hand moved to her throat, making it hard for her to breathe. Her vision swam, but she refused to break eye contact. She brought her hands up to the arm that was holding her, digging her fingers into his wrist. He let go, intertwined his fingers with hers and brought them above her head as she gasped for air. With his other hand he lifted her left leg over his shoulder, biting the side of her calf, never once pausing the steady thrust of his hips.

Ailith held onto their entwined fingers as if they were the only anchor keeping her sane, moving her hips with him, her back scraping across the stone floor.

"You are mine, little thief." His voice cut right across her. "Even when you leave here, you'll be wearing my collar, bearing my scars on your body." He moved his face even closer, pushing her leg back further, somehow allowing for even deeper access to her body. Ailith whimpered, unable to speak, her free hand digging into his shoulders. "No touch will ever equal mine." He sped up. "No name will taste as sweet as mine."

"Arkhael." She barely managed it. He grunted and she could feel him shudder, could feel him restrain himself. His eyes bored into hers, burning with a possessiveness that took her breath away.

"Come with me, little thief. Show me how much you love it when I fill your body."

Fuck.

As soon as she came, she felt him let go and release inside her, heard him call her his. Her cries of pleasure died on his lips as he kissed her through her climax. She shuddered in his arms, wave after wave of pleasure crashing into her. He was there the entire time, until her body all but collapsed onto the stone floor.

Barely had her vision returned before he pulled her up. True to his word, her legs nearly buckled under her. But he was there to catch her and take her by the hand.

"Come."

She followed him on unsteady legs as he led her to his bed, pulling her in with him.

"When are you expected back?"

"By breakfast at the latest. Just after sunrise." She looked at him confused, her mind not quite yet functioning.

"Then rest. There are a few hours left yet." He raised a hand when he saw she was about to protest.

"Your body is giving up on you, and I need you alive."

Ailith frowned. She didn't want to sleep. This night had been a dream she did not want to wake from. She knew there wouldn't be others, and that thought made her sadder than she wanted to admit. But she also knew Arkhael was right. The rough treatment of her body and the late hour were taking their toll, loath as she was to admit it. Was she safe to sleep here?

There is no safer place.

It was an odd realisation. She knew he needed her. If anything, he would protect her while she was with him. And who would dare attack him? So she relented and hesitantly lowered herself onto the mattress.

Arkhael traced the side of her cheek, down her neck, to the necklace.

"Worry not. If fate didn't have other plans for you, I would make you mine again." His eyes were dark, a hungry smile on his face. "Now sleep."

Every fibre of her body screamed at her to keep her eyes open. And she couldn't help but tense when she finally did close her eyes, ready for something, anything, to happen. Then the exhaustion caught up with her. She thought she heard Arkhael murmur something, but sleep took her before she could respond.

Despite the late hour of her bedtime, Ailith woke with the dawn. Years of watchfulness woke her up when the odd yellow light of a Hellish dawn filtered into the room.

Unmoving, she slowly opened her eyes. Next to her, Arkhael lay still, other than the rhythmic rise and fall of his chest, his eyes closed. She yawned, then squeezed her eyes shut again, wishing she could go back to sleep. There was no point; she never could. Instead, she gently turned over, careful not to move too much. Arkhael stirred, but his eyes remained shut. She took the opportunity to watch him.

Sharing a bed with a devil. You've truly reached peak insanity.

Her hand went to the necklace. Was that why people went mad? Because it felt so good?

Of course it felt good to have sex with a devil. He himself had said as much last night.

Then why had her stomach tightened every time he called her his? Why had it been so easy to give in, to tell him that he was right? Why had it *felt* so right?

Because he's alluring and intoxicating. Because you wish you could spend more time here with him. Because when he holds you, you feel special.

Because all you have thought of the last few days was the look on his face when you woke in his chambers, when he was convinced you had died.

She shook her head at herself. Foolish thoughts, all of them. Soon, they wouldn't matter. Though after last night, she was certain that she would never enjoy another's touch like she enjoyed his.

Fuck, what has he done to you?

She rubbed her temples. She was letting her emotions run away with her. Time would eventually dull all feelings, whether they were lust or something else brought on by being intimate for a night.

And what if it doesn't? Never before have you— She cut the thought off, determined to enjoy the present regardless of what the future might bring.

So she continued drinking in the sight of his body. So many parts of it she hadn't explored yet, but he seemed oddly guarded about where their touches went, and she felt no need to push the matter, lest she lose what little she had for the short time she had it. And even the thought of that alone was enough to set her body aflame.

Arkhael stirred, his eyes blinking open, meeting hers.

"You were supposed to rest. Why are you awake?" His voice was even more husky in the morning.

Ailith shrugged. "I woke up, figured I might as well enjoy the view."

"With only your eyes?" He smiled that dangerous smile of his. The one that meant she just had to rise to the challenge. So she rolled on top of him.

He was ready—of course he was—immediately guiding her down. Ailith gasped, slowly rocking her hips on top of him as she adjusted to the feeling of him inside her. Her body still equal parts sore and sensitive from the previous night.

"If your role weren't so crucial, I would tie a leash to you and keep you here." His words were interrupted by a grunt every time she rocked forwards. Ailith was about to retort when a better thought came to her. She paused, long enough to mutter under her breath and gesture with her left hand, ignoring Arkhael's wary expression. Vines trailed down from the ceiling, wrapping themselves around her wrists, holding them suspended above her. She wrapped another around her neck.

"Like this?" She cocked an eyebrow at him and was rewarded with a stunned expression on his face, claws digging into her hips. He licked his lips.

"Exactly like that." His voice was hoarse with desire.

She moved atop him, using her vines as leverage while she couldn't use her hands. He seemed entranced, not taking his eyes off of her once as she sped up. The fire in his eyes seemed to set her body aflame with its intensity. For all his intimidating presence, all his physical strength, she held him captive in that moment. The rush of it was too much. Even when her body started shuddering uncontrollably, she did not break eye contact, holding him in her gaze, moaning his name with what little breath she had. She watched him struggle for control and lose, slamming into her, releasing inside her. His head thrown back into the pillows, his horns tearing the fabric as his fingers dug into her hips. The image alone made her curl her toes.

Slowly, Ailith released her vines, letting herself fall forwards into his waiting arms. He held her tight, shuddering inside her still.

They stayed there until their breathing evened, the inevitable drawing ever closer. A thin layer of fine dust covered her back as her vines slowly crumbled. Ailith sighed against his skin, lifting herself, only for Arkhael to pull her back down into a kiss. It was messy and full of procrastination, and she wasn't at all surprised when she felt him harden again inside her.

What is an extra hour?

When they finally parted, her entire body hurt again, pain she refused to heal.

Arkhael was first to get out of bed. She watched him get dressed and leave the room.

Time to go. Nimbly, she slid off the bed and opened his wardrobe, putting on one of his white shirts. She did not expect the smell of coffee to greet her when she left the room.

"Are you having breakfast?" she asked incredulously, walking over to where he sat in his big chair.

He looked at her over his cup. "A most lucrative agreement made long ago." He gestured at the second cup on the table.

Actual fresh coffee? Ailith couldn't recall the last time she had had a proper coffee, and took a grateful sip. He also pushed a plate with an assortment of pastries her way.

She chuckled. "I can't remember the last time I had this decadent a breakfast." She nestled herself onto the chair across from him, catching him staring at last night's marks on her legs. "Thank you."

He shook his head, meeting her eye.

"My pleasure," he said before unfolding a paper across from her. He had a stack of them, she realised. Some from capital cities, others with a name or language unknown to her.

In silence, she nibbled on her food. It was of excellent quality, although she expected no less. Occasionally, she caught Arkhael glancing up from his papers, eyes trailing her body. It should have been so much weirder to drink coffee with a devil. And even if it was far from normal, it was oddly peaceful. Briefly, she closed her eyes. How she wished she could stay. It was so easy to forget about reality with him. But reality wouldn't forget about her.

Finishing her coffee, she stood up to finally gather her clothes and dress herself. The bodice of the pretty dress she had bought only the evening before was torn in the back. There was no salvaging that. She turned to Arkhael.

"Do you have a dagger or anything sharp lying around?"

He looked up from his papers and eyed her curiously.

"Second drawer in the desk."

Ailith walked over to the dark wooden desk, feeling like he had allowed her to catch a glimpse of who hid behind the facade. She opened the drawer and resisted the urge to smile. A variety of writing equipment lay inside it. Everything was so carefully sorted, so clearly had its own place. She retrieved the small dagger, the dark material of the blade unfamiliar to her, and carefully tore it through the fabric of her skirt, separating it from the bodice. Throwing it over her head, she dropped the skirt to her waist, tucking Arkhael's shirt into it and twisting a knot in the green fabric. She didn't ask him if she could keep his shirt. Ignoring his eyes on her, she walked over to the mirror.

Her thrown-together outfit worked if one didn't look too closely. The shirt just about didn't fall off her shoulders, the wide sleeves were so long on her, they had to be rolled up. She left the top few buttons open, knowing full well it would draw his eye. The uncovered marks on her shoulder and cleavage stood out starkly, the golden necklace sparkling above them. The wounds around her chest where he had dug in his nails would scar if she didn't heal them now. Yet she hesitated, then abruptly turned around, refusing to think about it, briefly touching the necklace. She would deal with the consequences when they happened. Resolutely, she threw the cloak over her shoulders.

It was time.

Behind her, Arkhael had risen as well. He quirked an eyebrow at her when she turned around, a faint smile on his lips as he took in her improvised work. His eyes lingered on her neck.

"You'll need a portal back, I presume?"

Ailith nodded, her throat suddenly dry. He snapped his fingers, then walked over to her, hand sneaking under the cloak to touch the necklace. Leaning forwards, he whispered in her ear. "Consider your favour paid." Then he walked off.

Ailith shivered but didn't look back, stepping through the portal instead.

CHAPTER 20

Ailith nearly tripped over Amelie when she stepped out of the portal, both women going down with a yelp.

"What are you doing in my room?" Ailith hissed, aware her face had gone entirely red.

Amelie only stared at her, her mouth open.

"Amelie, please close your mouth."

Amelie did. Her eyes took in Ailith's torn skirt, the white shirt that barely fit her under the cloak she was wearing. "Tell me you did not do what I think you did."

"And why not?" Ailith turned her back on the other woman, looking for the new clothes she had bought the night before.

"Ailith . . ."

She turned around at the disapproving tone in Amelie's voice.

"Tell me why not, Amelie? What I did with the devil doesn't affect the two of you, nor does it endanger us. Why care that I didn't go to a bordello last night?"

Amelie gave her an incredulous look.

"I'm not stupid, Ailith. I have noticed how distracted you are. Both of us have. He's got you wound around his little finger." She shook her head. "Did he summon you?"

Ailith raised her chin. "No, I went of my own volition. To thank him for saving my life."

"Oh, don't be stupid, you know he needs you to get his reliquary. Of course he saved your life."

The words stung, even if she knew Amelie was right. Ailith sighed and lowered herself onto the floor. "I know. Don't worry, I do. There's just something about him, Amelie." She looked the other woman in the eye. "He makes me feel alive, truly alive, like nothing ever has. Even if it is some devilish charm, is it really so bad if I enjoy it when I might die in a few days?"

Amelie walked over to sit next to her and laid an arm around her shoulders.

"You know what Jay would say." She imitated the wizard's pragmatic tone: "*Every piece of information you give him is something he will use against you.* He's right, Ailith. What if the devil shows up to kill you after we break into the vault?"

Ailith stared at the bare wooden wall. Amelie was right. They both were. And yet, she didn't think Arkhael would. But how was she to explain to them that a devil had seemed tender when he kissed the palm of her hand?

Or had that just been a facade as well? All part of a plan that she was willingly playing the victim of? Finally, she shrugged.

"It's not like we'll have time to relax anyway. Time is my adversary, remember?"

Amelie pulled her close. "I know. And we'll get into that vault. In the meantime, no other deals, okay? I don't care what naughty business you got up to in that very fancy cave-house of his. Just promise me that."

"An easy promise. I wasn't planning on it." Ailith squeezed Amelie's hand and got up to dress for the day. "So, what *were* you doing in my room?" she asked as she removed the cloak.

Behind her, Amelie groaned. "Woman, do you have a death wish? You thought you would just quickly nip over to the Hells *while wearing the jewellery you stole from him*?!" Despite her words, there was a hint of admiration in her voice.

Ailith allowed herself a giggle, and when Amelie giggled with her, the tension broke. "You have to tell me how he reacted to that."

"About as well as you would expect," Ailith admitted, reluctantly taking off Arkhael's shirt and replacing it with her own. It covered most of the skin his shirt left exposed, and only part of the necklace peaked out above it. "And now I can't take the bloody thing off."

Amelie snorted. "Can't say you didn't get what you deserved for that one." She rose as well. "I was looking for you just as you stumbled back into your room. Jay and I had both already returned, and you are not usually one to be late. I didn't really expect to find you here though, especially not doing the walk of shame."

Ailith rolled her eyes, fastening her armour over her shirt and donning her cloak again. As long as she wore that, no one had to see that she was wearing jewellery she would never be able to afford.

Following Amelie downstairs, she found Jay studying a map, a piece of bread in one hand. He waved at her without looking up.

Curious, she joined him at the table, and he pushed the paper in her direction. "One map of where the Chambers are, and one of the Chambers itself, although it seems regrettably useless so far."

She pulled the map of the Chambers closer. It looked to have been made for visitors, marking statues of interest within the building.

"Anything that indicates where there *could* be a vault?"

"Nothing I can find. If it is big enough to hold three doors, logic would dictate an entrance on the ground floor and a basement-level vault. Breakfast?" He pushed a plate over.

"Thanks, but I've eaten already." Ailith ignored the quizzical look he gave her. "So are we going there today? To scope it out?"

Amelie joined the other two at the table. "No use in waiting? See what we can find and learn, then buy the tools we need. Quick in, quick out. Done." She exchanged a look with Jay, who shook his head almost imperceivably. Ailith pointedly looked at the map, pretending she hadn't seen it. *Best not to know, just in case.*

"You and Jay good to be on lookout in that case? I'll watch the people, distract if needed."

Both nodded.

"We're nearly there." Ailith smiled at them. "A few more days, and we can have a proper holiday."

"Ailith . . ." Jay hesitated. "Amelie and I have been talking. Should you fail, should the devil come for you, what do you want us to do?"

Not the question she had expected. What *did* she want them to do? If she was successful, she was certain that Arkhael would leave her in peace, regardless of what Amelie might think. However, she also had no doubt that failure on her part would be punishable by death.

"There is no world in which I would ask you to risk yourself for me against him." The answer seemed obvious. "If he comes for me, you run. You don't look back. You don't try to rescue me."

What would *she* do if he came for her? Ailith pushed the thought away. She couldn't think about failing him, not with the contract in place. And she had already been prepared for the worst before she signed it.

"Are you sure?" The concern in Jay's voice was touching after how cold he had been with her.

Ailith nodded. "Before I struck that deal, he very nearly incinerated me, and physically he is much stronger than any of us. The chance of one of us not making it out of a fight with him is too high."

"But you think you'll survive by yourself?" Amelie huffed.

"I don't." Ailith smiled at her. "But I know his moves well enough by now to hold out while you get away."

"It is decided then." Jay nodded once and folded the maps away. "We can scope out the area around the building and plan a potential escape route tonight. While we still have the day, we should visit the Chambers itself."

The Chambers was an impressive building. The white stone reflected what little watery sunlight managed to penetrate the clouds, making it stand out amongst the wood and brick of the buildings around it. Even though the building had only two floors, its peaked roofs and arcs made it seem taller than it was.

Yet where it seemed grandiose on the outside, it was even more intimidating on the inside. The entrance doors led directly into a large hall that seemed to occupy most of the ground floor, tall pillars supporting a high arched ceiling.

Throughout the centre stood rows of benches, all facing a statue in the very middle of the room. A tall, armoured lord hewn out of white marble towered over kneeling figures. His face was stern, and in his hand he held a mace, the head of which was made of gold.

The sides of the large hall were equally decorated with statues, alcoves, plaques, and other items of religious importance Ailith didn't recognise.

She made her way in first, pretending to be one of the many visitors in awe of the display, following the general flow of people. The moment she walked in, a shiver went down her spine. Consecrated ground. This space was protected against creatures of fiendish nature. From the corner of her eye, she saw Jay enter, knowing Amelie would follow in a bit. As she walked along the pillars, she made sure to pay special attention to who was present in the temple. The number of visitors, the religious attendants, and those who looked like they might have a grasp of divine magics. Several of the Children walked around the hall, many in armour that looked as functional as it was ceremonial.

A sudden yell drew her attention. She resisted the urge to immediately draw on her magic, knowing it would only risk discovery. In one of the alcoves, a small group of people had knelt down, their backs exposed and bloodied. In front of them stood a figure in religious garb, preaching by the looks of it. At a gesture of their hand, each of the devotees raised a rope and brought it down on their own backs. Ailith's jaw tensed at the sight. She knew that the Children were fanatics; she hadn't known how extreme their practices were. The preacher caught her looking, and she quickly averted her eyes, following the masses again. At least this one person had access to divine magic, its aura radiating off of him.

She continued her walk, making sure to keep an occasional eye on both Jay and Amelie. At the end of the hall stood a large altar, and many of the visitors sank down to their knees in front of it. No one walked behind it, she noted, and one of the Children very clearly guarded the area. A middle-aged man with auburn hair kept a constant eye on the crowd.

On her way back to the entrance, she caught Amelie's eye. With her hands near her waist, she pointed at the altar, then followed it up with two other quick gestures.

"Look there. Can you investigate?"

Ailith left her herd of people, walking over to the statue in the middle so she could continue to monitor the other woman, catching Jay's eye in the process to let him know something was happening.

As Amelie followed a similar route to the altar, she signalled back to Ailith.

"Guard. Problem."

Ailith surveyed the area. With Amelie's talent for blending with the shadows, she had no doubt that the woman could manage to sneak behind the altar if the guard was gone.

They needed a distraction. Ailith chewed the inside of her cheek. What could she possibly bring to one of the Children that they would leave their post for? Too big a ruckus might draw the attention of more than one of them, and she did not fancy messing with them before they had even started their mission. With a resigned sigh, she walked over to the man, schooling her expression into one of badly masked fear and naivety. Sometimes plain old stupidity was distracting enough.

"Excuse me, sir? I have a matter of some urgency that I would like some advice on."

The man regarded her warily. His crossed arms were muscled, she noted, and his stance told her he knew how to fight, even if he appeared unarmed in the moment.

"Talk to my colleague," he said with a gesture towards one of the priests walking around through the halls.

Ailith lowered her voice. "It is more of a dangerous matter, sir, and you look like you could fight. It concerns a devil." She made sure to whisper the last word.

The man gave her a sceptical look. Before he could speak, she continued.

"I have seen him, sir. He's got wings, and horns, and dark red skin. He offered a deal to someone I know, and I would like to help them before it's too late." Ailith knew she wasn't a great liar, but she was phenomenal at spinning the truth in her favour.

The man raised both his eyebrows, but her choice of topic had at least gained her his attention. "Where was this, woman? Devils are rarely seen in these parts. We make sure they are kept clean of any fiendish filth."

She shrugged. "One of the farms not too far from here, sir." Before he could continue to ask questions that she had no answer to, she added, "My friend says he's charming. Do devils have a charm, sir? Like fey creatures do from the stories?" She glanced around. Amelie was nowhere to be seen. *Just a little longer.*

"They do. But a devil's charm only works if there is already sin in your heart. You would do well to send your friend here. We can cure her of both sin and devil."

Inwardly, Ailith rolled her eyes at his answer. How very unimaginative. She wondered how much the man actually knew and how much was regurgitated propaganda. He had started to turn, thinking the conversation finished. She needed to say something, quickly.

"So you think a devil cannot be nice, sir?" *Nothing like discussing philosophy with a religious extremist,* she thought wryly.

The withering look of disdain he gave her made her stomach crawl.

"Listen, woman, whatever notion you or your friend have in your head, you would do well to let go of it. Why do you think devils hunt us so endlessly? They have no souls of their own. It's why they crave those of mortals. And the more sinful the soul, the better." The haughty look he gave her told Ailith everything she needed to know about what he thought of her soul. "And because they have no souls, they do not feel. All they show is what you need to see to be lured in by their charm. So, no. I *know* that a devil cannot be nice."

He signalled one of the nearby priests. "This woman is in some distress, and I am worried for her soul. Would you mind listening to her?"

Something in his tone told Ailith she had no desire to stick around for what they considered to be soul searching. She gave a respectful bow to both.

"Actually, this conversation has been most enlightening. Thank you so much for your time, good sir."

Amelie had better have finished her investigation.

Ailith didn't linger. Once she found Jay, she signalled to him she was leaving and walked back outside. She had drawn enough attention to herself.

The moment she walked back into the cold air, she immediately felt better. Despite the grandeur of the Chambers, it had felt claustrophobic inside.

Amelie joined her not much later, and together they waited for Jay in silence. When he finally emerged, his face was grim.

They walked away from the cathedral, finding a quiet place to discuss their findings.

"Anything?" Ailith started, but she already knew the answer from her friends' faces.

Jay shook his head. "A lot of magic. None of it guarding or hiding anything, as far as I could tell."

Amelie nodded in agreement. "I couldn't see anything either. Not even behind that altar of theirs."

They fell quiet.

"So, what now?" Amelie finally asked.

Ailith touched the necklace under her cloak. What indeed?

She sighed. "We try elsewhere. Jay, I know there is not as much time as you would want, but try the local library. Learn anything you can. Amelie, I know you hate this, but could you try to speak to some local guild members? A city like this is bound to have some form of underbelly. They might have information, even if it is just a rumour. Anything would be helpful at this point."

Amelie grimaced but nodded.

"I'll get in touch with Nial. Ask him if he has heard anything, or if he knows anyone. We reconvene at our little shack for dinner. Any questions?"

Nial proved to be equally unhelpful, scoffing at her for the mere suggestion that he might have set foot inside the Chambers.

"It's not that I don't want you to succeed, Ailith." He sighed. "Once you have some form of proof for me, I will use what influence I have here to get it to the correct people within the government. If anything, I am aware that it is in my best interests for you to succeed as well. Until then though, I simply don't have the resources you are looking for. I tried looking into this Dorian fellow for you, but I found nothing on that front yet either."

Ailith ran a hand through her hair. One of her friends had to be successful today if she was not.

"Nial, while I am here alone. As an archdruid, could you explain something?"

"Of course. What is your question?" His tone changed entirely, from one of political pragmatism to actual interest.

"If there is a touch of divinity in our magic, is it possible to channel this purely?" Ailith had always felt somewhat insecure when asking others about her own magic, always worried that they would be able to see the shortcomings and lack of education in her words. Nial was one of the few who she dared voice such questions to.

He nodded. "There are a few ways. The easiest, and the one you would probably find most accessible, is by channelling moonlight." He moved to stand next to her. "Copy me."

Nial was right. It took her only a few tries to understand how to separate the strands of her magic and pick out the small pieces of divinity in them, directing them from her hands in the form of moonlight.

Nial didn't ask what she needed it for, and she didn't offer an explanation.

"As I thought." He nodded, looking pleased with himself. "Your affinity for the more plant- and air-based magics means this was hardly a challenge." He grabbed her by the arm. "Don't mistake my callousness, Ailith. I cannot help you, but that doesn't mean that I don't want you to succeed. Even if I disagree with the choices you have made for yourself, I wouldn't want to see harm come to you. If you or your friends do not find anything today, then lie in wait at the Chambers tomorrow. When one of the Children leaves, you take them and you question them. Whatever you need to do. Make sure you get those answers swiftly."

"I will." She smiled sadly. "I would be lying if I said I wasn't terrified. I haven't dared to meditate and look at my own body properly for days."

"Understandable. But avoiding the truth doesn't make it less true." Nial moved his hand to her shoulder and squeezed it. "You're strong. You've got this. Since I cannot give you the information you seek, here is my advice instead. Go to the Chambers and watch their movements; look for a pattern. Get whatever information you can via observation."

"I will. Thanks." She nodded at him.

"And after you have succeeded, come back to me, Ailith. You've grown strong. There might be prospects for you here."

Ailith raised an eyebrow as she walked to the door. "You know I don't want to settle, Nial. And certainly not in a city like this."

He shrugged as she left. "There's no harm in at least listening to the offers."

Ailith did as he had suggested. She returned to the Chambers and simply watched, memorising the patterns of those leaving and arriving, learning of a servant's entrance at the side of the cathedral. Yet she found it hard to focus while she was not actively pursuing something. She caught herself fingering the necklace, her stomach fluttering as she touched it. Under her breath, she cursed the devil's charm, but even as she did so, she knew her words to be lies. She hadn't seen many charms in her life, but she knew herself and her magic well enough, and unless a devil's charm was nearly undetectable, she was under no such effect. The near obsession was hers, and hers alone. Ailith huffed. She wasn't entirely sure if she alone was to blame. *More of a team effort.*

That didn't make it any less foolish or stupid. He had nearly killed her.

But only after you broke in.

She shook her head at herself. He was actively extorting her, had forced her into an agreement. Had all but let her know that he was looking to invade her Realm someday. She should be disgusted with him. And yet, every spare moment her thoughts went to him. Not just to the way he had made her beg for him, although her body felt aflame whenever she thought of that. How often he had desired her, had made her his in one night alone, sent a shiver down her spine. But the way he had kissed her hand, the way his eyes seemed alight when he looked at her, the casual arm around her shoulder in that wonderful bath of his—those were the memories she lingered on the most. The ones she was well aware were the most dangerous.

With a sigh, she got up. The day was slowly fading into night. She truly hoped the others had had more success.

CHAPTER 21

A ilith's hope ran dry the moment she saw the faces of her friends, and dinner was a tense affair.

Jay's visit to the library had been fruitless. Although there had been plenty of books on the Chambers, there was no mention of a vault. He had ripped another map out of one of them, but none of them could see anything on it that they didn't already know of or that would hint at there being more to the building than was visible to the naked eye.

Amelie had managed to get in touch with the city's underbelly, but they had laughed at her questions and claimed that if such a vault existed, they would have known of it and already found a way into it.

Ailith repeated Nial's suggestion. "We can try and corner one of them tomorrow. I've been watching their patterns. If we manage to get our hands on one of them in the morning, it gives us all day to get the knowledge we need."

"That leaves us with precious little time left to actually prepare," Jay noted.

Ailith ran a hand through her hair.

"Do we have any other ideas? Anything at all?"

"Right now, we don't even know where to start." Amelie leaned against the wall. "I don't want to explore that entire building by night and risk my life not even knowing if I am in the right place."

"Easy for you to say." Jay's voice was getting more aggravated by the minute. "You don't have mere days left to live."

"That doesn't mean we should risk her life needlessly." Ailith scowled at him. "I understand the fear, but taking it out on each other will get us nowhere."

"Do you understand the fear, though?" Jay's eyes darted between them. "You've been working with a devil since the very beginning. What other deals have you made when we weren't watching? What else do you do for him?"

Both women looked at him with open mouths.

"That is unfair," Amelie said quietly.

"I didn't ask for the devil to follow me around," Ailith hissed at him.

"Maybe not, but it's mighty convenient for you, isn't it?"

"What do you want from me, Jay?" Ailith threw her hands up.

He narrowed his eyes. "Why don't you run to your devil and pray to him for help, hmm? Maybe do him some other favours while you're at it?"

"ENOUGH!" Amelie stood up. "Both of you, pick a room at either end of the house and go cool off. Sleep, ideally. Tomorrow, we will rise early. We will plan and prepare when we are fresh and tempers have cooled."

Jay stormed off almost immediately. Ailith got up much slower.

"Sorry." She put a hand on Amelie's shoulder. "And if you don't want to join us, I don't begrudge you that either."

Amelie scoffed. "How are you going to get the vault doors open without me? By trying every individual pin? I'm coming. I just wish we had more to go on."

"I know." Ailith pulled her into a hug. "You're a good friend. I'll go get some air."

She found a room with a small balcony and stepped out onto it, pulling her cloak tight against the night's chill.

The noise of the city seemed more distant during the night, and she wrinkled her nose. If only the smell lessened too.

Resting her arms on the balustrade, she looked at the distant sea. It was as dark as the night sky. Nothing betrayed what life lay below the surface. She traced the necklace. Could one pray to a devil? She had never been religious, had never prayed to anything. Folding her hands together, she looked up at the sky, never having felt more stupid.

"Dear Arkhael. We're pretty fucked. Please help." Sceptically, she looked at the rising moon. "The end?" Then she laughed. Maybe she was going insane. Maybe the disease was slowly starting to eat away her sanity. It would certainly explain the last few days of risky decisions.

Her back itched, and she resisted the urge to scratch it. She had decided not to heal any of the wounds that Arkhael had given her, at least not magically, knowing that some of them would turn into permanent scars. It was a silly and sentimental decision, and once she had made it, she refused to think about her reasoning.

The hair on the back of her neck stood up as hands appeared on either side of her on the balustrade, the sudden warmth of his body causing a shiver to run down her spine. She didn't need to look behind her to know it was him.

"I don't believe I have received a prayer in over two centuries," Arkhael murmured in her ear, "let alone such an eloquent one."

"You weren't actually meant to hear it." Ailith sighed, the cold of the night suddenly not so bad anymore.

"But I did. So, what is it you need help—" She could feel the sudden tensing of his body behind her. "It seems you are not the only one who was praying." There was a sudden urgency to his voice as he laid his hands over hers.

The landscape in front of her changed. No longer was she looking out over the city at night. Instead, the air was warm around her and the sky entirely dark as she stood on a different balcony, only occasionally lit by flashes of red. Wind pulled at her hair. Was she becoming a regular house guest?

Behind her, Arkhael let out a long breath.

"Did you know about this?" His hands tightened over hers.

"About what?" Ailith couldn't have been more genuinely confused if she tried.

His grip relaxed, but he didn't let go of her hands. "Someone else in your home just had their prayers answered. Ah, but that is not important now. What could you possibly need my help with?" His thumb traced circles over the back of her hand, and Ailith found herself leaning back into him, closing her eyes. She was so tired, and he felt warm and safe.

"The bloody Chambers. If we had more time, I'm sure we could find a way in but as it stands . . ." Ailith shook her head. "We've got nothing. Not even a lead, other than your claim that the vaults exist."

"What do you need?"

"Ideally? A map." She tried not to sound as desperate as she felt. "But even knowing where the entrance to the vaults are would be a start."

Behind her, Arkhael was quiet. She tilted her head to look up at him. His beautiful face was pensive as he stared off into the dark sky. Her eyes went to his lips, and she couldn't stop the intrusive memories of how they felt on her skin. How they had commanded her.

She ground her hips against him, watching him blink and pull his focus back to her.

"Don't be cheeky, thief." A faint smile played across his lips, and Ailith could feel the immediate response of his body as he pressed into her.

"I believe it was you yourself who made sure I wouldn't be able to forget you."

He growled quietly behind her, his hands tightening around hers. "Did you think of me when you returned?" His quiet voice only fanned the flames that burned in her.

"Every second," she whispered back and closed her eyes again, wishing she could forget about everything and just live in this moment.

"We shouldn't do this now." He sounded strained.

"Why not?" Ailith pressed herself against him more forcefully, shivering when he moaned in response.

"Because you shouldn't even be here." One of his hands went to her throat, pressing her against his chest.

"Because I'm a mortal woman who shouldn't be in the Hells?"

"And because you should be resting. You are clearly exhausted, and you will need a sharp mind."

"You don't seem like you want me to leave."

He laughed hoarsely.

"I want nothing more than to bend you over and make you shout my name until all in the Hells know you are mine."

Ailith gasped.

"But neither of us has time for that." He stepped back slightly, peeling his hands away from her throat, though Ailith could tell he wanted to keep them on her body as much as she wanted him to. She turned around in the space of his arms, looking up at him.

"I won't be able to sleep either way."

His hand came up to her face, gently stroking her cheek.

"Go back and rest. You need it. Tomorrow, you will go into town and prepare. Buy whatever you think will help you, whatever you think could possibly be useful. Make sure to return before the dinner bell."

Ailith raised an eyebrow. "You're helping us?"

"I'm helping myself to finally acquire what I have worked centuries for. Don't wait any longer, Ailith." His face grew serious. "Do as I say, then fulfil the contract before the next daybreak. Else I'm afraid you won't get to fulfil it at all."

Ailith swallowed hard. Being reminded that the disease could claim her at any moment was too terrifying to think on. So she leaned back against the balustrade, choosing to ignore it.

"Fine. I'll do as you say. As long as you know I am not happy about it."

"Neither am I." He closed the space between them, pressing her into the balustrade and bringing his face close to hers. "I would tear those clothes off of you. Keep you here for myself rather than sending you into the lair of the Children." His hips pressed against her, and she moaned at the friction. "If I had the time, I would make you forget your own name."

To her surprise, he pulled her into a kiss, one of his hands moving her hips more forcefully into his. Ailith melted into him as he explored her mouth, hungering for more.

How can you be so desperate for him when you are so near death? It has only been a day.

When he finally pulled back, they were both breathless.

"That should help with the cold for a little bit," he said. The smug confidence on his face a sharp contrast to his laboured breathing. "Now go, before we do something we'll both regret."

"Not likely," Ailith whispered. But she let go of him, stepping through the portal he conjured for her, back out onto her own balcony.

Instinctively, she pulled her cloak around her, only to realise that the wind had lost its chill.

Fucking devil.

But the curse she threw his way was a grateful one.

That night, she slept better than she had in ages, despite the stiff mattress and ticking clock, an otherworldly glow protecting her from the cold, the memory of his touch protecting her from her own nightmares.

CHAPTER 22

Ailith was almost chipper as she prepared breakfast, ignoring the grim set of Jay's jaw when he joined her at the table. His eyes went to her neck and narrowed, but he said nothing. Cursing inwardly, she realised she had been so comfortable overnight, she hadn't donned her cloak that morning.

Oh well. He's judging you already; he might as well judge you more.

"I have a plan," she announced when Amelie finally joined them. "Or more of a . . . strong suggestion. I followed your angry advice, Jay. Turns out one *can* pray to a devil."

Jay frowned at her but refrained from commenting.

"Since it is also in his best interests that we succeed, he offered his help. He advised that we go into town and buy whatever we deem useful and to return before the dinner bell. Seeing as we don't have a better plan, and he doesn't have a reason not to help us, I am more than happy to follow his suggestions." She fought down a guilty blush as the other two stared at her. "If either of you have a better plan, I am all ears."

Amelie shook her head. "This has changed from trying to escape a devil into taking his orders, even if they are disguised as help, and I don't like it. But sleep did not bring me any bright ideas. At least it is a plan. And you're right, there is a weird kind of trust we can put in his support."

Jay had been frowning the entire conversation. Both women looked at him.

"It's a plan," he admitted. Ailith had never heard him sound so resigned. "I don't like it either, but it's our biggest chance of success. Much as I am loath to admit it, I trust the devil to keep its word more than I am convinced we can successfully capture one of the Children and get them to talk within a day." He sighed heavily.

"At least we have enough gold to afford whatever equipment we want." Amelie attempted a smile. "And if we need any last-minute additions, we should have a little bit of time after the dinner bell to try and get ourselves organised."

As they got ready to leave, Ailith took Jay aside. "He also said we should act before the next daybreak or we would be too late."

Jay's face paled. "But the full moon is not for another night."

"Do you want to risk it?" Ailith looked him in the eye.

He shook his head. "No. I don't. Thank you for telling me."

She hesitated before speaking again. "I know you've been unhappy with me, Jay, and even if I don't fully understand why, you're still my friend." She squeezed his shoulder. "Please tell me you have a plan."

"You know I can't talk to you about that, Ailith. We can't risk it." But he nodded as he spoke.

She pulled him in for a hug, ignoring his surprised protests. She had tried her best not to think about what would come *after* they destroyed the box, fully trusting that Jay had understood her hint days ago. Knowing that he had was a weight off her shoulders. Slowly, he returned her hug.

"Ailith, I don't know what your motivations are." He pulled back to look at her. "But please tell me you're doing what you're doing because you think it is going to help us. The woman I used to follow took risks, some of them I questioned, but this?" His eyes went to the golden chains around her neck. "This is madness."

She almost lied to him, the pleading look in his eyes tugging at her heartstrings. But she had never been a great liar. "My chances of survival are even slimmer than yours, Jay. Why begrudge me a little fun?"

"It's a devil, Ailith. It's not even human. And it's a murderer on top of that. We saw the man in its prison." He almost hissed the last words.

"Yes, and I was the one to snap his neck." Ailith clenched her fists. "Our hands aren't clean either, Jay."

He opened his mouth to speak but shook his head instead. "Don't say I didn't warn you." And with that, he left her to get ready.

"Hypocrite," she murmured as he left. Out of the three of them, it was only Amelie who could say her hands were truly clean. But Ailith couldn't help the niggling feeling that he was right.

She had gone to bed with a murderer. Knowingly. What did that say about her? Could she truly turn a blind eye to *what* he was simply because she hadn't seen him commit the crimes?

Ailith shook her head. Soon, those dilemmas wouldn't matter anymore. With a heavy sigh, she followed Jay and Amelie.

Maybe they had gone overboard with their shopping. They had certainly bought more than they could ever take with them. Amelie had insisted that they buy more or less every available tool that could help with the disarming of traps, just in case. In addition to that, Ailith had bought an arsenal of small poisons, gasses, darts, and other instruments of subterfuge. She was less worried about the vault itself, and more worried about encountering any of the Children. The last thing she wanted was to have to confront them head-on. Only Jay had not insisted on buying anything. He seemed distracted, but Ailith dared not ask him what with.

They returned well before the dinner bell, opening the door to their lodgings in anticipation. Arkhael had said he would help. He hadn't specified how. They had no idea what to expect.

It became clear the moment they stepped through the door. On their little dinner table lay a large piece of rolled-up parchment.

They exchanged a look. Then Ailith rushed over, dumping her purchases on the ground, and carefully unrolled it. It was a map. Hand-drawn, she realised. As she unrolled it entirely, a small note fell out. She unfolded it.

The map is correct, but I cannot vouch for the accuracy of the traps. Make haste.

"He got us a map?" Ailith could hear the hint of gratitude in Amelie's voice as she looked over her shoulder.

"No, he *drew* us a map." She gently touched the neat lines on the paper. In every meticulous stroke, every carefully drawn symbol, every perfectly written word, she recognised Arkhael's hand.

"Can't argue with results." Amelie pulled over a chair. "Let's get ready then."

The map was more than Ailith had expected. Not only did it show them the entrance to the vaults and the layout, it also detailed where and what kind of traps to expect. All three layers of the vault were drawn out, each connected by a set of downwards stairs. The stairways and rooms themselves were narrow. In Ailith's experience, that meant a gratuitous number of traps. And from Arkhael's neat handwriting, she could tell she wasn't wrong. They ranged from simple razor wires to traps of a more magical nature. Those were the ones she worried about most. It would be up to her, not Jay, to detect them. Most frustrating, however, was not the many traps. It was the entrance.

Their hunch had been right. The top of the altar could be lifted to reveal stairs. Amelie let out a string of colourful swear words, unsure how she had missed it and annoyed that she had.

The bigger question was how they would get in unnoticed.

"Knowing there is a crack, I could open the space," Ailith offered, "but how are we going to do it in a room that will likely have people in it? Even if we were able to sneak by unnoticed, lifting such a big piece of stone is going to make noise."

"Unless we count on being discovered." Both women looked at Jay. His eyes were distant. "Give me a moment. I'm trying to calculate if we'll have enough time."

They watched in silence. Ailith could almost see the gears in his brain working before he blinked, focusing on the map again.

"I could create an illusion that muffles the sound and hides what we are doing for a short amount of time. With the number of traps in that vault, we are bound to set off one of them. No offence, Ailith, but even if you are at your best, the amount of magical protection around the last door looks nearly impossible to avoid. But we are not here for a big haul. Ailith, you carry the feather, you destroy the box while Amelie and I take the reliquary. All we have to do after is get out. If the illusion drops and the open vault is discovered by then, we'll have already done the most important part. Even if we get arrested, at least we won't be on death's door. We'll have time to escape."

"Somehow, these Children don't seem like the type to let intruders live," Amelie said drily.

Ailith pondered his idea. Jay gave her a pointed look, and she realised there was more to his plan than he was letting on. She would just have to trust him.

"Alright, we focus on getting in quietly until the third door, where we start to focus on speed instead. How do we get out? An alarm goes off, your illusion drops, they know someone is in their vault. Best case scenario is that they will send regular guards. But they have holy warriors on location. I would rather not tangle with them."

Jay nodded. "Agreed. You bought a year's worth of poisons today. Do we have anything that could neutralise a large group?"

"Multiple things." Ailith grabbed the vials from her bag and started preparing them.

It was the oddest plan she had ever created with her friends. They discussed the first steps meticulously, only to entirely ignore how to escape. Tension hung between her and Jay as much as mutual understanding. For everyone's safety, secrets were being kept that they both pretended not to be aware of. Poor Amelie was caught in the middle of it all, looking more confused by the second but not asking any questions.

Once they had all agreed on the plan, Ailith rolled the map back up and left it on the table. If things went horribly wrong, Nial could find the map and maybe pick up where they left off with a more official investigation.

Before they left their little temporary abode, Ailith called both of her friends over, her throat suddenly dry.

"I, ehrm . . . I want to thank you both. For the last few years. They were amazing." She swallowed away the sudden lump in her throat. "I think we can all agree that there is a chance I might not make it out tonight. So, you know, thanks. I couldn't have had a better crew to work with. And wouldn't have wanted one even if it existed." With a smile, she looked at both Jay and Amelie, blinking away the unexpected tears.

Surprisingly, before Amelie could even react, Jay pulled her into a hug. "I never agreed with everything, Ailith, but you are a good woman. It's been an honour." The solemn finality of his words sent a chill down her spine.

He knows you will not make it out.

She pushed the thought away.

The moment Jay let her go, Amelie jumped into her arms.

"Whatever you do and wherever you end up, don't die, Ailith."

Ailith smiled. "Never without a fight."

With a sigh, she wiped her eyes and headed for the door.

She would miss these people.

CHAPTER 23

The Chambers were just as impressive in the dark as they were during the day. It was shortly after midnight when they approached the building, the streets around it almost eerily quiet. Their way in would be the servant's door at the side of the building. Although there was definitely a chance of people still being in attendance, it would be less conspicuous than trying to enter through the large main doors.

They quickly fell back into practised habits. Amelie unlocked the door for them and quietly opened it.

"Hello?" A man sitting next to a large fireplace got up from his chair at their entry. "Who are—"

Ailith shut him up with a quick dart to the neck. She had selected a potent sleeping draft to take with them. Almost immediately, the man fell back down. Catching him before he had a chance to fall and make a ruckus, she lowered him back onto the chair and removed the dart.

Hopefully no one would immediately miss this man. It would be a few hours before he would wake.

Jay and Amelie had already moved on.

Quietly, they made their way through the dark hallways and into the large hall they had scouted the day before. The moment they stepped in, Jay muttered under his breath and conjured up an illusion. The shimmer of the air in front of them was the only indication something had changed. However, she knew that to anyone on the other side of his illusion, the area would look exactly as it had been, without the three of them in it. It was a strategy Ailith would never get comfortable with. It felt too exposed.

There were indeed still people in the room. Two of the Children were wandering around, tending to the hall.

Praying Jay's illusion was as good as he made it out to be, Ailith rushed over to the altar. Both she and Amelie started trailing the outside of it with their fingers, looking for any cracks that might indicate that the stone could be lifted.

It was Amelie who found it: a barely noticeable gap between the top and the rest of the stone structure.

Ailith looked at Jay.

"*Ready?*"

He nodded, and with a barely audible mutter, the air shimmered again. Whatever noise she now made would be inaudible to those on the other side. Even with that knowledge, her heart hammered as she called on her own magic and summoned one of her vines in the crack of the stonework. With a loud screech the plant slowly pushed the stone apart, revealing the rest of the seam and forcing the top of the altar off the lower half. Once the outlines of the door were clear, Amelie helped her shove it to the side, both of them wincing at the sound.

Ailith looked up at the Children in the room. Jay's illusion was working; neither of them looked in their direction.

Slowly but surely, a stairway was revealed inside the altar. When they had created enough of an opening that they would fit through it, Ailith went down, gesturing for Jay and Amelie to follow. The top of the altar they moved back as well as they could from inside, but if anyone looked at it too closely, they would definitely notice it was open.

Their timer had started.

Ailith disarmed three traps on the first stairway alone. Two of them had been marked on Arkhael's map, and she found and unravelled the magic strands without too much difficulty. The last one she almost missed. Stepping forwards, her skin suddenly began to tingle, and she withdrew just in time before setting off the magic. Focusing on it, she found the barely visible strands in the air and started tearing them apart. One room in and already she had nearly made a mistake. She let out a long breath.

At the bottom of the stairwell, they were faced with their first door. The first vault.

Arkhael's map proved correct again as Ailith reached out to find magic woven over the door handle. The unravelling of the strands took her longer than she wanted it to. With every careful tug at the magic, she was aware of the limited amount of time they had. With her heartbeat in her throat, she tore through it and stepped aside to make space for Amelie.

It wasn't long before Amelie gave the all-clear sign and started picking the lock. For once, the woman actually had trouble with it. As she was working, she called Ailith over.

"Hold these," she murmured quietly, gesturing at the lock-picks she had carefully inserted into the keyhole.

As Ailith held the picks in place, careful to keep the tension the same, Amelie flicked something on the door to reveal a second lock. How she had seen it Ailith didn't know, but she had never been more glad that Amelie was with them than in that moment.

Tongue between her teeth, Amelie set about working on the second lock, until that, too, clicked.

Surprisingly quietly, the door opened.

All three of them audibly gasped at the wealth that lay behind the door. Jay held a small magical light in the palm of his hand, revealing the amount of gold that lay in shameless piles against the walls. The big open chests with jewels that stood next to it seemed almost small in comparison. It was without a doubt the biggest vault the three of them had ever been in, and this was only the first room. If Ailith hadn't been so worried for her own survival, she would have been sorely tempted. As it was, her eyes immediately focused on the next set of stairs.

They continued deeper down. Ailith had just unravelled and disarmed the first trap when a slight tremor in the air alerted her that she had missed something.

"Down!" Jay shouted behind her. A barrage of golden feathers shot through the stairwell, the quills unnaturally sharp.

At his cry, Ailith threw herself down onto the steps, but not before she felt one of the feathers graze her cheek as another pierced her shoulder. She swore quietly.

The moment the barrage stopped, she looked at her friends. They appeared unharmed. Being a step behind her must have given them the extra second they needed to dodge the trap. Getting up slowly, she carefully touched her shoulder. The magical feather had cut right through it, causing a small but steady trickle of blood to drip from the wound.

"Are you okay?" Amelie's forehead creased with concern.

Ailith nodded. "I have had worse."

She gritted her teeth. She could heal the wound, but with the amount of magic she needed to sense and disable the traps, she didn't dare risk it. Instead, she tried to simply apply pressure to her shoulder as she continued moving down the stairs, on high alert for the next magical traces in the air.

They passed both magical and physical traps as they continued down, most of which Ailith remembered from Arkhael's map.

She wiped the sweat from her brow. The constant unravelling of magical threats was almost as straining as actually casting magic, and it certainly required more concentration. They made it past and through the second door, but not without Amelie nearly breaking a set of lockpicks and nearly missing the razor wire that zipped through the hallway the moment she opened the door. Jay pulled her back just in time, the wire leaving an ugly slash down the side of his arm.

Ailith turned to heal it, covering the wound with her hand and whispering quietly. They needed Jay in one piece. If it came down to a fight, they should at least have one fully capable magic caster.

"Fuck," she heard Amelie whisper, "that would have been bad."

Jay nodded at her tersely. "Halfway there."

The moment they entered the second vault, Ailith became aware of an increase in magic around her. Closing her eyes, she inhaled deeply. Trying to find the source of it made the hair at the back of her neck stand on end.

The consecrated ground.

It was more intense, more powerful in this room. Stifling, almost.

How had Arkhael withstood it?

They walked through the next room. It was only slightly smaller and filled with weaponry and armour of different kinds. If Jay's gasp was anything to go by, it was all magical.

Only one more staircase to descend. Ailith's stomach burned with nerves.

No, not nerves.

Alarmed, she looked at Jay. Sweat coated his forehead.

"I feel it too," he whispered in response to her unspoken query. They were running out of time. Closing her eyes briefly, she made for the last stairway.

Between the increasing pain, the knowledge that she was dying, and the buzz of divine magic around her, it was hard to focus and find the threads of the magical traps. She felt magically blinded, and had to entirely trust Arkhael to not disappoint with his map. If it weren't for his help, she would never have been able to pick out the strands of magic through the ringing in her ears.

They all felt the vibration through the floor as something heavy was dropped far above them. They had been discovered.

Quickening her step, Ailith hurried down the last few stairs. The final door was within reach.

With shaking hands, Ailith watched as Amelie set to work. Fear gripped her heart as the burning inside her increased. Had they come so far only to fail at the threshold?

Next to her, Jay's legs buckled.

"Ailith, I'm sorry. I need you to hold these again." Amelie didn't even bother to be quiet.

Trying to keep her hands steady, Ailith took the picks that Amelie had inserted into the lock. The mechanism looked complicated, far beyond her comprehension.

Her vision turned blurry. She thought of Arkhael. Of the few fleeting moments of happiness that she had known with him. Of how he had shared his bed with her so she could rest.

She practically fell through the door as it suddenly swung open. If the consecrated ground had been stifling before, it was positively oppressive in this room.

Behind her, she heard a thud as Jay fell to the ground. Ailith clenched her fists.

So close.

"The box," she croaked at Amelie as she scanned the room. Black spots danced across her vision as she fought to remain upright.

"There!" Amelie shouted.

Ailith followed her finger. It was sat on a small table, entirely unassuming. Struggling to remain focused, she limped over to it. Her insides were on fire. Her body shook as she was eaten alive.

She fell against the table and just managed to snatch the box off it before falling to the ground. The moment it left the table, she felt a ripple in the air, and a loud bang warned her that the vault door had closed. Uncaring that she had just set off a trap, she slammed the box shut and pulled out the feather Arkhael had given her, stabbing it into the top with the little strength that remained in her shaking hand.

It pierced the wood as easily as a hot knife sliding through butter.

Nausea gripped her, and before she could stop it, she retched. Black smoke fell from her mouth onto the ground. She retched again and again, her body convulsing with pain as she forced out whatever had infected her. It seemed alive as it fell to the floor, shuddering as if it, too, was in pain, before suddenly turning into dust. Even after the smoke had left her body, she couldn't stop herself from bringing up more bile. Shakily, she turned her attention inwards, focusing on herself properly for the first time since the disease had set in. The dark teeth were gone. Relief washed through her, despite the pain wracking her body. With great effort she concentrated on her stomach, calming it down, stopping it and her muscles from spasming.

Slowly, her vision cleared. Behind her, Amelie was holding onto Jay. He seemed to be retching up blood. Quickly, Ailith moved over to him, rushing her healing magic through his body.

With teary eyes, he looked up at her.

"We did it," he said hoarsely.

Ailith smiled at him in relief. "We did it."

A loud noise sounded behind them. All three looked at the closed door.

"And we need to move. Quickly."

Chapter 24

Had she made it? Arkhael refocused his attention. The new scrying mirror he had obtained was smaller than his last had been, and he already regretted the purchase. But he had needed one on short notice, and this was all he had been able to get.

The stairway darkened. Arkhael shifted his gaze. The third vault door had closed.

Had they set off a trap?

Is she still alive?

Frustrated, he stared at the empty stairwell, the lack of knowledge grating at his pride. The first two vaults had been difficult enough to get into for him, but that the consecrated ground had been strong enough to stop him from getting into the third had never irked him more than it did now. He had nervously watched her stumble through the door, but even with this magical device, he could not see into the last vault. As he was about to shift his gaze again, light flooded the stairwell. Armed fighters ran down the stairs, weapons pointed at the closed door. He saw their mouths move, knew that something was being shouted, before they all took a defensive position and waited.

Together with those on the stairs, he held his breath, waiting for the door to move. When it finally did, he tensed with them.

The door opened just a little bit before all hell broke loose in that tiny space. A cloud of fog roiled out of the vault, and Arkhael saw what the mercenaries could not.

Under the cover of the fog, small bottles were rolled into the room, releasing what he could only assume to be some poisonous smoke. It took maybe a second before the effects made themselves known. He breathed a sigh of relief when he caught a glimpse of pale fingers. At least she had survived.

One of the men opened their mouth in a silent battle cry and jabbed their sword at their comrade. And with that, the room seemed to suddenly be in combat with itself. The tight formation broke, and the people scattered, allies fighting allies or illusions that only existed in their mind.

Even Arkhael almost missed their emergence from the vault. Her two companions came out before she did.

But her hands are empty.

A bright flash filled the space. Something else had appeared in there with them. Through the fog, he could barely make out a figure consisting almost entirely of light. It seemed to reach for the wizard, who handed it a small satchel.

The reliquary.

Only then did it dawn on Arkhael what was happening. He roared, filled with sudden rage, and transported himself into the room, ignoring the burning of his skin as he forced his way past the divine barriers. It hurt. Every fibre of his infernal being urged him to run, to turn around. A lesser devil would have, but he resisted the ugly light trying to turn him away. With a grunt, he found himself at the top of the stairwell. His skin was burning. He wouldn't be able to withstand the divine magic for long.

The chaos was so much worse than it had appeared in the mirror. Beyond the obscurity of the fog, he could hear fighting and shouting, the smells of blood and dying souls heavy in the air.

He was too late. Just as he appeared, the blinding light faded.

He screamed.

She had betrayed him.

Through the slowly clearing fog, he saw their silhouettes—her silhouette. Her gaze met his, and he read the admission in her eyes. *She knew.*

She said something to her companions, possibly warning them. He didn't care.

He only had eyes for her, and because of it saw the telltale signs of her magic when no one else did. Not caring that he was revealing himself to the mortals in the room, he spread his wings and flew upwards.

Just in time.

As the wizard drew a magical door in the air that he stepped through with the other thief, Ailith's eyes flared green. The ground transformed. What had been stone turned into small jagged wooden spikes. He watched the men around him unlucky enough to be hit by them keel over, foaming at the mouth, before the ground turned to stone again. Behind him, the other two thieves emerged from the magical door. He ignored them, his eyes solely focused on Ailith. Someone made it to her, weapon raised. He hurled a ball of hellfire in the fighter's direction. The woman died instantly, another soul for his collection. Ailith hadn't moved from her position on the stairs. She was staying behind to fight.

She was prepared for this.

It only angered him further. He flew at her only to be hit by lightning mid-flight, taking him down momentarily. She was looking directly at him, even as she dodged a halberd swinging her way. The man who wielded it was hit by the lightning soon after.

The storm roiled around him. He paid it no heed. Illuminated by the erratic flashes of lightning, her face seemed oddly serene. He wanted her to cower as he moved towards her. Instead, she seemed almost sad.

Ailith shook her head, and even though he couldn't hear her voice through the screaming, he understood her plea.

"*Please don't.*"

If she thought she could escape his fury, dodge the eternity of pain she deserved, she was wrong. He beat his wings, advancing, and realised that her eyes had changed from violet to a white-yellow just before she brought her hands up in front of her and released a beam of bright white light.

It hurt. He could not recall when he had last, in his many centuries, felt such pain. Behind him, he heard the death cries of the mortals caught in it, the smell of scorched flesh suddenly strong in the air. She couldn't kill him. She had outsmarted him, much as he was loath to admit it, but she couldn't kill him. Their contract still held. But she could disfigure him beyond healing, beyond recognition.

How dare she?!

She might be a strong spell caster, he held the physical advantage. Grabbing one of the fallen mortals to hold in front of him, he charged right at her, ignoring the pain, knowing the flesh on his left shoulder was starting to sear away.

Just a little closer. He reached forwards blindly and found purchase. The moment his claws closed around her arm, he jerked it downwards. The beam dissipated instantly. He heard her gasp as he pulled her towards him, saw the resignation on her face as he felt her cease her struggles. She knew he had won; he could see it in her eyes. *Are those tears?*

He teleported them out. Out of the chaos and the fighting, out of that damned consecrated ground. Straight to his prison.

"How could you?" he yelled, holding her wrists in one hand, slapping her across the face with the other. She didn't respond, even as a small trail of blood dribbled from her lip.

"Argh!" He took a deep breath and lowered his voice. "You will know my wrath until you wish you had never been born."

Still she said nothing.

Infuriating.

With his free hand, he opened a set of the manacles that hung on the wall and chained her up. Over her fingers he closed a metal clamp lined with small spikes on the inside. That should stop her casting any spells. The chains he hoisted up above her head until she could barely stand on her toes. He stepped back and looked her over. Her tunic was torn from the fighting, and the braid she had put her hair in was fraying at the edges. Pathetic.

A glint of gold caught his eye, and he reached behind her neck, heating the metal until he could tear the necklace off her.

She whimpered. It was the first noise he had heard from her. Somehow, that only angered him more. He turned.

Leave her. She is not the immediate priority.

He would be back for her. First, he needed to confirm the new location of the reliquary. Even if he suspected the worst.

CHAPTER 25

H e didn't return to her for days, even though her betrayal left a constant bitter taste in his mouth.

The reliquary was well beyond his reach. The wizard had traded it to one of Celestia's inhabitants. There was no chance, no hope, of him getting to it again. Not even Ailith, for all her skill, would be able to break into that Realm. He still couldn't believe he had been outsmarted by such a simple plan. All they had done was find another party to make a deal with, and by planting the seed for the idea but not getting involved, the druid had never breached contract.

Arkhael growled. He hadn't even been able to take out his anger on the wizard. Whoever that man had made the deal with, they had offered him shelter on consecrated ground. If Arkhael truly wanted to, he could break through that protection. But it would draw too much attention to him, attention he had already drawn when he appeared in

228

the Chambers, and he would be breaking several infernal laws by doing so. The reward of petty revenge wasn't worth the risk.

The only other option he had for petty revenge was chained up in his dungeon, and every day he found new reasons not to visit her. He needed to decide on an appropriate punishment. Or so he kept telling himself.

It certainly had nothing to do with the memories of her naked body under him. Or her sleeping form in his bed. The way she had leaned against him to shield herself from the cold.

He shook his head with a frustrated growl. He deserved his revenge. It was expected of him. If only he could get her out of his head.

Which was why he found himself in the Second Circle, Xandia's realm of lust. He detested it. In his eyes, it was the epitome of short-term gratification, lacking any pretence of long-term commitment or ambition. Yet here he was, standing in the middle of a rocky valley. The dark red sand around him whirled with the strong wind that always blew here.

His presence caused an immediate stir. Even if none of the local inhabitants had shown themselves yet, he was aware of their chatter nearby, the curious stares aimed in his direction.

"I am in need of your services." His voice was quiet. He didn't need to raise it to make himself heard.

Out of the shadows and from behind the rocks stepped shapes. Succubi and incubi, all of them beautiful. Their naked bodies made to charm and allure before they killed. But he was no mere devil. For any of them, it would be an honour to serve him, a chance to climb up the ladder of the infernal hierarchy.

One of them stepped forwards. "How can we serve, my lord." The succubus's voice was soft and melodic. He looked over the group that had emerged.

"Kneel."

Without question, they went down, and he felt a surge of satisfaction.

At least some creatures still know their place. This might just work.

He walked between them, looking at their shimmering features. They had no real fixed appearance, not until they knew what was desired of them. Yet even in their changing stage, there was a sense of beauty about them. As he walked between their rows, one of the incubi looked up from its kneeling position, meeting his gaze.

"You." He pointed at it. "The rest of you can go."

The creature stood up proudly. "How can I serve you, my lord?"

With barely concealed disgust, he raised an eyebrow at it. "In the only way you are capable."

To its credit, it barely flinched at his harsh tone. "Of course, my lord. Do you have an image of your desires for me?"

"Better. I have the person in captivity." He ignored the incubus's look of surprise.

Effortlessly, he brought them both back to the plateau in front of his home, briefly adjusting the wards around it to grant it passage. It had cost him decades to learn how to create them, safety nets that kept any unwelcome fiends out of his abode. Never had he thought that he would need to ward his home against a group of thieving mortals.

In silence, he escorted the creature through his halls, pausing only before he opened the door to his prison.

His plan had seemed solid enough: bring the incubus home, get it to change into her, get rid of the distracting hold she had over him, then finally get his revenge. Yet now that he was on the threshold, he didn't know if he wanted to face the state she might be in.

Ridiculous.

He pushed the door open and walked into the room.

Ailith's figure hung from the manacles almost exactly where he had left her. His stomach turned at the sight, and he looked away quickly, his gaze resting on the incubus. The creature took one look at her.

"That is how you want me to look?"

Arkhael nodded. "Can you do it?"

"Of course." The incubus scoffed.

Arkhael turned on his heel. "Then we are done here. Follow me."

He all but fled the sight of her.

He brought the incubus to his chambers, looking at it expectantly.

"Do you wish for me to look like her with or without her wounds?"

"Without." He cringed at how quickly the response came out.

The creature obliged. If it had thoughts about what he had asked of it, it wisely kept those to itself. It transformed into a perfect physical copy of Ailith. Arkhael walked over and put the necklace Ailith had stolen from him around its neck. He could almost imagine it being her. But then it knelt and looked at him, and the illusion was broken.

"How can I serve, master?"

231

If he wasn't so angry, he might have laughed at how ridiculous the thought of Ailith calling him that was. He growled instead.

"Use my name. And get up. Defy me."

"Of course, Arkhael." He hated how his name sounded from its lips. "You can try and catch me?"

It coyly stepped backwards. A longing stirred in him as he looked at Ailith's body moving away from him. For a mortal woman, she was so beautiful. But the longing he felt was a sad one, and as the creature moved, all he thought of was her unmoving body hanging from the chains he had put her in. All this time, he had avoided her, and now she wouldn't get out of his head. It was too much, the farce too ridiculous.

He caught the incubus by the throat. Its skin was too hot to be hers, its smell entirely wrong. The fear in its eyes was something he had never seen in hers.

"You aren't her. You can never be her." His voice was full of quiet anger. Anger that, even now, she still had a hold over him.

With the creature in his hand, he conjured up hellfire. Listened to the screams until only a pile of ash and a heap of gold remained. It was somewhat cathartic.

With the sound of death still in his ears, he left the room. His wings carried him back to the prison, until he stood before her once more.

She looked awful. Her skin was pale and gaunt, even more so than usual. Her head hung, her breathing raspy. He lifted her face by the chin. Was she even aware of him? Her eyes were almost closed, her body unresponsive.

He dug a claw into her shoulder, watching the blood well up around it. Still no response. Withdrawing his hand, he walked over to his torture implements, retrieving a set of manacles. She owed him, and she was not paying that debt by being down here.

He undid her chains and watched her drop to the ground. Without ceremony, he manacled her hands behind her back, ensuring the clamps around her fingers were still firmly in place, then placed a collar and chain around her neck. He had thought of doing this with her so many times, but the current circumstances brought him no joy. He teleported them both straight to his bedchambers, then called for his chamberlain.

"I want her rinsed off and cleaned. And whatever she's being fed, improve it. Pain won't work on her if she's dead. When you're done, you can chain her to the ring. Sit her next to my bed." He pointed at the brass ring on his headboard. With that, he stalked out of the room.

When he returned later that day, he found her cleaned and propped up in a kneeling position, the chain around her neck securing her to his bed.

How? How could any torture ever match what she had done to him? He lowered himself down in front of her on his haunches, just watching. No movement. It was then he remembered her words. She had learned to withdraw from her body during torture. Was that what this was? How could he get her focus back? If he could give her a false sense of safety, would that bring her back to herself?

He loosened the chains, creating more space for her to move her arms. Lifting her gently, he unfolded her legs from under her, leaning her against the bedside with straightened legs and propping a pillow behind her back. She felt even smaller than usual, and her skin was clammy. He quickly withdrew his hands.

It took her five full days to come back to herself. Five days during which Arkhael nearly paced a hole through his floor. He didn't want to leave his home in case she woke and he missed it. Instead, he worked away at his desk, starting early and finishing well after the sky had darkened. But his mind was unfocused, and he couldn't stop himself from constantly rising from his chair and walking to his bedchambers, where he would just watch her. Wishing for her to open her grey eyes again.

It was when Arkhael was resting, the room cloaked in darkness, that he heard the sudden rattling of chains. His eyes shot open immediately.

She is awake.

Carefully, he got up out of the bed, getting down on his haunches in front of her as he had done so many times in the past few days. He could see her search for him in the dark, knowing she would only be able to see his silhouette, whereas he could see her clearly, but her face betrayed nothing other than exhaustion.

"You know," he said, breaking the silence, "torture was never my speciality. Too crude for my liking. But"—he got up, slowly walking towards her—"it has its uses."

His words might as well have been air. She barely acknowledged him. Rather than saying anything, Ailith crossed her legs and straightened her back, slowing her breathing, gaze distant.

Anger coiled in his stomach. *How dare she?* After everything she had done to him, how dare she ignore him? But he realised his opportunity was starting to slip. He could see her withdrawing inside herself again.

234

Arkhael swore. He couldn't lose her. Not now that she was finally awake.

So he did the one thing he thought might hold her attention. Rushing over, he pressed his lips to hers, felt her tense against him before she responded by opening her mouth with a small gasp of surprise. She was still with him. This was his chance.

Yet he didn't stop. He didn't want to stop. She was a fresh spring in a desert, and he was a parched man who couldn't get enough. And *finally*, she was responding to him. If he had known all he had had to do was kiss her so he could torture— The thought broke off.

Abruptly, he broke away from her, walking out of the room and slamming the door. Ignoring what sounded like quiet sobbing behind him.

CHAPTER 26

The next two days were some of the most productive he had had, working even through the night. Ten new contracts signed, new contacts acquired, fingers on different pulses.

Yet when he finally returned home, Arkhael was full of rage. His heart hadn't been in it, and his thoughts had never left his bedchambers. She had moved what he desired most entirely out of his reach and now prevented him from enjoying his work. And his shoulder was still sore.

But this time, he was prepared. He slammed open the door to his bedchambers.

Good. She is awake.

Ailith's gaze followed him through the room, coming to rest on the small bundle he carried. For a moment, he thought he saw a flash of apprehension on her face.

Finally. He knelt down in front of her, unclipping the chains that held her wrists behind her back.

"I've been thinking. If you have taken my life's work from me"—he unrolled the small pack—"why would I not take yours from you? It would seem only fair, don't you think?"

In the pack lay two blunt sticks and a hammer. He watched her gaze flicker over them, saw the look of recognition in her eyes, but then she turned her face away.

Really? Nothing?

He grabbed her by the chin, forced her to look at him, voice full of disbelief and anger.

"You are just going to let me do this?"

Finally, she spoke. "What do you want from me, *devil*?" Her voice was hoarse, barely audible. "Do you want me to beg so you can pretend to humour me, only for you to then take that hope away at the last moment? Is that how you enjoy your victims? Or maybe you want me to be outraged at you for using such personal knowledge against me? You're a devil. It's what you do. I won't grant you the satisfaction."

Arkhael stared at her. The absolute gall on this mortal woman.

Blind with rage, he grabbed her left hand, lined one of the sticks up with her palm. He picked up the hammer, brought it back for a swing.

The damage this would do to her hands would prevent her from ever using magic again. She knew, and still, there was nothing. He roared. Then brought the hammer down.

Next to her hand.

He watched her face. She had squeezed her eyes shut, that was it. No scream, no gasp. Nothing. And he, too, felt nothing. No joy from seeing her suffer, nor satisfaction.

The anger and frustration were still with him. He roared. She turned her head towards him, confused. But he could already see the resignation setting in on her face, expecting the worst.

Why could she not just give him the revenge he wanted? That he deserved? Why did she make everything feel so hollow?

He swung the hammer again. Not onto her hand but against the side of her head, knocking her out with one blow to the temple. Realising he was breathing heavily, he closed his eyes and put the hammer down.

What did he want with her? He couldn't kill her; the contract prevented that. And he couldn't break the contract without her consent. Unless they both agreed to nullify it, he was as bound by it as she was. But he could leave her somewhere where her death would be guaranteed and not his responsibility. She could be gone.

No.

No? Why not? He looked at her unconscious form. What good was she alive? Her presence had only brought him torment.

She is strong, smart, powerful. She could be used.

Force her to serve him? An ironic retribution, and a prospect that stirred something within him for the first time since he had captured her.

But what of her punishment? She deserves the pain and the torture.

He looked at her unconscious form. No, he deserved what *he* wanted. And the thought of forcing her to serve him enticed him more the longer he thought about it.

Finally, he would have her sign a contract of his design. No matter how much she might challenge him, she would be forced to do his bidding in the end. And this time, he would put her soul on the line. Arkhael left the room, for the first time in weeks feeling motivated again.

It was one of his better works, he made sure of that as words burned into the parchment. She would serve him until she had paid off a debt similar in value to her theft of the reliquary. And as far as he was concerned, that debt was big enough that it could never be paid off. It also included the cancellation of their previous contract and forbade her from using any magic against him. And her soul would be payment for any breach. Rereading it one more time, he nodded, then stowed it away.

He had her.

Returning to his bedchambers, he looked at her slumped form. He just needed her to sign it.

A sense of security and comfort.

He needed to avoid her withdrawing into herself at all costs. Carefully, he unlocked her collar and manacles and removed her chains. Only the clamps on her fingers he left on. Lifting her up, he gently laid her down on his bed.

Now the waiting began.

He didn't have to wait long. That natural druidic healing, he suspected. Leaning against the wall, he watched her move, watched her slowly regain consciousness. With her eyes still closed, she moved a hand to her head, only to wince as the metal clamp hit the skin instead of her own fingers.

Arkhael moved over, sitting down on the edge of the bed next to her. "I can remove those for you."

Ailith's eyes shot open, but her gaze was unfocused.

Maybe you were too forceful with the hammer.

"You can, but you won't?"

"I can, and I might."

Her eyes closed. "You're not getting my soul, *devil*."

He clenched his jaw at the way she said the word, at her constant defiance. Taking a deep breath, he chose to ignore it. Instead, he simply answered, "I'm not asking for your soul."

Ailith opened her eyes again, and this time she seemed to take in her surroundings. Confused, she looked at the bed, at her unchained hands. He saw her try to sit up, arms shaking with the effort. Gathering some pillows to support her, he helped her upright.

Immediately, she was suspicious.

"Let's cut to the cha—" Her sentence was interrupted by a fit of coughs. With some concern he noticed a trickle of blood in the corner of her mouth.

"This is where you pretend to be nice," she continued after wiping her mouth, "and offer a way out. You entice me with something in exchange for what you truly want of me. So what is it you want?"

Arkhael shook his head.

"I offer you something more . . ." He paused for effect. ". . . mutually satisfactory. You can repay me for losing my reliquary—and you *will* repay me—but you can do it in suffering. Or"—he conjured up the contract—"you do what you already did. You steal, you spy, but you do it for me."

Ailith stared at him, her expression incredulous. He watched her open her mouth to speak, then close it again.

She sighed and reached for the contract. He could see her struggle to read it, to focus, before she put it down again.

"Summarise it, please." She sounded exhausted.

So close. He was so close to having her.

"You pay off your debt through servitude, until I believe said debt is paid off. It voids our previous contract. No attempts on my life. No divine magic. Any breach, and your soul will be mine."

He watched her frown, could see her consider. She opened her mouth to speak, but he cut her off. "There will be no amendments. It's this or nothing."

"So it's no choice, really?" Her face was grim.

"It never is. Only the illusion of choice."

Arkhael conjured up a quill. She laughed mirthlessly.

"I don't think my hands would be capable of writing, even if you removed these monstrosities."

He took her left hand in his, held the quill for her, felt her fingers tremble under his. *From fear or from pain?* Her skin was cold. More so than usual, and he had to resist the urge to wrap her hand in his entirely.

He looked at her. The set of her jaw was defiant, despite everything. How she possessed such strength was beyond him. He wanted to pull her towards him, to take her from the world for himself alone. He pushed the thought away. *How foolish.*

Ailith took one deep, shuddering breath, then brought her hand to the paper.

And with her hand in his for assistance, she signed.

He wanted to roar, to scream. To let all the Realms know of his victory.

She is mine.

Instead, he only took a restrained breath and rolled up the contract. It vanished from his hands, safely into his vault.

Ailith shook her head at him but said nothing. He took her hands and, no longer having to fear her magic, undid the clasps.

For the first time, he got a proper reaction. She wasn't quite fast enough to hold back the cry that fell from her lips when the devices came off.

Her fingers were a bloody mess, what skin was left on them was purple and swollen, and a rancid smell filled the air. Arkhael watched her look at her hands in disbelief, saw her fight back the tears.

"What do you need?" he asked her. His stomach wrenched at the look on her face. After everything, it was only now that she displayed the fear he had tried so hard to induce. He didn't care for it one bit. *Why is it so hard to find joy in her suffering?*

She shook her head.

"I don't—" She took a deep breath. "Water. A bowl of water to clean them."

He called for his chamberlain. "Get her whatever she needs."

With that, he left her to it, pretending that he wasn't fleeing the room at the sight of what he himself had done to her.

CHAPTER 27

She didn't see much of him during the days that followed and was too preoccupied to think much of it. Seeing the state of her hands had been a shock, to say the least, and initially Ailith had been convinced there would be no saving them. It had been hard to hold back the panic when Arkhael removed the clamps, and once he had left the room, she felt herself spiral into anxiety.

She had been in precarious situations before, and she had always believed she could find a way out, always been convinced that she could find a solution. And she always *had* found a solution. In all her years of thieving, she had never truly believed that she would find herself in a situation that she couldn't come back from. Yet the consequences had never seemed so real as when she stared at the mess of skin and blood that were her hands. Instinctively, she tried to flex her fingers to call on her healing magic, only to realise that the joints were too swollen to move, and that, more than the pain, brought tears to her eyes. Without her hands, she couldn't use her magic. Without her magic, she couldn't heal her hands. And if she didn't heal the slowly spreading infection . . . That thought alone nearly had her hyperventilating, and it was only because Arkhael's chamberlain arrived with a bowl of water for her that she didn't throw up on the bed, emptying her stomach in the bowl instead.

Desperately, she reached out to the space around her, but there were no plants in the room that she could use to ground herself, to calm herself. Black spots danced across her vision as she tried to get a hold of her breathing.

Inhale. Immediate exhale.

Her body refused to work with her.

Inhale. Hold for just a moment. Exhale rapidly.

And then what? She didn't want to focus on what she felt. Or what she could see.

Inhale. Hold for longer. Shaky exhale, but slower.

Without magic, she would be nothing in a world of devils. If she wanted to live, she had to try. Or she might as well give up altogether.

So, struggling through her tears, she assessed the damage, trying to pretend that these weren't her hands she was looking at. Most urgent were the infections and the threat of necrosis at the fingertips. If that wasn't treated soon, it would be irreversible.

Cleaning the wounds was a painful process, made more difficult by her pounding head and the occasional feverish shivers that wracked her body. The chamberlain had been more helpful than she expected. She recognised the man as the one who had opened the door for her. That visit seemed a lifetime ago. Once she realised that "whatever she needs" had been a very literal command, she had instructed him to acquire a variety of herbs and walked him through the steps of making several disinfecting poultices and compresses, as well as a tea that would help with the fever. She didn't ask how or where he acquired the ingredients, and was barely aware of the man otherwise. Her mind was solely focused on the healing of her hands. It had to be. Any thoughts outwith that seemed too big, too terrifying to contemplate just yet.

The injuries were serious enough that they needed more powerful magic to be healed, so her highest priority became getting her fingers moving again. Once they were, the healing would become a lot more straightforward.

In between the cleaning and the changing of dressings, she rested. Sleep was one of the body's best ways of recovering, and she was grateful to be lying in an actual bed after the last few weeks of chains.

If she had been more lucid, she might have wondered why Arkhael had laid her there, but between the panic, the concussion, and the effort of treating herself, those thoughts went unacknowledged.

By the end of the first day, the swelling in her fingers had visibly reduced and some of the wounds had started to crust over. It was all she could really have hoped for before she passed out from sheer exhaustion.

It took her two days to regain some semblance of mobility in her hands and enough lucidity to be able to focus on calling forth her magic. During those days, her waking moments felt like a fever dream, and maybe they were. She healed herself as best she could with what little energy she had, until she finally regained the movement in her fingers.

Once she did, she ignored the pins and needles that came with it, and properly got to work.

She drove out the remaining infection and knitted flesh together where muscle and skin had broken. The healing magic, now called forth, raced through her body. Most of her had been weakened by lack of proper nutrition and movement; magic wouldn't heal that. The fracture on the side of her skull, however, she carefully moulded back together. She was lucky none of the bone there had splintered. It was exhausting work, but she felt better than she had in days when sleep once again claimed her.

It was the next day that she finally left the bed. Her steps were small and wobbly, but her fever had broken, and her head felt clearer. No longer needing urgent medical care, she became aware of the other demands of her body. Carefully, she made her way over to where she knew Arkhael's bath was, desperately needing to clean herself.

Almost mechanically, she went through the process. Now that her life was no longer in immediate danger, reality threatened to force its way in. Ailith aggressively pushed it back out. It was easier not to think about what had happened, to focus on the black stone of the walls as she washed herself.

Only when she left the bath did she lose the control she had strained to hold onto.

Her clothes were ruined beyond repair, but she had nothing here. No bathrobe, no dressing gown, not even a spare tunic. She could wear one of Arkhael's shirts, but the thought almost repulsed her.

Arkhael . . . She had not seen him these past few days and had carefully avoided thinking of him. He wasn't a challenge she wanted to provoke anymore. He had changed himself from her secret desire to her captor, and as long as he could order her around with her soul as his hostage, she could never give herself to him.

And with that realisation, finally, came the tears. Tears for everything that had happened. The stress. The hardship. Tears for everything she had lost. The pain. But mostly tears of heartbreak. Knowing that, despite everything, she still cared. Knees pulled to her chest, still naked from her bath, she sat next to the pool and cried. Until eventually, the tears ran dry.

She didn't hear the door open and jumped when a towel was draped around her. Arkhael lowered himself next to her, the expression on his face unreadable through her bleary eyes, extending her a hand. She let herself be pulled up and dried her face with the back of her hand. Immediately, she was on her guard.

Compose yourself. Don't show weakness.

"I sent Marius to get you new clothing similar to what you had. Come."

She followed him back to his bedchambers, towel wrapped around her. Leggings and a green tunic had been laid out on the bed for her. It might have been similar in appearance, but upon lifting the tunic, she realised the quality was better than anything she had worn in her life. Pushing away the panic at the number of changes happening in too short a time, she turned to face Arkhael.

"So, what now?"

"Now you heal." That same odd expression was still on his face. "You can't work for me in this state. Once you have regained some strength, I have a job for you."

She refrained from pointing out that her "state" was his doing. It felt so wrong to see him as a . . . A what? She refused to call him her master.

She settled on employer instead. And he had a job for her already. She knew that it had been wrong to have sex with the devil. And yet that had seemed more right than whatever was going on between them now.

Ailith dropped the towel to dress herself and saw his gaze flicker down briefly.

Does he even still desire you? The thought that he might not hit her like a punch in the stomach. She had been responsible for the loss of his life's work. As much as he had hurt her, she had dealt him a blow just as big.

I would hate me too.

Her throat tightened, and she was grateful she didn't have more tears to spill. Coughing to hide the sob that threatened to leave her, she quickly dressed herself.

He gestured for her to follow him, and her stomach rumbled as the smell of food greeted her once he opened the door.

However awkward Ailith was feeling, the moment she saw the food laid out on the small table in his chambers, all she could feel was the hunger of someone who hadn't had proper nutrition in too long. With careful restraint, she sat down, waiting for Arkhael to start before she put food onto her plate. Her table manners were terrible. She was aware of it, could feel Arkhael's look of disapproval, and she couldn't have cared less.

Only halfway through her meal did she start paying attention to what she had been eating. Some form of fragrant stew. Ailith didn't recognise the ingredients. A type of root vegetable, judging from the texture? It was wonderful. She slowed her eating, looking across the table.

Arkhael leaned back in his chair, one leg swung over the other, quietly observing her. Judging from his plate, he had eaten, but not much. Ailith wondered if he needed to eat at all or if it was simply indulgence for him. When the chamberlain cleared the table, she folded her legs under her, nestling further into the chair. A rosiness settled over her despite the awkward silence. For the first time in a while, she was washed, comfortable, and had eaten properly.

Arkhael got up, and she followed him with her gaze as he walked to one of the large bookshelves, collected some books, and brought them back over to her.

"While your body recovers, I want you to read these. Pick others that you think might be relevant when you're done. I won't have you idling around here."

Ailith pulled the pile towards her. Books on the Hells, the power structures, other devils of note. She picked up the top one, *Fundamentals on Infernal Contracts*. It did not sound riveting, but she had no doubt the knowledge would be vital to her survival in this new position.

She awoke with a start to sudden movement next to her and the sound of rustling sheets. Arkhael had gotten out of bed. Ailith blinked in confusion. The bed? When had she fallen asleep? Her last memory was of opening the book, of the soft chair and how warm the room was. *Ah.*

Then how had she ended up in bed? She didn't want to think about it. *How embarrassing.*

Rolling over onto her side, she watched Arkhael get dressed. His left shoulder moved awkwardly, she noticed as he walked off. *An injury?*

With a groan, Ailith got up as well. By the time she had made it out of the room, Arkhael was gone. But there was coffee and food on the table, as well as the book she had attempted to read the previous night.

As she ate her breakfast, she considered her situation. Why had she awoken in his bed? With a start, she realised he must have shared it with her every night. How had she not noticed this sooner?

She blamed the concussion.

But why? She knew his touch well enough to know nothing had happened while she slept. So why would he want her there?

Shaking her head, Ailith finished her breakfast. Time to get her strength back.

The first night she retired was nothing short of awkward. She was uncertain where to go. Arkhael had very gracefully allowed her to sleep in his bed while she recovered, but surely he didn't intend for her to stay there.

Almost shyly, she asked, "Where do you want me to sleep? Do you have servant's quarters?"

He never even looked up from the parchment he was reading. "You'll sleep where you have been sleeping."

That gave her pause. Why would he want her in his bed? Unless . . .

The thought made her sick. No matter how attractive and alluring he was, she would not give herself to a man who forced her. She was about to open her mouth to say as much when she changed her mind. Not once in the last few days had he touched her. Hells, she hadn't even realised she had been sleeping in his bed until lucidity returned to her. From under her lashes, she observed him and caught him glancing her way. Could she trust someone who had had her in chains only a few days ago?

It's not like you have a choice.

Resolutely, she turned around, hoping her hesitant faith in him was not misplaced.

"And druid, I won't have you dirtying the bed with your clothes."

With gritted teeth, she kept walking, magic sizzling at her fingertips. She could easily imagine the natural look of authority on his face as he said it, the expectation of blind obedience. If her soul hadn't been on the line, she would have turned around and told him exactly what she thought of that. As it was, she didn't want to give him the satisfaction of her outrage. Instead, she dropped her clothes next to the bed in petty vengeance. She knew he disliked messes.

As she got into the soft bed, she wrapped the sheets tightly around her body, ready for the worst. But when morning came, her apprehension proved to have been unfounded. She awoke where she had fallen asleep, the blankets still tightly wrapped around her. Only the clothes had been folded away, she noted with a hint of satisfaction. As relieved as she was, it was another mystery to add to the growing turmoil in her mind. For someone who held her life in his hands, Arkhael was being strangely considerate.

The days that followed blended into a not entirely unpleasant blur.

Being an early riser, she would wake with Arkhael and more often than not have breakfast with him. Then she trained. Returning to the most basic martial training she had received as a druid, she would put her body through various poses until she could barely walk, after which she would read.

Arkhael left most days, and when he was at home, she would usually find him working at his writing desk. She never spoke to him when he sat there, too frightened to interrupt him while he was working, even though she was full of questions. She was uncertain of how to start a conversation, and he didn't initiate one either. Yet she caught him looking her way often when he thought she wouldn't notice.

Despite his silence, she saw small glimpses of the devil hiding behind the facade. He worked hard, almost constantly. That didn't surprise her. What did surprise her was when she caught him reading a theatre script on his sofa one night, and when she hesitantly queried if he was working with a theatre, he simply replied that he "enjoyed the arts when he got the chance to do so."

Marius brought in a small cabinet one day. It was beautifully crafted, the lacquer work complimenting his other furniture beautifully, and Arkhael spent a good hour positioning it just right. When it was finally in place, he offhandedly told her to feel free to use it, and to her delight she found that it was filled with different teas and included a teapot and a burner with a small magical flame. She had never seen him drink tea.

And every morning when he left the bed, she would watch him through her eyelashes. Admire the shape of him. Her body still full of yearning, even if her heart was broken.

He continued to carry his left shoulder awkwardly, but the dim morning light and her half-lidded eyes meant she never caught what caused it. Whatever affliction plagued him, his normally quick healing seemed to have no effect on it.

Ailith's body, on the other hand, was quickly regaining strength. Between her exercise and the luxurious lifestyle she was suddenly enjoying, there was little to stop it from healing. Her mind, however, was a different matter. As the exhaustion slowly started to fade, the nights began to torment her.

It started with a dream in which Arkhael took her to his bed, carrying her in the midst of passion. Her arms were tight around his shoulders, head against his chest, as she breathed in the scent of him. She had missed being close to him, feeling his body against hers, and now that he held her, she almost clung to him. But once he had her down on her back, his face showed only revulsion as he laughed at her. And with that all too familiar flick of his fingers, pain shot through her as he tore at her soul, slowly separating it from her body, like she was nothing more than a meal to him. Laughing as she tried to reach out for nature in a home made of stone, trying to cast magic with fingers that wouldn't move.

She screamed and shot up in the bed, clamping a hand over her mouth as she frantically tried to calm herself down, lest she wake the devil next to her. Quietly, she flexed her fingers, confirming that they were still working, calling her magic to her hands to feel its comforting presence. Her breathing came out in shallow gasps, and she could feel tears brimming in the corners of her eyes.

Squeezing them shut, she carefully lay back down, forcing her breath to slow. Arkhael hadn't moved. She couldn't tell if she had woken him or not. An almost physical pain ripped through her chest. She wanted nothing more than for him to wake up and take her in his arms. And yet, she was terrified of waking him, of causing him the slightest inconvenience and watching her nightmare become reality. So instead, she hugged herself, trying to find sleep again in a bed that seemed both too large and too small.

When the nightmares became a nightly occurrence, she knew that the turmoil in her soul had become too great. So she waited until Arkhael was out of the house, then did what she always used to do to ground herself. She focused on the nature around her.

Ailith sat herself down cross-legged on the warm stone floor, extending both hands to the ground. Closing her eyes, she let her awareness roll into the mountain. Nothing but rock greeted her. The stone was old and dense. Not for the first time, she wondered why Arkhael had chosen to live here. It must have been a colossal effort to excavate. She let herself travel further through the rock and found running water, realising that this must be the spring he drew from. To her greatest surprise however, she found nothing around the water. There was no life at all to be found within the mountain. Not even the smallest bit of moss had tried to wedge itself into a crack near the spring. It was overwhelmingly devoid of anything. It felt suffocating. Not at all like the gentle embrace she had hoped for.

She tried to claw back out of the darkness, away from this void of pure *nothing*, only to realise she couldn't find herself. There was nothing she could hold onto, nothing to ground her back in her own body. Desperately, she tried to summon her vines, anything at all that would feel alive. But her own summoned plants were merely an imitation of nature, a gentle flicker of life before they withered and vanished. Distantly, she was aware that she had lost control of her breathing. Had she screamed? She couldn't tell. Her teachers had warned her she could lose herself in the forests if she lingered too long. Never had she been told that the pure absence of everything would be so much more dangerous.

Warmth.

There was a warmth in the darkness. Something almost too hot to bear. Finally, she touched life. Ailith clung to it as if it was her beacon back to sanity, using it to find her way back to herself. She became aware of her cramped muscles, her erratic breathing, her clammy palms that she had pressed against her temples. Two large hands held her by the shoulders.

Arkhael.

She focused on the heat of his body. The steady rhythm of his breathing.

In. Hold. Out.

With great effort, she tried to match her own to his. After the sheer abundance of nothingness, the sound of it was deafening in her ears, her own heartbeat more akin to a battle drum.

In. Hold. Out.

Her hands found his arms, and she tore her fingers through the fabric of his clothing, sighing in relief when she felt his hot skin under her fingertips.

In. Hold. Out.

He was alive. And so was she. With a trembling breath, she opened her eyes. Even the warm glow of torchlight seemed too bright, and she squeezed them shut again twice before she felt safe to keep them open.

"Better?" His voice was so quiet, so full of concern, that for a moment, she wrote it off as a figment of her panic. But his expression mirrored his concerned tone. His fiery eyes searched her face with something almost akin to alarm.

She nodded, and the moment she did, the expression was gone, replaced by the hard mask he always wore.

"Then tell me, what were you doing?"

"Nothing lives here." Her words still came out through panted breaths.

Arkhael raised an eyebrow at her, withdrawing his hands and walking over to one of his cabinets. Ailith almost reached out for him, the absence of his touch leaving behind a cold that reminded her too strongly of what she had just felt. She barely managed to refrain, the rational part of herself reminding her she had shown him too much weakness already.

"Is there nothing that grows in any of the circles of the Hells?"

Drink in hand, Arkhael sat down on his sofa, quietly watching her before he shrugged. "Not this deep down, no. It bothers you that much?"

"It feels like . . ." She barely managed to speak the words. "Like looking for something that should exist in a sea of nothing. There is no place in our Realm that feels so . . . hollow. Even the stone cities that people love so much have moss creeping on the sides of buildings, weeds that find a crack to live in. This is just . . . empty." A shiver ran through her body.

"Get up off the floor. It's no place for you to sit."

Ailith's eyes shot to him at the change in tone, and she struggled to get her legs working again. He beckoned as she walked over to sit next to him.

Arkhael put his goblet down and took her hands in his, slowly unfurling her clenched fingers and gently rubbing them between his own.

"How do you manage to be cold here?" His voice was quiet as he shook his head at her. "There is life here. You are here. I am here. But you are right; that is all. It is why I live here. Nothing to bother or threaten me. As quiet a location as you can find down in the Hells."

Warmth slowly returned to her hands, the tremors subsiding ever so slightly before Arkhael let go of her.

"Did you actually build this place?" she asked, trying to get the empty feeling out of her mind.

"Is that so hard to believe?" He smiled as he took a sip from the goblet.

"You with a pickaxe in hand? It's hard to imagine." Despite herself, she returned his smile, feeling a little more herself again.

He handed her his goblet. "Drink. It will warm your soul."

The liquid burned down her throat, tasting of strawberries and other sweet fruits. She coughed at the strength of it, even as a warm glow spread through her core.

"You would be surprised how much I am willing to do if I want something." Arkhael took the goblet back from her, ignoring her sputtering with a distant stare. "And I desperately wanted a quiet home."

Ailith said nothing, feeling like he was letting her in on something personal, scared to disrupt whatever had prompted him to lower his mask.

His eyes came back to rest on her. "Should you not have been doing something other than whatever this druidic magic is?"

The moment was over. Ice had returned to his voice.

She swallowed heavily. "Of course." She scrambled to get off the sofa, more than a little confused by his change in demeanour.

Arkhael walked in on her one morning as she went through her exercises, watching her without comment.

It was unsettling, but she continued through the various poses, determined not to let him distract her. Even as her body regained its strength, she continued the training, convinced she needed all the strength she could muster. Only when she was finished, panting and sweating heavily, did she raise her eyebrows at him.

He simply nodded at her. "You are ready. Talk to me once you've cleaned up."

She found him where she usually did: working away at his writing desk. Ailith stood next to him, waiting for him to speak.

"I'm not sending you on a difficult job." He turned to face her. "I need you to find someone for me in a small convent to the Grace Mother. I suspect that amongst the Sisters, there hides a young woman on the cusp of adulthood. She would be dark of skin and bear herself well. You have an excellent eye for reading people. If she is there, I expect you will recognise her immediately by how she carries herself, like a swan among chickens."

Ailith nodded as he spoke. It seemed simple enough.

"Do you want me to make any contact with her, do anything?"

"Just confirm her existence for now." He handed her one of the rubies and gestured next to his table. "I still have the pack you brought with you to the Chambers. Speak to Marius if you need anything else. I will send you out tomorrow morning. It goes without saying, I presume, that you don't mention me or your reason for being there, should you speak to anyone."

Ailith nodded again. "Naturally. Can I know who she is?"

Arkhael shook his head. "It is better if you don't."

"Alright."

The silence hung.

Then they both spoke at once.

"Is your shoulder—"

"I am late for—"

Ailith smiled awkwardly. "You must be busy. I won't keep you."

She turned around to find the book she had been studying to avoid looking at him. Only when she heard him get up and leave for the day did she relax.

CHAPTER 28

Arkhael stepped out onto his balcony. This high up, the wind never entirely died down, but it felt especially strong that night. Running a hand through his hair, he stretched his wings, staring off into the distant glow of fires, watching other winged figures fly through the sky. They stayed well away from his mountain. His reputation had been carefully built. The terrifying recluse. The quiet schemer. No one dared to anger the puppet master.

He had burned entire circles of the Hells to the ground without batting so much as an eye. Even his own family had come to fear him for how cold he was. His lack of compassion was legendary, his devotion to himself widely known. It was a reputation he was proud of. It proved he was so much more than his brethren, than the other devils that gave in to their every whim and desire, that lacked all self-control. It wasn't just his source of pride. When he had renounced everything, his reputation, his self-control, had become the very foundation of his power and authority.

So why did that iron grip seem to disappear the moment she stepped into the room? Why did the way she spoke his name haunt him so? Why was it her grey eyes that met him when he closed his?

Clenching his fists, he cursed. It wasn't his fault that the druid kept crawling under his skin. He didn't even know how she was doing it. Walking over to the edge of the balcony, he gripped the balustrade, remembering how she had stood there between his arms not long ago.

He should never have allowed her in. Now every part of his home smelled of her, reminded him of her. And he couldn't let her go either. Of that he was certain. It wasn't his fault that the burning need to own her was almost as hot as his desire for her. That he needed her in his home as much as he needed her in his bed.

His claws dug into the carefully sculpted stone as he thought of how absentmindedly she played with those long silver strands of hers. Like she knew every flick of them tightened the noose she had around his neck.

With a crack, the stone under his hands broke.

Devils were supposed to enchant mortals, not the other way around. He cursed again. Her presence was a constant torment, her careful tiptoeing around him even more so.

He wanted to hurt her, to break her, to punish her for what she had done. Her betrayal stung him more than it should have. She wasn't the first to try to break a contract with him. She wasn't even the first to succeed, although she was the only one he had let live.

But she was the first whose betrayal had hurt.

Because she was mine.

There were plenty of creatures—mortals, devils, and otherwise—who had presented themselves to him willingly. But never had he met someone who made his blood run so hot, and who met him with equal fire and passion. He had believed her when she said that she was his; there had been no lie in her words or in her soul. So why would she betray him? *How could she?*

With a cry, he grabbed the stones of the broken banister and hurled them into the distance, where they quickly disappeared into the fog below.

It made no sense to him. She made no sense to him. And yet, even more than he wanted to hurt her, he wanted to own her again. To experience that unique pleasure that she had gifted him with such passion.

With a frustrated sigh, he sat down. Even now, when she should have been his, when he all but held her soul, she gave him neither pain nor pleasure. She was an enigma walking around his home, a reminder of what he could and should have.

Maybe he should just get rid of her.

His stomach churned at the thought.

Why? Why are you so desperate to keep her around if all she brings you is unanswered longing?

He had no answer to the question.

Annoyed, he walked back inside and into his bedchambers. His eyes immediately found her sleeping form.

Why do you have her sleep in your bed?

Again, the answer eluded him. Every night was an exercise of careful restraint. Even thinking of giving in to the desire to simply hold her threatened to break the iron grip he had on himself. She broke the perfect rhythm that he had lived his life to, the perfect command he had over everything. He despised the feeling.

And yet, he wanted to have her near so that he could watch her delight in discovering how many teas he had gotten her, or watch the soft rise and fall of her chest when she lay down to rest.

Reaching out, he gently stroked her hair. She stirred under his touch, and he quickly withdrew his hand, not wanting to wake her. But all she did was mutter something intelligible in her sleep. With a heart full of regret, he stepped away from her, his fingers burning where he had touched her. He balled his hands into fists. Every night, it became harder not to reach out for her.

If only he knew how to get his thief back, the one who challenged him at every turn, who demanded as much pleasure as she gave. He would do anything to have that woman returned to him.

Quietly, he slipped under the covers on the other side of his bed. With his eyes closed, he only felt more aware of how near she was to him. The soft sound of her breathing quickened, and he gritted his teeth. Terrors seemed to plague her nearly every night. It was hard to listen to, and even harder not to ask her what caused them. If it had been his torture of her, throughout which she had appeared so deceptively unaffected, or if it was something else entirely. But he never asked. It had nothing to do with him not wanting to hear that he might be the source of her fears, and everything to do with her deserving the hardship after what she had done to him.

Next to him, Ailith tossed in her sleep, a quiet gasp leaving her mouth. *Hells, she sounds so scared.* He was about to turn his back to her so that he couldn't accidentally open his eyes and see her torment for himself when her hand shot out and grabbed his arm. Immediately, he tensed, his eyes on her, ready to ask her what she thought she was doing. But she appeared oblivious to the world still. Oblivious to her own actions. Stuck in whatever fear she was reliving. His skin almost itched where her fingers pressed into his arm, a strange glow emanating from them. Then Ailith sighed, her body relaxing ever so slightly before she withdrew her hand. Leaving Arkhael frozen in his own bed, wondering how to react. Seconds flew by, quickly turning into quiet and peaceful minutes as Ailith's breath evened out.

It was only just before dawn broke that he decided not to act at all, not to tell her of what she had done in her sleep. It most definitely had nothing to do with him possibly being the cause of her fear, and *certainly* nothing to do with the warmth he felt knowing he was her comfort.

CHAPTER 29

A ilith had packed as she would for any job. Most of her belongings were still intact and in good condition. Touching them conjured up a wave of nostalgia. She wondered how Amelie and Jay were doing.

With a sigh, she ensured everything was in place. Although she didn't expect to need them, she had cleaned her lockpicks and the few spare knives she always kept. The blowgun she had bought was still in the bag as well, but the vials of poison had dried completely.

She rose quickly that morning, not wanting to keep Arkhael from his other work, and was ready before he had finished his coffee, oddly nervous to leave his home. With the usual snap of his fingers, a fiery portal was conjured up for her.

She was about to step through when Arkhael suddenly grabbed her wrist, his claws digging into her skin.

"Come back to me." The intensity in his voice surprised her, and she searched his face. Whatever emotion lay behind his fiery yellow eyes, he hid it well.

"Even if I didn't want to, I don't think I could disobey now that you've ordered me to," Ailith said with a wry smile, trying to ignore how even this small amount of contact set her body aflame.

He let go of her immediately, as if her skin had burned his hand, and for the briefest moment, something flashed across his face. *Hurt?*

But then it was gone again, and he merely nodded at her.

She stepped through.

Fresh morning air.

It felt cold on Ailith's skin. Her eyes strained against the light of a rising sun. She couldn't say she had missed it.

Arkhael had dropped her off just off a small forest road. The air was full of birdsong and the smell of morning dew. As she inhaled deeply, a smile crossed her face. She might not be a great druid, but she still relished the sudden reunion with nature. Laughing out loud, she walked over to the nearest tree, placing her hand upon it. To her surprise, all signs of blossom had faded, bright green leaves crowning the branches instead. How had spring transitioned into summer already? With the absence of seasons, she had not realised how much time had passed while she stayed in the Hells.

"Hello, tree," she murmured. "How are you? I've had a wild few weeks."

The tree's leaves rustled in the wind. Ailith closed her eyes. Life was good for this tree, she felt. Its roots went deep, and its leaves caught the sun until late afternoon. She leaned her forehead against the bark, following the roots down, branching herself through it to the next tree. And the next. Until she was one with the forest. Arkhael's home wasn't bad, but by the gods did it feel good to lose herself in a root network again. Reluctantly, she drew herself away from it.

"Thank you," she whispered, then opened her eyes and walked to the road.

Looking around, she immediately spotted the convent. Her portal hadn't brought her far from it. It lay at the end of the road, bathed in the light of the morning sun: a quaint little building of yellow brick.

Habit made her approach it practically. Two stories high. Long stained-glass windows that didn't look to open on the ground floor. Windows on the second floor that possibly could. The brick wall could offer potential climbing opportunities. A small gate shielded the grounds from the rest of the forest. It seemed more ceremonial than practical, yet as she stepped through it, something tightened in her stomach. *Some form of magic.* Then it hit her. Consecrated ground. Of course. This was why Arkhael needed her. He couldn't enter the convent.

You could escape him here.

A few Sisters were out in the garden. Ailith barely noticed them, still reeling as she walked into the building. It was quiet inside. The morning sun bathed the interior in a golden light. There were no decorations other than the statue of a woman holding a sword in one hand and the sun in the other. The Grace Mother.

Ailith sank down onto one of the pews in front of the statue. It seemed to glow. *Magic or a trick of the light?* She was unsure. Piety had never been her forte, but for once, Ailith found herself bowing her head.

What should I do?

The Grace Mother would tell her to stay there, of course. If she remembered her religion correctly, followers of the Grace Mother were less extreme than the Children of Illumination. Only in their hunt for fiends could they rival one another.

What do you want *to do?*

Before she could give the question too much thought, one of the Sisters sat down next to her. An older woman, her hair covered by a scarf, with stern wrinkles on her face.

"Can I help you, dear? You look troubled."

Despite her appearance, the woman had a kind voice.

Ailith smiled. "Trouble with men, I fear. Nothing worthy of the Grace Mother's time."

The Sister tutted at her. "All those who come here and look as troubled as you do are worthy of her time."

Ailith hesitated. *Why not?* "There is a man who I used to see from time to time. He is powerful, almost frighteningly so. Definitely frighteningly so. He shared with me his greatest desire and—" Ailith chose her next words carefully. "In an attempt to do right by the world, I took away his one chance to get it." She wrung her hands. It was weirdly hard to admit, even to a stranger.

"Now he has taken me on in servitude to repay him for what I did. What I don't understand, though, is why he still shares his meals with me as if I were a guest rather than an indentured servant. Why he shares a bed with me . . ." Her voice trailed off.

She looked up at the Sister, who had raised both her eyebrows, then realised the implication of her words. "Not like that. I mean . . ." A slight blush crept up her cheeks. "Previously, it was somewhat like that. But now he just has me sleep next to him. I . . . don't understand."

A frown had appeared on the woman's face as she spoke.

"So, if I understand you correctly, you had a lover who confided in you and whose trust you betrayed. And by the sounds of it, your young man still cares enough to offer you a place in his home." The woman's voice was stern. "Have you apologised yet?"

Ailith looked at her in stunned silence. That was certainly one depiction of the truth. She almost laughed as she imagined Arkhael's reaction to being called a young man.

"It isn't that simple," Ailith said incredulously. "There was no 'caring for' in the beginning, and there certainly isn't now."

"That's not what it sounds like to me, dear." The Sister tutted again. "Why else indeed would he choose to keep you near? Try taking responsibility for your actions." She got up. "That is the Grace Mother's wisdom."

Ailith watched her go with an open mouth. She had quite possibly saved the world by removing the reliquary from the field, and this woman wanted her to apologise for that? After what he had done to her? And Arkhael hadn't entrusted her with some big secret; she had pledged that service to him in exchange for her life. He knew that as well as she did.

Right?

Ailith's thoughts were interrupted by a young woman walking quickly through the hall. Her gait wasn't pious. She walked briskly, basket in hand, dark skin warmly illuminated by the light of the morning sun. Ensuring her pace was different enough, Ailith got up and followed her back out into the gardens.

Ailith pretended to admire a rose bush while observing her. The woman was gathering herbs, but her scissors did not move particularly meticulously. Her actions were rushed and sloppy. There was clearly something else she would rather be doing. *Interesting.*

Arkhael had told her to just confirm the woman's existence, but she couldn't resist the pull of curiosity. Slowly, she made her way over, timing her pace so that they nearly collided when the woman got back up.

"Oh, excuse you!" She was beautiful—not just because her face was pretty but because of how she carried herself. *Noble born, at least.*

Ailith nodded respectfully. "I am so sorry."

As she moved out of the woman's way, she noticed one of the Sisters watching her. *A guard in disguise?*

Although this woman wore robes like the other Sisters, her stance was almost aggressive. She was ready for violence. And there was something about her, something that made Ailith's hair stand on end. Averting her gaze, she made her way off the convent grounds, walking back down the forest path. The feeling of unease lingered. Was she being followed?

She walked over to a thick tree near the path, hoping to break line of sight in case someone was behind her. Once behind the tree, she dropped down, crawling further away from the road through the underbrush, magically urging the plants around her to grow denser and shield her from wandering eyes. The road remained clear, yet Ailith didn't move until the feeling of unease subsided. If there was one thing she had learned over the years, it was to always trust her gut.

Only then did she realise that she may have just run away from her one chance at freedom.

Would it have been freedom, though?

She would have to stay within the confines of the consecrated ground. Was that what she wanted? Moving away a small spider that tried to climb up her cheek, she pondered.

What do you want?

She held her hand above her, watched the spider lower itself from a small thread.

Freedom.

The idea of being trapped in a convent seemed awful. And she had no doubt Arkhael could find a way to bring it down if he truly wanted to. Dropping the spider onto a small branch, she took the ruby out of her pocket.

But he had tortured her.

No, he hadn't.

He had had plenty of opportunity to torture her, but he hadn't.

He still starved you, imprisoned you, and forced you into servitude. If not torture, it certainly was abuse.

She looked at her fingers. Not a single scar blemished the skin, nothing to reveal the horrors of how she had nearly lost them.

It was torture.

What was she trying to convince herself of? She didn't have a choice in the matter anymore.

You want to go back.

Ailith stiffened. Did she? Yes. She wanted to go back. To the Arkhael from before the contract. That taunting, arrogant, powerful devil who had looked at her with hungry eyes. Who had refused to kiss her but then seemed unable to get enough of her. Who had shown moments of surprising tenderness.

But he was gone. Something had changed him. Had it been the contract?

Or your betrayal?

She wanted to go back, she realised, because somehow, she held out hope that she could find that devil again.

And then what? You're still no more than a slave, even if he treats you well.

The contract had to go. She couldn't be someone's property. Every step she took around him, every word she uttered, reminded her of what was at stake. Yet she wasn't sure she could destroy it.

Then why not rewrite it?

Could she? Would he let her? More importantly, was she seriously planning a potential future in the Hells?

Ailith looked around. The road was clear. She shook the twigs and leaves out of her clothing.

Apparently so.

With muscles stiff from the cold, she crushed the ruby, returning to her gilded cage.

His front doors remained a challenge to open. With a grunt, Ailith made her way from the windy plateau back into his halls. To her surprise, Arkhael was already home, sitting in his usual spot at his desk.

Holding onto her newfound resoluteness, she approached him. He barely looked up at her.

"Report."

"I found your woman. Noble born, at least. Certainly not pious."

Arkhael smiled at her words. "As I suspected. Anything else of note?"

"She had a bodyguard who's masquerading as a Sister."

He nodded. "That makes sense."

Without any further ceremony, he turned back to his paperwork.

It stung. Even though she knew that her life was now in his service, she hated how he treated her like she was nothing more than a messenger. Blinking back the unexpected tears, she threw her bag in a corner, grabbed the book she had been reading off the table, and walked outside onto his balcony. He didn't need to see her cry.

Only when dinner was served did she go back inside, eating the food in silence and avoiding Arkhael's gaze.

"I need you to go back to the convent." Arkhael's voice cut through the awkward silence.

She looked up from her food but said nothing.

"I want you to break in tomorrow and plant something for me."

Ailith set the bowl down on the table, a quiet anger starting to bubble below the surface.

"No," she said resolutely. Arkhael raised his eyebrows at her, but before he could speak, she continued, "You out of everyone, should know that I need at least a little bit of time before I break in somewhere. There's no way I can do it tomorrow."

"You managed to break into the Chambers with only, what, two or three days to gather information? I have no doubt you will manage a small convent."

Ailith hissed at him. "I had help when we broke into the Chambers. Your map was invaluable. Do you have a similar one for this building?"

"It's happening tomorrow. If you are worried about it, I suggest you start preparing yourself."

"You truly are just like any other arrogant nobleman, aren't you?" Ailith snapped, the earlier disappointment and anger finally bubbling over. "Thinking you know better when you have no idea what you are talking about."

Arkhael narrowed his eyes at her. "Those noblemen who hired you are nothing compared to me." She could see him take a deep breath. "Regardless, if I didn't think you capable, I wouldn't have ordered you to do it."

Was that a compliment?

It completely caught her off-guard, taking the venom out of her anger.

"It's not like I have a choice either way," she muttered, mostly to herself. Then she continued a bit louder, "So what exactly is it that you need me to do?"

"Find out where the woman you saw sleeps. Once she's asleep, I need you to deposit a letter under her pillow. That is all."

Ailith refrained from commenting. Instead, she asked, "Do you have any information about the place at all? Any idea of the internal layout? Of where she sleeps?"

When Arkhael shook his head, she groaned in frustration and leaned back in the chair, going over what she had seen during the day. The size of the hall of worship meant that there couldn't be much space for anything else downstairs. Certainly not sleeping quarters. But where upstairs would this lady sleep? And how would she get there?

If she waited until dark, she could scale the wall undetected, as long as no one walked outside and looked up. But then what?

She looked up to catch Arkhael watching her intently.

"You don't happen to have any spare sleeping potions on hand?"

He raised an eyebrow at her. "I believe you have daggers in your pack?"

Ailith huffed. "I am a thief, not a murderer."

Arkhael's response was instant. "The man I held in my prison would disagree."

She could feel a blush creep up her cheeks at that. "At least I don't enjoy it," she muttered. The poor man hadn't been the first who was in the wrong place at the wrong time, but she had always tried to avoid killing as much as she could.

"I don't need you to enjoy working for me, I need you to do your job well." Arkhael regarded her coolly.

"I won't kill for you," Ailith all but snarled at him.

"Oh, I think you will." He snapped his fingers, a rolled up piece of parchment appearing in his hand. "Or do I need to remind you of the consequences should you disobey me?"

Her stomach churned, and she swallowed hard, biting back her response. Narrowing her eyes at him, Ailith got up from her chair. "Excuse me. I need to do some unexpected planning."

Fuming, she made her way back out onto his balcony. Anything to not be in the same room as him. Gripping the balustrade, she tried her best to calm down her erratic heartbeat.

How dare he?

She hated the hold he had over her, hated that he would threaten to abuse it. But most of all, she hated that she couldn't hate him. It was ridiculous.

Maybe he knows. Maybe the hope of seeing that other side of him again is exactly what he wants you to feel to keep you obedient.

She shook her head. It changed little.

With a sigh, she went over her lack of a plan again. Climb up at night, find a window so she could sneak through when everyone was asleep, and hope they didn't have anyone staying up for a night shift. If she ran into anyone . . .

She hoped she wouldn't.

Chapter 30

Although Arkhael had requested that she break into the convent during the night, Ailith asked him for a portal in the middle of the afternoon. She wanted time to scout the building from a distance, hoping for a last-minute miracle that might give her anything more to work with.

To her surprise, she found a small vial next to her bag when she gathered her tools. Carefully, she removed the stopper and sniffed the contents. She immediately recognised the strong, acrid smell of the herb mixture. A poison that, when injected directly into the bloodstream in the correct dose, would instantly put the victim into a deep sleep. She said nothing as she put the vial in her pocket, within easy reach, but she couldn't help the small smile on her face.

There is still hope.

With a last check of her gear, she made her way over to Arkhael, who handed her both ruby and letter before summoning her a portal.

She searched his eyes, but his expression betrayed nothing. He could pretend to be callous all he wanted; she knew at least a part of him cared.

"Don't worry," she said with a slight smile, "I'll be back."

She caught both his raised eyebrows but made sure to step through before he could respond. Whatever mask he was trying to wear around her, whatever facade he was trying to hide behind, she could still crack it.

At least she had to believe that.

Ailith spent a good few hours just observing the convent. She had remembered correctly that the upstairs floor had small windows she could use all around the building. Scaling it would be strenuous, but certainly not impossible. Unfortunately, however, she was unable to see through the windows or learn anything from a distance. So she found herself a hidden spot in the surrounding forest and waited patiently till nightfall.

After the sun set, she gave the convent a few hours to quiet down. One by one, the lights started to dim. When she was fairly certain no one would come back outside, she walked over, jumping over the fence onto the consecrated ground. The moon was out, which meant she had to make sure to find a spot on the shadowed side of the building.

Finding herself a dark corner, she carefully summoned a vine out of the brickwork above her. Without a sound, she brought it lower until she could wrap it around her hands. Pressing the soft soles of her boots against the wall, she started to climb. The darkness should have made the journey slower, but to her pleasant surprise, the brickwork was weathered, making it easy to find grip with her feet. Still, by the time she had climbed to the small windows, she was covered in a thin sheen of sweat. Rather than stopping, she conjured a vine slightly higher and used it to ascend to the roof, allowing herself a brief moment to catch her breath. The roof was slanted, but not steep enough that she risked rolling off it immediately.

She had been hoping to find a hatch or some other form of roof access. With careful step she scouted the space. Roofs were notorious for carrying noise. By the time she had searched the entire roof and come up empty-handed, her mood was sour. In her head, she cursed Arkhael for not telling her of this assignment the first time she visited. If only she had known, she would have kept a better eye out.

Grumbling, Ailith made her way back over to the edge and dangled her legs down. The last thing she wanted to do was enter the convent through a window and search every room from the inside. The risk of running into someone was too great. And although she had her sleeping poison, it was a last resort. She didn't want to have to drag any unconscious bodies through hallways.

Biting the inside of her cheek, she mulled over her options. She could try and peek inside every individual window. It would drain her magic and take a stupidly long time with only a very small chance of her gaining the information she needed. Yet she preferred that option over all others. Arkhael be damned; she was not going in there blind only to risk discovery and having to fight her way out. She knew there was at least one capable fighter inside; there was no telling how many others there might be.

Throwing another curse in the devil's general direction, she walked over to the far corner of the roof and summoned another vine from the stonework.

With gritted teeth, she slowly climbed down next to the first window, pausing to listen for any noise. Quiet, muffled voices reached her through the glass. She leaned to her left, peeking through it and praying none of those inside looked out the window at that exact moment. The room was small, with a few tables and chairs strewn about. Three Sisters sat in a corner with sewing equipment. Ailith ducked back again. It wasn't what she was looking for.

The next few windows she looked through were sleeping quarters, but there was no trace of her mystery woman. Her arms started to burn with the strain of the constant climbing, and she hoisted herself back onto the roof to allow herself a break and to rub her arms. Unfortunately, muscle fatigue could not be healed away.

She looked up at the sky. The moon had progressed its journey quite a bit, she guessed it to be past midnight.

There was still time.

With a quiet groan she descended again, ignoring the burning in her arms. Luck favoured her this time. When she glanced through the next window, she found her mark. The room seemed to be a private one, with only one bed. And the young woman was currently sitting on it with one of the other Sisters, their quiet voices carrying a hushed conversation through the window.

Moving to the side again, she twisted her vine into a loop and sat herself in it. It wasn't comfortable, but at least her arms got a break. She would wait there until the women went to sleep and then look at opening the window to slip the letter under the woman's pillow. Easy and straightforward.

Or so it should have been. If she had thought luck favoured her before, she now realised that Arkhael couldn't have chosen a worse time. As she listened in on the younger women's conversation, she quickly realised that they were not meant to be still awake. Their voices held a hint of mischief, as if they were young girls staying up past their bedtime. The more Ailith listened in, the more she realised the conversation wasn't innocent either.

She learned that the young woman's name was Meredith, that she greatly disliked having to stay in the convent, but most intriguingly, she learned that Meredith and the Sister were thinking of running away together. Arkhael would be very interested in that piece of knowledge. In her experience, the sons and daughters of noblemen were seldom allowed to marry freely. There was always some ulterior motive, some profit that needed to be gained from the union. She doubted that Meredith's family would approve of her marriage to a Sister of the Grace Mother. Eventually, the voices quieted. Just as Ailith was about to glance through the window again, a soft moan reached her ears. With a grumble, she resigned herself to a long night of waiting.

Her luck did not return. The longer she waited, the more she felt like she was sitting in on a secret date night. Hesitation began to set in. What if they stayed up all night? She didn't dare return to Arkhael and report failure. But the moon was already starting to set, and sunrise couldn't be too far off.

The choice was made for her.

A noise sounded from the garden below: the heavy thud of large doors being opened. A quiet pair of voices emerged.

Damn these pious folk and their early-morning habits.

Ailith's mind raced. If she waited here, she would still have to figure out how to open the window after the women had gone to sleep—if they were planning to sleep at all—and then she would somehow need to leave the grounds without being seen. With a curse, she climbed back up to the roof. There was no way she would manage to complete the job this night, but neither did she dare return empty-handed. Quietly, she scrambled further up the roof, balancing herself on the ridge as she lay down and threw her cloak over her. Resigned, she prepared herself for a day of discomfort and hoped that no one would look at the roof too closely during the daytime. Her muscles were cramped from hanging in the same position all night, and her body ached with fatigue.

Would Arkhael be looking for her? Would he try to claim her soul for not returning to him? Closing her eyes, she prayed that the holy ground would stop him from doing so, and tried to get some semblance of rest.

It was hard. She had been in awkward positions for jobs before, but this topped the list. The cloak she had thrown over herself to stand out less became stifling to breathe under. Yet despite the hot air, a cold seeped into her bones and muscles from lying still against the shingles of the roof. Hunger gnawed at her stomach, and her throat felt parched. And even though she was exhausted, sleep refused to come. The discomfort and her nerves kept rest at bay, until, when the sun finally set, she felt like she had never been in a fouler mood.

As darkness fell, she slowly pulled the cloak off her face. The cold air pricked her cheeks, and she inhaled deeply.

One more try.

Very slowly, she started to move, trying to rub some warmth into her body, while a muscle pain from the previous night set into her shoulders.

She lowered herself down to the window again, trying to ignore the burning in her arms. Thankfully, Meredith did look to be asleep in her bed. Feeling like she could cry with relief, Ailith observed her for a few moments, making sure the rhythm of her breath was definitely that of a sleeping woman. Only when she was certain did she inspect the window. There was no lock or other security on it, just a simple handle that kept it closed. Drawing on her dwindling reserve of magic, Ailith put her hand on the wood, willing the shape of the handle to change and smooth. This part of the job was almost laughably simple compared to the previous night. With ease, she moulded the wood until she could carefully pry the window open. Ever so quietly, she slipped in and put the envelope under the sleeping woman's pillow. She cast a quick glance around the rest of the room. There was nothing else of value or note in it. Simply a plain desk and chair. Whoever this woman was, whatever made her so special to Arkhael, nothing in the room betrayed her identity.

With nimble feet, Ailith climbed back out again, pressing the window shut before descending down the building.

The sooner she left this place, the better.

Ailith sighed in relief when she finally returned to the plateau, the sky behind her already dark. She was hungry, sore, and she desperately wanted a bath.

Report first. With that thought, her nerves returned. She could honestly say she had done her best. All she could do was hope it would be good enough.

Arkhael wasn't at his desk or in his usual chair. There was, however, a bowl of grapes and other fruit on the table, of which she gratefully partook.

Where was he usually this time of night? She realised she didn't know; she was usually asleep by this point.

If she couldn't find him, he would get his report in the morning. She couldn't be bothered roaming the halls for him, and she craved a bath and her bed.

Dropping her clothes to the floor as she went, she opened the door to his bath. And paused mid-step.

"You are letting all the steam escape."

No matter how many times she had seen his naked body, it never failed to steal her breath.

Ailith closed the door behind her, carefully keeping her gaze averted. She was here now; she might as well commit.

Walking to the other side of the pool, she lowered herself into the water, then looked up, trying her best to ignore the nerves and making sure to keep her eyes trained on Arkhael's face.

"I wasn't sure you would return."

Ailith scoffed, suddenly angry. She had not sat cramped on a roof all day to be insulted now.

"If you weren't so worried about me breaking your precious contract, you might actually find that you can trust me to do my job." She narrowed her eyes.

"Like how I trusted you with the reliquary? I think not." His voice was quiet.

She could feel his anger, sense the danger, and said nothing.

"Report."

She did. She shared with him all information she thought he might find important, including Meredith's midnight lover.

He sat with his chest above the water, she noticed as she spoke. Unusual. The few times she had seen him in here, he had lain back more. Her eyes trailed despite herself, and she clenched her fists.

Do NOT think about touching him.

Trying to stop her breath from hitching, she finished her report.

He listened attentively, then nodded, pondering her words. Again, Ailith noticed how he favoured his right side.

"What's wrong with your shoulder?"

It was out before she could stop herself.

"Nothing you need to concern yourself with." His voice left no room for argument.

Maybe her confidence had healed with her body, or maybe anger and annoyance were finally starting to outweigh caution, but she slowly waded over to him. Her eyes caught by his. Her heartbeat in her throat.

Biting her cheek—*Please don't let me lose my soul over this.*—she looked down and hissed despite herself. The usually dark red skin was pink. Parts of it were covered in blisters, and the parts that weren't seemed to be oozing. Why wasn't this healing? She gently touched his arm below the wound, moving it so she could get a better look. The affected area was bigger than she had initially thought, covering his entire shoulder as well as the top of his arm.

"What did this?"

"You did."

Ailith looked up, caught the flicker of pain on his face.

The moonlight.

She hadn't meant to . . . Hadn't wanted to . . .

"I . . ."

Hadn't she, though? She had known that the beam of divine light could be fatal to him. Yet somehow, he had seemed so strong, so invincible to her. The thought that she could scar him seemed inconceivable. No wonder he had been so paranoid about keeping her fingers restrained.

Arkhael opened his mouth to say something, but before he could speak, she gently put her fingers on his lips.

"Please. Let me."

She didn't wait for his response, too worried he might say no, and not in the mood to argue. Instead, she put one hand on his chest under the wound and closed her eyes. Briefly, her focus was drawn elsewhere. His firm, hot skin, his quickened heartbeat. She pushed the thoughts away, called for her healing, and let the magic travel via her hand into him.

He felt different. She knew he did, knew it from when she had reached out for him in the emptiness of his halls. But never had she felt it in this much detail. The makeup of his skin was unlike anything she had felt before.

She found the wound. The top layers of skin had been burned away, and whatever natural regeneration his body possessed was gone from the area. Without magical attendance, this wound wouldn't heal.

Gently, she nudged the skin at the edge closest to his neck, encouraging it to knit itself together with the skin next to it. Drawing on more magic, she examined his healthy skin, then slowly tried to restore the regenerative properties to the injured areas. It was a slow process.

The creation of new skin was so much more complex on him. And once created, it was as if it refused to heal and merge with the skin next to it until Ailith drew on more magic to connect it together. Yet she kept at it, focusing on one small piece at a time.

And then there was no more magic to draw on. Her resources were depleted.

Bracing for the headache she knew would follow, she opened her eyes, blinking away the black spots that danced across her vision.

Complete magic depletion felt worse than a hangover.

She ignored the thumping that had started in her temple and examined the freshly healed skin. Despite her efforts, she felt as if she had not even managed to make a proper start at healing the wound, but the new skin looked good.

Carefully, she ran her fingers over it. It was slightly lighter in colour and would remain a visible scar when completely healed—she couldn't help that—but the skin felt supple and warm to her touch. A good sign.

Only after she had withdrawn her hands and clenched her fists did she dare look Arkhael in the eye again.

His jaw was tense, but he didn't seem angry. At least, no more than usual.

Ailith averted her gaze. "I'll continue tomorrow," she said and turned to leave.

"Wait."

She froze. He moved behind her and grabbed her shoulder. Panic coiled in her stomach as he pushed her down slightly into the water, pulling her head back. But then he scooped water over her head, combing it through her hair. Ailith relaxed as he repeated the process, shivering slightly whenever his claws touched her skin. His hands moved from her head to her shoulders, rubbing them slightly. Then he gently pushed her away.

"You would have made the bed dusty," he murmured.

Ailith said nothing, not knowing how to react, and didn't look back as she walked out of the chamber, heart pounding.

An aggressive headache awoke Ailith the following morning, making reading nearly impossible. Instead, she claimed one of the balcony chairs and watched the horizon, tea in hand. Occasionally, she would see the shadows of other devils flying across the yellow sky, lit by the sporadic fires below. Distant screams carried on the wind.

It was the one thing she missed most: trees. As the pain continued to assault her, she longed for nothing more than the gentle sound of wind through leaves. She wondered if any could grow in the Hells.

Only when the sky darkened did her headache subside.

Neither she nor Arkhael spoke about the previous night, and she retired shortly after dinner, despite no longer needing an early night. Avoiding the awkwardness of the drawing room, she took her book with her to bed. It wasn't until she heard his footsteps followed by the quiet sounds of moving water that she put it down again, staring at the door.

She had promised to continue the healing, and he hadn't told her not to.

With her heart in her throat, she left the bed. Only when her hand was already on the door handle did she feel suddenly bashful, aware of her nakedness. Things were too different between them for her to walk in there without clothes. Yesterday had been accidental. If she did it today, it would be deliberate.

So she walked over to his wardrobe, put one of his shirts on for lack of a dressing gown, then pushed down the door handle before she could change her mind.

Even though she carefully looked at the floor, she could feel his eyes on her. Quietly walking over, she sat down on the floor next to him, never speaking a word, and closed her eyes.

"Wait."

She opened them again to look at him.

"I don't want you exhausting yourself again. You're useless to me when you're unable to even read." The stern tone of Arkhael's voice didn't quite match the look of slight concern on his face. "And I don't want you unable to defend yourself," he quietly added.

Ailith nodded in response, trying her best to focus on the task at hand. On the feeling of guilt when she looked at his shoulder, rather than the rest of him so close to her. Trying her best to not look further down. Gently, she placed a hand on his chest and returned to her arduous task.

CHAPTER 31

S he came to him like this every night after, the door barely making a sound as it opened, her footsteps quiet as she walked over to him. Arkhael found himself wondering if she was such a good thief because she was naturally quiet or if years of practice had ingrained this in her. Often, he found himself uncharacteristically curious. There was so much about her he didn't know.

Every night, she knelt down without a word, healing the damage she herself had done to him. He could tell it was taking its toll.

He had said nothing when she nodded off while reading, dropping his book to the floor. He also didn't mention that she was technically disobeying his orders. Instead, he made sure to be around, to watch over her when she fell asleep on his balcony chair.

At least the exhaustion meant she was too tired to wake from her nightmares, even if she did still occasionally reach for him in her sleep, and for that he was grateful. It had been excruciating to watch her try to silence herself. But whatever plagued her in her dreams, she showed little of it as she visited him in his bath.

Every night, she wore his clothing. The steam plastered it against her body, the shirt not covering anything when she crossed her legs. And every night, it became a little bit harder to not tear it off her.

Her gentle touch was its own torture, his skin aflame wherever her fingers ghosted over it. He was almost grateful for the pain her healing brought, distracting him from the thought of her body so close to his. All he had to do was reach out, and she wouldn't be able to refuse him.

But then he saw the way she averted her eyes, and his desire died. Even though she was his, she still eluded him.

He needed her to want him, to say his name like it was ambrosia, to give herself to him fully. The memory of her breathless plea came to him. He focused on the pain.

Most of the wound was healed now. He didn't think she knew how great a service she had done for him by healing it. It wouldn't have healed on its own. Arkhael was well aware of that. And no one else with this kind of healing power would have deigned to heal a devil.

Yet he dreaded the end of their nightly ritual. Despite the torture, he enjoyed having her this close. When she healed him, he glimpsed the woman he missed so much, who wasn't constantly guarded around him, and he was loath to see it end.

He looked up briefly. She looked serene like this. Her back straight, eyes closed, mouth whispering quietly. She let down her long silver hair every night, and it curtained her face perfectly as she sat next to him. The hand on his chest glowed ever so faintly.

Part of him had been surprised when she had returned from the convent. He knew she was smart enough to realise he couldn't easily reach her there. And yet, she had returned. Twice.

Clearly, she preferred his prison over theirs.

The pain faded. Ailith no longer had her eyes closed. Instead, she was touching the newly formed skin, examining it critically.

"I believe that's it healed," she finally said quietly. "Just make sure not to strain it too much over the next few days." Her eyes were still trained on the floor as she got up.

He realised she was falling before she did.

He watched her get up, saw how shaky her legs were and watched her lose her balance. Without a second thought, he caught her as she fell into the pool with a yelp, protecting her head from hitting anything.

Spluttering, she righted herself, and Arkhael almost laughed at the look of indignance on her face. But then he realised how the water took away any illusion of decency his shirt had pretended to give her. The fabric that clung to her body all but transparent, outlining every curve. And she was right there, already practically in his arms. All he had to do was close the distance.

He would have. Had she not finally looked at him. Her grey eyes bore such sadness, it halted him in his steps.

Why care? She is just a mortal woman. One who betrayed you, at that.

"Why? Why did you do it?" Immediately, he regretted asking the question. She, of everyone, did not need to see any more weakness in him.

Ailith threw up her arms. "It was a forced contract, never a voluntary choice. What did you honestly expect?"

He shook his head. *But you were mine!* he wanted to scream at her. He didn't.

"I'm a thief, remember?" She smiled sadly. "Scheming is part of the job."

"Did you ever even consider it?"

Why pursue this line of questioning? The answers will only be more disappointing, more hurtful.

Ailith hesitated. "I never wanted to. I may not hold much love for most people, but I do think our world is generally better off not being ruled by some devil." She winced at her own words.

He knew it would sting, but he had still been unprepared for how deeply those words cut. Staggering backwards, he sat back down, the water somehow not warm enough anymore.

"Some devil. Is that what I am?" *What else did you expect to be?*

"No. You are my captor."

"And before?"

He watched her struggle to formulate an answer, staring down at her fingers. When she finally spoke, her voice was even quieter.

"You were my first thought in the morning, the name on my lips when I closed my eyes. You plagued my thoughts and haunted my dreams. I did what I had to do, but I don't think I will ever recover, knowing that it gained me your hatred." Ailith looked back up again, and even though her cheeks were flushed slightly, he swore he could see tears in her eyes before she turned around to leave.

"If only I could hate you," Arkhael whispered after her.

CHAPTER 32

H e did not come to bed that night.

Ailith spent the night tossing and turning, and when a yellow light finally filtered through the windows, breakfast was set for only one. The chamberlain informed her that, "Master Arkhael will be gone for a few days."

Being in Arkhael's home without him was odd. She felt like an intruder, an interloper. Someone who didn't belong in the space she was in. Initially, she felt a small bit of excitement. Knowing he wouldn't return home, she could explore the place to her heart's content. But the excitement quickly faded. There was nothing in his home she hadn't seen already.

Sinking down on his sofa, her thoughts went back to the look on his face the previous night. For the first time, his composure had properly dropped, and she had seen behind the facade. He wasn't happy either.

The disappointment and pain had been palpable. And seeing it on his face stung her more than any wound ever had.

Enough.

She had had enough of this misery. If this was to be the remainder of her days, she might as well risk eternal damnation to try and improve it. What did she have to lose?

Your soul.

She bit the inside of her cheek. It was a risk she was willing to take. Stupid, of course. A lifetime of sadness would be shorter than an eternity of damnation.

Just make sure you play your cards right.

Ailith walked over to Arkhael's bookshelves, snorting slightly at the level of organisation. He would hate the chaos she was about to create. She pulled out multiple books on infernal contracts, as well as some on the more prominent figures in the Hells, and spread them out on the floor, dropping herself in the middle. If she was going to attempt this, she needed to be certain of every step of her plan.

After two days of note-taking and cross-referencing, Arkhael still hadn't returned. Strained as their interactions had been, Ailith had to admit she missed his presence. Without him, his home felt empty. And with no nature nearby, she thought the silence might drive her insane.

If anything, it made her more determined. As long as he stayed gone for another day, she would have her plan ready. She had barely slept the last few nights, reading well into the early hours to be as prepared as she possibly could be.

She also had another look at his vault.

Anyone with a vault door so big and ostentatious was just begging to be robbed. She had thought so the first time she saw it, and she still thought so now.

The lock had been replaced, but it was the same style of pickable lock. She made a mental note to talk to him about that. *If you're still alive then.* No additional security seemed to have been added, magical or otherwise.

The next day, she went to work. Packing quill and parchment, Ailith brought her tools over to the vault doors. Last time, it had been a fairly simple job. Would she risk raking the lock?

No, better to take longer and do this properly. *Just in case.*

Tongue between her teeth, she started gently applying pressure to the pins. *Click.* Tutting, she put her picks away. She had picked more complicated locks. *Because no one is foolish enough to attempt to rob a devil. Twice.*

Carefully, she opened the door. There was no resistance, nothing that indicated a trap bound or linked to the door. Creating a gap just big enough to fit through, she peered inside.

"Ah, that's new."

A small tripwire was suspended just behind the door. Bringing her tools over, Ailith gingerly stepped over it, examining it from the other side. An alarm spell, a fairly common magical trap. Disarming it would be more work than just leaving it.

She lit a lantern and moved deeper into the vault. Unable to resist her curiosity, she peeked into some of the chests in the room and couldn't help but be impressed. Arkhael had wasted no time refilling his coffers since she and her team had emptied them.

But it was not what she was here for.

That was at the very back of the room. The cabinet full of scrolls. Of contracts.

She had been worried about being able to find hers but quickly realised there was no need. It had its own shelf, next to a long piece of something gold. The necklace. *He kept it here?* Carefully, she picked it up. What had happened to it? The metal was slightly deformed in places, almost as if it had been exposed to high heat, but otherwise was still as beautiful as when she had first stolen it from his vault. She smiled sadly at the wave of longing it conjured. That had been just as foolish as what she was doing now. Putting the necklace back, she unrolled her contract, sat down on the floor, and started to read.

Ailith barely remembered most of it from when Arkhael had shown it to her. With the knowledge she had now, she could appreciate how well-written it was. The contract couldn't leave the vault without Arkhael's consent, and she couldn't destroy it. So she took out quill and parchment, and started writing. Right there. On the vault's floor. A new contract to present to him.

She tried her best to keep the wording similar, even if she didn't have Arkhael's gift for flowery language. If she changed too much, he would never be open to the changes she wanted him to accept. The repayment of debt, the fine print about not working against him, all of that she kept intact. But she removed any hold it gave him over her soul. Instead, she offered up her life. He could kill her if she actively worked against him, but not for any small disobedience or disagreements. And, nervously, she proposed that she should be more than just an obedient servant.

It was a daring plan. Ailith was well aware that she was taking a big gamble.

Half of it had been carefully written when she heard a noise. Marius. *Fuck.*

He stepped through the doorway. "Miss, you shouldn't be here."

Ailith didn't look up. "At your feet, there is a silver tripwire. Did you break it?"

From the corner of her eye, she saw him look down. The sudden panic on his face confirmed what she had feared.

"Then you have just set off the alarm. I imagine Arkhael will be home soon. Leave now and I won't tell him you were here."

With that, she went back to her writing, doubling her pace. She had expected to be caught eventually; no doubt Arkhael had left orders to keep an eye on her.

Still, she wanted to face his wrath with as finished a proposal as possible.

Her heart was racing as she heard footsteps approach, heard the distant, "I tried to tell her, master!" Her hand shook above the paper.

All or nothing. This was it.

CHAPTER 33

"Really . . . again?" His voice was quiet.

She was familiar with the tone by now, knew she would see anger on his face even before she looked up.

Arkhael still looked human, though no less imposing as he emerged from the shadow into the light of her lantern, eyes glowing yellow in the dim light. It almost felt like old times, only the stakes were so much higher now.

Ailith put down her quill, resealed the bottle of ink. "I —"

"Quiet!"

She shut her mouth. He looked at her little setup.

"I didn't think we would need to go back to the chains, but clearly you cannot be left alone."

She bit her tongue. Now was not the time to be defiant.

"Do you have any idea what you called me away from?"

"Marius set off the alarm, not—"

"QUIET!"

"I would have closed the door behind me and left everything as it was."

She couldn't stop herself. Ailith had gotten up, matching his angry gaze.

Arkhael raised an eyebrow. "That was an order, not a suggestion."

Ailith swallowed and clenched her fists. She should have kept her mouth shut; this was not a good start to a negotiation.

"You will gather whatever this is and then follow me."

She obeyed. There was no point in angering him further. Returning her contract, she carefully rolled up the new version she had written and put everything in her pack, following him out.

He walked her to his chambers, sat down, and rubbed his temples.

Ailith said nothing. He seemed to be teetering on the edge, and she didn't want to push him over it. So she stood in front of him, biting the inside of her cheek, waiting for him to speak.

Finally, he looked up. "I thought I had been more than generous with you," he sighed. "You have one chance to explain yourself, and only one."

Ailith chose her words carefully. She needed to pique his curiosity, lead him away from this anger. "You seemed unhappy."

"And, keeping up the pretence that you care for a moment, breaking into my vault again was your solution to this?"

Ailith dug her nails into her palms.

All or nothing.

"I do care." She sank down onto her knees in front of him, her voice trembling slightly. "I think you wanted me to be yours. And I don't think you realised that I already was. Only when you made me sign that contract did you lose me."

Her heart seemed to be beating out of her chest. She had to keep going. If she stopped now, she would never find the courage again. "I think you might still want me, but you cannot convince me that whatever we have going on currently makes you happy. I haven't changed anything about the debt I owe you. I tried to . . ."

Words failed her. She held up her proposal. Suddenly it felt silly. Stupid. Inadequate. She was a mortal trying to play chess with a god. Without a word, Arkhael took it, unrolling the parchment and reading her work as she knelt in front of him.

For a long time, he said nothing. Ailith was sure he had finished reading by now, but when she looked up at him, she couldn't read the expression on his face. So she remained where she was, waiting for his judgement.

Finally, he huffed. "It's a bit rough around the edges, and of course unfinished, but not a bad first attempt."

She looked up. Was he mocking her?

He met her eye, eyebrow raised. "Consort?"

"There have been several devils of note who had consorts throughout history." Ailith straightened herself. "I refuse to be a servant."

She had raked through the books he had available. Devils didn't share power. The only time the literature ever spoke of equals was when they took someone as their consort. And even then, the relationships were questionable. But it had been the only solution she could think of without outright asking for her freedom. And she knew he would never agree to that. Her nails dug deeper into her palms. She hoped she hadn't asked for too much.

Arkhael stood up, walking over to his writing desk, and gestured for her to follow. She did. Pins and needles shot through her legs as she got up from her kneeling position.

At the snap of his fingers, quill and parchment appeared before him. He rolled her contract out on the table, sat a paperweight on it to stop it from curling up again, and started copying it. Letters burned into the paper.

"You won't 'actively' work against me? That means you can still passively work against me?" His quill paused as he looked up at her.

"I meant that . . ." She tried to find the right words. "I guess removing 'actively' works?"

He nodded and resumed writing. "Add flare, maybe a little whimsy, not loopholes."

Ailith nodded awkwardly as he schooled her. As if she hadn't put herself in the most vulnerable position.

He finished the contract she had started, then read it over.

"You break into my vault, and I am supposed to reward you with more autonomy and lose the hostage of your soul." He chuckled mirthlessly. "Why, pray tell, would I let you sign this?"

Ailith's stomach dropped.

Of course he would let you think there's hope only to take it from you at the last moment . . .

No, she refused to give up now. She had seen the hurt in his eyes, the pain of betrayal. He *had* to care.

"Look me in the eye and tell me that this is truly what you wanted. That my presence here, like this, brings you whatever your equivalent of joy is. But if you need reasons, then because I can improve your vault security better than anyone else." She sat down on the armrest of his chair and brought her mouth to his ear. "And because this is the only way you'll have me."

She saw his hand tighten on the quill before he handed it to her, grabbing her wrist with his long fingers.

"If you make me regret this, you *will* know it."

Ailith nodded, pulse racing. For the third time, she watched her name get burned into paper. She inhaled deeply. *Freedom.* A long breath out.

Arkhael rose.

"As much as I would love to stay and learn exactly what you think *consort* means, I was meeting with King Aldwin about his daughter's future." He narrowed his eyes. There was still anger there. "I expect a proposal for my vault's improvement ready upon my return."

And with that, he was gone.

Ailith stared at the empty space.

Then she laughed out loud.

She was free. The terms she had agreed to were all hers.

Her joy didn't last long. He hadn't believed everything she had said; that trust had been damaged. He had allowed her this because, like her, he had had nothing to lose. She would show him, show him she was sincere and worthy of being his partner. And show him that she cared.

"How did you do it?"

She looked up at the sudden voice. The chamberlain stood in the doorway, his voice filled with venom. Jealousy?

Ailith shrugged, suddenly wary of the man. "I just made sure that what I had to offer was interesting enough."

The chamberlain shook his head. "I offered him everything he could ever need. Forever. And it wasn't interesting enough."

Ailith winced. So many ways to exploit that offer. No wonder the man was such a good servant. There was no way he couldn't be tending to Arkhael's every whim.

She shrugged again. "Just play the game better."

She couldn't bring herself to feel pity for the man, the rush of adrenaline and relief still too fresh.

He narrowed his eyes. "You're not worthy of him."

And with that, he left her.

It couldn't spoil her mood. Sitting down in Arkhael's chair, she pulled some parchment over and started the work on the improvements to his vault security.

A false lock would be a good start. *Less ostentatious doors?* That would never happen. She wrote it down anyway. It was well after dinnertime before she had finished her proposal.

A better lock, a decoy one, more traps, and a better alarm system.

Satisfied, she left the papers on Arkhael's desk for him to find upon his return.

When would he come home? Then what?

She was well aware that she had taken a leap by suggesting she be his consort. Her stomach had been aflutter with nerves of a different kind ever since he had left, and even though the sky outside had darkened, she was still wide awake. She picked up one of the books.

What *did* it mean to be his consort? Other than as close to his equal as she could get, the books had been annoyingly vague. Did it matter? Any position was better than the one she had been in.

After rereading the same page three times, she decided to give up on the book and retire to bed.

Sleep must have taken Ailith at some point, for she woke up to the bed dipping next to her. Immediately, she was wide awake, heart beating so loud, surely Arkhael had to hear it. She wanted to speak to him, finally talk to him without having to hold back. To reach out for him in the dark. But where to start? She felt uncertain in this new dynamic she had created for them.

"Your thoughts are loud."

She froze at the sound of his voice. "Sorry, I didn't mean to keep you awake." Suddenly, she felt shy. "Were you successful? With the king?"

He sighed. "Yes. We will be attending a midwinter ball, which he'll use to introduce potential suitors for the princess. The man is becoming stubborn in his old age."

"We?"

"Unless you're already regretting your decision?" Ailith didn't need to see his face to recognise the challenge. Familiar territory. *At last.*

She rolled over, smiling slyly at Arkhael's dark silhouette next to her. "Depends. I went to a court ball once. It was incredibly boring."

"You? At a court ball? I find that hard to believe."

"I'll have you know, I was an excellent guest," she retorted with mock offence in her voice. "And my dancing was—"

"What did you make off with?" he interrupted.

Ailith laughed. "The king's sceptre and a kiss from the queen."

She heard Arkhael turn in the dark.

"That was you?" He chuckled. "With hindsight, that makes sense."

They fell quiet. She wondered if he was watching her, tried to discern where his face was.

All or nothing. Just jump.

She reached out a hand, found his arm. In the dark, she followed it up to his shoulder, finding the places where the skin was thick and leathery, tracing it to his collarbone. He took her hand, opened it, and kissed the palm, then pulled her closer.

With that, the dam broke.

He kissed her. Hungrily. Greedily. And *fuck* had she missed the taste of him. The way his tongue felt against hers, against her lips, the sharpness of his teeth. She moaned into his mouth, pulling him on top of her, parting her legs for him.

All the frustration, the waiting, the wanting. In that moment, all she needed was to feel him inside her again. She hooked a leg around his waist, urging him forwards.

He didn't need encouraging. Slowly he entered her, one hand under her back, pulling her against him.

Ailith brought her hands around him, holding him tighter. Feeling like it was still not close enough, even as he pushed all the way inside her.

Almost as if scared that this would turn out to be a dream they could never return to, they took their time. Mouths roamed, their bodies never far apart as Arkhael held her close in an iron grip. His thrusts were short, barely withdrawing before entering her again. She felt his teeth sink into her collarbone while she dug her nails into his back and raked them down. He groaned in response, grazing his teeth over her shoulder, her neck, her jaw. Her skin burned wherever his mouth touched it.

There was so much that they needed to talk about, so much between them that was unspoken. But in that moment, neither of them wanted to face the last few weeks. Instead, Ailith allowed herself to finally lose herself in his embrace. She wanted it to last forever. Just that moment of passion. The way he made her feel so full, the way their bodies seemed to perfectly fit into each other. His mouth on the most sensitive areas of her neck, his breath hot against her skin. But her body betrayed her, letting her know exactly how much she had missed him as her hips began to tremble.

He noticed. And sped up until her body was shuddering against his, muscles contracting around him, his name on her lips.

She felt his claws dig into her back as it brought him over the edge. His hips thrust once, twice, thrice more before he buried himself inside her and held her close.

She was his.

Exhaustion hit Ailith. Everything seemed to suddenly fall into place. She felt as if she had been swimming against a current that had finally dissipated, and only now was her body allowed to feel the fatigue.

She gasped as Arkhael slowly pulled out of her, the inside of her thighs wet with both of their pleasure.

He still held her tightly to his chest as he rolled over. Neither of them spoke. It could all wait. For the first time in ages, she felt content. Happy to just be held. Eyes closed, she allowed herself to doze off.

She woke with Arkhael. But this time, it was not to him leaving the bed.

She woke to his roaming hands, a quiet moan leaving her mouth before she was even properly awake.

He was exploring her body. His hands wandered over her shoulders, her arms, claws raking through her hair, pulling it slightly, causing her to arch her back. Down again. Down her side, her hips, to her thighs. Ailith's breath quickened, sleep rapidly leaving her.

His hands seemed to be everywhere. Everywhere but where she needed them to be.

Finally opening her eyes, she scowled at him, even if she couldn't stop the faint smile on her lips. His fiery eyes caught hers, glittering as he challenged her to maintain eye contact when he stroked the inside of her thigh.

Ailith bit her lip, holding back her frustration and meeting the challenge, then gasped in surprise when one of his fingers slipped between her legs.

He smiled, sharp teeth just visible, eyes wicked as he slowly applied pressure, her hips moving into his hand despite herself.

The tension inside her built up quickly as he continued his ministrations. Ailith wasn't surprised he was good with his hands, but *fuck* was he good with his hands. She could have melted into that touch, the way he looked at her, that smile.

That smile.

She wouldn't give in *that* easily. With her left hand, she reached between them, found his hard lid. The smile on his face faltered slightly as she started slowly moving her hand around him. Her turn to be smug.

Eyes still locked with his, motions faltering every time he moved his fingers, she sped up slightly, tightening her grip on him as she did so, rubbing her thumb over the sensitive tip. His smile was lost to a moan, his eyes no less wicked as he slipped one of his long fingers inside her. Nearly she let her eyes close as she arched into his touch.

But she wasn't done yet.

In response, she let go of him and moved her fingers to her mouth, never breaking eye contact. Slowly, she closed her lips around them, moving them in time with his hand. His eyes narrowed at her.

She had him.

Withdrawing her hand, she brought it back down between them, trailing it down her own body, her breasts, the scars he had left there.

Arkhael seemed entranced, eyes on her fingers until she gripped him with them.

Imagine my mouth on you.

She knew he was. He groaned and closed his eyes. A surge of victory coursed through Ailith. She might be his, in that moment, he was hers.

As if hearing her thoughts, Arkhael's eyes shot back open. She had won the round, but she knew well that victory would be short-lived. His pride wouldn't have it otherwise.

His gaze darkened as he grabbed her wrist. Forced it above her head while rolling them over.

Ailith couldn't resist smiling, even as he reached for her other hand and restrained it too.

"Now what?" she challenged him, knowing full well how much stronger he was. He brought her hands together in one of his, pinning them down, tracing her lips with his free one.

"Now, I will use your mouth until you realise that every part of you belongs to me."

Well fuck.

She shivered at the intensity in his voice, not even pretending to struggle against him as he moved up, holding her shoulders down with his knees. Then he let go of her wrists to grab her by the back of the head instead.

He pressed against her mouth, hot and hard against her lips, before he pushed forwards.

"Mine," he grunted as she parted her lips for him, felt him fill her. He tasted of salt and of fire, and she moaned around him as he took her mouth. She dug her nails into his thighs, needing something to hold onto as he moved back, then filled her mouth again, down into her throat.

She barely had time to adjust as he found a rhythm, moving her head to meet his hips. Through half-lidded eyes, she watched him above her. His usually perfect hair was plastered to the sides of his face, horns curling up behind him, wings spread slightly, a feral look in his eyes. That perfect composure entirely shattered.

He was the perfect image of hellish temptation, *and she was his.*

The thought took over everything else. In that moment, time meant nothing, pride meant nothing. All she knew was that she wanted to be his. In all ways, any way he wanted to have her. She felt almost drunk with the feel and the taste of him. How heavy he was in her mouth, how hot he was in her throat. His rhythm was starting to falter, his breathing getting more erratic, clearly entranced by the sight of himself in her mouth. Finally, his hand in her hair tightened, holding her as he released down her throat, head thrown back, wings spreading fully behind him.

His eyes sought hers.

"Mine," he said hoarsely before slowly withdrawing himself. Ailith gasped for air as he released her. Her mouth was on fire, her throat burning, the taste of him strong on her tongue. Something had been different, and not just because he had never let their mouths go anywhere below the waist. Something in his face. In his voice. It set her heart racing.

She watched Arkhael compose himself. Watched how he barely noticeably shook his head before swinging his legs over the side of the bed. Realised from the sly smile he had regained that he was planning to leave her with that.

Still catching her breath, Ailith rolled over. She still needed him; he wasn't leaving yet.

With a deep breath, she reached out a hand and changed the ground at his feet. Stones became small, jagged spikes, the tips covered in a paralytic poison. His body froze in place. She doubted it would hold him for long with how quickly he healed. It didn't need to; just long enough. Moving over to him, she swung a leg over his hips, straddling him.

Already she could see his fingers start to twitch, muscles straining against the magic, eyes full of fury.

"You don't get to leave me here, wanting you." She moved herself so he could feel exactly how much she wanted him. How much she had enjoyed what just happened.

"If all of me belongs to you, then you'd better use all of me," she whispered in his ear, releasing the magic, the floor turning back to stone. Leaning back, she cocked an eyebrow, waiting, watching the poison wear off now that the magic was gone. The moment control came back to him, he grabbed her by the throat. Ailith had expected no less.

"I should punish you for that." His voice was quiet, dangerous. Full of indignant anger. But his eyes were dark with desire, and she could feel him stir under her.

"You could. But I don't think you want to." She leaned into his hand, kissed him ever so lightly, flicking her tongue across his lips, giving him plenty of opportunity to move away. He didn't.

The hand on her throat went to the back of her neck as he pulled her closer, forcing her mouth open with his. When they parted, he was hard again, pressing against her.

"You've barely swallowed the taste of me, and it's still not enough for you?"

Ailith moved her hips, just enough to take the tip of him inside her, body trembling with need.

"If it's just me who hasn't had enough, then feel free to leave."

He narrowed his eyes at her, seeing the challenge for what it was. But then he took her hips in his hands and brought her down, slowly sheathing himself in her. Ailith gasped, shaking with the effort to hold herself still when all she wanted was to move.

"Tell me what you want," Arkhael whispered against her neck.

Trying to keep her voice steady Ailith responded, "I want you to take me again, to fill me again. Make me yours."

She felt his hands tighten on her as he bit down on her neck.

"You *are* mine."

With that, their game was over. She set the pace this time. It was fast, all earlier pent-up need finally finding a release.

His mouth was on her shoulders, her collarbone, her breasts. Ailith arched into his touch as he bit down on a nipple, flicked it with his tongue, while she moved atop him. Taking him entirely every time she sank down. One of his hands moved from her hips to her mouth, opening her lips with his thumb. She felt his fingers slide in and out in time with her hips, a reminder that all of her belonged to him.

It was too much. She rode the waves of euphoria, moaning around his fingers.

She felt him release inside of her, withdrawing his fingers so he could hold her hips down on him. As he relaxed his grip, she let herself fall forwards, leaning her forehead against his. Only when her breathing started to even out, did reality return to Ailith.

She could feel her cheeks redden, and bit her lip.

Did you actually just say all that?

Worst of all, she immediately knew it to be true. She had enjoyed being his, challenging him until he lost control of that perfect facade. The way his arms tightened around her afterwards, almost as if he was worried she might disappear.

Arkhael leaned back, stretching his wings, and narrowed his eyes at her. "I believe I just made the mistake of rewarding bad behaviour rather than punishing it."

Ailith smiled at him, face full of mischief and victory.

"And you loved every second of it." Her expression changed to one of shock as she realised her voice was entirely gone.

Arkhael laughed, lifting a hand to stroke her lips, and the sound of it set her stomach aflutter. *Oh fuck.*

CHAPTER 34

There was no sunset in the Hells. Yet the sky still darkened during the nighttime. Ailith didn't think she would ever get used to that. It felt oddly unnatural.

She had sat herself down in one of the chairs on Arkhael's balcony, a book on infernal history forgotten in her lap. The more she read, the less she realised she knew about the Hells and what she had gotten herself into. There were nine layers, nine circles to the Hells, that much she had been aware of. And each circle had its own ruler, its own prince. What she hadn't known, however, was that there was one devil who ruled all of the nine circles: Moloch. In addition to him, several other names kept repeating throughout history, the princes who ruled the individual circles, important lieutenants who had changed the tide of battles, influential figures who seemed to be involved in every major event. Never had she known that the Hells were so full of politics, that it was so rife with culture, even if it was so completely different from her own.

She had been surprised at the lack of Arkhael's name. He was never mentioned despite how powerful he seemed, and at first, she thought she had made a major lapse in judgement, thought of him as more powerful than he actually was. But the more she read, the more she saw his hand in the events described on the pages. Armies being delayed or arriving slightly faster than they should have; items appearing or disappearing at crucial moments. It fit the image of the devil she had come to know, one who preferred to pull the strings from the shadows until he knew victory could be assured. One who kept up a tightly controlled image of perfection, who disliked anything that would disturb the order he so carefully maintained.

Except for her. And the fact that she did not understand the *why* frustrated her to no end.

What made her so special?

She understood his initial interest in her. Her group had been perfectly suited for the job. She also understood why he had brought her back after she cost him the reliquary, although she still couldn't fathom how he had ever thought she wouldn't try to thwart him. She understood keeping her around for the sex, even if she was certain he could get whomever he wanted. But the sudden possessiveness he showed towards her she did not understand. *Is it something to do with my soul?* It was the only thing she could imagine him being possessive of, and the one thing she knew she had no knowledge of.

The last traces of yellow disappeared from the sky before it went black entirely, but no chill set in. Finally, she got to enjoy sitting outside at night. If only she could combine this with the sound of trees and crickets around her, the comfort of nature at her fingertips, she would get the best of both Realms.

Her gaze went from the sky back to the balcony. Only then did she notice the crack and long grooves in the otherwise perfect balustrade. That hadn't been there before.

Yet another mystery.

Her thoughts circled back to Arkhael. He had been possessive from the beginning, but she had blamed that on the odd situation they had found themselves in when she signed the first contract.

This felt . . . different somehow. The way he had explored her body that morning had been new, and not only because he always seemed so very strict about where he kept his hands. Again, she wondered why. For a moment, he had done away with the facade without her even trying to break it. What had caused it?

And why did it leave you so . . . Even in the privacy of her own mind, Ailith struggled to come up with the right word for the feeling.

She could feel her cheeks flush in the darkness.

The first time he made her beg, it had been in the throes of passion. He had demanded it of her, and his argument had been . . . very convincing. Just the memory of it made her blood run hot. The rest of that night, they had simply continued on the path that they were already on.

Had that truly been all?

Ailith shook her head at herself. It didn't matter. It still didn't explain what had come over her this morning. She closed her eyes. His hair undone, wings spread, the way he had looked at her . . . Immediately, she opened her eyes again. The image was branded in her mind.

But one pretty man, devil or otherwise, should not be able to have so much control over her. She had wanted to be his. Truly wanted to be his. And not just in body. She wanted him to care.

With a groan, she pinched the bridge of her nose. It was not that long ago that he had threatened to repeat one of the worst acts of torture she had ever endured. How could she be so quick to forgive that?

In her head, she knew she shouldn't be, yet in her heart, she found it hard to hold onto the anger. Especially as she knew how real the pain was that he had felt at her betrayal.

"No historical book justifies the angry glare that you are aiming at the horizon."

Ailith jolted upright, hoping he hadn't noticed the colour in her cheeks. She had been so lost in thought, she hadn't heard him walk over.

Unfolding her legs, she rose from the chair, choosing to ignore what he had just said. She watched his eyes sweep over her body, knowing full well how much he enjoyed seeing her in just his shirt.

"You're home late today."

"I left home late today."

He walked over to the balustrade, watching the darkened sky with her.

The peace was broken as her stomach growled quietly.

"You haven't eaten yet." It wasn't a question.

Ailith shrugged. "I got distracted."

"You know you can order Marius to bring you food. And as my consort, he will have to obey you."

She grimaced. "I'm not used to having servants. And he loathes me."

Arkhael quirked an eyebrow at her. "I didn't think that would stop you."

"Blame it on years of looking over my shoulder, but I don't usually let people who dislike me prepare my food." *Fuck*, but it was nice to talk to him again without holding back.

"He can't harm you. And I thought you druids couldn't be poisoned."

"I know. Force of habit." She turned and smiled at him. "And it's not that we cannot be poisoned. We are trained to be aware of how our bodies should function, so anything that interferes with this we learn to pick up on immediately and eradicate from our system. Poison shouldn't kill a trained druid, but getting rid of it can still be . . . a nuisance."

"Interesting. Is it a magical ability?"

Ailith's smile turned wry, and she averted her gaze. "I don't think I should tell you that."

Arkhael laughed. "A fair response."

She shouldn't have told him any of what she had just said. It was easy to forget that his intentions for most people were less than honourable. That any information she gave him, he could, and would, use if he thought it would benefit him. That he took pleasure in the suffering and pain of others.

And you share a bed with him.

What did that say about her?

His hand on her arm interrupted her thoughts. *How much blood is on his hands?* But when she looked up, his eyes seemed full of concern.

"Did something happen while I was gone? You seem pensive."

She shook her head at him. For someone so objectively evil, he seemed oddly caring. *For you as a person? Or for his property?*

"I . . ." She hesitated, then opted for at least partial honesty. "The line between telling you about myself and giving you information you can use against others is very thin."

He withdrew his hand as if she had burned it. "Because you would never take an advantage like that?" The concern in his eyes had been replaced by anger, and guilt hit her in the stomach.

She had, but she knew he was referring specifically to when he had told her about the holy weapons.

"We spoke about this. I thought I was doing the world a favour." She averted her eyes, unable to meet his gaze.

"So the end justified the means?"

"I never meant to use that knowledge against you."

"But you did." His voice was quiet. "Look me in the eye and tell me honestly you wouldn't repeat your actions."

Ailith looked away. He was right; she couldn't.

"Mortals and their double standards." The contempt in his voice chilled her to the bone as he turned away.

"I'm sorry."

He paused, looking back at her. This time, she met his gaze. No matter how it tightened the wrench around her heart.

"Genuinely. You're right. I thought I was doing the right thing. And I would do it again if we turned back time, even knowing how much it would hurt you. But I took no joy in it, no satisfaction. If there had been a different way, I would have taken it. I didn't see one. So I am sorry. Truly."

She realised she was rambling and shut her mouth.

Arkhael sighed. "I am not asking you to trust me. But do not disrespect me. When you handed me that contract, you knew who you were giving it to. I haven't asked you to change your nature. Do not ask me to change mine."

He held out his clawed hand. A peace offering.

Ailith laid her hand in his. "I do trust you," she said quietly. "Maybe not with the lives of others, but unconditionally with mine. Is that stupid of me, after everything?"

His fingers closed over hers as he pulled her in, kissing the top of her head.

"I have no desire to hurt you. And I will kill anyone who does." There was a tone to his voice she couldn't quite place. She didn't question it. Instead, she closed her eyes and listened to his heartbeat as he wrapped his arms around her. In that moment, she didn't care how much blood was on his hands. Out of everyone, it was a devil that made her feel more cared for than she had ever felt before.

"It's not magic." She looked up at him. "The control over our bodies, the way we feel how it is connected to the world around us, how we can connect ourselves to that world — that is what makes us druids. The magic stems from that. It's . . . hard to explain."

He stroked her hair. "You didn't have to share that. I don't begrudge you your secrets if you wish to protect your people."

"I know." But if he had shown her more care than most people had, were they really "her people"?

She reached up to his shoulder, where she knew she had scarred it. Even through the fabric of his clothing, she could feel the difference in the texture of his skin. "Does it still hurt?"

He took her hand and smiled lightly. "Mostly in my pride."

Ailith looked at their entwined fingers, at the stark contrast between their skin tones. She ran her magic into her fingers, watched them glow a faint green in his hand, and briefly allowed herself to draw strength from how alive and near he was to her.

The unspoken question finally tumbled off her lips.

"Why did you leave me in your prison? Why did you never come for me? Or even torture me?" Her words were barely audible as she spoke.

Arkhael's voice was equally quiet when he answered.

"I didn't know how to enjoy your suffering." He closed his hand around hers. "No matter the punishment I devised, the thought of enacting it on you never brought me the satisfaction I craved."

Ailith swallowed past the sudden lump in her throat.

"Why not?" she asked, her eyes still carefully averted.

The grip he had on her hand tightened. Lifting her gaze slightly, she gently laid the other on his chest. The heartbeat under her palm was rapid. Finally, she hesitantly looked up. His fiery eyes met hers with such a forlorn look, she knew the answer before he spoke it.

"I don't know," he whispered.

Ailith moved her hand from his chest to his cheek. As she was about to speak, her stomach rumbled again. Embarrassed, she looked away, and he chuckled, the moment broken.

"Come, let's get some food in you." He pulled her back inside.

"Can I ask you something else?" Ailith hesitantly asked.

Arkhael rang the small servant's bell. "If I said no, would you let it rest?"

She smiled. "Not likely." As he ordered Marius to bring them some food, she sat down in the chair opposite his. "I thought all devils were hedonists, but you seem to be constantly at work. Do you ever sit back to enjoy the fruits of your labour?"

He hesitated. She didn't think her question had been a difficult one. The silence lingered as Marius walked back in with a platter of flatbread and small dips. Only when the chamberlain had left the room again did Arkhael speak.

"Nothing I have ever set my sights on has been achievable in a day's work. It took me centuries to locate the reliquary, decipher how to use it, and then nudge all the pieces into place so that I could hire a thief to steal it for me." He narrowed his eyes at her, but there was no malice in his tone.

Ailith's heart skipped a beat. Maybe, just maybe, there was a chance for forgiveness. "Is there anything I can help with that doesn't end in the subjugation of the mortal Realm?"

Arkhael's hand halted as he brought a piece of flatbread to his mouth, a flash of surprise washing over his face before he composed it again. "That's exactly what you are being employed to do."

She rolled her eyes at him, catching a crumb before it could fall to the ground. "I'm serious, Arkhael. Share some of the burden and give yourself a break. I might not have your flair or way with words, but surely there is something I can take off your hands?"

He gave her a long look and, to her surprise, smiled. "Let's see how you fare at King Aldwin's ball, and maybe I will bring you along to more meetings."

"Meredith is his daughter, isn't she?" It was a hunch, nothing more, and with how wide his reach was, she might well be looking for a connection where there was none. But the thought had come to her earlier that morning, and she hadn't been able to shake the suspicion.

Arkhael's smile grew sly at her words. "You'll find out come winter. Until then, study. I'm not making you read for nothing. If you wish to be useful, you need to know exactly how the game is played."

Only mildly annoyed, she nodded, chewing her food. Would she dare ask him?

"I know the contract states 'until my debt is paid off,' but what of your forgiveness?" Carefully, she inspected another piece of flatbread. "Do you think that could ever be gained?"

With his long fingers Arkhael took the piece of food from her hand and pulled her off her chair to stand in front of him. Only when he took her chin in his hand did she meet his eye.

"After what you did, I should make you beg for it." Ailith almost looked away at the intensity of his gaze and the strained note in his voice, but he tightened the grip on her chin. "There are very few who dared betray me, and none who did survived to tell the tale." He stroked her cheek with his thumb. "You are the first who I let live, and the first who ever offered a genuine apology. I would be lying if I didn't say you were mostly there already."

Ailith let out a long breath. It was easy to get used to his presence and forget how intimidating he could be. He pulled her closer until she had no choice but to straddle him on his chair. Immediately, she was aware of the heat of his body, his breath, the steady drum of his heartbeat. And all the while, he held her captive with his eyes. She thrilled at the intensity of him, her body responding immediately.

Arkhael chuckled quietly. "I think I will make you beg for other things tonight."

CHAPTER 35

I t was unorthodox, to say the least. Arkhael didn't think she realised quite how unorthodox, didn't believe she truly understood what it meant to be a devil's consort. He shook his head as he watched her dress. It was a position of power, true enough, but consorts were never truly a devil's equal. They were always kept for a very specific reason, and once they had fulfilled that purpose, they joined the other souls that were trapped in the Hells. Arkhael knew that wasn't what she had in mind, but he didn't feel the need to correct her either.

To the Hells with tradition. She was finally his. Truly, this time. He could hear her conviction every time she moaned his name. And he ensured she did so often.

After that first day, he had taken her to the tailor he had in his employ, Laudus. The man had sold his services to him long ago, and his work was nothing short of excellent. Despite the man's aversion to Arkhael, Ailith seemed to get along with him wonderfully. The moment he had introduced her and told her she was to design better clothes for herself with the tailor, she had lit up with an almost childish delight.

Even though he could acknowledge the practicality, Arkhael had never liked her garb. It was plain. Too unassuming. If she was to be his consort, she would have to look the part. He had left her and it in Laudus's capable hands. There was much he needed to do, and she had already made him late.

Just as she is doing now.

He watched her hurry over, face still slightly flushed, pear in one hand. She preferred fruit for breakfast, he had discovered, and he made sure there always was some. The juice was dripping onto the ground as she walked through the room. Arkhael shook his head. He despised mess, hated how careless she could be. And yet, it was not anger that stirred in him as he watched her bring her hand to her mouth to lick the drop that was about to fall off her fingers. With an outstretched hand, he beckoned her over.

She took it without question as he pulled her close, onto his lap, taking the pear from her hand.

"I thought you said we were already late?" she said with a cocked brow. He was known for his punctuality, for his decorum. Still, he pulled her in to kiss her. She tasted of pear, of earth. And of him.

How she was so intoxicating he did not understand. She was only mortal. She should have been a carnal indulgence once. Twice at the most. Instead, she had become an addiction.

We really don't have time. Hurried fingers moved trousers just enough. She sank down on him. No matter how often she did so, she was bliss. Tight enough around him to make him lightheaded.

He watched her face as she threw her head back and closed her eyes. Small beads of sweat glistened on the odd colour of her skin, her lips parting as he moved inside her. She was beautiful. He tightened his grip on her hips, felt her muscles tighten around him.

"Arkhael." There was something about the way she said his name. As if she touched the very core of his being. But hearing her moan it made everything disappear. It was just her, taking his very essence on her lips. He shivered.

"Again," he demanded hoarsely.

She opened her eyes, and he could tell she *knew* from the look she gave him, how she caught him in her gaze.

"Arkhael."

He lost himself in her, his world reduced to their unity. She was his. He filled her. Held her tight. His alone. His druid. He slammed into her again. His thief. Again. Until he knew she couldn't be more his. Ailith shuddered in his arms.

We should really be leaving. And yet he couldn't resist holding her against him for just a little longer. Relishing in the way she calmed her breathing, rested her forehead against him. Reluctantly, he pulled back, only to have her pull him in for another kiss. Aggressively. He didn't resist. Her slender fingers crept under his shirt, her touch slightly cool on his skin until she dug her nails into his chest, the sting of it an immediate threat to the little bit of control he had just regained.

When she finally let go of him, he could feel her quickened heartbeat against him, her breasts pressing into his chest. His fingers clenched as she got off of him, pulling up her trousers and combing her hair back with her fingertips as she put it back up.

Before she had the chance to distract him further, he took her by the hand and teleported them to Laudus's shop so she could pick up her order, handing her a ruby and enough gold to pay for a lifetime of clothing.

With that, he left her to go on his own errands. His client was late. It left him as irked as he was relieved. At least he himself wasn't seen to be late. Their meeting location of choice was a rather upscale tavern. Much more upscale than the man he was meeting could afford. He had ordered himself an expensive mead, swirling the drink in the glass as he let his gaze wander through the room. It was busy. Despite the hour, the tavern's reputation meant it was well filled with people. Judging by their clothing alone, most people here had excess money to spend. Yet listening to their desires, he mostly found petty greed. Some things never changed.

He sipped the sweet liquid. There wasn't truly a need for him to partake in the food or drink of mortals, but they had quite refined the craft over the centuries.

Ailith liked mead. She wasn't much of a drinker, unless he offered her the honeyed wine. She generally had something of a sweet tooth, he had noted with amusement. Watching the alcohol cling to the glass, his thoughts went to her unexpected offer to help him and her apology. It had been genuine, which had made it all the more surprising. He had detected no lie in her words.

Anger still simmered in him at her betrayal, and the memory of her knowing look as the reliquary was taken away from him still boiled his blood. It was hard to accept that that had been the same woman as the one he had desired so. His own refusal to torture her still rattled him to the core. It was so unlike him. He *always* had his revenge. Always.

And yet he could not deny that their current arrangement, odd as it was, brought him infinitely more pleasure than the thought of seeing her in pain ever had. He would never admit it, but he had been glad for her disobedience. Grateful that she had gone against his orders, even with him holding her soul hostage. *And she apologised.*

With such earnestness. If anything, she had almost seemed ashamed of her own betrayal. And never had anyone offered their services to him so willingly. At least, not without ulterior motive or mindless infatuation.

Arkhael sighed. So many complications, all because of one woman. He wondered how she was getting on. Part of him had wanted to stay with her, watch Laudus do his job. There was no need, of course. The man was perfectly capable, and she was perfectly able to protect herself. And yet.

She conjured up a protectiveness, a greed in him that was almost frightening. He had thought such intense desires were something he had long since left behind him. But every night, he woke her when he joined her in his bed, and found that she responded with the same fire that rushed through his veins. And every night, he held her in his arms as she fell asleep, holding her close, as if she might be stolen away from him at any moment. It stirred something in him, something unfamiliar. Something too immense to fathom.

He pushed the feeling away as he watched his client finally walk through the door.

Getting the man to sign had been almost too easy. An aspiring artist who wanted fame—tale as old as time. It would take little effort to find him a patron. His art was genuinely good, and Arkhael was convinced that if the man had been willing to put in more work himself, he could have found his own. As it was, it had been an easy soul to collect. Too easy, almost. He usually didn't bother with those, but the man had a way with words that impressed him. Either he could be of use in the future, or it would indeed just be an easy soul. Regardless, he came out on top.

He finished his mead. They truly did make a good vintage here. Perhaps he should take a bottle home, he mused. He could share it with Ailith, watch her cheeks flush the more she drank. With a sigh, he got up and walked over to the bar, trying to focus his thoughts. It was ridiculous how obsessed he was with her.

When he finally arrived home, he found her curled up and asleep on his sofa, a book under her cheek, a new cloak pulled tightly around her. Her hair had come loose from whatever messy do it had been in and fallen over her face, now softly moving with every breath she took. He resisted the urge to tuck the strands behind her ear or take the cloak off of her. Less than a day with her new clothing, and already she had found a way to wrinkle it.

The mead could wait for another day. Quietly, he walked through the room, letting her rest as he unfolded his writing desk and sorted his day's work. Maybe he shouldn't be waking her every night. She was only mortal, after all, and her body needed more rest than his. With practised motion, he conjured everything he had accumulated throughout the day—proposals, contracts, information gathered—and went through the process of sorting and filing it.

Behind him, he heard Ailith move, his stomach clenching as he heard the unmistakable sound of tearing paper.

She was a menace to his home.

He didn't look up from his work, although he had to read the same contract twice before he managed to focus again.

Ailith's quiet footfall was barely audible as she walked over to him.

"What do you think?"

There was an unusual lilt to her voice. *Is she nervous?*

He looked up and nearly dropped the quill he was holding. Laudus had outdone himself. Gone were the thief's scrubs. Instead, she wore well-fitting black trousers with a high waistline into which she had tucked a dark green blouse. The fabric was patterned, the brocade matching the gold embroidery on his vests. The sleeves she had already rolled up, he noted with amusement. But mostly, his eyes lingered on the neckline. It plunged deeply, clearly showing where he loved to rake his claws down from her throat. The entire outfit radiated quality, and he had to commend Laudus for making something so simple look so good, and for the way her clothes so subtly mirrored his in style. A perfect harmony between her preference for subtlety, and his requirement for quality. *And a little bit of her audacity.* He swallowed hard and got up from his chair.

"Laudus has truly outdone himself," he repeated out loud.

Ailith scoffed. "I think you will find that the blouse you are so shamelessly staring at was a collaborative effort." But despite her tone, he noticed some of the tension leave her shoulders. She *had* been nervous.

With a single claw, he followed the lines he had made that morning, watching a thin line of blood well up in its wake. He bent forwards, following the same trail with his mouth. Ailith shivered under him, her hands gripping his arms.

With a smile, he brought his mouth up to her ear. "Only you would design a piece of clothing to constantly tempt me."

Even though she kept her face schooled, he saw the glint of mischief in her grey eyes.

"How else will the world know who I belong to?"

He froze. The words cut right through him. Something in him responded almost instinctively. He pushed it away, even if he could not contain the possessiveness that followed those words. Instead, he focused on the way his body responded, a much safer and more familiar feeling. With a barely contained growl, he lifted her by the hips, pinning her against the wall.

"There should never be a doubt in anyone's mind that you are mine," he all but hissed.

That glint was still in her eyes, and from the smile she gave him, he knew she was about to challenge him. And he knew he would rise to it, regardless of what it was.

CHAPTER 36

L ife was good in the Hells. Ailith had never imagined something so absurd, and she was well aware of how unique her situation was. But she couldn't deny that she was living more luxuriously than she ever had. Most of her time was spent reading, trying her best to remember the convoluted rules and politics of her new home, although she had made her morning exercises part of her routine as well. Living lavishly was one thing, but she didn't want to become stagnant and lose the fitness she had.

Even so, she didn't have to worry about food, accommodation, or even the law trying to catch up with her. She couldn't remember the last time she had been able to entirely take her mind off survival. It was all too easy to forget that she was contractually obligated to stay with Arkhael when life with him was so deceptively easy. And with her basic needs taken care of, it was something she now had the time to worry about.

Life with him was almost *too* easy. She had to constantly remind herself that, despite the sudden change in their relationship, he still had a hold on her, even if her soul was safe. Every word she uttered was one he could use against her; every moment she let her guard down was one in which he could end her life. By proposing to be his consort, she had evened the power balance a little, but she was well aware that he could tip those scales with one of those annoying flicks of his fingers. She had safeguarded her soul—or at least she hoped she had—but she had no illusions that much else had changed. Every difference since was because Arkhael had wanted it to be so and not because she had written it down on paper.

And yet . . .

Ailith groaned. And yet she let her guard down constantly, unable to resist the thrill of challenging him, unable to resist his allure. She had thought that the initial excitement would have been tempered by now. It hadn't been. The mere thought of him alone woke the slumbering fire that he had lit within her.

It shouldn't.

She still couldn't entirely reconcile the memory of what he had done to her with the desire she felt for him, no matter how often she went over it in her head. She should be disgusted with him, or at the very least, she should be angry. Instead, she found herself annoyingly understanding. She had hurt him. Deeply. And he had responded to that pain the only way he knew how. She vaguely remembered the distress on his face as he threatened to torture her. He hadn't gone through with it. That had to mean something. It was the only way she could justify her quick forgiveness of him.

Ailith turned the page of the book she was reading. It was old and the writing was archaic, even for Arkhael's collection. The book was so worn, parts of it were entirely missing or unreadable. Yet the topic was intriguing. Moloch, the King of the Hells, and the exact grip he had on the Realm. If she understood the old writing correctly, his reign of the Hells was not just symbolic. Something prevented the other fiendish denizens from so much as hurting him. How exactly it worked, she didn't quite grasp, and she made a mental note to ask Arkhael about it. No wonder Moloch had held the throne for so long, despite how power-hungry every devil seemed to be.

Her thoughts wandered. Arkhael hadn't sent her back out again after her two trips to the convent. The new contract had changed nothing about her debt to him, and she doubted that he lacked work. Again, she pondered how possessive he seemed and wondered if it was the value of her soul that made him seem to care so much for her. It was something she had turned over a million times in her head, but the answer was no clearer.

She flipped over onto her stomach with a sigh as she stretched out on the sofa, tucking her cloak in around her and leaning on her elbows, trying to focus on her reading again. Behind her, the door opened, and she smiled at the familiar footsteps. He was home early.

Before she had a chance to turn around, the cloak was pulled off of her.

"Honestly, woman, why do you insist on wrinkling the material? Cloaks are for wearing, not reading under. And you'll bring dirt onto the sofa."

She bit back a chuckle at the exasperation in Arkhael's voice and turned around to look at him. It wasn't the first time he had told her off for something so small.

"Don't worry, I made sure it was clean."

Arkhael rolled his eyes, her cloak draped over one arm. In the other, he held a large bundle. She eyed it curiously.

He snorted and handed her the bundle. "Hopefully it will stop you from using your cloak."

Curious, Ailith unfolded it. In her hands she held a large, finely woven blanket, softer than anything she had ever felt. An intricate pattern of leaves and branches was woven through the material. It was beautiful. She looked up at Arkhael, but he had already wandered off to his desk.

"Thank you," she called after him, "this is beautiful."

She watched him lay out his work as he did at the end of every day and shrug.

"Think nothing of it."

But it meant the world to her. With a fluttering stomach, she wrapped it around herself as she picked the book back up again. A comfortable silence filled the room, only broken by the occasional turning of a page and Arkhael's scratching quill. She heard him close the desk much sooner than he usually did, looking up as he walked over to her.

"We're going out tonight." He extended a hand and pulled her off the sofa, giving her a once-over and straightening her blouse.

"Out? Out where?" As she asked it, she realised he still looked human.

"To a theatre." Before she got a chance to ask more he continued, "And it's a reputable establishment. Fix your hair before we leave."

Ailith scoffed. She had loosely tied it back and out of the way in the morning, but the bun had come loose throughout the day.

"Fine, how do you want me to wear it?"

Reaching behind her, Arkhael pulled the pins out of her hair, letting it fall down. He tucked one of the strands behind her ear, his face uncharacteristically soft.

"Beautiful," he murmured quietly before straightening himself and extending his arm. His features schooled back into the familiar arrogant mask as if nothing had happened.

Ailith tried her best not to stare at him—loose it would be—and hooked her arm through his.

She found herself in a narrow alley next to a large building, music and loud voices spilling out of the windows as Arkhael led her to the entrance. She didn't recognise the cityscape. The buildings were made of a light, near-white stone, many of them with large windows, in front of which hung large baskets with colourful flowers. The warm nighttime air was heavy with their different scents, sweet and floral without being overpowering in a way that only nature could provide. Ailith inhaled deeply, losing herself in the flowers for a brief moment before the stench of a large city caught up with them. Stagnant water, food waste in warm weather. Either early summer had progressed into late summer, or she was much further north than she had ever been.

With a gentle squeeze of her hand, Arkhael brought her focus back to the theatre they stood in front of. In awe, Ailith watched as the personnel clearly recognised him and escorted them to a private booth. They were seated at a small table on the second floor with a perfect view of a large stage. She barely noticed Arkhael order drinks. In all her years of thieving, she had never seen a room as decorated as this theatre. Every banister, every chair, every table was gilded. It glistened in the dim light of the candles and wall sconces. The audience seemed equally lavish, fine silks and jewellery sparkling at her. She couldn't resist thinking through the many ways she could walk away from the establishment richer than she had ever been.

With difficulty, Ailith tore her eyes away from it all, only to find Arkhael watching her closely.

"I have never been to a theatre before," she admitted quietly.

Arkhael smiled. "Consider it my pleasure, then, to take you to your first play. Although I don't believe that is what caught your eye."

Ailith ignored the knowing look he gave her and pretended she wasn't blushing slightly.

"Is this something you do often?"

"Not often." He poured her a glass of wine when it was brought into their private booth. "But occasionally I try to make time for it. This playwright does particularly good tragedies."

Ailith barely had eyes for the play when it started. Never had she imagined Arkhael enjoying something so mundane in a room full of normal mortal people. Yet here he was, watching the stage with great interest. When he had said he enjoyed the arts, this was not what she had had in mind. She had just assumed there must be an infernal equivalent.

He caught her staring and raised an eyebrow at her.

She simply shook her head and looked back at the stage with a smile. Every time she thought she had him figured out, he proved her wrong.

There was so much more to him than just lust for power. And she found herself dangerously enjoying every discovery.

Arkhael brought his mouth to her ear.

"Your thoughts are loud again," he whispered.

"Sorry," she whispered back.

Rolling his eyes at her, he pulled her chair closer and laid an arm around her shoulders, pulling her against him.

Trying not to show her surprise, Ailith rested her head against his shoulder. It wasn't often that he showed affection so openly, and she certainly didn't expect him to do so in public. With difficulty, she tried to focus on the play and not the butterflies in her stomach.

Chapter 37

To Ailith's annoyance, the butterflies decided to stay. She was all but counting the days, waiting for them to leave, every night convincing herself that it was the fresh mango he had brought her for breakfast that kept them around, or the earrings he had gifted her, or the way he had woven his hands through her hair that day. After more than a fortnight had passed, she was reluctantly forced to admit to herself that she was running out of excuses. That perhaps there was more to it than the small acts of tenderness. Arkhael had always taken her breath away. But now his every touch left her stomach in knots. She huffed as she put her empty cup of coffee down. *How very silly.*

Ailith had barely finished her breakfast when Arkhael told her, "We're travelling today."

"Where to?" she asked curiously. He hadn't taken her out since their one outing to the theatre.

"The Second Circle. Someone there needs reminding of their place." His tone was grim.

She was accompanying him in the Hells?

Ailith rose from her seat. "What do you want me to do?"

He walked over to her, gaze travelling over her body, and tucked a strand of hair behind her ear. "We will be seen arriving together. That's all I need from you." Arkhael held out an arm, and she hooked hers through. It felt strangely formal. With a snap of his fingers, he transported them.

They found themselves on a long, yellowish path that led to a large, distant house. Ailith looked down. Hollow eye sockets peered back at her.

"Really?" she said quietly to Arkhael. "A path of skulls?" She rolled her eyes.

The corner of his mouth tilted slightly. "Tacky, isn't it?"

Odd brown shapes stuck up out of the ground around them as they walked down the path, towering over them. They reminded her of—"Trees?"

"Of a sort." She felt Arkhael tense next to her and looked for what could have caused it. Shapes moved in the distance. He turned to her. "I am continuing alone from here. Anything comes close, use that lightning of yours. No divine light unless your life depends on it. Don't hesitate; kill immediately. If you don't make it clear what happens to anyone approaching you instantly, you *will* get swarmed. I expect to find you here when I return, unharmed and uncharmed."

Uncharmed? Before she could ask what he meant, he beat his wings and flew down the path away from her. She watched him go, watched the distant winged shapes follow in his path, then turned to the trees next to her.

He hadn't needed her here at all. He had brought her to a forest.

Of sorts, at least. Whatever passed for a forest in the Hells.

She left the path, wandering through the odd landscape. The ground was a brackish grey colour, and the brown trees around her looked dead. She picked a big one and sat herself down, leaning her back against it, carefully sending her magic into the ground.

Her heart skipped a beat. They *were* trees. Like none she had ever encountered before, but nevertheless very much alive, with roots stretching deep into the ground. She followed them, wondering what could sustain them in this climate. Decaying organic matter rotted far below. Drawing herself back a bit, she followed the root network to the next tree, and to the next, until she felt herself stretched out over the entirety of the forest.

Ailith drew a deep breath. For all its strange properties, it felt wonderful to be part of an organic whole again.

Through the ground, she felt tremors near her. Something had landed. A set of footsteps, followed by another. Wings stirred the leafless branches.

"One step closer, and I will obliterate you," she said quietly before opening her eyes.

A group of three devils lurked around a tree, staring at her. They were beautiful. Their features shimmered and changed constantly, but there was something undeniably alluring about them. Their skin was a brighter red than Arkhael's, their horns smaller. And they were very much unclad, their naked chests looking almost oiled.

Incubi.

They looked at one another at her words. One of them stepped forwards.

"We're only—" A loud crack resounded as Ailith called down her lightning. Where the devil had stood, a pile of ash remained.

Maybe a bit much, she thought wryly as her own body shook slightly with the force of the impact.

The two remaining devils looked at her in stunned silence. She raised her hand again in clear warning until they both took a step back. One of them turned, whispered something to its companion, and ran before taking off to the sky.

The one that remained eyed her curiously.

"You came with Lord Arkhael, didn't you?" His voice was honeyed, smooth and alluring. Her stomach coiled at the sound of it, torn between immediate wariness and an arousal that had nothing to do with her own feelings.

"What of it?" she responded coolly, holding onto the lightning.

He circled her, careful to maintain the distance between them.

"What could he offer a mortal woman that I couldn't?" the devil mused out loud, then grinned at her. Ailith struggled to remain in control of her breathing, narrowing her eyes at the creature.

"By status alone, a lot more I believe."

He leaned against the tree opposite her, arching his back into it, shamelessly showing her exactly what he could offer.

"But what of your deepest desires? Do you know those . . . Ailith?"

She didn't question how he knew her name. "Peace and quiet are high on the list. Something you are rudely taking from me." Despite herself, her voice came out strained. With her free hand, she touched the tree behind her. *Breathe. It's only a devil's charm.*

He sank down on his haunches to be at eye level with her. In front of her, his face transformed. It should have been grotesque, but instead, she watched mesmerised, until Arkhael's face looked back at her. The devil gave her a wicked smile.

"The lord himself?"

She laughed, his charm suddenly broken. "That is your big play? To tell me what I already know?"

The creature put its knees on the ground, kneeling for her, lifting his chin. "But I offer you a chance to live those desires. Feel them like your lord will never let you."

Heat spread through her, no matter how hard she tried to remain unaffected. His body was an almost perfect copy, and even the mere illusion of Arkhael kneeling for her made her head spin.

"I don't think he will appreciate you wearing his body," she managed to force out through gritted teeth.

The devil crawled forwards, just a little, testing her boundaries. "He is not here, though, is he? And I am."

Ailith managed a smile. "I don't think you can give me anything he doesn't give me already, devil." The moment it was out, she realised she had made a mistake.

He grinned at her. "So, the cold Lord Arkhael has finally found a mortal to heat his frozen blood?" Leaning back, he spread his legs in front of her, and she struggled to keep her eyes on his face. "How much does he give you, I wonder? All of his body? You can tell me, you know. Maybe I can make up for his flaws?"

The devil bent forwards again, crawling closer. She was vaguely aware that other winged figures had landed nearby. A safe enough distance away, but near enough to be watching.

Kill him. Set an example. He knows too much.

She realised she had dropped the lightning from her hand.

"He has no flaws. Now leave me in peace."

The devil came closer, close enough to touch her, and sucked in an audible breath.

"You don't just desire him, do you, mortal?" His laughter was cruel, and yet she couldn't bring herself to summon the lightning again. She felt a need between her legs and an ache in her heart at his words.

He reached out a tentative hand. "Lord Arkhael doesn't feel, even less than the other lords do. I could provide you that warmth. I could love you—"

Lightning crashed down on him, filling the air with the smell of burned flesh. Ailith was breathing heavily, the desire suddenly gone. The other winged figures took off again.

She rested her head back against the tree. That had been too close.

By the time Arkhael returned, she had calmed down. He found her with her legs crossed under her, hands on the ground in a meditative pose, a faint smile on her face. No other devils had approached her.

She opened her eyes at his familiar footsteps and saw him raise an eyebrow at the pile of ash next to her. "Don't ask."

"I did tell you to—"

"I know." She got up, refusing to look at him.

He held out his arm. "Should I know about it?"

Ailith hooked hers through, looking pointedly ahead. "It's probably better you don't."

With a familiar snap, she found herself back in his chambers, but as she made to walk away, Arkhael grabbed her wrist painfully tight.

"Who did they show?"

There was a tightness to his voice Ailith couldn't place, and she raised her eyebrows at him.

"With that tone? Even less of your business."

Roughly, he pulled her towards him. "I'm making it my business now."

"And then what?" She met his gaze with an angry one of her own. "What will you do when I tell you?"

"I will kill whatever mortal you think can offer you more."

Is he jealous? The thought was so ridiculous, she laughed.

"And if you continue to taunt me, I will make sure you endure the same pain."

Ailith brought a hand to his face, ignoring the flash of anger in his eyes. "There is no need for threats, you idiot." She smiled softly, even as the hand on her wrist tightened. "It was you he changed into." She ignored the heat creeping up her cheeks.

Arkhael looked at her in bewilderment before he let go of her wrist. He cleared his throat. "That shouldn't have fooled you."

"It didn't. His charm was immediately gone."

"Then why let him get close to you?" The steely tone returned to his voice. "What did he offer you that I would not?"

Ailith bit her lips nervously, and she withdrew her hand. That was something she herself wasn't even willing to face yet.

"Something you would find beneath you," she offered instead. It wasn't entirely a lie. Arkhael would never kneel for her.

"And did you desire him in that moment? Did you let him touch you?" His voice had gone quiet. The dangerous kind of quiet.

She rolled her eyes at him even as a shiver ran down her spine at his tone. "Don't insult me. I desired *you* in that moment. I wanted to see *you* naked and on your knees in front of me, not his shallow imitation. And yes, that got to me. Lest you forget, I am only mortal." Ailith turned on her heels, her face hot.

How could she tell him what the incubus had shown her if she herself didn't even know what to do with it? The very thought of bringing love into this strange relationship tied her stomach in an uncomfortable knot. It was stupidly impossible.

"Don't leave." Arkhael's voice halted her step. "Come here."

She briefly considered ignoring him, but she immediately recognised how petty that would be. So she sighed and walked back over to him.

"What do you want?"

He beckoned her to come closer, and she took his outstretched hand. Let herself be led as he walked them to a chair and pulled her onto his lap, one leg on either side of him. Arkhael took her chin in one hand, forcing her to look at him.

"Tell me why this fantasy has you so upset."

Ailith narrowed her eyes. "It doesn't, your behaviour does." It wasn't the entire truth, and she could see in his eyes that Arkhael knew.

"You know better than to lie to me, little thief."

"Why do you care so much?" she spat back, avoiding the question.

He let go of her face and ran the hand through her hair instead. "Is it so hard to imagine that I might care without ulterior motive?"

"It is." Ailith looked away. His hand tensed briefly in her hair at her words. For someone with no soul and no feelings, he could be so disarmingly tender.

"Fine then," he sighed as he leaned back. "Contractually, you have made yourself my consort. It is only natural for me to have some measure of care for the wellbeing of the person who has bound themself to me. Is that ulterior motive enough for you? I could think of another few if you want me to."

She hated the faint trace of hurt in his voice.

"The incubus implied something." Clearing her throat she continued, "That I don't quite know how to handle." Ailith met his gaze. "It implied something about me that I don't feel comfortable with."

Arkhael shook his head. "I shouldn't have taken you."

"No, you should have."

"You clearly weren't ready."

She took his face in her hands. "Bringing me to a forest was a gift. Rude incubi included. I wish I could share that feeling with you." A soft smile spread across her face. "Even though the trees were different, they were alive. Tapping into that is like . . ." She sought for the words to describe it. "Like thinking you are lost, only to find an unexpected home. It's becoming a part of something peaceful when your own mind is in turmoil. It's the realisation that, in the grand scheme of it all, you are no more than a small branch in an unending system. It's a healing balm for the soul. I am incredibly grateful. Truly."

Arkhael stared at her as she spoke, his eyes unreadable.

"I am glad it wasn't spoiled for you," he said finally, then took her hands in his. "A word of wisdom. Devils cannot lie. Whatever that incubus said to you, make your peace with it. If they believed it to be true, it likely was." He huffed. "They are annoyingly perceptive little bastards."

Ailith moved her hips slightly closer to him. "Do they show you anything?" she asked curiously, a hint of mischief in her voice.

Arkhael raised an eyebrow at her. "You are unwilling to share what was shown to you, and yet you expect me to answer?"

"I already shared the fantasy with you." Ailith felt fire creep up her cheeks, but she made sure to answer his raised eyebrow with one of her own. "And you were a lot less nice about it."

"No, not good enough." The smile he gave her dared her to offer more.

"Fine, what would be good enough?" She ground her hips into him, looking at him from underneath her eyelashes.

"Show me." He leaned back and crossed his arms, giving her a toothy grin. The challenging facade was only slightly marred by the involuntary moan that left his mouth.

"Show you what?" Ailith leaned forwards, ghosting her lips over his.

"Show me your fantasy, what you thought was beneath me."

She stilled. "And then you'll show me yours?"

"No, I'll *tell* you what the incubi show me."

"That seems unfair." Her words lacked conviction as she traced her tongue down his neck.

She heard Arkhael's breath catch, but his words remained full of arrogance. "You lied to me. I think you owe me one."

Ailith hissed against his neck. "Fine." She moved off of him. She would show him exactly what the incubus had shown her, and nothing more.

Walking away from Arkhael, she took off her blouse and dropped it to the ground, not looking at him as she removed the remainder of her clothes. He wanted a show, he would get a show. Naked, she walked over to the nearest wall and turned around, making sure to look Arkhael in the eye. Then she slid herself down it, spreading her legs.

"He asked me if I knew my deepest desires. Of course I do." A twinge of nerves twirled through her stomach as she put herself on display. Putting her knees to the ground, she lifted her chin. One look at Arkhael's face destroyed any reservations she may have had. His mouth was open, his eyes dark. Even from her position, she could see his hands gripping the armchair. Without breaking eye contact, she brought her hands to the ground, crawling forwards, torn between shame and satisfaction as she watched him suck in a breath.

Her own heart beat in her throat. Yet despite the nerves, her body ached as she moved. The air on her skin seemed like fire, and it was almost as if she could feel the power of his gaze caress her body. She yearned for him with a sudden need that made her hands tremble. She didn't just want him. She wanted him to *use* her.

Only when she was near enough to touch Arkhael did Ailith lean back again, spreading her legs.

"I imagined you in this position for me." To her surprise, her voice came out slightly breathless as Arkhael's eyes flicked down, and she knew a blush had coloured her cheeks. She could almost feel the tension in his body.

"Although I preferred the image of you kneeling with your head high." Assuming the pose, she smiled. "Your turn."

He blinked once, twice, thrice, before he answered, and Ailith could see him struggle to form words. "And what would I do in this position?"

She raised an eyebrow. "I'm afraid the incubus was dead at this point, so you'll have to imagine what comes next."

A smile appeared on his lips, even though his expression remained slightly pained and his voice was hoarse as he spoke. "Details, my little thief. You agreed to show me your fantasy, not just what the incubus had shown you."

Ailith took in a sharp breath, narrowing her eyes at him. That's what she got for playing games with a devil.

"Unless, of course, you wish to stop there and not learn the answer to your question?" He knew too well she wouldn't back down from a challenge, but she could tell he was also desperate for her to continue.

"Stand up."

Before he could question it, she interrupted him.

"You want to see my fantasy? You stand up."

She noticed his legs were shaking when he rose, but it did not diminish how impressive he was when standing. Kneeling before him sent a tremor through her body, her own need, which she had tried to ignore so far, making itself known aggressively. Digging her nails into the palms of her hands, she tried to regain some control.

She lifted herself up slightly and moved her shaky hands to the buttons of his trousers, slowly undoing them. Wondering how, after everything they had done, she could still feel that flutter of nerves.

Because, despite everything, he never lets your hands or mouth wander this freely.

Arkhael groaned as she removed the garment. She took hold of his hands and brought them to her hair.

"Don't let go," she whispered breathlessly, "because I wouldn't." He wove his hands through the strands but otherwise didn't move.

With a last look at his face, Ailith refocused her attention, bringing her hands to his hard lid instead. The claws in her hair tensed as she brought her mouth up to tip of him, moving her tongue over it slowly, then sucking it into her mouth. Arkhael let out a strangled moan as she started working her hands and mouth in unison. She could feel his hips rocking involuntarily against her as she took him down further, trying to relax the muscles of her throat.

Withdrawing to catch her breath, she used both hands instead, casting her eyes upwards. Arkhael's mouth was open, his eyes trained on her, and the moment she looked up, he growled.

"I want you to worship me," Ailith managed between panted breaths, "the way I am worshipping you now." Maintaining eye contact, she moved her tongue over his length and watched the remainder of Arkhael's self-control crumble. Tugging on her hair, he pulled her forwards, sliding himself into her open mouth.

Ailith moaned around him, moving her hands to his hips as he held her head. She struggled to breathe, her eyes watering with the effort of accommodating him, her nails digging into him, her own hips trembling with desire.

"Touch yourself." His voice was ragged above her.

Ailith obliged immediately, moving one of her hands between her own legs, spreading her own wetness around while she pleasured herself to him taking her mouth. Moans spilled around him as she spread herself and looked at his beautiful face. The dark red of his skin gleamed in the light of the room.

Any embarrassment she might have felt at exposing herself so was entirely drowned out by the desire he sparked in her as he used her.

"Come, my little thief. Worship me with ecstasy on your face."

She did, the low timbre of his voice adding to the fire that was already blossoming inside her. Her constant moans muffled by his length as she let herself come on her fingers before him. Worshipping him.

Arkhael let out one long moan as he buried himself down her throat, her mouth filling with the taste of him. He didn't pull out. Instead, he continued rocking his hips even after he finished until she had swallowed all of it.

Only then did he withdraw, pulling Ailith up by her hair, his mouth on hers immediately.

"By the Hells woman, will you ever be enough?" He pulled her against him, one hand between her legs, coating his fingers in her pleasure.

Before Ailith could respond, his fingers were in her mouth, and as he led her back to the chair she knew that, no, even eternity would not be enough for her.

By the time they were both sated, they had made it to the sofa. Arkhael lay atop it, his eyes half lidded, one arm still around Ailith, the other behind his head.

Ailith had barely moved from where they had finished. Her legs were still on either side of his hips, her head resting on his chest, her hand tracing the long lines her nails had left behind. Occasionally, she let her fingers trail over the fresh wounds, eliciting a hiss from Arkhael before she brought them to her mouth.

"So tell me." She cleared her throat, her voice hoarse from his rough treatment. "What do the incubi show you?"

His arm around her tightened slightly. "You won't enjoy the answer."

Ailith lifted herself up just a little bit, enough to look at his face.

Is it someone else?

"I kept my end of the deal."

"Fine, fine." The look he gave her was strangely smug. "They show me nothing."

"What?" Ailith shot up. "We made a deal!"

Arkhael merely raised an eyebrow at her in response. "You showed me your fantasy, and in return, I told you what they show me. It is not my fault you didn't specify the details of the deal and believed it to include something that was never agreed on."

He was right. Of course he would be; this was his domain after all. She couldn't believe that she had fallen for the oldest trick in the book.

"How dare you!" Indignantly, she brought her nails to his chest, raking them down hard.

Arkhael hissed in response, grabbing her wrists. Despite knowing she would never win that battle, Ailith still tried to break free from his grip, squirming in his grasp.

"You. Filthy. Tricking. Devil," she panted.

If anything, it only made Arkhael look more pleased with himself.

He tutted. "You should really have known better."

Ailith growled at him. She should have, but that didn't mean she would concede easily. His amusement at her struggle only made her redouble her efforts. With her wrists restrained, she brought her mouth down instead, trying to bite his shoulder.

He barely stopped her in time, letting go of one of her hands to grab her hair. Immediately she used the opportunity to try and slap him in the face. He laughed as she made contact. Ailith's heart skipped a beat at the sound. He *never* laughed so freely. It almost made her stop her struggling. *Almost.*

"Alright, alright. Peace, Ailith."

"Not until you answer the bloody question." She narrowed her eyes at him, even as he pulled her head back by her hair. No matter how charming he was, she had a point to make.

When she brought her hand back up, he suddenly pushed her to the side. With a yelp, she fell off the sofa, landing on the hard stone floor. Before she had a chance to move, he was on her, pinning her down with his body.

"You know you cannot win this." He laughed again, holding both her wrists next to her head.

It was hard to stay annoyed at him when he was being so genuine, so *himself* with her. Even as she glared at him, she could feel a smile tugging at her lips.

"Fine, but don't think I'll be forgetting this." She relaxed her arms, and Arkhael's grip on her wrists loosened slightly.

"Incubi cannot see the desires of other devils." He brought his face closer to hers. "But I don't think you need them to know what I like, do you?"

"Is that so?" She resisted the urge to close the distance and kiss him. Her body was still tender from how often he had made her see stars, and yet already, it ached for him again.

Arkhael smiled, his eyes glittering. "You tell me."

"Well . . ." Ailith bit her lip, pretending to consider his question carefully. "I do believe you quite like it when you see me on my knees. Or when you hold me down, like you are doing now."

Arkhael's hands twitched briefly. She ignored it, making sure to maintain eye contact with him.

"I think you like it even better when I fight you and you force me to submit to you."

Ailith could tell her words were getting to him as his breath quickened, his grip on her wrists tightened again, and she felt him stiffen against her. He seemed as insatiable as she was. She lifted her hips ever so slightly.

"But what I believe you like most, is owning me. Leaving scars on my body so everyone knows who I belong to. Hearing me say that I am yours, that I want to be yours. I don't know what's stopping you, but I think that, if you could, you would take me to the highest peak in the Hells and have me shout your name in ecstasy so all other devils would know who owns me. Am I wrong?"

She was not. Arkhael's grip had increasingly tightened as she talked, until his nails were digging into her skin. Vaguely, she was aware that he was barely missing the artery in her wrist, and she kept her healing magic close, just in case. She watched him take a shuddering breath and felt the familiar addictive surge of adrenaline run through her as she saw him struggle to regain control of himself.

"No, my little thief." He licked his lips. "You are not. And the thought of those incubi trying to tempt what's mine with their bodies makes me want to incinerate them all until they are nothing but ash."

Ailith brought one of her legs up and hooked it around his hips, pressing him into her.

"Tell me, Arkhael, why my body keeps yearning for you. Is this some devilish charm you have bewitched me with?"

He huffed, even as his voice came out strained. "What do you take me for? I don't charm my prey into submission."

"Then tell me what this is." The words came out breathlessly.

The look he gave her was so tormented, it almost scared her.

"I don't know," he whispered, letting go of her wrists with one hand to bring his arm around her, pressing her against him.

A shiver ran down her body at his admission. If it wasn't of his doing, then what had caused this? Never in her life had Ailith felt such intense, unending desire.

Her thoughts were interrupted by the shift of his hips, and she tilted her own to meet him. His eyes were still on her.

"Tell me you are mine."

"Yours."

Slowly, he pressed into her.

"You won't let anyone else touch you like this."

There were implications to what he was saying, but Ailith barely noticed them in the state she was in.

"I won't," she gasped as he pushed in entirely.

He snarled, baring his sharp teeth. With his wings unfolded behind him, there was no mistaking his fiendish nature.

And yet Ailith gave herself to him, letting his claws rake down her body so all could see that she was his.

CHAPTER 38

S he was fast asleep by the time he retired. He sank down against the pillows, careful not to disturb the mattress too much. He had noticed that she was usually a light sleeper, but she didn't so much as stir when he lay down.

No surprise after the day she had had. Between the incubi and himself, he was surprised she was still standing after dinner.

Laying on her side, breathing softly, it was easy to forget the power she held. In that moment, she seemed so serene, so vulnerable. A sudden urge of protectiveness overcame him. As it did every night when he looked at her.

What is wrong with you?

He tore his eyes away from her sleeping form and ran a hand through his hair. She had thrown his life into disarray with her chaos, and he found he couldn't care about it. In the privacy of his mind, that was frightening.

Let go, a quiet voice in his head urged him. He ignored it.

He had a reputation to maintain. If any of this got out—and he had no doubt it would eventually—it would ruin his standing. Would ruin everything he had worked so hard to acquire. Just the other day, he had seen a figure fly past his windows. Although his home was entirely warded to prevent most other devils from entering without his permission, he knew that he was being watched even closer than usual at the moment. His attempt at the Hand of Saint Argon had drawn eyes to him. They had already watched him fail at that; he didn't need to be seen debasing himself below his status. He couldn't afford to lose his reputation. Couldn't afford to lose the authority it granted him. And his pride couldn't suffer yet another blow.

Next to him, the sheets rustled as she shifted in her sleep, sighed, and settled again. The blanket had slipped off her shoulder, revealing the earlier marks he had left there. Suddenly the opinions of his brethren seemed less important. And he was certain she would challenge them if they so much as looked at her wrong. She could hold her own. She had proven that today. His anger at her had been irrational. He had known it, and yet he couldn't stop himself from lashing out when he had learned that she had nearly let one of those disgusting creatures touch her.

His thoughts went back to her earlier questions. If he hadn't been so entranced by the spell of her body that it was almost painful, he might have considered his answers better. Instead, he had answered her without thinking, caught up in the story she had been weaving him. But she had struck a nerve by asking.

Why was he so obsessed with her? His every thought went to her, and every fibre of his being seemed to long for her touch constantly. If he didn't know any better, he would have agreed with her and blamed the entire thing on a charm being at play. But the thought alone was ridiculous. He doubted she was easily charmed.

It was then that realisation hit him. She *could* hold her own.

She had to be one of the more powerful casters of her time, and he had seen her soul. Any devil would be willing to fight for that if they thought they could win. He narrowed his eyes at her in the darkness. The sheer value of her.

It explained why she had such power over him. *Of course.* It explained everything.

He scooped her up and pulled her close to him. Laying her head on his chest, one arm around her waist. The need to protect her settled, and he gently brushed his lips against her hair.

His little thief.

He followed the line of her slightly pointed ear to her jaw, her neck, her throat. All it would take was one flick of his claws.

She knew. And yet, here she was.

It was exhilarating. He could feel himself stir at the thought.

No, she needs her rest.

But his breath had already quickened, and his mind wandered. To how tight she felt around him. To her wandering hands. Every inch of exploration they engaged in. That they shouldn't engage in. That he shouldn't allow.

It might be wrong, but his body constantly yearned for her regardless. He wanted her. Every second of the day, every moment of the night. It was overwhelming.

Closing his eyes, he wrapped his free hand around himself. It was all too easy to imagine it was hers instead. Not breaking eye contact as she grabbed him, asking him to cover her body.

He sucked in a sharp breath.

Quiet.

He imagined her hand joining his. Her grip slightly less strong than his, her hand slightly colder as she followed his rhythm. She would look at him with her grey eyes, full of mischief and satisfaction, trying to remain in control, while the noises escaping her mouth would betray the lack of it. Entirely uncaring of how wrong it was what they were doing.

Her hot breath was on him before she took him in her mouth. The very tip at first, her tongue moving over the sensitive bits there.

Arkhael's eyes shot open. Just in time to watch Ailith take him in her mouth entirely.

When had she woken up? When had fantasy become reality?

He wove his fingers into her hair, unsure if he was guiding her movements or trying his best to hold on as she slowly undid him. Her hands covered him when her mouth did not, her tongue moving over him every time she took him back in.

His hips moved of their own volition as the world spiralled. Control was a distant illusion. Groans left his mouth at her command, his gaze transfixed on the sight of her mouth on him. She moaned; he felt it as much as he heard it. Knowing that she enjoyed it when he took her mouth made him tighten his grip on her hair. How she managed to break him he did not know. But she managed it every time, cutting right through his facade and the control he so carefully exerted over himself like it was nothing.

He could feel himself nearing the edge, hips thrashing. And then the world exploded as she took him down her throat.

He swore and rolled them over. Withdrawing from her mouth as he came. Watching his seed land on her body.

Only his wings stopped him from falling forwards, knees trembling.

She was a sight. Lips slightly swollen. Cheeks flushed. Her naked body glistening. Chest rising rapidly. Eyes looking for him in the dark.

Something snapped in him. He *needed* to claim her. To make her his. In every way possible.

He reached next to the bed, found the rope in the nightstand, and looped it around her wrists through the ring at the headboard. The surprised gasp she let out was music to his ears, and he took a moment to admire the struggle she put up as she tried to figure out how exactly she was bound.

Finally, he let himself do what he had wanted to do since he had first laid eyes on her. What he had denied himself.

To the Hells with decorum. To the Hells with the rules.

He let his mouth explore her body. Let himself indulge in all that was forbidden. Bit the collarbone he was so familiar with. Moved down from there, tasting himself on her breasts, rolling a nipple between his lips.

Ailith had stopped her struggles, instead arching into his touch. He continued his path downwards. Kissing the scar on her stomach, anticipation coiling in his own. This was unknown territory to him. And so very forbidden.

His tongue traced her hip bones on either side. The inside of her thighs. She was so unique. So perfectly suited to him.

He bit down, watched the soft flesh slowly turn red, felt how tense her muscles were with anticipation.

Until, finally, he let himself taste her, his tongue teasing, playing around her entrance. The noises she made only fuelled his fire as he held her hips down. Slowly, he pushed his tongue inside her, savouring the taste of her, revelling in the way her body shook as he did so repeatedly. If he had known that this would be her reaction, he would have done it much sooner. And now he never wanted to stop.

He pulled back just enough to watch her, and knew in that moment he would do anything for her.

Never had she seemed so at his mercy. The ropes around her wrists were taut, and he could see she had dug her nails into them. Her body was slick with sweat, trembling uncontrollably, eyes squeezed shut.

He dug his nails into her hips to regain some modicum of self-control, torn as he was between wanting to continue until she came on his tongue, and wanting to take her right then and there, knowing how wet she would be for him.

Keeping her down, he flicked his tongue past her entrance to the bundle of nerves just above it. The headboard creaked with the force of her reaction. He felt it in his very core. He repeated the motion. Revelled in how her body shuddered in response. At the strangled moan she let out. Again, he moved his tongue over her, applying more pressure this time. Until he could tell from her spasming muscles that she was close to losing it.

"Fuck, Arkhael. Please."

His own breath hitched at her unexpected plea. He obliged.

There wasn't truly a choice when she moaned his name like that. Her muscles tensed around him. Fighting his hands holding her in place.

Fighting the restraints as she came. He moved his tongue, needing to taste the pleasure he had given her.

Before she had even finished riding the waves of her orgasm, Arkhael moved up to thrust into her. He understood now that time she had forced him back into bed. Watching her come undone under his touch only made him want her more, if that was even possible.

He never got the chance to find a rhythm. His thrusts became frantic as soon as he entered her and felt her muscles contracting around him, pulling him in further until he came inside her. It wasn't enough. And part of him again wondered if he would ever truly get enough of her.

How long they continued he didn't know. When his legs finally gave out, they were both drenched in sweat. His hair had escaped its ties, sticking to the side of his face.

Ailith's breath came out raspy after the time she had begged him to cover her and cried out his name. Her eyes were closed now, chest moving rapidly. His seed covered her nipples, her breasts, her thighs. Her body was littered with fresh claw and bite marks, and her thighs were wet with how often they had found pleasure in one another. Desire flared in him at the sight of her. Again. But he doubted even his wings could lift him at this point.

Instead, he leaned forwards to burn away the rope that held her hands, not bothering with the knots. Shakily, Ailith brought her arms down. The skin on her wrists looked raw from the strain. Arkhael let himself fall back onto the bed next to her.

He knew he should tell her to clean up. Letting her sleep like this would ruin the sheets. But he didn't. He pulled her close to him. Stroked her hair while she took shaky breaths.

In that moment, all her usual bravado seemed to have vanished. She almost clung to him.

Neither spoke. Their shared vulnerability a secret between them that words might betray.

Gently, he lifted her chin, and her eyes found his in the dark before he kissed her. Softly, without pressure. She returned it, equally as tender. He tasted both of them and the sweet tang of blood in her mouth. And the promise that this moment was their secret to keep.

"Sleep, my little thief," he whispered as he leaned into the pillows. Utterly exhausted, and aware that he had just made a grave mistake.

CHAPTER 39

Something had changed. Ailith didn't know what had come over Arkhael, but he hadn't so much as kissed her since that night. Instead, he kept a forced distance that grated at her. For the last five mornings, she had awoken with his arms around her, her body pressed against his, his desire for her obvious. Yet every morning, he had pulled away before she had a chance to do anything, turning his head away the moment she looked up at him. In the evenings, he came home late and submerged himself in his work. And whenever he thought she wasn't looking, she caught a hunger in his eyes that contradicted his behaviour entirely.

She wasn't completely oblivious to the emotional turmoil he was trying to hide from her. It was in his clenched fists, in the tightness of his jaw as he worked, in how close he held her to him throughout the night. After the first two days, she had stopped pressing him, realising he was working through something and respecting his need for space.

But his lack of communication was starting to vex her, and she couldn't stand that he was avoiding her.

With a sigh, she closed the book she had been reading. If he didn't talk soon, she would start asking questions. Her body ached for him. *Especially* after that night. Whatever restraint he had been exercising, whatever had held him back, he had abandoned it and let himself go in a way she had not seen of him before. The mere thought of it made her shiver with desire. His mouth had been all over her body. She clenched her thighs at the memory of it. And she suspected that was exactly what bothered him so. The initial refusal to kiss her, the refusal to explore their bodies further, even the very first time when he had forced her down on the bed and taken her mouth, she remembered him shaking his head afterwards. What she just couldn't understand was, *why*?

With a huff, she got up off her balcony chair, walking back inside to find herself a new book. It only took her a second to realise she was not alone. He was home early.

Arkhael sat in his large armchair, leaning back into the cushions, one leg swung over the other, eyes trained on a piece of parchment held in one hand. His eyes flicked to her briefly as she entered the room, but otherwise he said nothing. Quietly, she walked over to the large bookcases and put the book she had been reading back on the shelf, grabbing a new one at random. It looked old. *The First Celestial War*, the title read. Turning around, she just caught Arkhael averting his eyes.

It stung, and her waning patience decided she had had enough of his silent treatment.

She walked over to his large chair, sat down on one of the armrests, and slowly let herself slide into his lap. Finally, Arkhael stopped reading.

He looked down at her, both eyebrows raised in question. With petty satisfaction, it was her turn to ignore him as she made herself comfortable, resting her head against his chest, legs swung over one of his. Opening her book, she started to read, pointedly not looking at him.

With a huff that was somewhere between amusement and annoyance, he went back to his paper, bringing his other arm around her so he could turn the page.

It may have started as a bit of petty revenge, but it didn't take long for Ailith to find herself relaxing against him as she tried to make sense of the archaic writing in the book. The closeness of his warm body felt oddly safe, and she realised that his free hand had started stroking her arm absentmindedly as he read. It made her heart flutter. It was easy to pretend she wasn't there because of a signed contract, that there was no awkward barrier of silence between them.

Stop daydreaming. It will only make reality harder to deal with.

But why shouldn't she allow herself this moment of happiness?

Arkhael's hand left her arm to turn another page, his arm tightening over her as he did so, before he rested it on her again. How such a small gesture could feel so possessive Ailith did not know, but it only increased the yearning in her heart.

She peered over the edge of her book at the documents he was reading. It took her some time before she recognised it as a negotiation of sorts. Details were laid out on how much was owed by an unnamed party, ranging from livestock to other goods, to even land.

"A peace treaty?" she mused out loud, immediately cringing at the sound of her own voice, worried it may have ruined the companionable silence they had been sharing.

Arkhael nodded. "Are you familiar with Oshador? I imagine it would be outside your usual hunting grounds."

"Never heard of it."

"They were on the verge of losing a war against Tibia when the tide suddenly turned. For all his cold-heartedness, the ruler there has only one heir to succeed him. Imagine his shock when said heir was suddenly in the hands of the enemy."

Ailith tilted her head to look up. "What an unexpected turn of events."

"Hmm, just so."

"So what are you getting out of it?"

Arkhael tutted. "You're smart. You tell me."

She looked back at the treaty. "You're reviewing the treaty, which means you are advising one side. I suspect Oshador, since you delivered them the heir. If you were any other devil, I would have guessed the soul of their ruler, but I would like to think I know you better than that. You care more about power and influence than you do about souls." Her eyes went back to his. "How many kings and queens do you actually have wound around your finger?"

He smiled at her. "Oshador sadly lost their queen in the most recent battle. Suddenly, her son was responsible for the safety of his people in a war that he was already losing, with no real experience to speak of."

"Desperate for someone trustworthy to help him and guide him."

"Exactly."

She shivered at the tone in his voice and fell quiet. Had he orchestrated the war? It wouldn't surprise her if he had, knowing that it would gain him another kingdom in the end. And with that tone in his voice, it wasn't hard at all to remember how ruthless he could be.

"You're frowning."

Ailith hesitated. It was hard to reconcile the devil who started and ended wars that easily, with the one who had just stroked her arms without thinking.

You have seen his cruelty firsthand.

How could she care for someone who caused so much suffering so easily? She looked up into his fiery eyes. There was a touch of concern in them as he looked down at her.

Because he had shown her more care than anyone, save maybe Amelie, ever had. Because he made her feel safe. Because he made her feel treasured, even if that was maybe only because of the value of her soul.

"If my soul was worth less, would you still have made me sign?" She bit her tongue. He had made her feel too comfortable; that didn't mean she shouldn't watch her words.

Arkhael sighed and carefully put the treaty down on the table. He plucked the book she had been reading from her hands and put that down next to it, then gently moved her so she could face him easier.

"This might be difficult to understand, since you don't *see* souls how I do. But a soul is not just a separate part of you that has its own value. It is the accumulation of all of you. If your soul was not worth as much as it is, you would be a different person altogether." He touched her cheek, and a shiver ran through Ailith, as if he had touched the very core of her being. "I can see your soul, touch it even, and since it is unclaimed, I could separate it from your body."

A sharp pain shot through her, and Arkhael smiled at her as he withdrew his hand.

"Then why do you need a contract at all? Why don't devils just go out and reap what they want?" Ailith ignored the drum of her heartbeat at what had just happened, her palms sweaty.

"Because a soul given is different from a soul that is taken. It is . . . complicated to explain." He tucked away one of the strands of hair that had fallen in front of her eyes. She wore it loose more often these days. "Imagine being famished. A taken soul would be like a single berry. The juice of it tastes good in your mouth. Sweet and tart. But once you swallow, it is gone and will have barely sated your hunger. A soul that is given, it is like a banquet. The richer the soul, the richer the banquet. And if you treat it well, it could last you an eternity."

Ailith considered his words.

"We also would not have the tenuous peace we do if devils started swarming the streets, harvesting souls whenever they felt like it." Arkhael chuckled. "The Celestials begrudgingly allow us our deals because, in the end, they are made through the free will of mortals. Any devil breaking that rule is a threat to all of us, and it is a strictly enforced rule. Does that answer your question?"

Ailith nodded, frowning slightly.

"But you still have another question."

She nodded again. "I feel it might be indecent to ask."

He cocked an eyebrow and smiled lightly. "Surely we are past the point of indecency?"

"That's *different*. Fine, just don't get angry with me for asking." She averted her eyes. "Is it true that devils don't have souls and that is why you crave them? That because of this, you can't truly feel?" *That you cannot love*, she wanted to add. She didn't. It shook her to her core that she had even thought of it.

"Who told you that?"

She felt him tense and shrugged. "Does it matter?"

He ran a hand through his hair. "When I look at my kin, I see nothing." His eyes narrowed at her. "Does that scare you? That we are soulless?"

She could tell she had struck a nerve, and she regretted asking. The answer could wait for another day. Straightening herself, she reached up with a hand and gently pulled his head down, brushing her lips against his.

"Have I ever seemed scared of you?" she whispered against him.

His arms came up around her, holding her close as he deepened the kiss. Ailith sighed into it. She had missed his touch. He bit her lip before he withdrew.

"Never as much as you should have been."

Ailith smiled. "I thought you arrogant and entitled."

He laughed at that. The sound sent little jolts through her. He didn't laugh often. Not genuinely, like he did now.

"I *am* arrogant and entitled."

At that, she laughed with him.

His face grew serious again. "I thought you were the most mysterious, challenging, and annoying prey I had ever gone after. Now I realise you are the most beautiful and enticing mistake I ever made."

Her breath caught in her throat. She tried to find a retort, but her usual wit had left her.

"What do you mean mistake?" she finally managed.

Arkhael traced her neck with a single claw, and she briefly closed her eyes, tilting her neck almost instinctively. He bent down to meet the invitation, kissing the nape of her neck, sinking his teeth down just below it.

"The deal was never meant for you," he murmured against her skin, licking up the trickle of blood. She could feel his arms tense around her as he spoke, could feel the forced restraint as he pulled himself away. "It was meant for the wizard."

"Really?! Why?"

"Figure it out." He cleared his throat as he leaned back, and she could feel him clench his fist behind her back as he created distance between them.

It took a moment for her thoughts to return to logic. But the realisation came to her as soon as they did.

"Because you knew he would have taken the deal. Maybe not at the first meeting." Her thoughts went back to Jay's mood after being in pain for days. "But certainly by the third."

Arkhael nodded, smiling slightly. "You'll make a fine devil yet."

"Jay wouldn't have been able to pull it off."

Arkhael's smile turned into a look of surprise. "He wouldn't?"

"I wouldn't have let him." Ailith shook her head at him. "He needed the team to break in. If he had shared the truth, I would have worked against him. In secret, if I had to, but I wouldn't have allowed him to succeed. And if he had lied, well." Ailith shrugged. "He's always been a terrible liar. We would have found out eventually."

"You truly do display humanity's worst quality sometimes."

"And what would that be?" She frowned at him.

"A moral compass." He gathered her hair in one hand and pulled, causing her to gasp as her head was forced back. "At least I would have had a soul. He wouldn't have challenged the contract like you did. Instead, I have a disobedient thief who has no manners and who continues to tempt me into breaking all sorts of ancient rules." With his free hand he reached under her blouse, tracing her breasts with his nails. He slowly trailed them down her stomach until he was fingering the waistband of her trousers.

"And which would you rather have?" Ailith managed to gasp with her head still pulled back. Heat coiled in her stomach as she quietly willed him to move his hands down. Through their clothes, she could feel him harden under her. Her desire flared.

"I'll take the thief any day," he murmured before he kissed her. It was forceful, and she gasped against him, parting her lips, enjoying the feeling of his tongue. She moved her hand to his trousers, palmed him through them, delighting in the sound of his moan and the way he moved his hips against her.

All of a sudden, both his hands came up and grabbed her by the shoulders, forcefully pushing her away from him. Ailith gave him a bewildered look.

Arkhael gasped. "No. I—we—shouldn't continue this."

Ailith frowned, breath still quickened. "And why not?" He seemed serious. "What's wrong?" She reached out a hand to touch Arkhael's face, but he grabbed it before she could get too close.

"What has been going on, Arkhael?"

"As I said, we should stop this." His voice sounded strained.

"Why do you keep turning me away? Do you no longer desire me?"

He shook his head. "It doesn't matter."

"Are you rejecting me?" She could hear the pitch of her voice rising.

"Not exactly like that."

Ailith's mouth fell open. The illusion that a part of him might care shattered.

"What happened? Did you want me because you couldn't have me, and with the thrill of the hunt gone, you have come to realise I'm not that special?" She could make no sense of his behaviour.

"Of course not," he scoffed.

"Then what?" She raised her voice in frustration. "You remembered I'm only mortal, so I'm no longer good enough?" When he didn't answer immediately, it was as if a knife was being twisted in her guts. "Really?!"

She couldn't get off the chair fast enough.

"I have a reputation to uphold, an image to maintain. I cannot be seen doing more than just taking pleasure from your body. It could ruin everything I have so carefully built up." The pleading in his voice left her cold in her anger.

Ailith was seething. "You are rejecting me to save your image? Fuck what others think. You're an archdevil. You can do whatever the fuck you want. If anyone disagrees, we'll kill them."

"Not everyone who would disagree can be so easily discarded." He had the gall to look away from her as he said it.

"Coward." She narrowed her eyes at him before throwing her hands up, laughing almost hysterically. "I should have known, though, shouldn't I? Nothing comes between you and your self-idolisation, isn't that right, *devil*? You disgust me."

Without waiting for his response, she stormed out of the room, slamming the door behind her, running past his vault, the dining room he never used, and through the hallway until she stood outside his front door. Wind whipped her hair around her. She looked past the plateau, into the fog below. Driven by rage and the raw pain in her heart, she summoned a vine from the side of the mountain, and jumped. Air howled past her, and for just a moment, she soared freely. Then the vine pulled taut, nearly pulling her shoulder out of her socket with the sudden jerk. The hand she had wrapped it around burned as the plant dug into her skin, and she felt a painful jolt in her back and hips as she slammed against the mountainside. It didn't stop her. She summoned a new vine next to her and wrapped it around her hand, discarding the old one, then pushed herself off again.

She had no idea how long she had been falling for. Her body was bruised and battered, both hands bleeding, when she found a small outcropping in the rock. She lowered herself onto it, leaning back into the mountain.

The pain in her body was a sweet distraction from the ache in her heart. Only when it faded into a dull throbbing did she focus on her surroundings. There was nothing around her but fog. She had descended low enough to sit in the mist, vague rays of yellow still filtering through from above her. Every so often, a faint cry from below would reach her ears, and she tried not to think of what was being done there.

Instead, she screamed into the abyss. The anger, but mostly the pain, she howled away, lightning striking with every heart-wrenching yell, until her anger and pain were burned out and there was nothing left but an emptiness and bone-deep exhaustion.

Leaning back against the mountain, she pulled her knees close and finally allowed herself to cry. Sobs wracked her body until even the tears had run out and she just sat, staring into the fog with a blank expression.

The yellow above her turned red, then darkened entirely, the fog occasionally lit by something beyond her view. Ailith didn't move. She had been a fool. A fool to let herself get comfortable. A fool to believe there was any care in his gentle touch. She groaned at herself. How could she have been so stupid? Why had she let her guard down so carelessly and forgotten who he was? *What* he was?

He had even admitted it himself. He had no soul, which meant he could never care for her. Right?

She wasn't sure. Matters of the soul were for the clergy to ponder over. *And devils, apparently.*

But if he didn't care, then why the tenderness? Why bring her to a forest?

Ailith's head pounded with the unanswered questions. Almost desperately, she reached for her exhaustion, for the numbness to take over again. Arkhael had made his stance clear. There was no point in questioning his actions.

She was still sitting there, leaning against the mountain, when the yellow rays started penetrating the fog again. Her rumbling stomach finally dulled the pain of her loss. She couldn't stay in her little alcove forever. Not only did she need to eat, she had a debt to pay that could not be ignored.

So she forced herself to her feet and started the arduous journey back up, summoning vines as high as she could see, wrapping them around her wrist, and using them to climb back up. The mountain offered her little support, and before long, her arms hurt from the constant strain.

When she could go no further, she wrapped one of her vines in a loop and sat in it, hanging against the mountainside.

By the time she rose above the fog, the sky had darkened, and day had progressed well into night when Arkhael's front door came back into view. She hoisted herself onto the plateau, sweating and shaking. His home was quiet. She imagined he was already abed at this hour, and for a moment, indecision paralysed her. Marius would have to supply her with food if she asked for it, but then what? She couldn't—wouldn't—return to Arkhael's bed.

Quietly, she tiptoed into his chambers and rang the servant's bell, praying it wouldn't wake the devil. Marius appeared in an instant, a sneer on his face.

"Bring me some food. Something light." She sat down in one of the chairs, the one Arkhael never used.

"Of course." With disdain on his face, he bowed, turned, and returned not too much later with a small platter of bread and dried fruits.

Despite her hunger, she ate slowly. The food tasted like ash in her mouth and sat like stones in her stomach. She looked across at the other chair. Arkhael's chair. Her stomach churned, and she pushed the remainder of the food away, suddenly feeling sick. Folding her arms on the table, she rested her forehead on them.

She had been so gullible, thinking that there would be anything more than selfish desire behind a devil's actions. But he had seemed so tender at times, so deceptively genuine. Tears that she thought had all been shed crept into her eyes. Quietly, she wept again and realised that all the stories and warnings she had heard about devils had turned out to be true. They hit you where it hurt you most, and where you least expected it.

CHAPTER 40

He found her in that same position the following morning and couldn't quell the rush of relief he felt knowing that she was safe. Three times he had nearly flown down the mountain to check on her, to remind her that the Hells had no safe places, that she could have been attacked at any point. But he had also known she was able to take care of herself and didn't need him to be there.

Instead, he had raged like he hadn't in centuries. He had travelled to the upper circles and wreaked havoc, killing lesser devils in a fit of uncontrolled fury. He regretted it, of course. His self-control was something he kept on a tight leash. It was his pride. It was what had gotten him his reputation. No matter how horrifying the situation, he kept his composure, fully aware that it was whispered that he had no feelings anymore.

His gaze went to Ailith's hands. Her fingertips were chafed, her wrists bloodied, her blouse torn near the shoulders. *What did she do to herself?*

She had never known the rumours about him, and she had immediately seen him for who he was. He shook his head. He never should have let her. Steeling himself, he brought back that familiar facade and shook her shoulder.

Immediately, she shot up and moved away from him, nearly knocking over the chair in the process. Her face was even paler than usual, and there were dark rings under her eyes. Yet they shone with a fury he had not seen in her before, and having it directed at him felt like a dagger to a heart he didn't know he possessed.

"Don't you dare touch me, *devil*," she spat at him, twisting the knife.

He couldn't stop his jaw from tightening as anger flared within him. Anger at how easy it was for her to break his self-control, but most of all, anger to drown out the pain.

"You're filthy. Go wash yourself."

Without a word, she stormed out of the room.

It was easier to ignore her that day than to face her, and when she told Marius she would have her food outside, Arkhael didn't protest.

Only when she lay down on his sofa in the evening, pulling the blanket he had gifted her over her, did he speak again.

"You are not sleeping on my sofa."

"Where else do you propose I sleep?" Her icy stare met his. "The floor? More befitting of someone of my station, maybe?"

A second dagger joined the first. He ignored it, turned the pain into venom.

"You will sleep in my bed, or you can join Marius in his."

For a moment, he thought she actually might, just to spite him. Her eyes flashed a violet-white. "Fucking make me."

Arkhael grabbed her left hand, the one he knew she preferred for her casting. Too late.

A blast of lightning knocked the breath out of him, his muscles spasming uncontrollably. With gritted teeth, he held onto her, bearing the pain, knowing there was only so much she could do before the contract would stop her.

"I told you not to touch me."

He ignored her angry words, willing his muscles to move, and yanked her closer to him. The lightning stopped abruptly.

"This was your choice, your contract. You chose to be my consort; you live with the consequences." His voice was quiet in his rage, and he watched her narrow her eyes.

She didn't need to know that no devil would ever share their bed with a mortal for anything other than sex. All she needed to do was believe that it was true.

With a grunt, she pulled her hand down. He let her go as the colour of her eyes returned to their usual cloudy grey. The lightning had stopped, but his body was still reeling. He gritted his teeth to hide it from her.

"If I feel you anywhere near me during the night, that lightning will be made of divine light." Her voice was almost as quiet as his before she turned around and marched out of the room. The satisfaction he might have felt at winning the argument was quelled immediately by the withering look of disgust she gave him on her way out.

At least he knew she would be safe at night and not out doing something foolish. The slight relief dulled the edges of his anger, and he made sure to give her time and privacy before he retired.

She was still awake when he entered his bedchambers, even if she kept her eyes pointedly closed when he entered. It was ridiculous how pleased he felt to see her there again after two nights of missing her, how relieved he was that she had returned to him. As he sank down on the mattress, he could feel her inch further away from him. A third stab in the heart. He ached with a pain that was entirely alien to him when he looked at her, so close yet so far from him. She had turned her back to him, blankets wrapped tightly around her. Only her silver hair spilled out from under them.

He closed his eyes, trying to bring his mind to rest. To no avail. He was aware of her every breath, every move, of how it took her way too long to find sleep herself.

He balled his fists. It wasn't his fault that she didn't understand. Was this not exactly why he told her to do so much reading? So she could understand the Hells and its customs better?

A quiet hiccup broke the silence. He pretended not to hear it, even as he could see her wipe her eyes with a corner of the blanket. His hands burned with the desire to reach out. Finally, he had broken her, and it ate at him like a cancer.

Why do you care so much?

Empathetic was the last thing anyone would ever have called him. Yet here he was, wanting to take this woman into his arms to stop her tears. It was exactly why he needed to create the distance. He couldn't risk being perceived as weak. Not by her, nor by anyone else. The moment he did, the vultures would descend.

So he hardened his heart until exhaustion finally pulled her into sleep, ignoring the pain and guilt in his chest.

"Send me out." Her voice cut through their silent breakfast.

He looked up, surprised.

"I am in your employ to work off a debt and I am not doing that by sitting around here reading books. Send me out."

A fist clenched around his heart at the thought of letting her go, but she was right. Those were the terms laid out in the contract; he could not deny her that.

So he nodded. There were enough errands for her to run. Ones that he had delegated to others purely so he could keep her in his home.

He hated it. Hated dropping her off in the morning and watching her come home as late as she could get away with. Hated how she reported to him as if he was nothing more than her employer, even if he knew that was precisely what he should be.

His plan was working exactly as he had originally intended it, and he hated every second of it.

CHAPTER 41

I t was odd to return to Dewhaven after everything that had happened. Arkhael had asked her to meet up with two of his informants to deliver orders, then to monitor a transaction in a tavern. She hadn't realised quite how many people he controlled and was involved with until he had begun sending her out, and she was well aware that he was skirting her away from some of his crueller dealings. It was a difficult truth to come to terms with. Knowing he was a devil and her own experience with him were one thing; seeing the number of people who danced to his tune, the sheer number of lives he used and abused for his own gain, was quite another. She would be lying if she said it left her unaffected. There was no joy for her in the suffering of others, yet knowing she helped cause it did not weigh as heavily on her conscience as she thought it would have. And that worried her more than anything. Little had she realised how jaded she had become. It was not something she liked about herself. Worse was the occasional small twinge of admiration she sometimes felt. He truly was a master at a craft she had only dabbled in with her small thieving crew.

The first time she had returned to his home, she had expected herself to look at him differently, to see him for who he truly was. Yet that night, and every night after, all she saw was the devil who had held her when she was scared, who could be so tender, who she so enjoyed challenging. No matter how far he sent her, no matter who she spied on or what terrible fate she learned of, it did nothing to ease her heartache.

So she tried to avoid it altogether. On the occasions he sent her somewhere she had never been to, she spent whatever time she had left after finishing her job exploring the area, feeling like a tourist who was trying to see a city in one day. Anything to delay her return.

But there wasn't much for her in Dewhaven. She missed Amelie, but had no idea if the woman was still in the city. And she doubted she would find the thief in the few hours she had remaining.

Her feet walked her to the large park. It only took her a minute to spot Nial, trowel in hand as he worked away in the dirt, waving aside the falling leaves as they threatened to get in the way. She sat down on a bench near him, waiting for him to finish. He nodded at her once to acknowledge her presence but didn't look up from his work. Nial had never been considered a warm person.

She waited patiently, wrapping her cloak around her, letting the dark material absorb the warmth of the early autumn sun.

"So, you're still alive." Nial finally joined her on the bench, wiping the dirt off his hands on his trousers. "A pleasant surprise."

"You didn't think we would pull it off?"

Nial snorted. "I was fairly confident you would manage to break into the Chambers. Less so that the devil would let you live after I confirmed with Jay how to get the reliquary out." He turned to face her. "How are you alive? And how are you?"

Ailith shrugged. "Arkhael let me live to pay off a debt that can never be repaid. Life with him is . . . complicated." She stared off into the distance, desperate for someone to share her heartache with. But Nial was not that person.

"Complicated?" He raised an eyebrow at her. "You know, Amelie came by not too long ago to return the key I gave you. When you weren't with her, I assumed the worst. But she told me you might yet have a chance with the devil. I thought she had lost it, but now you are saying life is complicated when I am expecting stories of torture."

Ailith ignored his unspoken query. "Amelie came by? How was she?"

"Fine. Sad but fine." Nial shrugged. "One of her friends might be dead, the other is basking in being hailed a hero. How would you feel?"

"Awful," Ailith said through gritted teeth. Poor Amelie. She deserved so much more. Maybe she could convince Arkhael to let her visit the woman. It was not a conversation she looked forward to having with him.

"Jay confirmed with you he got the reliquary out. Were you in on his plan?"

Nial nodded. "He came to me one night and explained how you had hinted at getting another party interested. A smart idea." He gave her an appraising look. "Your friend's biggest fear was not getting in, it was getting out. I agreed to have an escape route ready for you all, should you make it out alive."

"If you knew of his plan, then why didn't you try harder to help us?" Ailith looked at him and knew she wouldn't like the answer before he even opened his mouth. The expression on his face was cold.

"As much as I wanted you to succeed, I would not help you in potentially delivering a powerful reliquary to the devil Arkhael."

It stung, but she couldn't pretend she didn't understand his motivations.

"You're familiar with him?" she asked instead.

"I know off him," Nial responded vaguely. "So, you want to tell me what is actually going on between you and the devil?"

"Not really." She gave him a wry smile.

"Then why are you here, Ailith?"

"Can I not be here to visit an old friend?"

He snorted. "We both know that's unlike you."

"Fine." Ailith rolled her eyes at him. "I am delaying my return because I don't want to go back yet, and I was curious how things were in the city after I left."

Nial's smug expression annoyed her unreasonably much. Maybe going to see him had been a mistake.

"To answer your unspoken query: The city moves as it always has. Most people are barely aware that something happened at the Chambers. An investigation into the Children is underway, but as with all things politics, it will take time for it to get off the ground, and I doubt much will come of it. Dorian Redwing is also being investigated as a person of interest."

Ailith blinked. She had entirely forgotten about the man who had initially opened and stolen the box. So much had happened that seemed more urgent, more important. His fate had left her entirely unfazed. It was disappointing to hear that the people who set out to kill a part of the population might not face justice, but she hadn't truly expected otherwise.

"What of the disease? Is that at least entirely gone?"

Nial nodded. "To the people here, it has been nothing more than a rumour. Little do they know . . ." His voice faltered briefly. "I felt it take hold the evening you and your group went to the Chambers, but I think I was alone in noticing it. There are no other druids here that match my skill, and we both know that users of arcane magic are almost blind to the wonders of their own body. I knew you had destroyed the box when my body became violently sick, and several others in the city appeared to have similar symptoms, like food poisoning. We were lucky. Few people had heard what happened down south, but I sent out birds immediately after your arrival. Many didn't make it, and those with symptoms that were out of control . . ." He shrugged. "You know what fear makes people do."

She did indeed.

"Thanks, Nial. I'll leave you to your garden." She got up off the bench.

"Ailith." At the quiet sound of his voice, she turned. He hadn't spoken her name like that in a long time, like she was more than just a student. "There are still opportunities here for you. If you can break free of him, I can provide you a home here."

Ailith bit her lip before she responded. "Don't judge me too harshly, Nial, but I don't know if I want to break free of him."

"I feared as much." He rose. "He's a *devil*, Ailith. You realise that him letting you live means he has a purpose for you?"

Ailith hesitated before she spoke. "I appreciate your warning, but I am aware of the risks I am taking."

Before she could leave, Nial grabbed her by the arm. Surprised, she looked at him.

"Think of the opportunities. Arkhael is powerful. He has just gained the enmity of an entire religious organisation. Why not use that? Find out what he wants from you, what his plans are. You could help rid the Realms of an incredibly powerful archdevil."

With a frown, Ailith yanked her arm free.

"You want me to work with the Children? After everything they have done?"

"You don't have to work with them. Use them. They owe you for what they have done to you."

The direction the conversation had taken was leaving a bitter taste in Ailith's mouth.

"You misunderstand me, Nial. I don't want to free the Realms of Arkhael. And the last thing I want is to have anything to do with the Children. As far as I care, they can all rot."

Nial narrowed his eyes at her, then nodded.

"If that is what you choose, so be it. If you will excuse me, Ailith. I have somewhere I need to go." With that, he nodded his farewell.

Ailith was glad when he left, glad she didn't have to see the obvious disapproval on his face.

He had never approved of the path she had chosen in life, but it stung more this time for reasons she didn't quite understand. Something felt off. The morose feeling stayed with her even as she left the city.

Maybe that was why she wasn't aware of her tail until she was well outside the city gates. Only then did she realise that the sound of hooves was keeping pace with her.

She palmed the small ruby. The portal took a few seconds to open, and judging by the sound of the hooves, her pursuers would reach her before she could step through. So she groaned and turned around.

Her blood went cold. Behind her rode five people on horseback. All five of them carried large shields bearing the emblem of the Children of Illumination, the large golden mace. Holy warriors. Those were not good odds, and she doubted it was coincidence.

"May I ask what business you have with me?" she asked, raising her voice.

One of them, a tall woman, rode forwards and dismounted. The others followed suit.

At least you'll be free of him if you die here.

She grimaced at the thought.

"Call forth your master," the woman at the head of the group ordered.

It was a trap for Arkhael. They weren't after her. Five holy warriors to try and catch a devil. She glanced over them. Three women and two men. All equally heavily armed and armoured. All looked ready for battle. Would he survive it?

She balled her left fist and cursed Arkhael's name and the grip he still had on her.

I hate you. And I might die for you here.

"I don't think I will."

The woman took a step forwards.

"Girl. There are five of us and one of you. We don't need you alive."

Ailith held up a hand. "That's close enough. I don't wish to be responsible for the death of the five of you. But one more step, and you'll have forced my hand."

She watched two of them exchange a look of sceptical surprise, a red-haired woman and a balding man. Their leader had no such misgivings. She stepped forwards and drew her sword.

Ailith responded immediately. If she wanted to have a fighting chance, there was no space for mercy. She called her lightning down in one concentrated bolt, sending another curse Arkhael's way as she did so.

I don't even know why I am protecting you.

The woman's eyes widened at the instantaneous reaction just before her corpse hit the ground, leaving the grass under her blackened and smoking.

The others moved immediately. They were no ordinary mercenaries, Ailith was quick to note. They were well practised and knew how to work together.

Before she had the chance to call forth another bolt of lightning, the red-haired woman had drawn a small crossbow, and Ailith had to duck to get to safety. The other three were on her in an instant. She barely had time to dodge a glowing sword that swung her way. From the corner of her eye, she noticed the two men trying to circle her. Being pincered would certainly mean death. She rolled backwards, away from the three of them, caressing the ground as she did so. Thorny spikes jutted upwards. The woman who had swung at her crushed the spikes below her with her shield, the thorns sizzling as she did so.

Fucking priests.

The balding man followed her example, but less successfully so. One of her thorns pierced between the armoured plating. He broke it off with a cry, but not before the paralytic poison had started its work. The man froze where he stood. Ailith summoned one of her vines and yanked him forwards by his feet. Unable to move, the man fell. She heard a gurgle as one of the thorns pierced his throat.

The second man however, had managed to jump forwards. She tried to move away from his blade, but a searing pain at the back of her knee let her know she had not been fast enough. Ailith tried to assess it as quickly as she could and became aware of the torn muscle even before her magic picked it up when she tried to stand on the leg and nearly fell over. It was useless.

Fuck.

A sudden force hit her in the shoulder as the red-haired warrior launched another bolt, too far away to be bothered by the thorns. Ignoring it, Ailith tried to steady herself and went for the man, aware that the woman trapped by her spikes was slowly making her way over as well. He was too close. She couldn't heal herself without giving him another free swing. So instead, she summoned her lightning again, bringing it down on him. Recognition flashed in his eyes, and he brought his shield up, gritting his teeth against the pain, his other hand spasming uncontrollably. Ailith saw the opportunity and conjured another vine to drag the sword away from him. Before she had a chance to capitalise on the opening, she noticed the woman had made it out of her thorns.

Instinctively, she took a step back, only for her torn leg to give out. She stumbled, and fell, pain shooting through her body. With an outstretched hand, she caught the blade that was coming for her throat, willing the skin of her palm to thicken like bark.

The blade did not cleave through her as it would have, but her right hand burned all the same, her arms straining with the effort of holding the sword up.

She heard the swing before it hit her. The man she had thought disarmed swung a small warhammer her way. It hit her in the back with a sickening crack, launching her body to the side with the force of the swing.

Don't come for me, Arkhael.

Chapter 42

Something pulled at his awareness. He ignored it as he pored over the details of Tibia's capitulation. Four times, he had forced them to revise it. But finally, he deemed it good enough.

The pull became stronger. Arkhael sighed and put the quill down, rubbing his temples. What was it Ailith had said? Something about him working too hard to be a hedonist? He looked over at her empty chair. He missed her. Even when she had just been quietly reading, she had brought a life to his halls. They seemed so empty when she was gone.

"Don't come for me, Arkhael."

He shot up, ink bottle clattering off the table. Something in her voice made his blood run cold. He focused on her. The moment he felt her presence, *and it was frighteningly weak*, he teleported himself to her.

He barely had a chance to take in the scene. Two dead. A woman aiming a crossbow, another walking over with a sword in hand, and a man whose hammer was inches away from Ailith's head. She was bleeding. Blood pooled around her legs, and she held herself at an odd angle. Her dazed eyes shot to him.

He raged.

Ash. He willed the man to be ash. Hellfire shot forth, incinerating the man before he could deliver the killing blow. Arkhael rushed over to Ailith, helping her up with one arm.

Shielding her with his body, he faced the approaching woman. As she lifted her arm again to bring down her sword, he rushed forwards, claws reaching for her face, only to be rebuked by an aura of divine magic. Even her armour appeared to be holy. But the sword did not hit him either. One of Ailith's vines held the woman's hand.

He felt coughs wrack her body as she whispered her incantation, and he couldn't help himself. Despite knowing he should keep his eyes on their enemy, he turned. The concern for her seemed to choke him. She was coughing up blood, but her eyes glowed green as she struggled to keep the vine in place. A whizzing sound warned him of an incoming arrow, and he curled one of his wings around her, feeling it hit the leathery membrane instead.

"Arkha . . . el."

Ailith's voice reached him just in time. The woman behind him, with her sword arm still restrained, had dropped her shield and replaced it with a dagger. Ailith's warning prevented it from hitting him in the back, but instead, it tore through the muscle and membrane of his other wing. With a loud roar, he turned to her. She, too, would be ash. Hellfire licked his fingers as he threw it at her, and without a shield, she had nothing to hide behind as it hit her in the chest, burning through the feeble protection her god had deemed her worthy of.

Before her body could hit the ground and burn, he felt an impact behind him. But no pain.

He turned to catch Ailith as she fell towards him, blood dripping from her mouth, a crossbow bolt sticking out of her back. Panic gripped him. He looked at the one remaining woman.

She deserved to die.

They didn't have time.

He transported them out, back to his home.

"Ailith. Ailith, look at me." He tried getting her attention, but her eyes had closed, her breath rattling.

"No . . ." he whispered. His heart refused to believe what he was seeing. *She can't die.*

Paralysed, he held her body, felt her breathing slow. He screamed, a guttural noise filled with anger. At the Children, but mostly at himself.

He wouldn't let her die.

But he could not heal this. His thoughts raced. No healers were in his employ or owed him favours. And what healer would help an archdevil?

He looked down at Ailith again. She had known one, but he had nothing on the man. Arkhael would have to bargain for his goodwill and accept whatever else might be asked of him. It was either this small chance or Ailith's death. Gently, he laid her on the floor.

"Don't die while I am gone, little thief."

Resisting the temptation to appear in Nial's living room, Arkhael made sure to look human again before he rapped on the druid's door. Nial seemed to take an eternity to appear and open it, and when he did so, there was a glint of recognition in his eyes.

"No," the elf said resolutely, trying to close the door again.

Before he could do so, Arkhael pushed it back open. "Ailith is dying."

Nial eyed him up warily, and he had no doubt that, like Ailith, Nial saw right through the illusion of his human appearance.

"Not by my hand." Arkhael paused and balled his fists. "Please, can you heal her?"

The druid's eyes widened slightly at his plea before he stepped out with a sigh, closing the door behind him.

"Never show up at my house again, devil." He held out a hand, and Arkhael could not rush them back fast enough.

Ailith was where he had left her, her body still.

She's a druid. She's hardy. She can't be dead.

He repeated it to himself like a mantra while Nial rushed over and let off a string of elven curses. His hands glowed as he examined Ailith's still form, then dulled again.

"I want a favour once she's recovered. Unconditional. In writing." Nial's eyes bore into his, and Arkhael briefly wondered if this was why devils never pursued druids. All of them seemed to be too stubborn.

"You are bartering now, druid? She doesn't have the time."

"Then you had better decide quickly."

Arkhael looked at the elf, looked at who he truly was. Cold. Pragmatic. Keen. *Too keen*. This Nial might not want Ailith to die, but he would let her if Arkhael did not agree to his terms. And he had come up with those terms awfully quickly.

There was little choice. Arkhael would have given him anything.

"Deal." He cringed inwardly as the word left his mouth, at the amount of power he had given this stranger. If Nial played his cards right, he could destroy him.

A problem for later.

"Tell me what happened while I work."

Arkhael gritted his teeth at the commanding tone.

"I don't know. When I arrived, two of the Children of Illumination lay felled on the ground. The three remaining had cornered her."

Nial's glowing hands stilled as he looked up. "She took on five of the Children?" He whistled between his teeth. "They were stupid to not go in better prepared and let her get away."

Arkhael narrowed his eyes but didn't question what the elf meant. Now was not the time.

Nial carefully rolled Ailith over. "I need you to pull out this arrow."

He did as he was asked, ignoring the tremor in his hands and Nial's querying stare.

Although the druid's magic was similar to Ailith's, Arkhael was surprised by how differently the two of them worked. Where Ailith's touch always seemed gentle and subtle, this elf's magic was almost harsh in the way that he moved his hands and chanted under his breath.

He balled his fists, hating that he couldn't help, that all of this was out of his control.

The healing seemed to last an eternity, and when Nial's hands finally stopped glowing, he could barely restrain his impatience. The elven man sat back, wiping the sweat from his face.

"The good news is that she will live."

Arkhael let out a long breath.

"The bad news is that I cannot heal her any further."

"What do you mean?"

Nial smiled grimly. "The Children are effective at what they do." He gestured at the left side of Ailith's back. "Most of the ribs on this side were shattered, and some had punctured the lungs. She was drowning in her own blood, and one of her lungs couldn't expand to give her the air she needed."

A coughing fit tore through Ailith's body.

"Shhh." Nial put a hand on her back, chanting quietly until Ailith stopped.

He looked back up at Arkhael.

"The lungs are healed. As is the internal bleeding caused by both the broken bones and the arrow in her back. The ribs are . . ." He paused. "Back in place. I have repaired the bones as much as I can. But they are fragile. Any overexertion, including this coughing, could break them again. She will need constant monitoring." His eyes searched Arkhael's face, and he could see the judgement in them.

"Are you able to provide her that, Arkhael? Can you be there for her until she wakes up and is able to heal herself? She will need someone to hold her down when she coughs. To wipe away the blood that she will continue to cough up. To ensure that she doesn't fall entirely unconscious and drown in her own saliva. I could take her home with me."

Arkhael nearly snarled at the elf. "She's staying here."

Nial narrowed his eyes. "I see. Interesting. In that case, I will need you to get the following."

He received a list of items that he immediately passed on to Marius.

Nial cleaned and bandaged Ailith's other wounds, assuring him that they were nothing to worry about. Then created a brace around Ailith's ribs and showed Arkhael how to make one himself. It was humiliating, and he bore it all with gritted teeth. Finally, Nial helped him move Ailith to his bedchambers. He noted the elf's raised eyebrow when he asked if Arkhael wanted to lay her on his sofa and he told Nial to bring her to his bed instead. Something about his behaviour irked Arkhael. He didn't trust the elf. The flavour of his soul was foul, and he seemed to know more than he was letting on.

Once Ailith was in his bed, the elf began muttering once more.

"Don't be alarmed," was all the warning he gave Arkhael as a bright light shone from his hands.

Ailith opened her eyes, and it was as if a warmth returned to his home after a long winter he hadn't been aware of. She truly lived.

Nial said something to her, and to his dismay, Arkhael could not understand the language. He had made a point of knowing almost all spoken languages, but this was something he was entirely unfamiliar with. Not a single word sounded close to anything he knew. When Ailith barely audibly responded in the same tongue, he realised it must be the sacred language of the druids. Inwardly he cursed their habit of not keeping written records.

Both druids stopped talking and looked at him, and he didn't need to know what had been said to know that he had been the topic of conversation.

A strange anxiety filled his stomach as he met Ailith's eyes, unsure what he would find there.

Pain. There was so much pain in that single look she gave him that he ignored Nial, ignored what the elf might see, and rushed to her side.

He reached out a hand to touch her cheek, then paused. Only a few days ago, she had told him not to touch her.

A few days ago, you were a fool.

He reached out, maintaining eye contact, and gently touched her cheek, a question in his eyes, looking for any sign of repulsion. There was none. Instead, she sighed as he stroked the side of her face. The tension in his stomach slowly unfurled.

He leaned forwards, brushing his lips over her forehead.

"You'll live," he promised her quietly.

Ailith opened her mouth to speak, but no words came out. With a sudden exhale, she closed her eyes, whatever energy had been granted to her by magical means leaving her body again.

He turned to Nial, who was giving him a quizzical look, and summoned parchment and quill.

"One favour. Unconditional."

Nial nodded, still staring at him. "Why did you want her saved?"

Arkhael narrowed his eyes. "That knowledge was not part of our deal." He snapped his fingers, conjuring up a portal for the druid.

Nial shrugged. "Suit yourself. I would rather she be your handful than mine." A small smile played over the elf's lips. "You should ask her about that someday."

With that, he left.

Arkhael let out a long breath. He may well have just toppled the empire he had worked so hard to build up. His gaze went to the woman in his bed. He would do it again if it meant she would live.

CHAPTER 43

Ailith woke as Arkhael held her down through another coughing fit, dabbing away the trickle of blood at the corner of her mouth.

Her eyes shot open.

"I thought I told you not to touch me."

As if she had burned him, Arkhael withdrew his hands.

"Where is Nial?"

Clenching his fist, he schooled his expression, hiding that she had added yet another dagger to his heart.

"He left after healing you."

Ailith narrowed her eyes at him. "And how long ago was that?"

"A few days," he answered coolly.

"Impossible."

He raised his eyebrows. "Are you calling me a liar?"

"Someone would have had to take care of me. And we both know that's beneath you."

He nodded. "You're right. It is." He leaned back in his chair. He didn't have the energy to argue this with her. She was smart enough to draw her own conclusions in her own time.

He had moved one of his big armchairs and the small table into his bedchambers so he could work while watching over her. Nial had been right about one thing: the last few days had been exhausting. He hadn't dared join her in his bed, lest the mattress move too much and he inadvertently hurt her. But even in his chair, he hadn't rested much. Worry kept him alert, and the few times he had closed his eyes, she had woken him.

"Are you hungry?" She would need food to regain her strength.

He watched her eyes flit to his chair and the table with paperwork next to it, then back to him.

"You look awful. Taking care of me looks terrible on you."

He quirked an eyebrow at her, relief washing over him when he noticed the hint of a smile.

"Pot, kettle. Nearly dying doesn't look good on you either."

She reached for him, and he carefully took her hand, closing his eyes in relief as her fingers entwined with his.

"Arkhael?"

He looked up at her as she spoke his name.

"This is the pain talking."

"Okay?"

"I missed you." She looked away from him as she spoke.

A warmth blossomed in his stomach. "I believe I should apologise."

Ailith shook her head, then groaned in pain at the motion. "Leave it. It can wait."

He squeezed her hand. If she wanted to wait, they could wait.

"Do you want any food?" he asked again.

"Not really." Ailith chuckled drily. "But I am a good enough healer to know when the body needs sustenance."

He ordered Marius to get her some broth and hesitantly brought it over to her.

"Do you need any help?"

"You're not spoon-feeding me, if that's what you're asking." Her tone was dry, but he could just make out the hint of shame that was in there.

Gently, he handed her the warm bowl, but he stayed near her. If she needed his help, he would be there. Silence fell over them as she forced herself to eat. He watched her like a hawk, taking the bowl from her when she indicated she was done. Barely had he put it down when coughs wracked her body again. He rushed over, gently restraining her so she couldn't hurt herself further.

"I'm fine." Ailith's voice was hoarse when she spoke up. "I'm awake, I can stop my body from destroying itself."

Reluctantly, he let go of her, not sure what to say.

"Why don't you take a moment for yourself?" She rubbed her temples.

"Are you sure?" He hadn't struggled through the last few days only to lose her to her own pride.

She gave him a small smile. "You look like shit. Go and wash. I'll be fine." As he was about to speak, she added, "I'll call you if anything is wrong. I promise."

Begrudgingly, he left her side. She was right. He looked and felt awful. Even so, he made sure to be quick as he freshened up.

405

When he returned, her eyes were closed, but he could tell she was awake by the sound of her breathing.

"Did Nial tell you how long I was supposed to stay in bed for?"

"Another two days at least," he responded as he put on a fresh shirt and tied his hair back. Walking over to the mirror, he admired himself, straightening the cuff of his left sleeve. Much better. Only the tightness of his jaw betrayed how tired he truly was.

"Curse that man." Ailith groaned. "Two more days will kill me with boredom."

Arkhael walked back to his chair. "Objectively, as a healer, is your prognosis different?"

From the frown on her face, he could tell that it wasn't.

"I would have trusted his judgement over my own regardless." Ailith sighed and reached out as he sat down. He took her outstretched hand and squeezed it, not understanding why it made him feel so much better.

"He hinted that the two of you have a history."

Ailith rolled her eyes. "Of course he would." Another coughing fit rattled her lungs. Arkhael held her down, ignoring her weak protests and stroking her hair until she had settled again.

"It's a . . . long story." Her hesitation was obvious. He didn't press it. Now was not the time to force things. But then Ailith sighed. "I guess I do owe you for saving my life. Again."

He wanted to tell her that she didn't need to, but she had already started talking.

"Remember when you asked me how a druid becomes a thief?"

He nodded, thinking back to how he had bent her over the side of his bath afterwards.

"I told you I wasn't born a druid? They took me in because they found me after the Nimble Weed had awakened a magic in me that they recognised as their own. However, I wasn't truly a druid, no matter how patiently and how long they taught me.

"Our grove leader grew impatient with me as I grew up with them. Some aspects of their training I excelled at, almost more than they did." With a quick gesture, she grew a vine down from the ceiling. It swiftly shrivelled and turned to dust. "No druid can create nature where there is none. I have never had an issue with it. But there were other aspects where my skills were lacking severely. I was never able to communicate with animals. They never liked me either. And I won't mention the disaster that my attempts at shapeshifting were." Another coughing fit forced her to pause.

"After years of impatience and failure, tempers rose. I was sick of being called weak simply because I was different. To cut a long story short, we had a falling out that became . . . magically violent. I tried to prove that some of my magic was stronger than theirs and I proved it too well. Their leader died. I got exiled." Ailith's eyes were distant as she continued. "I became a hermit. Druid groves have ways of communicating. There was no other grove that would take me in, so I decided to train by myself, to get stronger." She laughed. "I wish I could say that I had some deep and profound spiritual revelation. But in truth, I got bored. I had never liked sitting still. Being a hermit turned out not to be for me."

Arkhael smiled with her. "And here I see you sit in the same chair for days."

"Odd, isn't it?" Ailith nodded. "That out of all places, I find my wanderlust settles here."

His smile faded. There was something in her words that made his heart stutter.

"Either way," she continued, "I came upon a small village and, obviously, I had nothing. So I stole a horse that had already been saddled. I still remember the adrenaline rush as I galloped away, the high I rode when I realised I had stolen something without getting caught. Jay and Amelie often accused me of being addicted to the high and to the gambling. They were absolutely correct." She cleared her throat.

"Many years and many scars later, I learned the hard way that I needed to know how to heal myself. It was one of the aspects of druidic magic that I had never mastered. Something even the children of the grove were better at than me. But I knew that no grove would teach me. Enter stage Nial. He's an odd one for a druid. More in tune with people than most, and perfectly suited for his role as ambassador between groves and city. We quickly became close. Very close." Ailith cleared her throat, and Arkhael felt a sharp pang of jealousy and anger towards the other druid. "And we fell apart equally as quickly." Ailith laughed again, grabbing her ribs as she did so. "I drove him insane with how restless I was, how often I got in trouble, and how often he had to bail me out. Equally, I hated how pragmatic he was, and how cold-hearted he sometimes seemed. Despite that, he agreed to teach me. I have never had a sterner nor a better teacher. He was more open-minded, more practical, than the druids at the grove and realised very quickly that my magic worked differently. He figured out how my connection with nature worked, how it differed from his own, and then taught me in a way that worked for me. If he hadn't agreed to teach me, I would never have made it this far in life." She fell quiet. "So, there's the answer to two of your questions."

Arkhael had barely dared to breathe, worried Ailith would stop her tale.

"I'm sorry you had to take care of me. You should have asked Marius. Or left me with Nial."

He looked up sharply. "Don't you dare apologise for that. I would entrust your care to no one else."

She was still avoiding his gaze.

"Tell me what happened, Ailith. How did you find yourself in that predicament?"

He stroked the back of her hand, trying to soothe some of the tension he felt in her body. How he wished he could take her in his arms.

"I'm not entirely sure." She frowned. "I was already out of the city when I realised I was being followed. At that point, I was on the road. I knew that if I started running or tried to return here, I would only give whoever it was an opening to strike. So I turned to see who was following me. I never expected to see five warriors behind me. They asked for you." Finally, she looked up at him. "They wanted me to get to you. I refused, and they wouldn't take no for an answer. What I don't understand is how they knew we are connected."

Arkhael furrowed his brow. "Did you tell anyone about me outwith the group you were working with?"

Ailith shook her head. "Nial. But no others. I"—she cleared her throat—"I saw him before the attack, but I doubt he would have done something so drastic that it could kill me."

Arkhael wasn't so sure, but he kept the thought to himself. She thought highly of the man, and he didn't need to add to her worries. "They could have seen me when I retrieved you from the Chambers." He didn't believe that would have caused the attack and made a mental note to have Nial investigated further. That the Children of Illumination now had an interest in him didn't surprise him in the slightest, but their knowledge of Ailith's connection to him was alarming.

"Did you kill them all?" Ailith had closed her eyes, but the sudden fire in her voice caught him off guard.

"No, one got away from me. It was either you or her. But once you have recovered, I will kill her."

"No!" Her eyes shot open. "Let me be the one to kill her. Please?"

"If you wish," he responded without hesitation. "I will keep an eye on her. After you have recovered, she will be all yours."

Ailith closed her eyes again, and he watched her drift off, her hand still in his. Even in her anger, she had refused to give him up, knowing that she might pay for it with her life. Why would she do that? Her actions conjured up all sorts of conflicting feelings in him.

CHAPTER 44

A ilith watched Arkhael's form as he rested in his chair. He hid the exhaustion well, but she could see it in every part of him. Guilt and shame crept into her stomach at the thought of him taking care of her for these past few days. Followed by an intense, burning anger. She conjured the face of the red-haired woman into her mind. Once she was able to move again, she would find her and inflict every ounce of pain upon her that she had felt these last few days. She would send a message to the Children so strong, they would not even consider coming after Arkhael again.

She could feel a cough coming on and tried to still herself, her body wracked with pain as her lungs contracted. Arkhael did not wake. His black lashes cast a shadow onto his high cheekbones. Her eyes travelled to his lips, his sharp chin, the rhythmic rising of his chest. She narrowed her eyes. One of his wings had a large tear in it. Again, she cursed the Children, and she vowed that she would heal it the moment her magic had recovered enough. Currently, it was taking all her energy to keep her own ribs from falling apart. Every bit of magical energy she had, her body sent inwards. Her druidic magic constantly trying to heal herself meant she barely had any left. It made healing a slow process, leaving her drained. Next time she woke, she would try to save her magic for him.

He shifted slightly, the horns on his head gleaming in the light streaming through the window.

She was still angry with him, but it had only taken one look to know that he had indeed sat next to her bed for days. Before she had told him to freshen up, he had barely looked like himself. His hair had fallen out of its bonds, his shirt had been wrinkled, and his skin had an almost ashen appearance. If his image was truly more important than she was, he would not have looked so dishevelled. Whether it was for the value of her soul or something else, he clearly cared. They would have words, and she still wanted to rage at him, but it could wait. Right now, she was content to simply bask in his presence.

She had been terrified when he showed up to save her, terrified that he would take a blow meant for her. And he almost had. Her heart ached at the thought.

Is this something that you should finally acknowledge?

Annoyed, she pushed the thought away.

You nearly died. Is this truly something you want to ignore?

With a groan, she closed her eyes. What difference would it make to acknowledge how she felt? He was an archdevil. A beautiful and tempting archdevil whose company she happened to enjoy more than she had enjoyed anything else in her life. In whose home she had managed to find a peace that she had found nowhere else.

Fine. It might be love.

Grumpily, she rubbed her temples. It made no difference. He would never be able to return the feeling.

Does he need to?

She considered Arkhael's sleeping form. Would his desire for her soul be enough in the absence of love?

It didn't matter. Love or not, desire or not, she was stuck with him until her debt had been repaid, and she was well aware that it likely never would be.

She might as well accept that he desired her in his own way. Yet she couldn't help but think that it felt like accepting scraps when what she truly wanted was to sit at a table she could never join.

With a sigh, she realised that just looking at him had set her stomach aflutter. She missed the feeling of his arms around her, his hands stroking her hair. The way he seemed to want to hide her away from the world.

Fine. Maybe you have it bad for him.

The moment her magic had recovered enough, she set herself the task of healing Arkhael's torn wing, ignoring his concern for her own health. The wound was much smaller than the one she had inflicted on him, and although the leathery skin was challenging to heal, she managed it in only a day. Withdrawing her hand from his shoulder blade, she took a deep, shuddering breath.

"You shouldn't have," Arkhael said with a frown, stretching his wing to test the new skin. "You should have used that energy on yourself."

"Let's say you owe me one?"

He glared at her. "Don't you dare haggle with me now."

Ailith rolled her eyes. "Fine. A question, then?" She continued before he could respond. "Stop sleeping in the chair? Your bed is big enough, and my bones are no longer so brittle that you shifting the mattress risks breaking them."

Rising from the chair, he sighed but conceded. "You're incorrigible."

Ailith didn't even pretend to avert her eyes as he undressed, cursing the Children once again for stopping her from reaching out and worshipping him like she wanted to. He caught her eyes on him and cocked an eyebrow as he joined her in the bed.

"You cannot convince me that your bones are strong enough for that." With a flick of his fingers, the torches in the room extinguished.

Ailith bit the inside of her cheek. This was dangerous territory. She had told herself not to bring any of this up yet, but he had broached the topic, and she was awful at backing down.

"I didn't think you would be interested." Despite herself, Ailith could not hide the venom in her voice entirely. She could feel him tense across the mattress.

"Lack of interest has never been the problem," he answered eventually.

"Then what is the problem? How could an archdevil doing whatever the fuck they want to do, be a problem for their reputation? Isn't that the whole premise of your existence?" She groaned as her angry shrug only increased the pain in her torso.

A long silence answered her query, until she was convinced that he intended to simply ignore her. But then Arkhael let out a sigh in the darkness next to her.

"I am not any archdevil, Ailith. I am Moloch's third son. Everything I do is being watched, being reported on to my siblings, to my father. Every move I make, every pawn I place on the board, has to be carefully considered. It *has* to be."

For a second, Ailith forgot to breathe. *He is one of the princes of the Hells?*

Arkhael either hadn't noticed her shock, or he decided to ignore it.

"Sure, any devil can seduce a mortal and enjoy their body. The upper circles are full of it, incubi and succubi that do nothing but partake in carnal pleasures. Someone of my standing? I could seduce you, but I certainly shouldn't enjoy you, let alone enjoy anything more intimate than just sex. Even if I—" He cut himself off.

"Even if you do," Ailith finished the sentence for him.

She stared into the darkness. His predicament made sense now. No wonder he had held back so much, that he had been so hesitant with his exploration of her body. He shouldn't have done any of it, and she could only imagine what the consequences of discovery would mean for his position.

"I'm sorry," she said finally. "I didn't know."

He shifted next to her. "You couldn't have known. I don't give that knowledge away freely."

Silence fell again. Ailith didn't know what to say. If he had been mortal royalty, she could have told him to choose love over duty. But if devils couldn't know love, then there was no point in demanding that of him. And she doubted the pleasure he got from her body was worth *that* much.

The mattress next to her dipped, and she tensed her muscles to stop herself from moving. But then his lips were on hers, and no pain in the world could have stopped her from enjoying that moment. The kiss he gave her was soft and careful, and only when she parted her lips for him did he push further into it.

When he withdrew, she was left breathless.

"You were right, though. Why spend centuries building up power if I don't get to reap the benefits of it? If my siblings can squabble and fight over their petty desires, why should I not allow myself the one thing I want? What were your exact words again? 'Fuck what they think'?"

Ailith didn't know what to say to that. Her heart was thundering in her chest, and breath seemed to have left her altogether.

She felt him draw back at her silence. "That is, if the subject of my desires can forgive me? I believe you called me a coward and disgusting." The hurt in his voice was poorly masked. It spurred her into action. She reached out in the darkness and squeezed the arm she found.

"If I could move, I would kiss you. As it is, you'll have to make do with my words alone." She smiled wryly. "Of course you have my forgiveness. I am yours, remember?" The arm she was holding relaxed noticeably. Her own heart had left her chest. Closing her eyes, she let out a long breath. *He still desires you.*

"Do you truly understand what that entails, though?" His hand stroked her cheek in the darkness. "I am cruel, Ailith. I extort, I torture, I kill. Anything for my own gain and ambitions. And I have never dreamed small. I take pleasure in the pain of others. Is that something you can live with?"

She had asked herself the same question. And every time, she had reached the same impossible answer.

"Just don't ask me to take joy in it," she said quietly.

"You may have to be ruthless. Life here is hard. You have only seen—"

"Arkhael." She cut him off. "Don't insult my intelligence. I knew I was visiting a devil when I donned that stolen necklace, and I did it regardless. Nothing has changed in that regard."

He took the hand she had put on his arm and brought it to his mouth, kissing the tips of her fingers.

"I'm still not sure if I am angered or impressed by that," he murmured, and she could hear the smile in his voice.

"Both?" she offered.

He chuckled, and silence fell between them again. A comfortable one this time. Arkhael was still holding onto her hand, and she was almost scared to move, lest he let go of her.

"This is so wrong, isn't it?"

He hummed in agreement. "In every possible way."

CHAPTER 45

Much as she hated feeling helpless, Ailith begrudgingly stayed in bed an extra day. Even with the constant healing, she was not confident in the strength of her bones yet.

The lines where they had been magically forced together still seemed too brittle to her, and she didn't want to risk having to start over again. That it was her own fault for spending the energy healing Arkhael's wing, she pointedly ignored.

She looked at his empty chair. He had reluctantly started going back out again after she assured him he didn't need to constantly be there for her anymore.

His concern was as touching as it was embarrassing, and even if she wanted to try and read, she couldn't focus with him so closely watching her.

Carefully, she tried to sit up, attention focused inwards. It hurt. But she could live with the pain and knew it would heal over time. More importantly, she felt confident that she wouldn't reopen or worsen any wounds by moving.

Smiling to herself, she slowly swung her legs over the side of the bed and stood up, immediately grabbing the bed as she remembered how badly hurt one of her legs had been. It had been healed, but between all the damage in her body and the constant bedrest, she had forgotten how weak the muscles would be. With gritted teeth, she righted herself, limping over to the bathroom door. Every step she took reverberated through her body until she found she could barely breathe. By the time she had reached the door, sweat coated her forehead from both pain and the strain of holding herself upright.

Only a little further.

The last few steps to his pool felt like some of the hardest she had ever taken, but once she sank down into the hot water, she decided it had been well worth it.

Exhausted, she leaned back with her eyes closed. Maybe she had overestimated herself a little bit.

Her head still reeled from what had happened over the last few days. There had been a subtle change after that night. Whatever restraint Arkhael had forced on himself had lessened. He would stroke her cheek in passing, kiss her on the forehead before leaving, and hold her hand as he rested next to her. Yet he was no less intimidating when he spoke of his schemes and ambitions, no less fearsome when he talked of those who tried to thwart him. It was an odd contrast, one she could barely wrap her head around.

And then there was the revelation that Moloch was his father. It certainly made everything that they did so much more precarious for him. There was no doubt in her mind that his father would not approve of their current arrangement. Yet she could not find it in herself to feel guilty. If anything, the last few days had only proven to her what her heart had long known. No matter how impractical, no matter the obstacles, no matter how wrong or how forbidden, the hold he had on her heart was as immutable as the change of the seasons. He had become the very reason she drew breath, and she would fight the King of the Hells himself for him if she had to.

The soft opening of the door and his familiar footsteps pulled her from her thoughts.

"You had me worried when I returned to find an empty bed."

"You worry too easily," Ailith responded without opening her eyes, a faint smile on her lips.

Arkhael did not reply. Instead, she heard the door close and open again.

Confused, she opened her eyes. He had walked in carrying a small tray with a variety of dried fruits, glasses, and a bottle of something.

She watched him set it down next to the poolside, then slowly undress and fold his clothes, tutting at the haphazard way she had thrown her own clothes down on the floor.

Finally, he turned to her.

"Get up," he commanded.

The natural authority in his voice still gave her shivers. Carefully, she rose, hissing slightly at the pain, an eyebrow quirked at him.

He ignored the question in her eyes. Instead, he got into the water and ever so gently pulled her into his arms. Ailith let out a deep exhale as she relaxed against him. She had missed this more than words could describe. For a long time, he just held her, his face buried in her hair while she was pressed against his chest. When he finally spoke, his voice was quiet.

"You should have waited till I was home before walking here."

Ailith wanted to roll her eyes at him, but she was too relieved to be back in his arms again to bother with the gesture.

"It was fine."

Gently, he lifted her chin. "You're a terrible liar."

This time, Ailith did roll her eyes at him. "Just because you decided that I am worthy of your attention again, doesn't mean you also get to decide what I do."

It came out harsher than she intended, and she could see his jaw tense.

"Sorry, that was uncalled for." She brought her hand up to his one holding her chin and took it in hers, kissing the knuckles in apology. "I just don't want you to think of me as weak."

"You took on five of the Children by yourself, Ailith. I would never think you weak." He stroked her cheek and leaned down to kiss her forehead. "Come." Carefully he pulled her down to sit next to him in the water, handing her one of the glasses.

The liquid smelled of honey and spring. She took a small sip. It was mead, an incredibly well-made mead. Looking up, she found Arkhael watching her expectantly.

"This is really good," she said, biting back a smile at how pleased he looked.

He smiled at her. "To your recovery."

She raised her glass in gratitude and let herself lean against him, enjoying the fruit and mead he had brought in in companionable silence.

"I missed this." It was out before she realised what she was saying.

His arm tightened around her, and he hummed in agreement. "I brought you something else. It is waiting for you on the nightstand."

Curious, Ailith cocked an eyebrow.

"You'll see," he said, sounding far too pleased with himself.

Ailith huffed. "Fine, keep your secrets, devil." Only then did she notice how the alcohol had gone straight to her head. "Were you intending to get me drunk?"

Arkhael chuckled in response. "No, although I do like the flush on your face."

"Hmm, I bet you do." She glanced down, her heartbeat quickening for an entirely different reason.

"You should heal more before even thinking of that." Arkhael's voice was quiet in her ears.

Ailith groaned in response. "Easier said than done."

"I know." His hand stroked her arm, knuckles brushing against the side of her breast.

"Tease," she grumbled.

"I don't want you to break your ribs again," Arkhael said, ignoring her complaint entirely. "We can be patient."

She huffed, but only for the sake of it. In truth, she was more appreciative and relieved by his patience than she was willing to admit. Despite the buzz in her head, she took another swig of the mead. Moloch's third son was willing to be patient for her. It was a dizzying thought. From under her lashes, she eyed him up, looked at all the parts of him that were so clearly not human.

Perhaps it was the alcohol that gave her the extra courage, but carefully she reached out to his shoulder, tracing a finger down to where the skin became leathery and transitioned into one of his wings, then following the muscular folded top. A soft tremor went through him at her touch. Even with everything they had done, she had never more than brushed against them. With Arkhael so wary of where his hands and mouth went, she had never dared cross that line. Nerves twirled through her stomach as her fingers danced over the surprisingly soft leathery skin.

She retraced their path back to his shoulders, then brought them up over his neck into his hair, moving herself onto her knees so she could reach up to where his horns were. Unlike his wings, there was nothing soft about them.

"Ailith . . ."

"Hmm?" She continued her exploration, fingers slowly following the curvature towards the back of his head, noting every bump and ridge under her fingertips.

"What are you doing?"

"Feeling how wrong you are," she whispered back, bringing her fingers to the side of his face, the unnaturally sharp cheekbones. Finally, she sat back down, letting herself lean against him again.

"And what did you find?" Arkhael brought his arm back around her, and she noted the tension in his body.

Chuckling slightly, she rested her head against his shoulder. "It seems I may have given myself to a devil. It is wrong in every way."

He huffed, but said nothing.

Ailith closed her eyes. It *was* wrong, and strange beyond belief. She nuzzled slightly further into him, not caring that their union was so incredibly forbidden.

Arkhael cleared his throat. "Tell me something, Ailith. Why didn't you call for me when the Children cornered you?"

Ailith tipped her head up in surprise, the world spinning pleasantly as she did so. "What prompted that question?"

"I simply wondered." He shrugged, and she watched his eyes flick from her own to her lips.

"Kiss me," she demanded.

In an instant, he had closed the small distance between them, his lips against hers, his hand coming up behind her head, claws digging into her hair. She gasped against him as he bit her lip and deepened their kiss, the taste of him mixing with the sweet taste of honey.

With a growl, he slowly withdrew and narrowed his eyes at her. "I'm not a virtuous creature, and you are not making it easy to be patient."

Ailith returned him a dreamy smile, her head swimming from his kiss combined with the mead. "Don't worry, devil, soon I'll follow you into sin as much as you want."

She watched Arkhael clench his jaw and reach for the mead with an almost unsteady hand. If her heart hadn't been racing already, it would have done so now.

"Just answer the question, you impossible woman."

Ailith blinked. "What was your question again?"

Bemused, Arkhael shook his head. "You're drunk."

"Whose fault is that?" she shot back. "And you know I am not as sharp when I am drunk, or I wouldn't be answering your questions without asking for something in return."

He laughed. She would never tire of the sound of it. "Guilty as charged. Now tell me why you took on the Children by yourself."

"They wanted to use me to kill you." Ailith shrugged. "There's no more to it than that."

"We could have fought them together," Arkhael countered. "You could have called for my help."

Ailith closed her eyes. She felt warm and drowsy, and Arkhael's hand was moving in small circles over her arm again. "They seemed like they had a trap prepared for you. I was too worried you would walk into it. I don't think they expected you to show up in my defence, though."

"I'm an archdevil, my dear. I can hold my own." But even though his voice was dry, there was a hint of something else to his tone.

"Or you can hold me." Ailith smiled.

He laughed again. "That's enough alcohol for you. Let's get you back into bed before you pass out."

With a gentleness that belied how strong his touch could be, he helped her up and out of the pool, wrapping a towel around her before supporting her back to his bed. Begrudgingly, Ailith had to admit that it was a lot easier to walk with his assistance, especially when the room started spinning. She had completely forgotten about his other gift for her by the time she finally reached the bed and noticed the strange thing on her nightstand. Even if she hadn't just partaken in more mead than she should have, it would have taken her a few moments to recognise what she was looking at. In a small pot stood what could only be described as a deformed stick with odd bulbous protrusions. The surface of it had an odd near-black colour, fading into a dark purple in the centre of each knob.

Although her mind wasn't as sharp as it usually was, her body *knew*. Almost without meaning to, her magic reached out to it, and she couldn't stop the sigh of relief that left her lips when it found life. Strange and entirely alien, but life nonetheless. Whatever it was, it was young. A shoot of something, with roots that were barely clinging onto the Hellish soil it was planted in. Ailith followed the small roots up into the stem. It needed more nutrients. The odd protrusions on it were flowers. But they were too young yet to open and too weak to grow properly.

"Ailith?"

Blinking, she drew herself back from the plant to find Arkhael staring at her with a look of concern on his face. With what little strength she had left, she brought her arms around him, standing on her toes so she could kiss him.

"Thank you," she murmured quietly, for once not begrudging him how smug he looked at her reaction.

"A warning, though." With one hand, he tugged some of her wet hair behind her ear. "The flowers are—"

"Poisonous. I know." She closed her eyes with a smile, leaning herself against his chest. "I can tell."

Arkhael huffed. "Of course you can."

"Thank you. Truly. You don't know how much this means." Ailith felt the world spin around her slightly before Arkhael caught her.

"I think I do." The words were so quiet, Ailith nearly missed them. She let him help her into his bed. The moment her head touched the soft pillows, the drowsiness took over. With one hand, she reached out to Arkhael, her fingers tangling in the still-wet strands of his dark hair.

He was beautiful.

With a start, she realised she must have said it out loud, because he laughed quietly.

"You are truly drunk, Ailith, which means you are far from recovered yet. Rest and get better."

Reluctantly, she let go.

"Am I truly your dear?" she asked as she closed her eyes. She could feel Arkhael tense next to her, but her head was too fuzzy to understand what it meant.

"I suppose, as my consort, you are." His voice was carefully neutral.

Ailith didn't care. If he said it out loud, it had to be true. With that knowledge, she let the comfortable darkness pull her back into sleep.

CHAPTER 46

As Ailith recovered, Arkhael felt his mood lift. With renewed fervour, he left his home to garner them more souls and influence, knowing she would be waiting for him when he returned. Being able to hold her again, a restlessness that he hadn't realised was there, settled. The moment she was able to walk, she resumed her reading, and he could tell she was happy to be doing something. Her limp was slowly disappearing, and every day, she moved a little bit easier.

And every day, his body ached for her with a need that dwarfed all his other desires. He was careful not to make her feel pressured in any way, aware that she was already overexerting herself. But a constant hunger gnawed at him to claim her, to make her his again. At times, it seemed almost unbearable. During those moments, he held her in his arms, contenting himself with the feeling of her body pressed against his, with the knowledge that the same hunger was reflected in her eyes.

He rubbed his temples as he tried to bring his attention back to the stolen missives he had been reading. A faint sweet scent tickled his nose. Ailith had moved the plant he had gifted her next to the couch, telling him it was more important to have it near her when he was gone than when he slept next to her. Hearing this had pleased him enough that he ignored how it offset the symmetry of the room, even with the small table he had acquired for it. Barely a few days after he had given it to her, it had started to bloom. Big dark purple flowers unfurled their petals one by one until they revealed a maroon centre. There was a beauty to it, he supposed, but he cared little for it. Much more important to him had been the light he had seen in Ailith's eyes when she found it at her bedside. Or the moments he found her sitting next to it with her eyes closed and a calm expression on her face.

Ailith's quiet footfall entered the room, and he looked up to watch her walk in, her hair slightly damp still.

Suppressing the need to bury his claws in it, he extended a hand. Gently, he pulled her onto his lap, against his chest, legs over his, like that day he nearly lost her.

He vowed to himself to keep her close. *Never again.*

She said nothing, but the way in which she settled against him was enough. Some things didn't need words.

The doors to his chambers opened. Marius bowed in the doorway.

"Elrannen is here to visit you, my lord."

Arkhael sighed. Leave it up to her to spoil a nice moment.

He nodded at Marius. "Bring her through."

In his lap, he felt Ailith tense as she tried to get up. He gently pushed her back down.

429

"If she insults you, strike immediately," he murmured in her ear. Even though he had pushed her back down, he could feel how tense her body was, and he couldn't deny that he, too, was somewhat wary. There would be no coming back from this.

Elrannen, Prince of the Seventh Circle, walked into the room shortly after. They were much alike in appearance. She was almost as tall as he was and just as dark of skin. And like him, she was one of the few siblings who took great care in her appearance. Her dark curling locks were pinned above her long white dress. Yet unlike him, Elrannen loved attention. She was one of the Hells' biggest schemers. Once, she had been one of his biggest rivals, both of them vying for every scrap of information. Now, she was mostly the one sibling who insisted on pestering him when all he wanted was to be left alone.

"Brother! I have news!" She paused mid-step, her eyes on Ailith. "Oh my, my, my. So those rumours are true."

He gestured her towards his other chair. "Feel free to sit, sister. What news do you bring?"

"You might want to send your little lapdog away first, dear." Elrannen wrinkled her nose.

"I'm feeling generous, so I'll let that one slide." Ailith turned a page, not looking up from her book.

She was always beautiful. But having her in his lap, so confidently talking back to another archdevil, he craved her with a sudden intensity that caught him by surprise.

Before Elrannen had a chance to react, Arkhael held up a hand. "You heard her. Now out with it."

She sucked in a breath.

He barely listened to her news. The politics in the Hells were as convoluted as they were pointless. Unless someone removed Moloch, there was no point in their petty squabbles. It was why he had renounced his position so long ago. Why fight over the scraps when you could make a play for the throne?

"I don't know why you are bringing this to me," he said without much interest. "I presume you are here for an actual reason?" Elrannen never visited without ulterior motive.

She leaned forwards. "I had heard rumours, Arkhael. About you and a mortal woman. What's your endgame, hmm? This is unlike you, brother."

He gave her a smile dripping with contempt. "My business is my own. As always."

"Oh, come on. She's what? A druid? She can't be that good a bed companion, and you never cared for that anyway. What could she possibly have that you would elevate her to a consort? Unless you think to use her against father?"

He regarded his sister coldly, ignoring the desire to tear her apart. "That, too, is my business and not yours."

Elrannen sighed theatrically and leaned towards Ailith. "Do you have anything to say for yourself, little plaything?"

He almost thought Ailith genuinely hadn't heard it, for she didn't so much as move a muscle before her eyes flared, and with a single word her lightning struck down, a resounding crack echoing through the room.

Elrannen shrieked as the blast hit her, throwing her forwards off her chair. Instantly, Arkhael brought an orb of hellfire to his hand, ready for however his sister might retaliate.

Ailith sat up slightly, and he could feel the tensing of her muscles, knew that holding that position must be agony for her. With a pang of regret, he noticed she was holding the hand which wasn't conjuring the magic slightly behind her back, shielding it from his sister. But if she felt fear, she showed little of it as she spoke.

"I gave you one free pass," she said to Elrannen. "Consider this a warning. The next one will be divine light. That is what I have to say for myself."

The light in her eyes changed from violet to a pure white. Even Arkhael tensed instinctively in response, but it was nothing compared to the look on his sister's face. Her eyes had gone wide with both pain and shock, her skin was scorched, and her wings had been pockmarked by the lightning. She would heal. But the strike had been enough of a warning that Ailith would follow through on the very real threat that she was making. Few devils would risk that.

He dropped the fire. Elrannen wouldn't retaliate. On her face, he saw the glint of fear as she looked at Ailith, *his* Ailith. Briefly, he saw the woman that his spies had reported her to be so seemingly long ago. The ruthless woman who led a trio of criminals and bargained with clients who cared little for her life.

His left arm came up around her possessively, and he rested his hand on her thigh while he looked down at the form of his sister.

Mine.

Elrannen narrowed her eyes at him and opened her mouth to speak, then closed it again with a look at Ailith.

With grim satisfaction, he noted how much effort it took her to get up.

"You have gone too far, Arkhael," she hissed at him.

He merely shrugged, and it was Ailith who answered for him.

"You insulted me in my own home. I let you off with a warning, and then with your life. That is nothing if not generous."

Her home. He felt almost lightheaded. She had called his halls *her home*. His claws dug into her thigh, and he felt her tense against him.

"This will never be your home, woman," Elrannen spat back.

"Enough. You have said your piece, sister. You insulted my consort and are still alive and unscarred. Take solace in that. But you have overstayed your welcome. Leave."

Glaring daggers, and eyes flitting to the divine light that still shone in Ailith's eyes, his sister turned and walked away. Only when she was in the doorway did she pause.

"Father won't let you keep her, Arkhael. Not a powerful and unclaimed soul like hers."

She left before he could respond. In his lap, Ailith sank back against him with a shuddering breath. He looked down at her.

"You did well."

His hands itched to turn her around and undress her, and the sudden possessive need to claim her and feel her around him was overwhelming. He tried to focus on the pain in her eyes, on the exhaustion she must be feeling.

"Not too much?" Ailith asked him with a grimace, and he chuckled.

"The lightning? Not at all. She needed to know that your threats weren't hollow. That you wouldn't hesitate to turn that lightning into something that could truly scar her. And she knew it too." He kissed her hair and inhaled deeply, trying to calm himself. "You were perfect."

"That's not what I meant." She sucked in a breath as she turned slightly to face him better. "Was it okay to call this my home?"

He couldn't resist. He leaned forwards to kiss her, relishing in the way she parted her lips for him in surprise. The way she met him with the same heat he felt. With a groan, he pulled back from her, trying to control the fire in his veins.

"This *is* your home," he murmured against her lips. Her hand came up to the side of his face, and he leaned into the touch, shivering as she slowly trailed it down to his neck, his chest, until she withdrew it again.

"And what of its owner?" she asked quietly.

He tensed. "What of him?"

"Could I call him mine too?" Her voice was barely audible. He could feel her rapid heartbeat as one of her breasts pressed against him. It was hard to think through the haze of lust.

Am I hers?

Part of him struggled to comprehend the question she was asking him, and was alarmed by it. Yet a small voice in the back of his mind grew stronger, tried to make itself heard.

Let go.

Her hand went back to his chest, slowly sliding down the soft material of his shirt until she found where it was tucked into his trousers. With her fingers, she trailed the waistband, then dipped one behind it. He hissed, trying to refocus his thoughts, trying to focus on the implications of what she had asked, on that voice in his head.

A second finger joined her first, and he groaned as her hand slipped under the material, finding his hard lid.

"Ailith . . ." He gasped her name, and she stilled, her grey eyes looking up at him in wonder. His nails dug into the side of his armchair. He wanted to tell her to move, wanted to tear her clothes off and ravage her. But was he *hers*? His hips moved despite his best efforts, pressing against her hand.

She must have seen the turmoil in his eyes, for she put her free fingertips against his mouth.

"Leave the questions for later." Then she moved the hand in his trousers.

Arkhael swore as he tried to hold still while she wrapped her fingers around him. His hips bucked when her thumb rubbed over his tip, spreading the fluid gathering there.

"Ailith." He grabbed her arm, breathing heavily. "Don't." His nails dug into her skin as she tightened her grip. "Your ribs," he barely managed to wring out.

Carefully and slowly, she repositioned herself, straddling him, her hand still around him.

"What about them?"

"I don't want to hurt you." He leaned his head back to avoid looking at her.

"Then don't." She moved her fingers around him, even as he held her arm still.

"You're making it increasingly difficult," he managed through gritted teeth. Her other hand had come down and was working the buttons of his trousers, loosening them one by one until he sprung free.

"Look at me, Arkhael."

He did as she asked. Her grey eyes were dark with desire, her lips slightly parted. She brought her fingers up, and as he gasped at the sight of her, she used the opportunity to slide them into his mouth, never breaking eye contact as she moved both hands to the same rhythm. His nails dug in further, no longer trying to stop her, but trying to force himself to keep still. She withdrew the fingers from his mouth, and he watched as she brought them down her own body, down her own trousers. He imagined the wetness she would find there and groaned, hips trembling.

"Move your hands above your head."

He raised an eyebrow at her demand, head swimming.

Ailith withdrew her hand from her trousers and brought the fingers back to her mouth. Enthralled, he watched her tongue wrap around them.

"Now move your hands, and you can lick them clean next time."

His mouth fell open. Pride tried to break through the desire-fuelled daze he was in.

Ailith wrapped both hands around him, her fingers still wet.

"I know you want to tear these clothes off me." She moved her hands down his shaft, then back up. "I know you want nothing more than to feel me around you." She stilled her movements. "Hands, *Arkhael*."

His hips jerked at the way she said his name. Almost without thinking, he brought his hands up, grabbing the back of the chair above his head, nails digging through the fabric into the wood. He gritted his teeth against the realisation but was too far gone to protest.

"Good." She resumed her ministrations. "Now close your eyes."

He glared at her, unable to find the words to tell her how ridiculous this was. She moved a hand to herself again and pressed her hips against him so he could feel how she was touching herself. A guttural moan left his mouth, and she moaned with him.

"Obey, *Arkhael*, and I'll let you taste me."

"You are torture," he brought out before he rested his head back against the chair and closed his eyes. Indignant anger simmered within him. Once she had recovered, he would punish her for this. He would bend her over the bed and—

The thought was interrupted by the feeling of her fingers pressing against his lips.

Hungrily, he sucked them in, savouring the taste of her. He almost whimpered when she withdrew them again. But then the fingers were replaced by her mouth, and he eagerly accepted the kiss she offered him, sharing her taste between them. The rustle of fabric sounded as she moved, and then both her hands were around him again. Her mouth moved away from him, kissing his jaw, biting his neck.

"I imagine you are angry," she whispered against his ear. "You don't obey, you order." Her hands sped up. "Yet here you are." Then stopped suddenly.

He growled, hips jerking upwards.

She moved, and he felt her weight leave him. Almost, he opened his eyes.

"Disobey and you won't get to feel my mouth around you."

The absolute audacity of this woman.

He groaned and tightened his grip on the chair until his knuckles ached from the strain. Then gasped as he felt her breath on him.

"If you move, this stops. If you disobey, this stops. Show me how good you are at following my orders, Arkhael."

The heat of her mouth around him was almost enough to undo him in that moment. Even with his eyes closed he could imagine the sight of her kneeling in front of him, her lips around him, cheeks flushed. His hips trembled, and he growled with the effort of keeping them still.

She drew back just a little. "Tell me what you want." Before taking him back in again.

He tried to find the words, the ability to speak, while she took him in deeper.

"I want to grab that silver hair of yours so I can see your face as I claim your mouth." Ailith moaned around him, and he shook with the feel of it, struggling to form words. "I want to drag you over this chair as punishment for your audacity and take you until—"

He gasped as she swirled her tongue around him and his hips spasmed of their own accord. Ailith stilled.

"Please don't stop." It was out before he could help himself.

Her voice was hoarse, and he could imagine the tears in her eyes from taking him so deeply.

"Only because you asked so nicely."

Arkhael cursed, but he kept his hands where they were and his eyes closed.

"What else do you want?"

He stilled himself as her mouth came around him again. *How does a mortal woman have so much power over you?*

"I want to hear you moan my name as I fill you. Watch it spill out of you." He shivered at his own words, at the thought of it. "I want to mark you so all will know that you are mine, and mine alone."

Almost his hips bucked again, and he squeezed the chair to hold them still as he felt her take him in further, realising she had taken all of him into her mouth. He needed to see her, wanted to watch her silver hair fall down her face as he disappeared inside her.

"By the Hells, Ailith."

In his mind's eye, he saw her look up at him as she drew back, then took him in again. Her tongue pressed against the base of him, and if she kept this up any longer, he would lose what little control remained him.

Slowly, she withdrew, noting the tension in his hips, and he shivered at the sudden absence of her. But then her weight pressed down on him again. Her hands came up over his, holding the chair, and he could feel her breath near his ear.

"Tell me you want me."

He gasped. "Ailith, I want you." He intertwined their fingers. "I need you to be mine. I need you."

His breath left his body when he felt her slowly sink down on him, shaking with the effort to hold himself still.

Ailith gasped. "I love how completely you fill me," she whispered in his ear, then lifted herself up again. His breath hitched with her slow movements.

"I love how it makes me feel owned by you." She sank down again and bit his neck. "I'm going to come with you inside me." He shuddered at her whispered words. "And then you can claim what's yours."

One of her hands went down, and he could feel her touch herself, moving her hips against him as he struggled to hold still, struggled to hold on. She was going to be his undoing first.

"Ailith, I can't . . ."

Her mouth was on him.

"You *will* hold on."

He groaned as he held back, gritting his teeth until his jaw hurt.

"Open your eyes."

He opened his eyes to watch her climax hit her, her face the perfect image of ecstasy as she tightened around him. Throwing her head back as she groaned his name, her hair falling lose around her face. Control left him at the sight. He let go, releasing inside her, hips trembling as he filled her body, wood creaking under his hands, his breath coming in short bursts.

Fuck.

Stars danced across his vision.

He felt Ailith lean against him, her body shaking while he slowly blinked back to reality.

What has she done to you?

With trembling hands, he let go of the chair. Only then did he notice the splinters in his hands, and he brushed them off on the side of the armrest. His chest was still heaving with unsteady breaths. Disbelieving, he looked down at her as she slowly lifted herself off of him, then leaned against his chest, her breathing laboured.

Worry warred with indignance and embarrassment, but neither won as she looked up at him, a sly smile on her face, cheeks still flushed. Instead, he felt himself bend down to kiss her head and stroke her hair. He could tell she had overexerted herself but said nothing, letting her rest against him and watching as she slowly nodded off in his lap.

Only when he was certain that she was asleep did he sigh and run a hand through his hair.

This impossible woman.

He looked down at her sleeping figure and brought an arm up around her without thinking. A shiver ran through him at what had just happened. If anyone found out . . .

Let go.

Let go of what? But what lay hidden behind that barrier was too immense to consider. He pinched the bridge of his nose.

She had handled his sister well. He doubted Elrannen would bother them again for a long time. But her threat had been real enough, and she was right. Their father would come knocking sooner rather than later. He had managed to keep up the illusion of being a passive player for long enough that Moloch had stopped seeing him as an active threat. It was a facade that had taken him almost as long to build up as it had for him to bring his attempt for the Hand to fruition. One that was threatening to crumble. His actions had drawn too much attention to him already. If Moloch believed that he was keeping Ailith around to use as a weapon against him, he was sure to come for her.

The idea had occurred to him, of course. A divine caster in the Hells, she could be the perfect opportunity. But almost immediately, he had discarded it again. The danger it would put her in would be too great, and after nearly losing her once already, he knew he would never risk letting his father get anywhere near her. As grateful as he was to Ailith for changing the contract he had written, she had been safer when her soul was still pledged to him. Rules dictated that devils were not allowed to reap souls in the mortal Realm unless a mortal pledged themselves to them of their own volition or gave first offence. But those rules said nothing about mortals who willingly travelled to the Hells. Ailith was fair game for anyone who dared to get close enough to her. The protection his reputation offered only went so far.

He frowned. He hadn't been surprised that Elrannen had visited. Even if she didn't have spies tracking his home, he had all but announced Ailith's presence by bringing her to the Second Circle with him. And he refused to regret that. She had needed the comfort nature brought her. It was a shallow excuse. Much more satisfying had been the whispers of others who had seen her arrive with him, reeking of him.

So very clearly his. Arkhael shook his head, trying to drive the memory of what she had done afterwards out of his mind.

He tried to divert his focus back to Elrannen, one of his hands gently stroking Ailith's back as she rested, replaying their conversation in his head. Insults, fishing for information, there was nothing unusual about that. His hand stilled. She had called Ailith his bed companion. He had heard the insult in her tone, presumed she had meant that he kept her for the sex. But why use those exact words? *What if she knows?*

How could she? What he did in his bedchambers shouldn't be known to anyone. There was only one possible answer to that question. *But how?* The man's soul was so bound to him, he wasn't even allowed to *think* about disobedience.

With a quiet groan, he tightened the arm around Ailith. There was nothing in Marius's contract about his consort. And why would there be? Arkhael had never considered taking one.

It was incredibly inconvenient. He would have to find himself a new soul as desperate as Marius had been. But the man couldn't stay. Not if there was even the smallest of chances that Marius could be used as a spy against him. Too much information had already gotten out.

Ailith sighed in her sleep, grasping the fabric of his shirt when he resumed stroking her back, and he couldn't help the faint smile on his lips as he looked down at her.

Resolutely, he decided she was worth it.

Let them find out, he thought grimly. He would let it all burn if he needed to. They would rise from the flames and build themselves a new empire.

CHAPTER 47

"I want to see my friends."

It had taken her a few days to find the courage to ask him, and even now, Ailith chewed the inside of her cheek as she spoke.

Arkhael looked up from the papers he had been reading. The remnants of their breakfast still stood on the table, and he scowled as his gaze travelled over it. Ailith hadn't asked what exactly he had done to Marius, but the lack of replacement was starting to grate on Arkhael's nerves. She hoped it wouldn't influence his answer.

"Absolutely not." He looked back down again, clearly believing that to be the end of their conversation.

He should have known better.

"Why not?" Ailith clenched her jaw, ignoring the disappointment she felt at his quick dismissal. She had expected it, but it still stung.

With a sigh, Arkhael put the papers away. "I nearly lost you last time you left. I am absolutely not letting you go again."

"I highly doubt the Children will attack me a second time." Ailith scoffed. "Plus, that was almost a fortnight ago."

"And what if you are wrong? What if they have a magic user looking for you, ready to alert them once they know you're back in their Realm again?" Arkhael shook his head. "I won't risk it."

"Then come with me." She gave him a pleading look.

"You don't even know where your friends are," he countered.

"No, but you do." Ailith wasn't certain he did, but she had made an educated guess. She did not believe for one instant that he had not continued to keep tabs on them for at least a little while.

Arkhael's restrained grimace told her all she needed to know.

"Please, Arkhael," she added. "I'm not some songbird you can keep in a cage."

He huffed at her. "While you are not fully healed, I certainly can. I don't want you going out. That's the end of it." Resolutely he stood up, avoiding her gaze as he walked over to his desk.

Ailith looked down at her hands. Despite knowing better, she had clung to the hope that he might change his mind. She clenched them into fists.

"Do you not care for my happiness at all?" she whispered.

Arkhael did not respond. From the corner of her eyes, she watched him sort his parchments.

How could he treat her as no more than a possession after everything? Dejected, she got up. Time to be a good little bird and sit nicely on her perch.

"Wait." Arkhael sighed.

She looked over at him as he put down his scrying mirror.

"I won't take you to see the wizard. Not just because I don't want to. I don't trust the man."

Ailith raised her eyebrows and watched Arkhael hesitate before he spoke again.

"Mister Lansith has been accepted by the College of Magus in Dewhaven. Not just as a student or aspirant; he has been accepted as philosopher."

The College of Magus was one of the most prestigious arcane organisations Ailith had heard of. She had tried to break in there once, when she was still studying under Nial. He had been the only reason she survived being caught. She knew that the locks on the front door were disappointingly mundane but that opening it without the correct passphrase set off an amalgamation of magical traps. That was as far as her knowledge extended. She had no idea what the rank of aspirant or philosopher entailed. The lack of knowledge must have shown on her face. Arkhael pinched the bridge of his nose, ignoring the offended look she shot him.

"The College doesn't usually accept thieves into their ranks, Ailith. Why would they suddenly do so?"

"I don't—" She stopped herself when Arkhael raised an eyebrow, rolling her eyes at him. "Fine. Nial told me Jay was being hailed as a hero after he escaped the vault with Amelie. He no longer possessed the reliquary at that point." Despite herself, she chewed the inside of her cheek. *So what did he have?* "But he did get a look at the reliquary," she said slowly. "Information."

"Information indeed." Arkhael's eyes shone with approval when she looked back up at him. "Information that could certainly buy you a position of power. Information so unique, it doesn't matter who you

445

were or what you did. Did you never wonder why he didn't come looking for you?"

Ailith narrowed her eyes at him. "I told Jay and Amelie not to come after me."

"And yet Miss Stirling still tried." Arkhael raised a hand when she opened her mouth to speak. "She failed, of course. You know my home is well hidden from those with magic, let alone those without. And, if my reports are correct, she was dissuaded by both Mister Lansith and your former mentor. But *her* angry cries certainly reached my ears."

The implication was painful.

"I'm sorry," Arkhael added softly when he saw Ailith's frown. "I did not wish to change the memories you have of your colleague, but I want you to understand why I won't take you to him. The man is surrounded by powerful casters and cares too much about his own gain. You are too valuable to bring into that situation."

Ailith wiped her eyes with her sleeve, biting back tears. Jay had travelled with her for years. Knowing he had dropped her that easily was a hard truth to swallow.

Arkhael sighed as he got up from his chair, extending a hand. "Your thieving companion, however, is currently having breakfast in an inn. I can miss an hour."

Ailith looked at him in hesitant disbelief, trying to blink away the tears.

"Truly?"

He grunted. "Don't make me repeat myself."

She ignored the hand he held out for her. Instead, she ran to him as fast as her injuries would allow and wrapped her arms around him. The prospect of seeing Amelie again lifted a weight from her shoulders.

"Thank you," she said quietly.

Arkhael rolled his eyes at her, but she saw the faintest hint of a smile on his lips before he returned her embrace. Ailith briefly let her head rest against his chest.

This fucking devil. He held far too much sway over her heart.

"One hour," he said as she stepped back, the sternness in his voice somewhat undone by the softness in his eyes. "Any danger, we leave. I will be nearby."

Ailith nodded at him as he held out his arm.

She didn't recognise the tavern nor the town he brought them to. Wherever Amelie had travelled to, it was further afield than she had ever been.

The inn itself was quiet but looked decent enough. Arkhael squeezed Ailith's arm as they walked in, then let go of her as he found himself a table in a corner.

Despite Amelie's talent for blending in, Ailith spotted her friend immediately. Her heart lifted as she walked over, and she had to stop herself from breaking into a sprint. Nerves fluttered through her as she saw Amelie look up. Would the woman be angry with her for leaving?

Ailith need not have worried. The moment Amelie spotted her, her eyes widened, and she shot up from her chair, rushing over.

Ailith held her hands out in front of her.

"Careful! Careful!"

Amelie barely slowed down. "One good reason for me not to hug you right now?" The joy on her face warmed Ailith's heart.

"I'm still recovering from some freshly broken ribs," she said with a smile that turned into a genuine laugh as Amelie carefully hugged her. Gods, she had missed this woman.

"Fuck, Ailith, it's good to see you. Look at you, being all fancy. What happened? How did you break your ribs? Come!" Amelie led her to the table she had been sitting at. "How are you here?"

Ailith simply smiled through the onslaught of questions. It was so good to see Amelie again. She leaned forwards, shielding her hands from Arkhael's view with her body, and gestured at Amelie.

"Look, there."

She pointed at where Arkhael was sitting at his table on the other side of the inn.

Amelie's eyes widened as she glanced over.

"Friend or foe?" she gestured back.

"Friend," Ailith responded with a smile and a blush.

Amelie raised her eyebrows. "I'm getting you a drink, and you are telling me everything."

Ailith did. She told Amelie how Arkhael had captured her but had seemed unable to torture her. She told her of the contract that he had made her sign and how she had rewritten it. How he had shared his bed with her and how he had rejected her after a night of passion. She told her of the fight with the Children of Illumination and how Arkhael had confessed that he desired her despite everything.

It was wonderful to speak to Amelie again. All the worries, the doubts that had piled on her, seemed lighter as she confided in her friend. When her tale was finally finished, she leaned back, taking a swig of the ale Amelie had gotten her. It was cheap, but with her throat dry from talking, she drank it gratefully.

"And what about you?" She eyed Amelie. The woman had dark circles under her eyes, but she seemed fine otherwise.

Amelie visibly hesitated, then sighed.

"It was hard after you were taken, Ailith. Jay shared part of the plan with me, but not all. He was worried I would accidentally tell you. We were offered shelter and safe haven for a few weeks, but I left after a few days. Jay was . . . changed, and I couldn't stand him."

"Power hungry?" Ailith wasn't surprised.

Amelie nodded. "I was wrong. I thought he was jealous of you because he fancied you. Now I realise he was jealous of you because the devil chose to talk to you. A few times he raved about you like a fanatic lunatic, spouting nonsense about wasted opportunities. He seemed like a changed man after we left the Chambers."

As Amelie said it, Ailith realised how true it rang. Especially after what Arkhael had told her. She hesitated, then decided to say nothing. There was no point in adding to the sadness Amelie clearly already felt at his behaviour. She reached across the table to squeeze Amelie's arm.

"I'm sorry."

Amelie shrugged. "It stung, but I've moved on."

There was a sorrow in her tone that broke Ailith's heart. "Tell me you at least got something out of it? I have heard that Jay was practically made into royalty. Surely that reward was split?"

With a loud *thunk*, Amelie put a water flask on the table. Ailith immediately recognised it as Jay's.

"Gold." She gave Ailith a wry smile. "You know I am not the talker that you are. So when Jay started speaking with big names, I asked for my compensation and left."

"That's it?" It seemed incredibly unfair, after everything they had gone through.

Amelie shrugged again. "I considered what I could do with political power behind me. I didn't consider it for long. There's a reason I ran away from home. Sure, I miss the comforts being rich brings occasionally, but I would rather continue to live on the road than return to that life." She paused before continuing, an almost melancholic look on her face. "I never checked to see if my family ever looked for me. I don't want to give them a reason to come and find me now. Jay gave me the bag as parting gift. I loaded it up and left. Either way, I tried some thieving, but it's not quite the same by myself." She smiled at Ailith. "So I'm looking for a guild, believe it or not."

"Really? I thought you had forsworn those after everything that happened."

"I'm planning to travel quite a bit before I join one. They can't all be bad, right?" Amelie winked, but Ailith couldn't help but notice that some of her original spark was missing.

She took Amelie's hand. "Whatever guild you end up with will be lucky to have you," she said sincerely. "I have no doubt that you will find a place you can call home."

"Enough about me. I'm a bit morose, but I'll recover." Amelie smiled before leaning forwards, lowering her voice. "He's quite possessive, isn't he?"

It was a poorly masked change of topic, but Ailith didn't comment. She respected her friend's need for time. Instead, she raised an eyebrow. "What makes you say that?"

"Ever since you took my hand, he has not taken his eyes off me. I think he would kill me if he could."

Ailith resisted the temptation to look over.

"He could. Easily," she said drily, then sighed. "I think I love him, Amelie. What's wrong with me?" Her voice was a whisper, barely audible, as if speaking the truth out loud might make it more real, as if he could hear her from the other side of the room. "He uses people. Kills them."

Amelie tightened the grip on her hand. "Does he make you happy?"

"I don't even know." Ailith shook her head in frustration. "On the one hand, he can be cruel and cold. He hides what he feels so well. And I am always wary of an ulterior motive. I don't even know if he cares for me or if I am just valuable. I thought devils couldn't feel. Yet at times he can be so tender and genuine." She felt a blush rise to her cheeks as she spoke. "The possessiveness and the sex, it is electrifying and addictive. But then he holds me during the night as if he fears that I might run away from him. He'll share little bits of his work with me that he takes pride in. He makes sure that there is fresh fruit for me every day. Fuck, he brought me to a fucking forest in the Hells, Amelie, because he must have known how much I missed nature." She groaned.

Slowly, Amelie had raised her eyebrows.

"Wow," she said when Ailith had finished, "you are *so* in love with him." A chuckle escaped her before her face grew serious and she covered Ailith's hand with both of hers. "There are few enough truly good people in the world, Ailith, and so many of them have blood on their hands. If he makes you happy, then screw this moral quandary. You deserve someone who cares for you like he seems to do. And there is little enough love in the world as it is."

Ailith sighed. With her exhale, she felt a weight lift off her shoulders. For so long, she had bottled these worries up and carried them alone.

"I'm sorry I wasn't there for you, Amelie. And I'm sorry I am having to abandon you again."

"Don't worry about it. We could never have lasted forever. Something would have caught up with us sooner or later." Amelie smiled. "Just don't forget who you are. The Ailith I know wouldn't enjoy killing."

Ailith huffed. "I still don't. To be fair, he has carefully steered me away from his darker dealings." She gave Amelie a grateful look. "I can't stay too long, but I would love to visit again when I can, if you don't mind."

"Of course. I will miss you, Ailith. Thanks for not forgetting about me." Amelie let go of Ailith's hand and took a final swig from her tankard. "Now, let's see how much your devil truly cares," Amelie said with a smirk.

Ailith regarded her warily. "Don't try him, Amelie. He might desire me, but he's still a devil."

Amelie merely rolled her eyes and got up, walking straight over to Arkhael's table. Ailith followed her hesitantly.

The closer Amelie got to Arkhael, the slower her steps became, her bravado dropping. Ailith vividly remembered how intimidating Arkhael had been when he had first approached her.

Even so, she watched Amelie put a hand on his table.

"Can I help you, Miss Stirling?"

Arkhael had not once taken his eyes of Amelie, and Ailith could hear the quiet anger in his voice. Almost instinctively she readied her magic, prepared for either one of them to do something foolish.

"I might not be as strong as you are." Amelie's voice hitched slightly as she spoke. "But if you hurt her, I will break into that vault of yours again. And I will burn every single contract you have in there. Understood?"

Ailith's jaw dropped, and she failed to stop herself from snorting.

The balls on this woman.

Before Arkhael even had a chance to react, Amelie turned around again. With every step she took away from the devil, confidence seemed to return to her.

"Fuck, I don't understand how you live with him," Amelie whispered. "Just being near him makes me weak in the knees."

Ailith looked over Amelie's shoulder. Arkhael scowled at her as he got up. She smiled and shifted her focus back to Amelie. "You get used to it."

"Let's see if we can spur him into action. You're clearly head over heels for the man; it wouldn't hurt for him to tell you he cares about you too." In the same whisper she added, "Goodbye, Ailith, till next time."

Before Ailith had a chance to ask what Amelie meant, the woman pulled her into a hug.

"I have missed you, and I love you." Amelie's voice was slightly louder than it needed to be. Pulling back, she winked and then pressed her lips against Ailith's.

Only then did it dawn on Ailith what Amelie had meant.

Arkhael is going to kill her.

She felt as much as she heard the growl and almost lost her balance when Arkhael pulled her towards him, his claws digging into her skin as he teleported them straight back to his chambers in the same motion.

"What was that for?" Ailith asked, grabbing his arm to stop herself from falling over. She knew. Of course she knew. But she wasn't going to let the opportunity Amelie had created go to waste.

Arkhael didn't answer her.

"Stay here," he commanded instead, then turned away from her.

Ailith tightened her grip on his arm. "Why? Are you leaving?"

He tore his arm loose.

"I am going to burn that woman alive," he snarled, "and that damned inn will burn with her."

Only once before had Ailith seen such clear anger on his face.

Shit, Amelie, you truly provoked the devil.

Ailith rushed forwards, grabbing his arm again before he could leave, her heart beating in her throat.

"You will do no such thing."

Furious, Arkhael turned around. "And why not?"

"I would never forgive you." Ailith looked him in the eye, making sure he could see she was deadly serious.

"She touched what is mine, Ailith! You cannot expect me to let her get away with that." As he spoke, he dropped the human appearance, his wings flaring out behind him angrily.

"If you hurt her, I will never let you touch me ever again."

With a growl Arkhael pulled himself away, fire sparking in his hands. "You care for her?" he spat.

Ailith nodded. She cared for Amelie more than she had ever cared for anyone. The woman was more than family to her. She said none of that. Instead, she felt oddly justified as she watched Arkhael rage. For once, it wasn't her who wondered whether he cared or not, whether she was just another soul in his collection. He had always been so confident, so convinced that she would want him. It was almost satisfying to see him experience some of that doubt.

The fire in his hands grew until he roared and hurled it at the black stone wall of his room. He started pacing in front of her.

"Why? What does she offer you that I do not?"

If Ailith hadn't spent so much time with him, she might have missed the utterly forlorn tone he tried to hide so hard from his voice. It tugged at her heart.

No, you cannot give in yet.

"At least Amelie admits she cares."

She was pushing him, but it was out before she could help herself.

With a roar, Arkhael grabbed her and slammed her into the wall, causing her to hiss in pain as she tried to hold the healing magic around her ribs in place.

"What are you implying?" One hand shot up, grabbing her by the throat as he narrowed his eyes at her.

She raised her chin. He may have intimidated her once, but that time was long past.

"You heard me."

His other hand slammed into the wall next to her head.

"I let you live here with me, show my sister that I consider you above her, share my bed with you. And you dare question if I care?" The last words were barely a whisper.

Guilt began to creep into Ailith's stomach. Maybe she had pushed him too far, been too unfair. But how was she to know if his actions proved that he cared when she didn't even know if he was capable of it? Just once, she wanted to hear him say the words. That she was more than just a valuable soul to him.

"You've never told me you do," she answered quietly, holding his angry gaze with hers.

Arkhael opened his mouth to speak, then closed it again, the hand around her throat loosening its grip. Hesitation flashed across his face so swiftly, she almost missed it.

"You know how many others have stayed overnight in my bed, Ailith?"

She shook her head, ignoring how her stomach tightened at the thought of others sharing his bed. He had centuries on her *and* he was a devil; she knew there had to have been others.

"None." Arkhael's eyes burned into hers. "Even when I did still have the occasional tryst, I made sure they left my home immediately after. None stayed the night. Never have I opened my home to anyone."

Ailith swallowed hard, but she refused to back down.

"Then tell me you care for more than just my soul. That I am more than just a contract to you."

Arkhael scoffed in response. "Don't be stupid. You are my consort." He bared his teeth before turning around, the anger returning to his voice as the fire returned to his hands. "And no one touches what is mine."

Ailith looked at his retreating back, then sighed. Maybe she was asking for too much, angry at the fish for being unable to fly. Yet she still felt a small stab of pain at his words. A part of her had clung to the hope that, despite his nature, he loved her.

As he stepped away, the fire in his hands grew, flames licking up his arms. Suddenly he turned back to her, slamming both hands into the wall on either side of her face. Ailith bit back a cry of surprise, calling for her magic almost instinctively at the sudden movement.

"Of course I care, you stupid woman," he roared.

She froze. Her heart raced, guilt mixing with elation.

He said it. He actually said it. Out loud. It has to be true.
But how?

And she was hurting him by pushing him so. What power she had over water and ice she summoned to her fingertips as she laid them on Arkhael's arm. It burned. The hellfire that wreathed his body cared naught for her protection. Gritting her teeth, she sent healing magic to her hand instead, trying to heal the burns before they could sear flesh from bone.

But she did not back down. She had caused this anger in the devil she loved; she would face the consequences.

With a deep breath, she stepped forwards, laying her other hand on his cheek. Even there, his skin burned to the touch.

"For me, there is only you, Arkhael. You have nothing to fear in that regard. Stow your anger."

As he looked down, he seemed almost surprised to see her hand on his skin. But then the flames slowly receded, and he wrapped his arms around her, his breathing heavy, his claws digging into her back. He held her with a desperation that was almost frightening. Carefully, Ailith brought a hand to his neck, stroking it soothingly, guilt gnawing at her stomach.

Only when he finally lessened his grip did she speak.

"Amelie is the only person who I have ever considered family. My partner in crime, literally. But there is no reason to be jealous of the love I have for her, or that she has for me. It is entirely different from —" She halted herself.

Arkhael's claws dug deeper into her back.

457

"She kissed you," he hissed into her hair.

Ailith opened her mouth, then closed it again. Perhaps admitting that Amelie had baited him was not the best idea right now. She chose her next words carefully.

"Only because she wanted you to be truthful with me."

The low growl he let out told her exactly what he thought of that.

"Calm your anger, Arkhael. Any other person that touches me you can burn alive. But not Amelie. She is no threat to you, and she is the only family I have left."

"Swear it to me." His voice was gruff. He still hadn't moved, hadn't let her go.

"I swear it."

Finally, she felt him relax slightly as he inhaled deeply.

"You have me hurtling down a path I cannot come back from," he whispered against her hair.

"I'm sorry," Ailith whispered back.

"You're lying."

She tried to draw back a bit so she could look at him, but he only tightened his arms around her.

"I'm not sorry you care," she admitted, "but I am sorry for the turmoil it causes. I wish it didn't have to be so hard on you."

He huffed slightly.

"Just don't make it harder."

Almost reluctantly, he let go of her, her back stinging as he withdrew his claws. He took her burned hand in his and shook his head.

"I shouldn't have lost control of myself."

"It's alright," Ailith said quietly. "I shouldn't have provoked you."

As she stepped back to look at him, she realised her cheeks were wet.

Are you crying?

Arkhael touched them with his fingertips, surprise clear on his face. "What's this for?"

"I don't know." Ailith looked away, embarrassed. "I guess I couldn't quite believe that you actually care." She wiped her cheeks, unwilling to admit how deeply his words had affected her.

Arkhael rolled his eyes at her. "For someone who reads people so well, you can be truly blind." His features were carefully schooled again, the arrogant, confident mask back in place. He pulled one of his chairs over to his desk and gestured at it.

"Sit. There is work that needs doing, and I have dallied for too long."

Ailith sat down. She didn't comment on him moving the chairs he always so carefully positioned. She didn't ask why he wanted her so near him or why he kept reaching out for her as he was working, as if to make sure she was still there. Instead, she allowed her heart to soar.

Damn, Amelie. I owe you a drink.

CHAPTER 48

Ailith was lounging in her chair, clad in nothing but Arkhael's shirt, book in hand, when the door to his chambers opened. She immediately recognised that the footfall wasn't Arkhael's.

But his home is supposed to be warded against intruders.

"One more step, and I will obliterate you," she said, raising her crackling fingers to emphasise the point, not looking up from her page to hide her nerves.

"I believe my son would be deeply disappointed if he returned to find nothing but ashes left of you, but I do encourage you to try."

Ailith looked up. Arkhael was imposing, but he was nothing compared to this figure. The devil's red skin was so dark, it was nearly black. A double set of horns on his head curled back and around his head. He was clad in nothing but a simple black robe. Yet his air of commandment seemed to dwarf the room. Ailith closed her eyes briefly.

Of all the times for him to visit.

She doubted it was a coincidence. So, pretending the visitor couldn't kill her within seconds and that she wasn't nearly naked while facing the King of the Hells, she sat up straight, biting back a grimace at the pain she still felt in her torso at the sudden movement.

"What can I do for you?"

He laughed, all malice and no mirth. The thundering sound of it rattled her heart. Confidently, he strode over, turning the other chair to face her, and sat down. She eyed his movements like a hawk, ready to act if she had to.

"Ailith, isn't it?" He leaned forwards. "Tell me, Ailith, what is it my son wants with you?"

She swallowed hard, resisting the urge to sink back further into her chair. Instead, she tried to keep her voice steady.

"Moloch, I presume?" With more confidence than she felt, she closed her book and put it on the table. He did not react. "I like to think there are many services I can provide for your son."

"Elaborate." The word was laced with command, and Ailith recognised the magical undertone. She wasn't easily charmed, but even so, she felt her stomach turn at the knowledge he could try.

"He would be able to do so better than me," she answered with a forced smile, purposely not answering his command to let him know she was aware of the magic. His eyes flashed at her.

"You gave my daughter one warning, so I will extend the same grace to you. I am not here to be disobeyed." Moloch's face was entirely impassive as he spoke.

Ailith wanted to tell him she owed him no obedience, but she swallowed the words. According to the literature she had read, all denizens of the Hells owed him their allegiance. As Arkhael's consort, that could technically include her. She didn't want to risk discussing fine print with the king of all devils. Instead, she opted for honesty.

"He has contracted me to work off a debt. If there are any other ulterior motives he has in mind for me, he hasn't shared them."

Her nails dug into her palms, and she shifted ever so slightly, one of her hands at the ready, the other shielded by her body. Gently, she reached out with the smallest amount of magic, searching for the small plant that Arkhael had gifted her. Anything to make her feel more confident in the face of this . . . what? Even "archdevil" seemed too inadequate a term to describe how much of a presence this figure carried. Yet regardless of how terrifying he might be, she refused to show him exactly how much he scared her. She was Arkhael's consort; she was determined to at least make him proud of her. So she looked Moloch in the eyes. They held a similar fire to Arkhael's but lacked all of the warmth. Even his voice seemed a mixture of silk and an ice that sent shivers down her spine.

"And what do you want with my son?"

Ailith hesitated. *I want him to love me.* But she couldn't say that to Moloch. That would be guaranteed to cost Arkhael whatever reputation he had left.

She considered her next words carefully. "I will work off my debt in whatever way he desires me to." It wasn't really an answer.

Moloch narrowed his eyes at her. "You test my patience. I don't care for it."

Ailith's muscles tensed. She could feel the change in his demeanour and readied herself. If he wanted a fight, she would give him one.

With a loud *THUNK*, the door to the room slammed open.

"Father, it has been some time." Relief rushed through her as Arkhael strode into the room. He almost managed to look casually confident, only the tension in the muscles of his jaw betraying him. As he approached, Ailith got up so he could take the chair. The back of his hand brushed her arm ever so lightly as he walked by, and her nerves settled slightly at the gesture. He was with her.

"Shall I leave you to it?" she asked, already backing up.

"No, stay." Her feet froze at Moloch's command. Clenching her fists, she walked back over to Arkhael, standing next to his chair.

"What are you trying to achieve, Arkhael? This is a new low, even for you."

Ailith watched as Arkhael's hands twitched ever so slightly at the insult, but his face remained otherwise stoic. She wondered if Moloch had even noticed it.

"She's talented and she owes me. It would be a waste not to use her."

Moloch laughed. It was a cruel sound, causing the hair on the back of Ailith's neck to stand up.

"She gave me a similarly evasive answer. Why is she truly here? I heard of your little failed stunt to acquire the Hand of Saint Argon. She should be trying to keep her innards in while imps slowly tear them out again. Instead, she sits unsupervised in this cave you call a home, wearing your clothing, acting as if she owns this place. Answer me." Moloch never raised his voice, but he might as well have shouted for the authority his words carried. An instinctive panic gripped Ailith's stomach. Only Arkhael's steady presence next to her stopped her from running.

"I enjoy her company." Arkhael's calm and deep response was a stark contrast to his father's snide tone.

Deafening silence followed his admission. Ailith could almost feel the surprise, followed by the disappointment and disdain radiating off Moloch. For a long time, father and son looked at one another, an unspoken battle being fought of which Ailith felt like an awkward spectator. She wondered who would strike first, from which direction the flames would come. But to her surprise, neither did.

Finally, Moloch responded, "You've grown weak, Arkhael. You truly are a disappointment."

Ailith glared daggers at him as he rose from his chair. He might have been more powerful than she was, that didn't mean she would let him insult Arkhael.

"Then let me be a disappointment and leave me in peace." Arkhael, too, had risen.

Moloch took a step towards them, and this time, Ailith raised her chin at him. Her anger slowly burned away the fear that was trying to cripple her body.

"You cannot truly believe you can keep her with her soul unclaimed like this?"

Arkhael's hand shot forwards as his father reached out towards Ailith's cheek, grabbing his wrist before he could touch her.

"She is *my* consort. I can do with her as I like."

"And you are wrong." Both of them looked at her as she spoke up, but Ailith only had eyes for Arkhael. "My soul is his."

She turned to face Moloch. "Try to take it from him, and I will kill you, or die trying. He might not be able to hurt you, but I most certainly can." Her eyes flashed white as she summoned moonlight to her hand. She prayed she wasn't wrong.

Moloch raised an eyebrow at his son. "So you managed to get yourself a devotee with claws." He met Ailith's icy stare. "Put that power away, girl. You don't understand who you are threatening."

This time, she didn't budge. "I believe I do, and I don't take kindly to your threats."

"Call off your lapdog, son, before I snap her neck."

She felt Arkhael's hand on her shoulder. "I have no plans to use her as a weapon against you, father. I can promise you that. But I will not stop her from defending herself."

At the squeeze of his hand, Ailith reluctantly dimmed the light in her palm, not letting go of it entirely. Then she realised what he was saying and the implications of it. The King of the Hells had admitted she could hurt him, and Arkhael had just promised she wouldn't be weaponised.

Moloch narrowed his eyes at them. "See that you keep her leash tight. I'll be keeping an eye on you. Both of you."

With the sound of roaring flames and a heat that scorched her face, he disappeared.

Ailith let out a long breath, finally letting the moonlight dissipate. Arkhael hadn't moved. She turned to look at him, her eyes searching his face.

"What's wrong?"

He let out a strangled noise and she reached out to him in concern. "Arkhael?"

"You shouldn't have. Not like that." The set of his jaw was tense, and there was anger in his eyes.

She raised her eyebrows at him. "Talk to me. What did I do wrong?"

He took her face in his hands. "Your soul. Hells, Ailith, I wanted it, but not like this."

Ailith laughed softly, ignoring the incredulous expression on his face. "My soul was yours long ago. You were just too blind to see it. It was about time for you to finally have a proper claim to it." Her expression grew serious. "Please, don't kill me now that you know."

His eyes bore into hers, unreadable. Then he bent down to kiss her. "You are impossible," he murmured.

She let out a shaky laugh. "So you keep telling me."

Arkhael drew back, hands still resting on her cheeks. Pain shot through her, like a knife had pierced her very core, her very soul, as he plucked at it. She gasped but didn't move away from him, gritting her teeth. All he had to do was tighten his grasp and pull to separate her soul from her body. Instead, she trusted him even as he held her life in his hands in the most intimate way. Meeting his gaze, she bore the pain, wordlessly giving him all of her.

His eyes were full of disbelief as she let him, and she felt him let out a shaky breath when he let go.

"You don't understand how big a gift this is," he all but breathed. "Name what you would have of me, and it is yours."

Ailith shook her head. There was only one thing she desired of him, and she still didn't know if he was truly capable of giving her that.

"That you stood up to your father for me is enough," she said instead.

The expression on his face hardened. "I didn't expect him to come sniffing so soon. Elrannen must have spoken to him already." With a sigh, he let go of her.

"Will he return?" Ailith asked hesitantly.

"Eventually." Arkhael smiled wryly. "But as long as he doesn't perceive us as a threat, it won't be anytime soon. As you can tell, his visits to me are never of a particularly social nature."

"Why does he dislike you so?" The enmity seemed like so much more than normal rivalry.

"His own son gave up his title and position as prince to live the life of a hermit. What parent wouldn't be disappointed." The laugh Arkhael let out was bitter. "He will never forgive me for the blow his ego suffered that day."

He touched her cheek again, and his gaze softened.

"It matters little. He has never understood the grander schemes I strove for. The less he cares, the better."

Ailith covered his hand with hers. She could feel how tense he was in the way his hand rested on her cheek, saw it in the set of his jaw. Understood that his desire to fight back against anyone who insulted his pride was warring with the knowledge that Moloch would quite likely win that fight.

"Is there anything I can do?"

Arkhael smiled faintly at her. "If I hadn't promised otherwise, you would have fought him, wouldn't you?"

"Without hesitation."

His other hand came to her waist as he gently pulled her against him. "You can recover quickly for me. Every day, the need to devour you grows."

Ailith bit back a moan as she felt exactly how pressing that need was.

The hand on her cheek moved to her hair as he pulled her head back. "Don't ever silence yourself for me," he whispered in her ear, his lips grazing her neck. "I want to hear exactly how much you want me."

"You want to hear how much I want you?" She sank to her knees, palming him through his trousers. "My body always yearns for you, Arkhael. That fire, that want for you, it never fades."

Chapter 49

As much as Arkhael had wished for Ailith to recover swiftly, when she told him she considered her body healed, a cold dread gripped his stomach.

He grunted as he put down the wine he had been drinking. "I wish you hadn't said that."

She raised her brows at him in confusion.

"It means I owe your druidic friend his favour." Taking her hand, he pulled her in for a brief kiss. "Do you wish to attend? It's a business meeting, but I know he was your mentor."

Ailith's eyes lit up at the offer. "I'll join you."

He had involved her in more of his business deals over the last few days, letting her read what he was working on and asking her how she would approach it. Her mind was keen, and the many books she had been reading were starting to pay off. She was softer than he was, which was to be expected, but she didn't judge him for his actions either. And occasionally, her different perspective provided him with valuable insight. He had never considered having a business partner, and even when she had presented him with the idea of becoming his consort, he had been sceptical. But slowly, he was coming to appreciate an entirely different side of her. A shrewd and cunning side that could be as merciless as he was.

To Arkhael's disappointment, Nial was quick to respond to the invitation, ready to meet that same evening. He had Marius bring wine to his dining room and received the elven man there.

The druid looked dirty, as if he had been tilling soil, and with distaste, Arkhael noted that he was trailing mud over his floor. But he was careful to put on a jovial face.

"Welcome again, Nial."

Nial barely acknowledged him. Instead, the elf's gaze went to Ailith. "It's good to see you recovered so quickly." He smiled. "How are you feeling?"

"Well, thank you." She rested her hand atop Arkhael's arm. "I was fortunate to be well taken care of."

"Indeed?" Finally, Nial acknowledged him. "I have to admit I was wrong."

Arkhael smiled coldly at him. "A mistake most don't have the pleasure to survive. Name your favour."

His spies hadn't found any concrete evidence linking Nial to the attack on Ailith, but he was still wary and distrusting of the elf. Nial reeked of ulterior motives. The attack on Ailith had been too convenient, too sudden. And despite Nial's initial reluctance to help him, he seemed to have an answer for Arkhael at every turn.

"I want Ailith. Five days with her."

Immediate anger rushed through Arkhael. The man actually had the gall to smile while he said it.

"Out of the question."

Pain like he had never experienced hit him the moment the words left his mouth. His throat was squeezed shut by an invisible hand. He clawed at it but found nothing as he gasped for air. Fire burned in him, hotter than anything he could conjure. Impossible.

He was in breach of contract.

Through a daze, he could hear Ailith's voice, feel her panic. The other druid said something. For reasons he didn't quite understand himself, he hated the elf. He would die before giving her up to him. Before giving her up to anyone.

Black spots danced across his vision as the heat inside him became overwhelming, threatening to spill out. Yet through all of it, he mostly felt regret. There was so much he hadn't told her yet.

". . . agree to your terms," Ailith's voice rang through the pain.

The heat slowly subsided. The hand around his throat lessened its grip. He gasped for air.

"Can you do that?" Nial sounded surprised.

She was making a deal without him. He tried to focus, to get the black spots out of his vision.

"As his consort, I can speak with his authority." She sounded so strong, so certain of herself. He would gladly die for her if he had to.

He froze at his own thoughts, even as the world slowly came back into focus, and struggled to redirect his attention. More urgent matters were at hand. Ailith stood next to him, her expression furious. Nial had crossed his arms but otherwise looked entirely unaffected by what had just transpired.

"Just tell me to what end."

"No," Arkhael gasped. He hated how quiet his voice sounded. Hated that this elf had seen him during this moment of weakness.

"No," he said again, louder this time.

Ailith sat herself back down next to him, her hand on his.

Nial ignored him.

"The Rite of the Never Ending."

He watched her go pale. The name wasn't familiar to him.

"Why would you want to take me through that?"

Arkhael interrupted her. "You're not going with him."

She finally looked at him, her face softening but her voice resolute. "You are not breaking any deals over five days of my absence."

He gritted his teeth. If she had agreed to the terms on his behalf, then she was now bound by the same infernal rules. He couldn't persuade her even if he wanted to.

"What is the Rite of the Never Ending?" He turned his anger towards Nial.

The older druid leaned forwards. "You might appreciate this, Arkhael. It is our most sacred rite. It would give you eternity with her."

Arkhael sat in stunned silence at the unexpected answer. Ailith could be with him *forever*? Beyond her mortal lifespan?

"If I survive it," Ailith added drily. "You know I am an awful student. What makes you think I could pass?"

Nial gave her a smile. "You finally have something to live for." He leaned back again. "You are more powerful than you were when you left my tutelage, Ailith. I am confident you can pass, else I wouldn't be asking it of you."

Ailith tightened her grip on his hand.

"And why would you be so altruistic?" Arkhael looked at the elf, looked beyond his face. There was very little altruism to him.

"Why indeed would I want one of our own to be the eternal consort of an archdevil? You tell me."

Ailith narrowed her eyes. "I won't be your spy."

Nial rolled his eyes. "Come on, Ailith, use that mind of yours. You were well on your way to becoming a force to be reckoned with, who could have done great things, before you were whisked away here." He glared at Arkhael. "Then the Children ruined any chance of you ever returning. But I like to think there is some virtue left in you. Having one of the Hells' most powerful devils tempered by that moral compass of yours, however questionable some people may find it, would still be a benefit to us."

Despite himself, Arkhael had to appreciate the man's shrewdness. It was a move he could have made himself.

Ailith's voice was low when she responded, "I think you will find yourself disappointed, then. Arkhael makes his plans regardless of my 'virtue', and I cannot work against him."

She was wrong. And he could tell the other druid knew. She was a weakness that Nial was perfectly exploiting. He gritted his teeth in frustration. Had this been the elf's plan all along? Was that why he had sent the Children after Ailith, or had this all been a very convenient coincidence? If only he had evidence. All he needed was the hint of a rumour, and by infernal law, he would be allowed to take the man's soul for potentially working against him. But he had nothing.

"If you touch her, I will kill you."

Nial rolled his eyes. "Neither of us desires that, fear not. The only touching will be when needed to teach her." He got up. "I'll wait outside for you."

The moment the elf was out of the room, Ailith turned to him, her face furious.

"Why didn't you tell me? How could you have granted him an unconditional favour?"

Arkhael raised his eyebrows. Was she lecturing *him* on how to bargain?

"You were dying. There was no time." He brought a hand to her face, stroking her cheek. "I don't like this."

Ailith snorted. "Nial might be cold, but he won't hurt me."

"That's not what I mean." He sighed. Five days was nothing; he was overreacting. "Tell me about this rite."

"I have nothing to tell." She shrugged. "I know next to nothing about the rite. There are archdruids who do not age. Or at least, they age so slowly that it is negligible. But only those who have partaken in it know what to expect, and I believe they are sworn to secrecy."

"There's a chance you won't survive it?" Arkhael tried to keep his voice even as he asked her the question.

"Most druidic rites come with a cost if you fail." Ailith shrugged again, but he could see the worry in her eyes. "I have heard stories, but I cannot tell you how true they are."

He didn't think he could live without her. "You shouldn't have to do this for me."

She knelt down in front of him and took both his hands in hers. "I would burn the world to the ground for you, Arkhael. All you have to do is ask."

"Don't let Nial hear you. He might regret his idea." Arkhael laughed wryly, standing up and pulling her up with him. Even after all this time in his home, she still smelled of the forest. He held her in his arms.

Let go. That voice stirred within him again. He quieted it. Now was not the time.

Ailith leaned against him, resting her head on his chest. It reminded him of the first time they had stood like this in his dining room. It seemed like a lifetime ago.

"Promise me you'll live," he whispered against her hair.

She let out a shaky breath. "I'll try my utmost. I still have a debt to work off, after all." Her cocky smile didn't quite reach her eyes.

"Remember." He lifted her chin and kissed her, pouring into that kiss all that he didn't know how to say. "You are mine." *And I am yours.* The words died on his lips as he looked into her grey eyes.

"Yours," she whispered against him. He watched her straighten herself, then took her arm, walking her out onto the plateau.

Nial was leaning against the mountainside, whistling a tune, appearing as if he was not deep in the Hells.

"Before I forget." He turned to Arkhael. "There is a sanctity to where we are going. I need you to exercise that infamous self-control of yours for the next five days. Do not try to get in touch. Do not watch her. Don't even scry on her." The elf narrowed his eyes. "She will die if you do. I will return her to you once the last light of the fifth day has disappeared."

Arkhael bit back a curse. "See that you do, Nial. Or an eternity of hellfire will seem tame compared to my wrath."

Ailith squeezed his arm, then gently unhooked hers.

"I'll be fine. Enjoy the peace and quiet."

She winked as he reluctantly let her go. With a heavy heart, he watched her walk to Nial and step through a portal of the druid's creation. A flurry of leaves later, she was gone.

CHAPTER 50

Ailith didn't think she would ever truly get used to the cold after living in the Hells for an extended time, and the autumn air didn't do her any favours.

Nial had brought her to a forest. Immediately, she was aware of the age of it. The trees were thick and tall, and the air under the canopy was taut with the most natural of magics. She inhaled deeply, laying her hand on the nearest tree. The connection was almost instant, like the forest was reaching back out to her.

Ailith looked up to find Nial watching her.

"This forest is magical, isn't it?" she asked him somewhat warily.

He nodded. "I'm hoping it will help you succeed."

Ominous.

"You truly think I have a chance of succeeding?"

Nial raised an eyebrow at her. "If you are so hesitant, why did you agree to this?"

She frowned at him. "Because you requested it as part of the deal. You know I had no choice in that."

"You could have let the devil burn when he disagreed. You didn't need to step in." There was a glint to the elf's eyes she disliked, a slyness to his tone of voice.

"You knew he would refuse." Despite herself, a part of Ailith hoped he would deny it. She didn't want to believe Nial could be that cruel.

The other druid shrugged. "He either would and you would be returned to us, or he wouldn't and you would be with him to keep him in check. What I didn't expect was for you to take on his deal instead."

Ailith bristled. "Keep him in check? I will do no such thing. I'm not your pawn, Nial."

The elf turned his back on her and began walking deeper into the forest. "I'm aware, Ailith. You've chosen to be his."

With a huff, she followed him. "I'm not his pawn either."

Nial said nothing in response. For a while, they walked in silence. The deeper into the forest they went, the more the air thickened, until it wrapped around Ailith like a blanket. She wasn't sure whether it felt comforting or suffocating.

When they reached a small pond, Nial stopped.

"This is where we will stay for the next few days."

Had the circumstances been different and her stomach not felt as if it was full of lead, it would have been a beautiful place. The trees parted ever so slightly to create a small mossy clearing next to the clear pond. The green stood out starkly against the deep reds of the freshly fallen leaves. Birdsong and the small hum of insects were the only sounds that disturbed the quiet.

Nial sank down onto the mossy floor, and Ailith followed his example.

"The Rite of the Never Ending," he began, "takes five days in itself. You will be learning it as you go through it." Out of a small bag, he retrieved a bowl and a collection of dried herbs. Ailith recognised some, but not all of them. What alarmed her was that the few she knew included painkillers and the infamous Nimble Weed.

He followed her gaze to the small bundle. "Let's hope that triggering whatever affinity the Nimble Weed has already given you helps with the rest. That a high dose of it will awaken whatever other magics might be lying dormant in you. This is the last time you will be fully lucid, so listen closely, Ailith."

She clenched her fists and nodded.

"Only the best of druids, those who are deemed worthy and who stand a chance of survival, are invited to partake. The rite involves a test of three skills: your willpower, your healing, and your ability to withstand pain." From the pond, he scooped water into the bowl and mixed it with the herbs. His hands shimmered slightly as he heated the bowl magically.

"Your ability to withstand pain is not something you need to train further. Your willpower is more than strong enough. What we will be focusing on is your ability to heal yourself. This has to become something you don't focus on, an instinctual action. Your body should be healing itself without your conscious input."

Ailith grimaced. She had become a fairly good healer over time, but it had not come easy to her. Then again, Nial had been the one who finally succeeded in teaching her.

"So how are you training me in that in only five days?"

"It's not going to be pleasant, I fear."

Ailith sighed. She had expected as much.

"We will talk, and I will wound you while doing so. You will need to heal the wounds while being otherwise occupied," Nial continued. "If you progress fast enough, I might teach you some other magics you are currently lacking, like how to travel to the Hells yourself, all while going through the same exercise."

That perked Ailith up a little bit.

"Once you take the final test, you either pass it successfully, and the knowledge will sustain you for life, or you fail." The implications of failure did not need to be spoken aloud. Nial handed her the now steaming bowl. "Let's begin. We are short enough on time as it is."

It was a vile mixture, and by the time Ailith had emptied the bowl, there was a thin sheen of sweat on her brow.

Nial had taken out a small dagger. "Let's start easy. Look at how my body heals itself when it gets hurt."

Ailith laid a hand on his wrist, sending her magic forth into his body as he drew a small line over his arm with the dagger. The response was instant. Rather than sending forth his magic, it was as if it was already there, ready to respond.

"Is it proactive rather than reactive?" she asked. Her tongue felt funny in her mouth.

"A little. See how the magic is already present? That is what you need to achieve. Not only will it heal your injuries, it will also stop the degeneration of the body."

Ailith sucked in a breath. That was the secret? It sounded so simple.

Nial reached over, dagger pressed to her skin.

"Focus on me, Ailith. When the knife cuts, continue talking, do not get distracted, heal without effort. I'll start by making it easy for you. How did you convince Arkhael, out of all devils, to nearly sacrifice himself for you willingly?"

She was stunned by the question. "How is that relevant?"

"It isn't. I'm distracting you with conversation. Now focus."

Ailith raised an eyebrow at him, her voice full of suspicion. "You seem to have previous knowledge of him. How are you acquainted?"

Nial smiled. "The devil and I had never met until your misfortune, but like him, I try to keep myself well informed about other players in the field."

Ailith didn't so much as blink as she felt the cold sting of metal across her arm. She let her magic run through her as she continued talking.

"I don't believe you play the same field. You live in a city, he—"

"Reactionary and too slow. The magic should already have been present," Nial interrupted her. "In some things, you are so naive, Ailith. I might live in a city, that doesn't mean I don't keep an eye further afield. Anyone with an interest outside of their own Realm knows of Arkhael, if only by reputation."

Ailith tried her best to maintain a constant grip on her healing magic whilst she paid attention to Nial.

"And why is that?"

He barked out a laugh before slicing the knife through her skin again. "He has been the only devil to ever rebel against Moloch, for one. Or at least the only one who rebelled and lived to tell the tale. It says something of his power."

Arkhael had never told her that particular detail. She wondered why not.

"If only a fraction of the rumours are true, he has watched people and devils fall and die for him, showing even less emotion than other devils, which makes him dangerous. And he is one of the few who has an interest in not just mortal souls but also mortal politics. A threatening combination," Nial continued as he looked at her arm. "Too slow again."

Ailith shrugged, struggling not to focus on the magic that should have been flowing so effortlessly. "I don't have the answer to your question. Ask him yourself if you want to know."

"He seemed greatly distressed when he believed the Children had killed you."

Another slice. Ailith gritted her teeth. Too slow again. She knew it before he said it.

"Do you love him?"

She looked up sharply. "Why does this feel like an interrogation, Nial?"

"Because it keeps you distracted and on edge."

"And?" Ailith didn't buy it.

"Too slow again. And because you need a reason to survive this rite. You're useless to me dead, and I don't think I will survive Arkhael's fire if I am responsible for your passing. There is no stronger reason to live than for love."

There was more to it. Nial didn't have many tells, but she had spent the last few months bargaining with a devil who had even fewer. It was clear the man was hiding something. Her hand went to her arm to rub the skin. The constant cutting and healing was making it itchy. As she looked down, her world spun, and she blinked to counter the sudden dizziness.

What was in that tea?

Why would it benefit Nial if she cared about Arkhael? Surely he did not believe that she would be his spy.

Unless it wasn't about her. With calculating eye, she observed the man.

"Better." His voice pulled her from her thoughts. Surprised, she looked down. The cut on her arm was poorly healed, the skin barely knitted together, but it was the first time she had ever healed herself without conscious effort.

She gave him a guarded smile. "So you already know the answer to your question. What do you hope to gain from it?"

Nial paused. "I suspected it to be true, but even I couldn't bring myself to believe that you are actually stupid enough to fall in love with a devil."

"He has shown more care for me than anyone in our Realm ever has." It was out before she could think better of it, and she immediately regretted it. Nial was clearly fishing, and if he was trying to gain leverage over Arkhael, she didn't want to help him with that.

"Anger is working well for you. Better again." He gestured at her arm. "You know he can never truly love you in return. It will only lead to heartache if you stay, Ailith."

His talk grew irksome to her. "It doesn't matter, Nial. As long as the contract stands, it is up to him to decide when I can leave, not me. Now stop your questioning. It is rude, and your implications are bothersome."

He did not relent. Instead, he continued to try and convince her that she should break free of Arkhael's grasp. By the time he finally decided that she was allowed her rest, Ailith felt prickly and tired from defending herself. Nial had been her mentor when the world had seemed to reject her. She had never questioned him then, but she was slowly starting to believe that his disappointment in her was not that of a tutor who saw their pupil take a wrong turn. No, she suspected his disappointment was because he had had plans for her, and she had refused to conform to them. It stung. A mental blow added to the physical exhaustion. Her body hurt from the constant pain and strain, and her magic felt nearly depleted. The only silver lining she clung to was that Nial had told her she had made good progress.

She wondered what Arkhael was doing. Would he be worried for her? Her thoughts went to the distress he had been in when Nial had named his favour, his immediate refusal. She shook her head. If anything, *she* was worried for *him*. Concerned he would do something reckless in her absence. It had been cruel of Nial to bring her somewhere he couldn't even look in on her. She knew that relinquishing control was not something that came easy to Arkhael.

If only she had a way to reach him.

You do.

"Nial, can I pray here?"

Surprised, he looked up at her. "I never took you for the religious type, but I don't see why not."

"You told Arkhael not to look in on me. I didn't know if this fell into the same category." Ailith shrugged, keeping her face carefully neutral.

Nial shook his head and waved a hand at her. "This forest reacts strongly to intruders. But we are not that. By all means, have at it."

Before she lay herself to rest, Ailith prayed.

Hey. I don't know if you can hear this. I hope so, because I feel really awkward thinking so loudly to myself. I'm not really sure what to say other than that I'm alive and made good progress, apparently. It's tedious and annoying, but manageable so far.

Nial is trying to get information on you. I don't know to what end, and I don't know if I will be lucid enough to watch my words. Sorry.

I hope you're enjoying some quiet time with me gone.

I miss you.

Today was tougher than yesterday, but I still live. The tea is starting to get to me, spinning the world when I lie down. But I made progress again. I still miss you.

Oh, I learned how to step between Realms. I think. I couldn't test it, but Nial told me I understood the theory.

Sorry, I think the tea is making me ramble. It's hard to keep my thoughts coherent.

Are you hearing these, or am I going insane and talking to myself? Maybe I am. I have started hearing voices, Arkhael. Is that not the first sign of madness?

Today was hard. My focus keeps slipping. There are shadows in the corners of my vision, but when I look, they are gone. It's so cold here. I miss your arms around me at night.

Nial thinks I make you weak. I hope not. I would hate that.

The voices belong to the shadows. They keep haunting me. But I live. I remember I need to tell you that, even if I don't know why. Did you know the world swings when I stand? If I turn my head, it swings harder. You would love it. So many people would fall over.

If you need me to topple them, just let me know.

I miss you. The night is so cold without your arms. All I want to do is sleep without the cold and the whispering shadows.

Nial keeps telling me to leave you. He seems convinced I can. He doesn't understand that only with you I have a chance at happiness.

Ailith grabbed at her head as the voices increased in power. She didn't want to hear them, but they kept plucking at her. Every insecurity she had ever had was bared.

A failed druid.

No, this was old. She was over this. Failed only in some aspects. Great in others. And she didn't care. There was no need to be a great druid.

A failed thief.

Her body convulsed as pain rushed through her. Her head hit something, but she was barely aware of what was around her. Ignoring the voices, Ailith tried to hide in herself, away from the pain. It followed relentlessly. She screamed at the whispers to leave her alone. She had stolen from a devil. There was no failure in that.

The devil.

The whispers bit down on her, echoing his name around her, through her head.

In love with a killer.
Not worthy of love.
You're a bystander to murder.
His crime is yours.
He's tricking you.
He's playing you.

With a heart-wrenching scream, Ailith opened her eyes. The shadow figure stood bent over her, reaching out towards her with a dark hand. She recoiled.

You are forever his slave.
You worship evil.
He doesn't care.
He cannot care.
He detests you.
He will never love you.

"No!" With a cry, Ailith called down her lightning towards the shadow, gathering all her anger into one single bolt. The lightning went straight through it, evaporating what she recognised as a fragment of her mind just before the full force of her own wrath hit her in the chest.

CHAPTER 51

Arkhael was pacing the plateau. The sun would be setting in her Realm right now. Whatever the rite entailed, she would be coming home soon. He refused to think of the alternative.

Her last prayer to him had not been reassuring. She had sounded less and less sane, and he worried what state she would be returned to him in.

Five days was too long.

He didn't care how stupid it was, how short five days should be when put into the perspective of his long life. Without her, his focus was gone. A constant dread filled his stomach, and his hands ached to hold her with an almost physical pain.

He clenched his fists as he continued his pacing. This was the last time he would let her leave.

Something pulled at him. One of his contracts. He conjured it from his vault. Ailith's name was ablaze on the paper. The embers slowly turned into flames, licking up the floating parchment until the entirety of it was alight. Bit by bit, it crumbled to an ash that was immediately whipped away by the never-ending gales that blew around the mountain. Gone were the words that made her his consort.

Arkhael stood frozen. He could not—would not believe that she had failed. She was too strong, too stubborn to die. Yet even through his disbelief, he became aware of a soul ready to harvest. Her soul, which she had so readily entrusted to him. He hesitated. And found that he couldn't do it.

Gritting his teeth, he resumed his pacing, ignoring the ice in his heart with resolute denial.

She can't be gone.

There were those who could thwart death. Clerics, mostly. The least likely group of people to be willing to deal with him. But if that was what it would take to get her back, he was prepared to speak to them.

Your father was right. She made you weak.

Furious, he growled into the darkening sky. No, she was strong. Together, they made each other stronger.

He turned his mind back to practical matters. Nial was to return her regardless, so he would have her body at least. If he didn't claim her soul, he would try to find someone to reunite the two. He would have to act fast. The longer soul and body were separated, the weaker the link between the two of them became.

He halted. The feeling of her soul had disappeared. That had never happened before.

Leaves whirled into existence further down the plateau.

Nial. He was going to kill the man.

The druid stepped through the portal almost before it was fully formed, carrying a limp body wrapped in a cloak. Arkhael's heart stopped at the sight.

It can't be true.

"She lives," Nial called out before he had a chance to move.

How?

It didn't matter. Immediately, he rushed over to the druid.

"Hand her over," he snarled through gritted teeth.

Torn between wanting to snatch her from the man and wanting to be gentle to keep her safe, he took Ailith's limp body in his arms. Her breathing was raspy, and she seemed oblivious to the world.

"She will recover rapidly. Within the hour, I expect." There was a smugness to Nial's expression that Arkhael wished he could claw off it. Moving Ailith slightly higher up his arm, he called hellfire to his hand. The man would die for what he had done to *his* Ailith.

"Death will be a mercy when it finally takes you," Arkhael snarled.

Nial merely laughed. "Careful. How will you explain my untimely demise to your woman?"

"She will have no issue with your corpse."

"I am certain she won't, but will she stay with you once you have explained why you killed me and she learns she can leave?"

Arkhael halted the fire in his hand and narrowed his eyes. "What are you implying?" He glanced at Ailith's drowsy form. The truth struck him like her lightning. "She doesn't know."

"Yet. She might find out. And are you confident that your shallow imitation of love will keep her with you, princeling?"

Arkhael gritted his teeth. "Leave. And pray you never lay eyes on me again."

The druid only smiled at his threats as he stepped towards his portal and turned to leave. "I thought you were known for your callousness. She has made you soft."

Arkhael clenched his fists with barely contained rage. He wanted nothing more than to kill the man. To tear him limb from limb for provoking him. To throw his soul into the ever-burning fires. But Nial had been right. If it risked losing Ailith, he would never do it. And knowing he had been outsmarted by the elf, that Nial was already using Ailith against him, had him shaking with anger. All he could do was watch as the portal slowly closed behind Nial. Only when the man was entirely gone did he turn back to Ailith. She was shivering in his arms. Why was she always so cold?

With a sigh, he lifted her up and carried her inside.

She stirred against him as he walked through his halls, one of her hands grasping his shirt weakly.

"Are you carrying me?" Her speech was slurred, but he breathed a sigh of relief at the sound of it.

"Do you want me to put you down?" The question was purely to give her a sense of control. There was not a chance of her walking in this state.

She shivered again. "Will you think me weak if I say no?"

"Never." He kissed the crown of her head and brought her to his bath. "Let's get you warm."

He carefully set her down at the side of the pool, undressing and folding his clothes before getting in the water and taking the cloak she was wearing off her shoulders. He inhaled sharply at the sight of her. Her entire body was covered in fresh burns, her usually grey skin an angry red. There was barely anything left of the clothes she had worn, the fabric of it scorched and torn. Gently, he removed the remainder of it, wincing as he realised it was almost melted to her skin in places. He barely succeeded in biting back a curse, but something must have shown on his face, because Ailith averted her eyes.

"Don't look at me like that." She tried to lower herself into the water, and he caught her before she fell forwards.

"Should you really submerge yourself with wounds like these?" Concern laced his voice.

Ailith shook her head. "It is already healing." She showed him her hand, and he could almost see the skin changing colour, turning from an angry red into a lighter shade of pink. "And don't worry, it won't scar."

He eased her down into a seated position, ignoring how she tried to shield her body from him with her arms.

"Even if it did, you would still be perfect to me," he whispered in her ear, simply holding her until he could feel her start to relax, slowly letting herself lean against him. "Tell me what happened."

"I did it. I passed. You have eternity for me to work off my debt." She looked up at him with a weak smile. "Or whenever you decide it's done."

Arkhael looked away from her. She truly didn't know.

"I thought you would at least be a *little* happy." Her voice was slowly starting to sound more lucid.

"There is nothing I want more than to spend eternity with you." He stroked her cheek.

The way she looked at him took his breath away. Then she lowered her gaze to her arms. The wounds on them were already healing. "I think I hurt myself."

"You did this to yourself?" He watched her grimace.

"I think so." She leaned her head against his chest. "Everything is such a blur. I remember the first day. The constant pain and the effort to heal it. The second day, he inflicted the pain while I practised magic. It was hard. Every day, Nial made me drink this awful tea. I knew it was a drug but"—she shivered against him, despite the heat—"it was vile."

She looked up at him. "Did you hear my prayers? I wanted to let you know I was still alive, to stop you from doing something stupid." And for the first time since she had returned home, she flashed him that cocky smile of hers. He kissed it before it could leave her lips.

"I would never do 'something stupid'. But yes, you smart trickster, every day."

"I can't even remember the last ones." Her face was pensive. "Never have I felt such cold in my life. I know I am prone to being cold, but this was . . ." She shivered again at the memory. "Like death itself reached for me with its icy fingers."

Arkhael tightened his embrace. She was smart. She would figure it out soon.

Nial's words echoed in his head. What did he truly have to offer her? He knew she didn't care for his wealth, and the home that he had worked so hard on suddenly seemed too small a gift for her. He had dreadfully little. Not once in his life had he doubted his own power, his superiority over others. For the first time, Arkhael feared he might not be enough.

"Something happened while I was gone." Her voice brought him back to reality. "You are quiet. Tell me."

He opened his mouth. Then hesitated, and swallowed the words. If she was going to leave him, he would at least see her recovered first. "It can wait. But you'll be interested to know that Tibia signed the peace treaty."

Ailith narrowed her eyes at him, but she didn't comment. Instead, she listened quietly while he regaled her with everything he had done in her absence. The new contracts signed, the few he had lost, and what information he had gained on the ones outstanding.

It felt so good to hold her again. He stroked her hair as he spoke and inhaled deeply, then paused. All traces of his scent were gone from her. She smelled of soil, of trees, and faintly of a burning that had nothing to do with him.

"What's wrong?" Ailith frowned as he stopped his hand, nudging it with her head.

"You have been gone for too long." A low rumble formed in his throat despite himself.

"Meaning?" She leaned her head back to look at him, a glint of realisation in her eyes.

"You smell different."

She knew. He could tell by the mischievous smile on her face, by the way she laid her hand on his chest and pressed the nails slightly into his skin. He shifted, his body immediately responding to her touch.

"Are you going to do something about it?"

Arkhael cleared his throat. "You can barely stand."

"I'll be able to again before you're done with me." Ailith lifted one of her legs and laid it over his. It would have been so easy to lift her up and move her into his lap. His breath quickened at the thought, but he resisted the burning temptation, ignored how hard she made him with nothing but a suggestion.

"Maybe I need you on your feet." If she would be leaving soon, this might be the only chance he would get.

He watched her raise an eyebrow at that and shivered as her nails dug in deeper when she raked them down his chest. "As long as it involves both of us in a compromising position, I think I can manage that." Her hand trailed further down, ghosting over his lid before she withdrew it.

Arkhael gritted his teeth and couldn't stop himself from giving in, pulling her onto his lap, barely resisting the temptation to lower her onto him, instead digging his claws into her legs to restrain himself.

Ailith gasped. "Whatever plan you have, if you don't execute it soon—"

He lifted her up out of the water by her hips, carrying her to where the pool met the wall so she had something to lean against, relishing the way she clung to him.

Gently, he let go of her legs, kissing her as he pushed her against the stone wall. She pressed herself against him immediately. The urge to claim her was still as overwhelming as the first time he had done it. He moved his mouth to her neck, loving how she bared herself to him. His hands trembled slightly as he moved his mouth over her collarbone, down to her breasts, frowning as he realised that the marks he left there so often had vanished. Something he immediately remedied.

Even in the privacy of his own chambers, he was hesitant to give in to his desire.

You can still change your mind. She would be none the wiser.

Briefly, he stilled against her, resting his forehead on her chest, warring with himself. She tensed under him.

"Arkhael?"

He clenched a fist against her hips.

Fuck what they think.

With a deep exhale, he looked up into her grey eyes and lowered himself to his knees for her.

Ailith gasped loudly, bringing a hand to her mouth, and he averted his eyes, trailing a shaking hand down her hipbones instead, down to her thigh. The burns were barely visible anymore. He pressed his claws down on her skin hard and watched the blood well up around them. Holding her still, he brought his mouth over and kissed it away. The strangled moan she let out above him released some of the tension in his stomach, encouraging him to move his mouth higher. He could hear Ailith's breath hitch as she parted her legs for him, and he trailed a single finger down between them. His breath stuttered as he realised how wet she was for him.

With his heart beating frantically, he looked up at her. Any lingering doubt melted from his mind. Her lips were slightly parted, eyes dark with desire as her chest heaved, her long silver strands covering her breasts. She had put her hands against the wall behind her, nails scraping slightly over the stone as if she was trying to hold onto some semblance of sanity.

Yes, Arkhael realised, *I could easily worship this woman.*

He took hold of one of her hands with his free one and brought it to his head. Immediately, she buried it in his hair, letting out a shaky moan.

He moved his finger over her again and watched her eyes close in response, felt the hand in his hair tighten. Desire rushed through him. He would worship her until all she could remember was his name.

Lowering his gaze, he brought his mouth down to join his fingers, breathing hot air over her. Her hips shuddered as he spread her apart, then bucked against him as he ever so slowly trailed her with his tongue.

"Arkhael."

He groaned against her as she moaned his name, applying more pressure with his tongue, the taste of her only fuelling his own need. The worries about his pride, his dignity, were drowned out by the sounds Ailith was making, and he would be damned if he didn't love what he was doing to her. What he was doing *for* her.

He lifted one of her legs over his shoulder, allowing himself better access, tracing the inside of her leg with his fingers before coating them in her arousal. Still working her with his tongue, he slid one of the digits inside her. Her reaction was instant. A second hand joined the first, grabbing onto one of his horns as she trembled against him. He almost paused. No one grabbed a devil by their horns.

Let go.

With his finger still inside her, he bit the inside of her thigh as punishment for her audacity, savouring the sound of her drawn out moan, but he didn't remove her hand. No one grabbed a devil by their horns—except for his Ailith. If this was his last chance to be with her, he would give her all of him. With his teeth, he nipped a line back up to where his fingers continued to work her and let himself savour her taste again. It mingled with the tang of her blood on his tongue, and he was certain he had never tasted anything better.

Finally, she gave in, letting her hips grind against him as he added a second digit to the first, curling his fingers inside her while he worshipped her with his mouth. The pull on his horns became stronger as she gripped him tighter, setting the rhythm for him. He let her, giving himself to her entirely and continuing the rhythm for her when her thrusts against him began to stutter, his name falling off her lips like a prayer. With a final gasp of his name, she pulled his head between her legs, giving him no choice but to take whatever she granted him. Greedily, he pushed his tongue in between his fingers as she tensed around him, drowning him in her pleasure.

Finally, the aggressive tremors in her body subsided, her fingers slowly uncurling themselves from his horns as she leaned against the wall, breathing heavily.

Arkhael felt drunk with lust, the scent of Ailith all-encompassing, the taste of her strong on his lips. Yet even through the haze, a voice was telling him to get up, that he knelt for no one, not even her.

With shaking hands, he moved her leg off his shoulder. But as he made to rise, she lowered herself to her knees instead, meeting him in the steaming waters.

Her eyes were so full of wonder, and there was something on her face that made his heart skip a beat. Something he didn't dare to name but that made her entire body radiate with it.

He would kneel anytime she asked it of him, if only to catch a glimpse of what he was seeing right now. The voice stilled, its power silenced.

And then she was on him, her mouth pressed against his, her arms around him.

Let go, a different voice whispered.

Finally, he did.

And by the Hells did it hurt. The intensity of the emotion that washed over him threatened to drown him. A maelstrom pulling him into a current he was entirely defenceless against now that he had let it in.

Only Ailith's touch kept him from insanity, and he clung to her, afraid he would be swept away if he let go. Until even her touch was too much to bear, and fire ate at his body, consuming him as he claimed her for himself.

CHAPTER 52

Ailith lay awake as Arkhael slumbered next to her, unable to find sleep despite her exhaustion. Too much had happened in one day for her to find rest.

Something irked her about the Rite of the Never Ending, but her thoughts were too muddled to figure out what exactly was wrong. Even though the drug was mostly out of her system, the unwelcome aftereffects lingered. In addition to that, Arkhael had been dancing around something ever since she returned. At first, she thought his strange demeanour meant he was unhappy that she had returned successful, but the thought had been quickly dismissed. She knew him well enough by now to know something was bothering him. And then, in a completely unexpected turn of events he had knelt before her and—*fuck*, just thinking about it made her lose her mind. She had seen the turmoil in his eyes almost stop him, but then his mouth had been on her and . . . Ailith lost her train of thought.

Arkhael shifted next to her, his hair uncharacteristically messy as it lay loose against the pillow, murmuring something unintelligible under his breath. She stroked his cheek, and he sighed, tightening the arm around her before he stilled again.

Something else had come over him. His expression had almost seemed pained when they joined their bodies, and if it hadn't been for how passionately he had—

She stopped her own thoughts. She had almost thought of him as making love to her. But damn her if it hadn't felt even more intimate than usual. If that was even possible.

A headache throbbed at the very edges of her consciousness. Ailith groaned quietly, closing her eyes again and trying to will her thoughts to slow. *Just breathe.*

She focused on her breath.

In. Hold. Out.

Listen.

Arkhael's breathing was quiet, his heartbeat under her ear steady as he rested. Why was he so unwilling to talk about what was bothering him? He had so blatantly been avoiding it.

Frustrated, she realised her thoughts were in too much of a spiral for her to focus on her breathing.

One thing at a time. Start with the facts.

From the moment she had regained consciousness, something had seemed off with Arkhael. Something must have happened when she was gone. In vain she tried to remember, cursing Nial in her head. He was a cruel teacher, and she could tell Arkhael despised him.

Her memories were a haze of Nial's voice and the vile drug he had given her. She remembered that he had told her to be more aware of herself, of her body. That had been vitally important. What for?

She tried retracing her steps and let her awareness spread through herself. It was so much easier now, as natural as breathing. Already her body had started to heal the claw marks Arkhael had left on her. She made a conscious effort to halt it, not willing to let go of them.

Then what?

"Too slow."

But why?

Because she would have only mere seconds to save herself. The rite would be fast and self-inflicted.

Ailith shot up as she realised what had happened. Next to her, Arkhael immediately woke, alarmed by her sudden movement, summoning flames to his hand.

"What's wrong?" His voice was filled with alarm as his eyes darted about the room.

She paid him no heed. She had *died*. Only briefly—her body had had enough energy to pull her back from the brink—but for a few moments, she had been dead. Her mind was racing.

That explained the cold, why it had taken her so long to warm up again.

Your soul.

Arkhael could have taken it. She had given it to him freely, and her death meant he could have made good on that offer. Why was she still in possession of it?

He knew.

Her head began to hurt with the implications of it all. *That* was why he had behaved so strangely.

"Ailith?" The hesitation in his voice confirmed everything she needed to know.

"Why didn't you tell me?" She couldn't keep the hurt out of her voice. Nial had known too. Of course he had. Arkhael's increased disdain for the man made sense now. She turned around to face him and was met with the last emotion she had ever expected him to show. Fear.

There was a change in his posture, ever so subtle, as he sat upright, the fire in his hand sizzling out. Was he *scared* of her?

"Arkhael?"

The devil cleared his throat. "I wanted to—" With a sudden cough, he grabbed his throat. She reached out for him in concern, and her heart broke when he turned away from her.

He can't lie.

But why would he? And why did he almost seem to be shunning her?

She wrapped the blanket around her shoulders as if it could defend her from his odd behaviour.

"I wanted to ensure you were recovered before leaving." His voice was carefully neutral.

Finally, it dawned on Ailith. An infernal contract only lasted as long as both parties were alive.

Which meant she was free to leave. No more debt to pay off. She was no longer his consort. And he was no longer protected from her. Her head swam.

Flexing her fingers, she looked at her hands. His posture was careful, defensive.

Does he not trust me?

She remembered the monstrous clamps he had used to ensure his safety. Surely he wouldn't do that to her now? For the first time since he had brought her home, she looked at him and saw the terrifying archdevil, the Prince of the Hells that others were so scared of.

Resolutely, she halted the direction of her thoughts. She refused to fear him now. If he had wanted to kill her, he could have done so the moment she set foot in his halls again.

Turning back to him, she reached out again, slowly this time, taking his hands in hers. "Tell me truly: Do you want me to leave?"

She saw him tighten his jaw, open his mouth, and close it again. His hands came around hers in an iron grip, almost painfully tight. When he finally spoke, his voice was hoarse.

"No."

Her heart soared. Gently, Ailith pushed him back down onto his pillows, aware of his constantly vigilant posture. She lowered herself down next to him and rested her head on his chest.

"Then why would I go?"

Ever so slowly, his arm came up around her again, and Ailith let herself relax under his touch, even if she could feel that his muscles were still tense against her.

"You are free to go. Why would you stay?"

Why would you? Do you want to?

The questions seemed silly, even in her head.

She leaned up slightly so she could look Arkhael in the face. "Because I thought this was my home. Is it no longer so?"

"Of course it is." His answer was brusque, and she had to remind herself to listen to his words and not just his tone.

She chewed the inside of her cheeks nervously.

"Because—" She cleared her throat. "Because I don't need a contract to keep me here. Because I gave my soul and heart to its owner."

The silence that followed was deafening. Ailith lowered her head again, refusing to look the devil in his eyes. Suddenly, the exhaustion caught up with her.

"Please, let me rest here? Just for one night, while you gather your thoughts?"

Still Arkhael didn't speak, but the arm around her tightened.

When his voice finally reached her ears, Ailith had already started drifting off. "As long as you need to."

Despite everything, Ailith slept soundly once sleep actually embraced her. For the first time in days, she was back in Arkhael's arms, and sheer exhaustion was quick to catch up.

When she finally awoke, a yellow light already filtered through the windows. She had slept in.

To her surprise, Arkhael was still in bed with her, his arms around her, one resting just above her chest, nails pressing down slightly on her skin. He was awake; she could tell from the tension in his body.

"You let me sleep in."

"You died yesterday. I thought you would need the rest." His voice was still terse.

Ailith sighed. Morning had not brought the answers and resolutions she had hoped for.

"You're tense," she said quietly, laying the palm of her hand on his chest.

"As are you."

She rolled her eyes at his guarded response. "I'm lying naked in the arms of a devil who has his claws resting on my heart and no reason not to kill me."

"You think I would kill you?"

Ailith could hardly begrudge him his short replies. If this was awkward for her, it had to be nothing short of alien to him.

Carefully, she brought his hand from her heart to her throat, pressing his long nails against the thin skin there. She felt a shiver run through his body.

"Was that a shiver of lust for murder?"

A wry laugh left him. "Lust certainly, but not for murder." He traced his nails over her throat. "You are insane."

Before she could respond, he brought the hand to her chin, lifting her face up towards him to press his lips against hers. As abruptly as he had done so, he pulled away again.

"This is so, so wrong."

Ailith laid her hand over his. "Tell me what you want from me." She squeezed his fingers. "Ask me, and it's yours."

Arkhael groaned in response, turning his face away from her.

"Why couldn't you just leave? I would have raged, I would have burned cities to the ground, taken it out on others. It would have been so much easier."

Ailith lifted herself up, leaning on her elbows to look at him. Hesitantly, he met her gaze. She could see the war he was waging with himself in his eyes.

"How is this different? What we were doing was already damnable."

He shook his head. "But we had a contract to hide behind. You were my consort. Now you are just a mortal woman who shouldn't be here in the first place."

"Ouch." Ailith grimaced.

His hand came up to touch her face, but he clenched it into a fist instead, dropping it down again and biting back whatever he had been about to say.

Ailith sighed sadly. "So what are we to do?"

"If we were sensible?" The laugh Arkhael let out was devoid of any mirth. "We would turn on each other right now. If I was quick enough, I could maybe restrain you before you had a chance to release any of that divine light on me and pluck the soul from your body. If I were too slow, you would turn me to ash." He paused and pinched the bridge of his nose. "I would kill myself before taking your soul." His voice came out ragged. "So, it is up to you, Ailith."

She slapped him in the face, ignoring the stunned glare he gave her.

"Don't be stupid," she hissed at him. "I thought I was clear enough last night, but let me spell it out for you. I love you, Arkhael. I am yours. All of me. Heart, soul, whatever you desire of me. I don't care that you lack a soul. I don't care if that makes me insane. I don't care how wrong it is. If you wanted to be rid of me, I would leave. But don't ask me to kill you."

"And what do you want of me, Ailith? To tell you that I love you in return? I'm a *devil*, remember? Be realistic." He raised his voice at her. "What could I possibly offer you here? A lifetime of reading books? Is that truly what you want, now that you have eternity lying at your feet?"

"To spend it with you? Yes, it would have been my first choice." She sat up and clenched her fists, trying to remain calm. "Tell me why you are so opposed to it. You don't want me to leave; you told me this is still my home. But every argument you have made since has been to convince me there is nothing for me here. You know that we are good together." Ailith narrowed her eyes. "I think you are scared, but I can't tell what you are scared of."

He sat up as well, wings flaring out behind him. She had hit home.

"Do not insult me." His voice had gone very quiet.

"Or you'll do what?" Ailith tried to stop herself from shouting. "Face the truth?"

With a snarl, he was on her, pinning her down to the bed below him. Ailith fought back, kicking and screaming until he restrained her legs with his and he swallowed her screams with his mouth as he kissed her.

She would spend eternity fighting with him if that was all he gave her.

"Tell me to stop." His voice was hoarse against her mouth.

"Never."

His mouth was on hers, and it was like the first time they had done this all over again. No preamble, just a desperate need as he entered her and she wrapped her legs around him, moving with him until there was no more space for anger, naught but the rhythmic movement of their bodies and that unending desire, until even that disappeared.

When they finally separated, Arkhael pulled her up abruptly. "Get dressed. I'm taking you somewhere."

Ailith didn't question him. Quietly, she put her clothes on, watching Arkhael from the corner of her eye. She couldn't help but sympathise a little. She had risked nothing but heartbreak admitting her feelings to him. He had everything to lose if he let her stay. It would be a gruelling task to keep his position and maintain respect with her by his side. And even though she was more than willing to fight for him, she wondered if her demand to let her stay was selfish of her.

Tying her hair up, she joined him in his chambers to find him already pacing. He extended an arm, and she took it, hooking hers through as if they were just going out for a formal walk.

CHAPTER 53

Before she had had the chance to blink, he had transported them. His quiet chambers replaced with the sounds of wind and screams. Ailith looked around her. They were standing on a barren hill, red dust blowing in her face with the wind. At the bottom, she saw figures, both with and without wings. The source of the screams. Quickly, she averted her eyes. Living in the Hells was one thing; she didn't need to see the torture enacted here.

Further in the distance, she spotted what looked like a fort, a large, dark building with high walls around it.

"Welcome to the Fourth Circle of the Hells." Arkhael pointed at the building. "That is where Annoth resides. Its current keeper." Ailith recognised the name from the books she had read.

He gestured down at the writhing bodies.

"And these all used to be under my domain. All creatures who sold their souls to greed."

Ailith's eyes flickered down briefly, before she trained them on him again. She knew who her heart had chosen. She knew that he did terrible things. She would not be so easily deterred.

Arkhael turned her around. Behind her up the hill stood a large house. Its facade was as beautiful as it was terrifying. Out of the stone pillars, statues had been sculpted, decorating the front of the building with people in various stages of agony.

The entire estate was enclosed by a high wrought-metal fence, and although most devils seemed to be able to fly, the grounds were empty. Its only visitors the broken statues that littered the space.

He walked her over to the gate. At his touch, it sprang open. In silence, he walked her to the large front door. The bottom of it showed a relief of people reaching upwards, towards a figure seated in a throne above the door. She watched Arkhael lay a hand on the door and hesitate briefly before it, too, opened for him.

Wall sconces stuttered to life in the hallway behind it. A smell of burning dust filled the air. As the door closed behind them, the sound of screams was immediately cut off. Ailith breathed a sigh of relief.

Still Arkhael didn't speak as he led her through room after room, each more decorated and lavish than the last, aside from the thick layer of dust that covered everything. Even so, it was hard to miss Arkhael's hand in everything, from the dark wooden furniture to the perfectly symmetrical placement of chairs. And every thinned tapestry and faded painting on the wall held an image of him watching over souls being tortured. He slowed every time they walked past one of them, not speaking, the set of his jaw tense.

Ailith broke the silence. "Do you think I am so easily horrified?" Her voice was weirdly muffled by the layers of dust around them.

Arkhael didn't so much as slow his step. "I am showing you how much of me you don't know."

"I might not know much of you, but I know you," Ailith countered. "I noticed the absence of your name in your books. I know that you are keeping secrets from me about your past, like how you alone rebelled against Moloch. You think I care?"

Arkhael flinched. If she hadn't been so in tune with his body, she might have missed it.

"How did you come by that information?"

"Nial told me."

He muttered something under his breath that sounded suspiciously like a curse aimed at the oral history of druids. Then he sighed and halted.

"If I am letting you in on who I truly am, then you might as well know of that too."

Ailith said nothing, noting the bitterness in his voice.

"Yes, I rebelled against Moloch. It was one of my most intricate schemes. You know I cannot harm him, but I had others who could indebted and bound to me. Despite all my planning and my preparation, I failed." He nearly spat the last word.

"You tried to dethrone him?" The very idea seemed absurd.

Arkhael shrugged stiffly. "A goal a lot more worthy than petty politics. Imagine what could be achieved from that seat of power."

She gave him a sidelong glance. "That dream hasn't faded, has it?"

"Never." Ailith could almost hear his teeth grind against each other with how tightly he clenched his jaw.

She squeezed his arm, knowing he hated failure, hated admitting to it. He pulled her along again, continuing the journey through his former home.

"How are you still alive?" Ailith finally asked.

Arkhael let out a dry laugh. "He owed me. The payment of that debt was that he could never kill me. He tried, of course, in roundabout ways. But after all his attempts failed, he stopped trying. Mostly because he couldn't be seen to lose forces against the dishonoured son. But also because I worked hard to no longer appear to be a threat to him. Why do you think all mention of me is gone from the tomes of our history? Why do you think you never knew who I was until I told you? As long as I am nothing more than a remote *disappointment* and a recluse, an almost forgotten name, I am not worth the attention and effort. All that has changed now." He sighed. "It will take centuries to regain that position before I can even begin to contemplate another coup."

Ailith said nothing. No wonder that relationship was so extremely strained. Or that Moloch had seemed so wary of her. For all he knew, she was Arkhael's new weapon against him.

And you could have been, if he hadn't made your safety his priority.

She looked up at the devil next to her. So many acts of horror lay in his past, and she doubted his future was going to be more peaceful. Yet she couldn't bring herself to see him differently. She knew the parts of him that he never showed the world. And she loved him for them. If he asked it of her, she would overthrow the King of the Hells with him. *And then?* Ailith grit her teeth. He was nowhere near succeeding in that. Whatever came after she would deal with when the time came. She would rather face that conflict than face the hardships of life without him. Resolutely, she gripped his arm tighter.

Finally, Arkhael stopped in front of two gilded doors, stroking the door handles almost lovingly before pushing them open.

A large room lay behind them, strangely empty compared to the previous ones. Arkhael pulled her through the doorway, and her breath caught as the sconces sprang to life. At the other end of the room stood a giant gilded throne on a raised dais, the gold still reflecting the light even under the buildup of dust. It only took her a second to recognise it as the throne from his painting.

She looked up to see Arkhael watching her.

"A thief's dream?"

Ailith smiled. "A thief's nightmare. So much gold and no way to transport it."

He laughed, and the sound of it lifted her heart. Still holding her arm, he walked her further into the room. "I used to hold court every other day. I received beggars, sinners, mortals, devils, some fey, even demons. Extorting them for their money, their influence, their servitude, their souls, until there was nothing left to desire." He halted in front of the throne, looking up at it. "And still it wasn't enough. I took until gold lost its shine and power its allure. All to prove to my brethren that I was the better one, the more powerful one, like they still do." He turned to Ailith.

"Only when I saw the futility of it all did I change my sights and ambitions. And even now, I cannot stop. You know I will always want more. It's the curse that comes with my heritage. *That* is who you claim to love. Are you certain about that?"

Ailith smiled at him. "I already loved you *while* you were trying to extort me," she laughed awkwardly. "You think stories of your greed will scare me away? Your sights were set on a reliquary guarded by the fucking Children of Illumination. I know you will never settle for less."

"You shouldn't love the person extorting you." His face was incredulous.

She rolled her eyes at him. "You think I don't know that? You think I haven't already tried to talk myself out of this long before last night? That I haven't told myself I shouldn't share a bed with a devil? Let alone one that kept me chained up to torture. One that nearly destroyed my hands." She sighed deeply. "If only it was that easy."

Arkhael looked at the throne for a long time before he finally spoke again. "Whoever you talked to was wrong." He looked back at her, and there was something in his eyes that she hadn't seen there before. It took her breath away. "We might be soulless, but we don't lack for feelings. If anything, we feel too much. Too much hate, too much jealousy, too much greed." He brought his hand to her cheek. "Too much love." Ailith's breath hitched. "I have never knelt for anyone. Let alone worshipped anyone." He pulled her closer. "If you stay, I will never let you leave me. I will never let you touch another or let you desire the touch of another. If you ever betray me, I will tear the soul from your body so slowly, an eternity of pain will seem short in comparison. And you were right, Ailith. I am scared. Scared of showing and telling you all this and watching you leave. But you have my word that right now, you have a choice. And if you choose to go, I will not come for you."

Ailith listened to him in stunned silence, and it took her some time before she realised that he was asking something of her. Her heart hammered, urging her to say yes. With difficulty, she ignored it, clearing her throat in an attempt to find her voice.

"Promise me you'll always give me a chance to speak first, before you go straight to torture."

With a clenched jaw, Arkhael nodded, his hand moving from her cheek to her waist.

"Devil or not, you ever lust after another"—the hand on her waist tightened in response—"I will kill you. And them." She tried to keep her breath steady as his other hand trailed down her back.

"Never," he answered quietly, "but understood."

"What of your family?"

Arkhael's hands stilled. "They will come for me. For us. I'm afraid that letting you stay with me without a contract will be the final straw. I have gone from a silent figure to one of public interest." She watched him swallow hard. "It won't be long before they challenge everything I have tried to build up. And they will test you. It will take years, if not decades, for me to get a fraction of my reputation back. But they will never accept you as my equal. Let alone theirs. Your life will never be safe. We will have to walk a fine line between negotiation and violence, not only to regain some semblance of peace but also to stop my father from seeing us as a potential threat. If he so much as suspects that we might be working against him, we will never be truly safe." His voice went quiet. "I hate bringing you into a potential future like that."

He was nervous. Ailith could tell from the way his hands clenched behind her, the tension in his jaw. But was he nervous about her answer or his family?

"Are you not going to regret this?" she asked him quietly.

"I would relinquish everything for you if I had to." His eyes bore into hers, the intensity of his gaze enough to take her breath away. "Are you willing to fight that battle by my side?"

Ailith nodded, her throat dry. "What place would I have by your side?"

The hand on her back pulled her closer still, pressing her against him.

"I have renounced my throne, but I would have gifted it to you."

She shook her head. "I don't want your throne."

"I have little to offer you, Ailith. The wealth in my vault is only a fraction of what I once had, and my home is barely the kingdom that you would be worthy of."

Ailith smiled at him, at the small lilt of nerves in his voice that he tried to hide from her.

"I have never wanted any of that. You, just you, are enough, Arkhael. I love you for you, not for all of this." She gestured around her.

There was a tremor to his voice as he spoke again. "Then, if you would have me, your place would be right here with me, as my partner, my equal, my one forbidden love."

Ailith trembled in his arms. She tried to think past his honeyed words, past the way his quiet voice alone filled her with need, past the way his warm body pressed into hers. If there was a hidden catch in the devil's words, she couldn't find it. Her heart was singing.

"Decide, my little thief. Or my lack of control around you will make the decision for us." His voice came out strangled, and she could feel his arousal pressing into her through their clothes.

She wove a hand through his hair, standing on her tiptoes to bring her lips up to his.

"Yours," she whispered against him.

He kissed her with such passion, she thought she might faint from it. When he finally let her go, the flames in his eyes were dark, and her own breath was fire in her lungs.

"Come back home with me, Ailith." Despite the command in his words, there was an unspoken query in his tone.

"Always," she whispered back at him.

He brought them back to his chambers. A place she realised had come to feel more like home than anywhere else had. His arms were still around her.

"Close your eyes." His voice was hoarse.

Ailith searched his face. It gave nothing away. Taking a deep breath, she obeyed.

His arms left her, and she heard him move away. Nervously, she waited for his return, and nearly jumped as she felt his hands around her neck, followed by a cool touch as he fastened something around her.

"I told you once these belonged to a queen. And I couldn't think of a queen more fitting." He spun her around and carefully walked her forwards. "Now open your eyes."

Ailith was met with her reflection in Arkhael's tall mirror. The golden necklace she had stolen from him glittered around her neck. But it wasn't quite the same, she realised. It hung lower, and the chains dangling from it formed more intricate patterns, extending as far down as the neckline of her blouse.

"I had it repaired and modified for better access." He tilted her head slightly, and in the mirror, she watched him bite her neck, arching her back into him as he did so, pressing her hips against his. He groaned and met her gaze in the mirror as he slowly brought his hands around her. His claws rested against her throat, trailing down to follow the necklace, down to her blouse, where they tore the fabric in two, exposing her breasts. Ailith shivered under his touch, watching as if in trance as one of his hands travelled further down.

"I can feel how much you desire me through your clothes," he murmured against her ear, and she couldn't stop the moan that rolled off her lips as he started slowly applying pressure between her legs, her hips moving into him of their own volition. "Tell me who you belong to."

Ailith moaned again as his other hand came back up to her breasts, trailing her nipples with his claws.

"You," she watched herself say and shuddered against his hand. He brought it up to the waistline of her trousers, his claws tearing at the fabric ever so slowly.

"Say it again."

"Only if you touch me." Her eyes met his in the mirror, a faint smile on her lips, even though her breath came out quickened.

With a loud tearing sound, he brought his claws down. The fabric around her waist fell open, and his hand was back between her legs.

Ailith bucked her hips against him as his long fingers slowly started circling her, pressing into her ever so slightly.

"Say it." He stilled his hand.

"I belong to you, Arkhael." Her voice was breathy, and she moaned as he finally pressed his fingers into her fully, his thumb circling the bundle of nerves, her hips trapped between his hand and his hard lid behind her.

His other hand moved to her throat, and the sight of it in the mirror made her lightheaded. She had never looked or felt more owned.

Arkhael's breath ghosted over her ear. "I am going to make you watch while you come for me. And then, I'll use your mouth until all you can taste is me." Ailith whimpered against him as his fingers continued working inside her. "And just maybe, I'll put my tongue where my fingers are now."

Moans fell off her lips at the image he painted her, at his fingers inside her, at the *sight* of his fingers inside her. He curled them slightly, and her hips shuddered against him as he sped up, his thumb continuing to send jolts through her body.

"Come for me, Ailith. Be mine."

Stars danced across her vision as she did, the sound of her name in his voice only enhancing the climax that gripped her. Arkhael kept working his fingers until her legs buckled and she had to grab his arm for support.

Satisfied, he slowly withdrew them, and through half-lidded eyes, she watched him bring them to his mouth in their reflection. She turned around to kiss him, tasting herself, her hands sneaking down to palm him through his trousers. He groaned as she applied more pressure.

"Kneel," he whispered against her. "Let me use you."

The sudden need in his voice spurred her into action. She all but tore the shirt off of him, hands on his trousers immediately after, until she found herself on her knees before his naked body, dark red skin gleaming in the torchlight.

Almost tenderly, she stroked the inside of his thighs, kissing the thin ridges of leathery skin before wrapping a hand around him. She revelled in the feel of him, how hard he was in her hand, how his entire body trembled slightly at her touch. Gently, almost teasingly, she moved her hand over the sensitive tip.

Arkhael shuddered, weaving his hands into her grey strands as she trailed her tongue from base to tip and back.

He was hers. Truly hers.

Ailith looked up and caught his fiery eyes, his mouth slightly open with his quickened breath. *Fuck he is beautiful.*

"I want to hear you say my name." She squeezed the base of him, earning herself a loud gasp.

"Ailith."

The sound of his low voice saying her name with so much reference went straight through her. It didn't matter that she had just come on his fingers.

"Beg me for it," she whispered.

The hands in her hair tightened, claws scraping over her skin as she gave him a firm tug. His eyes narrowed at her. Again, she moved her hand, her grip tight as she stroked him slowly.

When he spoke, his voice was hoarse. "Please."

She inhaled sharply, the nails of her other hand digging into his thigh.

"Have you ever begged anyone for anything before?"

He growled above her. "Ailith . . ." There was a hint of warning in his voice. She ignored it.

"Tell me," she breathed. Looking him in the eye, she brought her mouth to the very tip of him, rubbing him over her lips.

She could feel his thigh tense under her hand, watched him bite his lip as dignity warred with lust.

"Never," his voice came out strained.

She had known the answer, yet the thrill she felt at hearing it was no less. Arkhael all but glared at her.

"Stop your teasing."

Ailith ran her mouth along the base of him, never stopping the slow movement of her hand. Maintaining eye contact, she brought him back to her lips, keeping her mouth closed as she raised an eyebrow.

The hands in her hair clenched into fists, almost painfully pulling at it. She tightened her hand around the very base of him, squeezing tightly.

He let out an involuntary moan and relented.

"Ailith, please." His voice was barely audible.

"I love it when you say my name like that," she whispered before slowly taking him in her mouth. He was close already. She could tell from the tension in his hips and the way he let out a strangled moan as she took him in. With her tongue, she applied pressure to the base of him as she moved her mouth, taking in a little more every time until she could feel him nudge against the back of her throat.

Looking back up at him, she relaxed the muscles, tears forming in her eyes as she pushed forwards until all of him lay heavy in her mouth.

Arkhael let out a pained sound as their eyes met. Grabbing her by the hair, he thrust his hips, not breaking eye contact with her until she felt his muscles contract and his hot seed shoot into her throat. She slowly removed her mouth as he climaxed, gripping him with her hand as she covered herself in his pleasure.

With a hand still on him, she coated her fingers in it, spreading it over her breasts, then slowly bringing them between her legs.

He almost staggered forwards, sinking to his knees to meet her, their mouths clashing as he guided them down. Breathlessly, she lay in his arms on the warm stone floor, his hands roaming her body freely.

"For all my governance of greed, I don't think I truly knew it until I first laid eyes on you back in that small cell."

She looked up at his words, and he gave her a pained laugh. "And now, just one look from you fuels the fire in my blood." He guided her hand to his lid, hardening again under her. "Your touch, the sound of your voice, this is the effect they have on me. All my schemes, my reputation, my self-control—one breath from you is all it takes for them to come crumbling down. This unending want for you might be my undoing, but I have never lost a fight so willingly."

How was she supposed to react to his words? Even if she didn't know, her body spoke for her. She could feel her face flush, her breath halt in her chest, her entire body tense in his arms.

She looked away, bashful almost. "You are annoyingly eloquent, and I am not used to receiving such declarations."

Arkhael rolled them over, positioning himself between her legs, his face full of arrogant confidence. "Get used to it, my dear." He pressed down on her ever so slightly, just enough to rub against her and make her gasp. With a groan, he got up, offering Ailith a hand. "The floor is not befitting a queen, let alone myself."

She let him pull her up. "So, what is befitting then, prince?"

He gave her an odd look. "Strange, to hear you say that when you wouldn't even say my name for so long."

"Of course not." Ailith grinned at him. "You seemed to hate it when I called you devil, and I loved getting under your skin."

Arkhael quirked an eyebrow. "Loved?"

She just flashed him a smile, and he lifted her by her waist in response.

"Befitting would be for me to take you to my bed so I can spend the rest of the day enjoying the moans leaving your mouth. Duty can wait until tomorrow."

Ailith wrapped her legs around him. "Really? The archdevil Arkhael is choosing lust over power?"

He dug his claws into her back, supporting her as he walked them to the bedroom.

"I think that having a mortal woman brave enough to stand up to Moloch himself moan my name in my bed, qualifies as choosing power." He sat her down on the edge of his bed and stroked her neck just above the necklace. "I thought about finally taking you out on my balcony and bending you over the balustrade."

Pretending her heart didn't skip a beat at his words, Ailith pulled him onto the bed next to her, kissing a trail from his hipbone to his neck as she pushed him down. "Why didn't you?"

"Because today is for us. I have all of eternity for you to moan my name loudly into the rest of the Hells, and I plan to use all of it to live every fantasy I have ever had about you." He pushed her hips down against his own, and Ailith moved to line herself up with him.

"Wait."

She halted, toes curling with need. His fingers were good, but her body was aching to feel him inside her.

"I want you to—" He stopped himself, biting his lip.

Ailith blinked herself out of her lust-filled haze, forcing herself to focus, her eyes searching for his.

He looked conflicted, and she recognised the look in his eyes. A conflict between centuries of pride and his want for her. She touched his cheek, holding his gaze. "Anything for you, my love."

"Let me—" He looked away from her. The hands on her hips tightened, then pulled her upwards. "Put your hands on the headboard."

Realisation dawned on her, and she swallowed hard. Mindful of his wings, she let him guide her, gripping the headboard tightly as he brought her hips to his face.

Despite the anticipation, the slight tremor going through her, she let Arkhael set the pace, giving him every opportunity to change his mind. She should have known better than to think he might, and the moment his mouth was on her, any reservations left her. A heat spread through her body that had nothing to do with the temperature in the Hells as his tongue slid between her legs, her nails digging into the headboard. A part of her tried to hold back, wanting the torturous bliss to last longer. But any attempt at restraining herself was lost as she heard a quiet moan escape him. She threw her head back and let go, her hips grinding into his face as he slowly unravelled her, forcing him to take her until her orgasm washed over her. His nails dug into her thighs as she cried out his name, pulling her down on him until she thought she might black out from the constant sensation of his tongue.

When he finally let go of her, she was breathing heavily. Her hair had long since escaped its restraints and was plastered to the side of her face.

With shaking legs, she lowered herself, sliding back down his body. Almost immediately, he rolled her over, placing her hands above her head and his legs between hers.

"You taste amazing," Arkhael murmured against her lips before kissing her. Ailith had barely recovered her breath enough to kiss him back properly, and she could feel him smile knowingly into it.

Smug bastard.

He pulled back a bit. "Knowing only I will get to savour you makes it even sweeter."

She groaned against him, well aware she was letting him get away with way too much. So she sought his eyes with hers and flashed him a smile. "You looked good below me."

Arkhael narrowed his eyes. "You looked good losing yourself to me." He moved his hips, rubbing himself over her.

Ailith groaned. Everything felt so sensitive; even the slightest touch halted her breath.

His mouth went to her ear. "You sure you want to play games now, Ailith? You know I will win." He licked her earlobe, moving his mouth to her neck. "You are too far gone already to challenge me."

"You want me just as badly." Her voice came out more shaky than she wanted it to.

Slowly, Arkhael pushed his hips forwards, his smile faltering briefly as he entered her. Just enough to give her a taste of what she wanted.

"I do." He bit down on her collarbone. "So just relent." And pushed himself in further.

Ailith gasped, clawing at the sheets at the feeling of him so soon after he had undone her, tilting her neck to give him better access. She almost growled at him as she spoke. "Just this once, I'll make it easy for you."

He felt too good inside her, and he was right: she was too far gone to challenge him in anything right now.

"Good. Because I will make love to you until you won't even so much as look at anyone else for the rest of your long life."

Ailith let out a shaky breath at his words. She didn't think she could have wanted him more, but her body yearned for him with a desire that was almost painful. She hooked a leg around him, trying to get him to move, while her lightheaded brain tried to formulate words.

"I already wasn't."

Arkhael smiled. "Eternity is a long time." He inched forwards.

"You underestimate me," she gasped.

"I always have," he murmured against her lips before he kissed her.

Tilting her hips, she shuddered as Arkhael pushed in the rest of the way, his hips flush with hers. He pulled back to look her in the eye.

"I love that you can take all of me." His breathless words sent fire through her body as he leaned back on his knees, hooking both of her legs over his shoulders. "Like your body was made for sin, for me."

Ailith writhed before him, unable to take her eyes off his figure. Her breath came out in short gasps, her earlier orgasm only heightening the feeling of him inside her.

When he finally moved, it was almost lavishly, his thrusts slow as she watched him look down to where their bodies joined and bite his lip at the sight of it. His confident facade finally faltered. With every thrust, her world disappeared a little bit more, until it was nothing but Arkhael. His fiery eyes, the light reflecting off his dark red skin, his hair now loose and falling over his shoulder. Suddenly, it wasn't enough. She reached out for him with a hand, and he obliged. Bending her legs back, he palmed both her breasts, using her as an anchor so he could quicken his pace, his claws digging into her skin.

527

Ailith crumbled under the new angle. Every time he filled her, she saw stars. Through her half-lidded eyes, she saw Arkhael look at her hungrily.

"Let go, my little thief." His voice was hoarse. "Come for me, Ailith. Give in to me."

Her hips shook under him, and her orgasm washed over her so suddenly, she thought she might faint from the force of it. Pleasure filled every fibre of her being as she arched her back further into Arkhael's touch, his name falling off her lips. He slowed his pace as she came undone under him, but he didn't stop. She was vaguely aware of his clenched teeth and the sweat rolling down the side of his face.

Is he holding back?

He moved her legs down, pulling her upright and on top of him. Instantly, she pressed herself against him, needing to feel as much of him against her as she could, her arms wrapped around his shoulders, lips on his in an instant.

"*Arkhael.*"

He moaned into her mouth as she breathed his name against his lips. Ailith couldn't tell if she was still riding the high from her last orgasm or if he was pushing her over the edge again already. This time, he didn't slow down.

"Tell me where you want me, my queen." His voice was barely audible as he drew back just enough to look her in the eye. A sharp pain shot through her as she felt him briefly reach for her soul. "My love."

Ailith nearly forgot how to breathe.

"Right here," she managed to bring out breathlessly.

His claws tore over her back as he pushed into her, muscles tensing as he finally let go with her.

When the world came back to Ailith, she was still in his arms, her head resting against his shoulders. Arkhael's naked skin was hot against hers, and she let herself relax against him as he stroked her hair, kissing the top of her head while they both tried to catch their breath. It was hard to believe that, after everything, he had truly called her his love. She closed her eyes, a single tear running down her cheek as reality settled in. After years of wandering, she had finally found her home.

In the Hells, of all places. And with a future ahead of her that only promised danger.

She tightened her arms around Arkhael, running her shaking hands over his shoulders to the leathery skin of his wings.

He *loved* her.

A smile came to her lips, and she lifted her head to kiss him. She would face whatever battle she had to with him. Her love. Eternity was theirs. And in his arms, she was finally, truly, happy.

Acknowledgements

What started out as a dream would never have turned into a novel if it weren't for some incredible people along the way.

For a start, an enormous heartfelt thank you to Jackie, who reminded me that there is nothing wrong with following your dreams.

A thank you to Liv, McKellar, and Katie, who all patiently listened to my constant self-doubt and anxiety, who got the first tastes of who Arkhael was going to be, and who were willing to read the first snippets of a very rough text. Even if it was accompanied by many giggles, "oh my"s, and made me want to sink through the floor.

A somewhat apologetic "thank you" to the ESFF community who were patient enough to listen to my complaints about italics and commas, and my general woes about author voice versus grammar.

A massive thanks to the legends at Midnight Tide Publishing for taking the time to actually read part of the manuscript and for judging a book by its content rather than query letter. You have all been a massive help in navigating the journey to publication and have made me feel so welcome!

And of course, my eternal gratitude to Meg Dailey who made the whole editing journey so much less daunting. Thank you for bearing with me through my too-many questions and awkward enthusiasm as I bumblefucked my way through editing a novel for the first time. For the infinite amounts of patience, reluctantly for the fry that went up my nose, and the incredibly stellar job you did with everything. I have an unending amount of respect for how good you are at your craft. Thank you for immediately understanding my vision for these characters and helping me fully develop them into their best (or worst?) selves. Arkhael would never admit it, but let's be honest, he might be a little indebted to you.

But mostly, thanks to my partner, my one true love, who supported me through the good but also through the very, very bad. Who was determined to be my number one fan, even when I couldn't love my own writing and was plagued by bouts of insecurity and imposter syndrome. Who showed me an absolutely impossible amount of patience and was willing to assist me every step of that way, from beta reading to marketing advice.

Thank you for never once complaining about the many nights I was being very asocial, the times you had to remind me that I do, in fact, need sustenance to survive, and the many "sorry I need to write this down" moments at 3 a.m. that you accepted without complaint. There is so much I am grateful for, I'm not sure how to bring it all into words.

But this book wouldn't be here without you. Thank you for being my love so unconditionally.

And finally, dear reader, thank you for reading this book all the way to the end. As the author of somewhat kinky scenes and very flawed characters, I do feel that I bear some responsibility to stress, *emphatically*, the importance of consent in all sexual scenarios and the healthy discussions of boundaries that should be had *beforehand* (maybe make sure your partner likes permanent jewellery before forcing it on them?).

I hope you enjoyed Ailith and Arkhael's journey as much as I enjoyed writing it, and I hope to see you back in the next book! And who knows, we might just catch a glimpse of these two again.

About M. Vixen

Storytelling is something M. Vixen (she/they) has done since she was old enough to speak. As a child she would retell stories she had heard until she was old enough to create her own. Living in Scotland with the love of her life, her overly active imagination combined with the beauty of Scotland's wild nature now feeds her passion for romantic fantasy and her ongoing Dungeons & Dragons campaign.

When she is not writing or daydreaming, she can usually be found doing one of her too many hobbies. She loves spending time with her love, prepping her next DnD sessions, painting miniatures, touching moss, reading (although she still has not recovered from Robin Hobb), feeding the local wildlife, or caring for her runt (said with love!) of a snake Jörmungandr, who is practising hard to eat the world one day.

Learn more about M. Vixen and sign up for her newsletter on www.mvixen.co.uk.

ALSO BY MIDNIGHT TIDE PUBLISHING

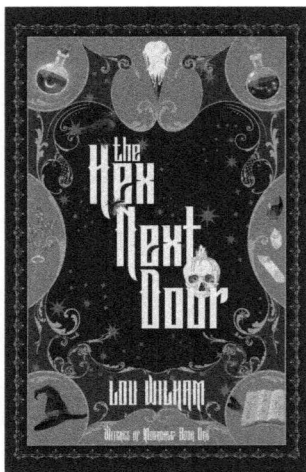

The Hex Next Door by Lou Wilham

What's a little necromancy between family?

For the Crow Witch, Icarus "Rus" Ashthorne, Moondale seemed the perfect hiding place. But like they always say, you can't go home again, and Rus finds out quickly that nothing is how she remembered, while at the same time very little has changed. Then she comes face to face with the only woman she's ever loved, Az Elwood, and... well, things get messier than she thought they ever could.

The Elwoods are a staple of Moondale, respected, feared, powerful, and Azure Elwood was always happy with her place amongst them. Happy to play the part of the good little witch, until Rus Ashthorne. Eleven years ago, Rus got on a bus and left Azure behind, but she's back, with two little girls trailing her like ducklings, and enough unspoken things between them to drown the town.

Now witch hunters are knocking at their proverbial door, the council of magic is being a real pain in the ass, and Rus wonders how much magic it'll take to protect the people she loves from herself and the danger following her.

9 781964 655284